The
HOUSE
of
LANYON

The
HOUSE
of
LANYON

VALERIE ANAND

MIRA®

ISBN-13: 978-0-7783-2502-4
ISBN-10:   0-7783-2502-4
B+T 24.95 11/07
THE HOUSE OF LANYON

www.MIRABooks.com

Printed in U.S.A.

First Printing: November 2007
10 9 8 7 6 5 4 3 2 1

ACKNOWLEDGMENTS

I am most grateful to the many people who have helped me
as I did the research for this book. My thanks go in particular to
Dolores Clew and Father Garrett for information on the medieval
church, and to Michael Grantham (Rector of St. George's in Dunster),
Laurie Hambrook (Churchwarden of St. George's), Mrs. Joan Jordan
(local historian) and Dr. Robert Dunning (County Editor) for
information on west country families and fifteenth-century Dunster.

This book is dedicated, most affectionately and gratefully, to all members of the Exmoor Society, and in particular to the members of its London Area Branch.

PART ONE

FOUNDATIONS
1458

CHAPTER ONE

QUIET AND DIGNIFIED

Allerbrook House is a manor house with charm. Three attractive gables look out from its slate roof, echoed by the smaller, matching gable over its porch, and two wings, with a secluded courtyard between them, stretch back toward the moorland hillside which shelters the house from northeast winds. In front the land drops away gently, but to the right the slope plunges steeply into the wooded, green-shadowed combe where the Allerbrook River purls over its pebbly bed, flowing down from its moorland source toward the village of Clicket in the valley.

Allerbrook is far from being a great house such as Chatsworth or Hatfield, but its charm apart, it has unusual features of its own, such as a mysterious stained glass window in its chapel—no one is sure of its significance—and the Tudor roses, which nowadays are painted red-and-white as when they were first made, which are carved into the hall panelling and the window seats.

The place is a rarity, standing as it does out on Exmoor, between the towns of Withypool and Dulverton. There is no other house of its type on the moor. It is also unique because of its origins. The truth—as its creator Richard Lanyon once admitted—is that it probably wouldn't be there at all, if one autumn day in 1458 Sir Humphrey Sweetwater and his twin sons, Reginald and Walter, had not ridden out to hunt a stag and had a most distressing encounter with a funeral.

There was no manor house there when, in the fourteenth century, the Lanyons came from Cornwall and took over Allerbrook farm. Then, the only dwelling was a farmhouse, so ancient even at that time that no one knew how long it had stood there.

Sturdily built of pinkish-grey local stone and roofed with shaggy thatch, it looked more like a natural outcrop than a construction. Around it spread a haphazard collection of fields and pastures, and its farmyard was encircled by a clutter of barns, byres, stables and assorted sheds. Inside, the main rooms were the kitchen and the big all-purpose living room. There was an impressive oak front door, but it was never used except for wedding and funeral processions and the hinges were regrettably rusty. It was a workaday place.

On a fine late September evening, though, with a golden haze softening the heathery heights of the moors and gilding the Bristol Channel to the north, there was a mellowness. That mellowness seemed even to have entered the soul of the man whose life was now drawing to a close in one of the upper bedchambers.

This was remarkable, because George Lanyon's sixty-one years of life had scarcely been serene. He had been an aggressive child, apt to bully his two older sisters and his younger brother, for as long as they were there to bully. The Lanyons had never, for some reason, been good at raising healthy families. All George's siblings had ailed and died before they were twenty. Only George flourished, as though he possessed all the vitality that should have been shared equally among the four of them.

As an adult, he had quarrelled with his parents, dominated his wife, Alice, and shouted at his fragile younger son, Stephen, until the boy died of lung-rot at the age of eleven. The grieving Alice, in her one solitary fit of rebellion, accused him of driving Stephen into his grave, and she herself faded out of life the following year.

Only Richard, his elder son, had been strong enough to survive and at times to stand up to him or, if necessary, stand by him. George also quarrelled with their landlord, Sir Humphrey Sweetwater, when he raised their rent. George had refused to see that this was dangerous.

"The Sweetwaters won't throw us off our land. They know we look after it. They were glad enough to have us take it on when Granddad Petroc came here, looking for a place, back in the days of the plague when everyone who'd lived here before was dead."

"That was then. This is now, and I don't trust them," said Richard. He was well aware that the Sweetwaters, although only minor gentry, were on social if not intimate terms with Thomas Courtenay, Earl of Devon, which was a double-edged blade. On the one hand, they considered themselves so far above their tenants that they could scarcely even see them. But on the other hand, if the said tenants tilled the land badly or wrangled over a rise in the rent, they were as capable of throwing the offenders out as they were capable of drowning unwanted kittens. You never knew. Richard loathed the Sweetwaters as much as George, but he was also wary.

The quarrel passed over. George gave in and paid the increase, and the Sweetwaters continued to regard the Lanyon family with disdain. Quietly the Lanyons began to prosper, though Richard considered that they could have done better still if only his father hadn't in so many ways been so pigheaded.

But now...

Extraordinary, Richard thought as he stood looking down at his father's sunken face and half-shut eyes. *Extraordinary.* All his life he had fought this man, argued with him and usually given in to him. And now, would you believe it, George was making a good Christian end.

Betsy and Kat, the two middle-aged sisters who cooked and cleaned and looked after the dairy and were so alike in their fair plumpness that people often mixed them up, were on their knees on the other side of the bed, praying quietly. At the foot stood Father Bernard, the elderly parish priest. "He's safe enough," Father Bernard said with some acidity. He knew George well. "He's had the last rites. Luckily you fetched me while he was still conscious. Lucky you had that horse of yours, too, whatever your father thought!"

Richard Lanyon grinned, fleetingly. Father Bernard lived down in Clicket village, in a cottage beside St. Anne's, the elegant little church built of pale Caen stone imported from France for the purpose by some pious bygone Sweetwater.

There was a long, sloping mile of Allerbrook combe between the farm and the priest, but George had asked for Father Bernard with pleading in his eyes and begged his son to hurry, and

Richard had been able to do so, because he had a good horse at his command. George always said he had lost only three battles in his lifetime. One was the squabble over the rent. Another, a very long-running one, was the way Richard, once widowed, kept on refusing to remarry and make another attempt to raise a family. The third was over Richard's purchase of Splash.

"Why can't you ride a local pony like everyone else?" George raged when Richard went off to a horse fair miles away and came back leading a two-year-old colt with a most remarkable dappled coat. The dapples were dark iron-grey and much bigger than dapples usually were, overlapping and running into each other so that he looked as though someone had splashed liquid iron all over him. "The ponies round here can carry a grown man all day and never tire *or* put their feet in bogs by mistake. What did you spend good money on *that* for?" Master Lanyon senior demanded.

"He's well made. I'm going to break him for riding and call him Splash," said Richard.

"I give you your cut from any profits we make," George bellowed at his unrepentant son, "but I don't expect you to throw it away on something as ought to be in a freak show!"

But Splash, with his long legs and his undoubted dash of Arab blood, had proved his worth. He was as clever as any moorland pony at avoiding bogs and he could outdistance every horse in the parish and beyond, including the bloodstock owned by the Sweetwaters. He had got Richard down to the village and to the priest's house so quickly that by the time Richard was hammering on Father Bernard's door, the dust he had kicked up as he tore out of the farmyard still hung in the air.

"Get up behind me," Richard said when the priest opened the

door. "Don't stop to saddle your mare. It's my father. We think he's going."

And Splash, head lowered and nostrils wide, brought them both back up the combe nearly as fast as he had carried Richard down it, and before he drifted into his last dream, George Lanyon received the sacrament and was shriven of his sins and given, thereby, his passport into paradise.

"I couldn't have done it without Splash," Richard said, and glanced at his father, wondering if George could hear and secretly hoping so.

But if he did, he made no sign and when Peter, Richard's nineteen-year-old son, came quietly into the room asking whether the patient was better, Richard could only shake his head.

"Keep your voice down now, Master Peter." Betsy, the older of the two sisters, looked up from her prayers. "Don't 'ee be disturbing 'un. Your granddad's made his peace and he's startin' on his journey."

Peter nervously came closer to the bed. As a child, he had seen two small brothers die, and at the age of eleven he had been taken to his parents' bedchamber to say farewell to his mother, Joan, and the girl-child who never breathed, and every time he had been stricken with a sense of dreadful mystery, and with pity.

The pity this time was made worse by the change in his grandfather. Petroc, the Cornishman who was George's own grandfather, had died before George was born, but his description had been handed down. He had been short and dark, a very typical Cornishman. He had, however, married a local girl, said to be big and brown haired and clear skinned. The combination had produced good-looking descendants, dark of hair and eye like Petroc, but with tall strong bodies and excellent facial bones. In life, George had been not only loud voiced and argumentative; he had also been unusually handsome.

Now his good looks had faded with his vitality. He had been getting thinner for months, and complaining of pains inside, though no one knew what ailed him, but the final collapse, into this shrunken husk, had come suddenly, taking them all by surprise. To Peter it seemed that the man on the bed was melting before their eyes.

George himself had been drifting in a misty world where nothing had substance. He could hear voices nearby, but could make no sense of what they said. His body no longer seemed to matter. For a change, nothing was hurting. He was comfortable. He was content to surrender to whatever or wherever lay before him. But in him, life had always been a powerful force. Like a candle flame just before it gutters out, it flared once more. For a few moments the mist withdrew and the voices made sense again and his eyes opened, to focus, frowningly, on the faces around him.

Father Bernard. Sharp-tongued old wretch. But he'd provided the last rites. No need to fear hell now. With difficulty he turned his head, and there was young Peter, his only surviving grandson, looking miserable. Why did the Lanyons never produce big healthy families? As for Richard...

Wayward boy. Been widowed for years; should have married again long ago. Should have listened to his father. *I kept telling him. Obstinate, that's what he is. Big ideas. Always thinks he knows better than me. Always wanting to try new things out.*

Oh, well. Richard would soon be able to please himself. His father wouldn't be able to stop him. Didn't even want to, not now. Too tired...

Weakly he turned his head the other way, and saw the white-capped heads of Betsy and Kat. Beyond them was the window. It was shut, its leaded panes with their squares of thick, greenish glass denying him a view of the world outside. He'd had the windows glazed long ago, at more expense than he liked, but he'd always detested the fact that Sweetwater House was the only dwelling for miles that could have daylight without draughts. Yet even with glazing, the daylight was partly obscured and the view scarcely visible. "Open...window," he said thickly. "Now. Quick."

Betsy got up at once. Kat murmured a protest, but Betsy said, "No cold wind's a'goin' to hurt 'un now, silly. We'd be doing this anyway, soon." She clicked the window latch and flung the casement back, letting cool air stream into the room.

She meant that, once he was gone, someone would open the window anyway, because people always did, to let the departing soul go free. George knew that quite well. He wanted to see where he was going.

The window gave him a glimpse of Slade, the barley field, all stubble now, because the summer had been good and they'd got all the corn in and threshed, as well. The names of his fields told themselves over in his head: Long Meadow, Slade, Quillet, Three Corner Mead...

He had been proud of them, all the more so because they were really his. He knew that in many places fields were communal, with each farmer cultivating just a strip, or perhaps more than one, but compelled to plant the same crop as everyone else and changing strips each year. Here in the southwest, it was different. Here, a man's fields were his own.

Beyond the farmland was a dark green line, the trees of Allerbrook combe, and in the distance strode the skyline of the moorland's highest ridge, swimming in lemon light. There were strange mounds on the hilltops of Exmoor, said to be the graves of pagan people who had lived here long, long ago. He'd like to be buried in a mound on high ground, but he'd have to be content with a grave in the churchyard of St. Anne's. He wouldn't even be able to hear the sound of the Aller-brook…well, no, he wouldn't be able to hear anything, near or far, but…

He was growing confused and things were fading again. But how lovely was the light on those moors. He'd never attended to it in life. Been too damn busy trying to control that awkward son of his. Now he wanted to float away into that glorious sky, to dissolve into it, to be part of it….

His eyes closed. The voices around him became irrelevant once more and then were gone. Father Bernard, gentle now, spoke a final prayer and Richard, also gently, kissed his father's brow and drew up the sheet.

"It was a good passing," he said.

The priest nodded. "Yes, it was. I will make arrangements for the burial. Will you decide when the best day would be, and let me know?"

"Of course," Richard said. "I shall have much to do."

And organising the funeral would be only part of that. To Richard—and though he didn't speak of it aloud, he didn't conceal it from himself, either—the golden light of the descending sun was a sign of golden opportunity. He would give his father a respectful farewell, as a good son should. But his mental list of the people he would invite included some with whom he particularly wanted to talk, and the sooner the better. He had plans, and now, at last, he was free to put them into action.

But *certainly* the funeral itself would, he trusted, be long re-membered as an example of well-organised, quiet dignity.

In the event, George Lanyon's funeral was unquestionably memorable and parts of it even dignified. But from that day onward, the conflict between Richard Lanyon and the Sweet-water family was more than a simple matter of dislike. That was the day when what had been merely dislike and resentment es-calated into a feud.

CHAPTER TWO

SHAPING THE FUTURE

I n the village of Dunster, a dozen or so miles away on the coast of the Bristol Channel, Liza Weaver, suitably grave of face, stood among other members of the extensive Weaver family and bade farewell to her father, Nicholas, the head of the house, and her mother, Margaret, as they set off on the long ride to Allerbrook for the funeral of George Lanyon.

She was a strongly built girl with warm brown eyes and hair that matched, although at the moment it was hidden under a neat white cap. Her big, florid father said cheerfully, "I'm sorry about George, and his family will miss him, but we'll likely bring back some good fresh bacon from the farm. It's an ill wind, as they say," and he leaned down from his saddle to kiss his eldest daughter. "Be a good wench. Help your little sister and—" he dropped his voice "—don't mind Aunt Cecy's tongue. She means no harm." He straightened up in his saddle, took off his hat and waved it to them all. "See you all soon!" he cried. Margaret smiled and turned her sturdy pony to follow him as he set off.

So there they went, thought Liza. Off to the funeral of George Lanyon. The two families were mostly linked by business, but there had been some social contacts, too. She had been to Allerbrook now and then—to Christmas and Easter gatherings as a rule—and she had met George. She had also found him rather alarming. She felt dutifully sorry for anyone who was ill, or had died, but she was young and the passing of Master Lanyon did not mean so very much to her.

On the other hand, the departure of her parents did mean something, of which they had no inkling. She had since childhood had a habit sometimes of going for walks on her own. Here in Dunster where everyone knew everyone else, it was safe enough and no one had ever stopped her, unless there was so much to do that she couldn't be spared. Aunt Cecy would probably say that with Nicholas and Margaret absent, there'd be too much to do just now, but it shouldn't be too difficult to give Aunt Cecy the slip after dinner.

And in the dell beyond the mill, where bluebells had been out the first time they met there, back in the springtime, a young man called Christopher would be waiting.

Autumn had declared itself. On the moors the bracken was bronzing and the higher hillcrests were veiled in cloud. It had rained overnight and there were puddles in the farmyard at Allerbrook. In the kitchen Betsy and Kat were busy by daybreak, preparing the food which must be served to the guests. When Richard came downstairs, the stockpot was already bubbling and there were chickens on the spit. The poultry population of Allerbrook had gone down considerably in George's honour.

Out in the byre Betsy's husband, Higg, was milking the cows while Kat's husband, Roger, fetched water from the well for the benefit of the kitchen and the plough oxen in their stalls. It should have been the other way around, since Higg was as broad chested as any ox while Roger was skinny and stoop backed from a lifetime of carrying full buckets and laden sacks. He carried buckets so lopsidedly that they usually slopped, but the cows, perversely, responded better to Higg.

Upstairs, guests who had had a long way to come and had arrived the previous day were still abed, but Peter was up ahead of his father and snatching a quick breakfast of small ale and bread smeared with honey. Richard sat down next to him. "Sleep all right? It'll be a long day."

"I didn't sleep much, no. It's strange without Granddad. Nothing's ever going to be the same again, is it?" Peter said.

Richard was silent, because to him, the fact that nothing was ever going to be the same again was a matter for rejoicing, but it would be quite improper to say so.

Under George's rule, life at Allerbrook had been the same for far too long. There were so many things that Richard would have liked to try, new ideas which he had seen put into practice on other farms, but his father was set against innovations.

It was always *Take it from me—I know best. No, I don't want to try another breed of sheep. Ours do well on the moorland grazing, so what do you want to go making experiments for? No, what's the point of renting more valley grazing? Got enough, haven't we? Nonsense, I never heard of anyone growing wheat on Exmoor, even if Quillet field does face south and the soil's deep.*

There were going to be changes now, and that was nothing to grieve about. He glanced at Peter again, and saw that the boy was hurrying his meal. "Take your time," he said. "Our guests'll be a while yet. Ned Crowham's never been one for early rising, I've noticed."

For a short time, Peter had been to school in the east of the county and Ned had been one of his fellow pupils. They had become friends, although they had little in common. A complete contrast to the Lanyons to look at, Ned was short, plump, pink skinned and fair as a newly hatched chick. He was also the son of a man as wealthy as Sir Humphrey, owner of several Somerset farms and a manor house twenty miles away, toward the town of Bridgwater. At home, young Ned was indulged. He had spent nights at Allerbrook before and shown himself to be a terrible layabed.

"And the Weavers didn't get here till after dark last night," Richard added. "Mistress Margaret was tired. It's only twelve miles from Dunster as the crow flies, but it's a heck of a lot more as a pony plods and she's not young. It was good of her to come. I hoped Nicholas Weaver would, for I've business with him, but I'm touched that his wife came, too."

"We'll have a crowd here soon," Peter said, swallowing his final mouthful. "Just as well Master Nicholas didn't bring his whole family! Poor Granddad used to envy the Weavers, didn't he, because of their big families? Father, why did you never marry again after my mother died? I've often wondered." Richard frowned and Peter hastily added, "I'm sorry. I didn't mean to say anything I shouldn't."

"I'm not offended, boy. I was just wondering what the answer was, that's all. I tell you," said Richard, man-to-man, "about three-quarters of the reason was that your granddad wanted me to marry again so badly! He kept on and on and the more he kept on, the less I felt like obliging him. So time went on, and it never happened. You'll gain! You won't have to share with others when you inherit the tenancy."

Another reason, although he was fond enough of Peter not to say this to him, was that he hadn't been very happy in marriage. Joan had been a good woman; that he wouldn't deny. Too good, perhaps, too gentle. He sometimes glimpsed the same gentleness in Peter and didn't like it. Peter was a Lanyon in looks but he had his mother's temperament, and that wasn't fitting for a man. It had even been irritating in a woman! He'd have liked Joan better if she'd spoken up more, the way Margaret Weaver sometimes argued with Nicholas: good-naturedly—there was no spite in it—but clearly, and often with very sensible things to say.

Joan was timid, scared of him and scared of George. She always had a bad time in childbirth and she was terrified of that, too. The fact that her last pregnancy had killed her had left Richard feeling guilt stricken. For some years now he had had a comfortable arrangement with a widow down in Clicket, a woman who'd buried two husbands and never borne a child. She did him good and he had done her no harm. He never discussed her with his family, though they all knew about Deb Archer.

"I don't think you'll be inheriting yet awhile," he said jovially to Peter. "I've a good few years in me yet, I hope. Do you want to see your grandfather again, for a last goodbye?"

George was in his coffin on the table in the big living room. After the funeral, the room would come back into use, with a white cloth over the table and the best pewter dishes brought down off the sideboard, but until then, the room was only for George.

25

Peter shook his head. "No. I...I'd rather not. I saw him yesterday but he doesn't look like himself anymore, does he?" He shivered. "I can't believe that what's in that box ever walked or talked...or shouted!"

"You're getting morbid, boy. Well, maybe before long I'll turn your mind in a happier direction. You just wait and see."

In another hour Father Bernard had ridden in on his mare, and shortly after that, Tilly and Gilbert Lowe arrived from the farm on the other side of the combe, accompanied by Martha, the plain and downtrodden daughter who was virtually their servant. The Lowes were followed by the Rixons and Hannacombes from the other two farms on the Sweetwater estate, and then a number of folk from Clicket village straggled in, all soberly dressed, some on foot, some on ponies, to pay their last respects and escort George down to the churchyard and his final place of rest.

Among them came Mistress Deborah Archer, forty-nine now but still buxom and brown haired. Richard kissed her without embarrassment and Father Bernard greeted her politely. Like nearly everyone in the parish, he knew of the arrangement but accepted it without comment, just as he accepted the fact that neither Richard nor Deborah ever mentioned it in his confessional. He had had a lapse or two of his own. It was even possible that Geoffrey Baker, steward to the Sweetwaters, was his son. No one knew for certain.

The Sweetwaters didn't come and no one expected them, though some of their employees arrived, including their shepherd Edward Searle, along with his son Toby. Edward Searle was a local personality. Tall, gaunt, dignified as a king and able to tell every one of his sheep apart, he was one of the few in the district whose baptismal names had never, unless they were already short enough, been chopped into nicknames. In a world where Elizabeth usually became Liza or Betsy and most Edwards became Ned or Ed, Master Searle remained Edward and no one would have dreamed of shortening it.

The other exceptions included the Sweetwaters themselves, Richard Lanyon (who refused to answer to Dick or Dickon and had long since squelched any attempts to make him) and Geoffrey Baker, who arrived on a roan mare and gave his master's apologies with great civility though Richard knew, and Baker knew he knew, that Sir Humphrey Sweetwater hadn't actually sent any apologies at all.

Sir Humphrey, said Baker solemnly, had guests, connections of Thomas Courtenay, the Earl of Devon. The Sweetwaters had promised to show them some sport today. They were all going hunting.

"Sir Humphrey's showing off, as usual," Richard growled to Peter.

Friendship with the Courtenays had brought one very marked benefit to the Sweetwaters, since Sir Thomas was the warden of Exmoor Forest. Clicket was outside the forest boundary, but only just. All deer belonged to the crown and no one hunted them except by royal permission, but a Sweetwater had distinguished himself so valiantly at the Battle of Crécy that he and his descendants had been granted the right to hunt deer on their own land.

Normally, they would not have been allowed to pursue them into the forest, which was inconvenient because the deer, oblivious of human boundaries, very often fled that way. Sir

Thomas, however, had used his own considerable powers and granted permission for the Sweetwater hounds to follow quarry across the boundary. Sir Humphrey never missed a chance of demonstrating his privilege to his guests.

By ten o'clock all was ready at the farmhouse. The Clicket carpenter, who had made the coffin and brought it up the combe strapped to the back of a packhorse, had solemnly nailed it shut while Father Bernard recited a prayer. The Lanyon dogs—Peter's long-legged, grey-blue lurcher Blue, Silky the black sheepdog bitch who had belonged to George, and Silky's black-and-white son Ruff, who was Richard's special companion—knew that they were not invited on this outing and lay down by the fire. How much animals sensed, no one could guess, but Silky had been pining since George died.

The six bearers, Richard, Peter, Higg, Roger, Nicholas Weaver and Geoffrey Baker, lifted the coffin onto their shoulders. They would be replaced halfway by a second team of volunteers, since the mile-long Allerbrook combe which must be traversed to reach Clicket was a long way to carry their burden, but to put a laden coffin on a pack pony would be risky. Ponies could stumble, or take fright. Nicholas, whose hair and beard were halfway between sandy and grey and who had grown hefty with the years, grunted as he took the weight, and cheeky Ned Crowham, who was one of the relief bearers—he had been got out of bed only just in time to join the procession—said that at least Nicholas's pony could now have a rest.

"True enough," Nicholas said amiably. "My pony's stout, but I reckon the poor brute still sags in the middle when I get astride him. That's why Margaret's got her own nag. Not fair to any animal to put me on him and then add someone else."

Father Bernard smiled, but Margaret said seriously, "Oh, Nicholas. We shouldn't make jokes, surely."

Richard, however, easing his shoulder under the weight of the coffin, said, "Oh, my father liked a laugh as much as any man and he wouldn't grudge it to us now. Are we all ready? Then let's start."

The bearers carried George ceremonially through the front door—the hinges, as usual, had had to be oiled to make sure it would open—and took the downhill path into the combe. They trod with care. The sun was out now, but the ground was soft from last night's rain.

The voice of the Allerbrook came up to them as they went. It was a swift, brown-tinged peat stream which rose in a bog at the top of the long, smooth moorland ridge above and the rain had swollen it. Some feet above the water, the track turned to parallel the river's course down to Clicket. The trees met overhead and the light on the path was a confusing mixture of greenish shade and dazzling interruptions where the sun shone through. There was no other track to the village. The combe was thickly grown with trees and tangled undergrowth and on the far side, the few paths did not lead to Clicket. The track was wide but in places it was also steep, and in any case the coffin lurched somewhat because Higg and Roger were among the first team of bearers at their own insistence, and Higg's broad shoulders were four inches higher than Roger's bent ones.

Father Bernard led the way on his mare. The bearers followed him and the crowd formed a rough and ready procession on foot behind the coffin. They talked among themselves as they went, for funerals were not such rare events, after all. Death was part of life. Father Bernard, in church on Sundays, often spoke of the next world and told them to be ready for it.

Halfway down, a steep path descended the slope to the right, met the track, crossed it and continued down to a ford. Water was draining down the path from the side of the combe and the crossing was extremely muddy. "Carefully now!" Father Bernard called over his shoulder, and steadied his mare as one of her hooves skidded. "The rain's made this a proper quagmire. Mind you don't slip."

"Keep in step!" said Nicholas. "And take it steadily."

Somewhere on the other side of the combe they heard a hunting horn and the voices of hounds, but, being concerned with their uncertain footing, no one paid much heed to it. The horn sounded again, nearer. And then, out of the trees on the other side of the river, came the stag.

There were two ways of hunting deer. If the purpose was simply venison, the hunt could drive the quarry into a ring of archers who would mow them down like corn. But if the huntsmen wanted sport and the pleasure of the chase and maybe a fresh pair of fine antlers to decorate a hall, then they would look for a grown stag and bring him to bay after a chase. Sir Humphrey preferred the chase. The hall in his manor house bristled with antlers and he employed not only a huntsman to care for his hounds but also a harbourer to keep track of likely stags and lead the hunt to them on request.

The harbourer had found them a fine beast this time. The animal which burst out of the woods, splashed headlong across the stream and came up to the crossways like a four-footed hurricane was in full breeding array. He had twelve points to his crown, six each side, tipped white as if with pearl. His nostrils flared red with the effort of running and his eyes were rolling. The horrified bearers were passing the top of the slippery path down to the river when he hurtled up toward them, fleeing in such panic from the hounds on his trail that he was not aware of them until the last moment.

Then he swerved, with a huge sideways leap, sprang past the nose of Father Bernard's startled mare, which reared in alarm, and was gone, into the trees and on up the hill, and at the same moment the hounds, brown and black and patch-coated, giving tongue like wolves, poured out of the woods opposite, and hard behind them came Sir Humphrey's huntsman and then Sir Humphrey himself and his twin sons, Reginald and Walter, on their big horses, closely followed by three riders who were presumably their guests, all hallooing nearly loud enough to drown the hounds and the horn.

Hounds and horses crashed through the ford, water spraying up around them. They scrambled for footholds on the path and tore upward. The cortege had stopped where it was as if paralysed, everyone having unanimously decided to keep still and let the uproar flow around them as it would around a line of trees. Most of the hounds veered as the stag had done, but three of them took the shortest route and went straight under the coffin and between the legs of the bearers. One collided with Richard's ankles and another bounced off Nicholas Weaver's shins. Both Richard and Nicholas lurched and their burden shifted.

The lurches were small and the shift in the weight was minor, but feet slipped on the perilous ground and the uneven weight of the tilting coffin made them slip still more. There were shouts of alarm. The riders, coming hard after the hounds, swerved their mounts around the head of the cortege, but one of them came too close. His horse saw the coffin, shied to avoid it and kicked out, catching Higg's hip.

Higg, knocked sideways, held on but stumbled, and the tilt of the coffin became dangerous. Then Richard, who was one of the foremost bearers, lost his footing altogether and sat down, still holding on but pulling the front of the coffin down farther still. The tilt became a slide toward the ground, tearing the other bearers' hands and breaking their hold. There were more cries of alarm. Margaret Weaver and Betsy called aloud on God, and people crossed themselves. Kat and Deborah screamed.

In a shaft of sunlight through the leaves, the funeral party had a fleeting glimpse of tall horses, reins with ornate dagged edges, spurred boots, richly coloured saddlecloths and tunics, bearded faces, one with a hunting horn held to its lips, velvet cloaks and exotic headgear, twisted liripipes bouncing on their owners' shoulders, and then they were gone, leaping over the path and crashing up the hillside.

As they went, the coffin slithered right out of the bearers' grasp, came down slowly but inexorably onto the path to the ford and then, gliding on the mud churned by the hunt, set off on its own, straight toward the river.

Father Bernard was off his horse on the instant. He threw himself after the coffin, clutching at it as he landed facedown in the mud, but its weight dragged it out of his grasp. Others scrambled frantically down through the trees to help. Deborah Archer, exclaiming with horror, got there first, tearing her dark skirts on the underbrush. She flung herself on top of the coffin as it went into the water and somehow succeeded in hooking one foot around the trunk of an alder at the brink. Held by her weight, the coffin sank where it was, and grounded in the shallow water of the ford, Deb lying on its lid and spluttering with her face in the stream and her skirts floating to each side of her.

Roger, rushing after her, waded into the water to get to the other end of the coffin and push it back toward land. Other helping hands were there. They picked Father Bernard up, lifted Deb and grabbed the coffin, dragging it ashore and hoisting it up again.

Richard, white-faced, had got to his feet and reached them in time to help with carrying his father's casket back up the slope to the shocked procession on the path. "It's all right. It hasn't broken open. Deb saved it. If the water had moved it off the shallows…"

It could have done. The Allerbrook had a strong current and downstream of the ford it became quite deep. No one wanted to imagine what could have happened next.

"Father Bernard, you're covered in mud!" Richard looked at the priest in distress. "You must brush it off. You must call at your house and put on something clean before the service. Can you find Roger here some dry things, too? He's drenched to the knees. And Deb, oh Deb, I can't be more grateful, but you're wet through and shivering. Here!" He pulled off his cloak and threw it around her. "That'll keep some warmth in. You can hardly strip your wet things off just here, so go home, Deb, *run,* to keep some heat in you, and put on dry things. We'll wait for you in the churchyard. But you must get dry or you'll take a chill. Go on—*now!*"

"I'm past the age for running and it's over half a mile!" said Deb through chattering teeth as she wrung out her skirts and clutched the cloak to her. "But I'll get home fast-like and see 'ee in the churchyard." Holding her wet gown clear of the ground, she scurried off and Richard turned his attention to Betsy's husband, Higg, who was flexing his right wrist and rubbing his hip, a pained expression on his seamed brown face. "What's the matter, Higg? You've hurt yourself?"

"One of their damned hosses well-nigh kicked me off my feet

and then my wrist went when I was tryin' to keep a'hold of the coffin," Higg said. "Hip don't matter—that's just a bruise—but it feels like my wrist's been twisted half off. Don't think I can go on as bearer. T'wouldn't be safe, and we've had trouble enough for one day."

"It's time for the relief bearers, anyhow," Richard said, and raised his voice to call the volunteers forward: Ned Crowham, the Searles, Gilbert Lowe, Sim Hannacombe and Harry Rixon. Far away in the distance the hunting horn spoke again and the baying of the hounds once more drifted through the trees.

"Bloody Sweetwaters," said Richard through his teeth. "I hope they all fall off their damned horses and break their necks and I hope the hounds bring that stag to bay and it gores every single one of them to death!"

"It went well enough in the end," Nicholas Weaver said to Richard later that day as they stood together, partaking of the generous food and the excellent cider that was Kat's speciality, and yet very conscious of the space in the household, the empty niche in the air which once had been filled by George. "That accident could have been much worse!"

"I daresay," said Richard. "But I'll never forgive the Sweet-waters. Never!"

"Likely enough they hardly realised what had happened," said Nicholas. "It was all so fast. By the time they'd seen us, it was too late."

"They had time enough! Had to get across the ford, didn't they? And all of us up there on the path. Couldn't miss us!"

"Ah, well. The light under the trees is always dim and we were all in dark clothes. Can't come to a funeral in festive red and tawny!"

"You're a good-natured soul, Nicholas," Richard said. "I'm not so even tempered as you. The Sweetwaters behave as if this were still the days of serfs and villeins and we were nothing but animals with no human feelings. Before I'm done, I swear I'll teach them different. I'd like to kill every last man of them. It would be a pleasure to see every Sweetwater head on a chopping block."

"You're so fierce!" said Nicholas, and adroitly turned the subject. "Well, there's talk of war these days. Plenty of people will get chopped up if that happens!"

A good many of the gathering were talking about the accident to the coffin, some of them with amusement, some with anxiety for the health of Mistress Archer, who had been soaked to the skin and had had to go a good half mile like that in order to get home and dry herself. For others, however, talking about the Sweetwaters and their connections had led to conversation about the wider world in general. Here in this quiet corner of the southwest, the power struggles of kings and lords didn't often impinge, but it had been known to happen, and for years the news had been disturbing. King Henry VI was said to be ailing in his mind, and his relative, Richard, Duke of York, who like the king was a descendant of Edward III, had been made regent for a while, but it was an uneasy state of affairs.

"Ambitious, that's what I hear. He didn't much care for it when the king got better. Could lead to trouble…"

"Some say all that's a tale put about by the queen. She don't like him. They say he's sworn his loyalty but she don't believe it. I've heard no good of her. When I were in Lynmouth and there were a ship in from London way, the men aboard said folk in the eastern parts are calling her Queen She-Wolf, ever since her

French friends burned Sandwich port last year. Bloodthirsty, they say she is."

"Yes, I've heard that." Ned Crowham was unwontedly grave. "We had a queen over a century ago, a French-born one, that used to be called the She-Wolf of France. They must have named this one after her and it's hardly a compliment. You could be right. I can see war coming."

"Pray God and the saints it don't come near us or call any of us away. If the Sweetwaters go to war…"

Nicholas had heard things, too. "If war does come," he said to Richard, "then the Luttrells in Dunster Castle will go, for sure, and they'll take some of the young fellows in my family. We're their tenants."

"And I'm a Sweetwater tenant! The last thing I want to do is die nobly fighting at their orders!" Richard said angrily. "Oh, well, it hasn't happened yet. My friend, there's something else I want to discuss." He took Nicholas's elbow and steered him into a quieter corner. "I've something in mind that could do both of us a bit of good. You might think a funeral's no place for fixing up a marriage, but nothing'll bring my father back and this talk of war's unsettling. I'd sooner think of things that can be settled by you and me, here and now, and might give all our thoughts a happier turn. Your eldest daughter's still not betrothed. I've been thinking…"

The Sweetwaters lived at the eastern end of the village on a knoll, in a house with a battlemented lookout tower. The Aller-brook, running close by on its way to join the River Barle, provided the house with a half moat in front, and there was a good ford for the packhorse trains carrying wool to market, and a set of stepping stones maintained by the Sweetwaters for the convenience of travellers in and out of the village.

Richard envied the house and approved of the stepping stones, but his father had been sour. "They put all the village rents up when they put in the stones," George had said. "Lucky they didn't put the farm rents up again and all!"

In the great hall Reginald Sweetwater, the elder by twenty minutes of Sir Humphrey's twin sons, helped his father off with his boots while Walter did the same office for their guests, and Geoffrey Baker, who had returned to his duties immediately after the funeral, came in with two young pages and served mulled wine. He did not let the women servants wait on all-male gatherings. Sir Humphrey and Reginald were both widowers, and Walter's wife, Mary, preferred to remain in her solar with her young daughter when male guests visited without their own wives.

"That was a good run," said Thomas Carew, one of the guests—and an illustrious one, since his mother had been a Courtenay. "You'll have a fine new set of antlers for your wall, Sir Humphrey." He looked appreciatively around at the remarkable collection already there. "Twelve pointer, wasn't he? Not bad. They hardly ever go over fourteen points in England."

"That one did." Sir Humphrey, a heavily built man, stretched a large pair of feet toward the warmth of the hearth and pointed to the impressive trophy just above it. "My grandfather killed him. Eighteen points. Almost unheard of for this part of the world."

"It was a sixteen pointer that chased a friend of mine up a tree one September," said Thomas.

"Damned lucky to find a tree on these moors," said Walter Sweetwater.

"It was on the edge of Cloutsham vale, over beyond Dunkery hill. Plenty of tree cover there. Up there two hours he was, with the old stag parading around and going for the tree with his antlers every now and again. It was in the rut. Stag must have thought he was a rival. Do you reckon a male deer can tell male and female humans from each other?"

The conversation went on an excursion around remarkable hunting stories and anecdotes about animal sagacity, and an argument between Walter and his father about the intelligence of sheep, Walter maintaining that according to the Sweetwater shepherd, Edward Searle, they weren't as stupid as most people believed, and Sir Humphrey complaining that Walter spent too much time in the company of the shepherd and should concentrate on practicing his swordplay instead. "Edward Searle may look like a prophet out of the Old Testament and stalk about among his sheep with his head in the air as though he were royalty, but he's only a shepherd and ought to remember it, and so ought you," said Sir Humphrey, who was himself slightly intimidated by Edward Searle, though he would have died before he admitted as much.

Thomas's young son, whose mind seemed to have been elsewhere all this time, suddenly asked, "Who were those people we almost crashed into after we crossed the river? I could hardly see them in that bad light under the trees. What were they doing there?"

"George Lanyon of Allerbrook's funeral party," said Reginald contemptuously. "Our steward, Baker, attended it." He looked around, but the steward had withdrawn and was out of hearing. Reginald laughed. "He said they dropped the coffin and it almost went into the river. But they got it up and it was all right. There was no harm done."

"George Lanyon's no loss. Maybe deer know men from women, but George Lanyon never knew gentle from simple," said Sir Humphrey. His eyes, which were grey and always inclined to be cold, became positively icy at the thought of the departed George. "Had the presumption to argue when his rent went up, as if rents don't have to go up now and then—it's the course of nature. Let's hope the son—what's his name...?"

"Richard Lanyon, Grandfather." Walter's eleven-year-old son, Baldwin, was also in the company.

"That's it. Richard. Bigheaded peasant who won't let anyone call him Dickon. We can hope he's less bloody-minded than George, but I doubt it. There's something about him. He doesn't like taking his cap off to me. He'll very likely be even worse than his father was. Ah, here's Baker back again. More mulled wine, Baker."

When he brought the wine, Geoffrey said, "I've ordered a fresh basket of firewood to be brought in. The weather's turning colder. It feels as if winter's on its way early."

"That ought to cool the talk of war," Thomas said. "No fun campaigning in snow and mud. Wonder if it'll come to fighting?"

"That's anyone's guess," Sir Humphrey said. "What makes me laugh is the way they use roses as their badges! A red rose for the House of Lancaster, a white rose for the House of York! As though they were carrying ladies' favours at a tournament! Pretty-pretty nonsense."

"Their ambitions aren't nonsense, though," said Reginald. "They're fighting over the crown."

CHAPTER THREE

THE BUSINESS OF MARRIAGE

Nicholas and Margaret Weaver's home in the coastal village of Dunster had a characteristic smell, a mixture of oiliness and mustiness with a hint of the farmyard. It was the smell of sheep fleece, and it pervaded the whole house, even the bedchambers. Which was natural, for wool was their world.

Rents from sheep farmers accounted for much of the wealth of the Luttrell family, who lived in the castle overlooking the village. The spinning of yarn and the weaving of cloth were the main trades of the village, and the monks of Cleeve Abbey, a few miles to the east, close to a village called Washford, were industrious shepherds who brought their fleeces regularly to Dunster and did so much business there that they had a fulling mill at the western end of the village and a house of their own in North Street. The abbots of Cleeve spent nearly as much time in Dunster as they did in their monastery.

The Weaver family, who had taken their surname from their trade generations ago, were as prolific as the Lanyons were not. Nicholas, who had had some schooling and knew many well-travelled merchants, said that he had heard of people in far-off places who lived in communities known as tribes, which had usually grown from an original large family. His own cheerful, noisy, crowded family, he was wont to say, was almost a tribe.

It was a fair summing-up. They all knew how they were related to each other and they all, more or less, lived together, although sheer necessity had obliged them, eventually, to spread first of all into the house next door when the tenancy chanced to fall vacant, and later to rent the house opposite, as well.

By that time Nicholas's cousin Laurence and his richly fertile wife, Elena, had a family of formidable dimensions and it was their branch of the tribe that moved across the road, where they took to carding and yarn spinning as distinct from the actual weaving. At one time, like many other families, the Weavers had bought yarn from other cottagers, who made their living by spinning. Until it occurred to Laurence that they had hands enough to do both jobs, whereupon he set his side of the family to creating yarn. Only the fulling and dyeing had to be contracted out. Otherwise, the family bought raw fleeces and did the rest themselves.

Under Nicholas's roof, only Margaret now spun yarn. She had a knack for creating a thin, strong woollen thread which she sold, undyed, on market days, a small but useful addition to the household coffers.

Renting the third house was a wise move from every point of view. The various cousins, uncles and aunts who had been squeezed in with Nicholas and Margaret could now occupy the next-door premises. Meanwhile, as time went on, Laurence and Elena brought their family to ten, plus a daughter-in-law and three grandchildren. As yet, the youngsters were too small to be useful, but they would soon be big enough to learn to spin. They would also take up space. Laurence eased the congestion as best he could by building a workroom on to the back of his house. Nicholas likewise constructed a weaving shed to the rear of his. These additions made little difference, though. The Weavers remained much as they always had been: amiably argumentative—and crowded.

With so many mouths to feed and three rents to be paid, their prosperity had to be carefully nurtured. They grew vegetables and reared poultry in the long back gardens of the three houses and Nicholas now rented a meadow on a hillside at the seaward end of the village, where he kept not only his three ponies but also two cows. He had built a byre-cum-stable there as shelter for the animals and somewhere to store tack and winter fodder. Margaret was good at dairy work as well as spinning thread, and they had cheese and cream for everyone.

It was also a family custom to marry their daughters off early, taking their youthful appetites for food into other people's households. Sometimes even surplus boys were exported. Nicholas and Margaret had two young sons and one of them, eventually, might have to leave home. "A good rose bush needs regular pruning" was the way Nicholas put it.

And the next one to be pruned, thought their daughter Liza, *is going to be me.*

From the moment her parents arrived home from George Lanyon's funeral, she had sensed that something was in the air, though at first it wasn't clear what the something was. The return of Nicholas and Margaret chanced to coincide with a busy time. New orders for cloth had come in, and there had been a problem at the Cleeve Abbey fulling mill, which the Dunster weavers used as well as the monks, to get their cloth cleaned with water and fuller's earth before dyeing. A thunderstorm on the moors had sent quantities of peat down the Avill River and polluted the water supply. "It's always happening. Nature wants us to dye all our cloth dark brown," Nicholas grumbled. "We'll have to send it somewhere else till the river clears. Can't go delaying orders from new customers. That's bad business."

But concerned though the family had been with these matters, there had been something else on their minds. Twice Liza had walked into a room to find her parents talking to other family members, and the conversation had stopped short the moment she appeared. And she had noticed her parents glancing at her, pleasantly enough, but thoughtfully, too, as though they were wondering…

Wondering what? Liza could guess the answer to that. Indeed, she had been through all this before and was fairly sure that she recognised the symptoms. They had a marriage in mind for her and were asking themselves whether she would be pleased with it or not.

She had been expecting something like this. After all, she was the eldest daughter. She was twenty-three now and should have been wedded long ago. Three of her younger sisters were married and the little one, Jane, the infant of the family, was single only because she was as yet only seven years old. Liza had stayed unmarried so far because first one thing and then another had interfered with her parents' plans. They had arranged a very good match for her when she was sixteen, but the young man inconsiderately died of a fever before the wedding day. Another proposal came in quite soon, but the prospective bridegroom, though well-off and good-natured enough, was nearly fifty. Liza objected and neither Nicholas nor Margaret were easy about the matter, either. The argument—put forward by Aunt Cecy, one of the older family members—that she would probably become a wealthy widow before long and could then please herself, failed to convince either Liza or her parents and the negotiations died away.

There had been others, too—a suitor who changed his mind and another whose parents changed it for him because they had found a better prospect. Time had gone on.

"And now," said Margaret indignantly when at last the business problems had been overcome and the family had gathered together—without Liza—for a full-scale discussion of the proposal which she and Nicholas had brought back from Aller-brook, "and now there's gossip. Folk have such vile minds."

She broke off to cough, because during the summer they did not light the fire in the big main room and now, when autumn had set in and they needed warmth, the chimney was smoking. She had pulled her spinning wheel out of the way of possible smuts, but was still using it, important though this gathering was. The steady whirr formed a background to the business in hand.

"Liza's a good wench," she said when the coughing fit was over. "And we've said naught to her about these hints we've heard, that she's been meetin' a man in secret, because hints is all it is, and we reckon they come from jealous old women with clatterin' tongues and naught better to do than make up nasty stories about young girls who still have pretty faces and all their teeth! But it's time we got her settled—that's true enough. She's got a right to depend on us for that."

★ ★ ★

I knew it. Flat on the planks of the floor overhead, with one ear pressed to a chink between two boards, Liza felt her stomach clench in fright. Earlier that day she had heard her name mentioned in a conversation among her elders and had without hesitation done some deliberate eavesdropping. She had guessed right, it seemed. Her marriage was being planned and it seemed that her future was to be discussed this morning, in her absence. Slipping away from duties in the kitchen, she had gone to her chamber just above the main living room, and then, having taken the precaution of bolting herself in, flattened herself to the floor to eavesdrop for the second time that day.

It wasn't the sort of behaviour her parents would have approved of in any of their daughters; in fact, they would have been appalled. But then, they would be even more appalled if they knew about Christopher, Liza thought, and by the sound of it, they had heard something. She could guess the source of the rumour, as well. That wretched woman who had the cottage down by the packhorse bridge. She had seen Liza and Christopher together and must, after all, have recognised them.

Lying flat, her left cheekbone in danger of being grazed by the floor, Liza felt tears pricking behind her eyes. She tried to blink them away. She had *known* this was coming. She had *known* that, sooner or later, arrangements would be made for her and all her dreams would be destroyed. She had thought she was prepared. But now…

Oh, dear God. Oh, Christopher, my dear love. I can't bear it.

A few feet away, below Liza, Aunt Cecy was staring coldly at Margaret, who stared back in an equally chilly manner. They all addressed Cecy as *Aunt,* but she was actually the wife of Nicholas's oldest cousin, Dick Weaver, who was the son of Great-Uncle Will, the most ancient member of the tribe. Her virtue was as rigid as her backbone, and her backbone resembled a broom handle. Her mouth and body were overthin, and alone among the women of the family she had had trouble giving birth. Her two daughters had been born, with great difficulty, eight years apart, with several disasters intervening. They had both been married off at the age of fourteen and had seemed glad to leave home.

"If that girl b'ain't wed soon," Aunt Cecy said now, "her pretty face'll get lines and her teeth'll start going. Margaret, do you have to keep on with that everlasting spinning when we're talkin' over summat as solemn as this, and what in heaven's name is wrong with that there chimney?"

"I think birds must have nested in it since the spring-cleaning. We'll have to clear it. The men'd better lop a branch off that birch tree in the garden to push down it. As for spinnin', I like keepin' my hands busy," said Margaret. "I can spin and talk, *and* listen."

Aunt Cecy snorted. Laurence, who had come across the cobbled road with Elena and others of his family, threading their way past the permanent market stalls which occupied the middle of the street, said reasonably, "Never mind the tales. Nicholas here says he's had an offer. If it's a good one, where's the problem?" He was very like Nicholas, with the same hearty voice and the same robust outlook on life. "Even if she has had…let's be charitable and say a friend—in secret—what of it? Who didn't, when they were young? All that'll be over. Who is it you've got in mind?"

"Peter Lanyon," said Nicholas. "Grandson of George, whose burial Margaret and I have just been to."

"Liza's older than Peter, isn't she?" Elena said. "Does it matter, do you think?"

"Er…" said their daughter-in-law, and her husband, Laurie, a younger version of Laurence, grinned. Laurence burst out laughing and so did several of Nicholas's cousins.

"Our Katy here's two years older than young Laurie and who cares? Didn't stop them having twin sons inside of a year!" Laurence said.

"Liza ought to be married," Nicholas said. "And I've called you all in here to discuss this proposal from the Lanyons. Peter'll do as far as I'm concerned. He's good-looking and good-natured, and Richard's offered me a deal. He got me in a corner at his dad's funeral and put it to me. I've a good dowry put by for Liza, but he's suggested something more. He wants to be cut in to our business. We've always bought about half his wool clip—he sells the other half when the agents come round from the big merchants. Now he says we can have the wool for a discount if he can have a regular cut off the profits when we sell the finished cloth and yarn. He asked a lot of questions and we went into another room and he clicked a few beads round his abacus, arriving at a figure. I reckon he's judged his offer finely. He'll come out on the right side more often than not. In effect, we'll pay more for his wool, not less, only not all at once, but…"

"Looks as if he's takin' advantage." Great-Uncle Will didn't like to walk far, so he spent his days sitting about. At the moment he was in a bad temper because the smoking fire had driven him from the settle by the hearth, where he liked to sit on chilly days, driving him back to his summer seat by the window. His voice was sharp. "We want to get Liza off our hands. He'll oblige if he's paid!"

"Quite. We'll have to look on his cut from our profits as part of Liza's dowry," said Nicholas. "Getting the wool cheap won't offset it, most years anyway. But he also pointed out that once we're all one family and one business, there are things we can do to help each other. Put opportunities each other's way—things like introductions to new customers, or brokering marriages. Word to each other of anything useful like new breeds of sheep. He's thinking to buy a ram from some strain or other with better fleeces. If he does, we'll gain from that after a while. Meanwhile, we'll have got Liza settled and she'll be eating his provender, not ours."

"You must admit the man's got ideas," said Laurence, and Dick Weaver nodded in agreement. "What of the girl herself?" he asked. "Has this been mentioned to her?"

"Why should it be?" demanded Aunt Cecy. "She'd be well advised to do as she's told."

"Not yet," said Margaret. "But she won't be difficult. When was she ever? She's a good girl, is Liza, whatever silly gossip may say."

"She'd better not be difficult. If 'ee don't get that wench married," said Great-Uncle Will, "she could get into trouble and then what'll 'ee do? Get her shovelled into a nunnery while you rear her love child? I've heard that there gossip, too, and if there's truth in it, the fellow can't wed her anyhow. In orders, he is. That's what the clacking tongues are saying."

The entire family, as if they were puppets whose strings were held by a single master hand, swung around to look at him.

"I've not heard this!" Nicholas said. "You know *who* this fellow is that Liza's supposed to be meeting? Well, who is he and how did you find out so much?"

"Gossip!" said Margaret, interrupting forcefully and snagging her thread in her annoyance. "Liza's a sensible girl, I tell 'ee!"

"She knows all the ins and outs of the business," said Nicholas. "I grant you that. She's handy with a loom and an abacus, as well. She understands figures the way I do and the way that the rest of you, frankly, don't! But she gets dreamy sometimes. Don't know where she gets that from. And now folk are asking why's she still single and is there some dark reason? Sounds to me as if there maybe is and the whispers have something behind them after all! Well, Uncle Will? What have you heard?"

"I sit here by this window on warm days and folk stop to talk to me," said Will. "I didn't want to repeat the talk. Not sure I should, even now. These things often fade out if you leave them be. Don't matter if she's had a kiss in the moonlight or a cuddle in a cornfield, as long as she don't argue now." The fire belched again, swirling smoke right across the room, and he choked, waving a wrinkled hand before his face. "Devil take this smoke!"

There were exclamations of protest from all around. "That won't do, Great Uncle!" said Nicholas bluntly. "If you know a name, then tell us. Who does gossip say the man is?"

"Young fellow working up at the castle, studying with the Luttrells' chaplain, that's who," said Great-Uncle Will. "I don't know his *name,* but I know the one they mean—he's stopped by to talk to me himself. Redheaded young fellow. In minor orders yet-awhile, but he'll be a full priest one of these days. So he b'ain't husband material for Liza or any other girl. You get her fixed up with Peter Lanyon, and quick."

"I can hardly believe it." Margaret had stopped her spinning wheel.

Aunt Cecy gave her a look which said, *I told you you couldn't keep on with that and attend to this business as well,* and said aloud, "Where *is* Liza, anyway?"

"In the kitchen," said Margaret. And then stopped short, looking through the window. Liza, far from being in the kitchen, must have slipped out the front door only a moment ago. She was crossing the road, going away from the house on some unknown errand.

Uncle Will turned to peer after her. "There she goes. Well, let's hope all she wanted was a breath of air and that she b'ain't runnin' off with her red-haired swain yetawhile. You take an old man's advice. Say nothing to her about him. Pretend we don't know. No need to upset the wench. But get her wed, and fast. Get word off to Richard Lanyon tomorrow and tell him yes. That's what I say." Another wave of smoke poured out of the fireplace and he choked again. "Can't anyone do something about this? Put a bucket of water on that there fire and get to sweeping the chimney!"

CHAPTER FOUR

ONE MAGICAL SUMMER

Peter'll do as far as I'm concerned. When Liza heard her father say those words, she had heard enough. She sat back on her heels, miserably thinking, while the murmur of voices continued below her. At length she rose quietly from the floor, picked up a cloak, unbolted her door and stole out. The stairs were solid and didn't creak. She went softly down them, glad that in this house they didn't lead into the big main room as they did in many other houses, but into a tiny lobby where cloaks and spare footwear were kept, and from which the front door opened.

She could hear a buzz of talk and a clatter of pans in the kitchen. If anyone saw her, she would probably be called in to help and chided for having left it in the first place. She opened the front door as stealthily as she could, darted through, closed it and set off, crossing the road, trying to lose herself quickly behind the stalls in the middle of it, in case anyone should be looking from the window.

Bearing to the right, past the last cottages and the Abbot's House opposite, she hurried out of the village. Then she turned off the main track, taking a path to the left, crossed a cornfield and emerged onto the track that led to the next village to the west, Alcombe, two miles off.

She felt uneasy as she crossed the field, for here, as at Allerbrook, the corn had been cut and a couple of village women were gleaning in the stubble. Although they were some way off and did not seem to notice her, she was nervously aware of them.

Beyond the cornfield stood a stone pillar on a plinth, a monument to the days of the great plague in the last century. Villages then had kept strangers out in case they brought disease with them, but commerce had to go on; wool and yarn, cloth and leather, butter and cheese, flour and ale must still be bought and sold and so, outside many villages, stone pillars or crosses had been set up to show where markets could be held.

"I'll be by the plague cross at ten of the clock on Tuesday," Christopher had said at their last meeting. "I'll have an errand past there that day. The Luttrells send things now and then to an old serving man of theirs in Alcombe. He's ailing nowadays. They often use me for charitable tasks like that, and lend me a pony. Meet me there if you can. I'll wait for you for a while, though I'd better not linger too long."

It was only just past ten o'clock, Liza thought as she slipped out of the field, out of sight of the gleaning women. Had he waited? Would he be there?

He was. There was his pony, hobbled and grazing by the

track, and there was Christopher, his hair as bright as fire, sitting on the plinth.

"Christopher!"

He was looking the other way, perhaps expecting her to come along the main track instead of through the field, but he sprang up at the sound of her voice, and turned toward her. She ran into his arms and they closed about her. "Oh, Christopher! I'm so glad to see you!"

"Are you? What is it, sweeting? Something's wrong, isn't it? I can always tell."

"Yes, I know you can!"

That was how it had been from the beginning, when they met in the spring, at the May Day fair in Dunster. It had been a fine day, and the fair was packed and raucous. There were extra stalls as well as the regular ones, offering every imaginable commodity: gloves, pottery, kitchen pans and fire irons, hats, belts, buckles, cheap trinkets, questionable remedies for assorted ills, lengths of silk and linen from far away as well as the local woollen cloth, sweet cakes and savoury snacks cooked on the spot over beds of glowing charcoal. There were entertainments, too: a juggler, tumblers, a minstrel playing a lute and singing, a troupe of dancers and a sword swallower.

And, creating an alleyway through the crowd and inspiring a different mood among the onlookers, an unhappy man stripped to the waist except for a length of undyed cloth slung around his neck. Splashed with dirt and marked with bruises, he was escorted by the two men who that year were Dunster's constables. Ahead of them walked a boy banging a drum for the crowd's attention and announcing that by order of the Weavers Guild of Dunster, here came Bart Webber, who had been mixing flax with his woollen yarn to make his cloth, and selling it as pure Dunster wool, and had been fined for it at the last manor court.

It could have been worse. The hapless Master Webber hadn't been whipped or put in the stocks, and the crowd was good-humoured and not in a mood for brutality. Many of them knew him socially, which inclined them to restraint or even, in some cases, sympathy. He was still drawing a few jeers, though, and an occasional missile—handfuls of mud and one or two mouldy onions, which had caused the bruises. His situation was quite wretched enough and his face was a mask of misery and embarrassment. Liza, distressed, turned quickly away.

Her parents had often told her she felt things too deeply and ought to be more sensible. They clicked regretful tongues when she persisted in going for walks on her own or when they found her in the garden after dark—"mooning after the moon," as her father put it—or being stunned by the splendour of the constellation of Orion, making its mighty pattern in the winter sky. Yes, Nicholas said, of course the moon looked like a silver dish—or a lopsided face or a little curved boat, depending on which phase it was in—and yes, of course the stars were beautiful. But most people had more sense than to stand outside catching cold, especially when there was work to be done indoors.

Sometimes Liza felt that she was dedicating her entire life to appearing sensible when inside herself, she often didn't feel sensible at all, but wild and vulnerable, like a red deer hind, fleeing before the hounds.

Now she wanted to get well away from poor Bart Webber. Elena and Laurence, who were with her, stayed to stare but Liza, abandoning them, edged back through the crowd. Then she realised that a young man who had been standing next to

Laurence had turned away, too, and was beside her and seemed to want to speak to her. She looked at him in surprise, and he said kindly, "You didn't like seeing that, did you?"

She stopped and studied him. He wore a clerk's black gown and a priest's tonsure. The ring of hair left by the tonsure was an astonishing shade of flame-red. "I know him," she said. "Bart Webber. He's dined with us. No, I didn't like seeing him—like that." It occurred to her that the young clerk had been watching her and that this was impertinent of him. With a rush of indignation she said, "You were looking at me?"

"Forgive me," he said mildly. "But when I saw you move away alone—well, in such a throng, you shouldn't be on your own."

"I was with cousins, but they're still back there. I've other relatives somewhere about, though, and my home is over there." She pointed.

"Let me walk with you to your door, or until you find some of your family." His voice was intentionally gentle, cooling her flash of annoyance. "You never know. There could be cutpurses about."

She let him escort her and as they walked, they talked. He was Christopher Clerk, halfway to priesthood, studying with the chaplain at the castle. She was Liza Weaver, daughter of Nicholas Weaver who, with his family, owned three Dunster houses and was head of a business which carried on both spinning and weaving. "Our cloth's quite well-known, and so is my mother's special fine thread."

"You sound as though you're proud of your family," he said.

"I am! And you must be proud of your vocation, and of living in a castle! Is it very grand, with paintings and carpets from the east and silken cushions for the ladies?"

"All those things, but my quarters are plain, as they should be.

I wouldn't have it otherwise. I felt called to be a priest, and once that happens, a man doesn't seek to live in luxury."

"Do you mean you give it up even though you miss it, or you somehow don't miss it because you don't want it anymore?" Liza asked, interested. She often caught sight of the Abbot of Cleeve and his entourage of monks coming and going from their house and had many times wondered what made them choose such lives. Were they happy, always wearing such plain white wool garments and never marrying?

"Some of us cease wanting the pleasures of the senses," Christopher told her, "and others give them up. They are the price. But if you really value something, you don't mind paying for it."

"But which group are you in?" Liza asked acutely, and privately marvelled at her own outspokenness. He might well accuse *her* of impertinence! Yet it seemed easy to talk to him, as easy as though she had known him all her life.

"I'm among those who have to make an effort. But as I said, the price is worth it." She turned her head to look at his face and he gave her a grin, a tough, cheerful, entirely masculine grin, and she found herself smiling back. His eyes, which were the warm golden-brown of amber or sweet chestnuts, glowed with laughter, and without warning, her breath seemed to halt for a moment and her heart turned a somersault.

"I won't say it's always easy," he said, searching her face with his eyes, and she knew, without further explanation, with a certainty that would not be denied, a certainty as solid as the simple fact that two plus two made four, that now, this moment, was a time when it wasn't easy. That he was talking, obliquely, about her.

About them.

About us. But we met only five minutes ago!

At that moment she caught sight of her parents, apparently arguing and just going in at their door, for dinner no doubt, since it was past noon. With a few words of farewell and thanks for his company, she took her leave of Christopher and followed them into the house, to find that an argument was indeed in progress, and that it was about Bart Webber.

"To my mind, Margaret, it's enough, what he went through today. There's no need to keep on about it and say we can't have him and Alison to dine or ask them to Liza's wedding when it comes...."

"I don't agree, Nicholas. I can't. I'm sorry for Alison and I'd sooner lie dead and in my coffin than be in her shoes, but have them at my table...no, it won't do. It's makin' out we don't take honesty seriously and we do."

"But..."

Margaret would win, of course. When it came to social niceties she usually did, and as other households often followed the Weaver lead, Liza now felt sorry for Mistress Webber as well as for Bart. Her parents broke off their wrangle when they saw her and greeted her, and to her surprise, they seemed to notice nothing strange about her.

Liza herself gave the Webbers little further thought, for she was engrossed with the astounding experience she had just had, and amazed that it had apparently left no mark upon her. She felt as though it should have done; as though the wave of hair which always crept from under her neat white coif should have changed from beechnut brown to bright green, or as though luminous footprints should appear wherever she trod.

But after all, what had really taken place? Nothing that anyone could have seen, and nothing that could be repeated. Very likely she would never set eyes on the red-haired clerk again. *Whatever* had happened, it would never be repeated. She had better forget it. That would be sensible.

No doubt it would have been, but a perverse providence seemed determined to reunite them. Two mornings later, going to the herb plot at the far end of the garden to fetch flavourings for dinner, she discovered a small brown-and-white dog industriously digging a hole under the mint.

"Here, stop that! Where did you come from?" said Liza, advancing on the intruder and picking it up. It yapped at her indignantly and struggled, while Liza stood with it in her arms, wondering how it had got in. Then she saw that there was a hole under the wooden fence which bounded the end of the garden. Beyond, meadowland sloped away, down toward Dunster's harbour. It was silting up these days. Just now, the tide was out and a number of small boats from the Dunster fishing community lay aground, waiting for the sea to come back and refloat them. The sea itself was a band of iridescent blue and silver, far away, with the coast of Wales beyond.

To the right, however, the meadow was bounded by the castle hill and its covering of trees. The Luttrells' black cattle were in the pasture, and a man was hurrying across it from the direction of the trees and the castle. He saw her and waved, and came on faster. "You've got him!" he said breathlessly as he came up to the fence. "Wagtail! You wicked dog!"

"Is he yours?" Liza asked. "He shouldn't be let loose to scrabble in people's gardens. Someone might throw stones at him or kick him!"

Wagtail barked again and struggled in her arms. And then she recognised the man. He was once more in clerical black, though this time in the more practical form of hose and jerkin, and he had pulled a dark cap over his fiery tonsure. Some of his red hair was visible, though, with an oak leaf absurdly clinging to it. Christopher Clerk, the young man who had read her mind and knew that she was sorry for the swindler Bart Webber.

"I hope he did no serious damage," he said. "He belongs to Mistress Luttrell—he's her lapdog—but he's forever running off into the woods. I think he thinks he's a deerhound! Can you hand him over the fence to me?"

Liza went to do so and his eyes widened. "Don't I know you? Aren't you Liza Weaver? We met two days ago at the fair."

"Yes, yes, I am. And you're Christopher." At the fair they had stood and walked side by side. This was the first time she had stood face-to-face with him and really studied him. He had a snub nose and a square jaw with a hint of pugnacity in it, the effect both tough and boyish and remarkably attractive. His red-gold eyebrows were shapely above his smiling eyes, and once more she noticed how beautiful and unusual their colour was. That amber shade was quite different from the soft velvet-brown of her own eyes, as she had sometimes seen them when looking in her mother's silver mirror. There were a few gold flecks in the amber, and his skin, too, was dusted with golden freckles. There was a slightly denser freckling on his chin, adding an endearing touch of comedy to his face.

The hands that reached to take the struggling dog from her, though, were beautiful, strong without being coarse, the backs lightly furred with red-gold hairs, the bones clearly defined beneath the skin, the fingers and palms in perfect proportion. She found it hard not to keep gazing at them.

On his side, he was having his first clear view of her. He took in fewer details, but the little he did absorb was enough—the deep colour of the beechnut hair showing in front of the coif, the candid brown eyes, the good skin. She was tall for a girl, and within the plain dark everyday gown her body had a sturdy strength. Not that either of them felt they were studying a stranger. It was more as though they were reminding themselves of something they had known since before they were born but had unaccountably forgotten.

"The bluebells are still out in your garden," he said. His hands were now full of dog, but he nodded to the little splash of blue next to the herb plot. "There are wonderful bluebells in a dell on the other side of the castle. You can get there by the path past the mill. A few yards on, there's another little path that leads aside, leftward, to the dell. Do you know the place? Anyone can go there."

"Yes. Yes, I know it. But how do you come to know it?" Liza asked curiously. "I thought…I mean, you have your work."

"I came across it a week ago—chasing Wagtail again! He's always getting out, and whoever sees him slipping off usually goes after him—page, squire, man-at-arms, maid or cook or groom! Not the chaplain or Mistress Luttrell herself, though. They keep their dignity. I found Wagtail among the bluebells and I've been back since to see them before they fade. Father Meadowes—the chaplain, that is—gives me a passage from the Scriptures to meditate on each day, and three times I've done my meditating while walking about in the dell after dinner. At about two of the clock."

He shouldn't be saying these things. Liza knew it and so did Christopher. He shouldn't, either, have lain sleepless last night, while the girl he had met at the fair danced through his mind, glowing with light and warmth so that all thoughts of priesthood and his vocation had melted like morning mist before a summer sunrise. Now the words he ought not to say had come out, apparently by themselves.

"I walk out to take the air sometimes, too," said Liza. She smiled. "There's a leaf in your hair. Did you know?"

"Wagtail's fault. He tore straight off through the woods below the castle and I went straight after him. But it's hard going if you don't take a stick or, better still, a wood-axe along with you," said Christopher, grinning, and because he was still holding the dog, he leaned forward across the fence and let her remove the leaf from his tonsure. It was the first time they'd ever touched. It made her inside turn somersaults again.

"I must go," he said, and she watched him walk away across the meadow. He was almost a priest and her parents wouldn't like this at all, but it made no difference. Something had begun that would not be halted. At the thought of seeing him again, her spirit became as light as thistledown, dancing in the wind. Around her, the scent of the herbs, the green of the meadow, the azure of the bluebells, the distant sparkle of the sea all seemed enhanced, brighter, stronger, as though her senses had been half-asleep all her life and now were fully awake at last. She felt about as sensible as a hare in March, or an autumn leaf in a high wind.

She *would* see him again. She must.

In the afternoon she slipped away, through the village, along the path that led to the dell, and found him there and they walked together.

Three days later, although the bluebells were no longer at their best, they met there again and this time they kissed. Then they sat down on a fallen log and stared at each other in consternation.

"I'm going to be a priest. Well, I already am, in a junior way. I've been a subdeacon and six months ago I was ordained deacon. Becoming a full priest is the next step, the final one. If I...if I abandon my vocation now, my father won't take me back. He has other sons to settle. He's a merchant in Bristol, successful but not rich."

"I see. Well, you told me to begin with that you were going to be a priest. But..." Liza's voice died away in bewilderment, mainly at herself.

Christopher thrust his fingers through his tonsure. "Liza, my father and mother are both steady, reliable people. They expect their children to be steady and reliable, too, and I thought I was! And then—we met at the fair, and you smiled at me and all my good sense has flown away like a flock of swallows at the end of summer! You make me feel as though my feet have left the ground and my head's among the stars. I don't understand myself!"

He stopped running his fingers through his hair and reached out to take her hands. "What I do understand is that my world has turned upside down. Liza, as I said, I'm already in the priest-hood. To get myself released from this would be horribly diffi-cult. I'd have to go to my bishop and he'd probably say I was committed for life. I've heard of men who've bought their way out, but I have little money. I suppose I could borrow some. I know I could make my way in the world, given time, but it would be very hard at first and perhaps I'd be in debt. Would you wait for me? Would they let you wait?"

"I don't think so. They want to get me married, and they'd say that a priest can't marry and that's the end of it."

Liza knew her family. They were good-natured as a rule, though liable to shout loudly in times of crisis—if, for instance, a pot should be spilled in the kitchen or a piece of weaving be damaged or if Aunt Cecy discovered a spider in her bedchamber—but with no real ill feeling behind the uproar. Nevertheless, for all their seemingly easygoing ways, they took their work seriously; nothing slipshod was ever let past. And they expected their private life to be properly conducted, expected that parents would arrange their children's future careers and marriages and that the children would concur. The arrangements would be made with affection and consideration, but made, just the same, and with a very keen regard for respectability. What Liza was doing now would not be tolerated. She would be seen as a wanton who had tried to seduce a priest from his vocation. Her mother in particular would be horrified. Margaret prided herself on holding up her head among the neighbours.

"No, I see. I'd say the same, in their place. Liza, *what* has happened to us?"

"It's as if…this were meant to be. I was reared to be steady, sensible, like you. My father talks to me about cloth-making because sometimes I ask questions about it and he says he likes to see his daughter being interested in practical things and her family's business."

If you're taking the trouble to learn about my business, you'll do the same about your husband's business when you marry, whether he's in the weaving trade or no. I'd sooner see you with an abacus than mooning at the moon. Nicholas had said such things to her several times.

"He's taught me to keep accounts, with Arabic figures, and an abacus," Liza said. "I've always tried to be what he and my mother wanted of me. I think my parents are like yours in many ways. But now…my head's among the stars as well."

They looked at each other helplessly, two earnest young creatures who had suddenly found that common sense wasn't enough.

"Except that it can't come to anything. Dear heart. Oh, Liza, what have I done to you, letting you love me, letting myself love you? It really is like that, isn't it? I mean—love?"

To Liza's distress, there were tears in his eyes. "Yes. I don't see how I can ever marry anyone else, but they'll make me!"

"Oh, my poor Liza! *Oh!*" He cried it out in anguish. "Why can't a priest be a man as well and live as other men do? Why are we condemned to this...to rejecting human love, to being so alone? It's cruel! And there's nothing, *nothing* I can do about it, for you or for me!"

"Hold me," said Liza.

On the way home, aglow from the feel of his arms around her and the feel of his body as her arms closed around him, she came face-to-face with a small, wan woman whom she recognised as Alison Webber, the wife of the unfortunate Bart. Bart was at least forty, but Alison was his second wife and she was still very young; indeed, not yet married a year. She had been a rosy girl with bright eyes like a squirrel, but now she went about like a shadow, and Liza, troubled at the sight of her, paused to say good-day. Whereupon Alison's haunted eyes blazed at her.

"*You* wish me good-day? Your mother's the cruellest woman in all Dunster. Won't speak to me in the street, as if it was all my fault, and it isn't! Your parents should have dined with us yesterday and they cried off. And what the Weavers do, others do! If she'd put out a hand to us, it 'ud be different. She's pushed us into hell and she's done it a'purpose and I've no word to say to you. Just this!" said Alison furiously, and spat at Liza's feet before pushing past and going on her way.

No, thought Liza miserably, all the glow gone, no, there was no future for her and Christopher. Margaret would never forgive her if she knew. Never.

But all through the summer she and Christopher went on with their stolen meetings, most of them in the dell. One, by chance, was on the stone bridge which had been built across the Avill River for the benefit of packhorses carrying wool to and from Dunster market. On the bridge, shadowed by the trees that bordered the river, they hugged each other and then stood to talk and look at the water, and Liza saw someone in the garden of a nearby cottage looking at them. Alarmed, she dragged Christopher off the bridge without explaining why, which annoyed him because he thought he'd seen a trout and was about to point it out.

"A trout!" Liza gasped. "The woman who lives in that cottage has the sharpest nose and the longest ears in Dunster! If she recognised us…!"

"Never mind her nose or her ears. Unless she's got the eyes of an owl as well, she couldn't possibly have recognised us in the shade of the trees! Acting guilty like that, you've probably drawn her attention. She'll *think* about us now and start wondering who we were!"

"Oh!" Liza burst out, stamping her foot. "How I hate this secrecy!"

"Good thing we're off the bridge. You might damage it, stamping like that," said Christopher, and as he pulled her into his arms, there, once again, was that tough grin which had turned her insides to water at the fair.

They had other small squabbles later. Liza never told him of the feeling of guilt toward her family, which often kept her awake at night; nor did he tell her of his own wakeful nights, when he wondered what he was about, how it happened that the studies, the prospect of full priesthood, which had once, to him, been the meat and bread, the sweet water and glowing wine of the spirit, were now nothing but yesterday's cold pottage.

But sometimes their secret misery, forced to dwell side by side with this extraordinary thing which had come upon them and bound them together and could not be altered, seemed to turn them into flint and tinder and sparks of anger were struck, though only to be extinguished moments later by Liza's tears and Christopher's kisses and that sudden, enchanting grin as his temper faded.

They never went further than kisses, though. Their stolen embraces woke a deep hunger in them, but the common sense to which they had been bred, and the knowledge, too, that they would be breaking Christopher's solemn, priestly promise of celibacy, protected them.

"I think sometimes that we quarrel because I want you so much but I know I mustn't," Christopher said once, after one of their brief arguments.

Cautious caresses were all they would ever have of one another and they knew it. They would have this one magical summer, but never would the enchantment reach its natural conclusion, and the summer would soon be gone. As it now was. From what Liza had heard that morning, the woman with the sharp nose and ears apparently did have owl's eyes, as well. Talk had started somehow and almost certainly with her. Very likely she knew them both quite well by sight. Their secret was almost out. Only her family's kindly trust in her had kept them skeptical, but it wouldn't last.

Now, standing by the plague cross on the Alcombe road, they recognised that their time was done.

"They are arranging my marriage," said Liza. "And they've heard talk. We dare not ever meet again. It's over, Christopher."

"Oh, dear God. Don't say that!" He closed his fingers around her upper arms so tightly that she protested and he eased his grip, but his face had gone hard. "It can't be…so suddenly, so soon!"

"But we knew it was coming," said Liza miserably. "We've always known. I can't defy them and if I did—even if we ran off together—I shouldn't take you from your vocation. I know that. Only, I don't know how to bear losing you. I just don't know how to bear it."

"Nor do I!"

He drew her into the shelter of some trees, out of sight of the track, and pushed her coif back so that he could kiss her thick brown hair, and then for a long time they stood there, clasping each other so tightly that they could almost have been one entity, as they longed to be.

Parting was so painful that they did not know how to do it. Liza, gazing into his face as though she were trying to memorise it, had a sudden inspiration and pulled a patterned silver ring from the middle finger of her right hand. "Christopher! Take this! It's loose on my thickest finger, but it might fit one of yours. Please take it and wear it. I want you to have it!"

"But…how did you come by it? If someone gave it to you as a gift, should you give it away?"

"It belonged to my grandmother. When she died, Mother gave it to me. But it's always been loose, as I said. I can say I've lost it. Mother will scold because she'll think I was careless, but nothing more. Take it, Christopher, please."

He did so, trying it on his left little finger and finding that it fit quite well. Then, at last, after one final and furious kiss, they let each other go. Christopher, looking over his shoulder all the time, went to reclaim his pony, and Liza, putting her hair back under its coif, found her hands trembling. She saw him mount and waved to him, but then couldn't bear it anymore. She turned away, brushing a hand across her eyes, and started back across the field.

The women were still there, gleaning, nearer to the path now, and they looked at her curiously. One of them—Liza recognised her as Bridget, the wife of another weaver—said, "Are you all right, m'dear? You look a bit mazed and sad-like."

That was when she realised she was crying. She wiped her knuckles across her eyes. "It's nothing." They went on staring at her and she told them one small part of the truth. "I think I'm going to be married but I don't know him very well and..."

"Ah, that'll come right soon enough," Bridget said kindly. "Don't 'ee worry, now. Nicholas'll not agree to anything but what's good for thee. Don't 'ee fret a moment longer. You'll be as happy as a lark, and think of all they pretty babes that'll come!"

"Of course," said Liza, now determinedly smiling. "Of course I know you're right."

Whatever happened she mustn't have red eyes when she reached home. With a frightened jolt she realised she had been away without explanation for quite a long time, and that her parents knew there was gossip about her.

She must find an excuse for her absence. She could say she had wanted to go for a walk and when passing through the lobby had overheard her father talking about marrying her to Peter Lanyon. That she hadn't meant to listen but had accidentally heard that much. So she had walked to St. George's church to pray for happiness in her future, and then walked back across the stubble field. Yes, that would do, and if Bridget should ever mention seeing her, it would fit in.

CHAPTER FIVE 🌀

UNTIMELY AUTUMN

With an effort that felt like pulling her heart out of her body, Liza arranged another smile on her face as she approached her home, only to realise, on reaching it, that she needn't have troubled. Her family was in the middle of one of its noisy crises. Dirk, the younger of the two menservants in the Weaver establishment, was up astride the roof ridge along with her cousin Laurie, doing something to a chimney, and she could hear shouting within the house while she was still several yards away.

As she stepped inside, the smell of soot assailed her nostrils and the shouting resolved itself into confused cries of annoyance from women in the main room, and a furious bellowing from the back regions, which she recognised as the voice of one of the older cousins, Ed, declaring that soot was blowing into the fleece store and would somebody shut that accursed door before the whole lot had to be washed a second time!

She walked into the living quarters and her mother and one of the maidservants, both liberally smeared with dirt, turned from the business of sweeping up a shocking mess of soot and disintegrated bird's nest, which had apparently come down the chimney and mingled with the revolting remains of a fire over which someone had tossed a pail of water. Above it, the filthy and battered remains of what had once been a thin tree branch waved and waggled, presumably because Laurie and Dirk on the roof were agitating it. "What in the world...?" said Liza.

"The chimney were blocked," said Margaret. "Where've you been?"

"I just went out to take the air. I went to St. George's and—"

"You and your walks." But Great-Uncle Will had advised them not to challenge Liza, and Margaret, distracted by domestic upheaval, didn't at that moment want to. "Find a broom and help us out. Fine old muddle this is, I must say. Spring-cleaning in October. I never did hear the like."

No need after all for excuses or lies. She'd got away with it. Thanking the saints for her good luck, Liza made haste to be useful. Later in the day, when order had been restored and dinner eaten, her parents called her to their room, and she felt alarmed, but their faces were kind. They simply wanted to talk about her marriage. Nothing less, but nothing more, either. If her absence in the morning had aroused any doubts, they evidently didn't mean to mention them—unless Liza herself was foolish enough to be difficult. She knew her kinfolk very well indeed.

"The whole family has discussed it now," her father said, coming to the end of his explanation. "We've agreed it's a good thing for you. Peter Lanyon is young and healthy. The business side is not ideal, but it may work out well. Anyway, we intend to say yes."

"I understand," said Liza nervously. Since she had not had to invent an excuse for her absence in the morning, she had taken care, throughout the interview, to look as though the notion of Peter Lanyon as her bridegroom were a complete surprise. She added, "It's a big thing for me."

"Naturally. Have you any objection?" Nicholas asked. Her parents were both watching her sharply. Well, she'd better allay their suspicions before they voiced them. She dared do nothing else.

"No, Father. I...I'm sure it's a good thing." She must, *must* be the sensible Liza her family wanted her to be. She shuddered to think of the storm of wrath the truth would arouse, and besides, Christopher might suffer. She made herself smile again. Would she have to spend the rest of her life forcing the corners of her mouth upward when all she wanted to do was cry and cry?

Well, if so, so be it. She had no alternative.

Christopher, on his way to Alcombe, felt like crying, too, but except for that one uncharacteristic fit of emotion during their first meeting in the dell, he was not in the habit of shedding tears. He must face it. He had lost Liza for good and what had been between them must remain a secret for all eternity. They had known it would be like this one day. It felt worse than he had expected, that was all. It was like an illness, but he supposed he would recover someday. And so, of course, would Liza. At the thought of Liza forgetting him, he did find tears attempting to get into his eyes, but with a highly unclerical oath he repressed them and rode on.

At that very moment, at Allerbrook farm, another unsanctioned love affair was disturbing the air. It had been secret until now, and its emergence into the light had thrown Richard Lanyon into a dramatic fit of temper.

"*Marion Locke?* Who in God's name is Marion Locke? I've never heard of her! You're going to marry Liza Weaver—it's all settled! Who's this Marion Locke? Where did you find her? There's no Locke family round here!"

Richard Lanyon stopped, mainly because he had run out of breath. He stood glowering in the middle of the room, the same room in which George's coffin had lain awaiting its funeral. He had shouted so loudly that the pewter on the sideboard rang faintly as if trying to echo him.

"She lives on the coast. In Lynmouth, Father. I met her at the Revel there, in June."

"*Lynmouth?* That's as far as Dunster, the other way. I remember you went to the Revel. Well, half of Somerset and Devon go to it—young folk have to enjoy themselves. I've no quarrel with that, and if you've had a loving summer with some lass there, I've no quarrel with that either. Young men have their adventures. I did, in my time. But that's one thing and marriage is another. How have you managed to visit her since? Oh!" Richard glared at his son. "*Now* I recall. Two weeks back, we drove the moor for our bullocks and somehow or other you got yourself lost in a mist, you that's known the moor all your life. Came home hours late, after the cattle were all in the shippon, and said you'd mistaken the Lyn for the head of the Barle and thought you were going southeast instead of north. I thought your brains had gone begging, and all the time..."

Peter stood his ground. "Yes, I saw her then. Other times were when I said I'd ride out to see how the foals or the calves were doing. It came in useful that we're allowed to run stock on the moor. I've seen her twice a month since we first met. Marion visits relations—a grandmother and an aunt—in Lynton, at the top of the cliff, on the first and third Tuesdays of each month. We arranged it so I'd meet her in Lynton whenever I could."

"Who *is* she?" Richard spoke more calmly and with some curiosity. After all, if this unknown Marion Locke were a more profitable purchase than Liza Weaver, it might be worth indulging the boy. Nicholas would be upset, but maybe he could suggest someone else for Liza who would suit her parents better than Peter. He raised an enquiring eyebrow. Peter immediately dashed his father's hopes by replying, "The Lockes are fisherfolk. They run a boat—the *Starfish*—out of Lynmouth harbour. They—"

"Her father's a fisherman?"

"Yes, that's right. He—"

"Are you out of your mind, boy?" roared Richard. "When did fisherfolk and farming folk ever marry one another? Fisher girls can't make ham and bacon and chitterlings out of a slaughtered pig, or brew cider, or milk a cow, and our girls can't mend nets and gut mackerel!"

"Are those the things that matter?" Peter shouted back. "Marion's lovely. She's sweet. We love each other and—"

"When you're living day to day then, yes, they do matter, boy, believe me, they do! When a girl can't do the things you take for granted, that'll soon see the end of your loving summer! The autumn leaves'll fall fast enough then, take my word for it!"

"Liza Weaver's not been farm reared, either!"

"She can bake and do dairy work. She'll soon pick up the rest. *And* she'll bring a pile of silver and a cut into the Weaver profits along with her. What sort of dowry has this Marion got, I'd like to know? Well? Tell me!"

"I never asked. Not much, perhaps, but—"

"I'll tell you how much! Nothing! Fisherfolk never have a penny to spare. They put all their money into their boats. Marion Locke, indeed! You can forget this Marion, right away. I'll—"

"Father, she's beautiful. And we're promised to each other." Peter raised his chin. "We're betrothed and—"

"Oh no, you're bloody well not!" shouted Richard. "Not unless I say so and you needn't go trying to get Father Bernard on your side, either! I won't have it and that's that. I'll see this girl's father and see what he has to say about it, and I'll be very surprised if he doesn't agree with every word I say. Who is he? What's his name?"

"He's well respected in Lynmouth. He's Master Jenkin Locke and he lives by the harbour in the cottage with the birds made out of twisted thatch along the ridge of his roof. He made them himself. The *Starfish* is one of the finest boats—"

"Be quiet! Just forget about Marion Locke, as from now! And...what is it?" Hearing a sound at the door, Richard swung around and found a timid-looking young girl there with bare feet, a shawl wrapped around her and a lot of straw-coloured hair trailing from under a coif that was badly askew. "Who the devil are you?"

"I'm...I'm sorry, sir. But the mistress sent me—Mistress Deborah. I'm Allie, sir, her maid...."

"Allie! Oh, of course! But what brings you...is something wrong? With Mistress Deborah!" Suddenly he was taut and alert, his eyes fixed on Allie, Peter's vagaries for the moment quite forgotten.

"Yes, sir, dreadful wrong!" Allie was near tears. "She's so ill, sir. I've called the priest. She took a chill the day after the…the funeral, sir, when she fell in the river, for all you give her your cloak, and she's worse and she's sent me to fetch you, sir. She wants to see you…."

Richard turned at once to his son. "Go and saddle Splash for me, while I get my cloak. Allie, is anyone with your mistress now—any other woman?"

"Yes, sir, our neighbour. But she'll not be able to stay long. She has children and—"

"She won't have to stay long. I'll take you down to the village with me on my horse."

"But sir, I've never been on a horse."

"You'll get up behind me and hold tight and we'll be there in a trice. She'll need you. Go with Peter and wait for me. Go on!"

CHAPTER SIX

THE LOCKES OF LYNMOUTH

"I swore I'd never forgive the Sweetwaters for crashing into my father's cortege," said Richard Lanyon grimly. "Now there's something else I'll never forgive them for, in this world or the next. They as good as killed Deb Archer, that's what! If Humphrey Sweetwater ever meets me in a lonely place, he'll wish he hadn't!"

"Master Lanyon, I don't like to hear you talking like that." Father Bernard had conducted Deb's burial service with dignity, tacitly accepting Richard's presence as natural without making any reference to the reason for it. In the priest's eyes, however, this outburst went too far. It had also been too loud. In the group of mourners now moving out of the churchyard, heads had turned and brows had been lifted. Father Bernard put a hand on Richard's arm to halt him. "It's not wise to raise your voice so much," he said. "What if the Sweetwaters hear of it?"

"Maybe it'll stir their consciences!" Richard was unrepentant. "Poor, poor Deb. Never harmed a living thing and everyone who knew her was the happier for it." He was going to miss her more than he had dreamed possible. She had been friend as well as mistress—someone to talk to and laugh with as well as to sleep with. "And now I've watched her being put in the ground, all because of the bloody Sweetwaters!" Richard thundered.

"I'm sorry, too, Father." Peter, who had been walking with them, had stopped beside Richard. "Everyone is."

"Her little maid, Allie, said she was chilled when she came home all wet that day," Richard said. "But she still went out again after she'd changed, so as to come to my father's burial. Sun was out, but there was a sharpish wind. Allie told me she fell ill next day. Looked like a bad cold at first, but two days after that she started coughing and in two more days, she was in delirium and Allie was sending for the priest and for me, and she died that night, with me holding her. All because the Sweetwaters...!"

Fury choked him. Shaking off Father Bernard's hand, he jerked his head at Peter to follow, and strode out of the church-yard, not turning toward Deb's cottage where the other neigh-bours were going for the funeral repast, but turning the other way instead, evidently making straight for home.

"He's grieving," said Peter awkwardly to the priest.

"Yes, I know. You'd better go with him. Look after him."

"If I can," said Peter, and set off in his father's wake.

Kat and Betsy had a meal ready in the farmhouse. Richard ate it in a stormy silence, which Peter decided not to break. After-ward, when the two women had left for their own cottages, father and son repaired to the big main room where a good fire had been lit. Some saddlery in need of cleaning lay on the floor, to provide occupation for the evening. They lit candles, since it was October and darkness was closing down already. With only the two of them in the house, it had an echoing, empty feel.

"It's time we had more folk about this place, more helping hands and a mistress for our home." Richard broke his silence at last. He picked up a bridle and put some oil on a cleaning cloth, but fixed his eyes on Peter, in no kindly fashion. "Now I've something to say to you. What with Deb dying, I've not spoken to you again about Liza Weaver, but nothing's changed. You'll marry Liza and I'll hear no more talk of this girl Marion. Understand?"

Peter, in the act of reaching for a saddle, put it down again and drew a sharp breath. "I'm sorry, Father, I truly am, but…"

"Look here, boy!" Richard glared at him and his voice became aggressive. "I want to *make* something of this family, to wipe the lofty looks off those damned Sweetwater faces, even if we can't chop their heads off their shoulders. Last century, before my time, let alone yours, there was a big rising in the southeast of England. It got put down, but it left its mark. Higg and Roger would have been villeins then, with no right to leave Allerbrook and go somewhere else, but they're free men now and they can go if they want to. The rising was because—"

"I thought it was the plague that set men free," said Peter. "So many folk died that villeins were left without masters and no one could stop them going where they liked—and asking wages when they found masters who had no one to work the land and weren't in any position to argue."

"The plague and the rising together made the difference, so I've heard," said Richard. He moderated his tone, trying to be patient. "The one made the other stronger. But the rising was about people like us getting bone weary of having people like the Sweetwaters lord it over us. *When Adam delved and Eve span, who was then the gentleman?* That's what the rebels used to chant. What makes the Sweetwaters think they're so wonderful? My father sent me to school, though he could have used my hands on the land by then, because he wanted me to have a chance in life and not speak so broad that no one could understand me that wasn't born in the west country. Later I sent you, too—and paid through the nose for it!"

"Yes, Father, I know, and I'm grateful, but—"

"No buts, if it's all the same to you. We can read and write, just about; we can talk proper English and understand the Paternoster in Latin; we can add up our accounts and we know a bit of history. What have the Sweetwaters got that we haven't? Land and money, that's all. Well, that's what I'm after, and seeing my only son hitch himself up with a fisher girl ain't going to help. Liza Weaver's another matter. We could gain a lot from that, could start saving. I'm relying on you making a good marriage to give us a leg up in the world. You can just forget Marion!"

"But, Father…" Peter, too, was now trying to be calm and patient. "We've said the words that make it a contract."

"Without witnesses, and her a maiden in her father's house? Those words were never said, my boy, and that's that."

"But they *were* said, and they're binding."

"I see. You'll challenge me, will you? The young stag's lowering his antlers at the herd leader, is he?" Richard abandoned patience, rose to his feet, laying aside his own work, and unbuckled his belt. Peter also stood up. He was taller than his father and though not as broad, he had in him the coiled-spring vitality of youth. The two of them faced each other.

"Father Bernard told me to look after you," said Peter seriously. "So I wouldn't want to hurt you, but if you try that, I might. I'll fight. I mean it."

"My God!" Richard stared at him. The candlelight was shining on Peter's face. "You've had her, haven't you? There's nothing turns a boy into a man the way that does. She's let you...and you still want to *marry* her?"

Peter was silent, remembering. September, it had been; not the day of the heavy mist, which had been a brief and chilly meeting, but the time before, which was in warm, sunny weather. They had met as usual close to Lynton, the village at the top of the cliff, and wandered into the nearby valley, with its curious rock outcrops. He had left his pony to graze while he and Marion took a goat path up the hillside, through the bracken, untroubled by the flies which in summer would have surrounded them in clouds.

On a patch of grass, hidden from the path below by a convenient rock, they sat down to talk and caress. They had done as much before, but this time it went further. Marion made no protest and soon he was past the point of no return, far adrift on the dreamy seas of desire and at the same time full of energy and the urgent need for pleasure.

The memory of it, of Marion, of her curves and warmth and moistness, her murmurs and little cries of excitement, her arms around him like friendly ropes, the rustle of a stray bracken frond under his left knee, the scent of warm grass and Marion's hair, which she had surely washed with herbs, and then the splendour of his coming, were beyond putting into words and, in any case, they were not for anyone else to share.

"Yes," he said now. "I want to marry her. I intend to."

"We'll see about that," said Richard. "I'm going to Lynmouth tomorrow, to find the Lockes. I'll see what they have to say! And now I'm going to bed and you can damned well finish cleaning the saddlery. And you can tell that priest that I don't need looking after!"

His father, thought Peter bitterly as Richard stalked out of the room, was turning out as big a bully as George Lanyon had ever been.

The sky the next day was dull but dry and Richard left Allerbrook at dawn, a nosebag for Splash on his shoulder. He rode down the combe, through Clicket and then out over the moor, following the ancient tracks made by the vanished people who had buried their chieftains in hilltop barrows and had raised the strange standing stones one saw here and there amid the heather.

The tracks led across the high moor and brought him at last to the East Lyn River—which his besotted son could not conceivably have mistaken for the Barle, since the high ridge known as the Chains lay between them. He rode downhill beside the tumbling stream, on a steep path through bracken and trees, came to a fork, took the branch that bypassed Lynton village at the top of the cliffs and went on down to its sister village, Lynmouth, at the foot.

Here there was a harbour, with a quay and a square stone building with a smoking vent, where herring were dried. The tide was in and so were a couple of big ships and a fleet of small boats, which were being unloaded. Both men and women were bringing netting and baskets of fish onto the quay, and buyers were already clustering around them. Close by stood the thick-walled thatched cottages of the fisherfolk.

He looked for a roof decorated with birds made of twisted

straw, and found it at once. It was one of the larger cottages, which suggested that the Locke family was comparatively prosperous. But still nowhere near as well-off as he was, he thought grimly. This was not the place to find a new mistress for Allerbrook farm, even if the girl Peter had in mind was respectable, which he doubted.

There was a hitching post beside the cottage. He secured Splash, loosened the girth and ran up the stirrups, gave the horse his nosebag and went purposefully to knock at the door of the cottage. It was ajar and opened when he rapped, but he paused politely, waiting for someone to come. The door opened straight into a living room and kitchen combined; he could see a trivet and pot, set over a fire, and a woman stirring the pot. Another woman was standing over a whitewood table close to a window, no doubt for the sake of the light, and gutting fish with a ferocious-looking knife. A third, broom in hand, was now advancing to ask him his business. He knew at once that this was Marion.

Peter had said she was beautiful, but it was the wrong word. Inside his head Richard struggled to find the right one and found himself thinking *luscious,* like the pears and plums which grew beside the southernmost wall of Sweetwater House. It was sheltered there, with good soil, and the fruit was always so full of juice that it seemed about to burst through the skin.

Village boys were employed as bird scarers and when the fruit was ready to harvest, they were paid with a basketful each. Richard himself, as a lad, had sometimes helped to frighten off the starlings, and been paid with pears and plums, the taste of which he had never forgotten.

This girl called them to mind. Her working gown was a dull

brown garment, but within it, her shape was so rich and full that he had hard work not to stare rudely. He saw, too, that her hair, which was not concealed by any cap or coif, was extraordinary. It wasn't so much curly as wiry and it was an astonishing pale gold in colour. She had pulled it back and knotted it behind her head, but much of it was too short for that and stood out around her head in a primrose cloud. It was clean hair, too. She looked after it.

Beneath it, her face was round, but there were strong bones within that seeming softness and she had long, sloe-blue eyes, full and heavy with knowledge and an unspoken promise to impart it.

And she was aware of him, of his dark good looks, and young as she was—sixteen, seventeen?—she knew something about men. He couldn't blame Peter for falling for this. But all the same...good God, Peter was welcome to his wild oats. No one in their senses grudged a young man that. But marriage—that was different.

"Are you Marion Locke?" It came out harshly, as though he were angry with her.

"Yes, that I be." Her accent was thick. Her looks might be remarkable but he doubted if she knew *A* from *B*.

"My name is Richard Lanyon. I believe you know my son, Peter. Is your father at home?"

"Aye. Down on the quay, he be. You want to talk to 'un?"

"I certainly do...ah!"

The woman who had been stirring the pot had put her spoon aside and come toward them. "What is it, Marion?"

"Gentleman axin' for dad. Name of Lanyon." Marion smiled beguilingly, as though she imagined he was here to settle the marriage arrangements. *You're wrong, my wench,* said Richard to himself.

"Then go and fetch 'un," said the woman. "He'm unloading the boat. You can take over from 'un. And ax the gentleman in!"

"I'll want to come back with 'un," said Marion querulously, standing aside to let Richard enter. "With Dad, I mean. I've met the gentleman's son and it'll be about me."

"All the more reason for you to keep out of it. Send your father back here and you stop down there and get that there boat emptied. Go on!"

Marion clearly didn't want to go, and pouted. Her mother stared at her fixedly, however, and after a moment she left.

"I don't want to offend anyone, least of all a man and wife in their own home." Richard, sitting by the fire with his hat on his knees, was conscious of being on someone else's territory. Not that it was much of a territory. It seemed to consist of this main room, half the size of the one at Allerbrook, an upper half-floor, reached by a ladder, where he could see some pallet beds, and a small back room, partly visible through a half-open door. In there, he could see a workbench with what looked like some half-made garment thrown over it.

A wise arrangement, no doubt, if one wanted to keep bits of thread out of the cooking and bits of fish out of the stitchery. Dried fish hung from the beams above his head, and there were scales and innards all over the table. His farmhouse was plain, but it had a decent oak front door and two spare bedchambers and even a parlour. They weren't used much, but they were there. *This* place was squalid. It also reeked of fish. The smell was far stronger and much more disagreeable than the woolly odours of Nicholas Weaver's home.

Manners, however, were manners. "I'm here on an awkward errand," he said, "but likely enough, you'll feel the same way as I do. You'll be Master Locke, I think?" He addressed the elder of the two men who had come up from the quay shortly after Marion had left. The younger one had the same pale, wiry hair as Marion. The hair probably came from the father, if the older man were he, though his mop was turning grey. "And you—" he looked at the woman who had been tending the pot "—are Mistress Locke?"

"That's right," the older man said. "That's my wife, Mary, and this here's my son Art and this is my daughter-in-law Sue." Sue was the one who had been gutting fish. She had left her work and joined the rest of them on seats by the fire. She had a smiling pink face, and by the look of her, was expecting a baby in a few months' time.

"And the wench who came to fetch us," said Master Locke senior, "is my daughter Marion. I've a notion it's her you want to talk about. She said it could be. She said she knows your son."

Art said glumly, "Here we go again."

"She does know him," said Richard, plunging straight to the point, "and it's difficult. But I'm Richard Lanyon from Allerbrook farm, far over the moor. I rear sheep and grow corn and sell wool. It's a different life from yours. My boy Peter met your Marion at last summer's Revel and he says they've agreed to marry but…there's no use going all round the moor about it. I've other plans for Peter. Besides, I don't think he's right for your girl, or she for him. What do you think?"

"I suppose the lad claims they've betrothed themselves?" said Master Locke. He didn't sound surprised.

"More or less, yes."

"That'll be the third time," said Marion's mother crossly. "All the lads go after her, she's got such a pretty face." Richard heard this understatement with amazement. Did these people, who lived together as a family, never actually look at each other? *Pretty?* A girl as striking as Marion? You might as well say the sea was wet.

"Aye, she'll promise anything to anyone and go further, very likely," Art said. "Reckon she did go further last year, with that young sailor off that ship from Norway that had some foreign name. *Fjord-Elk,* that's it. Dunno what it means. She's in port again now. I wouldn't be surprised if Marion isn't on the lookout for that young fellow now this minute."

"You don't need to worry," Master Locke assured Richard. "She needs to be married and soon will be, but to someone like ourselves. There's a likely boy in Porlock, along the coast. Too many folk round here are cousins of ours and the priest won't have that. You did right to come and warn us, but nothing's going to come of this. Two silly young people get together and say things, but we don't need to take no notice. I say nothing about your son, but Marion's always saying things to young men, mostly the wrong ones. Will you take a dish of stew and a drop of ale with us?"

"I'll take our share down to Marion," said Art, "and we'll eat and drink together and I'll tell her I'm tired of her foolishness."

"It's natural, at her age. She's barely seventeen," his father said tolerantly. "We're an easy-natured lot," he said. "We don't watch each other. Marion's daft and the boys round here turn her head with their sweet talk, but I'll see it don't come to anything."

"She b'ain't in the family way yet," Mistress Locke said. "That I do know. And she'd better not be, till she'm wed."

"He meets her in Lynton when she goes visiting there, so my son says," Richard said cautiously, concealing his relief at learning that Peter had at least not got his sweetheart into trouble. He had wondered, but it was a difficult question to ask.

"Aye." Marion's father nodded. "My mother-in-law and my wife's sister that's crippled with the joint evil live up there—they've got a cottage and a bit of land at the far end, just outside that valley with the funny-looking rocks in it. Maybe you know it...?"

"Yes, I went there once," said Richard. It had been long ago, when he was young and had gone to the Revel, just as Peter had done in the summer. He'd taken a girl into the Valley of the Rocks, as many people called it. "I know where you mean," he said.

"Marion takes fish to my mother and sister twice a month and brings back eggs and goat cheese for us. They keep hens and pasture a few goats in the valley—there's others do the same—and their maidservant does the milking and makes the cheese," said Mary Locke. "I wouldn't like to stop Marion's visits. They'd be hurt if she didn't go regular, as they're fond of her, and they like the fresh fish. And *we'd* miss the eggs and cheese. I've no time to go up there, mostly, and Sue here can't just now. But don't fret. It'll lead nowhere. It don't do for fisherfolk and farming folk to marry. We don't understand each other's lives. That pot of stew's about ready. It's not fish." She grinned, displaying gaps in her teeth but a wealth of good nature. "Last time Marion went, she bring down a nice plump chicken as well, all plucked and drawn ready. Chicken stew, this is. Sue, get the ale."

Richard reached home to find that Peter's friend Ned Crowham had ridden in and that as usual, Kat and Betsy, impressed by his velvet doublet and silk shirt and the polish on his boots, had put him in the parlour, lit a fire especially for him and plied him with mutton pie and the best cider.

"Good day, sir," said Ned civilly as Richard walked in. "I thought you might be out driving ponies off the moor or something of that kind at this time of year, but I took a chance and I found Peter here, though he's had to go out to the fields now. Kat and Bet said I must eat before I set out for home again." He chuckled. "As though I hadn't flesh enough already! They said you'd gone to Lynmouth."

"Yes. You'd nearly guessed right about the ponies, though. We'll be bringing them in tomorrow. We fetched the cattle two weeks back." Richard helped himself to cider.

"I heard from Betsy that congratulations were in order and that Peter's going to marry Liza Weaver. I told him it was a good match."

"Did you, now? And what did he say?"

"He thanked me. What else would he do?"

"Hah! Well, if he's out on the land, he won't overhear anything." Richard planted himself on a settle and unburdened his soul. "You're his friend and I fancy you're no fool. I wish you'd try and talk sense into him. Liza's the right girl for him, but he doesn't think so. I've been to Lynmouth today to see the family of a girl—a fisher girl, would you believe it?—that he's got himself mixed up with. They agree with me that it won't do, but how the boy could be such a wantwit...!"

"Mixed up with? You don't mean...?"

"No, she's not breeding, though I've a feeling that that's just luck!"

"No wonder he was so quiet when I congratulated him," Ned remarked. "But I doubt if I can talk to him, you know, sir. I don't think he'd listen to me. I'm fond of him, but..."

"He's got an obstinate streak. You needn't tell me! You youngsters!"

"You're not so old yourself, Master Lanyon," said Ned with a smile. "Will you think me impertinent if I ask if you've ever thought to marry again yourself?"

"Not impertinent, though not your business either. I've been content enough single." Ned knew nothing of Deb Archer and Richard saw no need to tell him. "What brought you here today?" he asked.

"Why, to ask both you and Peter to my own wedding. My family have found me a lovely girl, from east Somerset, near where Peter and I went to school. We're to marry in the new year. If Peter and Liza are married by then, he must bring her, too."

The Luttrells heard Mass each day in the castle, said by Father Meadowes, but on Sundays they and their household came down into the village and joined their tenants in worship at the fine church which Dunster shared with the Benedictine monks of St. George's Priory. It was an uneasy partnership, with frequent arguments about who could use the church when, and who was to pay for what, but the Luttrells—mainly by dint of donations to the priory and regular dinner invitations to the prior—did something to keep relations smooth between the villagers and the monks.

To the villagers, they were familiar figures: fair, bearded, broad-built James Luttrell, putting on weight in his thirties; his wife, Elizabeth, who had been born a Courtenay, no longer a young girl but still good-looking because of her well-tended complexion and the graceful way she managed her voluminous, trailing skirts and the veiling of her elaborate headdress; their well-dressed young son, Hugh; their household of servants and retainers, and the castle chaplain, always known as Father Meadowes because he did not like the custom of addressing priests by their first names, along with his assistant, Christopher Clerk.

All the week, Liza had said to herself, *On Sunday Christopher will be in church. On Sunday I shall see him.*

She was seeing him now. The Luttrell family had benches near the front while the rest of the congregation stood behind them, but Christopher had placed himself to one side, and was able to glance over his left shoulder and scan the body of the church without it being too noticeable. He caught her eye and let a smile flicker across his face. Liza smiled, too, when her parents weren't looking.

Afterward, when the service was over, everyone trooped out as usual through the round-arched west door built by the Normans who had founded the priory, and gathered in sociable clusters among the graves, exchanging news and dinner invitations with neighbours. The Luttrells were accosted by the prior, who wished to complain that some unknown person, presumably from the castle, had carved a pattern into one of the benches and he wanted the miscreant brought to justice.

Mistress Elizabeth shook her head gravely, although the fact that she had her little brown-and-white dog under her arm, and he was struggling to get loose, somewhat spoiled the effect. Father Meadowes had also stopped to listen to the prior's complaint but Christopher, who had been walking respectfully in the rear, moved unobtrusively aside and stood looking up, as if studying a gargoyle on the church roof.

Her own family had fallen into conversation with a group of neighbours. Liza, grown cunning through desperation, drifted gently away as if to approach a group of chattering girls, all acquaintances of hers, but passed them and used them as a shield as she came to Christopher's side and paused, also looking upward.

"That gargoyle," said Christopher, pointing, "is supposed to be the face of the prior who was here when the church was being partly rebuilt, not so long ago. So Father Meadowes says. It isn't very flattering, is it?"

"No, it isn't. I should think the stonemason hated the prior."

"I think that, too, but Father Meadowes doesn't know any more. Liza, I can't bear it. I can't go on to become a priest. I've made some enquiries, discreetly. It's unlikely that I can get legally free of the church but I can still run away from it. Will you run away, too, and come with me?"

At any moment the group of girls might move away and her family would see her talking to a young man. Christopher, pointing up at the roof, was apparently instructing her on history or architecture, but that would be a poor protection if the whispers her parents had heard had hinted at the identity of her illicit suitor. But she couldn't answer him quickly, not over a thing like this. She must say, "Christopher, I need time to think." She must be sensible....

Christopher...

The sensible thing to do was to say, *No, we mustn't. It's wrong. The church would hunt us down. My family would never forgive me. I'm sorry, but I can't.*

Unfortunately—or fortunately, and only time would tell which estimate was the right one—she had lost the fight to be sensible. Liza-in-Love and Liza-the-Sensible had striven one with another all through the summer, and Liza-in-Love had won. She and Christopher belonged together. They had met as though they had been moving toward each other since the beginning of time and there was nothing to be done about it. And yet—to leave her family, to abandon her good name for an unknown future with a man she could never lawfully marry... that was as terrifying as jumping off a cliff. Even though she would be hand in hand with Christopher.

She stared at him, poised equidistant between two opposites and unable to speak.

"We could make for London," he said. "I'll have to shave this tonsure off on the way—and keep a cap on wherever I go till my hair grows again. I do have *some* money, if not much. I've been saving my pay all summer...half planning. We'll get to London. London's very big. We'll be lost in all the crowd. We might even marry eventually, though not yet because they'll be looking out for us. The church has a very long arm. We'll have to find a small church to attend on Sundays and stand modestly at the back. We'll take new names and for the time being we'll just say we're married. Or we might go to France. I speak French well. Sweetheart, don't be afraid. I'll make my way. I understand merchanting. I was brought up in the midst of it. I'll find a merchant somewhere who needs a clerk. Believe me, I *will* make a life for us!"

There it was again, that vigorous grin. "It'll be just lodgings at first, but one day we'll rent a little house. Here or in France, we'll manage. There'll be children. Just an ordinary, everyday life, but we'll be together. If that's what you want."

"It's all I can imagine wanting," said Liza. And closed her eyes for a moment, so as not to see the rocks at the foot of the cliff, and jumped. "Yes," she said in a low voice. "I'll come. But Christopher...even if we can't marry, can't we at least take vows?"

He glanced around. The girls were still chattering together; beyond them, the prior was still monopolising the Luttrells and Father Meadowes, and Liza's family was still deep in conversation with their friends. Rapidly, in a low voice, he said, "I, Christopher Clerk, promise before God that I take thee, Liza Weaver, as my wedded wife."

Also rapidly and in an undertone, Liza said, "And I, Liza Weaver, promise before God that I take thee, Christopher Clerk, as my wedded husband. There!"

"It's not valid," said Christopher. "Not in the eyes of the church. But it's valid for me, my love. When and where can we meet? I'm often free for a while after dinner, just as I always was, though I do more study now, so the best time would be later than it used to be. About three of the clock would be right, I think."

"Won't we need horses?"

"Horses!" For a moment he looked appalled. "Horses—of course! My wits are going, I think. Well, one thing I daren't do is steal horses from the Luttrells. Can you get hold of any horses?"

"My father has three ponies. We all use them. They're family animals…as much mine as anyone's. I don't think they'll come after us for horse theft! But Christopher, they suspect something—they watch me these days. Yesterday they wouldn't let me go out for a walk alone. I can go into the garden, though!" She was thinking aloud. "I could get away over the meadow at the back. That's easy for you to reach, too. You mean we'd set off at once?"

"Yes."

"We could meet and go straight to the paddock. Tomorrow?"

"No, Tuesday. Mondays I do some study with the chaplain after dinner and if I don't appear, he'll look for me. We need a head start if we're to get away safely. But Tuesday, yes, unless it's pouring with rain. If it is, then the first day when it's not. If Tuesday is dry—then that's the day."

CHAPTER SEVEN

FLIGHT

N ed stayed overnight but didn't broach the matter of Peter's love affair. Richard did not discuss his visit to Lynmouth, either, and Peter, though he knew well enough where his father had been, asked no questions. The next day Ned left. Peter still asked no questions. Richard, grimly, knew what the boy was up to. He was just going to blank Liza Weaver out of his mind and pretend she didn't exist. Well, that ploy wasn't going to succeed. Even if Liza had never been born, Marion Locke was an impossibly unsuitable bride for Peter Lanyon. It was time to talk to the boy again.

This, however, was the day when they and their neighbours went to fetch the ponies in from the moor, to check their condition, separate the foals from their mothers and choose the ones to be sold. It meant rising early and snatching breakfast on one's feet, with no time for family wrangles. Afterward they would dine with the Rixons, whose farm adjoined theirs farther down the hillside. It would be a late dinner and they'd come home tired, with a dozen chores to do before a hurried supper. There would be no good opportunity in the evening.

However, the matter was so urgent that Richard finally blurted it out when he and Peter were riding close behind the herd as it trotted, all tossing manes and indignant white-ringed eyes, through the narrow lane that led to the Clicket pound. Just then, they were out of earshot of their fellow herdsmen, who were some way behind. Richard seized his chance.

His son's reaction was pure outrage.

"You're lying!" Peter said fiercely. "Telling me that Marion's betrothed herself to others beside me! She wouldn't! She couldn't! Betrothal's serious—it's nearly as binding as marriage, and—"

"I've seen the girl and I've talked to her father. I don't blame you for going head over heels for her, boy, but she's not for marrying. What you've got," said Richard brusquely, "is an attack of sex. We all get it. It's like having the measles or the chicken pox. If you wed her, the day would come when you'd be sorry. She's a lightskirt. I tell you—"

"No, I'll tell *you*. If when you were betrothed to my mother someone had called her a lightskirt, how would you have felt? What would you have said?"

"No one would have said such a thing, that's the point, you damned young fool—can't you see it? Why, your mother'd hardly as much as kiss me until we'd both said *I will*. Can you say that of Marion?"

"I'm not going to talk about this. I'm betrothed to her and that's the end of it," said Peter, and spurred his mount up onto the verge alongside the track, shouting at the herd to hurry them up, his face averted from his father and likely, thought Richard bitterly, to remain that way for a very long time indeed.

It was all the more annoying because the fury emanating from Peter had almost intimidated him, and Richard was not going to tolerate being bullied by his own son. He knew he would be wise not to try physical force to make Peter obey him, but there were other methods. One way or another, Peter, that ill-behaved pup, must be brought to heel.

And he was beginning to see how he might achieve it. Since her death, he had more than once dreamed at night of Deb Archer, but oddly enough, last night she'd turned into Marion halfway through the dream.

Maybe that cheeky, overweight, well-bred friend of Peter's, Ned Crowham, was right. Maybe he ought to get married again after all.

There'd be no advantage, socially or financially, in marrying Marion Locke, but now that he'd seen her...

Peter hadn't got her with child, but probably that was because he hadn't had chances enough. That didn't mean she wouldn't have babies once she was a wife. It would be a pleasant change for Allerbrook to have children about the place. His and Marion's; Peter and Liza's. Peter's marriage would be the one to bring the material benefits. And it would show Peter who was master. Oh, yes indeed.

It wouldn't do to have Peter under the same roof as Marion, of course. No, that would be daft. But there was a good-sized cottage empty just now, over on the other side of Slade meadow, where Betsy's son and his wife and children had lived before the young fellow took it into his head to go off to the other side of Somerset because he'd heard life was easier there, away from the moors that were so bleak in winter. And off he'd gone, depriving Allerbrook of two pairs of adult hands and several youthful ones. George had been alive then and he hadn't been pleased. He'd said that all of a sudden he could see the point of villeinage.

Still, the cottage was there, and once Peter was installed in it with Liza, he needn't come to the farmhouse often. He wouldn't come at all, except when his father was there; Richard would see to that. Once the boy had settled down and seen what Liza was worth and got some youngsters of his own, and Marion had a few as well, wanting her attention, getting underfoot and thickening her midriff, Peter's infatuation would die away.

Marion would probably breed well. She looked strong, quite unlike his poor ailing Joan. It was an idea.

It was a most beguiling idea.

"Where's Liza?" Margaret called to Aunt Cecy as she came down the stairs from her bedchamber. "In the weaving shed? It's time we were talking of her bride clothes, and I must say I'm surprised that Peter Lanyon hasn't been over to see her. A girl's entitled to a bit of courting."

"Farm folk are different from us," said Aunt Cecy. She was patching one of Dick's shirts, though because her eyesight was faulty nowadays, she had Margaret's small daughter beside her to thread needles. "She'll have to get used to a lot that's different, out there on Allerbrook. She's not in the shed. She went into the garden with a basket—said something about fetching in some mint."

"I'll call her," said Margaret, and hastened out through the rear of the house.

Five minutes later she returned, frowning, and once more went upstairs. Great-Uncle Will, back in his familiar winter seat beside the hearth, remarked, "Looks as if Liza's not in the garden. Funny."

"She'll have slipped off somewhere," Aunt Cecy said. "She's always had a fancy for going walking on her own, but Margaret told her she wasn't to go out by herself anymore."

"I did indeed," said Margaret, reappearing on the staircase. "But she's not in the garden and not upstairs, nor is she in the kitchen or at her loom. I've looked. And I've just been into her chamber and her toilet things are gone—the brush and comb and the pot of goose grease she uses for her hands. So I opened her chest and I could swear some of her linen's missing. I don't like it."

Aunt Cecy said, "I can't see so clear as I used to, but I thought I saw her talking to a fellow in the churchyard when we came out of the service on Sunday. He were pointing out something on the church roof. Looked harmless, but..."

"She might have gone across to see Elena for something," said Margaret uncertainly.

"And she'd take her linen and toilet things for that, would she? Better look for her," said Great-Uncle Will. "And fast."

"So she's not in any of our houses," said Nicholas, who had been hurriedly fetched from the inn at the other end of the village, where he had been talking to a potential buyer of his cloth. "You've made sure, you say, Margaret. And she's not in any of our gardens and some of her things are gone." He turned to Will. "Great-Uncle, you said that according to the gossip that's going about, she's been meeting a red-haired clerk from the castle. I think I've seen him at church with the Luttrells."

"That's him. And that's what's being said, yes," said Will.

"The fellow I saw her talking to on Sunday were outside the church and he had his cap on. But he were all in black, like a clerk," said Aunt Cecy.

"I wish we knew his name," said Nicholas, "but I think we know enough. I'm going up to the castle. Now."

"Why is it," grumbled James Luttrell, standing in his castle hall, wishing he could sit down to a peaceful supper and irritably aware that any such thing was out of the question for the time being, "why is it that trouble is so catching? The whole world's disturbed these days and it spreads like plague. There's no good government in the land, with all this squabbling between the king and these upstart cousins of his, Richard of York and his sons. What's it matter if the king is weak in his mind? He's been crowned and anointed and that ought to be good enough for any man."

"But the point is..." began Father Meadowes, normally a stern and self-confident priest but unable to stem James's irrelevancies.

"No one has any proper sense of their duty anymore. Even priests aren't staying on the right path, it seems!" Abruptly James abandoned his excursion into national affairs and returned to the real matter in hand. "Are you *sure* Christopher Clerk has vanished, Father? He hasn't gone on an errand and forgotten to let you know? Something urgent, perhaps?"

"I regret to say this, but I don't think so," said Meadowes. "He went out to meditate in the open air as he often does, but I expected him to return later and there was a matter to do with his studies that I wished to discuss with him. He hasn't come back, and personal things are missing from his room. There has been village gossip concerning a girl. I took him to task and he assured me there was nothing in it, that he had merely escorted her home when she was accidentally separated from her family at the May fair and exchanged the time of day with her after church once or twice out of courtesy. Villagers do have a talent for making something out of nothing and I believed him then. I warned him to be careful and left it at that. Now, frankly, I wonder. Earlier this year he asked me some odd questions."

"What sort of questions?" Elizabeth Luttrell asked. She was seated, working at an intricate piece of embroidery while Wagtail snoozed at her feet. "He always seemed so earnest," she remarked.

"Yes, he did," Father Meadowes agreed. "But the questions he asked were about leaving the church if a man changed his mind about his vocation. I asked if he were having doubts about his own and he said no. Now I'm wondering!"

"He's always seemed very quiet and conscientious," said James. "Too much so, perhaps, for a young man."

"Yes, I felt that, too, sometimes," Elizabeth said. "He was— is—so very…very self-contained, yet I sometimes felt that there was a side to him that was hidden."

The two men looked at her with interest. Elizabeth, usually a quiet woman, had a knack of occasionally making very acute remarks. *Sharp as an embroidery needle,* her husband sometimes said.

She smiled at them. "All the same," she added, "need we be anxious so soon? There could have been a misunderstanding…or even an accident."

She broke off as the gatekeeper's boy arrived in the hall at a breathless run and barely sketched a bow before exclaiming, "There's a Master Nicholas Weaver from the village, zurs and

101

mistress! He's axin' to see Father Meadowes and he says it's that urgent—can Father Meadowes see him now, at once. He looks that worried, zurs!"

"Nicholas Weaver?" said James. "I know him. Hardworking man and a hardworking family, that's him and his. It's you he wants to see, is it, Father Meadowes? Maybe he's got something to say about this mystery."

"Christopher was talking with a girl after the service on Sunday," murmured Elizabeth. "It looked quite innocent, but...I wonder..."

"The gossip," said Meadowes ominously, "concerned a daughter of the Weaver family."

"Fetch Master Weaver along, boy," said James.

Nicholas came in with a firm tread, which concealed a secret hesitation. He had never been inside the castle before, never hitherto walked up the steep track from Dunster to the gatehouse with the castle walls and their towers and battlements looming ahead of him, and although he was not a man with a poor opinion of himself, he felt intimidated. At the gatehouse the porter had greeted him politely, but with an air of surprise. Villagers, even well-to-do ones like Nicholas Weaver, didn't often call at the castle and certainly not to insist that they must immediately see men who held such dignified positions as castle chaplain.

Despite his secret misgivings, Nicholas had been resolute and he had been admitted, but now that he was actually inside, he was awed by the scurrying of the numerous servants and by the great, beamed hall, with its huge hearth and the dais where the family dined. Thick rushes underfoot silenced his footfalls, the rosemary sprigs strewn among them gave off their scent wherever one stepped and the walls were hung with tapestries: a huge, dramatic one of Goliath being downed by a gallant little David, and a pretty one with a background of flowers and a lady in the foreground with a unicorn beside her.

The fact that he had been led into the presence not only of Father Meadowes but of the Luttrells as well added further embarrassment. However, he bowed politely, murmured a conventional greeting and looked at the chaplain.

James took control. "This is Father Meadowes," he said. "At the moment something is making him anxious and we're wondering if your visit is to do with the same matter. Is your business by any chance connected with one Christopher Clerk, Father Meadowes's assistant?"

"It may be," said Nicholas. "If Christopher Clerk has left the castle. Has he?"

"Yes. He's vanished," said Meadowes. "He went out after dinner as he often does. I had set him passages of Scripture on which to meditate, and in fine weather like today he likes to do that out of doors. He went off across the pasture that slopes down to the sea. I saw him go. But he hasn't come back and we can't find him anywhere."

"Does he have red hair?"

"Very much so," said James. "A tonsure like a sunset, as a matter of fact."

"My girl Liza's vanished, as well," said Nicholas. "And so have two of my ponies! I thought to look before I came here. And there's been talk, about her and a young fellow with a red tonsure, possibly Christopher Clerk. We didn't want to make a to-do over a bit of flirtation, even with a clerk, especially as we weren't sure there was anything in it but silly tattle. We always thought Liza had some sense. We told her we'd found her a marriage and she seemed agreeable. We reckoned if there'd been any nonsense, it was just sweet talk and that she'd put it behind her. Now we think otherwise. We're afraid she's run away from home and if so, she'd hardly go on her own. Now you say this red-haired clerk…"

"He's a deacon," said Meadowes.

"Is he, indeed? Well, you tell me he's missing. Have they run off together?"

"It's possible," said Meadowes slowly.

"So what can be done? I want my girl back. The marriage we've arranged is a good one and by that I mean a happy one. I'm a careful father, I hope. I've got her welfare at heart and a runaway priest isn't what's best for her."

"And you want to get her back before anything happens and before the young man she's betrothed to finds out what she's done," said Elizabeth helpfully. "Father Meadowes, where might Christopher have taken her? Where does he come *from?* That might be a guide."

"Bristol," said Meadowes. "But his father's a highly respectable merchant there. He won't have gone near his father! He studied in Oxford, but—no, I doubt if he's gone there either. It's hardly the place for a runaway couple to go to for sanctuary. I'd guess they'd make for a city, but they'd be more likely to choose Exeter or London."

"Three directions," said James, thinking aloud. "London by way, to start with, of Taunton or Bridgwater, or south over the moor to Exeter by way of Tiverton. One of those."

"Bridgwater's likely," said Meadowes. "Christopher knows that road well. I've several times called on friends there and taken him with me. I doubt he's ever been to Taunton."

"I could be quite wrong," said Nicholas unhappily. "But Liza's *gone,* and taken linen and toilet things. There's been talk of her and a red-haired clerk, and we'd just told Liza about the marriage we'd planned for her. That could have been the spark in the straw. I *hope* I'm wrong. I want to be, but..."

He looked at James with a question in his face, and James answered it. "I'm sorry for you, Master Weaver, and I doubt very much that you're wrong. We'll go after them. Meadowes, are you joining us?"

"Of course. I can still sit a horse for a few hours, despite my grey tonsure," said the chaplain. "And the boy is my student as well as my assistant. I feel responsible for him. I should have pressed him harder over the rumours about Master Weaver's girl. I fear I've been remiss."

"The more helpers we have, the better," James Luttrell said. "Weaver, you and Meadowes can take one of my men and try the Bridgwater road. I'll send two men by way of Taunton, and myself, I'll take another two and ride for Exeter. Light's going, but the sky's clear and the moon's nearly full. We'll fetch them back, never fear. Young folk in love can be the very devil and their own worst enemies, but we'll see if we can't save these two from themselves. You can borrow one of my horses."

He turned to the gatekeeper's boy, who was still in the hall, listening openmouthed with excitement. "Get to the stable, my lad, and tell them to saddle eight horses. My Bay Arrow, Grey Dunster—he's hardly been out today—and whatever else is fit and not tired. Then send the garrison sergeant to me and after that, get back to your post. Hurry!"

CHAPTER EIGHT

HUNTERS AND QUARRY

The daylight was going. Grooms held up lanterns while the horses were brought out and saddled. Picking up the smell of urgency from the humans, the horses fidgeted and tossed impatient heads while their girths were tightened. James Luttrell, who seemed to have the entire map of the west country in his head, was giving final instructions, complete with landmarks, to the men who were going by way of Taunton. Nicholas, Father Meadowes and Gareth, the Welsh man-at-arms who was to accompany them on the Bridgwater road were all familiar with their own route.

The mood was that of a hunting party, albeit an unusually unsmiling one. Father Meadowes actually said as much to James Luttrell as they clattered down the slope to the village below. "If we had hounds with us, this would feel like a chase. Except that

THE HOUSE OF LANYON

I've never gone hunting after dark before and never had a man as my quarry before, either. It's a strange feeling."

At the foot of the slope they turned left, to circle the castle hill on its inland side. The first group to peel off was Luttrell's. "Good luck!" he called, taking off his hat to wave farewell to the others as he led his party away, bound for Exeter through the town of Tiverton on the south side of the moor. "I just pray somebody catches them before it's too late!"

Christopher and Liza rode eastward through the fading day. The Channel was dulling into a misty grey and shadows were gathering in the hollows of the inland hills. "You're safe with me. I hope you know that," Christopher said suddenly. "Believe me, I haven't quite abandoned my upbringing! There's a lot to be said for being steady and reliable, and I mean to be that for you. I shall take the greatest care of you. It was clever of you to think of taking the ponies. We'll send them back eventually."

"Yes, of course. I hated taking them, but we needed them so much." She did feel safe with him. They were doing a crazy thing, a wrong thing in the eyes of the world, but it was a right thing, as well. It was right because Christopher was Christopher and they belonged with one another.

"Will anyone guess where we've gone?" she asked. "They'll be after us as soon as they know."

"They might guess at London. If they do, they'll probably think we began by making for Taunton. It's the more usual road. But I know the Bridgwater one and just because it's not so usual, I think it's the safest one for us."

"I wish it could be different," said Liza. "I wish we could be married with everyone congratulating us and pleased with us, approving of us and wishing us luck. I feel like a hunted deer. I keep straining my ears to hear the hounds! But all the same, I'm so very glad to be here with you."

"And I am glad to be with you, sweetheart. I hate the thought of being hunted down, as well. We just mustn't be caught, that's all!"

At Allerbrook Peter was not exactly refusing to speak to his father, nor was Richard making it too obvious that he was furious with his son. Neither had any wish to expose their disagreement to the world. Conversation of a sort had taken place around the Rixons' table, mostly concerned with farming matters. It had been generally agreed that the field known as Quillet might well support a crop of wheat, but ought to be fenced.

"You've only got ditches there and wheat'll invite the deer in as if the Dulverton town crier had gone round calling them," cheerful Harry Rixon said. "You'll get they old stags lying down, the idle brutes, squashing great patches of it and snatching every ear of wheat within reach afore they get theirselves up and stroll off to find some nice fresh wheat to squash and gobble."

"The Sweetwaters won't like it," Gil Lowe prophesied glumly. "You've mostly used Quillet for pasture, haven't you? I've noticed they put their milking cows there now and then. Are they supposed to?"

"No, but when did that ever stop them?" enquired Richard sourly. "I pay rent on that land. I'll plant it if I like. Reckon you're right about the fences, though."

All that was normal enough, and if few words were actually exchanged between the two Lanyons, it was hardly noticeable, for the crowd was considerable. It included everyone who had helped in the pony drive, farmers and farmhands alike. Roger and Higg were there along with their employers. Higg alone seemed to sense something strange in the air. Higg looked and sounded slow, but he was nowhere near as slow as he seemed and Richard caught a thoughtful glance or two from him. He looked away. He was thinking.

All of a sudden Richard Lanyon was unsure of himself. All very well to decide that after all he ought to marry again and why not Marion, but there were things to consider. For instance, it was quite true that farm life would be strange to her, far stranger than to Liza, for Liza's father dealt a lot with sheep farmers and she knew farmers' wives and had some idea of how they lived.

Still, Marion was young enough to learn, and not squeamish. Fisherfolk were never that. Gutting a herring, or gutting a chicken; there wasn't much difference really, and Betsy could show her the dairy work.

The lack of any respectable dowry was a worse drawback, but that might be offset if she produced sons to help on the farm, and daughters to be married off into useful families. Taking the long view, even a Marion Locke might provide a step or two on the upward ladder.

Yes. He *could* take Marion to wife and still remake the future in the shape he wanted. And put Peter in his place.

What would be harder would be convincing her parents that the proposal was a good one, especially as he and they had already agreed that such marriages wouldn't do.

But, by God, he *wanted* her. He'd desired her from the moment he first set eyes on her. It was sheer desire that had overridden the old way of thinking, the taking it for granted that fisherfolk and farmers didn't intermarry, the lack of dowry, the embarrassing fact that his own son had probably had her first. The wench was by all the evidence about as steady as a weathercock in a gale, but he didn't care. He knew now that he wanted her more than he'd ever wanted Deb and about ten thousand times more than he'd ever yearned after Joan. He wanted to get his hands on her, to make her his, to surround and bemuse her so that she could see no other man, think of no other man, but himself.

The proper thing to do was to see her father, but instinct said no. Instinct said *win the girl over first*. Go hunting and bring her to bay; tame her to his hand and maybe she could help him tame her parents.

Today was a Tuesday, the second in the month. Next Tuesday was the third one, and she'd be going to Lynton to see her grandmother and aunt. Her mother had obligingly mentioned where her relatives lived—close to the mouth of that strange valley where he'd had a youthful romance long ago. He'd find the cottage easily enough. He meant to be open and honest. He'd call and ask to see the girl. Maybe he could coax her to stroll with him, alone, so that he could talk to her, persuade her...

And he'd make damned sure that Peter couldn't get away that day. Yes. One week from now. That was the thing to do.

It was a hunter's moon, shining ahead of the pursuers, low as yet, disappearing at times beyond shoulders of land as they came through the Quantock Hills, but when visible, bright enough to light the track in front of the horses, even to glint in the eyes of a fox as it darted across the path. They could see their way.

"Where are we?" Nicholas asked Gareth as they cantered their horses up a gentle hill and drew rein, looking down on the moonlit world. Somewhere in the distance was the fugitive twinkle of candlelit windows in a village. He knew the countryside east of his home, of course, but he had never ridden through the Quantock Hills after dark before.

"Nether Stowey, that is," said Gareth's Welsh voice at his side. "They'll have gone straight through there, I fancy, if they ever came this way. If I had all of us on my heels, I wouldn't stop till my pony fell over, indeed to goodness I wouldn't."

"Liza'd never push a pony too hard," said Nicholas, and to his own annoyance, found his eyes pricking. He had been proud of his daughter, proud of her glossy brown hair and her smile and her kindness. She was good with the ponies. Yes, and better at catching them than anyone else because they would come to the field gate to meet her! How could she have so misused her gift with them, and done this to her parents?

"We'd better do some pushing on ourselves," said Father Meadowes. "As fast as the moonlight will let us."

They pressed on. Presently, as they came into a shallow dip, he checked his horse again, and the others slowed down with him. "What is it?" asked Nicholas.

Father Meadowes pointed ahead, to the top of the little rise in front of them. "See? Against the skyline? Two riders…there, they've gone over the crest." As he spoke, his horse raised its head and whinnied. "If they're on the Nether Stowey road ahead of us," Meadowes said, "those two could be them."

"They've been dithering along the way if it's them," said Gareth with a chuckle. "I wonder what for?"

"You mind your tongue," said Nicholas.

Father Meadowes shook his steed up again. "Let's catch up. Heaven's been good to us—we can see where we're going, just about. We can gallop here."

"What are we to do tonight?" Liza asked. She was strong, but the day had taken its toll, and they weren't covering the miles as fast as they should. They had taken a wrong track three times, once heading for the shoreline by mistake, and twice in the fading light as they made their way through the Quantocks. Time had been particularly wasted on a steep, pebbly path which turned and twisted and finally tried to take them back westward.

They were on the right road again now, Christopher said reassuringly as they came out of the hills, but she was growing tired and she was very conscious of having left her home and all familiar things behind. This black-and-silver moonlit land was unreal, alien. And she was cold. There was a chill in the air after nightfall in October.

"We'll have to find somewhere to sleep, but if we can, we should avoid looking for lodgings or rooms at an inn," said Christopher. "We don't want to leave a trail behind. Maybe we should have gone another way, across to Devon, to Exeter. We'd have been that much harder to trace. But London will be easier to find than Exeter. I've been there before, as a lad, with my father. Exeter would be quite strange to me."

"But tonight, Christopher?"

"I think we should try to find a barn with hay in it. I've got some bread and cheese with me. I managed to take it from the kitchen when no one was looking. We can eat."

"But can we find a barn in the dark?"

"Oh, yes, I think so. Look, that's surely a farmhouse over there.

See—where the lights are? There'll be barns there. Let's walk the ponies. There ought to be a track turning that way."

"But what if we *can't* find a barn?"

"If we can't find one here, we'll find one somewhere else— on the far side of Nether Stowey. There are farms beyond it."

"Is Nether Stowey far?"

"Only a mile or a little more. Take heart, love. I know where we are well enough."

The search for a barn was unsuccessful. They found a lane to the right and before long they could distinctly smell a farmyard. But the lane seemed to be leading straight into it and if there were barns at a safe distance from the house, they couldn't be seen because the lane was a sunken way between high banks with brambles on top, which hid anything on the far side. To make things worse, the darkness became intense because the direction they had taken had put the moon behind a hill. They heard sheep bleating, and then, alarmingly, a dog began to bark. Christopher pulled up, reaching a hand to the bridle of Liza's pony, too.

"No good. If we go any farther we'll have people coming out to meet us and we'll have to explain ourselves. Turn round. We'll have to go back. Sorry."

"Oh, *Christopher!*"

"Don't let's have a wrangle here," he said wryly. "Let's quarrel later when we can enjoy it!"

"All right!" said Liza, and tried to sound as though she were laughing. She was beginning to feel frightened. They were losing so much time, and the pursuit must surely have begun by now.

They went back. Presently they were on the Nether Stowey road again and once more had the help of the moonlight. "Not far now," said Christopher. "I *think* I know where we'll find a barn, once we're through the village. And the bread and cheese are fresh. Take heart."

"I'm certainly hungry," said Liza, determined to be cheerful. "I'll enjoy our supper."

Her new, if somewhat forced, cheerfulness had five minutes to live. At the end of that time, as they cantered to the crest of a rise and paused briefly to look ahead, she saw her pony's ears flick backward, and then behind them, some way off but not nearly far enough to be comfortable, they heard a horse whinny.

"Christopher…!"

"Maybe it isn't them," said Christopher.

"It is! I know it is. I don't know how I know, but I do!"

"All right. Well, let's be on the safe side and assume it is, anyway," Christopher said. "Come on! Let's ride for it! We'll look for another side lane and try to dodge into it and let them go past. If it *is* them. Come on!"

It was the best plan he could make. He had kept his voice steady, but he too was now afraid, for her as well as himself. He could endure whatever they did to him for this, but what would happen to Liza? He had done horribly wrong in bringing her away, but what else was there to do, other than let her go forever?

Side by side, alert for a secondary track, they urged the ponies into a gallop, taking advantage of the moonlight. But providence wasn't with them. There was no break in the banks to either side, no escape from the track, and sturdy though their ponies were, their short strong legs could not match the stride of the Luttrells' big horses behind them. They heard the hoofbeats catching up, and then a rider swept past them and swung his horse right across the track to block their way. They found themselves looking up into a dark, square face which Liza did not recognise, though Christopher did. "Gareth!" he said.

"Look round," said Gareth, grinning, and they turned in their saddles to find that Nicholas Weaver and Father Meadowes had pulled up behind them.

Nicholas rode forward. To Liza's astonishment he didn't even look at her, but instead made straight for Christopher. "Have you taken her? Is that what slowed you down on the road? Come on! I want to know!"

"We kept missing our way and then turned aside to look for shelter," said Liza in a high voice. "We've taken vows to each other, but we haven't...Christopher hasn't..."

"I'm glad to hear it, but no doubt it was just a pleasure postponed," said Nicholas. He spurred his horse right up to Christopher's pony and his fist shot out. It landed with immense force on Christopher's jaw and the younger man reeled sideways, out of his saddle. His pony plunged. Christopher, who had clung on to the reins, scrambled up again, his spare hand pressed to his face.

"Father, don't!" Liza cried it out in anguish. "Oh, please let us go! Let me go with Christopher! I can't marry Peter Lanyon. I can't. I tried, so hard, to make myself willing to marry him, but I can't do it. It has to be Christopher...and we've bound ourselves...oh, why won't you understand?"

"I understand that you're talking nonsense and one day you'll know it, my girl. I've come to take you home," said Nicholas.

CHAPTER NINE

REARRANGING THE FUTURE

"Go to her, Margaret," Nicholas said. "Bring her downstairs and get her thinking about her bride clothes. She's got to at some point. Saints in heaven!"

His normal robust heartiness was dimmed. He was sitting by the kitchen hearth while Margaret and Aunt Cecy helped the maids with supper, and he could hear his young sons, Arthur and Tommy, laughing over some game or other in the adjacent living room, but just now these pleasant things could not comfort him. His shoulders were hunched and his face drawn with misery, and the two maids, aware of it, were unusually quiet.

"We never had this sort of trouble with either of our girls," said Aunt Cecy righteously. "Maybe that was because we walloped them when they needed it instead of bein' soft, the way you two are."

"We haven't been soft this time!" Margaret snapped, and continued obstinately stirring a pan of pottage.

"No, we haven't!" Nicholas agreed irritably. "But at least we had good reason. Cecy, you used to slap your girls for a bit of careless stitching or a speck of flour dropped on the floor, as if there weren't worse things! Reckon they were glad to be pushed off when they was barely ripe!"

"Well, really!" said Aunt Cecy. Nicholas ignored her.

"There's never been anything really truly *bad* in this house in my time, till now. I never thought our Liza would do this to us! I never thought I'd... I've never raised a hand to her, all her life, afore this and to have to take a stick to her...it broke my heart and I'm half afraid it's broken hers."

"Then the sooner she's married and away, the better," Aunt Cecy said sharply. "We'll all be happier, her included."

"I wouldn't have believed it of her either," said Margaret, still stirring. "It's a mercy we got her back in time and that there's been no more gossip." She eyed the maids, who had become very busy about the cooking. "And if I hear of you tattling, either of you, you're out! I mean it."

"If you ask me, half of this business is Peter Lanyon's fault," said Nicholas. "And you've said it, too, Margaret. He should have come to see her and done a little wooing! Margaret and I hardly knew each other before we were betrothed, but once it was agreed between the families, I came courting, didn't I, Margaret? You had your share of stolen kisses. I don't know what young Peter thinks he's about, and that's the truth!"

"Bah! She ought to do as she's bid, with wooing or without. A few more days in the attic 'ud do her no harm," said Aunt Cecy. "And Margaret here thinks the same, even if she won't say so."

"I don't care what either of you think!" shouted Nicholas. "I'm her father and I'm the one who's giving the orders this time! She's had enough days up there, enough time to study her conscience and get over things, so do as I tell you, leave that damned pan you're stirring, Margaret, and fetch her down here, and let's *pretend* things are normal even if she don't ever smile at me again. Go on!"

"Oh, very well," said Margaret, threw down her spoon and went.

When she entered the small room under the thatch, where Liza had been locked in now for six days, she found her daughter, as she had found her every time she went up there to take food in or remove the slop pail, lying on the bed and staring at the wall. "Time to get up," she said. "Your father says so. He's heartbroken, let me tell you, over what he had to do to you. To run off like that, and with a priest…well, I always thought I was the one who cared about bein' respectable, but the state your father's in—sayin' he's heartbroken is hardly sayin' enough!"

Liza looked at her miserably but said nothing.

"Forget all about this clerk," Margaret said. "He's to finish his studies in St. George's monastery. Your father and I have seen him—went to the castle and all, and he said to us that he was sorry for the grief he's caused us all. So that's the end of it."

"We swore oaths, taking each other as man and wife…" Liza began, but her words sounded empty, even to her.

"Moonshine and you know it!" Margaret snapped. "A man in orders is no more free to swear oaths about marriage than a married man is. Now then. Master Richard Lanyon's sent us a message by that big hulkin' fellow of his, Higg. He's sorry that Peter's not been over to see you, but there's been so much to do on the farm. We've fixed a weddin' day in November. So you get off that bed, and put on fresh things and come down to supper. No one'll say anythin' to you. No one knows outside the family, or ever will. We've not gossiped and the maids daren't, believe me. Master Luttrell's promised he'll order his men not to talk. Everythin'll be just as usual. You'll see."

There was a long pause. Then Liza said, "You don't understand how it was between Christopher and me. What it was like. What it *is* like!"

"Maybe not, but there's something you don't understand either, my girl." Margaret's tone was kinder. She could not, she found, turn against her own daughter as she had turned against the Webbers. "You think you'll never love Peter, but you wait till you've lived with 'un awhile. The day'll come when he'll be tired and frettin' over something and you'll look at his weary face and your heart'll ache inside you with sorrow for him, and wantin' to put it right, whatever it is. Marriage has its own power. Now, you comin' downstairs?"

"I don't want to go to Allerbrook," said Liza dismally. "It'll never be home."

"You'll be surprised. Now, there's things to talk about—or do you mean to take your vows in old clothes?"

There was a silence. Then Liza sighed and, at last, sat up. She did it because she had to. To get up from this bed meant giving in; it meant yielding herself to the stream of wedding preparations and, ultimately, to Peter Lanyon, but she had known her fate from the moment her father had caught up with her and Christopher outside Nether Stowey. Nicholas hadn't had to explain; there were things one knew. If she refused to marry, she would either be shut up in this room until she gave in, or else she would be deposited in a nunnery. Those were the customary methods of dealing with wayward daughters. Her face was stiff with unhappiness, but nevertheless, she slid off the bed and stood up.

"All right," she said.

She didn't say it gladly or willingly or even submissively. It came out in a flat tone that might have meant anything. But she said it.

The week that Liza had spent in her parents' attic, Richard Lanyon had spent making his mind up and then unmaking it again.

It was all very well to rearrrange the future inside his head, but what if seventeen-year-old Marion didn't take to the notion of marrying thirty-eight-year-old Richard Lanyon? Or even if she did, *would* her parents allow it? And *if* she did and they did, what if Peter kicked up, refused to marry Liza, and set about wrecking his father's new marriage?

Well, let him do his worst! Good God, no decent lad ever made eyes at his own stepmother; it was against all the laws of God and man. Peter might rage and scowl and slam doors, but he'd know that Marion was out of reach. He'd come around.

At this point in his inner dialogue, something inside Richard would snap ferocious jaws, like a pike catching a minnow. Peter would damned well have to come around. Peter was going to marry Liza Weaver, and why should he object to her? He'd known the girl most of his life and she was a fine-looking, good-tempered wench. He was lucky to get her and it was to be hoped that he would have the simple good manners not to sulk to her face. Liza was for Peter and Marion was for Richard and that was that.

Whenever he thought of Marion, he felt as though a hot, damp hand had clutched at his innards, both maddening and weakening him. At the idea of approaching her, he became anxious, wondering what to do, what to say to her, how to please her. He was like a youth again, bewildered by those strange creatures, girls.

On the Monday following Richard's visit to Lynmouth they fetched the sheep in from the moorland grazing, and having done so, counted them, because on these occasions there were nearly always a few missing. Sure enough, the count was half a dozen short. *Good,* thought Richard. *I can make use of that.*

That evening, in the farmyard, he took Higg into his confidence.

"Tomorrow I'm sending Peter out to look for the strayed sheep and I want you to go with him and make sure he *looks* for the sheep and don't go slipping off anywhere. I've had a bit of worry with him. There's a girl in Lynmouth that he's being a bit foolish about."

"Yes, Master Lanyon," said Higg, and from his tone, Richard gathered that Higg, Roger, Betsy and Kat all knew the situation and were probably discussing it avidly out of his hearing.

"Most young men have their adventures before they get wed," Richard said offhandedly. "But Peter's getting married soon and it's time this stopped. Tuesdays are likely days for him to go dodging off to Lynmouth, so I'm charging you to see he doesn't. Understand?"

"Ah," said Higg, grinning, and added a comment for once. "Could work out well. A bride's best off with a groom as knows what he's about."

"I daresay," said Richard coldly. "Go over Hawkridge way and search there. I'm going the other way, up to the high moor. Between us, we'll find them, I hope."

In the morning he gave his orders, watching Peter intently. Peter glowered, opened his mouth as if to protest, but then shut it again as he met his father's stern eye. He shrugged, and after breakfast went off with Higg as instructed, taking Silky, the sheepdog bitch, with them. "She's still mournful, missing my father," Richard said. "The more work she does, the better. Leave Blue to guard the house."

When Peter and Higg were out of sight, Richard asked Betsy for some bread and cold meat—"I could be out of the house at noon, if the sheep have wandered far." He then saddled Splash, swung himself astride, called his own dog Ruff and set off westward, to the coast and Lynton.

It was a mild day, the sky a mingling of blue patches and good-natured brown-and-white cloud, carried on a light west wind. The rolling moors, which from a distance looked so smooth that their colours could have been painted on them, were patched pale gold with moor grass and dark where the heather grew. Here and there were the green stains of bogs, and in places there were gleams of bright yellow, for always there was gorse in bloom somewhere.

Splash was fresh and they made good time. Richard found himself almost at the Valley of the Rocks while the morning was still quite young. He drew rein and looked round. That must be the cottage where the grandmother and aunt lived, standing a little back from the road; he could see its thatched roof, just visible above some apple trees. He hesitated. Would Marion be here yet? She would have quite a long walk from home, up the steep path which linked Lynmouth to Lynton, and then through Lynton itself. Should he wait, or go straight to the cottage and knock, or...?

Then he saw her, walking toward him, her basket on her arm. He knew her at once. It was as though during that one brief meeting a week ago he had memorised her, head to footsoles, every line and movement of her. He rode toward her.

"Marion Locke!"

She stopped, looking up at him in surprise, and he saw that she didn't recognise him and was startled, although, as she looked into his face, he also saw appreciation there. Marion responded to the sight of a handsome man as instinctively as a flower opening in the sun. Ruff ran up to her, wagging his tail, and she stooped to pat him.

"I'm Richard Lanyon," he said. "Peter Lanyon's father."

She'd recognised him now. She straightened up and smiled and he doffed his cap. "You saw me last week, when I called at your parents' home. I brought you a disappointment, I think. My son is betrothed already, my dear. But I wish to talk to you. Will you ride with me a little way before you go to see your grand-mother?"

She got up behind him without the slightest hesitation and neatly enough, despite the basket on her arm, putting her left foot on his and accepting a hand to help her on. For the first time he touched her, and the contact burned him like white fire. More prosaically, a smell of fish arose from the basket and Splash snorted disapprovingly. "Your horse don't like the scent of herring," said Marion, laughing. "But they taste all right."

"Not to him," said Richard, also amused. "Hold tight!" He put Splash into a trot on purpose, so that she would have to hold on and he would feel her hands grip his waist.

"Where we goin'?" Marion enquired.

"Into the valley. We can get down and stroll awhile and have some private talk, if you will. It's a pleasant morning."

Marion laughed again. Bumping and jogging, they made their way along the rough track and into the valley, with Ruff running at Splash's heels. Once there, Richard drew rein again, dismounted and helped Marion down. He removed Splash's bridle and hung it on a small tree, eased the girth, hobbled the animal's forefeet and told Ruff to stay on guard. He offered Marion his arm. "Shall we walk?"

In the priory of St. George's in Dunster, Christopher Clerk stood in a small monk's cell, looking about him. He had made it plain that he had no intention of taking vows as a monk, but Father Hugh Meadowes hadn't cared.

"Take vows as a monk or not—that's up to you as long as you take vows as a priest. That's your business in life and you know it. You've a vocation, my son. I know one when I see one, and what will your father have to say if you abandon yours? He's proud of you! You're not going to let him down and you're not going to let me down and above all, you're not going to let God down. You young lunatic! If you hadn't been willing to swear on a crucifix that you didn't sleep with the girl, I'd have had to go to the bishop. Do you realise how serious that would have been? Forget her! Forget any oaths you thought you swore. Forget you ever thought you loved her. I doubt it, myself. What sort of a life were you going to drag her into? She's going to marry someone else, who'll give her a better future than you ever could!"

"I'd have made my way. I'd have made a life for both of us!"

"And one day your call to the priesthood would have risen up and poisoned it. I know about these things. You'll finish your studies in the priory and then you'll stay there and serve the monks and the parishioners. Liza Weaver won't be among them. She's leaving the parish. No more argument, my son. I don't want to repeat what I had to do when you were brought back to the castle, but if I have to, I will."

His back was still marked from Father Meadowes's whip. He could only hope that Liza had not been similarly treated. He had not dared to ask, not even when her parents came to see him, to hear him apologise and promise to put Liza from his mind forever. He had had little chance to say anything beyond the apology and the promise. Nicholas had done most of the talking. Some of his remarks had burned more bitterly than Meadowes's lash. *Callow young wantwit. Trying to lead my girl into a life of concealment and poverty. She doesn't know enough of the world to realise what was ahead. And you say you loved her. Bah!*

But all the time, all through that diatribe from Nicholas, and all through Meadowes's beating, he had prayed inside his head for Liza, hoping that God would let him suffer for them both.

He sat down slowly on the hard, narrow bed. He was thinking about the past. At the beginning it had been his own idea to enter the church. He believed he had been called. Their own parish priest, back in Bristol, had given a homily one Sunday on what a privilege a vocation was; how it was like a summons to a holy army, and how priests and monks followed the banner of Christ just as knights followed the banner of their overlord. The soldiers of Christ fought battles of the spirit, not of the body, and their purpose was to save the souls of their fellow creatures from damnation. There was no nobler calling on earth, said the priest ardently.

Christopher had thought about that homily many times during the following weeks and he had gone to talk to the priest privately, and before very long he had become convinced that he was among those who had been summoned to take Christ for his suzerain. His father had been delighted.

His mother, a practical woman, was less so, and expressed regret that her second son would not marry and have a family.

They were willing to help him, she said; he could go as an apprentice to another merchant and could in time become a merchant in his own right, could succeed in the world. But he shook his head and said he must leave the world, in that sense, behind, and his father told her to stop making objections; this was a great honour and he was proud of Christopher.

And he, Christopher, had been proud of himself, sure of himself, had thought of himself as a good soldier of God. And then, as he'd roamed through the fair at Dunster on that spring day, he'd stopped to watch as a dishonest weaver was paraded past for swindling his customers, and realised that the girl standing beside him hated seeing someone put on display like that. She had left the people she was with and walked off alone into the crowd and he had followed, concerned for her in such a gathering, with so many strangers about. She had suspected his intentions and looked sharply around at him, and he had spoken to her, meaning to show kindness, as a priest ought to do, and their eyes had met, and the whole world had changed.

He had known then, in that moment, that his vocation was a horrible mistake, that he was made for the ordinary life of a man, that he was on the wrong path entirely. He'd fought the knowledge off and might have won the fight if Elizabeth Luttrell's wretched little dog hadn't run away, and he hadn't found himself chasing after it and coming face-to-face with Liza Weaver once again. After that, there was no more resisting. His vocation had been nothing but a dream, a youthful ardour trying to find somewhere to put itself and making the wrong choice.

And there was no way back.

He looked around him, at the stone walls of the little cell, at the prie-dieu in the corner, with its embroidered cloth—the only splash of colour in the room. Whatever revelations had struck him when he met Liza, he had ended up here. His vocation might seem unreal to him now, might have faded into nothingness as far as his emotions were concerned, but he was bound to it just the same, a soldier plodding across an arid desert, sworn to the service of his lord whether he liked it or not.

Liza was lost to him and he had been a fool ever to think they could escape together and create any kind of life worth living. She had been rescued from that and from him and probably it was the best thing for her. He understood that now.

What none of them knew, however—though God presumably did—was that what he felt for Liza, and what she felt for him, was real and would remain real all the rest of their lives, even if they never met again. They were sworn to each other, whatever Father Meadowes and the Weavers might say. He said aloud, "I will go on praying for her all my days."

Yes, he would! And there was nothing anyone could do to interfere with either his private prayers or his memories.

Meanwhile, this priory and this cell were to be his home. Very well. His future had been ruthlessly reorganised and his life sold away. Soldier of God? No, he was a slave, and for life. But his love was unchanged and would remain so until he died.

CHAPTER TEN 🪷

CLOUD BLOWING IN

The Valley of the Rocks was a curious place. On the moor and among its surrounding, greener foothills, the water had sculpted the land and was still doing so. Streams ran through nearly every one of the deep, narrow combes that dented the hills as though a giant had repeatedly pressed the side of his hand deep into a collection of vast and well-stuffed cushions. The valley, by contrast, was dry.

It didn't run down to the sea, but lay parallel to it. Its floor was flat and broad, but on either side, hillsides of bracken and goat-nibbled grass rose steeply to curious crests where grey rock outcrops, weathered into extraordinary shapes, adorned the skylines. Richard knew that the hills to his right were a thin wall between valley and sea, with a drop of hundreds of feet from the hillcrests to the water, most of it sheer cliff with broken rock at its feet.

Ahead, the seaward hillside broke in one place, though even

from there, the drop below was still hair-raising. The heights resumed with a tall conical hill topped by an extraordinary mass of rock which looked, from a distance, so like the ruins of an old fortress that most people called it Castle Rock.

There was no one about, except for a goatherd encouraging his flock from one piece of grass to another, up on the slope to the left. He was high up and moving away from them, and showed no sign of having seen them. He certainly wouldn't disturb them. "Mistress Locke," said Richard, "as I said, I wish to talk with you. I came here today to find you. I have something to tell you and something to ask you. I hope you will listen."

"Well, what might all that be about?" asked Marion.

She said it with a smile in her voice, and provocation, too, and when he turned to look at her face, that provocation was in her eyes, as well. The white fire leaped again, shockingly, filling him up. Her hand burned on his arm. He hardly knew how to go on just talking to her. He wanted to throw words and politeness and every last vestige of civilised behaviour away and her clothing with them and his own as well and turn this bleak, lonely valley into a Garden of Eden, with him and Marion as Adam and Eve.

To steady his mind, he quickened the pace, leading her toward the foot of the goat path that wound its way up and around Castle Rock. With a great effort he kept his voice normal as he said, "Mistress Locke, you must understand, even if it disappoints you, that I've plans for my son Peter and that there can be no question of a marriage between you. However, I can see very well why he's lost his heart and his head over you. You are as lovely a wench as I ever saw."

It was a poor description of her, he thought, nearly as inadequate as when her mother called her pretty. Marion Locke was no conventional beauty. His first impression had been the right one. She was *ripe,* like a juicy plum. She gave off the very scent of ripeness, of readiness.

"Tell me," he said, still keeping his voice even with the greatest difficulty, "what if I asked you to think about me instead? I'm a widower these many years and I'd like a wife. Specially, I'd like a wife like you."

"Oh," said Marion, and dropped her hand from his arm.

"Why *oh?*" He caught her hand back and drew her to him. "Come! I'm older than you, but I'm hale enough. You'd get used to farm life, though it's different from what you know. Marion…"

"But I…no, please," said Marion, shaking her head and pulling her hand free. She edged away, arousing in him a sudden huntsman's instinct to give chase.

"Now, don't shy away from me, sweeting. There's no need. I just want you to listen to me." He stepped after her, repossessed himself of her hand and then changed his grasp to her elbow, drawing her back to him, clamping her to his side and walking her steadily on. "There's nothing to be afraid of. I'm not an enemy. Just listen, my dear."

Marion didn't know what to do. The young men she'd flirted with and, well, given way to once or twice—and she knew that she'd taken a risk and been lucky that no harm had come of it— had been easy to manage, even a little shy. She had never felt out of control. She had never encountered anyone like Richard Lanyon before. He was handsome, but he had an aura of danger, something new to her. Besides, this wasn't decent. She had made love with this man's son, and here in this very valley, at that. It wasn't *right.* Marion's morals were broad, but not broad enough for that.

But she couldn't break Richard's hold and if she did, she knew she couldn't outdistance him. She could still see the goatherd but he was far away; there was no help there.

They had reached the foot of the path up the Rock. "Let's climb a little way and see if we can see the coast of Wales," Richard said, and steered her upward. The path wound, bringing them to the seaward side of the Rock, giving them a view across the Channel and westward down it. He looked down at her, smiling, but then, unable to stop himself, suddenly swung her in front of him, bending forward to kiss her.

His forebear Petroc, the one who had brought the Lanyons to Exmoor, had started life as a Cornish tin miner. That meant a free man, even in the days of villeinage, but it was a hard life of digging and panning, which produced men with muscles like steel ropes.

Petroc had hated it and given it up to breed sheep, though with poor success at first, for Cornish pastures were thin and sheep reared on them grew poor fleeces. However, when the Black Death tore holes in the population and opened, for those who still lived, chances hitherto unimaginable, he had snatched his opportunity and travelled to Somerset, where the grazing, even on the moors, was far better. Here he found success at last with his sheep. But if he had left the harsh days of failure behind him, he hadn't lost his tin miner's physique. To those of his descendants who survived, he had handed it down. Richard Lanyon had the thick shoulders and knotted muscles of his ancestors and he scarcely knew his own strength.

Marion, feeling his fingers grip her like pincers of steel, cried out, turning her head away from him. "Master Lanyon, don't! You're frightenin' me!"

Realising that he must have hurt her, he let go. This was no way to go courting. "It's all right. Don't be afraid." Better keep walking; it gave his overheated body something to do. He turned her and guided her onward and up. "Watch your footing—the ground's rough," he said, and used that as an excuse to put a heavy arm around her shoulders. "I'd treat you kindly," he assured her, "and you'd eat well, on the farm. Not so much fish, but much more cream and good meat. The farmworkers' wives would show you how to do this and that, and…"

"Weather's changin'," said Marion.

It was. It was growing colder and the west wind was strengthening. There was no more blue in the sky and the high brown-and-white clouds had given place to low grey ones, flowing in from the far Atlantic. The path had brought them quite high up by now and wisps of cloud were blowing around them, bringing a hint of drizzle. Wales, which had indeed been visible at first though neither of them had paid any attention to it, had vanished.

Marion was shivering, partly with cold, partly with what was now serious alarm. When Richard had come to Lynmouth to see her parents, he'd been just Peter's father, a farmer in a brown wool jerkin and a hooded cloak, darker than most Somerset men were, and good-looking—she was never unaware of good looks in a man—but all the same, one of her own father's generation and not, in her mind, a potential lover. But now!

His dark eyes were like Peter's as far as shape and colour went, but their expression wasn't the same. Peter's eyes held an essential kindness, but Richard's were hot and demanding. He wasn't offering her love. What he wanted was possession. He wanted to hold and control and enter her, not for her pleasure but only for his own, and he meant to have his way.

Beneath the outer layer of sheer sexiness which enveloped Marion like a rich velvety cloak was a girl who not only had at least some moral sense but a knack of understanding people, too. It had been part of her attraction for young men. She always looked at them as though she knew them quite well already and longed to know them better still.

She said carefully, "You're kind, Master Lanyon, payin' court to me like this. But I couldn't. I mean, I don't think it 'ud be fitting. My father wouldn't like it!" The last sentence was an inspiration. It was surely the one thing that might impress this man.

"I'll talk to your father." They were nearly up to the rock outcrop on top of the Rock, although they could hardly see it, for the cloud around them was thickening swiftly. "I'll make him an offer he'll look at twice, or maybe three times. Marion!" He stopped and swung her to face him once again, grasping her upper arms. "Can't you see I've fallen as deep in love as a man can fall? I've fallen further than if I jumped off one of these here cliffs. Don't let me land on the rocks! Say yes!"

"I can't! I'm sorry, but I can't!" Marion was really petrified now. She could not have put into words what she sensed, but if someone had said the words *snapping pike* to her, she would have said at once, *yes, that's it.*

"Why not? *Why not?*" He hadn't meant to get angry but the anger rose up in him by itself. He'd never wanted anything or anyone in his life as he wanted this girl. He hadn't even known one *could* hunger like this. "What's wrong with me, eh? What is it about me that's not good enough for the likes of you?"

"Please! Please don't. Let me go!"

"No. Say yes. Marion, say *yes!*"

"Oh, please let me go. I want to go back. My grandmother

and my aunt'll be waiting!" She tried to free herself, and the basket of fish, still dangling from one arm, swung wildly to and fro.

"We're not going back yet. Not until you say yes. Not even if we have to stay up here all today and all tonight. I've got to have you, Marion. You're a temptress and I can't say no to you, any more than you can say no to me. Let me prove it!"

"No! Let *go!*" Marion shouted it at the top of her voice and jerked backward, kicking him on the shin in the process. Richard swore and released her, but remained planted like a wall between her and the downward path. She wanted to get away from him so much that she found herself turning and scrambling on uphill instead. He came after her and caught her up at the foot of the outcrop. It towered above them. There was grass beneath their feet, and a wide place to stand, safe enough close to the outcrop, but perilous at the edge, for here they were immediately above the sea and the grassy space ended at the edge of a cliff.

"I said, *let me prove it.* Let me show you!" He had hold of her again and when Marion tried once more to shout *no!* he muffled the sound by crushing her mouth with his. Not that there was anyone who could have heard her, anyway, for the goatherd was now out of both sight and hearing, even if the cloud all around them hadn't become as dense as a damp grey fleece. "There!" said Richard, lifting his head at last. "Doesn't that tell you all you need to know? Don't you know now that you can't refuse me?"

"No, I don't!" Marion shrieked, kicking him again. He pulled her hard against him and this time she lowered her head and sank her teeth into his wrist. He swore, and she stamped on his foot. They wrestled, swaying back and forth. The cloud, as much drizzle as vapour, got in their hair and their mouths and confused their vision. For one moment, with the greyness all around them, they couldn't even see the looming wall of the outcrop. It was only feet away, but they couldn't have told in which direction. Marion, struggling, kicking, shouting, "No, no, *no!*" at last broke free and threw herself sideways to avoid his clutching hands.

And then was gone.

It was as sudden, as total, as incredible as that. One moment she had been there, a crazed harpy, fighting him; the next, he was alone on Castle Rock, in a world that seemed to be made of blowing cloud and wetness. But not a silent world, or not immediately, for as she felt herself go over the edge, the rock and grass vanishing from under her feet, Marion screamed.

Till the day he died, he would never forget that scream. Throughout all the years to come, it would echo in his ears. It went on for what seemed an eternity, fading downward but continuing, continuing—and then abruptly ceasing, as though a blade had cut it off.

Seconds ago she had been here, with him, alive and shouting and struggling against him. He couldn't believe that she was just—gone.

And gone forever, at that. The capricious wind tore a rent in the vapours and he walked, trembling, to the edge to look downward. Stupidly, pointlessly, he shouted her name. "Marion! *Marion, Marion!*" There was no answer. Between the wisps of cloud blowing past beneath him—how unnatural, to look down upon cloud!—he glimpsed, briefly and horribly, the sea and rocks at the bottom. His head swam. He staggered backward to safety, before that yawning drop could drag him to oblivion, as well. It occurred to him, thinking of that final struggle, that it could have been him just as easily as Marion.

In which case, he would have been dead, as she was. No one could survive that fall. The tide at the cliff foot was rising; he had seen the white foam boiling in over the fallen rocks, which were a peril to ships all along this coast. Marion had fallen into that. The rocks had broken her and the sea had swallowed her up. She had been wiped out of the world, and if he hadn't actually pushed her, well, he had frightened her into falling. It was a poor distinction.

He slumped down with his back against the outcrop. The cloud closed in again. He still struggled with disbelief, but the silence slowly brought it home. He was, as near as made no difference, a murderer.

No one knew he was here, though. He had not told anyone he was coming here; he was supposed to be out looking for sheep. He had ridden over the moor, taking the shortest way, and not seen a soul on the way. He hadn't ridden through Lynton, either. And in this weather he wasn't likely to meet many people on the way back. In fact, he'd be glad of Splash's homing instinct. People got lost in mists easily, but horses didn't.

He could go home. He could pretend he had never come near Lynton or this valley. At least there was one thing. He couldn't marry Marion now, but neither could Peter. He almost felt a sense of relief, as though she had put a spell on him, which was now lifted. Perhaps she had been a witch, and in that case the world was well rid of her.

He repeated this to himself, firmly, several times. Then, careful of his footing in the bad visibility, he started down the winding path around Castle Rock. Down on the floor of the valley it was drizzling, but it was below the cloud itself and he could once more see where he was going. He glanced back once at the

Rock. It stood tall, wreathed in the drifting vapours, but with an air of menace, as though it was aware of him and was ill-wishing him. Hurriedly he turned his back and made off to where he had left Splash. Ruff was lying down but got up at his master's approach, whining with pleasure. Splash, too, seemed glad to see him. He bridled the horse, removed the hobbles, tightened the saddle girth and mounted, to begin the journey home.

It would take time but that was all the better, for his hands had trembled as he bridled his mount. He needed time to recover. Thank God no one had seen him. Thank God no one knew he had ever been here.

The goatherd, a lad of fifteen, had in fact seen Richard and Marion arrive, leave the horse and walk on along the valley to start climbing the Rock. He had noticed that the woman had remarkable hair, and a very attractive, not to say come-hither way of walking, and that they had a dog with them and that their horse was an odd colour, with dark grey dapples all running into each other. He had never seen any of them before as far as he knew. Most of his life was spent in the valley, along with his master's goats; even Marion had not hitherto crossed his path. Few people ever came into the valley. He wondered what they were doing there, but his business, after all, was to look after the goats.

The horse and dog had gone when, after settling his charges on fresh grass and attending to a cut on the leg of a limping nanny, he came down the hillside to escape the weather and eat his midday bread and cheese in a little shelter he had built for himself. The strangers had presumably come back, collected their animals and left.

A month or so later, local gossip reached him about a Lynmouth girl who had run away from home, but he made no connection between the gossip and the couple he had seen.

Richard's route home took him high onto the moors and back into the mist. He let Splash take his time and ate his bread and meat in the saddle. As at last he approached Allerbrook, he was both surprised and pleased to come across his own missing sheep, their fleeces spangled with damp, nibbling dismally at the thin autumn grasses and not at all unwilling to be rounded up by Ruff and shepherded home to the better pastures lower down.

Another half hour and he was there, riding in with them, a respectable farmer and shepherd who had gone out on the moor to look for missing stock, found them and brought them back.

Peter came home shortly afterward, complaining that he had not found any sheep. Richard described how he had searched in vain in the mist for hours and then discovered them just after he had given up trying.

All the rest of that day the talk was of nothing but sheep. In the morning, however, Richard remarked to Peter that they ought to ask Nicholas Weaver to bring Liza over for a visit to her future home, and a formal betrothal.

Peter, without answering, swallowed his final mouthful of breakfast and stalked out of the kitchen to go about his day's work. Richard glared at his son's retreating back, but for the moment held his tongue. Clearly he would have to think about this.

"The master's got something on his mind," Betsy said to Higg three nights later as they settled to sleep on the straw-filled mattress in their cottage. "He's been goin' around all grim-faced and hardly hears what's said to him. He don't look like he sleeps at night. And it's plain as the nose on your face that him and Master Peter b'ain't hardly on speakin' terms."

"Not much we can do about it," said Higg tersely.

"I don't like the look of things. Peter don't want this marriage the master's planned for 'un, and you know what Master Richard is like for getting 'un's own way. Just like his father, he's turning out to be. He'll have his way, mark my words, but whether it'll be a happy house afterward or not, I wouldn't like to guess."

"Let's worry about that when it happens," said Higg stolidly.

The fact that Marion no longer existed meant that she couldn't now marry Peter, but Peter didn't yet know this. Somehow or other he must be informed, and then coaxed into standing before a priest with Liza Weaver. But how? Richard asked himself, lying awake on his bed.

It was all too true that he was sleeping badly. Hour after hour, every night, slumber eluded him, while he relived that ill-fated walk through the Valley of the Rocks, and when at last he did sleep, he dreamed of it. Night after night, Marion's last scream echoed for him again. What had it been like for her, throughout that long fall, knowing that she was still herself, healthy and alive, but would in the next few seconds be smashed and dead and that there was no miracle in the world that could save her? Sometimes he dreamed that he was the one who was falling.

She had died because he had tried to force his will on her. It seemed that compelling people to do one's bidding could be disastrous. How then was he to force his will on Peter? Well, once Peter knew that Marion had disappeared, he might decide to be sensible of his own accord. With luck, he would. But how on earth was he to be told?

No one must suspect that Richard knew more than he should. Only, time was pressing and mustn't be wasted. The betrothal to Liza ought to happen soon or Nicholas would be raising his eyebrows, and he'd expect the wedding to take place soon after. How much time would Peter need to get over the shock of learning that Marion was gone forever?

He'd killed her...no, she'd died in an unfortunate accident last Tuesday. Bit by bit, a scheme emerged.

On October 27, the following Saturday, as he and Peter went out after a breakfast at which neither had spoken to the other, he said, "Look here, boy, I'm tired of your dismal face round here. So be it. You go to Lynmouth and see Master Locke and ask him for Marion if you're so determined. I don't fancy he'll agree and it'll be for him to say. But maybe after you've talked to him, you'll see that she's not for you, and you can stop treating me as if I were a leper."

"And what if he says yes?"

"Then he says yes. But you'd better bring her here before you handfast yourself to her. She might not like the look of Allerbrook. No betrothal until she's seen what she's coming to. Saddle your pony and go."

Fifteen minutes later Peter was on his way, with a leather flask of spring water and a rabbit pasty for his midday meal, and hope in every line of his retreating back.

He returned in the afternoon, riding slowly. Richard, who had arranged to be close to the farmhouse all day, wandered into the farmyard to meet him as he was unsaddling. "So you're back. How did it go?"

The face that his son turned to him was the face of grief, bloodless and stricken. "I can't believe it. I just can't believe it."

"Can't believe what?"

"She's gone! Just gone. The last time she went to take some herrings to her grandmother and her aunt, she never got there! But last year she was seen at times with a sailor from some Norwegian ship or other, and that ship's been back in Lynmouth harbour lately and Marion was seen talking to the sailor again, on the quay. Seems his ship sailed on the very day that Marion set out and didn't come back. They reckon she's gone with him. Her father said she was flighty. He said he'd rather she *had* married me—at least it would be an honest marriage into an honest family! But it's too late now. She's...*gone!*"

And you don't know how thoroughly and completely she's gone, Richard said to himself.

"And even if she ever came back..." Peter said, but couldn't finish the sentence.

Richard, carefully, said, "I'm sorry. You mightn't believe me, but I am. You're taking this hard and I'm truly sorry." *You have no idea how sorry or why, and pray God you never will.*

"She never..." Peter began, and then stopped short again.

"Never loved you?" Richard said it quietly, though.

"Can't have done, can she?"

"You'd best come inside. Did you eat your rabbit pasty?"

Peter took off the bag he had slung onto his back. It still bulged as it had when he rode away. "No."

"Let's see what Betsy can find for you. You need a hot meal."

"You're talking to me like a mother!" said Peter, half-angrily.

"Well, your mother's not here, after all. Come on, boy. You fill your belly with good victuals. The world won't look so dark after that." He did not mention Liza. There was no need. The right moment would come.

It came three days later. "I suppose," said Peter, late in the evening, when he and his father, having made sure that the poultry were shut up safely where foxes couldn't get at them, were lighting candles so as to see their way to bed, "I suppose I may as well marry Liza Weaver. She's a nice enough wench."

"Yes. She is. You won't regret it, my lad," said his father.

Nor, thought Richard, will you have a chance to back out, boy. I'll ride to Dunster tomorrow and have the Weavers and Liza back here the day after. We'll get the betrothal official and start having the banns called next Sunday.

CHAPTER ELEVEN

NEW BEGINNING

There came a time, Liza had realised, when one could no longer fight. Christopher was gone. Not far in the physical sense, since he was only a few minutes away in St. George's Priory, but it had been made clear to her that she would never see him face-to-face again, not if her parents and the Luttrells and Father Meadowes had any say in the matter.

She thought of Christopher often. Inside her head she talked to him, even raged at him for letting himself be knocked out of his saddle instead of somehow seizing her mount's bridle and getting them both away. But at other times he seemed unreal because everyone around her kept behaving as though he had never existed. She might never have fled through the night, never have been fetched back and dragged up to that horrible little room under the thatch, never have been made to weep with pain and grief, never bolted in as a prisoner.

She was a bride-to-be. The ceremony, her mother told her as they stood in the bedchamber Liza shared with her little sister Jane and looked at a roll of light blue silk, would take place in the third week of November. Her mother sounded as cheerful and fond as though Liza were insanely in love with Peter Lanyon and could hardly wait for the wedding day.

"When you've taken your vows, everyone'll come back here for the feast, and your father and I'll move downstairs for the night so as you two can have our chamber. It'll be too far to get back to Allerbrook that night. You'll ride off in the morning. Now, this silk is for you to wear to church. Cost a fortune, bein' silk and blue bein' such a costly dye, but we don't grudge it. I'm having a new gown, crimson, but using our own cloth and having it dyed by this new man Herbert Dyer who's come to Dunster from Taunton and taken over our old dyer's business."

"I heard that Hal Redman wanted to give up," Liza said listlessly.

"Yes, poor old man. He can live on the money he got for the business and this man Herbert charges less than Hal did. Now, the wedding feast. I'll need your help with the cooking."

"And Cecy can't make light pastry if her life depended on it. I can hear you sayin' it even if you *aren't* sayin' it," remarked Aunt Cecy, putting her sharp nose in at the door.

"Well, you can't," said Margaret matter-of-factly. "Though I never can see why not. It's not that difficult."

"I can never see why it matters. My weaving's good enough," said Aunt Cecy, and walked away.

It was all, Liza thought bemusedly, so normal, so ordinary. For as long as she could remember, her mother and Aunt Cecy had had exchanges like that. It was part of the atmosphere of home, of everyday life, the same everyday life which was rolling over the episode with Christopher Clerk like a team of harvesters scything their way across a barley field. When the harvesters were done, the field was nothing but stubble.

She went like a sleepwalker through the rituals of preparation for marriage. There was a flurry of coming and going between Allerbrook and Dunster. On the last day of October Richard Lanyon came to visit the Weavers, and on the following day Liza and her parents rode back with him to Allerbrook for the betrothal. They dined at the farmhouse and in the presence of Richard Lanyon and Liza's parents, who were all beaming, Peter took her hand, promised to marry her and kissed her. He was the Peter Lanyon she had always known, looking older now and oddly tired, as indeed did his father. She supposed the work on the farm had for some reason been extra hard this year.

They both said how welcome she would be at Allerbrook. "You won't have to work in the fields much," Peter assured her as they sat down to dinner, "except that everyone lends a hand at harvest time if they can. But otherwise, it'll be taking care of the chickens, and helping with dairy work and bread making. Betsy'll be glad of an extra pair of hands."

"Won't you mind me coming in and...well, interfering?" Liza asked doubtfully, looking at Betsy.

"No, that I won't," said Betsy, handing her a platter of oatcakes and cream. "I've got too much to do and so has Kat. If 'ee can make butter and set the cream, I'll see to the cheese. Can 'ee milk a cow?"

"Yes. Father has two cows and I often milk them."

"All the better!" said Kat, and gave her a smile.

They were kind, those two flaxen, middle-aged farm women who looked so alike. Perhaps it wouldn't be too bad.

The first banns were called the very next Sunday. Her parents were wasting no time in getting her to the church door, Liza thought ironically, unaware that Richard Lanyon was hurrying Peter to the point with equal anxiety and for similar reasons. On November 20, she changed her name to Lanyon.

Peter and his father spent the eve of the wedding at the inn in Dunster, and on the day itself, wearing their best clothes, were waiting in the churchyard amid a crowd of the Weavers' interested neighbours when Liza and her family arrived. Gleaming in blue silk, with a train which small Jane had been allowed to carry on the way to the church, Liza stood at the church door beside Peter and in front of the priest who had led the Sunday prayers for so many years of her life. Christopher was somewhere near, within these very walls, but another bridegroom stood at her side and there was no escape.

She said, "I will." Peter put a ring on her left hand, the priest pronounced them man and wife and another stone was added to the wall that divided her from Christopher, this one a wall of law and religion and society, not tangible like stone but just as strong. The priest was jocularly encouraging Peter to kiss the bride. Someone in the throng of well-wishers remarked that he'd be doing a lot more than that before another day dawned and everyone laughed, including the priest. Liza managed to smile. She even managed to smile at Peter. There was no point in being sullen. He would be a power in her life henceforth. Whatever went on inside her head must remain known only to her. Besides, she and Peter were old acquaintances, if not close ones. At least, she thought, trying her hardest to overcome the scared, lonely feeling which had been growing on her all day, she wouldn't be left alone tonight with a stranger.

The crowd that returned to the Weavers' home for the feast

seemed enormous. "If I've forgotten to invite anyone I should, they've turned up anyway," Nicholas remarked as the rooms filled up, the older folk occupying every last settle, stool and window chest while the younger ones sat on the floor.

Bart and Alison Webber were not there, but they were gone from Dunster anyway. Bart, only two weeks ago, had had an accident with an axe while chopping down a dead tree in his garden, or perhaps it hadn't been an accident. At any rate, he had sliced the great artery in his left thigh and died of it, and Alison had gone back to her parents in Dulverton. They were still subjects of gossip, but not today. Today everyone's attention was on Liza and Peter.

The feast was generous, including roast pork and a saddle of mutton, a fruit pudding with figs and raisins and honey (Margaret had gone all the way to the county town of Taunton for the figs), and another pudding made of bread, eggs, wine and spices, and with real sugar in it.

Cider and ale were on the board, and for the Weavers and Lanyons and their chief guests even some French wine. Liza's two little brothers acted as pages and helped to serve the guests. Liza was glad of the wine, because despite all her efforts to encourage herself, the sense of dread and loneliness was still increasing.

Dancing followed the feast. Nicholas's friends included people who could play pipes and lutes and drums and between them they formed an impromptu band. The bride and groom opened the dancing and then Liza danced with a dozen different partners at least, before the moment came when her mother and Aunt Cecy and Elena quietly cut her out of the gathering and led her up to the room where her parents usually slept. It was the wrong time of year for flowers, but it had been decorated with evergreens and some sprigs of gorse which were still in bloom, and the air had been sweetened with dried lavender. Candles were alight, and there were clean sheets on the bed beneath the white fleece coverlet.

"There's nothing to be afraid of. Just make up your mind you're goin' to be happy, and you will be," her mother whispered as they settled her in the bed. Liza, giddy with the wine she had gone on drinking between dances—though in her opinion, not nearly giddy enough—dutifully whispered, "Yes, of course. Thank you for everything." Then they went away and left her alone, but not for long.

All too soon she heard masculine footsteps and laughter on the stairs and then Peter was brought in, draped in what, so far as Liza could see in the flickering candlelight, looked like one of her father's loose bedgowns, a casual affair of brown wool that Nicholas tossed on if he wanted to move about the house before he was properly dressed.

The priest followed the men, and the women came back, too, for this final stage of the ritual. Peter was inserted under the sheets beside her and the priest said a short prayer, largely inaudible because of all the ribald jokes which were being thrown about. Like Liza herself, most of the company was rather drunk.

It was Peter, apparently less drunk than anyone, who, as soon as the priest had finished, proceeded to shoo everyone out of the room. He did it quite commandingly, even pushing his own father through the door. Having emptied the room, he slammed the door with vigour and shot the bolt.

"That's got rid of *them,*" he remarked, coming back to her. "You must be tired out, Liza, and no wonder. I feel as if I'd been squashed in a cider press." He sat down on the edge of the bed and looked at her. "It's not as if we're strangers—there's that to be thankful for. This is a new beginning. I hope it'll be all right. I mean, I hope I can..."

He stopped. Liza studied him. The woollen gown had fallen open—she could see the paler brown cloth lining and yes, he had borrowed it from her father; there was the place where she herself had mended a small tear. She could see his bare chest with a scattering of dark hairs like the hairs on the backs of his hands. His hands were quite different from Christopher's—longer and narrower, though very sinewy, and browned by the weather. She wondered why he had stopped speaking in midsentence and noticed that he had turned his head away.

"Peter?" she said uncertainly.

He turned back to her. "I'm sorry," he said. "I've said *I will* to you, and I mean it. I'll be as good a husband as I can. I promise."

"But?" Liza pulled herself more upright. Through the haze of wine she had sensed that something was amiss, and knew she ought to find out what the something was, and try to put it right. "What is it? Peter, tell me."

"I can't do that, Liza. It wouldn't be right. I think we should..."

"Were you—are you—in love with someone else?" Liza asked bluntly, and the wave of scarlet that ran up into his face was answer enough. He did not have to speak.

"I'm so sorry," said Liza gently.

"I wanted to marry her. I thought we were betrothed, but her parents told my father that she'd promised herself to others before me, so her promises were empty. Then she ran off with another man. That's all," he said at last, with difficulty.

"Oh, Peter."

She was genuinely sorry for him. She of all people knew what it meant to be compelled to turn your back on the one person you truly wanted.

But she must never tell him about Christopher. He could speak of his girl, but she must not speak of Christopher. If she were to build any future with Peter Lanyon, and build one she must, then Christopher must remain her secret. She must be Peter's refuge, the rock on which his house could be founded. That was what a sensible girl would set out to do.

She shook herself inwardly, to disperse the wine fumes, and said, "I *am* most truly sorry. But here we are, together. I'll be coming back to Allerbrook farm with you tomorrow. I'll do my best for you. What else can I say, or do?"

"You can be my friend. Will you try to be that?"

"Yes, of course. But…"

"No, I know. We have to be man and wife as well and everyone downstairs is expecting us to get on with it. They're probably looking at the ceiling and listening for, well, interesting noises."

"If they're still drinking," said Liza, "they'll be too fuddled before long to listen for anything. Some of them won't get home tonight, or if they do, it won't be in a straight line. Soon we'll hear them going zigzag and singing along the street."

It worked. Suddenly he chuckled and Liza, thankful to see his face crease in amusement, chuckled, too.

She, like Peter, had said *I will*. This was indeed a new beginning, and yes, it was better not to look back through the gates of Eden. "I would like to be friendly," she told him, and, a little shyly, held out her arms.

Peter leaned forward. "I forgot to pack a loose gown. Your

father lent me this and the damned thing itches. Take it off for me, will you?"

She took it off. There was nothing unpleasant about his body. It was young and clean and hard and it would have been a very strange wench who didn't admire it. He took hold of her, strongly but not roughly, and his warmth was pleasant.

Peter himself was realising that Marion, who had hurt him so badly, had at least done him one service. She had taught him his business. He knew what to do, how to caress and persuade, so that when the moment came, it would be easy for Liza, and not frightening.

There was one absurd moment, about ten minutes later, when his left knee missed the edge of the bed and the two of them nearly fell off. Peter shot his right hand out, clutched at the bedpost behind Liza to check their fall, and hauled them both back to safety, whereupon they found themselves laughing aloud.

Downstairs, a number of people, including Nicholas, Margaret and Richard, did indeed hear the laughter, and smiled at each other.

"It'll be all right," Nicholas said. "Sounds as if it already is."

"God be praised," said Richard, rather overfervently, to Margaret's ears. She wondered why. She and Nicholas had reason to feel like that, but why should Richard? Had Peter been difficult?

Oh well, what if he had? He clearly wasn't being difficult now, and nor, thank heaven, was Liza.

PART TWO

BUILDINGS AND BATTLES
1458–1472

CHAPTER TWELVE 🔊

DEMISE OF A PIG

It was all very well, borne on the emotional wavecrest of a wedding day and more than slightly drunk on strong red wine from France, to take resolutions about putting the past away and dedicating one's life to being a rock and a refuge for someone for whom you had no feeling beyond mild friendship.

At the time, Liza had thought *well, I have to do it, somehow,* and believed that because she must, she could. She had roused up her courage and for a while she felt brave, like a knight, ready to sacrifice herself for a noble cause. But what it actually amounted to was day-to-day life in Allerbrook farmhouse, and getting used to that, she sometimes thought, was going to take her a lifetime.

It would have been better if she and Peter had had a home of their own, but although there was an empty cottage on the farm which Peter's father admitted he had thought of giving them, they were living in the farmhouse after all.

"There's plenty of space here," Richard told them. "You two can have the room my father had. You'll be more comfortable and it's best if we're all together. I'd feel lonely, rattling around in the farmhouse with no family round me and I'm planning to plant some extra crops, so it's always possible I'll take on more farmhands one day. They might need the cottage. I could afford to pay them. Your dowry was generous, Liza."

Her father had increased it, perhaps to reward the family that had taken his erring daughter off his hands, perhaps to do what he could to see that she was valued by the Lanyons and well treated! Nicholas must have dug deep into his coffers, even though he had already agreed to share his profits with Richard Lanyon. She thought with longing of Christopher, but also, now, with guilt. Her father and mother had brought her up, loved her and cared for her and even given her some schooling, which many girls never had, and now her father had been very generous indeed with her dowry. Running off with Christopher hadn't been much of a way to repay them.

Christopher. What are you doing, now, at this moment? Are you thinking of me?

She must put such thoughts out of her head and knew it, but it was a tiring struggle and after only a few weeks at Allerbrook, she was already tired enough. Going to bed every night with Peter Lanyon, waking up beside Peter every morning and then working...*working.* She was strong and healthy enough, but despite Peter's reassurances beforehand, she had never, physically, worked like this.

At home she had helped with spinning and weaving, had

shared the task of milking the cows, had made cheese and butter and shaped bread. Here, although there was a loom, once used by Peter's mother, and a spinning wheel, too, she had so far had no time even to touch them. Here, the dairy work and the bread making were only a small part of a much more arduous regime, which involved carrying fodder to the oxen and buckets of swill to the monstrous pig that was being fattened in a sty next to the farmyard, caring for the poultry, searching for eggs and gathering firewood in the combe, as well as helping Kat and Betsy to get the meals and clean the house while, even at this season, the vegetable plot needed some attention. The onions and cabbages could be invaded by weeds at any time of year.

And at other times she would, she was assured, be busier still, for she would have to help with both the harvest and the lambing, and lend a hand in gathering the apples from the little orchard below the house, in order to make cider. Betsy would show her how, Peter said.

Even now, in winter, she was out of doors much more often than she had ever been at Dunster, at times in rain or bitter winds, with heavy leather boots on her feet to protect them from the mud. At night she was usually so weary that she swayed as she went up the stairs, and then Peter's embraces still lay between her and the blessing of sleep. She was often out after dark or before dawn, but she never, now, looked up to wonder at the moon or the stars. She hadn't the time.

The greatest relief came on Sundays when they went down the combe to attend the church in Clicket, after which, in dry weather, most of the menfolk would spend the afternoon at the archery butts set up on the green, close to Sweetwater House.

All able-bodied men were supposed to practise archery regularly, and although down here in the southwest they were well away from the quarrels between the ailing King Henry's warlike wife and his cousins of York, that could change. Families like the Luttrells and the Courtenays and Carews and the Sweetwaters, too, had their allegiances. For the moment, however, in Clicket, as in Dunster, the men—even though one at least of the Sweetwaters usually joined them, to make sure that their tenants attended—regarded the archery as sport, one of their few relaxations, except for occasional social gatherings at the various farmsteads.

Gatherings there had been, as the neighbouring farming families were friendly enough, and wanted to make the new bride at Allerbrook feel welcome. There had been Sunday dinners and Christmas celebrations with the other tenant farmers of the Sweetwater estate, the Hannacombes, the Rixons and the Lowes.

The Hannacombes, Sim and Anna, were quite young and had two small sons, one aged two years and another just two months. They were a good-humoured, broad-built, pink-complexioned pair who kept their fields well weeded and drained. The Rixons and their four children, whose ages ranged from two to eleven, lived squashed into a very small farmhouse but were jolly by nature and very musical. Gatherings at their home always meant singing and even dancing, cramped though their main room was. Harry and the elder of the two boys could play the guitar, Harry's wife, Lou, could perform on the flute and Lou's widowed mother would tap a hand drum to give them a rhythm. Going to the Rixons was enjoyable.

The Lowes, Tilly and Gilbert, on the other hand, were much less likeable, though they didn't seem to realise it. Tilly was skinny and as sour as turned milk, while Gil was an ugly little

man with dirt seamed into the lines on his face and most of his
teeth gone, the rest being mere yellow stumps. They had their
byre and stable under the same roof as themselves, with only a
central passageway between the humans and the animals, and
hens wandering in and out of the kitchen. They were older than
the others and had reared only one child, their daughter Martha.

"A very suitable name!" Richard said. "Poor wench is only in
her twenties yet, but with no looks and no portion, she'll be an
unpaid servant to those two, till either she dies, or they do."

The Lanyons had held a party of their own at Christmas. Liza
found a stock of almonds in the house, and as she knew how to
make and mould marchpane into simple shapes, she made a
marchpane ram for the occasion.

"In honour of the shepherds who were visited by the angels
and the sheep that matter so much to us," she said, which met
with approval from all quarters. She was asked to make another
as a gift when in January they journeyed across the county to
attend the wedding of Peter's friend Ned Crowham. Those, at
least, were occasions when she felt like a success.

Usually, however, any pleasure in these social get-togethers was
limited because the talk was nearly all to do with farming, which
as yet was not familiar to her. It was all so different from the wool
trade society of Dunster that she sometimes felt she was listening to a foreign language.

She told herself not to complain. Peter was gentle in his love-
making, and Kat and Betsy seemed to like her and had shown
her how to cook dishes that Peter and Richard especially enjoyed,
including the illicit rabbit pies which were a regular feature of
the Lanyon table.

Rabbits were game in the eyes of the law and not to be taken without permission, but Richard and Peter, whatever their other disagreements, were as one when it came to hungry rodents in the cabbage patch. They set snares, made pies of the victims and carefully hid all the traces if anyone called who was employed by or simply too well in with the Sweetwaters.

Liza had worked hard to master the art of a good rabbit pie, and then achieved another small success when she showed Kat and Betsy her own recipe for verjuice, the sharp sauce made from unripe apples, which gave flavour to so many dishes.

Kat's husband, Roger, was a little shy of her but always polite, while Higg, who had some skill at woodwork, made her a Christmas gift in the form of a decoratively carved wooden platter for use at Sunday dinner. She couldn't say that she hadn't been made welcome.

But nevertheless, she knew that Peter's mind was still detached from her (as hers was from him, although she hoped she was concealing it better), and though he was always courteous, Richard Lanyon intimidated her. Everyone jumped to obey his orders just a little too quickly. And then, one cold, overcast January morning, she understood why.

Ever since Christmas, Richard had been talking about putting up fences around a south-facing field called Quillet, because he intended to use it for wheat this year instead of leaving it as meadowland, and it would need better protection from deer than the existing ditches could provide. The field sloped and the ditches drained rainwater off into the combe, which was useful, but they were hardly an obstacle and anyway, the ditches here and there ran through culverts so that people and animals could have a way into the field. Liza had already seen the ox team take the plough in to tear up the rich grass of Quillet. Henceforth, the entrances would be guarded by gates.

On that chilly winter morning, Richard and Peter, who had spent the previous two days in the wooded combe cutting poles, decided that they had enough for the first stretch of fencing.

"They'll be at it all the time it's light," Kat told Liza. "They won't want to stop till dusk, so you'd better take some dinner out to 'un. I've got some bread and hot chicken pasties ready. I'll put the pasties in a crock with a lid and wrap it in a cloth to keep them warm—and there's a drop of cider in this here flask."

Liza duly set off with a bag containing dinner for her husband and father-in-law and found them hard at work. "A hedgerow 'ud be better, like we've got round the fields near the house," Richard said as she admired the first few yards of fence. "But hedgerows take a man's lifetime to grow. Might plant some brambles or hazel, though, to get one started. We'd get nuts and blackberries that way, too."

Peter said, "I think we've got company. It looks like Sir Humphrey."

It was. Astride his big bay gelding, he cantered toward them, embroidered saddlecloth flapping and a brooch in his velvet hat gleaming in the dull light. He slowed to a trot, pulled up beside them, put one hand on his hip and then scowled. Liza hastily curtsied and after a moment's pause, her menfolk removed their caps. "Good day, sir," said Peter politely.

"I'm not sure that it is a good day," said Sir Humphrey. He pointed with his whip at the fencing. "What's all this, then? And why has this field been ploughed?"

"It looks to the south and the soil's deeper than in most places hereabout," said Richard. "It's more fertile, too. It's my belief that this field could rear a crop of wheat and I'm going to try. Only I've got to keep the deer out."

"You'll also keep my cows out, I see!" Sir Humphrey snapped. "And stop me riding over the land when I'm hunting. This *is* my land, let me remind you."

"I rent it from you, sir," said Richard, quietly, but with an undertone which Liza found alarming. "And it's my business to make the best of it. Wheat's a valuable crop."

"Barley's good enough for the likes of you. Wheaten bread's not for common folk. If any wheat's planted on Sweetwater land, it'll be on our home farm. We'll eat the bread and take the profit if any goes to market. Well, you've ploughed—you may as well plant. But make sure it's rye or barley and put the land back to meadow afterward. And take that fencing down. I'll have no fences getting in my way on my land."

Liza stared at him in astonishment and his cold gaze fastened on her face. "You're looking at me as though I had two heads, young woman. May I know why?"

"I just...wondered..."

"Yes, well? What did you wonder?"

"If a field has crops in it, Sir Humphrey...I mean...surely you wouldn't hunt across any crop, whether it's fenced or no," said Liza, quite seriously.

Peter gasped, but Richard laughed, although it was a mirthless sound. "My wench, a hunt goes where the hounds go and the hounds go where the quarry does, and find me the stag that solemnly runs round a field instead of across it!"

"Quite right." The bay fidgeted restlessly, but Sir Humphrey checked him with a rough hand on the curb. "I'll forgive her for her impertinence this time," he said. "She's new here, I believe.

But teach her to guard her tongue. Put your mind to breeding children, my girl, fine healthy sons to make the best of my land, but not to fence it. I'll be out here again tomorrow and I'll expect that fencing to be gone. My horse needs exercise, and standing here in the cold will do him no good. Good day to you all."

He swung the bay around, cantered it in a semicircle, jumped the ditch beyond the end of the new fencing and rode off across the ploughed field, veering away at the other side and heading downhill toward Rixons.

"What the devil," said Richard furiously to Liza, "did you want to go and say that for? We'll have no peace for months now. He's taken umbrage!"

"I think he'd taken it already," said Peter mildly. "The fencing's upset him much more than Liza did. We'll have to remove it, you know."

"I'm damned if we do! We'll finish the job, boy, and that's that."

"We can't," said Peter. "Do that and he'll send men up here to take it down for us. You know he will."

"God damn him and all the Sweetwaters. The only good Sweetwater is a dead one. Him and his two sons—I hate the guts of every single one of them. Why should they have everything and us hardly anything and not even the right to better ourselves? And why should he have two sons when it was all Joan could do to give me one? And when are *you* going to have some news for us, Liza?" His angry eyes appalled her. "Near eight weeks you've been wed and it's time there were signs. What have you to say for yourself?"

He took a step toward her and for a moment she thought he would strike her. "Father..." said Peter protestingly.

She did not know if he said more than that. Terrified by her

163

father-in-law's fury, she dropped the dinner bag and cider flask on the ground and turned away and fled.

By nightfall the fencing was down, but Richard at the supper table was like a thunderstorm in human form. He shouted at Betsy that the pottage was too salty, which it was not, and berated Higg, who had hurt his wrist during the accident with George Lanyon's coffin and had wrenched it again while helping to cut fencing poles, as wrathfully as though Higg had done it on purpose.

Liza did not dare speak to him and scarcely even ventured to look at him. Next morning his temper seemed no better. Breakfast was nearly as frightening as supper had been.

When it was over, she fed the fowls and the pig and then went off to walk up the combe to the ridge above, abandoning the work of the house, taking—or stealing—one of the solitary walks she loved and hadn't had since she came to Allerbrook, desperate for escape from the atmosphere of rage which seemed to fill the house like smoke.

It was cold, but solitude was a blessing. She reached the top of the combe and paused, thankfully breathing the free air on top of the ridge, beside the bog where the Allerbrook rose.

The bog itself was a long stretch of virulent green amidst dark heather, with clumps of reeds here and there. It spread along the hillcrest in wet weather, sometimes even spilling over the edge, something Liza had witnessed in a rainstorm during December.

The slope of hill between ridge and farm was not smooth but undulated like the folds of a curtain. It wasn't perpendicular—sheep could find a footing there, and a few stunted trees clung to it, but it was certainly steep. During the December rainstorm, the overflow had poured down one of the creases and formed a new stream, which raced past the farmhouse about a hundred yards from the front door, to find its tumbling way eventually into the combe and the Allerbrook. It was quite a dramatic sight.

The bog was not overflowing just now, however. Liza turned northward along the ridge, climbing a little, and rounded an oval-shaped mound she now knew was called a barrow and was thought to be the grave of some ancient chieftain who had lived here before the name of Christ was ever heard in these parts. Peter had told her that there were many such barrows on the moor, and most were said to be haunted, at least after dark. This one seemed wholesome enough in daylight, though. Liza paused beside it, looking back and down, to the thatched roofs of Allerbrook. The place where she lived, though she did not think she would ever call it home.

She shouldn't be here, of course. If Richard noticed her absence, it wouldn't do much to improve his temper. But it was comforting to see the buildings of Allerbrook, where she sometimes felt like a captive, dwindled by distance to the size of toys.

Raising her eyes from the farm, she looked northwest. There, in the distance, was Winsford Hill, where there were more supposedly haunted barrows, and far, far away beyond that rose the highest hill on the moor, Dunkery, where a beacon would be lit if any enemy invaded.

Just below Dunkery, though she couldn't see it, was the valley of the Avill River, which flowed to the sea through Dunster. Even though she couldn't, at this distance, glimpse as much as a trickle of hearth smoke, she knew where her home village was. Beyond it, lost in haze and therefore, today, just an emptiness, was the Channel. She missed it. At home, the sea had always been close at hand. If she was unhappy at Allerbrook, it was probably because she was homesick. Would she have been homesick living—in France, perhaps—with Christopher?

She didn't think so. Christopher was where she belonged. She had only to think of him and it was like a homecoming.

And she must not stay here too long, thinking about him. She was sure to be needed for something. She hoped to heaven that Richard was now out on the land and unaware of her idle wanderings.

As she took the path down the combe she noticed that while she had been out, someone had moved the cattle and horses from their housing in the farmyard and put them in a field, where they were making the best of the poor winter grass. She wondered why. A few moments later, as she neared the yard, she heard the scream.

It was the most hideous noise she had ever heard in her life, earsplitting and full of frenzied terror. Horrified, she began to run. As she rushed into the farmyard, the sound seemed to wrap itself around her. Raised voices were mingled with it now. That was Peter, shouting, "Not like that, you bloody fool!" and her father-in-law, clearly not out in the fields after all, bellowing, "Hold on, *hold on,* can't you? Damned slippery brute... *Higg!* What in hell's name are you doing? You've done this job before...."

"Can't hold 'un with this bloody wrist...!"

"You and your poxy wrist! Hold *on,* you and Peter, give me a chance...!"

The screaming crescendoed just as Liza arrived in the yard. It seemed to be coming from an outhouse which hitherto she had never entered. The door was half open. She ran to look inside and then stopped, staring, breathless and revolted.

Richard, Peter and Higg were all there, and so, hanging by its hind feet from a pulley in the roof, was the huge pig she had fed only that morning. The pulley rope stretched down and was made fast to a bracket in the wall, and immediately below the pig was a wooden bucket, empty. The pig was shrieking and struggling as Peter and Higg tried to hold it still. Richard was standing ready with a glittering knife in his hand. As she watched, the others finally stopped the pig from twisting its head and lunging with its front trotters, and Richard struck.

There was a final scream, which died away into a gurgle. Blood spurted all over the three men and then settled into a scarlet stream, which poured into the bucket. The pig jerked convulsively, not yet quite dead.

Richard, glancing around, caught sight of her and said quite amiably, "Oh, there you are. Stupid animal—put up a fight. Only made it harder for himself. But we'll get a good pork joint and some fine salted meat and chitterlings out of this one. Kat'll teach you to make chitterlings. She chops up some of the innards and fries 'un with bread crumbs and onions. She's a great one for them."

The pig was still now, dead at last. But the blood reeked, sweet and metallic and completely disgusting. Retching, Liza fled to the back door of the farmhouse, dashed inside and found a basin.

The kitchen was hot, full of steam from a vast cauldron bubbling over the fire. There was a bucket of fresh water under the table, however, and Betsy, clicking her tongue in concern, dipped a beaker into it and brought it to Liza as she leaned against the wall, basin in hand, and threw up what, to her, felt like her entire insides.

"Here, when you're sure you're done, wash your mouth out with this. What was it, seein' the pig killed? Meant to warn 'ee they were plannin' that for today since they can't go on with the fencin', but 'ee'd slipped off somewhere. Never seen it afore, I expect. You'll get used to it."

"Get *used* to it? It...it shrieked!"

"Who wouldn't?" said Kat, unconcernedly beating eggs for a pudding. "It's mostly quicker and quieter than that. Get it right and piggy's dead afore he knows he's even been hoisted off the ground. You only get that racket when whoever's holding 'un b'ain't got a proper grip. Roger ought to have helped instead of Higg, until that wrist's properly better. Pig should have been killed back afore your wedding, anyhow, to my mind, but Master always keeps one goin' till the New Year, so as to have fresh bacon and hams still hanging when everyone else has run out."

"Why isn't Roger helping?" Liza asked, and then retched again. When the spasm was over, she added, "Where is he?"

"Out clearing a ditch. Higg said holding a pig would be easier if he strapped his wrist, but it looks like he was wrong," said Betsy. "Dear Lord, you do be upset. Here, sit on this stool."

Liza was still sitting on the stool and sipping water when Richard came in, carrying a stack of empty buckets. She looked around once at his bloodstained form and hurriedly turned away, swallowing.

"Kat, is that cauldron boiling yet? Liza, you'd better come and learn how to get the bristles off a pig...what's the matter?"

"She's been sick. Gave her a shock, walkin' in on that," said Betsy.

"Oh, I see. Well, having something to do ought to put that right. Come along, Liza. Come and help. Betsy, Kat, that water."

He and the two women between them scooped water from the cauldron and bore the buckets away. Liza emptied her beaker, wiped her mouth on her sleeve and followed them reluctantly back to the outhouse. No one seemed to have noticed how long she'd been gone—there was that to be thankful for, at least. The cattle and horses must have been moved in case the screaming and the stench upset them.

Inside the shed, the pig still swung from the hook in the roof, but the bleeding was over. The pail of blood had been put aside and a piece of wood placed over it, while a large barrel had been placed under the pig instead. Peter had climbed, by way of a ladder, onto a stout timber ledge in the nearby wall and Higg was standing sulkily at the ladder's foot, saying that this was his job rightly and his wrist would be all right. "Bucket won't clobber me with its trotters and twist about."

"We're not risking you losing hold and emptying boiling water over us by mistake," said Peter brusquely. "Ah. Here's the water. Hand me up that bucket, Kat."

"Stand back," said Betsy to Liza—unnecessarily, since Liza had halted nervously in the doorway. Kat passed her pail up to Peter, who emptied the contents over the pig. The water sloshed down into the barrel and Peter handed the empty pail down through clouds of steam to Higg. Betsy gave him her full one and he doused the pig again. Liza found the first empty pail being passed to her.

"Fetch another lot of hot water," Richard said. "Quick! It needs to be boiling. It strips the bristles off. Didn't you know?"

"No. What...what do we have to do after this?"

"Scrape him down, get any leftover bristles off, right down to the skin. Couple of days and we'll start cuttin' him up and getting his meat salted and whatnot. Betsy and Kat'll show you what to do."

Liza slept badly that night, dreading the tasks that lay ahead. Her parents had bought their meat from a butcher who did his slaughtering out of sight and sound of the village. This close contact with it was something for which she hadn't been prepared. "I wish someone had warned me," she said that night to Peter.

"It's just the first time that's upset you," said Peter calmly. "Next time, you won't mind so much and the time after that, you won't mind at all. You'll see." Liza, who had eaten little that day and still felt nausea clenching at her stomach, hoped he was right, but doubted it.

But two days later, when the next stage of the work began, her tasks weren't too unpleasant after all. The good-hearted Higg had said that morning that the gutting and cutting up should be done out of Liza's sight. "The mistress b'ain't used to such things yet. It'll take a while."

Liza therefore stayed in the kitchen while the pig was dealt with in a barn. Under instruction from Kat, Liza peeled onions and grated bread for the mysterious product called chitterlings. Presently, Betsy brought in chopped-up intestines for the purpose, but they didn't look much like insides and therefore weren't particularly horrid. When they were fried with the crumbs and onions, the smell was appetising.

Nor, when larger cuts of pig were carried in, did she mind the business of laying down hams and bacon in troughs of salt with juniper berries and dried bay leaves. However, all the chopped intestines hadn't gone into the chitterlings. When Kat, quite forgetting Higg's warnings, went to the icy-cold shed where she had left the bucket of blood, after stirring barley and oatmeal into it, fetched it in, added the rest of the chopped-up innards and tipped the whole lot into a pan, saying that this would make a fine black pudding, Liza was overtaken anew with uncontrollable sickness, and Richard, once more choosing the wrong moment to walk in, said, "Oh, for the love of heaven! Not again! What's wrong with the wench? You're on a farm now, my lady. These fine airs won't do!"

Liza, sitting miserably on a stool and clutching another basin, said, "I can't help it!" and burst into frightened tears, punctuated with further heavings. Betsy, coming over to her, leaned down and whispered a question.

Liza looked up. The nausea subsided a little. "Oh! I'm not sure. I think it should have come three days back, only it hasn't."

Betsy asked another question and Liza nodded. "Yes. Always regular, till now."

Kat had come over as well and was listening. She and Betsy then turned to Richard and surveyed him unitedly and with so much authority that Richard actually subsided and said quite quietly, "What are you women muttering about?"

"Babies," said Betsy shortly. "I'd bet the next clip on it. It's got nothin' to do with putting on airs. She's expectin' or I'm Queen She-Wolf, and that I'm not."

"You are? Oh, Liza! *Liza!*"

For the first time, Liza found her husband looking into her eyes with something like joy, as though she actually mattered to him. "I'm sorry I upset everyone over the pig," she said. "I'll be more sensible another time—I'll get used to things."

"Never mind about any of that. We've got to look after you now. This is the best of news."

Peter himself was surprised by the comfort it brought him. Marion had enchanted him and then failed him, but here was this sensible, honest Liza, trying to please him, trying to please everyone, and carrying his very own child. Liza wouldn't betray him and nor would their offspring.

Richard, his temper now magically restored, said that Liza must do no work at all that was in the least heavy. It wasn't the time of year for butter making, but when the cows were in milk again in the spring, Liza was not to do any churning, nor was she to help with the lambing, not this time.

"You were brought up to weave, weren't you?" he said. "Try and get my wife's old loom and spinning wheel working again. You'll come to no harm with that. Nor with making rabbit pies," he added with a grin.

For two weeks there was peace in the house, albeit with a little nervousness because Richard had decreed that wheat would be planted, whatever the Sweetwaters said; he had the seed and would brook no argument. Then came the morning when Liza woke to find an all too familiar ache in her lower stomach, and by the end of the day she knew the hope of a child was gone.

CHAPTER THIRTEEN
THE HOWL OF THE SHE-WOLF

"So that's that! Twice!" said Richard furiously, standing beside Liza's bed and looming over her, his face dark with fury. "Twice! You've gone and lost another and before you'd got well started, at that! The wheat's sprouting in Quillet, but what's the good of the wheat growing if the family doesn't? You've let us down, wench!"

Liza, her hair tangled and streaks of tears on her pale face, shrank away from him, wishing she could bury herself in the sheets. It was May, and warm, and she felt not only wretched but feverish. But there was no pity in her father-in-law's angry eyes.

"I'm sorry. How could I help it?" she said wretchedly.

"What's wrong with you," Richard demanded, "that you can't do a simple thing like this? You're as bad as my wife Joan was. You were a good strong girl, I *thought*. You do your work and you go off walking on the moor as well—funny sort of habit, that, but it looked as if you were healthy. All right, you lost one, but it was the first—these things happen. I reckoned that this time it 'ud be all right, but no, it's hardly begun and then this!"

"It wasn't my fault!" She made herself try to fight back against the bullying. "You tell me how I could have helped it! What did you expect me to do?"

"Father!" Peter strode into the room. "What's this? Leave Liza alone! Betsy and Kat say she's had a nasty time and she's still bleeding. I won't have you shouting at her and blaming her! Go away!"

"You don't order me out of a room in my own house, boy!"

"Out of this room I do!" Peter retorted. "She can't get better with you standing over her, shouting. Do you think she did it on purpose? It'll be all right in the end. Betsy had the same thing happen to her, but she had children later."

"All right. I hope you're better soon, girl, and I hope next time'll be different." Richard gave Liza a last glare and walked out of the room. Peter followed him and tramped angrily down the stairs behind him. At the foot, Richard turned to face him.

"Sometimes I almost wish I'd let you marry Marion Locke."

"It's not Liza's fault! She's heartbroken. She prays each night, on her knees by our bed, asking God and Our Lady for a healthy child. We thought her prayers had been heard when we knew she'd quickened again. It's no help when you say things to her like *hope you'll finish the job this time* and *what we need is half a dozen sons.* You ever thought it might be something in us? Happens sometimes with animals, so why not people? Remember that ram that kept siring weakly lambs?"

"You're strong enough." Richard's voice, however, was suddenly tired. He had realised that his feelings had just betrayed him into mentioning Marion, and that was something he should never do, ever. The trouble was that now and then, he didn't seem able to help it.

He still sometimes dreamed of her death and heard her scream inside his head. Again and again he told himself that in the eyes of Peter and her family she had run off with another man and that he should tell that story to himself until he believed it. Except that he would never believe it. Always and forever he would know it for the lie it was, and one day he was afraid he would talk in his sleep and somebody would overhear.

More quietly he said, "You can tell her I spoke in the heat of the moment, and that I mean it when I say I wish her better." He led the way into the living room and added, with a change of tone, "Seen the wheat in Quillet? Looks good, if we can keep the deer out. The ditches just aren't wide or deep enough."

"Let's go and look at it," said Peter, willing to make peace if his father would, and also thankful to get his father away from Liza.

Long ago, when the Norman conqueror, William, first made Exmoor a royal forest, the land now occupied by the Sweetwater farms had been already under cultivation, and at that time it had lain outside the boundaries of the forest, as it did now. But in between, another Norman king, King John, had greedily enlarged the forest, moving the boundary so that the farmers on what was now the Sweetwater land found themselves inside, and subject to forest law, under which fences were forbidden. Deer must be able to move about freely and if this inconvenienced anyone, Norman kings didn't care.

When the boundary was changed again and the Sweetwater estate once more fell outside it, the law against fencing lapsed, but the Sweetwaters had made it plain enough that they held the same views as the Norman kings had done. Richard and Peter stood beside the growing crop, looking at the ditches which were allowed for purposes of drainage but which weren't nearly enough to discourage hungry and determined deer. "When the corn starts to ripen, could we tether the dogs out here?" Peter suggested.

"Deer aren't stupid," Richard said. "They'll soon work out how far the tether stretches. Then they'll take whatever they can out of the dogs' reach. It's growing well, though. I was right about the soil." He hesitated and then said, "Think Liza'll be well enough to get to church in Clicket on Sunday? It's the May Day competition, if the weather'll let us shoot this time. A bit late, but we'd have drowned if we'd tried to have the contest *on* May Day. Wettest first of May for years, I'd say."

"I hope she'll be up and about in time. I worry about her."

"So do I! I like the wench. If only…"

"Let's drop the matter." Peter did not wish to start the quarrel again and his eye had been caught by something in the sky, high above the barley. "There's a falcon up there, hovering. Can you see?"

"Where? Oh, yes. It's not a kestrel. Looks like a peregrine. There it goes! It's after that wood pigeon! Look at that! What a strike!"

The falcon had swooped, vertically, headfirst, a living arrow, straight onto the back of an incautious pigeon and borne it down to the ground. At the same moment there came a thunder of hooves and two riders came tearing up from the combe.

"Oh, damnation!" said Richard.

Coming level with the Lanyons, they checked and curvetted around them, colourful scalloped reins gripped in gauntleted hands, spurred boots gleaming, fantastic headgear on well-barbered heads. Richard and Peter gritted their teeth but removed their caps, since arguing with these two arrogant young men was unwise.

Then Reginald and Walter Sweetwater laughed, swung their horses away and put them at the ditch. The big horses leaped it side by side, manes and tails flying, and galloped on, headlong, this time across the wheat, to slow down in the middle and stop, while one of them dismounted and went to pick up the falcon.

"They did it on purpose!" Richard snarled, glaring across the field at them. "They know wheat when they see it and I daresay they know their father told me not to plant it! So they trample it for their sport and to put me in my place. Showing off with a damned great peregrine falcon, too. I swear," he added, "I *swear* that one of these days I'll turn things round. One day *they'll* take off their caps when they see *me* coming!"

"You won't be well enough to go to Clicket on Sunday." Betsy said. "You lie flat and still and, except when nature calls, you stay in that bed until that there bleeding stops. Wretched time you've had."

"And nothing to show for it," said Liza, turning her head away. *"Nothing!"*

"Sleep you need," said Betsy firmly, "and no goin' to church this week, let alone hangin' round they butts watchin' longshafts fly!"

Liza tried to take an interest in the archery. "I think they're having a crossbow contest, as well. Father-in-law is good with the crossbow."

"We'll bring 'ee all the news. Kat's said she'll stay here on Sunday, so she'll be within call." Outside the room, encountering Kat, who had just come up with a posset, she said, "The mistress is brightenin' up. Showin' interest in the shootin' next Sunday. That's a good sign. Just keep Master Richard out of there, that's all."

Liza thanked Kat for the posset, and once left alone, tried to sip it quietly and be what she knew her mother would have called "sensible." Tears and self-pity would worry Peter and annoy his father more than ever. She was grateful that Peter had not been angry. After Betsy had told him that it was all over, he had come to ask how she fared and done so in a kindly tone of voice. Later he had ordered his father to leave her alone, and got Richard out of the room, for which she was infinitely grateful.

If she had never set eyes on Christopher she could easily have loved Peter, and in a way, she did. The glittering spark that had been between her and Christopher wasn't there and nothing could put it there, but Peter was her real world, the company she would have to keep until one of them died, and there was much in him to value. Except that nearly all the time, Peter was ruled by his father. It was Richard who counted most in this house.

She lay there, puzzling over her own feelings, wondering why what she felt for Christopher was so very different from the mild affection she had for Peter. It was the difference between a leaping waterfall and a placid meandering stream; the difference between a bright fire and a dull red ember.

With Christopher she could have had a healthy child. She knew it.

The spring had been wet, but the following Sunday began with sunshine. Liza, lying on her bed after everyone except Kat had gone off to church and the archery competition, taking midday food with them, imagined how the grass and the cow parsley would be springing along the sides of the sunken lanes. In the most sheltered places there might even be some early foxgloves, adding their soft red to the green and white of the verges. Birds were singing. They were nesting.

Oh, dear God, they were nesting, rearing their young. Only Liza Lanyon, apparently, was not allowed to do that. She heard Kat coming to look in on her and turned on her side, closing her eyes. Kat was apt to want to talk and Liza didn't feel like it. Better look as though she were asleep.

She let Kat give her a meal at noon, but said she was still drowsy and put on another pretence of sleep to keep Kat at bay. The sunshine had gone by then and rain was beating on the windows. She wondered if it had spoiled the archery competition. She fell asleep in earnest then, but woke later to find that the bleeding had almost stopped, and that there were hooves and voices in the farmyard below. Then came the tramp of feet on the stairs. Pulling her pillow up behind her, she propped herself into a sitting position just as Richard and Peter came in.

As cheerfully as possible, she said, "I am better. I'll be up soon. Did you have your archery in spite of the rain?"

"I won the crossbow competition," said her father-in-law. "Harry Rixon won the longbow final, with Sim Hannacombe second. Peter here only got third. The rain started just afterward. We've something to tell you, though."

They came to her bedside and looked down at her, their faces solemn. Richard said, "Father Bernard made an announcement at the end of the service. He said that news has come that the king's mind has gone cloudy again but the queen, Queen Marguerite, is raising a host in his name, to keep the York family out of power. The She-Wolf is howling for the pack to gather, that's what Father Bernard said, and the Sweetwaters will answer the call. Sir Humphrey and Reginald are going, Reginald being a widower with no children, while Walter's got a wife and young-sters. Walter's staying home. But Master Humphrey's calling up men from the Sweetwater tenants."

Liza stared at them.

"They all came to the archery butts—the Sweetwaters, I mean," Peter said. "They watched the competition and then called us together. Just then the downpour started, so they hurried us all off the green, just as if they were herding a flock of sheep, and right into Sweetwater House to talk to us in their great hall."

Richard nodded. "I've never been inside that house before. From outside, you can see the gatehouse and that lookout tower with battlements round the top, and there are all those windows like lance heads, all with glass in, but it's plain inside. The hall's quite small! There's panelling, but nothing fancy about it, and only a couple of tapestries. The rest of the wall's full up with a lot of antlers, and weapons hanging in patterns. I got the feeling the Sweetwaters aren't as rich as they'd like us to think. Just hanging on the skirts of the gentry, that's them."

Liza, wondering if her father-in-law had paid any attention whatsoever to what was said or done inside the Sweetwaters' hall, or had spent all his time there memorising his surroundings, said, "But when you were in there, what happened?"

"They sorted us out," said Peter. "They still want their land tilled and the village trades to go on, so they're not taking all the men. But they're taking Edward Searle's son Toby. Geoffrey Baker's going and so are Harry Rixon and Sim Hannacombe, and some of their farmhands and from here at Allerbrook, either I must go, or Father. They don't want Higg or Roger."

"Both too old," Richard said, "and Roger too bent-backed

anyhow. But even with Higg and Roger still here, we'd be short-handed if Peter and I both went. We haven't men enough on this farm as it is, since Betsy's boy took his family away. All Kat's young ones were girls. The Sweetwaters know all that. We'll just take one of you, Sir Humphrey said to me, meaning me or Peter here. We can choose which. Generous of him! Dear God, we've got to follow the Sweetwaters to war whether we like it or no, just because we rent their land! It's enough to make a man puke."

"But which of you...?" Liza's mouth had gone dry. Peter was the younger man, the stronger one. The thought of being left at Allerbrook with her father-in-law and no Peter for an unknown length of time was terrifying.

"I said I'd go," Richard told her. Relief flooded through her, only to be stemmed a moment later when he added, "I'm fit enough and Peter's got work to do here. I said to him, you stay home and make a few more efforts to get this place populated. I'll do the fighting. My father went to war a couple of times and there's an old helmet of his somewhere. I've got my crossbow and I've been given a dagger. They handed out weapons from the ones they had hanging on their walls. We leave in two days."

It was more than two years before he came back, and by then they had all but given him up for dead.

CHAPTER FOURTEEN 🙠

HOPE AND FEAR

Throughout those two years they rarely had reliable news. They never knew for sure what was happening or where. Scraps of information filtered in sometimes, of course. Since her marriage, Liza had managed to get away from the farm only on rare occasions, and before Richard went away she had visited her parents in Dunster only once. However, Nicholas came to Allerbrook each year to collect his wool, sometimes bringing Margaret, too. They both came during the first summer of Richard's absence, a couple of months after his departure, and they had a little news.

"We get ships in Dunster harbour," Nicholas said. "Smaller than they used to be, on account of the silting up, but some of them have come from London. The rumour is that Queen Marguerite means business and hates the Yorkists and wants to see every last man of them dead. King Henry's woollier than your sheep and has nothing to say in the matter, and the Yorkists claim they're loyal to him, but if they can't convince Queen Marguerite of that, it won't help them. Our cousin young Laurie has gone to join her forces, my dear," he added to Liza, "and two of his brothers and a couple of our other cousins. The Luttrells called them up. She-Wolf or no, Luttrell said, while the king's ill, the queen represents him and the Luttrells follow their legal lord. Or lady, as the case may be."

But none of that amounted to much, and after it came a long silence until Walter Sweetwater received word from his father and brother, and passed the information on to Father Bernard to announce from the pulpit. It was unhappy news. There had been fighting in the southeast of England and Harry Rixon would not return to his home. Nor would the two farmhands who had gone with him.

A full two years had passed before Father Bernard announced one Sunday that the war was over, that they were now ruled by Yorkist King Edward IV, that King Henry VI with the wandering wits was a prisoner in the Tower of London, that the She-Wolf had fled the country with her son and the conflict was at an end. But still no word came from or about Richard Lanyon of Allerbrook, and the Sweetwaters did not come home, either.

Meanwhile, a number of things had happened.

The depredations of the deer at the first wheat harvest were nearly disastrous. They sold every last ounce of what was salvaged but made a loss, and even Liza understood why Richard had been so angry at being denied fences. Shortly after that, however, Walter Sweetwater told Peter that he could plant wheat in Quillet and fence the field, provided he didn't put up any other new fences. The results were highly satisfactory.

"We're making money from the wheat now," Liza said. "Walter Sweetwater's not all bad."

"No," Peter agreed. "I suppose not. The new bridge is useful, I must say."

Another innovation for which Walter Sweetwater was responsible was a packhorse bridge he had had constructed over one of the streams to the northeast of Allerbrook. The stream in question was deep, and the ford which had been its previous crossing place was unreliable. The area was so apt to flooding that packhorse trains from the Sweetwater manor usually took the long plod down the combe when they wanted to take their wool to Dunster, always the best market, if not the nearest.

The new bridge was built of stone and looked very like the one at Dunster, being long and narrow but high sided, to protect the packs when the river was in spate, and solid enough underfoot to reassure the most jittery pony. It made the journey to Dunster much shorter. Every time Liza saw it she recalled the Dunster bridge and knew a secret heartache, for it reminded her of the time she and Christopher had met there by chance and had their first tiff.

"I grant you," Peter said, "that there are things on the credit side of Walter Sweetwater's account." Then they both laughed, because Liza had learned double-entry accounting from her father, and introduced it at Allerbrook, which had impressed Peter considerably.

"Just as well your father-in-law's away," Margaret had said during the visit to pick up the wool. "Now you and Peter can settle down without him pokin' his nose in."

Liza knew very well what her mother meant, but it was a long time before she had any fresh hopes of a child. Peter at least refrained from nagging, for which she was grateful, and he tried to be considerate about the amount of work she had to do. She knew that although to her the outdoor work of Allerbrook was hard, the Lanyons—Richard included—expected less of their womenfolk in that way than most of their neighbours did. Everyone helped with the harvest, but Lanyon women weren't expected to do the winnowing, which meant standing on an upland field in the wind, no matter how chilly it was, and tossing grain into the air. Nor did the Allerbrook women carry manure to the fields on their backs as Tilly and Martha Lowe, Anna Hannacombe and Lou Rixon did, but loaded the smelly stuff in panniers and took them out on the backs of the oxen.

Not that Lou Rixon would be carrying any more manure out to the fields, for she had left the district, taking her children and her aged mother with her. She had been in despair when she heard of Harry's death, having already found that she could not manage the farm with the two elderly hands who were left. She had, however, been offered a chance to marry a widowed farmer on the other side of the moor who had somehow avoided having his helpers taken away to the war, and she seized the opportunity.

"I've been thinking about the Rixons' farm," Peter said to Liza after Lou's departure. "I reckon we should take the place on and pay the rent to Walter Sweetwater."

"But we can't look after Allerbrook *and* Rixons, as well!"

"We won't," said Peter, grinning. "We sublet it and make it pay its own rent. The Rixons ran sheep and Lou's selling the flock. Your father knows every family on the moor that runs sheep. Somewhere there'll be a young couple wanting a place and willing to buy the flock and work like demons to see that it pays. And so it will."

"But why shouldn't this young couple of yours just pay rent to Walter Sweetwater? You'll have to, and if you're to make a profit, you'll need to charge them higher, won't you?"

"I might let them have Three-Corner Mead in the bargain. It's our smallest field and we never use it much, but it marches with Rixons. We can do without it and they can pay extra for it. It won't be a big profit, but it'll be one just the same."

At lambing time a year after Richard went away, the weather was unkind and some of the ewes had trouble. Peter had bought a new ram with a magnificent fleece but, unfortunately, a magnificent set of horns as well and a massive skull to support them. Some of his lambs were too big in the head to give their mothers an easy time.

Liza, taking part in this year's lambing, found that she had some instinctive skill. Her fingers were sensitive to the shapes and movements of lambs which had got themselves into awkward positions, or tangled up with their twins, inside the ewes. She could very often free a little leg that was caught up with one from another lamb, or feel a tiny hind hoof which had come forward too soon and guide it gently back so that the lamb could slide safely into the world.

But halfway through that lambing season she was overtaken with sickness, just as she had been at the pig killing, and messy as lambing could be, the reason was nothing to do with that. Once more, Betsy was asking questions and passing the answers to Peter, who said, "No more getting up in the night for you, my girl. We'll see to the ewes without you."

This time let it be a success. Liza was never sure what she thought about God, and had been less sure still since He'd taken Christopher away from her. It did not seem right to her that strong young men should give all the urges of nature away to this invisible deity, or what the said deity wanted with the said discarded urges when He'd got them.

"You didn't time this too well," Betsy said, poking up the brazier that heated Liza's bedchamber, making sure that the window was fast and trying to cheer Liza along with jovial talk. "Nearly Christmas, and who's to make the marchpane fancies, with you abed like this? And what weather! Just look at it out there!"

"Well, who can choose these things?" said Liza between gasps. The thick window glass didn't reveal much of the world outside, but she knew well enough what it looked like: smooth-backed hills covered in snow, with only the tops of banks and bushes showing here and there, and a sky the colour of lead. Beneath it, the white covering was as bleak as a shroud. Nearer at hand, rows of icicles hung from the eaves of the outhouses and the water trough was frozen like stone. More snow was on the way.

"If it's a boy," said Betsy, "you'd best call 'un Jack, for Jack Frost."

"If it's a girl, we'd better call her Jill, then," said Liza, and then cried out as another pain seized hold of her. "Maybe he or she's in a hurry!" she panted hopefully when the spasm had passed.

The child was not in a hurry. It was the evening of the next day when Liza's exhausted and anguished body surrendered its burden at last. "Just in time," Betsy muttered to Kat as she lifted the little thing away from the bed. "The mistress couldn't have stood much more."

"Is it breathing?" asked Kat. "Which is it?"

"A boy," said Betsy sombrely. "And he's not."

They did their best with warm towels and massage, but it was no use. Jack Lanyon had been dead before he left the womb.

"But he was formed, a proper boy child." Peter tried to hide his disappointment, and indeed, it wasn't so hard, because only a monster would have denied pity to such white-faced misery. "You went your full time with this one. The next one'll live. You'll see."

Liza, speechless, just nodded. There would be a next time; of course there would. A man like Peter couldn't live like a monk. There would be another time and then another and then another…

Or would there? Next time she might well die! She tried to stop them, but the tears squeezed themselves out of the corners of her eyes and ran down her temples onto her pillow. Peter looked at her in consternation. "Liza? Are you in pain?"

"No. Not much, not now."

"What is it, then? Liza, you mustn't grieve like this. There'll be another time." Liza shook her head from side to side and the tears came faster. Peter, frightened, strode to the door and shouted for Kat and Betsy.

They pounded up the stairs and arrived breathless. "What is it? Is the mistress worse?"

"She's upset. I can't comfort her. She'll make herself more ill than she is now!"

Betsy went to the bedside. "Now, what be all this, then? These things be the will of God, and there are more babes born than ever live to grow up—we all know that. Hush, now. Hush."

"I'm so tired," Liza sobbed. "I wish I could go home."

"She's wandering in her mind!" Peter burst out. "She *is* at home. You're here in Allerbrook, Liza. *This* is your home!"

Liza, speechless once again, closed her eyes but the tears went on oozing from under her eyelids.

"You'd best leave her now, Master Peter. Worn right out, she is. You're feelin' let down, but she's been let down more than you have, let me tell 'ee. If she don't feel this is her home, it's because she's got no living child here. Where she rears her family, that's the place a woman calls home. She needs her children. But like I said last time, she needs a rest first and it's for 'ee to see she gets it. Longer than last time. You know what I mean!"

"We're doing very well indeed," said Liza. She was sitting at the parlour table with a small abacus in front of her. On the table were several tally sticks and also a writing set consisting of ink, paper, quill and sander. Her father had not only taught her to keep accounts by double entry (which the Lanyons had never heard of until she joined them, but which Nicholas had said was invented by Venetian merchants, long ago), he had also taught her the modern Arabic figures, which had begun to seep out of the east in the days of the crusaders and were now making rapid headway. Peter still recorded weights of fleeces and pounds of cabbages and bushels of grain by cutting notches in tally sticks, but Liza would translate them into figures on paper and have them totted up on the abacus the very same day.

"The wheat's promising again," she said, "and the bit of extra rent that comes in from Three Corner Mead is very useful, and the wool we kept for ordinary sales to merchants' buyers has brought in more than it normally does. I wish our new ram didn't have such a heavy skull. That's lost us two lambs. But I fancy that when we get our share from the cloth making, it'll be a healthy one this year. If only the weather holds for the harvest."

July had brought hot weather. The window was open on a vista of ripening grain, peacefully grazing cows and blue-hazed hills, but the room was stuffy, all the more so because it was slightly cluttered. Liza had acquired a bigger loom and put it in the corner of the parlour, and beside it was a basket of carded wool and her spinning wheel. She spun and wove whenever she got the chance and the Lanyons had both yarn and cloth to sell at Dunster market.

Wool and hot weather didn't mix, however. The mere presence of wool in quantity seemed to create heat. Liza herself was wearing a thin undyed linen gown and had thrown her crimson overdress aside. She had woven the crimson material herself, from yarn so fine it was more like silk than wool, but it was still too hot in weather like this. Even the linen gown had a damp and crumpled air. She rubbed a hand over her wet forehead, failed to notice the ink on her fingers and left a dark smear across her brow.

Peter, who had just come in with some extra figures for her to include, from the sale of surplus hay, burst out laughing. "You look so funny! You have ink in your eyebrows!"

"Have I?" Liza rubbed again and made things worse. Peter laughed again and looked at the discarded overdress, which Liza had tossed over the back of a settle.

"Why were you wearing your best overdress in order to do the accounts?"

"Because it isn't my best any longer," said Liza. "I washed it, very gently, after the Easter party Anna Hannacombe gave, because there was a gravy stain on it, and now it's gone streaky. The dye didn't hold as it should. See?" She reached out to pick it up and Peter saw that in places its colour had faded to pale red with pinkish streaks.

"That's a pity. Who did the dyeing for you?"

"Herbert Dyer of Washford, Father's usual dyemaster. He used to be in Dunster, but he moved to Washford a year ago. He does a lot of work for the monks of Cleeve and says he likes to be near them, though in his last letter Father says he can't understand why because the Cleeve monks send their wool to Dunster for weaving and fulling anyway! Herbert Dyer does good work as a rule. I must have been unlucky. Father still uses him, though nowadays it means taking cloth and yarn to Washford. I'm making another overdress for best and I'll have it dyed green. This will do for everyday when it isn't too hot to wear it! How much did we get for the hay?"

She picked up her quill again, added in the amount that Peter gave her and studied her totals. "I think that when your father comes back, the amount of money in our coffer will please him."

"If he comes back at all," said Peter. "Where is he? There's been no news of him or anyone else from round here, for months. They should all be home by now. If any of them are still alive. I've heard," he added, "that Walter Sweetwater is ailing with worry over his father and his twin."

"News must come in the end," she said. "Surely it must. *Someone* will let us all know what's happened. Won't they?"

"Who's to say? We're a long way from the heart of things here. I've heard of men going off to war in times past, and no more was ever heard of them, and no word ever came back." He stopped, gazing past Liza as though into some imagined scene. She looked at him enquiringly.

There was a long silence, though it was friendly enough. Since the loss of poor little Jack, Peter had slept in his father's old room instead of with Liza and oddly enough, the absence of lovemaking seemed to have brought them closer as friends. She was relieved because she need not watch for signs of pregnancy, to dread the outcome if they appeared or dread, with equal force, Peter looking disappointed when they didn't. She and Peter talked to each other more easily than they had ever done before.

"What is it?" Liza asked at last.

"I'm making a fair success of being master of Allerbrook, I think," Peter said at length. "Aren't I?"

"Yes. You are. That's very true." Liza studied him gravely. "Oh, Peter, I don't want any harm to come to your father and I know you don't, either, but I rather dread the day he comes back and takes the reins away from you."

"So do I," said Peter glumly. "It's a dreadful thing to say, but so do I. Better not to think about it, Liza. Better not to talk about it, either."

"Then we won't," said Liza, and then became alert, cocking her head. "The dogs are barking. Someone must have ridden in…Peter!"

"What is it?"

Liza had risen and gone to the window that faced toward the yard. She turned to Peter, her eyes wide. "The day has come, anyway. It's your father," she said.

CHAPTER FIFTEEN

DEAD DRUNK ON A HALF-STARVED HORSE

Springing up, Peter ran to join her. "He's still riding Splash! But why is he lurching in the saddle like that? He's sick or hurt!"

Together they made for the kitchen and the back door, shouting to Betsy and Kat, who were cleaning the dinner things, to come with them. As they all spilled out into the farmyard, Higg and Roger, who had been in the fields and had recognised Splash from a distance, rushed in to join them.

Richard was still sitting on Splash, who was standing still, head drooping. Except that his curious dark dapple coat was the same, the horse would have been unrecognisable, so gaunt had he become, with ribs and hips jutting. Richard too was as lean as a pole, burnt brown by wind and sun, and his clothes were patched and dusty. He had gone away with a crossbow slung on his back but must have lost it somewhere, although his father's helmet hung behind his saddle and he had acquired a sword.

"Father!" Peter gasped. "You're home...but what's wrong? Are you ill...wounded?"

"Neither. Jusht worn out," said Richard in slurred tones. He breathed out as he spoke. Liza and Peter exchanged quick glances and Richard emitted a short laugh. "Yesh, drunk as well. Shtopped at the White Hart in Clicket. Got some shider...cider. Had money. Picked up two sh...swords on the field at Towton. Sold the other. Walter Sweetwater gave me shome money, too. For bringing the news. No one else to do it."

They helped him down, and then Higg and Roger, one on each side of Splash's head as though he might fall down without their guidance, led the horse to the trough to drink while the others took Richard indoors.

Kat, eyeing his condition with disapproval, shook her head at him when he ordered her to bring cider, and said she'd brew a herb-and-honey posset. "More cider on top of what he's had already," she muttered under her breath to Liza, "or even a cup of my elderflower wine, and he'll drop unconscious. Wouldn't be surprised if he does that anyhow!"

"Shorry about this. No way for your father to come home, dead drunk on a half-starved horse," Richard said as Peter steered him to the parlour settle. "I've come from the north. I—we were with the queen. God'sh...God's elbow, is that what queensh are like? Winning, losing, going here, going there. Up to Shropshire, down to the Midlands, westward to Harlech, back east again to Yorkshire, shouth...south to attack London, back again north... zigzagging round the country like a bluebottle in a panic, and the thingsh she let happen!"

"Let me get your boots off," said Peter, kneeling to ease his father's feet free of their worn footwear, while Liza fetched some slippers and Betsy adjusted cushions behind Richard's back.

"I was ashamed, I tell you," Richard said as the slippers were put on his feet. "Queen She-Wolf and no mistake! Army wanted food—men just took it. Army wanted billets or horshes or wine, men took them. I did, too. Shtole…stole food, drink, fodder. Got to eat. Horse got to eat. I didn't rape any women, but some did. Anyone argued, he'd get his home and fields burned and a pike through his innards. Granaries emptied, fieldsh burned…no getting away, though. I was an archer with the Sweetwaters and deserters got hanged if they were caught. What'sh this muck?"

"Camomile and honey," said Kat firmly, presenting her posset. "That's what 'ee needs, after ridin' in that hot sun."

"We've seen to the horse," said Roger as he and Higg came in. "He'll be all right, given time and a few good feeds."

Richard was suddenly seized by aggression. "I hope sho. It'll take more than that to put me right!" His voice went up to a shout. "Bring me cider!" he bellowed and struck out, knocking the goblet from Kat's indignant hand.

"No cider, and none of my elderflower wine either. I'll brew 'ee another," she said, picking up the goblet. "Lucky this is pewter and not damaged," she added.

"You'll bring what you're told, woman!"

"Bring the elderflower wine," whispered Liza, "but water it."

This seemed to work. Richard growled but accepted the homemade wine in lieu of cider and didn't seem to notice that it was weak. More quietly, and more clearly, he said, "There were battles. I got through 'em all and so did the Sweetwaters, right till the end. It was in Yorkshire, Towton it was called. That's where the Yorkish…Yorkists did for us. The queen got away, went to Scotland, took her son—Prince Edouard, they call him, French-fashion—with her. We've got a King Edward now—so they shay…say."

"Yes," said Peter. "King Edward the Fourth. But there was no word of you, or Sir Humphrey Sweetwater or Reginald."

"No. They won't come back." Richard leaned back and closed his eyes for a moment. When he opened them again, he said, making a determined and obvious effort to speak clearly, "Sim Hannacombe's come home with me—Toby Searle, too. We were together—parted just outside Clicket. They couldn't face Walter Sweetwater. Us three, we're the only ones to come back. Sir Humphrey, Reginald, all the other men they took, they're dead and…Liza, I'm sh…sorry to carry bad news here as well, but five of your kinfolk went to war along with the Luttrells, and they won't come home, neither."

"Young Laurie?" Liza whispered. She had always liked Laurie, the son of her father's cousin Laurence and his prolific wife, Elena. Laurie and his own wife, Katy, had been a fond couple, both skilled at the yarn making which was the speciality of their side of the family and anxious to teach their trade to their own three children.

"Katy'll live on and find another, I daresay!" Richard snapped harshly. "What else *can* she do? Harry Rixon died early on and most of the others at this place Towton. Geoffrey Baker, too." His voice grew heavy and slurred again. "I shaw his body and Reginald Shweetwater's. They were on foot, not in heavy armour. Dear God, what a big axe can do to a man! I didn't know. Never 'magined. Horrible! Reginald…chopped near in half. Baker'sh head two yards from his body. I saw the Weavers, too, when I was getting away afterward. They was all together, in a heap. As for Sh...Sir Humphrey..."

He gulped at his drink and once more forced his speech to clear. "I used to want to murder all the Sweetwaters. Once said I'd like to see all their heads on chopping blocks. Don't feel like that now." He fell silent, apparently lost in some dreadful memory.

"What happened?" Peter asked at length.

"The Yorkist soldiers, they did Humphrey and Reginald in for me," Richard said, "and Walter Sweetwater can stay alive, far as I'm concerned. Death like that—it's shick...sickening. I didn't know! But someone had to tell Walter Sweetwater. See now why I want this wine? I went to Father Bernard first. They were in his flock, and it put off seeing Walter—only I didn't say much about Geoffrey Baker, just in case that old tale's true...."

"What tale?" asked Liza.

"Oh, you didn't know about that?" Betsy, with a sudden chuckle, interrupted. Richard didn't seem to mind, but closed his eyes again. "Geoffrey Baker's mother—Annet her name was—was widowed young, went to work as housekeeper to Father Bernard, and there was talk. Then all of a sudden she says yes to Jimmy the Baker, who'd been askin' her for months and bein' stood off, on account of he got hisself done for putting chalk in his bread flour the year before."

"Probably true, too." Richard's eyes opened again. "Too well dressed for a baker. Made more money than he should by the look of him."

"Jimmy got away with it for a long while," Betsy said, "but in the end he went too far, put too much chalk in and folk could taste something wrong. Harry Rixon's dad was parish constable then, and had Jimmy marched through the village with a loaf of chalky bread hung round his neck and put him in the stocks for half a day. Annet said he was no man for her. But all of a sudden she changes her mind, and less'n eight month later she tripped over a step goin' into her house and Geoffrey was born. Who's to say? He didn't look like either Father Bernard or Jimmy, but that's the tale."

"Father Bernard believes it, I reckon," Richard said. "Turned the colour of old cheese when I told him Baker was dead, and I didn't say about his head being cut off, even. I think I hoped he'd go to the Sweetwaters for me, but he looked so stricken…couldn't ask him to. I had to be the one. Not pleasant, bringing news like that to a man's son, a man's brother, even Sweetwaters! Walter's wife and youngsters were there, too. The boy Baldwin's an arrogant brat, but he's only about thirteen and his sister Agnes is younger. She was there, with her mother. She's pretty…."

He paused, plainly unwilling to come to the point of Sir Humphrey's death. Then he said, "Mary Sweetwater and Agnes both cried, hearing the news. They're decent enough women-folk, I suppose. Baldwin just went white. Cocky, like I said, but I pitied him then. Didn't tell them all of it. Couldn't. Must tell someone, though."

They were listening intently now, and in silence. Richard braced himself. "Sir Humphrey, he was up on a great big charger, in full armour. Horse was killed and he tried to run. Can't run fast wearing a lot of iron plates. Pack of Yorkist infantry caught him. Knocked him over, took his armour off. Hardly took 'em a minute—they knew how to do it—then one of them shtuck… stuck…a sh…sword in his guts and…and dragged it…he screamed and screamed. Like drawing a pig but not killing it first. I saw his insidesh spilling out…."

"Oh, no. Oh, don't!" Liza was appalled. Kat stood with a hand clamped over her mouth. But Richard had begun at last to empty the horror out of himself and now couldn't stop. His voice grew slurred again as he remembered. "Shaw…saw…his legs jerking about and the blood shoot up. I wash…was…hiding in a ditch, quite near. Didn't see the finish. Cowered down, let the long grass droop over me. Couldn't help him. Eight or nine of them, there were. Told his family he died quick. Thass what you have to shay. Everyone sh…says it, breaking news like that. Shome-times it's true. Sh…sometimes not."

Liza was trembling. Betsy had an arm around her. "Master Walter looked sht…stunned when I told him his father and his twin wouldn't be coming back," Richard said. He tried to steady his voice again. "Messengers bringing bad news aren't welcome mostly, but he was polite—I'll shay that for him. Paid me for my trouble. Gave me a drink and I gave him back the dagger his father lent me. Me and Sim and Toby, we've been monthsh…months—three or more—getting home from the north. Didn't have much money then—everything'd been in a muddle for so long; Sweet-waters couldn't pay us. Toby got sick on the way, too. We had to stop. Sold the spare sword to buy food—didn't like shtealing, but some places, where we'd passed through before, there weren't much left to buy *or* steal! Folk were trying to get back on their feet. Twice we stopped to help on farms where there was some provender going, got our keep and a bit more to take with us, moved on. That way I could keep shome of the money I got for the sword. Slow journey…dead shlow…"

He fell silent again and seemed about to fall asleep, but roused himself. "Give me your arm upstairs, Peter. I'm giddy and I want my bed."

Liza's stomach turned over and she saw Peter gnaw his lip, but Richard was already getting shakily to his feet. There was nothing Peter could do but help him up the stairs. Liza watched them go, hoping that Richard was too fuddled to notice that someone had been using his room, and that while he lay asleep, Peter could tiptoe around him and remove his own belongings.

It didn't work. Even when drunk and dazed with sleepiness, Richard was still remarkably observant. Liza, waiting nervously downstairs, flinched when she heard the roar of rage.

"What's this here, boy? Looks like one of your jerkins! You been using this room while I've been gone?" Then heavy footsteps—under the influence of fury, Richard had evidently recovered his sense of balance—and a door banging and another roar. "But Liza's still in here, seemingly! Ain't you two been shleeping together?"

She heard Peter's voice, quieter, trying to explain. A word or two reached her. "...last December...nightmare business...born dead...Betsy said..."

"To hell with Betsy, interfering old cow! You get your things and get back where you belong and do your duty and see Liza does hers! Fine sort of a stud you make, boy! Bad enough she's made a pig'sh ear of it again and again, but if you're not even trying...should have let you wed that Marion! Wager she'd have had a baby nine months after the wedding!"

Peter was annoyed enough to raise his voice in answer and the reply came clearly down the stairs. "I daresay Liza can hear you, Father. Just as well that she knows about Marion...."

Richard rumbled something, on a questioning note.

"Yes, I told her myself! And I'm damn glad I didn't marry Marion. Maybe she *would* have had a baby straightaway, and I'd never have been sure it wasn't fathered by a Norwegian sailor off a ship called *Fjord-Elk!*"

Betsy and Kat came to stand beside Liza at the foot of the stairs. "Now, don't 'ee worry," said Betsy, while Roger, embarrassment written all over his lined face, scurried out of sight. Higg stood where he was, shaking his head in concern. "Master'll calm down after a sleep," said Betsy, "and as for the other, well, a man needs his wife. Nice rest 'ee've had. Likely enough everything'll go right next time."

"I've one piece of good news for you." Peter's voice drifted down the stairs.

"Have you indeed?" Richard barked. "And what might that be?"

"Money. We're doing well and Liza's got more to offer than you think. You need new clothes and she's weaving cloth now, from our own wool and she'll see to it without paying a tailor— not that we couldn't pay a dozen tailors if we wanted. You wait till you see inside our coffer!"

"Really? Bloody good news, boy, given you and she provide us all with somebody to leave it to!"

"*Oh!*" said Liza in a desperate voice. Betsy put an arm around her. "Crying's no use," Liza said. "I know that. But just what does he think I can *do* about it?"

The Lanyons were not the only ones to receive news that day.

"My lady," said the gatekeeper's boy—a younger one this time, since the youth who had once announced the arrival of Nicholas Weaver had followed Sir James Luttrell to join Queen Marguerite's army—"my lady...there's a man to see you. He's got a string of knights with him."

Lady Elizabeth Luttrell knew that already. She had been in the grounds, not doing anything in particular, just roaming here and there and thinking about the past. Her son, Hugh, was at his studies. Her husband, James, Sir James, knighted at the end of the previous year after distinguishing himself in the service of the Lancastrians, had enjoyed his knighthood for seven weeks and then died in his next battle.

She was still struggling to grasp the two great changes in her life—the fact that she was now Lady Elizabeth Luttrell and the fact that she was also a widow. She had had no say in her husband's choice of allegiance, but she knew enough about the kind of passions which swayed both York and Lancaster to be afraid.

Then she heard the horsemen arrive, hooves clattering and striking sparks from the cobbles of the steep road up from the village to the gatehouse. She hastened to the walls, to a place from which she could see what the visitors looked like. One glance at the standard-bearer who led the way was enough to tell her that her fears were justified. The new king himself wasn't likely to be calling upon her in person, but his representative most definitely was. The standard displayed the badge of York, the spectacular Sun in Splendour.

She made for the hall to take her seat on her dais, the lady of the castle in her own kind of splendour, ready to receive defeat and dismissal with dignity.

Her visitors marched in, clanking as they came, since they were all in armour, with swords at their sides and spurs on their heels. Their leader gave her his name and rank, which was high, but somehow she was never afterward able to remember who he was. It didn't matter. It was what he said that was important.

"By order of King Edward, fourth of that name, the estates of the late Sir James Luttrell are forfeit to the crown. They will be granted to those who have shown loyalty to the house of York during the past few years."

"You are disinheriting my son?" said Lady Elizabeth.

"His father disinherited him, my lady. Blame him, if you wish to blame anyone."

"Frankly," said Lady Elizabeth, sitting very still and keeping her voice very calm, "I blame this new king, who takes vengeance on a young boy who has done him no harm and is not responsible for the actions of his father. Is that justice?"

"You have a right to your opinion, my lady. It makes no difference. You are required, forthwith, to pack your belongings, take your maid, your chaplain and one manservant and your son's tutor if he has one..."

"Father Meadowes tutors him."

"All the better. You and the boy and three companions, then. You must leave this castle. You may take horses for your son and the two men. You and your maid must travel pillion. You may take a pack pony."

"One pack pony only? There will be clothes, plate...."

"No plate or valuables beyond a little personal jewellery are to be taken. What you can't put in saddlebags or on the pony, you must abandon."

He looked with dislike at the woman sitting in the carved chair on the dais. She was more slender and softer of feature than Queen Marguerite, but reminded him of Marguerite all the same. She had the same knack of leaning regally back in her chair, with her forearms resting on the chair arms and her hanging sleeves sweeping the floor. Marguerite always had a thronelike chair, complete with arms and high pointed back, in her baggage so that she could hold court impressively wherever she chanced to be, even in the middle of a field. Lady Elizabeth looked as though she were holding court now.

He did not know that behind the dignified facade Lady Elizabeth Luttrell felt as though her inside were weighted with lead, and was holding back tears of longing for her husband, wondering tormentedly whether he had suffered much before he died, and making such an effort to hide her feelings that her body was rigid from crown to toes.

After a silent moment, however, something of the anguish in her still figure communicated itself to him, and more civilly he said, "You have somewhere to go? Kinfolk?"

"Yes. I have kinfolk."

"Good. You have today to prepare. You must leave tomorrow."

Edward Searle, his shepherd's crook in his hand and Drover, his black-and-white dog, at his heels, strode down the path from the moor where the Sweetwater flock was grazing, toward the home farm where three ewes he had recently bought for Walter Sweetwater were in a field along with their lambs. He would introduce them to the flock on the moor in a few days' time. A good year, except...

At the gate of the field he found Walter, standing with one foot on the lowest rung of the gate and resting his elbows on top. He was staring at the ewes and their frisking offspring, but not as though he was really seeing them. Searle moved quietly alongside him and also leaned on the gate.

After a while Walter said, "My father and my brother, both

gone. And from what I hear, it could be my home as well, when the Yorkist king gets round to it. I have my son, at least. Thank the saints that we all agreed Baldwin was too young to go to war. But what will happen to his inheritance, God only knows. You may have to work for a new master, Edward."

"Aye. It's a strange new world we're living in," said Searle.

As a boy, Walter had made friends with the shepherd, who was only eight years older than he was, but then they had talked only about sheep. Now, however, their conversation moved as smoothly into the sphere of power politics as though they had met there in the first place.

"Seems to me," said Searle, "that it's nothing to most of us whether it's York or Lancaster sits on that old throne in London. All we want's a bit of peace to get on with things as matter, like shearing and reaping and all of that. Pity they can't settle their squabbles without dragging us into 'em."

"It seems that they can't. My father and brother were dragged in and now see what's happened. They fought for Lancaster but York won, and this Edward of York is vengeful. He even wants revenge on the dead."

"If I were you," said the gaunt man at Walter's side, gazing straight ahead, blue farseeing eyes fixed on the distant outline of Dunkery Beacon, "I'd get in first. You'll know who to tell. I wouldn't, but you do, likely enough. Tell 'un you never went with your father and brother because you didn't agree with 'un. Say you're Yorkist and offer to…what's the way you folk put it? Swear your fealty. Offer 'un your sword for the future. See what happens."

"Hmm," said Walter. The ache of bereavement did not ease, because only time would ever relieve that, but the despair which had settled on him as word got out concerning the way the York-ists intended to treat those who had upheld the enemy thinned a little. "I've not much to lose, when all's said and done."

At breakfast on his first morning at home, Richard was silent and Liza found herself eyeing him nervously, but he seemed pre-occupied rather than angry. After the meal, he went out with Peter to ride around the farm. Peter came back ahead of him and walked into the parlour where Liza was weaving. His mouth was tight. Liza glanced at him and stopped her shuttle. "Peter? What is it?"

"My father," said Peter, "ought by rights to be lying in bed with a wondrous hangover. Instead, he's out on the land finding fault with every decision I've taken while he's been away—my God, I've made Allerbrook prosperous and not a word of real thanks has he uttered! I tell him our coffers are full and all he says is *bloody good news, boy, given you provide somebody to leave it to!* Sometimes I think that if he calls me *boy* again, I'll…I'll…*burst!* And now he's having revelations!"

"*Revelations?* Whatever do you mean?"

Peter rolled his eyes heavenward and cast himself into a settle. "I left him outside that old cottage—the empty one he thought of giving to us at one time. He has plans for it now. The sight of it has inspired him. After what he saw during the fighting, es-pecially at Towton, he no longer wants to see all the Sweetwa-ters dead, and anyway, two of them already are! But that doesn't mean he likes them. He's pleased that Walter's given us permis-sion to grow wheat on Quillet and fence it round so that he can't ride across it, but why, Father wants to know, should we need his permission or have to be grateful because he won't be tram-pling it down anymore? Walter, he says, has just as much conceit of himself as his father and brother—he just shows it differently. And as for what happened at my grandfather's funeral, and to Father's friend, poor Deb Archer—you know about her?"

"Yes, you told me long ago."

"Well, for her, he'll never forgive any of them. Trampling our wheat was nothing by comparison."

"They can't have meant any harm to Mistress Archer," said Liza. "That was just misfortune."

"He says it doesn't matter, that it was their fault and that's that and he's going to get the better of them for it. Not by killing them, no, not now. He's thought of another way. We're going to prove ourselves as good as they are. We're going to rise in the world. He said aloud, the day they rode across the wheat field, that one day they'd take off their caps when they saw *us* coming! He's been brooding over ways and means ever since, apparently, and now he's made up his mind. The first step, he tells me, is to build ourselves a fine house. Folk judge a man by the house he lives in."

"But we can't afford—"

"No, we can't afford to do it all at once, he says, but we can make a start, and to begin with, that old cottage is built of very good stone. It was looking at that cottage that gave him the idea. He wants to knock it down and use the stone, along with some more that he'll have to buy—saying thank you chokes him but I think he's a *little* bit grateful to us for tending our finances so well—and build a new wing for the farmhouse."

"But we don't need a new wing!" Liza protested.

"You try telling him that. It'll contain a hall, a proper dining hall like the one the Sweetwaters have. And one day he'll build on more rooms so that the hall will be part of the splendid new house he's inventing inside his head. He's as excited as a child going to a fair for the first time. Walter Sweetwater's going to hate this, he says, but we're not asking permission, and though the Sweetwaters ride across our land as if they owned it—"

"They do own it," said Liza reasonably.

"—they don't come right to the house or ride into the farmyard and with luck, the wing'll be finished and ready before they realise it's there. It'll cost the earth. We'll be begging alms from the parish by then, if you ask me," said Peter bitterly.

CHAPTER SIXTEEN 🔊

HOUSEWARMING

"Beginning to look like something, that is," Richard Lanyon, feet astride and hands on hips, said to Peter as they surveyed the new wing of the farmhouse. One day, as he had told his disapproving son, he hoped it would form part of a much bigger house, but this would do as a first step and as far as it went, it pleased him.

His satisfaction wasn't total, because Liza never these days bulged around the middle and was never sick at a pig killing. Nagging her was useless—he'd grasped that, and he couldn't help liking her, but his disappointment was still there. Betsy said it was the will of God. Richard would have liked a few words with God.

Peter found no satisfaction in the building work at all. "This new wing, it's got hold of him like a disease," he had complained to Liza, back in the early days of the work. "And according to him, this is just the start. And it's all because he wants to make a show in front of the Sweetwaters. Even if Walter Sweet-water does ride round with his nose in the air as though he were a lord of creation, what of it? He's less trouble than his father was!"

To Richard, that made no difference. Walter had been in that hunting party which had disturbed George's funeral and led to Deb Archer's death, and if Deb had lived, dear Deb, who had meant more to him than he knew until she was gone, perhaps he himself would not have become entangled with Marion and doomed to a lifetime of guilt. Only, that was not something that could be told to anyone. Ever.

"Well," Liza had said, "we'll have to help *your* father, whatever he does, to keep him happy. Life's easier that way."

She and Peter had been out in the yard during that conversation, watching while Richard prowled around the site, making sure that the masons were following their instructions properly. She had spoken distractedly, because something about that late October, the feel of the autumn weather, the look of the drifting clouds and the way their shadows moved across the hillsides had reminded her unexpectedly of the day she and Christopher had tried to run away together.

She had had no idea what kind of life lay ahead for the two of them, but she had believed that it would be a life with Christopher, and not with Peter and Allerbrook. But here she was, and it looked as though she always would be, but somehow or other, to her surprise, she wasn't miserable. Christopher's memory was always there, but the commonplace happiness of day-to-day living had come to lie over it, like a warm coverlet over tired limbs. She sometimes thought that it wasn't so much a matter of missing Christopher as missing her own longing for him. She didn't long for him much now. It felt like disloyalty, but it was true. She had too many other things to do, for one thing.

And one of the things she had to do was keep her father-in-law in a good temper as far as she could. Her husband, and for this she was grateful, had not blamed her for failing to produce the much-wanted family, but she knew very well that it was always in Richard's mind, a provocation ready to break out into temper at any moment.

She would be wise to be as helpful as possible over this unnecessary new wing. Anything, as long as it kept Richard Lanyon sweet.

As time went on, she discovered that she actually had a knack for good ideas. Richard admitted as much, and thanked her for them quite graciously. There was plenty of time to discuss her suggestions and put them into effect, because building the new wing took much longer than anyone expected. It was five years from the beginning to the day when Richard planted himself in front of it, put his fists on his hips and said that it looked like something now.

After studying the ground, Richard had settled that the new building should extend from the old farmhouse at right angles, along the side of the farmyard closest to the hill above. The farmyard sloped a little, and the new wing should stand at the higher, drier end. There was ample room, as the ground flattened out just there, extending back some way before the hill soared up again. The new wing, being a little higher than the rest of the house, was linked to it inside by a short flight of steps. It contained a single high-roofed hall, over thirty feet long, which as far as Richard could reckon from memory was longer than the one inside Sweetwater House.

The stone from the demolished cottage was pinkish-grey like

that of the farmhouse, which was as well, for Richard had decreed that the new wing and the old house must match. This, however, concerned more than just the colour of the stone. In George Lanyon's time the door to the dairy had been widened, revealing that the farmhouse walls were actually double, the space between being filled in with rubble. Richard could remember looking at it.

The new wing must be exactly the same, he said, which meant that after the hired workmen had dug out the foundations, rubble and extra stone had to be bought and fetched over the moor from a quarry six miles away.

Wheeled vehicles were of so little use on the moor that no one bothered with them as a rule. Stone could hardly be moved any other way, but it was half a century at least since any new building had been done locally and Richard's ox-drawn waggons therefore aroused great interest, not to say hilarity.

It was summer at the time, but the waggons still managed to get bogged down in muddy patches and wedged in narrow sunken tracks. On steep uphill stretches, loads had to be brought up piecemeal, which was slow, and one waggon lost a wheel while crossing the ford two hundred yards below Walter Sweet-water's packhorse bridge, the bridge itself being too narrow for any kind of cart. The vehicle had to be unloaded and hauled onto the bank and a wheelwright fetched from Taunton to repair it. After that the stone had to be loaded once again. It meant two days' delay and the farmer who accommodated the oxen in a field meanwhile cheerfully charged for the grass they ate as though (complained Richard) it had been best-quality oats. "As if I haven't had expense enough, buying stone and hiring the waggons and extra oxen, the loads being so heavy," he grumbled.

"Aye, the stone's heavy," Peter growled to Liza. "Which is more than you can say for our coffers nowadays!"

Once the shell of the building was in place, the next stage involved oak timbers for the roof beams, and slates for the roof itself. "Won't thatch do?" said Peter, but Richard would have none of it. "Good modern slate, that's what I want, boy!" he declared. "And planks for the floor. A thatched roof and floors of cobbles and earth are good enough for the old house, but not for this."

Work stopped once the walls, roof and floor were in place, because at that point the money ran out altogether. The next stage had to wait for a year, while the Lanyon coffers were replenished.

It was Liza (if only she functioned as well below the belt as she did above the neck, Richard thought but had the consideration not to say) who pointed out that if they were to eat meals in the new hall, then the kitchen ought to be next to it. Was food to be carried from the existing one at the other end of the old house, either through the rooms or across the farmyard when dinner was to be eaten?

"We shall just end up doing all our eating in the kitchen," she said.

"We do that now," Peter pointed out.

"But I don't want us to go on doing it," Richard snapped. "I want us to eat in the hall. Liza, what's in your mind?"

"Well, we won't just eat in the hall, surely, Father-in-law? Won't it be our place for living, whenever we're indoors? Like the big living room is now? We'll want to use it, enjoy it, won't we?"

"Yes, of course. Go on."

"Our cider press room is at the end of the house that joins the new wing. It's at the front. Why not turn it into a dairy, and make most of the present main living room into a kitchen and larder? The rest of the main room and the present dairy can all be knocked into one and if you agree, I can put my spinning wheel and loom in there and my accounts table and make a really good workroom of it. Then the parlour can be a proper parlour again. In case any ladies ever come to call! Any house of standing should have a good parlour, but I've fairly ruined ours, with my baskets of wool and my ledgers and all the rest."

"Where's the cider press to go, then?"

"Where the old kitchen is now. The new hall will still only need two doors—one into the farmhouse, and now it can lead straight into the new kitchen, and one into the farmyard."

"It's going to mean more trouble and more expense," said Peter.

"It's a good idea, though," said Richard, and went ahead with it.

It did indeed mean trouble and expense, and on top of all that, Richard insisted on glazing for the windows. This meant another delay while yet more funds were gathered. The glazing was made in Taunton and delivered with each window entire, wrapped in fleeces and roped on pack ponies, which could use packhorse bridges. But there were still places where streams had to be forded, and fords could mean trouble for ponies as well as waggons. Early in one journey a pony lost its footing while crossing a stream and fell. That was the end of one whole window. It had to be made again and transported again.

Peter, this time, said outright to his father that if only Richard didn't dislike the Sweetwaters so much, the new wing need never have been built and think of all the money they'd have saved. Richard retorted that he was just sorry that the new king hadn't thrown Walter Sweetwater off his land.

Walter was still on his land because he was a sprat compared to the Luttrells, who were much bigger fish. Sir Humphrey's title had not been hereditary and Walter had never been knighted. He was still only plain Master Sweetwater, a fact that in itself made him unimportant in royal eyes.

Before the king's clerks had worked their way far enough down their list of possible victims to reach Walter Sweetwater, Walter had reached the royal secretariat with a respectful message of submission, willingness to uphold the house of York henceforth, with his sword if need be, and the offer of a healthy fine in return for being left where he was.

King Edward was not particularly anxious to snatch a manor of Clicket's modest proportions. He accepted the fealty and the fine. Walter was left hard up and cursing, but still in possession of his property, and he even managed to negotiate a marriage for Baldwin, which would bring four farms, scattered around Devon, into Sweetwater hands.

After the fiasco with the glass, however, the Lanyons were hard up, too. There was another wait, another shearing and another payment from the Weaver profits before any furniture or panelling could be installed. Panelling was essential, Richard said, and so was a big new table with benches to go around it, plus a high-backed chair for him to use at the head of the table, and so, too, were three lidded chests-cum-settles, with lift-up seats and storage beneath, to go into the window nooks. The Lanyon coffers just barely succeeded in paying the Clicket carpenter.

"Well now," said Richard, turning to his son and daughter-in-law, when at last, after five stop-and-go years, the work was finished. "What about a housewarming?"

"Do we invite the Sweetwaters?" Liza asked, but Richard shook his head.

"Not yet! Not just for this. One day…but that's far ahead. This time," said Richard, "just our friends. There's a long way to go before we bid the Sweetwaters to dine."

"Richard Lanyon's invited us to a feast," Margaret said. "Because of this new hall he's added to the farmhouse. Will you feel up to going?"

"I'd like to," said Nicholas. "Only…"

His decline had started, Margaret thought, at the time of Liza's marriage, though the death of five family members during the recent fighting had assuredly made things worse. He had mourned especially for Laurie, of whom he had been very fond, literally mingling his tears with those of Laurie's wife, Katy, because when she heard of her husband's death, she had cried in his arms.

But Katy had left the household now, having married a saddler who had a workshop in West Street, at the other end of Dunster. He was a widower, much older than herself. His own children were grown and gone and as he hadn't wanted to take on her two boys, though he didn't mind her little daughter, the boys were still with the Weavers, learning to work looms. They were welcome, since so many pairs of hands had been lost, but Katy's departure had been another blow to Nicholas, who had had a tenderness for her.

But Liza's behaviour had begun the damage, of that Margaret had no doubt. "I feel betrayed," he said to her, not once but frequently. "If she'd fallen for a proper fellow, with a proper future, I'd have listened to what she wanted, but to lose her head over a half-fledged priest—and then to bolt with him! I never would have believed it of her, never, and what I had to do to her, it went to my heart, Margaret."

He had worried about it, wrinkled his brow over it, stayed awake at nights over it. Margaret tried to distract him by pointing out how well the business was doing, which it was. Despite the dividends that had to be paid out to the Lanyons, the union between the families was working. The Lanyon fleeces were so good these days that they were set aside for the manufacture of a particularly light, warm cloth, much of which was dyed red and yellow, because Master Herbert Dyer, whose competitive rates had so pleased Nicholas, specialised in those shades.

Herbert Dyer seemed to be a restless man, since he had come to Dunster from Taunton and then moved on to the village of Washford. Nicholas was not the only one to wonder why, and a member of the local Dyers' Guild, which watched over standards of work in Dunster, had been heard to say that he'd heard a thing or two from the Dyers' Guild in Taunton. "It's been hinted that he cut prices for favoured customers by charging others too much and that all his work wasn't good. Could be that a few folk in Dunster have started noticing things," he said. "We've had no formal complaints, but I've a feeling we might have started en-quiring if he'd stayed. Well, he's someone else's problem now."

Nicholas, however, had no complaint of him and he was a large, genial soul who visited the Weavers quite often and made cheerful conversation. Margaret, who liked him, was grateful for it. After one of his visits, Nicholas always seemed more like his old self.

The effect never lasted, though. Gradually Nicholas's hair had changed completely from flaxen to grey and he had begun to lose weight and complain, at times, of odd pains. Margaret, worrying about him, tried to encourage him to take life quietly, but he preferred to go on attending to his business, and still tried to fill his normal place in the family.

"It's just that I get tired the way I never used to, and Aller-brook's such a long ride away," he said as they lay in bed the night after the arrival of the invitation. "It's good of Lanyon to ask us, considering."

"Considering what?" Margaret asked. "They don't know about Christopher Clerk."

"Considering that there's been no child. Richard Lanyon wanted grandchildren. I know that."

"It could still happen. Cecy went four years once with nothing—after she had such a time with that first little girl and then that string of miscarriages—and then, all of a sudden, there was another little girl."

"Girls won't please Richard Lanyon either," Nicholas said. "Though he ought to be grateful for anything by this time! How long have they been wed? Getting for eight years come November, surely? I often fret about her, wondering whether we did right, pushin' the marriage on like that, and not givin' her more time. Still, she and Peter seem to get on, what I've seen of them. I wish we could see her more often, but there's hardly ever time for ridin' out all that way and I reckon it's the same for her. Women on farms always have work to do. I've decided, Margaret. We'll go."

The work on the new wing had been finished in early August, before the corn harvest but comfortably after the haymaking and the shearing. It was a convenient time for a feast. The weather was sultry, however, and Kat and Betsy, working with the kitchen door wide open, grumbled as they swatted flies, trapped wasps in a bowl of honey and water, and sweated over the creation of rabbit pie and a mighty pan of custard. However, by the previous evening, most of the work was done; all that remained was to roast the chickens and the saddle of mutton next day. The household retired early.

That night, Richard slept badly. The heat plagued him, forcing him to leave the window wide so that gnats came whining into the room, looking for blood, and the light of a full moon streamed in with them. When at last he fell asleep, he was again on Castle Rock, in swirling mist, and Marion Locke was there. As in real life, he had hold of her, but this time she didn't struggle against him but laughed in his face and made him angry and he threw her from him.

She fell backward through the vapours and then she was gone and only her scream remained, echoing in his ears, jerking him awake, except that he wasn't awake but had only been jolted into another layer of dreams. He was in his bed, but he was lying in a shaft of moonlight that held him down, like a mouse under the paw of a cat, and he knew it was holding him there so that Marion could come back and find him. In the mysterious way of dreams, he was in two places at once, both on his bed and staring down from Castle Rock at what, this time, was a clearly visible moonlit sea, from which Marion, white as bone, was rising toward him, coming for him, fingers curved as if to strangle him, with droplets of moonlit water falling from her fingertips.

He tried to call Deb's name, but his voice wouldn't work and Deb didn't come. Then he was really awake, heart pounding and sweat pouring off his body, but safe in his bed, though he was indeed lying in the moonlight. He got up and went to the window. The world lay hushed and still, a vista of shadows and whiteness, blanched corn, dark moorland marching against a silvered sky. Castle Rock was far away. Yet what would that matter to a ghost? It would be easy to believe that Marion's pallid shade was travelling toward him, floating over moor and peat stream, farm and woodland, just as birds did, searching for the man who had killed her.

He went back to bed and lay facedown, shuddering, waiting for the sanity of dawn.

It was a good gathering, even if everyone who accepted the invitation hadn't done so out of admiration for the new wing, or affection for the Lanyons, as the Lanyons would have known, had they been in the White Hart tavern in Clicket the previous evening.

"Can't think who he thinks he is, buildin' a great hall, as if he were a Sweetwater," said Sim Hannacombe.

"Vyin' with them, that's what he's up to," said Gilbert Lowe, spluttering slightly through his yellowed stumps of teeth. "'Member when they knocked his dad's coffin into the Allerbrook?"

He then added (because Gilbert always considered that his own personal grievances were the most interesting topics imaginable, and was skilled at twisting any conversation around to them) that it was a pity some folk couldn't stop where God had put them.

"That girl of mine, Martha, thirty-four she is now and you'd think she'd be past any girlish nonsense, but do you know, she went and took a shine this year to a travelling minstrel that stayed over one night with us! He hung round the district awhile and she took to slippin' off to meet him! Tilly followed her one day and found them having a cuddle, of all places, in St. Anne's Church, here in Clicket. We soon had her home and made her understand she'd got to stop there. Would you believe it!"

"Yes. Sounds natural to me. You should have got her wed years ago," said Sim disapprovingly.

"We need her at home and there she'm stayin'," retorted Gilbert.

"I daresay. Does the work of three, don't she?" said Sim.

"What's this about a coffin being knocked into the Aller-brook?" Young Will Hudd, who was now the tenant of what was still called Rixons, hadn't heard the story and thought it sounded more intriguing than the details of Martha Lowe's shattered romance. Information was duly supplied from several willing sources, including Edward Searle, who, along with Toby, often called in for a tankard of ale.

"I was at George Lanyon's funeral," Edward said. "I'd have offered to be a bearer, only I'm taller than most and I'd have unbalanced it. It was bad enough with Roger and Higg being different heights!"

"Then the hunt came by and unbalanced it well and truly," said Toby, amid laughter.

"If you ask me," said Adam Turner, who was the landlord of the White Hart and responsible for its name, which was in honour of an albino deer that had appeared in the locality twenty years ago, "the Lanyons have always thought they were above the rest of us, or ought to be. George Lanyon, he sent Richard to school and Richard sent Peter, and because they can read and write, they think they're special. Why, even Liza Lanyon can read and write and how many women can do that? But I wouldn't go challengin' the Sweetwaters—no, I would not. Do that to the gentry and you get trodden on, soon or late."

Turner, unlike most of his customers, was an indoor man, as his pale complexion and his stringy build clearly showed. He was a morose individual and none too fond of his fellow men. He wasn't even particularly fond of his own wares. His long nose had no red tip or broken veins. He was a good businessman, however, and the White Hart provided him with a steady living.

"I've been invited," he remarked. "But an innkeeper can't go gaddin' here and there, though I doubt I'll get much trade tomorrow. You'll all be drinkin' for free at Allerbrook."

"Don't grudge us a free mouthful of cider for once, Adam." The Clicket carpenter had joined the crowd, his day's work over.

"You've made more'n enough out of they Lanyons, what with panelling and furniture," said Turner glumly, and everyone laughed again.

Nicholas and Margaret were the first to arrive next day, having stayed a night with friends in the village of Winsford, which was on their way. "It made the journey shorter for Nicholas," Margaret explained as they were getting out of their saddles in the farmyard.

"I can't ride any distance nowadays," Nicholas explained, "and it's that hot and sticky. Thunder soon, I'd say."

Others presented themselves within the next hour or two: the Hannacombes, the Lowes, the Hudds, a number of villagers and Father Bernard. Betsy and Kat strove in the kitchen, mopping wet brows as they turned the chickens and the mutton on the spit, prepared sauces and sharpened carving knives. There was no breeze and the sky was beginning to dim from blue to a curious shade of bronze.

Liza and Peter put finishing touches to the new hall, decorating it with garlands of wildflowers made by Liza, spreading the table with white cloths and setting it with bowls and platters, spoons, ladles and an elaborate silver salt, a marvel of little salt and pepper pots and tiny engraved spice trays, which Ned Crowham had sent.

The Crowhams couldn't come, but this, said the letter their

messenger had brought along with the salt, might make up for that. It was the most handsome piece of tableware that Liza had ever seen. They had plenty of tableware otherwise; harvest suppers were always big occasions with most of the parish there, and the Lanyons were proud of the fact that they had ample spoons and dishes and didn't have to ask people to bring extra.

Shortly after midday the feast was under way and Richard, seated with dignity in his high-backed chair at the head of the table, with Peter and Liza one on each side of him, regarded the scene with complacency. They had got it right. He had thought of having a dais for the family, but both Peter and Liza had objected, saying that it would cut them off from the others, on days when everyone ate together.

"I wouldn't be easy," Liza had said. "I'd feel uncomfortable." And Peter had added that even if the dais were there, he probably wouldn't be able to bring himself to sit on it.

For a moment Richard had been angry and inclined to tell the pair of them that they'd do as he told them and like it, but realised in time that at heart he didn't want to cut himself off from Higg and Roger and Betsy and Kat, either. For one thing, farm-house meals were opportunities for useful conversation. *Should we slaughter that cow that isn't giving good milk anymore? When do we decide to cut the hay? The bay pony's had colic again—how much root ginger have we got? The rain's getting in at the corner of the big barn— better see to it, Higg.*

Decidedly, it was better to keep the household together, maintain normal farmhouse life but with a bit of extra dignity. Liza was admirably dignified, in a long green linen gown with hanging sleeves. It could have come from the finest dressmaker in Taunton, but hadn't, because Liza had bought the undyed linen, had it dyed to her own choice of colour, made the dress and embroidered it herself. She'd chosen green, she said, because crimson always seemed to run in the wash and she'd had much the same trouble with a tawny-yellow gown, too.

The green didn't suit her as well as the warmer shades, but she still looked handsome in it. She could have had silk for best; he and Peter wouldn't have minded. She'd chosen a good linen instead because she was thrifty and sensible. She'd be an ideal daughter-in-law, except for...

No use thinking of that now. He looked around at his guests instead and saw with satisfaction that they were making short work of the roast meat, the big rabbit pie, the beans in sauce and the cold ham and salad, and were interestedly eyeing the bread pudding that would follow, adorned with clotted cream and a sharp-tasting preserve which Kat made from the barberries that grew up on the dry part of the ridge, north of the barrow. The guests were enjoying themselves. Even Father Bernard, who had grown frail since he'd heard of Geoffrey Baker's death, was talking animatedly to his neighbour.

Richard reached for the cider jug, replenished his tankard, recommended his guests to try the elderflower wine as well, and was wondering whether to propose a toast to the future prosperity of Allerbrook Farm or whether he ought to ask Father Bernard to propose it instead, when beyond the new leaded windows, all of them open to let in some air, a movement caught his eye.

"Who's that coming up from the combe?" he said. "Thought we were all here."

Peter stood up to look, gazing across the farmyard to its open gate and the path beyond, which led down to the combe. He sat down again with a thud. "It's the Sweetwaters," he said.

CHAPTER SEVENTEEN
ONE COMES, ONE GOES

"The Sweetwaters?" Richard was indignant. "They weren't asked. Have they gone and invited themselves?"

"They've a nerve. Which of us got invited when Walter's son got wed last year?" said Sim Hannacombe. "And Sir Humphrey never even put his nose in at mine and he *was* asked to that."

"That's right. They don't goo axin' us to their affairs or come to ours." Gilbert Lowe's spluttery voice was heavy with disapproval.

His daughter Martha, who was wearing a plain dull gown as she always did, even at church, probably because she had no others, muttered, "What affairs do we have for them to come to? We don't build halls *or* have weddings," and was silenced by her mother Tilly's sharp elbow.

"Well, they've come to the feast this time," said Peter, standing up again to look. "There's Mistress Mary on Master Walter's pillion, and Baldwin with Mistress Catherine behind him, and a groom on a pony."

"I'll go out and welcome them," said Liza, and hurried off, murmuring, "Get that rabbit pie out of sight" into Betsy's ear on the way. Betsy hastened to obey. Peter, rising to his feet, said, "I'd better go with Liza, hadn't I? Father...?"

"Yes, you go, boy," said Richard. "And you, Higg. Give the groom a hand with the horses and bring him in for some food and drink."

The three Allerbrook dogs—descendants of Silky, Blue and Ruff—who had been panting in the shade of the stable all got up and barked as the newcomers rode into the farmyard, and Liza and Peter had to quieten them before turning to their guests. The groom was already helping the ladies down. In the farmyard surroundings the Sweetwaters looked incongruous.

They had dressed for the occasion or, possibly, just to put their hosts at a disadvantage. Mary and Catherine were in flowered brocade gowns that had to be held clear of the farmyard dust, and headdresses draped in white silk which would be ruined if the threatened storm broke while they were out of doors, while Walter and Baldwin, both fleshy and perspiring in velvet doublets, had jewelled brooches in their caps and gems in their dagger hilts, and looked as though they had come from a world unknown to the Lanyons.

Peter and Liza, both feeling demoted by these unwanted guests of honour, bowed, curtsied, were graciously polite and secretly angry.

There were other difficulties, too. Welcoming the Sweetwaters involved some hasty rearranging of people around the table. Roger beckoned to Sim Hannacombe and Will Hudd, and between them they brought an extra table and benches from the parlour to extend the hall table so that space could be made near the head for the landlord and his family. Betsy, returning from the kitchen where she had hidden the illicit rabbit pie, moved the salt so that Margaret and Nicholas should not find themselves unexpectedly below it, which would never do. "Thank you," said the flustered Liza as she passed Betsy while leading the unwanted guests to their places.

"So," said Walter Sweetwater once he had been seated, "this is the new Allerbrook hall that the whole village has been agog over these past five years. If you thought we didn't know about it, you were mistaken, Master Lanyon. A most ambitious project. To tell you the truth, I didn't think you'd ever manage to finish it, which was why I left you alone. There's a saying about give a man enough rope and he'll probably hang himself. But you've confounded me and done it after all, and all without ever dreaming of asking my permission."

Walter had the same bushy brown hair and thick brows as the other Sweetwater men, though he was not quite as heavily built as his father and his twin had been, or as Baldwin already showed signs of becoming. He was more subtle than his father and his twin, and now it was hard to tell whether he was sneering or admiring or both of them at once.

Baldwin, however, just turned nineteen and full of himself, looked about him and said, "It's a fine hall enough, but at home we have two pages to serve us, kneeling, with linen towels over their arms so we can dry our hands after using finger bowls, and we have rose-scented water in the bowls."

His father nodded in agreement, and Baldwin's quiet little wife, Catherine, who, with her small pointed chin, the dark hair just showing under her headdress and her almond-shaped blue eyes, looked like nothing so much as a kitten, gazed at him in admiration. Baldwin caught her eye and preened. He was fond of her and had actually been heard to call her Kitten, in tones of real affection.

Of his family, only his mother eyed him reprovingly, but he paid no attention. There were no finger bowls on the Allerbrook table, with or without rose water, and certainly no pages on bended knee with towels.

Neither Richard nor Peter seemed sure what to answer. Liza found that she was now frightened, to the point of feeling trembly and actually rather unwell. These Sweetwaters were dangerous. They had too much power.

Drawing a deep breath, she remembered that long ago, as a child, she had heard her mother say that it was the duty of a hostess to keep guests content. The idea of even trying to intervene made her feel more trembly than ever, but Margaret had always been particular about the details of hospitality. She was looking at Liza now, obviously expecting something of her. Shakily Liza rose to her feet, picked up a dish of carved mutton slices and offered it to Walter, saying, "We meant no offence by building this hall. We're plain farming folk with plain farming ways. We just wanted a good-sized room for our harvest suppers."

Richard almost glared at her, since this was not at all how he saw his hall, but realised that she was trying to smooth a difficult moment over, and checked himself. Liza did not notice the momentary scowl, indeed could hardly have seen it, for the bright noonday was rapidly fading to a livid half-light. Beyond the window the sky had turned leaden and, in the distance, there was a flicker of lightning. Nicholas's storm was on its way.

Liza's effort won her a little smile from Catherine and an approving nod from Mistress Mary, but these too were lost in the
gathering gloom and her valiant attempt hadn't, unfortunately,
managed to impress Baldwin.

"This new wing has added to the value of the farm, whatever
the reason for building it," Baldwin said to all the Lanyons impar-
tially, and then addressed his father. "I don't say we should order
them to pull it down, but shouldn't their rent go up to reflect the
increase in the worth of the place? Wouldn't you say?"

There was a startled hush, except for an intake of breath, a
communal gasp, which seemed to go right around the table.
Richard, in the act of lifting his cider tankard to his lips, banged
it down again. Then he broke the hush. "I paid for every last
stone, every slate, every inch of timber in this hall. *I* paid for it.
No Sweetwater did."

"My son has a point," said Walter, though his voice held a hint
of mischief. He took some of the meat Liza was still patiently
holding out to him and began to eat it. He had an air of private
amusement.

"It's Sweetwater property, though," said Baldwin, persistently
and quite seriously. "Rents should be charged to fit the nature
of the property. It'll come to me one day and to my son John
after me," he added, and there was a trace of self-satisfied em-
phasis on the word *son*.

"Baldwin. We are guests here!" His mother spoke quite
sharply. Catherine glanced from her mother-in-law to her husband and back again, bit her lip and clearly didn't know which
opinion to hold. She looked down at her platter and kept silent.

"If I've put up the value of your property, Master Sweetwater," said Richard, "Master *Walter* Sweetwater, that is, for your

son has nothing to say in this matter—if I've raised the value of your property, that's no good reason to fine me for it! You do that, and I *will* pull it down! I'll burn this damned hall to the ground again and take my biggest hammer and knock down what won't burn! What do you say to that?"

"It might be as well for you to remember," said Walter Sweetwater, "that I am indeed your landlord and that your right to occupy Allerbrook rests with me, and therefore to remember your manners."

There was a pause. The light by now was very bad, except for the flicker of the distant lightning. Thunder growled, low but almost continuous. The air felt scanty in the lungs, so that breathing seemed difficult. It was full of a huge tension, half of it nature's contribution and the other half emanating from the people at the table.

Betsy, seated below the salt, said frankly, "Now, that's not fair!" and another voice, male and anonymous, muttered audibly, "Aye, remember poor George Lanyon's coffin goin' in that there river?"

Walter peered along the table, but could see only a row of expressionless bucolic faces. He had sense enough not to ask who had said that last sentence. No one would tell him. All the same, he couldn't let the insult pass.

"I'll need to think this over," he remarked. "I must consider how much the value of the house has been raised by this addition, offset, of course, by how much the stock could have been improved if you had spent your money differently, Lanyon."

"The animals are mine, same as the hall!" said Richard angrily.

"But the right to run stock on the moor goes with the farm. Pretty sight you'd make, Lanyon, if you had to leave here. There you'd be, driving them along the tracks, with no idea where you were going or how to feed them on the way."

"Master Sweetwater," said Liza, getting in quickly before Peter could join in, "please…you surely don't mean any of this?" She had put the meat dish down on the table and resumed her seat, rather quickly, because her legs now felt very weak indeed. "You wouldn't harm us, would you?" She looked at him pleadingly. "We've been good tenants, have we not?"

"Yes, we have!" Peter snapped, joining in anyway. "And if anyone tries to turn us off our land—yes, I did say *our* land because we till it and seed it and cut the corn and it's our hands that work it, no one else's—then we'll find some authority to appeal to!"

"And if we left, you'd be hard put to find folk as good and hardworking as us to replace us!" Richard shouted.

"Don't speak to my father like that!" Baldwin was on his feet. He had had his dagger out to cut his meat. Now his fist was holding it at a threatening angle, straight toward Richard Lanyon.

He was not within arm's reach of Richard, and it was a gesture rather than a threat, but Richard, infuriated, instantly shot to his feet as well, pushed back his chair and started around the table. Mary Sweetwater looked horrified and Catherine, her eyes enormous, clapped her hands to her mouth to stifle a shriek.

Then several things happened, in rapid and shocking succession. A huge flash of lightning filled the hall with blazing blue light, causing people to cry out in alarm. It was followed almost instantly by a gigantic crash of thunder, so loud that the building seemed to shake.

And Liza Lanyon, tilting slowly forward, slumped over the table, slithered sideways off her bench and fell to the floor in a faint.

"It's all right. It's all right!" The lightning and the noise had passed and the hall and its occupants were all apparently undamaged. Richard, forgetting Baldwin, had dashed to the outer door to look at the rest of the house and that, too, was still standing, even its chimneys unharmed. As he stood there, rain came down, sudden and heavy, as though the lightning had released something inside the dark sky. He shut the door and came back. "Can't see any damage. It was just a big flash. I'll have to look at the cattle when the rain stops, though.... What's amiss with Liza?"

Betsy had already gone to Liza's aid and so had Margaret Weaver. She was coming around. They helped her up and settled her once more on the bench and Kat, who had hurried out to the kitchen, came back with a jug. "Well water. That's what she needs."

"I'm sorry," said Liza. "Sorry." She looked at the three women and suddenly smiled. Then she said something, very quietly. Margaret, her eyes widening, also whispered something, and Liza replied.

Standing up again, Margaret turned to the worried gathering, most of whom, now that they had realised that the lightning hadn't killed any of them, were looking at Liza in consternation. She turned to Richard. "Master Lanyon, pour me some wine! Quickly, now! There's a reason!"

Richard, bemused by her sudden air of command, did as she asked and handed her the goblet. Taking it, she raised it high.

"Everyone, listen! You, too, Master Sweetwater and you, Master Baldwin. This is no time for threats and quarrelling. It's a time for congratulations to the Lanyons, especially to Liza and Peter. God willing, there will be a child in this house by next spring."

"What? What's this?" Nicholas had gone scarlet with excitement, looking more like his old self than he had in years. "Is Liza...are you saying...?"

"Yes, I am," said Margaret strongly, "and I hope there'll be no more talk of turning folk out of their homes because they've toiled like slaves, which they're not, to grow good corn and improve their houses! What's wrong with that?" She gave a fierce glance to Walter and Baldwin, but then swung her attention back to the rest of them. "Fill your cups, every one of you, and drink to their health and to the baby's safe arrival and to good luck to this house!"

Mary Sweetwater unobtrusively put a persuasive hand on her husband's arm. Walter Sweetwater looked at it and at her, and then said, "Oh, very well. This changes things—I grant you that. I'll drink the toast, and so will you, Baldwin." Catherine, who had clearly been wondering what to do, took the hint and filled her own goblet. Goblets and beakers were raised all around the room.

"To Liza and Peter!" Richard bellowed.

The thunder rumbled, like an echo. Kittenish Catherine giggled. Walter looked at her and then laughed. Around the table, the atmosphere lightened.

Richard, thankful enough to find friendly relations restored, played the genial host until all the guests had gone, except for Liza's parents, who were staying the night. But when Liza had been put to bed by her mother, and the Weavers had retired, and Richard was alone in the parlour with Peter, he gave voice to his real feelings.

"They could have killed her! With the trouble she's had in the past, those threats could have made her miscarry again and who's to say she'd have come through?" he said furiously, sounding for all the world as though he had been Liza's earnest defender and protector since the day she'd come to Allerbrook. "That would have been Liza as well as Deb! How dare that young devil Baldwin point a dagger at me, here in my own home, at my own table?"

"He's just young," said Peter, wishing his father would calm down.

"He's the same as Sir Humphrey and that bully Reginald were, and so is Walter—just not so crude, more sly. I reckon most of all that talk about throwing us out was just cat and mouse, reminding us of his power. Inviting themselves, pushing their way in, throwing their weight about…"

"The storm's lost us two cows," Peter said, trying to change the subject. "I was afraid that lightning would get something."

"Yes, and one of them was Clover, our best milker," Richard growled. "It would be! See here, Peter, it's good news about Liza and that was a clever move that Margaret made, proposing that toast, but considering what's happened in the past, it's too soon for rejoicing. I just hope we don't have any more storms or trouble from the Sweetwaters."

"We'll take good care of Liza," said Peter. "We'll all pray for a good healthy child this time and may it be a son. There's still a long way to go."

"And not only as far as Liza's concerned," Richard remarked.

"How do you mean?"

"I'm talking about the Sweetwaters. So we've got a hall as good as theirs. But that's just the beginning, boy. I've told you before. One day we'll have a house as good as theirs, as well. That's my next step, however long it takes."

"Father, we've no need of such a house. We—"

"Don't make any mistake," said Richard grimly. "I mean it."

"As easy as though she'd been oiled," said Betsy joyfully, coming down the stairs to give the good news to Richard and Peter. "Not a problem in the world. Wish mine had come as quick and smooth. The mistress'll be ready to see 'ee soon, Master Peter. Kat's givin' her a wash. And the baby's as pretty as a newborn lamb and I don't know what's sweeter than that. She's got a tuft of brown hair, just like her mother's."

"She?" queried Richard.

"Yes, it's a wench," said Betsy with an air of challenge. "But strong, healthy, bawling her lungs out."

"Now that there's been one child, there could be another. Maybe a boy next time," said Peter. "After what's happened in the past, I'm glad there's just a strong baby and that Liza's safe."

"Humph!" Richard shrugged. "What do you want to call her?"

"We'd have called a boy either after you or Master Weaver, but if it was a girl, Liza said her mother's mother was called Quentin and she liked the name and could we use that?"

"Margaret Weaver's mother? I met her when I was a boy, I think." Richard was mildly interested. "Carroty-haired woman. Good thing Liza didn't inherit that. I don't call it pretty. Call this one Quentin if you like. If you ever get that boy, call him Nicholas. We don't want two Richards under one roof—too confusing. But get on with it. Time's going by."

★ ★ ★

"At least he lived long enough to know about Liza's daughter," said Margaret, struggling to find comfort as she looked down at the emaciated image which had been her husband. He was only three hours dead and already a terrible remoteness had laid hold of him. "One comes and one goes—b'ain't that the sayin'? Well, I'm glad that it was over quick, when it came to the point. Only three days from when he was took ill, to this."

"I fancy he'd had pain he didn't talk about. He was gettin' thin and lookin' drawn and not eatin' right, for a long while," said Aunt Cecy.

"What a cheerin' soul you are," Margaret said. "Always ready with a few words to make folk feel better. Did your mother make a habit of walkin' through graveyards when she was carryin' you?"

"No need to be nasty, just because this is a sad day. Oh, what is it?"

The last sentence was addressed not to Margaret, but to Elena, who had poked her head around the door of the bedchamber where Nicholas lay, awaiting the arrival of the coffin maker.

"It's Master Herbert Dyer from Washford. He'd like to see Aunt Margaret, to give her his condolences."

"How did *he* get to hear of all this, away in Washford?" demanded Aunt Cecy before Margaret could speak.

"Laurence called at Cleeve Abbey two days ago," said Elena, who wasn't intimidated by Aunt Cecy. "He called on Master Dyer as well, out of courtesy, and must have let on that Cousin Nicholas's illness looked serious because Master Dyer set out today, to see how he was faring. I've just told him what's happened."

"I'll see him," said Margaret.

She was glad, on descending the stairs, to find Herbert waiting alone in the main room. He was so big and cheerful, darker than the flaxen Nicholas but similar in type and he had a wide, kindly smile.

It seemed quite natural to say, "Oh, *Herbert,* this is dreadful. Nicholas is gone and I can't believe it!" and walk into his arms for comfort.

CHAPTER EIGHTEEN
DREAMS ARE SECRET

"You have a fine place here," Herbert Dyer said, standing respectfully in the Allerbrook hall, velvet cap held politely in his hand. His lavishly pleated tawny doublet was probably meant to conceal his well-fed stomach, but didn't quite succeed. Shrewd blue eyes scanned his surroundings.

"Those fine horses that I saw in the pasture along with some ponies are yours, I take it? Very unusual colouring, I noticed—one's a striking dark dapple grey and the other's piebald. They were never bred out on the moor."

"No, they weren't," said Richard, rather shortly. "They're both mine. I like a horse with looks. The grey's old now. He's never rightly got over being half-starved on the way south when I came home from Towton. He lives out at grass except in bad weather and takes his ease. Magpie, the piebald, is a Barbary horse.

Four years old and full of fire is Magpie, though he needs a stable and corn after a day's riding. Peter prefers a moor pony. Plume, he calls his, because of its great thick tail. Surely you didn't come here to talk about horses?"

"No, I came to talk business, but it's a chance to see Mistress Liza, too. You weren't at the wedding, Mistress, and I did wonder…"

"I'm not upset," Liza assured him. "I'm sure Mother knows what she's about. But it's a long way in lambing time. We're always busy then."

"My daughter-in-law has a way with ewes in trouble," Richard said. After considering the matter, he had decided that the birth of Quentin, even though she was only a girl, was a sign that Liza might yet fulfil her real purpose as a wife. Where there was a healthy daughter there might in due course be a son, as well. He had warmed very much toward Liza. Quentin was now two, and so far there had been no hint that a brother for her might be on the way, but it wasn't all that long since Liza had stopped feeding her. For the time being, he was willing to be patient.

"We did send a gift," Peter said mildly. "There's been no bad feeling here, sir, don't fret about that."

"I always liked your mother, in the most proper manner," Dyer said to Liza. "And after my Bess died, I used to think, well, Nicholas is a lucky man. But he's gone and there are things you very likely don't know, things your mother told me. I'm family now, so I suppose I can talk of them to you—I wouldn't otherwise. But your aunt Cecy as you all call her fairly made your mother's life a burden to her after she lost your father."

"Aunt Cecy?" said Liza. "Yes. I can imagine."

"Your father," said Herbert, "was the eldest son in a line of eldest sons. He was the head of the house, since your great-uncle Will sat back and said he was tired of running it, and that made your mother the first woman in the house, as well. But after Nicholas went, Aunt Cecy started saying she was the senior woman and she took to giving orders and countering what Marge—"

"Marge?" said Liza.

"My name for your mother, my wench. My pet name." Herbert Dyer's luxuriant brown beard fairly bristled with merriment. "Aunt Cecy would change Marge's orders—over what to cook for dinner, and who was to work at which looms and who was to tend the garden. All sorts of things. It was hard for Marge to bear."

"Aunt Cecy always did have an edge on her tongue," Liza agreed.

"Edge! Like a saw. I was glad to take Marge out of it. I gave her time to mourn, but then I went courting and she was happy to say yes. I'm six years younger than she is but that doesn't worry either of us. She's got a good home with me and no heavy work, and her younger children are off her hands. Your two brothers, Arthur and Tommy, are both grown up and working in the weaving shed. Tommy's so handy there, everyone marvels at it. And your little sister Jane's been married to a weaver in Timberscombe, just up the valley from Dunster."

"Yes, I know," Liza said, somewhat acidly. "I hear news of my family often. After all, we work with them, supplying fleeces and so on."

"Well, then. Your mother's well-off with me, I promise." The glance his deep-set eyes gave to Liza, who had come from the dairy in an undyed gown and the old, streaky pinkish-red overdress she used when working, and with her hair pushed into a creased coif, suggested that in his opinion, Liza might well envy her mother.

"I've got servants," Herbert said, "and my sons are grown up and gone, except for the eldest, Simon, and he's my partner in the dyeing workshop. I'll take care of Marge, I promise. Well, I'm your stepfather now, and if you ever need anything..."

"She won't need anything while she's here with us." Peter had noticed that disparaging glance and his tone was stiff.

"I'm sure of it. That was just a few words of goodwill. And now perhaps we can talk business. That's what I came for, mainly. My workshop and the Weavers' workshop and your sheep are linked together, after all, like a chain. I've been thinking. Now, I've always tried not to overcharge my customers. I'm not a greedy man," said Master Dyer. Peter's eyes roamed over Herbert's stomach, but its owner, oblivious to this cynical scrutiny, swept on.

"As it happens, though I get a good weight of cloth and yarn through my workshop, I could handle more. To tell the truth, business has dropped a little in the last few months. If the amount of cloth from the Weavers' place could be increased, I might be able to offer them a discount and still come out on the right side myself. I've had a word with them on the matter and we reckoned that since it's my scheme, I ought to be the one to come and see you and talk to you about fleeces. They said they could manage extra work, but you can't weave extra cloth without extra wool. Now, you supply a regular quantity of wool to the Weavers at a competitive price. If that quantity could be increased..."

Richard frowned. "I think we need to take a good hard look at what it all means when it turns into money."

"I've got some estimates here." Dyer produced a roll of parchment from inside his doublet. "I worked out my costs and prices before I came. You were bound to want them. We're all men of business."

"Very well." Richard nodded. "Come this way. Come along, Peter. And you, too, Liza."

"But this is business," said Dyer, disconcerted. "It'll hardly interest a lady."

"Liza is better with figures than either of us," said Richard unconcernedly. "And handier with the abacus. This way."

Some time later, when business had been discussed at length and Peter and Liza had gone out to the lambing pen, Richard called Betsy to bring some cider, and then sat down to drink it in private with his guest.

"I think our deal should work well," Herbert said, "if you can withstand the delay in income at the very beginning. Normally, you'd have sold those extra fleeces for their full value. But there should be a better profit for you when the finished cloth is sold—profits for all of us. I'm glad to see that you're prosperous, I must say. You have a good family life, too, I notice. Your son and his wife seem well suited. I've had trouble with my son Simon, though it's over now."

"Indeed?" Richard said, refilling Herbert's tankard.

"God's teeth, yes. I've got him married now to a good wench, but before he was wed, he was always getting wild notions about impossible girls. There was a Gypsy lass, going about with her wandering folk, hawking silly gewgaws and playing a tambourine, and then there was a milkmaid over at Withypool, pretty enough but not a penny piece to go with her...no one knows the struggle I had to bring him to his senses."

"Young men are like that," said Richard. "Peter had wild ideas, too, at one time—fell in love with a fisher girl at Lynmouth. Marion Locke, her name was." It still happened. From time to time he found himself impelled to speak of Marion, as though she were an itching scab he felt he had to pick. "I went to see her family," he said in offhand fashion. "I had a look at her. She was pretty, in her way. Extraordinary hair, she had. Close up, it was like gold wire but from a distance like a pale mist."

He managed to laugh. "It isn't only young men who have wild fancies. I wasn't going to let Peter throw himself away on her, not with Liza there, ready to marry him, but do you know, I had a notion for a while of marrying her myself. She ran off with someone else before I could do anything about it, though. Peter and I were both well out of that, I think."

"He didn't want me there," Liza remarked later, when Master Dyer had taken his leave and the Lanyons were gathering in the hall before supper. "He didn't like talking to me about my accounts, or watching me use the abacus. I think he couldn't really believe that I understood figures!"

"Well, most women don't understand them," said Richard, willing to be amused, and wondering, within himself, *why*, now and then, he still had this frightening need to speak of Marion. Why in the world had he, this time, actually admitted that he had once thought of marrying her? Saying that, he had stepped dangerously close to the edge of a cliff. The trouble with cider was that it mellowed a man and loosened his tongue.

"I can't really like Master Dyer," said Liza, "though no doubt my mother does. I hope she'll be happy. I didn't say so at the time," she added, "but some of his figures puzzled me. I learned a lot about these things from my father. He said once that I was better at figures than anyone else in the family except himself, and he's gone now. I think Master Dyer could have shown those estimates to my folk in Dunster and they might not have seen how odd they were. But some of the prices he was assuming for dyes and mordants..."

"Mordants?" said Peter. "I saw those listed on his estimates, but what are they?"

"Things to stop the dye from running. Yarns and cloths are soaked in mordants before being dyed. The amount he expects to pay for them struck me as low, and his estimates for what our cloths and yarns will fetch seemed rather high. They vary each year and if you're trying to work out profits in advance, it's best to be careful." Liza frowned. "There have been a few stories about Dyer, you know. My father never complained, but..."

"What stories would those be?" said Richard sharply, forgetting all about Marion Locke.

He and Peter listened thoughtfully to what Liza had to tell them. "So that's why you prefer green gowns to red or yellow ones!" said Peter.

"I don't, really. But in the cloth trade, everyone knows everyone and if I sent cloth to be dyed red or yellow to anyone but Herbert Dyer, and then my family heard of it, they'd wonder why. I didn't want that, because, as I said, my father never had any complaint. But it looks as though he's lost a few customers lately. He said business had dropped, didn't he? And now, of course, my mother's caught up in it. She's married to him! But this deal he's offering to my family, those figures of his—I don't like them. I don't believe he ought to be able to afford that discount. I think," said Liza sternly, "that he's trying to pull wool over all our eyes!"

Richard laughed. Peter said, "Go on."

Awkwardly, Liza said, "Look, here at Allerbrook we've done well, so far, out of the arrangement you made with my father. We sell fleeces at low prices and then have a percentage paid to us when the cloth's made and sold. Sometimes we gain and sometimes my family in Dunster gain, but mostly we're the lucky ones...." She hesitated, and Richard grinned.

"Your father saw it as part of your dowry."

"Yes, he did," Liza said. "Anyway, the market's been good. My family in Dunster haven't lost much by it. But if Herbert Dyer is up to something, well...I've a feeling that we'll be selling more wool at a discount and relying on good cloth sales to make up for it. And my family may be selling cloth that...I shouldn't be saying this without proof, but..."

"This is a private conversation," said Richard. "Speak your mind."

"What if my family find themselves selling cloth that isn't all it should be? What will that do to their good name, to their sales in time to come?"

"Just what is it you suspect?" Peter asked.

"I'm not sure," said Liza slowly. "I could make guesses—but I just think something's not right. Those figures weren't right."

"We'd better be cautious," Richard agreed. "Especially since that crafty bugger Walter Sweetwater put our rent up!"

Liza smiled. "There's rabbit pie for supper again. I hope you won't mind."

Her father-in-law threw back his head and laughed. "Liza, I'd never go calling you a vixen, but you're damn near as foxy and cunning as Master Sweetwater is."

"We ought to recoup if we can," said Liza reasonably.

Walter Sweetwater had exacted his toll for the building of the hall. Since the housewarming, the Sweetwaters, when hunting, had three or four times cut a swath through the Lanyon barley and once, after a gale had blown some of the fencing down, even galloped across a corner of the wheat. Richard swore it was intentional. Nor was that all.

"You built the hall at your own expense, as you said," Walter had said, stepping to Richard's side one Sunday as they came out of church. "Well, I accept that. You're entitled to benefit from it. In fact, I think a man with a hall so handsome should have some special rights to match."

The right he had in mind, it emerged, was permission to kill and eat rabbits on Allerbrook land.

Only, of course, such permission didn't come free. The rent had gone up ostensibly to cover it, and since rabbits had been on the Allerbrook menu since the fall of man in any case, everyone there was furious. For a time, in order to get their money's worth, the outraged Lanyons had eaten so much rabbit—stewed, roasted, fried, minced up to be seethed in cream and spread on toasted bread, and of course served in the familiar pies, mixed as usual with onions and mushrooms—that Peter said if they didn't stop it, they would all grow long furry ears.

After that, their diet returned to something like normal, but not quite. Rabbits still featured oftener than in the past.

After a pause for laughter, and Richard's agreement that as they hadn't had rabbit pie now for nearly a week, no one would object to it today, they reverted to the subject of Herbert Dyer. "I'm truly worried about Mother," Liza said. "I keep thinking of that story that Betsy told, Father-in-law, when you came back from

Towton. About Geoffrey Baker's father or stepfather or whatever he was."

"No one knows for sure which," said Richard. "But what's
he got to do with Herbert Dyer?"

"Betsy said he got into trouble for putting chalk in his bread flour.
And I remember once in Dunster seeing one of our own neighbours shamed for putting flax threads in his woollen cloth—"

She stopped short, while they all looked at her enquiringly.
To her own surprise, the memory of Bart Webber had sprung
into her mind with such vividness that for a moment she had
been transported back to that day. When she had turned away
in distress from the spectacle of Bart, and found Christopher
beside her. She had believed herself reconciled. She hadn't
thought that a reminder like this would hurt so much, as though
it had opened an old wound.

"What is it?" Peter asked. "What's the matter, Liza?"

"I *hated* seeing that happen, to a neighbour, to someone we
knew!" Well, so she had; it was true enough. "And it caused
misery to his wife. I couldn't bear to see Mother embarrassed
because her husband had been been put in the stocks for cheating
his customers. I'm afraid for them," she said unhappily. "I keep
thinking of the trouble I had with his red and yellow dyes. He
wouldn't play games with my father, but he may have cheated
me—just one farm woman sending home-woven cloth. Oh, I
may have been born Liza Weaver, daughter of one of his best customers, and later on his stepdaughter, but I'm a Lanyon now, and
I'm living out on the moor, away from my family, and he thinks
women are all fools. He'd take advantage of me the same as he
would of any woman among his customers. I fancy there may
have been many of us."

"This hall should have made him think again about farming folk," said Richard.

"It did," said Liza. "So did Splash and Magpie, when he saw them in the field. I think Allerbrook made him uneasy. I don't trust him. It seems to me that he wants to increase his business and is trying to use family connections to help him. I fancy he's waved figures in front of my family and got them to believe that he has benefits for all of us in mind, but all he's really after is benefits for him, at our expense if it comes to it. And I just don't see how he'll get really worthwhile benefits even for him, unless there's some sort of trickery going on."

"I think," said Peter slowly, "that when the lambing's over, we should pay him a visit and look round that workshop of his. No reason why Liza shouldn't visit her own mother and take an interest in the workshop while she's there, now, is there? And she knows something about the business. Liza's the one who must go. I'll take her."

"You'll do that?" Richard asked, looking at Liza.

"Yes, I will," said Liza. "We'd better find out, though what we can do about it, with my mother caught up in it now, I can't think."

"Leave that to me," Richard said. "Let's get at the truth first."

It's strange. I'm really not unhappy. I care about Allerbrook, and having Quentin makes a difference. A great difference! She's beautiful. I tried to do what Mother said, to make up my mind to be happy, and now I more or less am, and even Father-in-law has stopped saying things, though if I don't conceive again soon I suppose he'll begin again. But Peter is kind. I'm as well-off as most women. Mother was right. Only, talking about

Bart Webber reminded me. It all came back. I thought I'd left Christopher behind, but...it seems I haven't. Will I ever? Can I?

It was now suppertime on the day of Dyer's visit, and Liza was not at table eating rabbit pie but instead was lying flat in a muddy lambing pen, with a bucket of water and a pot of goose grease beside her and one arm inside a distressed and bleating ewe, trying to work out through her fingers which of the tangle of legs she could feel belonged to which lamb. There were certainly two of them, and sorting them out without being able to see what she was doing was always a challenge, and she was hungry and this was as messy a job as God ever invented.

It was useful work, though, and she seemed to have a talent for it, and if she succeeded this time, there would be beaming faces everywhere. Hence the thoughts now coursing through her head.

She had little to complain about. She was the wife of Peter Lanyon, a respected farmer of Clicket parish. Her home was better than most farmsteads were, now that the hall was part of it; she had plenty to eat and clothes to wear; she even, now, had a child—not the son everyone had hoped for, but the son might follow yet.

And Peter was a good man. Many women, bullied women, beaten, overworked women, envied her and she knew they did. It was shameful to discover that deep within her the little flame was still there after all, still burning, the flame that was not for Peter. When first she came to Allerbrook she had dreamed of Christopher at night, quite often. That hadn't happened for a long time, but she had a feeling now that the dreams might return, wakened by talk of Bart Webber and the reminder of that day at the fair.

Well, dreams were secret. If Christopher did come to her in her sleep once in a while, no one need know except herself...ah! She had traced that little foreleg back to its rightful owner, and got it out of the way of the lamb lying in front...now, if she let the ewe push...poor thing; she was bleating so. If she were human, she would be crying out for help. The lamb was coming forward, sliding toward the light. Here it came. And its twin was following. "All done, you poor thing," said Liza to the ewe. "Look, lovely twin girls."

The ewe, much relieved, was struggling to her feet, turning to inspect her progeny, and Peter came into the pen just as Liza was plunging her greased and bloodied arms into the bucket of water.

"You've done it!"

"It was a difficult one. I was afraid we'd lose them all."

"Far from it, by the look of that." The ewe was nosing at her offspring and beginning to wash them and the lambs were already attempting to stand up. Peter fetched the towel Liza had hung over the gate and handed it to her. "You really have a way with you, Liza. Liza..."

"Yes, dear?" said Liza, rubbing her arms as clean as possible.

"I'm not one for too much talking about such things, but I really love you. It's a wonderful thing, having a wife one can trust, really trust."

"I'm just ordinary," said Liza, very busy with drying herself. "Not special in any way."

"Oh, but you are," said Peter, laughing.

Dear God, said Liza inside her head, *make the flame spring up for Peter. Make it! Why won't it? I thought all this was over. Why is it that after all, I still burn for Christopher?*

★ ★ ★

"I have no objection," said the prior of St. George's Benedictine monastery. William Hampton was a calm individual, not given to making objections for the sake of it. "I don't own the man. He has never taken vows as a monk, although he has become a priest. In that capacity, he's useful to the brothers and to our vicar, Will Russell. He takes services on occasion when Russell is away, or falls sick. We sometimes send Father Christopher out to other churches as well, when their vicars need help. In fact, we've lent him to the castle once or twice. There are chantries attached to this church—not based here, but controlled from here—and when there's a vacancy, the vicar and I had intended to recommend him as a chantry priest. But you say you really need him at the castle for good?"

"Instructions from my lord of Pembroke, sir," said Master Miles Hilton, the steward of Dunster Castle, sipping wine in the prior's sanctum. He was elegant and relaxed, legs stretched out in front of him, ankles crossed. "We have no chaplain at the moment. We have had difficulties with chaplains ever since the Luttrells left and took their own man, Father Meadowes, with them, and the Earl of Pembroke became the landlord."

"Yes, your chaplains do come and go, don't they?" said Hampton. "Every time I dine at the castle there seems to be someone different in the chaplain's seat."

"We've had three!" said Hilton with feeling. "The first was a career man who soon found himself a deanery in Gloucestershire. The second one went on an errand to Winsford, lost his way in a moorland mist, found himself on Winsford Hill instead, thought he saw a ghost on one of the old mounds up there, came back hysterical—his horse brought him…sensible animals, horses—and left next morning."

"Did he really see a ghost?" asked Hampton, intrigued, offering his guest some more wine.

"Possibly," said Master Hilton. "People say that ancient kings are buried under the mounds—barrows, they call them hereabouts—and that they don't like to be disturbed. Or he may just have caught sight of some deer-poaching peasant slipping out of sight, or even merely a deer. Mist makes everything look strange. Anyway, he couldn't get back to what he called civilised parts quick enough."

"And the third one?"

"Went on an errand to Porlock, up the coast, took a path over Dunkery, got thrown by his pony, fell into a bog and came home on foot, hours later, soaked to the skin. Dead in a week of lung fever. And that's when I remembered hearing that you had a one-time chaplain here in this very monastery and I thought, my lord of Pembroke's the landlord of Dunster and has a right to him if anyone does. And at least your man knows the district. Presumably, *he* won't get panic-stricken if he's caught in a mist on Winsford Hill, or go falling into bogs on Dunkery."

A belated sense of responsibility overtook the prior. "You do know how Father Christopher comes to be here?"

"Oh, yes. The servants left at the castle when I first came spoke of it now and then. Some trouble with a girl, wasn't there?" Master Hilton didn't sound as though he attached much importance to this.

"It was quite a serious matter," Hampton said. "He was a deacon at the time, studying with Father Meadowes, and helping him. He and a local girl ran off together, though they were caught before they'd gone far and it seems that they did not actually commit fornication. Still, as I said, it was a serious piece of mis-behaviour for a man in orders."

"Where's the girl now?"

"Oh, she was married off and left Dunster. I think she went to Clicket—you know where that is?"

"Right out on the moor, I believe. Has Father Christopher given any trouble since?"

"None whatsoever. He keeps the Rule more carefully than some of the brothers do and when he prays, he looks as if he means it. I'd call him a devout man. We'll miss him," said the prior, refilling their goblets for the third time. "But as I said, I don't object if you don't. It's for him to say."

"I can but ask him. My lord is right—there should be someone to hold daily prayers in the castle. It's only proper. We'll all still come to church on Sundays."

Prior William Hampton, who dined at the castle fairly often, thought privately that though it was admirable of the unknown Earl of Pembroke, to whom King Edward IV had presented the Luttrell lands, to concern himself about the souls of those who looked after his Somerset castle, it wouldn't be at all a bad thing if he concerned himself a little more about the castle itself. The earl had never as much as visited it. He took the rents from the village and the farms attached to it, but the castle, it seemed, could fall down from neglect for all he cared.

In the time of the Luttrells, black grapes had ripened on a vine on its southern wall and it had been customary to send a few bunches to the priory each year. Nowadays, no one bothered to harvest them and the walls around the vine were streaked with the droppings of glossy and gluttonous starlings. The prior itched to let a hawk loose among them. The harbour was silting up faster than ever, too, and no one was even trying to do anything about it.

"I'll send for Father Christopher," the prior said.

Christopher was in the small walled garden where the monks grew their herbs, culinary and medicinal. During his years within the priory he had discovered in himself an unexpected knack for gardening. It was peaceful to be here, weeding, on a soft spring evening like this, with the rooks circling and cawing above the trees on the tall hill, Grabbist, that overlooked the village, and hearing the sound of someone in the church, practising the organ.

While he worked, his mind could drift as it would. He had become quite learned by now in Latin and Greek and theology. The novices regarded him with awe, and the novice master said that when Father Christopher toiled alone in the garden, he shouldn't be disturbed, for he was surely meditating on a theological problem or seeking the truth behind an ambiguous translation of a Greek text.

Sometimes he was. The years had made his enforced vocation easier, even against his will. He had resisted at first, wanting to grieve, to yearn, to remember Liza every moment of every day, but gradually reality and day-to-day living had their effect. When he'd believed himself to have a vocation, he had perhaps not been entirely mistaken. He had, eventually, begun to find satisfaction in his studies, and had embraced priesthood with something like sincerity. If he could not have Liza, well, there was much to be said for this—the beauty of ritual, the fact that he could offer help and comfort to others, the intellectual pleasure that Greek and Latin and theological problems could give.

Always, though, before going to sleep, he said a private prayer for Liza. He had promised himself he would do that, on the day that he came to the abbey, and sometimes, especially in this garden, especially in the evening, especially on one such as this soft, green April evening, with the scents of mint and lavender so very disturbing to the senses, then Liza's memory would come to him, clear and vivid still and not blurred by time.

When her parents had come to see him, after he and she had been brought back from Nether Stowey, they had told him of their plans for her. What kind of life did she have now, Liza Weaver who had become Liza…Lanyon, wasn't it…and gone to a farm out on the moorland? Was she happy? Did she have children? Did she love her husband? Were the Lanyons kind to her?

Did she still remember Christopher Clerk or was he just a youthful escapade, even, perhaps, embarrassing to remember? He hoped not, and at this point in his thoughts he would slip a hand inside the habit he wore although he had not taken a monk's vows, and find the thin silver chain he kept hidden under his clothes, and trace it down to the patterned silver ring which hung from it. No one knew of these hidden thoughts, of course. Dreams like this were secret.

He was in the depths of one when a novice came hastily but nervously through the gate to call him to the prior's lodging. "I'm so sorry to disturb you, Father, and of course I wouldn't, except that Father Prior sent me. I don't know what it's about, but he wants you to come at once. The steward of the castle is taking wine with him."

"The steward?"

"Yes. Shall I clean your tools and put them away for you?"

"If you would. Thank you." He stood up, brushed some earth

and bits of weed off the habit and hurried to answer the summons. He found, on arriving, that the castle steward, whom he had met when, now and then, his services were borrowed by the castle, was sitting with Prior Hampton, and that there were three goblets on the table, along with a flagon of wine.

"Here he is," said the prior. "You know Master Hilton, of course, Father Christopher. What have you been doing, Father? Gardening?"

"Yes. Weeds sprout overnight, at this season. Good evening, Master Hilton."

Hampton filled a goblet and handed it to him. "Sit on that settle there, Father. Master Hilton wishes to make you an offer. How would you like to go back to the castle as the official chaplain?"

"Go…and live there, you mean?"

"Most certainly you would have to live there," said Hilton, and began to explain, all over again, about the instruction received from the Earl of Pembroke, and the misfortunes of the chaplains he had employed hitherto. There was more, about the stipend he would receive, and the fact that he would have a free hand in restoring the castle chapel. He listened as attentively as possible, but his mind was leaping ahead, on a path of its own.

He would be living outside the monastery. Not just making occasional excursions, usually with a lay brother as servant and companion—or guardian—but living, all day and all night, right outside.

He had probably been free to go ever since Father Meadowes went away with Lady Elizabeth, but he wasn't sure. Meadowes had said that if he set foot outside the priory unaccompanied, he would find his behaviour with Liza reported both to his father in Bristol and to higher church authorities as well, and he did not know whether, before leaving Dunster, Father Meadowes had, as it were, passed the threat into the hands of the prior.

He had made no attempt to find out. He couldn't, in any case, see the point of going out into the world again when he had an assured and very comfortable life where he was. The Dunster Benedictines never had interpreted their vows of poverty too literally, for which Christopher was grateful. In his opinion, deprivation wasn't as good for the soul as some believed. It often made people unhappy, and unhappy people, in his experience, were often unkind ones, too.

So he stayed where he was, made no protests, kept the Rule and never made enquiries about a young woman who had once lived in Dunster, just in case the prior found out, and had, as it were, been left on guard.

Now, however, Hampton was setting him free. The castle would be very different from the priory. Hilton was in charge there and he couldn't see Hilton bothering to act as watchdog.

At the castle, no one would supervise him. He wouldn't approach the Weavers directly, but there would be people, in the castle itself, no doubt, who knew them but knew nothing about Christopher and Liza's little scandal. It was more than ten years ago now. At last he might come by news of Liza. That was all he wanted. Just to know that all was well with her. Then he could forget that he had ever let his feet walk on air, forget he had ever had his head among the stars, and give his heart and mind to being a good priest for the rest of his life, as was now his duty and his wish.

The steward had stopped talking and was looking at him expectantly. So was the prior. They wanted his decision. "But of course," he said. "If I am wanted at the castle, naturally I'll come."

CHAPTER NINETEEN

A GOOD SENSE OF SMELL

A crow, flapping steadily across the moors and the tangle of lower hills and combes between the heathery heights inland and the Bristol Channel, would have found the distance between Allerbrook and Washford to be about fourteen miles. Earthbound riders, who had to go over hills or, on occasion, around them and take detours to find fords and bridges and avoid bogs, needed to travel half as far again.

"We ought to take Quentin," Liza said. "Mother's never seen her."

"With Quentin along, you'll want the quietest pony and you'll be tied down to a walk," Richard said. "Take Mouse. And I think you'll need to spend a night on the way."

"Ned Crowham owns a farmstead about halfway," Peter said. "They'll put us up."

The farmstead was somewhat farther than halfway. It seemed

a long ride the first day, going at the slow pace imposed not merely by Quentin but also by Mouse, who from a filly had been the gentlest and most responsible of ponies, and seemed well aware that the woman on her back had a two-year-old child in her arms and must be treated with care. But it was a pleasant ride through the May sunshine with lark song sparkling in the sky, and by putting in the extra miles, they shortened the second day's journey. It was only just after noon when the little party rode past the gatehouse of Cleeve Abbey and on along the track to Washford village, where Herbert Dyer's combined home and workshop stood, a little back from the road.

The house, recently thatched and looking as though it had a golden pelt, was in front, with the slate roof of the workshop rising behind. There was a patch of front garden, with a few flowers coming into bloom.

"And someone's weeding," Peter remarked as the ponies plodded toward the gate.

"It's Mother!" said Liza.

Margaret had heard the approaching hooves and straightened up to look over the fence. "Liza! Peter—my dears! What brings you here? Nothing's wrong, is it? Oh, is that my granddaughter? You've brought her all that way?"

"Yes. We...we just came on a visit because I wanted to see you and I thought you'd like to see Quentin," Liza said carefully. "The weather's good and she's been no trouble. The pony's pace just sends her to sleep."

"Oh, give her to me!" Margaret held out her arms and Quentin, waking up, laughed. "Come along, poppet, let your grandmother look at you. You named her for my mother—that was sweet of you. But she hasn't got my mother's hair," said

Margaret, laughing, too. "She has yours, Liza, the very same pretty brown. I am very well, I'm glad to say." She lowered Quentin to the ground. "Good girl. Nice and steady on your feet. Oh, you're all so welcome. Down you get. I'll call someone to see to the ponies and you can come in through the garden."

She hurried to the right-hand fence and shouted, and a groom appeared around the side of the house, presumably from a stable-yard somewhere. He took charge of the ponies and the Lanyon family followed Liza's mother indoors.

"She looks happy," Liza whispered to Peter when they had been shown into a low-beamed parlour with padded settles and an agreeable smell of beeswax, and Margaret had bustled off to tell Herbert they were there. "I'm grateful to Master Dyer for that, but if, after making her happy, he goes and spoils it all…!"

"He's never got into trouble yet."

"I smelled trouble in those figures. I couldn't see how he was turning a profit. I *know* that some of the materials he was buying in should cost more than his estimate. Why did he leave Taunton and then Dunster, I wonder?"

"The Guilds?" said Peter.

"Yes, maybe. They keep a close eye on the tradesmen in both places. My father was part of the Dunster Guild of Weavers and used to attend meetings and have other Guildsmen to dine. But…" Liza frowned. "I do remember them saying sometimes that the Guilds weren't active enough in some villages. Maybe Washford is one of them and maybe that's why he came here! And isn't it true that the longer folk get away with things, the bolder they get? Like the man who was supposed to be Geoffrey Baker's father and…and the clothier I mentioned, in Dunster.

I've sometimes thought maybe we snared a few rabbits too many and Walter Sweetwater somehow got to hear of it."

"Sssh. They're coming back."

Margaret came in, pink and excited, followed by Herbert Dyer, who was calling over his shoulder for someone to bring wine and pork pasties to the parlour. He strode in, beaming, and also burping slightly; clearly he had only just finished his dinner. "Welcome! Have you dined? No, don't tell me, you haven't. Why would you, when you were nearly here? I'll see you right. And what about the little lass, eh? What would she like?"

"She likes oatmeal porridge and minced meat and little squares of bread with fruit preserves on it."

"Say no more." He went to the door and shouted a second time, which produced a bobbing maidservant. Herbert gave instructions. "And now," he said, turning back to his guests, "all your family news, if you will. Marge here will want to hear everything. She often talks of you, Liza, and she's as proud of your girl as if no little wench was ever born before...."

"I should have ridden out to see her long ago, but first there was Nicholas and I just never could get up the heart, and then there was Herbert's proposal, and arrangin' the weddin'..." said Margaret.

"So we've come to you, instead," said Liza.

Overwhelmed with hospitality, it was an hour and a half before Peter finally managed to say, "Now that we're here, could we look at the workshop? I'd be very interested to see what goes on and I know Liza would. After all, she was born into the Weaver family."

The meal was finished and Quentin had gone outside, where she was playing in the garden with one of the maidservants. Herbert glanced through the window at them and smiled. "All your family spin and weave, don't they, Liza? When she's a little older, I suppose you'll have Quentin sitting at a loom, instead of toddling about being a household pet. But surely, even in your family, the womenfolk didn't concern themselves with what went on when the cloth left the premises for fulling and dyeing. Why should they?"

"My wife," said Peter, "takes an interest in everything round her. She's learned the work of the farm better than some girls who're born to it."

"Ah, well, farming folk are different. Everyone has to join in. But Marge here, why, she's hardly set foot in the workshop and I wouldn't want her to. I want her to have a life of ease and luxury, unless she likes to embroider, or maybe spin and weave a little for her own amusement."

"I'd be *very* interested to see the workshop," said Liza in steely tones. "And so would Peter. Please show us."

"Well, if you're sure. Excuse me, I'll just go and see what's being done in there now, and tell my men to expect visitors."

He went out. With Margaret there, Peter and Liza couldn't turn to each other and say *what's he hiding?* out loud, but they could and did exchange glances which said it silently.

Herbert came back a few minutes later. "Well, if you'll come with me… Marge, are you coming, too?"

"No, I thank you," said Margaret comfortably. "I've weeding to finish and I want to play with my granddaughter. She's a pretty one, Liza, no doubt about it. And I'll see the kitchen knows there'll be extra mouths for supper. You'll stay the night, of course."

They reached the workshop by a covered passage. "I had the works adjoining the house in Taunton and again in Dunster, but the smells used to get in," Herbert said. "I used to think I was drinking alum soup."

"Alum?" Peter queried.

"A sort of clay. Comes from the Mediterranean and it's scarcer and more costly than it was," Herbert said, pushing open the door at the end of the passage. "It's used to make a mixture—a mordant, we call it—to soak cloth or the yarn before it's dyed."

"To make the dye stay put?" said Peter, airing his recently acquired knowledge.

"Exactly. Then it won't run when it's washed. As I was saying, when I came here and had this workshop built, I thought, this time, things will be different. I put it away from the house, but I made this passage in between so as to get in and out without getting wet in the rain. Here we are."

The workshop was big, built of stone, with three louvred roof vents, beneath which were big open hearths where cauldrons full of strange substances were bubbling. Materials were apparently soaking in them, and perspiring youths—all the workforce seemed to consist of youths except one young man who appeared to be in his twenties—were pushing them about with poles. From one cauldron, a couple of lads were lifting red-dyed cloth on their poles and draping it over a rack. Crimson drops, looking rather gruesome, fell into a drip tray below. Over another rack, some hanks of scarlet yarn had been draped.

Built into the wall was yet another hearth, which seemed to be heating a giant oven, and also, set into the floor so that they were completely stable were a number of wooden vats, most of them full of liquid of some kind and some of them steaming. Materials were soaking in these, as well. The heat was colossal and an extraordinary mingling of smells, some nasty and some merely peculiar, filled the air.

"No," said Peter thoughtfully. "You'd hardly want your soup smelling like that!"

"Now this dye," said Herbert instructively, leading them to a bubbling cauldron, "is made from madder, *rubia tinctoria* a scholar would call it."

"Latin," said Peter. "Meaning red colouring."

"You know Latin?" Dyer looked surprised.

"I learned some at the school I went to for three years or so."

"And where was that?"

"It was run by a schoolmaster in east Somerset. He used to take a dozen boys or so at a time, house and feed them and give them a bit of learning. My father was sent to him and he was still in business when I was growing up, so I was sent there, too. Some schools wouldn't take boys from an ordinary farm, but he did," Peter added.

Out of courtesy to Liza, he didn't also add that according to Richard, though the schools run by churches were often less particular, they were apt to turn boys into monks and priests and keep them from breeding families.

"Seems you remember what you learned," said Dyer, not sounding over-pleased about it. "So. I buy the madder root ready dried and ground and it creates the shade of red you see here. The cloth inside is being moved around to make the colouring even."

"What's in there?" asked Liza, pointing to the sunken vats.

"Oh, those are the alum tubs. That's the first stage, before the dyeing proper begins." Herbert, however, did not offer a closer inspection but led them instead to another simmering cauldron. "Now, this dyebath is a different shade of red. Madder was the basis but it was mixed with brezil wood. That's costly—comes from India. Mix it with madder and you get a stronger red that wealthy folk'll pay for. We're not doing yellows today. Simon, come here and tell my guests all about our work!"

He beckoned to the one fully adult member of the workforce. "This is my son Simon, who'll take over from me one day when I get too old. He knows all the jobs in the workshop and sometimes fetches consignments of dyes for me that come from abroad by ship. Simon, meet my stepfamily. My stepdaughter, Liza, and her husband, Peter Lanyon."

Greetings were exchanged. Simon was a solidly made fellow, with a beard which, although fair, grew in exactly the same way as Herbert's. At the moment he was dressed in red-splashed and sweat-stained garments, and was crimson with heat. He seemed glad enough to desist from prodding linen around a tub with a long pole in order to talk instead.

"I heard Father telling you about madder and brezil wood. There's a very rich scarlet dye made from insects, too—see those hanks of scarlet yarn? That's what we used for them. We don't do much work with it, though. It's too expensive. Uses up fuel, too. You literally have to boil the material in it. That comes from an island to the south of India. Yellows we're not doing today, as Father says, but for them there's a berry that's said to come from Persia or else there's saffron from India. The best dyes nearly all come from faraway places—that's why they're so expensive."

"Where do you keep your ingredients for dyes?" Liza asked Herbert.

"Oh, over there in that press against the wall. Not that they'll mean much to you. Half of them don't look like much, raw. You'd hardly guess what colours are hidden in them."

Liza wandered off, peering into cupboards and then into the mordant vats, before coming back to join her husband and step-father as they left Simon to his poling and moved on to a door at the far end of the workshop, which opened onto a drying yard, where what seemed like miles of cloth swung on lines, in the breeze.

"Nothing like a natural breeze for drying," Herbert said. "In bad weather there's space enough at the end of the workshop to hang cloth for drying and it's warm there, but give me God's good winds any day."

"It's so interesting," said Liza. "I really must thank you. I knew a little about your work before, but I didn't know the dyes had to be brought from such distant lands."

"Yes, I've got contracts with a couple of merchant captains based in Lynmouth and meeting ships there is part of our lives. They send word when they're in port. Minehead or Porlock would be nearer, but the captains I use know my trade and can do the buying for me. Simon and I don't mind the journey. It saves paying for the ship to make an extra call and it's an outing for us now and then," said Herbert Dyer cheerily.

Christopher set foot inside the hall of Dunster Castle and for the moment forgot about Liza, or any notions he had had of making enquiries about the fate of his former love. It was some time since he had last come to the castle, and though he hadn't liked what he found even then, it hadn't been his business. Now, however, he had come here to live, and things had clearly dete-riorated further. His scandalised and cringing nasal tissues were protesting.

In the days of the Luttrells the castle had been kept sweet, with lavender and rosemary always strewn among the rushes on the floor of the hall and beeswax rubbed into the furniture. Applewood had burned in the hall fire, and Elizabeth Luttrell liked rosewater perfume.

The present landlord, the Earl of Pembroke, had been absentee from the start, though not entirely through his own fault. At the moment he was said to be in attendance on King Edward and not likely to leave the court, as Christopher knew. Prior Hampton received news regularly and Christopher was aware that the court had been in an uneasy state for the past few years, ever since Edward had wrecked his cousin Warwick's scheme to arrange a marriage between the king and a French princess by blandly announcing that he had married a widow called Elizabeth Woodville.

"He's poked Warwick in the eye and no mistake," the prior had told Christopher in a gossipy moment. "And now, it seems, the new queen's got enough relatives to populate a city and they're out for all they can get. Edward's giving them good positions with one hand and wealthy marriages with the other and I heard that Warwick's as mad as a forest fire. There'll be trouble one of these days. As if the land hasn't seen enough of that!"

No, the state of Dunster Castle was probably not Pembroke's fault, but that of his steward, who had done nothing to correct the bad habits of the slovenly caretaker servants. No one had polished the furniture for years and years, or put as much as a single sprig of scented herbage among the rushes. It seemed doubtful that anyone had even changed the rushes.

The place stank, of dogs, dead mice and something suspiciously like ordure, and whatever was smouldering in the hearth of the great hall certainly wasn't applewood. The fire was smoking, and it reeked as though someone had tried to dispose of canine droppings and old chicken bones on it. Christopher looked down and saw that there actually were bones among the rushes, tossed to the dogs, no doubt. He had nothing against dogs, but the Luttrells had made sure that someone cleared up after theirs.

He stood looking around him, appalled. The beautiful tapestries were still there, but they were dimmed, unbrushed, and the pretty flowered one with the unicorn and the lady had moth holes in it. He had been brought in and told to wait for the steward. He wandered up to the dais to look more closely at the table. Its dull surface was not only dusty but also marked. Careless people had been putting hot serving dishes down on it without a cloth in between.

Well, he wasn't here as a steward. But God's teeth, this was a disgrace. Very well! Steward or not, his name wasn't Christopher Clerk if he didn't, somehow, kick and prod the idle louts here into doing their jobs better than this. A few homilies on the virtue of doing the work you were paid for, a few clipped ears when the steward wasn't looking…. Well, someone ought to bring this crowd of lazybones to heel!

"So," said Peter when at last he, Liza and Quentin were alone in the spare bedchamber they were to occupy that night. Quentin was asleep, in a crib beside the curtained bed. "This is the first time I've been able to talk to you without anyone else listening. You've been very quiet, as if you were thinking. Were you?"

"*Thinking!* I've been seething since we came out of that workshop. I've been longing to talk to you, as well. Never in all my life…!"

"Never what?"

"Alum!" said Liza witheringly. "Alum indeed! There were

three mordant vats and maybe one of them had alum in it. One of them had vinegar—cheap cider vinegar by the smell of it—and what was in the other, well, I hardly like to say!"

"I think you must, love. What was it?"

"Fermented piss."

"What?"

"I really do know something about the cloth-making business. Much more than I let Master Dyer realise! I was always interested, more than some of the boys in the family were, and Father used to talk to me, and he'd talk frankly. Before people found out about alum, which is much better, they used fermented urine or vinegar to fix cloth so that dyes would hold, except that neither of them worked all that well. They're out of date now because alum's much better."

"But...are you sure that Master Dyer is...?"

"When I went poking in that press," said Liza, "there were three vinegar barrels stowed under the lowest shelf. I put my nose down and sniffed at them. And as for what was on the shelves! Persian berries and Indian saffron, indeed! He had barberries there."

"Barberries? What Kat makes that bitter jam from sometimes?"

"Yes. They're another out-of-date thing. They used to be used for making yellow dyes, but no good dyeing works uses barberries now! Oh, there were Persian berries and saffron there as well, but I suspect that somebody's paying for good dyes and getting cheap ones, and that a lot of people are getting cloth where the dye's not fixed as it ought to be. I think that's what happened to me, when I used to send cloth here to be coloured red and yellow. He's making a profit—and offering my family a big discount because he's saving on dyestuffs and mordants. He's getting away with it because whatever local Guild keeps an eye on Washford, it isn't very thorough. Father would never believe any ill of him, though there were whispers when he was in Dunster. Well, I think the whisperers were right! No wonder he keeps moving from place to place!"

"Dear saints. But what are we to do? If he's really cheating his customers like that, then it's only a matter of time before he's caught! It's a wonder he hasn't been caught before."

"He was more careful at first, probably."

"Well, it can't last!" said Peter, horrified. "It won't even need a Guild to find him out. All it needs is one resentful customer with enough knowledge to work out what he's doing! Then a complaint will be lodged with the parish constable. And that will be the end of him."

"I don't know *what* to do, Peter. He's married to Mother now! I wish we hadn't come here. Or that we'd found out long ago and reported him ourselves, before she was tangled up in it. We can't do that now! I thought we'd find something amiss, yes, but not this much! This is…it's *awful!*"

"My father wanted us to find out what we could. Well, we have. Now we have to tell him what we've found and leave it to him, like he told us. He'll do his best to protect your mother; I think we can trust him for that. Don't upset yourself. Maybe we can make Herbert stop this. Then he'll be safe and so will your mother. Think of it that way. You're a marvel. My nose would never have told me half what your nose has told you!"

"Your nose can smell different things. I think you can smell a rabbit in the cabbage patch from the other side of Winsford Hill."

Peter laughed. Quentin made a little squeaking noise as though she were dreaming and then settled quietly again.

"Liza...?"

"Dear love." Liza moved against him, feeling the hard pressure of his need, pushed back the covers, which were heavy, and drew him on top of her.

"If you're not tired..."

"I'm not tired."

"Dear, dear, clever Liza..."

Good kind Peter, whom I ought to appreciate much more, whom I ought to love, really and truly, from the very depths of me. He protected me from his father when Master Lanyon was angry with me. And he trusts me to love him. Oh, God, I've tried to love him. Make it so! Help me to be what he thinks I am. Let me have a son for him. Let us make a son tonight. Please.

CHAPTER TWENTY

ESTRANGEMENT

"So now," said Liza to her father-in-law, "we know what he's doing. I'm as sure as I can be that he never swindled my father. Father was an important client. But I suspect he's battening on smaller clients. Like me! He's been getting away with it because it takes time for this sort of thing to become obvious. Any dye will run sometimes—if the water's too hot or the soap's too strong. It takes a while for the word to get round that cloth dyed in such and such a workshop runs more easily than cloth dyed somewhere else! It does get round in the end, of course. I'm quite sure that's why he moved from Taunton to Dunster to Washford!"

"Yes." Richard was grim. "So far he's kept one step ahead of the hunt, so to speak."

"Yes, just that!" Liza was animated and indignant. "And now I think he wants to prop up his business by getting work from my family, who'll do it because now they're his family as well, in a way, and he can pretend to be doing them a favour with his discount while he makes up the difference—and probably more, by a nice little margin—by charging for mordants he didn't use! My family's reputation, or their profits, in the end, don't matter to him. Oh, it makes me so angry!"

"Did you say anything to him?"

Liza shook her head and Peter said, "Not with Liza's mother there, but we're worried for her sake. If he gets caught, and he will if he goes on like this, she won't be able to look her neighbours in the eye."

"It would matter so much to her. She'd never get over it. We had to tell you, but don't go to the parish constable. Please, Father-in-law, don't do that!" Liza pleaded.

"Don't worry," said Richard grimly. "There are other ways of dealing with Master Dyer, without the constable. Well done, Liza. Very well done indeed. I'll saddle Magpie in the morning."

Richard, riding alone on a long-legged horse, left home early the next morning, used shortcuts over the moorland and covered the miles to Washford easily by midday. There was an inn in the village, where he dined and Magpie could have a manger. "I doubt if Master Dyer will ask me to dine," he had remarked to his family before starting out.

He was back by nightfall, though he had lengthened his journey by travelling via Dunster and at first seemed more inclined to talk of Dunster and the Weaver family than to report on his meeting with Herbert.

"There's a steward in the castle these days. The Earl of Pembroke—he's the castellan now—has never been near the place and the farmland's going back to the wild. I saw two great fields with brambles spreading out from the hedges and clumps of bracken where there ought to be crops, and as for the harbour! Nowadays the sea's going back so fast that half the quay's out of use altogether. If the inside of the castle is as bad, then it's nothing by now but a great big hovel."

"But what about...?" Peter began.

"And I thought," said Richard, refusing to be interrupted, "that you'd like news of your family, Liza. Your cousin Laurence seems to know what he's about. He's looking after it for your brothers while they learn the business all through. Your great-uncle Will's still alive, though frail as thistledown nowadays, poor old fellow, and hardly stirs from his chair."

"How does Elena manage Aunt Cecy, I wonder?" Liza said, setting his place for him at the table in the hall, while Betsy fetched his supper. The rest of them had eaten theirs.

"Laurence told me all about that," said Richard, grinning. "Said Elena just got on with her spinning and told Aunt Cecy if she wanted to run the household, she was welcome. Left it all to Cecy, and the old girl soon got tired of having to work out what was to be cooked for dinner, listing what was to be bought and worrying over whether the flour bin was going down too fast, and chivvying the maids on washday. Cecy's handed the task back to Elena and the worst she does now is carp now and then just for the sake of it, and Elena takes no notice. If your mother had thought to pull the same trick, she'd maybe still be in Dunster and Herbert Dyer could take his own road to hell and do no harm to her."

"Well, it didn't turn out that way," said Peter. The weather had turned chilly, as it sometimes did in May, and he was sitting by the fire with his favourite dog, Rusty, who had been the most beautiful puppy in Silky's last litter, between his knees. "Father, *did you see Master Dyer?*"

There was a moment of silence. Betsy came in with food and put it in front of Richard, who took a spoonful of broth and broke some bread before saying, at length, "Yes, I saw him, and it weren't pleasant. I made him take me round the workshop and I did a bit of sniffing at this tub and that and then I said to him, let's talk outdoors. Why, says he. You'll see when we're out there, I told him. So we went into that drying yard he has at the back and I said my piece. Then he said his. I won't repeat it."

"About us?" said Liza. "Well, what else could we expect?"

"He didn't give in easy," Richard said. "Blustered and shouted and swore and called us the sort of names that would make the air stink if I spoke them. And—I'm sorry, Liza—but in the middle of it all your mother came out to us. She'd heard the noise. He told her I was insulting him and making up slanders about his work, and he said that you two had been prowling and sniffing round when you came to visit and then she started calling us—all of us—names as well.... I don't like telling you this...."

"Calling *Liza* names?" said Peter indignantly.

"Herbert's her husband," said Liza, her face stiff. "If only my mother hadn't heard the shouting. What happened next?"

"I'm sorry for her," Richard told her. "She's a decent woman and she'd had a shock, but when I heard her saying things about you...well, I lost my temper. I reckoned she ought to know who was telling the truth and who weren't. My nose told me what yours told you. I could tell which vats had piss and vinegar in them and you've explained the meaning of it. I grabbed her by the arm and walked her into the workshop and told her, you just sniff at that there vat. Pushed her head down to make her breathe the smell in, as a matter of fact. And this one as well, I said…"

"Father-in-law, you didn't!"

"Yes, I did. Herbert had told her what I was accusing him of and he'd denied it. I made her know it was true. I tell you, I wouldn't stand hearing you and Peter abused like that. She started crying and broke away and ran into the house and I finished dealing with Herbert. I told him what he could expect if the constable got to hear of it, and said that if it didn't stop, the constable *would* hear of it, from me. And I said, don't think you can fool me. I'll know if you cheat. I'll be visiting once in a while, unexpected like, and I'll look at this workshop and you'd better let me in because if you don't, that'll send me straight to the parish constable, too. He said he'd do no more business with me, but then I said, well, that means not doing business with the Weavers either, which might be quite a loss, and what'll folk say when word gets round that you've parted company with your wife's own family?"

"I wish I'd been there," said Peter.

"I'm glad *I* wasn't," said Liza.

"Anyway," Richard said, "I told him, if you refuse to work with us, maybe that's another thing might send me to the authorities. I left him cursing but not before I'd made him swear, on the crosshilt of my dagger, to give up using cheap dyes and mordants and stop charging customers for what they hadn't had. I swore, too, that I wouldn't tell on him, as long as he stayed honest. That was for your mother's sake."

"She'll be saved from trouble in the end," Peter said to Liza. "Whatever she feels now, think how it would be if he were taken up for cheating! Why, the men in his workshop must all know. What if one of them were to turn nasty?"

"They were all very young, didn't you notice?" said Richard. "Hardly a boy over fourteen and one or two of them almost simple, I'd say. I doubt if they know what's in the mordants, or what ought to be, either. Cunning bugger, that man Dyer is. He guards his back."

Liza looked miserable. "I know it's best for my mother that he stops cheating. But I hate to think how it is with them now. They may be quarrelling. I wish I knew she was all right."

"He was scared when I started talking about penalties," Richard said, reaching for a chicken leg. "He's quite a personage in Washford. He didn't fancy having a vat of bad dye poured over him and then being marched through the village covered with it."

"Please, don't!"

"It won't happen now," Richard reassured her. "There's nothing to worry about, Liza."

Margaret arrived the following day, tearful and furious.

They were at dinner, all the household, eating quickly because in May cows needed milking three times a day, weeds grew in the fields between dusk and dawn, and paths vanished under overhanging grass if left untended for a week. The day was dry and most of them would be out of doors again the moment the meal was finished. It was Richard, busily mopping up gravy with the last of his bread, who glanced through the hall windows and said, "We have visitors. Got a packhorse with them, too. Liza! It's your mother!"

"What?" Liza, who had been helping Quentin with her food, twisted around to stare through the window. Quentin, perched in a high chair Higg had made for her, wailed. "There, there, you've finished anyway," said Liza. Hurriedly she wiped her daughter's mouth and ran out just as Margaret and Simon Dyer, leading a pack pony, came to a halt.

Simon was better dressed than when they had seen him last, but with a face as hard and closed as a bolted oak door, while Margaret had tear streaks on her face. The pack pony was hardly visible under the bundles and hampers strapped on its back.

"What on earth…?" Liza began.

"Here you are." Simon ignored her and spoke over his shoulder to Margaret. "Get down." He made no move to assist her. Margaret, who had been riding astride but without breeches to protect her legs from the stirrup leathers, scrambled painfully off.

"What *is* all this?" Liza hurried forward and Simon, acknowledging her existence at last, thrust the pony's leading rein at her.

"Here. The pony's your mother's, same as the mare she's on. I shan't take them back. I've brought Mistress Dyer safely here. I'll go home and say I've done my errand. Good day to you."

"But won't you come in? There's water in the trough for your horse and—"

"No," said Simon shortly. "I won't. The Allerbrook's good enough for any horse. *Good day!*"

"Ohhhh!" wailed Margaret, and burst out crying, though in a way which sounded as much like rage as grief.

The others were outside now, some of them with their mouths full, all exclaiming. Higg led the pony and the mare away and Liza went quickly to Margaret's side. "Mother? What's the matter? What's wrong?"

"*Wrong?*" screamed Margaret, and struck her an openhanded blow in the face, with such force that Liza staggered away with a cry of pain and bumped into Roger, who grasped her supportingly and said, "Here, what's all this? There's no call to go on like that, Mistress!"

Peter got in between mother and daughter just in time, as Margaret lunged after Liza and tried to hit her again. "Stop it! What's the matter with you? Mistress *Dyer!*"

"Yes, none of that!" Richard grabbed Margaret's upper arm, shouted, "Get inside!" and hustled her roughly through the door into the hall. He bundled her to a settle and shoved her into it, not letting go of her until she was seated and more or less imprisoned because he had planted himself in front of her. "Now then!" Richard bellowed. "Let's hear the meaning of this!"

Margaret, scarlet in the face and rubbing her arm where Richard had gripped it, let out a screech of fury and misery mingled, and then stopped rubbing in order to point a shaking finger at the horrified Liza, who had stumbled through the door after them, with Peter's arm about her. "It's her fault! Interfering, nose-poking, smug, righteous, nasty little bitch!"

"*Mother!*" Liza was weeping now and holding her face, and to add to the chaos, Quentin, abandoned at the table, began to howl. Kat and Betsy, hurrying indoors on Liza's heels, hastened to her, clucking.

"What the devil are you talking about?" Richard thundered.

"I was happy! I was happy bein' Mistress Dyer and she's gone and spoilt it all. I can't stop there anymore. I can't bear it!"

"Can't bear what?" demanded Richard.

"It's because of *Herbert,* you fool!" shrieked Margaret. "First of all, *they* came to see him, Liza and your Peter, and they pried and peered and asked questions and then you came and…and… all because that little…"

"Don't call my wife names!" shouted Peter.

"Because *Liza,* dear, sweet, adorable little Liza, my favourite daughter, with her saintliness and her base-metal halo, sniffed round the workshop and found that my husband was…was…"

"Using cheap methods and materials while charging for expensive ones," said Peter coldly.

"And now I can't stay there anymore! I can't! Nicholas was always honest and I can't live with a man who isn't. I was always that proud that there wasn't a word anyone could say against me or mine! But I'd have been happy if I'd never known about this and it's broken my heart but I can't stop with him, I can't, I can't, and it's all her fault and…"

"No, don't, please!" begged Liza as Richard's right hand came up.

"She's hysterical. *Mistress Dyer!* Be quiet or I'll make you!" The threat was enough. Margaret subsided, hiccuping and glaring at Liza.

"You would have known before long," said Liza, sobbing. "He'd have got caught. We've saved him from that, and saved you, too. No one knows what he's been doing except us."

"You ought to thank Liza," said Richard. "Her keen nose and her knowledge of cloth making told us the truth and you ought to be grateful!"

"Grateful? *Grateful!* My life's ruined and I should be *grateful?*"

"Yes, you should. If he'd been caught, half Somerset would have known," said Richard. "You couldn't have held your head up, ever again."

"He'll be honest from now on," Peter added. "He swore to that and we'll keep him to it. It's all right, Mistress Dyer. You can go back and live with him…he wants you to go back?"

"Not now! I said such things to him, I was so angry with him. I never thought—there had been stories, but Nicholas always said he'd treated us fairly and I never dreamed…he said if I hated him so much, I'd better go. I wish I'd never found out! He's been kind to me. I didn't *know*. I never went into the workshop. But *she* used to ask her father questions and he told her more than he ever told me. I'd never have known but for her—it's all her fault!" wailed Margaret, from whose mental processes any kind of logic had clearly taken wing.

"Didn't you hear what Peter said? You would have known before long. I'd take my oath on it," Richard snapped.

"But where are you going now?" said Peter icily. "Because I tell you frankly, Mother-in-law, you're not welcome here, not after this. Are you going back to the Weavers in Dunster, or to your own kinfolk, or where?"

"Stop here? With her? I'd sooner die!" Margaret bawled.

"I did it *for you!*" shouted Liza, and was rewarded with a shriek of fury. Margaret, still virtually imprisoned in her seat by the looming Richard, actually drummed her feet on the floor in rage.

"How can I go back to Dunster?" she screamed. "They'd ask why, and I can't tell anyone—he's my husband! Folk would point fingers, and anyhow, a woman can't betray her husband, even if he sprouts horns and a tail and she can't stand to live another day with him! As for my kinfolk, there's none left that I mean anything to and if I had, I couldn't tell them either! I can't be like that Alison Webber was, sayin' it's nothing to do with me! She got wed again, we heard, in Dulverton. Well, I can't do that either. I'm still wed and there's no gettin' away from it. I just wanted to come here to tell *her* what I think of her and her nosy ways! I'd like to kill you, Liza, I'd like to…!"

"Where do you want to go?" demanded Richard. "Just tell us and we'll see to it!"

"There's a women's abbey in Devon. They've a guest house and Nicholas and I stayed there sometimes, when I travelled with him. They'll take me in. Herbert gave me money. He said I'd better go but he'd make it easy for me. At the last minute he said he'd take me back if I liked, but I won't like! I can't!"

"Very well," said Richard. "You'll take some food and a night's rest, I trust?"

"I'll neither eat nor sleep under your roof. I brought food with me. We left at dawn and I ate in the saddle. Simon's gone to the inn at Clicket and then he'll go back to Washford. He hates me for his father's sake and I don't want to ride another yard with him and I told him as much. You'll just have to lend me a man and I'll start for Devon at once. Now!"

"You won't," said Richard. "Your horse is tired. You'll rest here till we say you can leave. Betsy, come here. Let Kat look after the child for a minute. Take Mistress Dyer upstairs...."

"There's one more thing," said Margaret. Her voice now was quiet, but in an ominous fashion. "Something I think you should know."

"And what might that be?"

"Dear Liza, that you think I ought to be grateful to, sweet Liza, that's wrecked my life, my whole life..."

"It was Herbert Dyer if it was anyone!" shouted Liza. "Stop blaming me!"

"You all think she's such a good girl," said Margaret nastily to Peter and Richard. "But afore she was married, she tried to run off with a half-baked clerk from Dunster Castle. Oh, we got them back in time. There was no harm done, but she was seein' him in secret, all that summer. And him in the priesthood! She'd have shamed us all if we hadn't stopped her. She's not quite the perfect angel you think. What have you to say about *that?*"

Richard swung around. "Is this true, Liza?"

"Yes." Liza had gone very white. "I was a young girl. I fell in love. But we were never...never lovers. I just tried to do a silly thing but I was brought home and—"

"God knows, I was sorry for her when her father beat her," said Margaret. "Now I wish he'd knocked the smugness and the cleverness out of her, too. I wish..."

"Mistress Dyer," said Peter, "I too fell in love with someone else before I married Liza. I've told her about it. My girl wasn't suitable, any more than I suppose this clerk was. What was his name, by the way?"

"Christopher Clerk," said Liza in a low voice. "But it was just a young girl's fancy. I've tried to be a good wife to Peter and forget all about Christopher."

"I wish you'd told me," said Peter. "I told you about Marion!"

"I wanted to!" cried Liza. "But I was afraid to! Men get forgiven more easily than women, and later on, it didn't seem to matter. Nothing *happened* between him and me! It *doesn't* matter, not now!"

"No, it doesn't," said Peter firmly. He looked his father in the eye. "She is telling the truth when she says that nothing happened. I can vouch for that."

"I'm glad to hear it. Ah, well, it's all over, years ago," said Richard. He was aware that he ought to be angry, to complain that he and Peter had been deceived, but there was no bigger deceiver in this hall than Richard himself and he knew it. "Young folk will be young."

He turned back to Margaret, who was gaping, astounded to see the aggressive Richard Lanyon, who should have turned on Liza in a fury, behaving like a lamb instead of a dark-maned lion. "If you thought I'd throw Liza out of the house because when she was a dreamy lass, she let some young fellow make up to her for a while, you don't know me. Now let Betsy take you to a bedchamber. You can stop there till tomorrow. I won't have you sharing meals with us down here. Betsy'll fetch food and hot water for you, all that, and tomorrow I'll escort you to this abbey of yours. It's a bloody nuisance this time of year, but I'll see you get there safe. You ought to be grateful to Liza instead of abusing her, yes you ought. But I damn well don't feel grateful to *you!*"

"What sort of place is it?" Liza asked when Richard returned two days later. "Will Mother be safe there? Happy?"

"I doubt if she'll ever be happy again," said Richard sombrely, "but that's her fault, not ours. The place is well enough. It's small—no more than a dozen nuns, but they look well fed, and they seem kind. They've given your mother a room in the guest house and a lay sister to wait on her. Your stepfather did give her some money and he's willing to send a yearly payment for her support. He's fond of her, I think. He's not entirely wicked."

"I'll have to visit her later. When she's settled. Maybe…"

"I wouldn't," said Richard. His nerves were still rasped from some of the bitter things Margaret had said about her daughter on the way to Devon. "I should leave her be. Your home's here, my girl. You're a Lanyon now. Come, don't look so down-hearted. There's work to be done."

"Yes, of course," said Liza, and went to do some hoeing, putting a good deal of energy into it because physical effort sometimes eased the discomfort of the monthly nuisance, which had come upon her that morning. Her downheartedness was only partly due to the estrangement with her mother. She and Peter had loved like mad things that night in Washford, but all in vain. There would be no child.

CHAPTER TWENTY-ONE

REBELLION

The year of 1469 wore uneasily on. Liza fretted a good deal. She had made up her mind that she must not think of Christopher, that he must indeed be consigned to the past, but instead she worried about her mother. Also, there was disturbing news from the outside world. From his pulpit one Sunday, Father Bernard announced that trouble had broken out in the north of England. In Yorkshire there was a rising against the king.

"It's a small affair," said Father Bernard. *"As yet,"* he added ominously. "But things could worsen. Just in case, every man who can shoot at all *must* be at the butts every Sunday, unless he's injured or ill. Those are the orders of Master Walter Sweetwater."

At first, matters rested there. June came, with sheep to be sheared and hay to be scythed, and Liza, her mind still on her mother's troubles, made an attempt to mend the breach. Following Richard's advice, she did not try to visit Margaret, but she sent Higg with gifts—a honeycake and a length of her own green homespun cloth, accompanied by a loving letter. Margaret could not read, but one of the nuns might read it to her. Higg came back with the gifts untouched.

"And the letter? Did someone read the letter for her?" Liza asked unhappily. Higg looked at her mournfully.

"Tell me," said Liza.

"Mistress, she…she tore it up."

"She needs more time," said Liza, trying to be calm, trying to be sensible. "Did she look well?"

"She said she wasn't ailing, Mistress. I didn't see her for long."

Liza worried afresh, but at this point, Father Bernard's gloomy forecast came true. The situation was indeed worsening. A new rebellion had started in Lancashire. "So far," said Father Bernard, "men have only been summoned to arms from the districts where the troubles actually are. We can but pray they come no closer."

The next report said that the rebellion was bigger than expected and was led by a relative of the powerful Earl of Warwick. The king had taken refuge in Nottingham Castle and the rebels had issued an alarming proclamation, condemning the queen and her family, the Woodvilles, and claiming that the Earl of Warwick was one of their own supporters.

July brought the news that Warwick had fled to France and that George of Clarence, King Edward's younger brother, had gone with him and had been married to Warwick's daughter Isabel. The air was full of danger. The southwest was still not caught up in it, but trouble was coming closer, like an incoming tide. The king had summoned the Earl of Devon to him, and the Earl of Pembroke, too, the same Pembroke who was lord of

Dunster Castle. The Duke of Somerset, however, was reportedly supporting Warwick, which now meant supporting the king's enemies. The Sweetwaters, who were now Yorkist and therefore on King Edward's side, came to the butts at every practice, and were seen watching the men of the parish with keen eyes, picking out the good marksmen.

The next reports were still more grave. Warwick and Clarence had landed in southeast England. They had marched through Kent, gathering men, entered London with a swagger and then set out northward to join their supporters. There had been fighting. And the Earl of Pembroke had been taken by the Lancastrians and beheaded. Dunster's absentee landlord would be an absentee forever now.

"I don't like it," Richard said over Sunday supper the day that Father Bernard made that announcement. "It's as if we're perched on a rock on a beach, watching the sea roll in!"

Further news was brought to Clicket by a seaman called Ralph Stubb, whose parents lived in the village. He had been granted leave from his ship, which had put in at Porlock, bringing goods from London. Having greeted his family, he had repaired to the White Hart to renew his acquaintance with old friends—Adam Turner's ale counted as one of these—and also to enjoy holding forth to a fascinated audience.

"Seems," Stubb said, "that whatever Warwick and Clarence are up to, King Edward's in London, and reigning. Only," he added, "there's another tale going round. It's old news now but some folk hadn't heard it before and it does make a man think. Some of them on the rebels' side...well, looks like they had a point."

"What do you mean?" demanded Father Bernard, who,

although now very pale and thin and assisted by an energetic curate who would take over from him eventually, was still, as yet, in charge of his parish, still liked his ale once in a while and was in the tavern that evening.

"Two years back," said Stubb, "that's when it happened. It's about the Earl of Desmond. You've not heard?"

"Nothing about anyone called Desmond. The Sweetwaters don't tell us everything they hear," said Father Bernard. "Not if it's against the Yorkists, anyhow."

"Well," said Stubb, "it's like this..."

It was an unpleasant story. The king's controversial marriage to the widow Elizabeth Grey, whose family of origin, the Woodvilles, now occupied so many splendid posts, was probably much of the driving force behind the rebellion, and with reason. The Earl of Desmond, who two years ago had been Deputy Lieutenant of Ireland, had paid a visit to England at that time. He had talked with the king and he had criticised the queen, who had learned of it and been angry.

Later Desmond returned to Ireland and lost the post of Deputy Lieutenant to the Earl of Worcester. "A friend of the queen, it seems," said Stubb. "He had Desmond arrested, for no good reason as far as anyone knows, and then had him beheaded. Worse! He had Desmond's two small sons beheaded, as well."

There was a stir, and a horrified murmur.

"One of them were no more than six years old and didn't understand," said Stubb. "Had a boil on his little neck and said to the headsman to mind it. That's what's being said."

"Wicked, that is," said Turner.

"We shouldn't be speaking evil of the king's own wife," said Father Bernard uneasily, but he was frowning. "But if that tale's true," he said slowly, "then it's a shameful thing. To murder two little boys!"

Father Bernard did not care for children in person, because he liked to read and pray or—these days—snooze undisturbed, and every child in Clicket knew better than to play near the vicarage. One incautious shriek and Father Bernard, who could still move surprisingly fast for someone of his age, would shoot out from his door, waving a stick. He would, however, have given his life without hesitation to protect any one of them from real harm. "This is ugly news," he said. "Pray God it's *not* true."

"But it is," said Stubb. "We gave passage to some of Warwick's men last year, had 'em on board for a week, going up north. They'd been at court the year before, when word got to the court from Ireland. They said the court was buzzing with it."

For the time being, however, quiet seemed to have fallen, even though Warwick and Clarence were presumably still at large. In the autumn Liza tried again to make peace with her mother, and sent Roger with two big mutton hams and two large cheeses. Another letter accompanied the offerings, this one not only loving, but pleading. When Roger returned, however, he brought the hams and cheeses back with him.

"I won't ask what happened to the letter," said Liza bitterly.

"Best not try again," said Richard. "You'll only upset yourself. Maybe it's because of all this that Quentin's still the only one."

He had begun, once more, to make digs. This was not the first. "Perhaps you're right," said Liza dejectedly. She felt heavy and tired and her head ached. The last thing she wanted just then was to be harried over her poor showing as a brood mare.

In fact, her out-of-sorts feeling was the harbinger of illness.

The autumn was damp and cold and it brought an epidemic—a cross, it seemed, between an ordinary cold and the sweating sickness. The sufferers were feverish and ached all over with violent coughs in the later stages. Liza was the first person at Allerbrook to succumb, but everyone there took it in due course, one after the other, and in the village there were deaths.

At Allerbrook they all recovered, although Higg never quite shook off the cough. In Clicket, however, just before Christmas, Father Bernard died. His erstwhile curate, Father Matthew, conducted his funeral and was confirmed by the Sweetwaters as Clicket's new vicar.

The winter closed in and a heavy snowfall cut off the higher farms and villages. Richard, these days, wasn't the good shot that he used to be with either crossbow or longbow though he was still accurate over short distances, but Peter's eye was straight enough, and he had the idea of putting out a few vegetables on the snow to tempt rabbits, or even deer, within range of his arrows. The rabbits, of course, were now legal, but the deer were not.

"Only, if we can't get down the combe to church through the snow, I doubt any Sweetwaters'll be clambering up it to see what we're up to," Peter said cheerfully, stepping into the kitchen one morning with a dead hind on his shoulder. "See what you can do with this, Liza."

The thaw made the Allerbrook spate and flooded some of the field, but at least it became possible once more to get down the combe from Allerbrook, attend church and hear Father Matthew give out the latest news, whenever there was any.

Father Matthew was a learned young man who believed in education and had started a small school for the Clicket children, though he was much given to homilies about the sinfulness of pleasure and the fires of hell, and his pupils found their lessons more depressing than inspiring. His face, though, had never been as sombre as it was when in March he announced that the time of quiet was over. Lincolnshire had risen on behalf of the imprisoned King Henry VI.

After that, for months, the news was a continual muddle as the warring factions went up and down on the wheel of fortune. "It's enough to make you dizzy," Richard said in disgust. "First one side's on top, and then the other. Where will it end?"

Everyone was relieved to hear that Warwick and Clarence had fled the country again, but in September the conflict at last rolled its first waves into the southwest, as the two of them brought fleets to Devon and landed.

"But they have set out straight for London," said Father Matthew. "Once more, the worst has passed us by."

It seemed to be so. King Edward and his youngest brother, Richard of Gloucester, were now the ones in exile. They had gone to Burgundy and King Henry was back on his throne. The queen was in sanctuary at Westminster.

"No business of ours," Richard Lanyon said as the winter once more clamped down. "I don't care who sits on the throne as long as they leave us alone. Let anyone have it!"

In March 1471, Father Matthew stood up in his pulpit once more and said the words they had all been dreading to hear. "The king is in England again. He is in the north, but he is mustering men and this time calling for aid from every able-bodied man in the country. All men of this parish are to assemble at the butts as soon as they leave this church. The women should go home.

The men who are to go will return home for one night before setting out with Master Walter Sweetwater and his son Baldwin Sweetwater tomorrow."

"I argued with them!" Richard said furiously to Liza as she stood, stricken and horrified, in the hall, while Peter, grim faced, put his arm about her. "I told them, take me, I've been soldiering before and I'm fit enough for all I'm fifty-one this year. But no! That sly Walter Sweetwater said he'd been watching me at the butts and I don't aim as true as I did over distances. Peter's to go and there's no appeal. God's teeth! If only we weren't Sweetwater tenants! I'm sick of being in their power, sick to my stomach of it!"

"I may not have to be gone long," said Peter. "It may be all over quite soon."

Liza, biting her lip, saw little Quentin looking at them wide-eyed from the doorway to the kitchen, with Betsy hovering behind her. For Quentin's sake, she mustn't give way. If ever there was a moment to be sensible, it was now.

"I...I must help Peter put his things together. Peter, you must have clean things...shirts, hose...."

"Yes, he must. Could find himself sleeping out in the damp. You've always got to have dry things to get into." Richard, though still burning with fury, hauled useful memories into the light. "And you'd better take the old helmet, and that sword I got at Towton."

"I don't know how to use it!" said Peter. "I'll have my bow."

"I daresay the Sweetwaters'll put you through some drilling before you get to the king. You take the sword, anyhow."

Liza, slipping from Peter's arm, went to Quentin and picked

her up. "Your dad's got to go away for a while, sweeting. You and I have to send him off with plenty of good stout clothes. Come and help!"

As she went out, taking Betsy with her, she heard Richard say to Peter, "I suppose there's no chance that you've left her with child?"

She didn't hear the answer, but the proof that no such thing had happened had come only two days before. It looked as though Quentin would be the only one forever. After all, she was now nearly thirty-six. If only, if only her father-in-law would just forget about it.

CHAPTER TWENTY-TWO

SHE-WOLF AND CUB

When men came home from war and sat warming their feet at the hearth and drinking ale and talking about their exploits, their descriptions of how armies met on the field made pictures in the minds of their families and friends. In their imaginations, these admiring hearers saw squadrons of horsemen with lances and swords, or a mass of determined foot soldiers grasping pikes, all shouting war cries and racing toward a cringing enemy.

What their mental pictures didn't contain was a confused collection of men, some in full plate armour, some light-armoured, some in chain mail handed down from bygone generations, and a number of unfortunates not in mail at all, some riding a variety of horses from massive destriers to wild-eyed ponies, and many others on foot, trying to keep out of the way of the horses, all sweltering hot and cursing the month of May for producing such a heat wave, and all so lost in a tangle of sunken lanes between banks and ancient hedgerows that they couldn't even find the enemy, let alone charge him. By the look of things, the Battle of Tewkesbury was going to be a disaster, though it wasn't yet clear for whom.

Peter Lanyon, in the middle of it all, was a horseman without armour, except for his helmet. He had his sword. He also had a destrier, which he had acquired just over two weeks ago at the Battle of Barnet, by grabbing the leg of the knight who was riding it, yanking him off and then sticking a dagger through a gap where his victim's armour was falling apart. This enabled him to fight on horseback, since ponies like Plume weren't used in battle, and anyway, he was fond of Plume and didn't want the poor animal to come to harm. Plume had been left behind the lines with the baggage.

He was now wondering, however, whether the enormous liver chestnut destrier was quite the prize he had thought. After Barnet, when the Captain of Archers he had been following saw that Peter now had a charger, he had been transferred to a mounted troop, but he had ridden Plume and led the destrier during most of the march from Barnet to Gloucestershire, and hadn't had much practice in handling his new mount.

He was now discovering that although he was strong and accustomed to horses, a trained war stallion was very different from even the most wilful pony. It had several times tried to bite him, even when he was offering it food, and now, with ears flattened back, it seemed to want to bolt, a desire he could understand but couldn't, just now, allow.

Richard of Gloucester, the king's youngest brother, the loyal one, who was in charge of this wing, had ordered them all to have their weapons ready, which meant that Peter needed his right hand for his sword. He had only his left hand for controlling the horse, and his left shoulder felt as though it were about to come out of its socket.

A pretty state of affairs it would be if he fell off the moment they met the Lancastrians. He would probably be killed and the Sweetwaters wouldn't care. Walter Sweetwater and his son Baldwin were both in this same company, among the lightly armoured riders but mounted on hefty chargers, which they handled with contemptuous ease, and they had already laughed to see him trying to manage his new steed.

It was a wonder he hadn't been killed already. This whole expedition was a nightmare, and not only that. Something completely unexpected had happened to him.

He was, after all, a vigorous man of thirty-two, a long way from boyhood. He hadn't expected to be seized with homesickness when he had been gone from Allerbrook only a matter of weeks. He was suffering from it now, and all the more because these deep lanes and high banks, where the grass was thick and the cow parsley was already in bloom, reminded him so much of the lanes of Somerset.

He kept on remembering Somerset. He was haunted by images of wooded combes with steep sides plunging down to swift peat rivers, of high moors where the wind whispered through the grass and gorse and over the dark heather and there were larks and curlews and ravens and now and then hovering kestrels or buzzards, searching the moor for prey.

He longed with all his heart to be back there, tending the sheep, watching the crops sprout, watching the calves and lambs grow, repairing ditches and fences. He was a farmer, not a soldier, but here he was, with no means of escape, trying to manage this horrible horse with one hand and wondering if Gloucester was ever going to get them out of this maze of lanes. He hated war, hated being away from home, and he was afraid.

Somewhere a cannon boomed, and just ahead of him a shower of arrows swished over the hedgerow to the left. Men fell, toppling from saddles; those with bows and quivers tried to return the compliment, shooting wildly over the hedgerows. Gloucester, who had already ridden past the place, turned back, shouting, and the trumpeter at his side blew a signal telling them to close up against the left-hand bank and use it as shelter.

Peter's stallion reared, snorting, and Peter stayed on only because he had acquired the saddle along with the horse, and a knight's saddle, with its high pommel and cantle, fore and aft, was designed to keep the rider in place. But he still wouldn't bet a single penny piece on his chances of ever seeing his home, or Liza, again.

They had set out as quite a sturdy force, fifty men all told from the parish of Clicket, led by Walter and Baldwin Sweetwater, who did indeed make opportunities along the way to drill them all in the use of various weapons, and bullied them pitilessly in the process. Long before they reached the king, north of London, Peter, whose dislike for the Sweetwaters was strong but had never hitherto been quite as violent as that of his father, found it becoming positively virulent.

They were part of a bigger company by then, having fallen in with others on the way. Ned Crowham had joined them for a while, still very much the same old Ned despite his added years— still pink faced, fair-haired, overweight and a terrible slugabed, much given to complaining when obliged to rise at dawn. They had skirmished with a few bands of men who were trying to link up with Warwick, but there were not many of these. They were small groups and easily routed.

As they went, they gathered news of the king's whereabouts, and by April 10 they had found him at St. Albans in Hertfordshire. There they found themselves being reorganised and allocated. Ned Crowham was sent to a force under the king's direct command and the Clicket contingent was handed over to Richard of Gloucester.

This was interesting, even rousing Peter at times from his fog of homesickness. The king, of whom he caught several glimpses, was a tall, blond, good-looking man with considerable presence and a broad smile, but the Duke of Gloucester was spare and dark and hazel eyed and though he was now the youngest brother of a king, in his boyhood he had more than once been a fugitive and at the age of twelve he had been riding around the country in armour, raising men and arms for Edward.

The result was that he looked older than his years. Gloucester had a worried face which rarely smiled and an overdeveloped right shoulder, usually visible because he preferred lighter armour, for the sake of mobility. He said that the thickened shoulder came from being determined from boyhood to learn to handle a sword as big as Edward's. He was known to have a great devotion to Edward. His motto was *Loyalty Binds Me.*

The news was that Warwick was on his way south to enter London, and had sent orders to the London City Council to be ready to receive him. Edward had sent spies into the city, who reported that the City Council were in a frightened dither and the mayor had taken to his bed with a (presumably) diplomatic illness.

"We'll see what they all do when I'm at their gates," said King Edward, addressing his troops, and when he tried it, what the City Council did was fling the gates open and welcome the king inside.

After that, Warwick arrived, and Easter Sunday, which should have been a day of rejoicing and church bells ringing and happy congregations singing praise for the resurrection, instead was the scene of the Battle of Barnet, outside the city to the north.

When he'd left Allerbrook, Peter had said to himself that if he had to fight in a battle, he would do his best. But he had never imagined either the horror or the sheer confusion of the reality. The Battle of Barnet, which had taken place in a thick morning fog on the edge of a marsh, had been as chaotic as this present campaign at Tewkesbury was.

Peter had been brought along as an archer, but archers were of little use in such bad visibility and when their lines were attacked, all sense of order was lost. Everything dissolved into mist and muddle. Standards appeared and disappeared and were mistaken for other standards. Friend and foe could hardly be distinguished in the confusion and men on the same side attacked each other. The fully armoured knights, who should have been kept back ready to ride down enemy foot soldiers once they were running, somehow got into the fray. It was at that point that Peter seized his chance and an armoured enemy leg and acquired the horse he now wished he'd left alone.

At the time, he was glad to get into the saddle because it felt safer. On foot, one was too vulnerable and too near, much too near the horrors that kept appearing and echoing out of the murk: the wet puddles which were not water but scarlet blood, the severed limbs, the piles of entrails, the trampled bodies, the maimed things that crept and wailed; all the dreadful sounds of despair and agony and death.

Then, somehow or other, Richard of Gloucester, though wounded in the arm, materialised from the vapours with his trumpeter and standard-bearer still beside him. Familiar trumpet calls pulled his men together and there was something like an organised charge on the part of the royal forces, and as the sun at last struggled through the mist, King Edward was triumphant.

And Warwick was dead.

Thank God for that, had been Peter's main thought. Now we can all go home. In a day or two, the king will disband us.

Forty eight hours later a frantic messenger rode headlong into London with the news that no one wanted to hear. There was another army to fight. Queen Marguerite had landed in Devon, with her son Edouard of Lancaster and a force of French soldiers. There would be no disbanding. They must march for the west, and at once.

Here at Tewkesbury they were supposed to be confronting the Lancastrian right wing, led by the Duke of Somerset (which to Peter felt odd, since he was a Somerset man himself). Still, unless they could escape from this labyrinth of sunken lanes, he couldn't see how they were ever going to confront anybody. However, a surge of movement ahead and a glimpse of Gloucester, his waving right arm beckoning them onward, suggested that their leader at least had some idea of where he was going. He was taking them into a lane going westward, toward a small wooded hill.

With a tightening of the stomach muscles, Peter saw glints of metal among those trees. There were armed men up there.

Then they were out of the lane, with almost open meadow between them and the hill, except for a few elm spinneys and clumps of bush. Trumpets spoke. Men sorted themselves out—horsemen this way, foot soldiers that way, fully armoured knights to the rear, archers to one side, front row down on one knee, back row standing, all with bows drawn or wound. Peter found himself near Gloucester, with the two Sweetwaters only a few yards away. "See you give a good account of yourself!" Walter Sweetwater shouted at him across the gap. "Seeing you've got yourself a warhorse when you ought to be on your feet like the rest of my lot!"

The stallion, sensing battle, plunged against the bit and Peter nearly replied that Walter could have the damned animal and welcome, but thought better of it in case he was taken at his word and summarily ordered out of his saddle so that Walter or Baldwin could have a spare mount and Peter be left once more among the foot soldiers, who in the eyes of mounted warriors were corn to be cut down.

There was no time for more. There were other trumpets, distant ones, among the trees. The glints of metal were moving, were coalescing, were emerging from the green shadows... were charging straight down toward them. There were enemy archers hidden somewhere, too, the same, no doubt, whose volley into the lane had done such damage. From a spinney to the north came another flight of arrows, intended to wreak havoc in Gloucester's forces before the main charge reached them. A shaft bounced off Peter's helm. Another went straight into the flank of Gloucester's horse, which reared with a scream and was at once struck by a second arrow, which went into its throat.

The horse fell, kicking, and Gloucester extricated himself just in time, snatching his legs clear and throwing himself aside before the horse could roll on top of him. He rolled almost under the hooves of Peter's stallion, which curvetted sideways to avoid him. Walter Sweetwater was one thing. Richard of Gloucester was quite another. Without pausing to think, Peter was out of his saddle. "You need a horse, sir. Take this one."

"My thanks!" Gloucester gasped, getting to his feet and grabbing the reins that Peter was offering him. "Who are you?"

"Peter Lanyon, sir, of Allerbrook farm in Somerset."

"I won't forget," said Gloucester, already up and astride. Then he was gone, shouting to his trumpeter, and a moment later the enemy was on them. Peter, dashing aside to join the foot soldiers after all, wondered why he had done it, but found himself more relieved to be rid of that diabolical horse than afraid of his fate on foot.

"Did you see that? Typical Lanyon!" Walter Sweetwater shouted to his son as the charge crashed into them. "I was going to give Gloucester my horse!" With a savage swipe of his heavy sword, he swept an enemy horseman out of his saddle. "Likely enough I'd have got another! Now Peter Lanyon's going to get commended instead of me...!"

"None of the Lanyons know their place!" Baldwin shouted back.

The scrimmage was short. Somehow or other Gloucester's forces held their shape, giving ground a little but not enough to matter. At the end of it, the Lancastrians retreated, Richard of Gloucester's trumpets sounded yet again and this time it was Gloucester who was charging.

Ten minutes later Edward of York's standard, The Sun in

Splendour, appeared behind the Lancastrians, borne at full gallop, with Edward and his standard-bearer leading a shouting, weapon-waving force straight at the Lancastrian rear.

The Duke of Somerset's forces wheeled in disorder, beset before and behind, broke and fled.

It was over. Peter was not at all sure how he had managed to survive but here he was, still alive, with dents in his helmet, other men's blood on his sword, a lot of bruises but otherwise a whole skin. On this warm, velvety May night he was not lying dead on the field, but sitting by a campfire with half a dozen other men, including Ned Crowham, who had been with the king in that final charge from the rear, and Sim Hannacombe, who had stayed with Gloucester's archers. Both had come through un-scathed. They had all found each other afterward and as dusk fell, they had made their own campfire and were frying veal steaks in a pan along with chunks of bread, knowing that no further battle awaited them tomorrow.

A figure loomed up from the twilight, cloaked and unre-markable except that its right shoulder was bulkier than its left. It squatted down beside Ned, who started, peered at the stranger's face and then hurriedly got up and bowed, exclaiming, "My lord of Gloucester!"

"Oh, sit down, all of you," said Gloucester as the rest of them started to follow Ned's example. "We're all tired soldiers, aren't we? We've all been frightened half out of our wits and wondered if we'd finish the day with our heads still on our shoulders." He touched his left hand to his right upper arm and Peter realised that the bulkiness under the cloak was partly due to a padded dressing, over the wound that Richard had received at Barnet.

He had marched to Tewkesbury and fought this long day through with a swordcut still not healed.

"The news will be proclaimed tomorrow," Richard said, "but I can tell you now that Edouard of Lancaster, the son of Queen Marguerite, is dead, and that the queen herself has been taken. She had fled to a house of nuns. The She-Wolf is caged and her cub is slain. The Duke of Somerset is a prisoner, too. Meanwhile, I am looking for a man called Peter Lanyon, of Allerbrook farm in Somerset."

"I am Peter Lanyon," Peter said.

"You gave me your horse."

"Yes, sir."

"It's a good horse and it's still alive and well. Do you want it back?"

"Frankly, no, sir. I am not a knight. I found the beast nearly unmanageable," Peter said, amid laughter from the others.

"I'll give you its price, then. Here." A hand came out from under the cloak, with a leather bag in it, and Peter heard the coins inside clink before he felt their edges through the bag. "But there'll be more, when we get to London. In giving me that horse, you rendered service far beyond the animal's value in the market. I've spoken to the king and there'll be a reward in accordance. We ride for London soon. You'll ride with us."

It was an accolade but also a command.

He was still homesick for his native combes, but he wouldn't be seeing them again yet. Ned Crowham, who knew him well enough to guess at his feelings, said softly, "It'll keep you from Allerbrook a while longer, but you won't be empty-handed when you get there. Well done."

"Thank you, my lord," said Peter to Gloucester.

"That's Lanyon that Gloucester's talking to." Baldwin Sweetwater, seated by a neighbouring fire with his father, nudged Walter and pointed. "I saw Gloucester's face in the firelight just now when he went to join them."

"And he's making a pet of Lanyon. God rot the Lanyons," said Walter. "Richard Lanyon's already got a hall the size of ours and a swollen head to go with it and the talk round Clicket is that he has dreams of one day building himself a house to outdo ours, never mind a mere hall!"

"I've heard that," Baldwin agreed. "But you're his landlord. You can forbid it."

"I certainly will! You know," said Walter, "it's high time we finally got your sister Agnes married. A good marriage for her could carry us up in the world and put us beyond the reach of any Lanyon impertinence. Negotiations have fallen through twice, but somehow or other it's got to be done. If I'd been quick enough to hand my horse to Gloucester before Peter Lanyon did, I might have asked for a rich marriage for her as a reward!"

"The Courtenays or the Carews might have a connection in the marriage market," Baldwin remarked. "Or there are the Northcotes in Devon—they're a wealthy family. We haven't tried in that direction, have we? We'll enquire when we get back."

"I wonder," said Walter thoughtfully, "what will happen now to poor deposed King Henry? If I were King Edward, I'd get rid of him. Just by existing, he's a breeding ground for trouble, like a corpse collecting flies."

"Poor old Henry," said Baldwin cynically. He added, "I wonder if the She-Wolf ever loved him?"

"I shouldn't think so. Love's for peasants—if it ever really happens at all, which I doubt," said Walter Sweetwater.

★ ★ ★

At Allerbrook the last tasks of the day were finished. Liza wanted to go to bed and made for the stairs, which meant crossing her workroom, since the stairs came down into one corner of it. She found Richard sitting at her desk and drawing something by candlelight.

She knew what he was doing, for she had seen him at this before. She sighed a little. Like her quarrel with her mother and her lack of a second child, this was one more thing to worry about. Richard had been doing this a good deal in Peter's absence and it would upset Peter if he knew. No, she silently corrected herself, *when* he knew. When he returned. "Are you designing another house, Father-in-law?"

"Yes." He didn't look up but with his quill and the straight edge of a box, began to draw a careful, straight line across the paper in front of him.

"But we have our beautiful hall." She spoke very gently and with caution, afraid of annoying him, but impelled to speak through sheer anxiety. "Do we really need any more than that? We...we're not..."

"Not gentry like the Sweetwaters, you mean? But I intend us to be one day, my lass." He tapped his drawing with the end of the quill. "I had some new ideas last night. If I can't sleep, I often refresh my plans for the house I'm going to build one day. I mean it, you know. It's the best way I can think of to make the Sweetwaters pay for the things they've done. In gnashed teeth, if nothing else!"

"But even if you do build it, Father-in-law," said Liza cautiously, "won't it cost a lot? And won't the Sweetwaters put up the rent? Or forbid you to build, even!"

"It won't be cheap, but I'm saving. It might take years but I'll get there in the end. You're right to fret about the Sweetwaters, though. I've been cudgelling my brains over them, my girl. Walter Sweetwater let me build my hall because he didn't think I'd ever finish it! When I did, he made his gesture with that rabbit rent, damn him, and left it at that. But a whole house…yes, he might well forbid me."

In view of the likely cost, Liza rather hoped so but wisely held her tongue.

"What I need to do," said Richard, "is buy Allerbrook from the Sweetwaters—buildings and land. The freehold, in fact. Then I can put up what buildings I like. Only I've still got to find a way of making them sell!"

CHAPTER TWENTY-THREE ❧

OUT OF THE PAST

"I s there any news of my mother?" Liza asked across the supper table.

Richard Lanyon, who had just returned from visiting Dunster, shook his head as he sat down. "Your brothers say they send gifts to her sometimes and get messages back—by word of mouth. She says she's well. But they have to send by a servant. She won't see family. Her messages say that she has a call to religion and is living in permanent retreat."

"She has a kind of loyalty to Herbert Dyer, I suppose," Liza said. "It's plain she hasn't told them what really happened."

"He still sends money to support her, to be fair to him," Richard said. "I fancy she's afraid to see her family in case they worm the truth out of her. Not that he's stepped out of line since then. How he hates the sight of me when I turn up in Washford.

I laugh to myself, watching him curdle like milk in thundery weather with the effort of being polite to me."

"Did all go well in Dunster, Master?" Roger wanted to know as Betsy and Kat served out the food.

"Aye, good enough. The Weavers are pleased with our clip and they've got two extra looms. I fancy our share of the profits could go up. I took a look at our hay meadow before I came in and it's about ready for scything. We'll have a surplus to sell if the weather holds. Pity Peter's not here to lend a hand."

There was a silence. Richard glanced across the table at Roger and Higg. Higg had lost weight in the past year or two. He was not the oxlike individual he had once been and his formerly tow-coloured tangle of hair was grey. As for Roger, his stoop was more pronounced than ever and his back was humped at the top of the spine.

"Peter ought to be here!" Richard said abruptly. "Fighting's over, so we heard, finished last month, and the Sweetwaters are home and so is Sim Hannacombe, but all we've had is Sim telling us that Peter hasn't been released from service yet. He's alive at least, which is a mercy. I'm thinking to ask Sim if his two younger sons could come and work here. They'll have to leave home anyway once they're grown. They're thirteen and eleven now and big enough to be useful and I'd pay 'em something. Not much because I'm saving, but something."

"That 'ud help," Higg agreed.

Richard started to say, "If only…" and then stopped, glancing at Liza and then to where four-year-old Quentin, who had had supper earlier, was seated in one of the hall window seats, solemnly experimenting with a spindle. A kitten was beside her and she was gently discouraging it from wanting to play with the thread. At four, Quentin already had a way with animals. Liza, recalling how the ponies at Dunster had come to her call, thought that Quentin was very much a Weaver, in more than one way.

Richard's mind seemed to be running on similar lines. "Looks like Quentin's going to be handy at spinning and weaving, Liza," he was remarking. "Just like you. She's getting to look like you, too. She's a good child. Maybe if that elder Hannacombe boy shapes well, we could make a match between them one day. Sim would like that. The boy's future would be made and if he and Quentin stop here, the Lanyon blood'll go on, if not the name."

"I think it's a good idea," Liza said. He had said no words of censure aloud, but she had heard them, just the same. Since Peter had ridden away she had tried hard to keep her father-in-law happy, and on the whole, by working hard, making sure that there was good food on the table at the right times and trying to agree with everything he said, she had succeeded. But the undercurrent was always there. *I like you well enough, Liza, but you should have had a son.*

Well, she would have liked one, as well, she sometimes thought rebelliously. What a pity Richard Lanyon never seemed to realise that.

However, he spoke amiably enough now as he said, "By the time Quentin's old enough to marry, I hope she'll have a fine house as her inheritance. Every time I see the Sweetwater place, I get new ideas."

Betsy said, "Well, well." Kat clicked her tongue, Roger grunted and Higg shook his head as if in sorrow at the insanity of an old friend. Liza decided to introduce a new topic.

"It's time I went myself to see my mother and tried to break through this...this wall she's put between us," she said. "I've been afraid to go in person before, but a lot of time's gone by. Maybe she's not so angry now. I can see why she won't see the rest of the family, but I know all about Master Dyer. She has nothing to hide from me, and after all, I'm her daughter. I ought to try, anyway. Father-in-law, may I go?"

"After the haymaking," said Richard. "Higg can go with you and you can come home by way of Dunster if you like. See your family and give them firsthand news. But don't go upsetting your-self over it, if your mother wants to keep up the feud. Just let her."

"Is that the place?" Liza said to Higg as the two of them rode their ponies over a low hill and came in sight of the little abbey in the Devon valley below. It was indeed small; a tiny church beside a cluster of thatched buildings. There was a vegetable plot where two or three black-clad figures were working and a patch of fruit trees, hardly big enough to be called an orchard. It was all encircled by a wall with a gatehouse at the nearer side, but a few fields, which probably belonged to the abbey, lay on the gentle slope of the hillside beyond.

"Yes, Mistress," Higg said. "That be St. Catherine's, where your mother is. Let's get on. Don't like this sticky heat. It takes it out of me."

The gate was closed but there was a bell rope, which Higg tugged. After a moment they heard footsteps, and then a shutter in the middle of the gate was opened and an elderly nun peered out. "Visitors, hey? Who might you be wantin'? Seen you afore," she added to Higg.

"I am Liza Lanyon, daughter of Margaret Dyer. She is living here. I've come to ask after her welfare," said Liza.

Bolts were pulled back. They dismounted and, leading their

ponies, they entered and followed the porteress along a path to one of the thatched buildings, where she knocked on the door. It was answered promptly by another nun and the porteress announced them. The second nun went away briefly and then reappeared. "Mother Abbess will see you. This is her study time, but she is willing to interrupt it for you. Mistress Lanyon, please come this way. Dame Porteress, show the lady's manservant the stables and then take him to the kitchen and see he's given food and drink."

The abbess's room was cool and dim, its stone walls and floor unadorned, but for that very reason it was a welcome haven in weather which, as Higg had said, was over-warm and sticky. Built into an alcove were shelves laden with parchment scrolls and several books and a supply of unused paper. Another book lay open on the plain walnut desk.

"You wish to see your mother?" It was hard to guess the abbess's age. Her pale face was unlined but her hazel eyes were knowledgeable and there were knotted veins on the backs of the thin hands folded at her waist. She had risen to greet her visitor and did not sit down again or invite Liza to do so.

"If I can," Liza said. "If she will not see me, at least, please, tell me how she fares."

"I will ask if she will see you." The abbess was a small woman and had to look up to talk to Liza. "But I can tell you that if she does, what you find may disquiet you. Oh!" Seeing Liza's alarm, she raised a hand in reassurance. "She is not sick. She sometimes occupies herself with spinning, which is useful, since we own sheep which are cared for and sheared for us by the brothers of a monastery not far from here, and we make woollen cloth to sell. But...well, let me take you to her. She lives in our guest house."

Much concerned, Liza followed the small, black-draped figure out of the room and then out of the building and across a cobbled space to another house. Again it was necessary to knock, but again a nun came at once and with a murmured "*Benedicite, Mother,*" she stood aside to let them in.

The abbess led the way up a twisting stone stair. The guest house was built around three sides of a small courtyard and a covered gallery, overlooking the courtyard, ran around all the first-floor rooms, which opened onto it. The abbess knocked at one of the doors and announced herself. A voice called to her to come in. Signalling for Liza to wait, the abbess did so, but moved a little to one side, so that from where she stood on the gallery Liza could still see into the room.

The room looked comfortable, with a bed and a table and stools, a window seat and, in one corner, a spinning wheel with a basket of wool beside it. Margaret Dyer was not using it, however. Dressed in a robe of unbleached wool, and with a plain coif on her head, she was seated, hands folded, on the window seat, half turned so as to look out at the rolling Devon country-side beyond.

"Mistress Dyer!" said the abbess, rather too heartily. "I am sorry to see you so dispirited again. On such a day it is pleasant to walk in the grounds. Sister Honoria would go with you gladly."

"I know, but I don't want to go walking," said Margaret, not rudely, but despondently. She turned from the window and caught sight of Liza, hovering just outside the door. "Oh, so you've come. Thought 'ee would one day. All right. You may as well come in. I no longer care enough to get up and throw you out."

"Mother—how are you?" Liza entered the room and wanted

to go to her mother and embrace her, but somehow dared not. Margaret's eyes, both dull and unfriendly, repelled such affectionate gestures. "I've thought of you so often," Liza said timidly. "And I've worried about you and so have the family in Dunster. I had to come, to know how you were, whether you needed anything...."

"I never wanted to set eyes on you again," said Margaret tonelessly, "but I knew it' ud happen in the end. Here you be, and here I be, and you can see I'm well. I'm doin' penance for my husband's sins. Someone must, since I know he won't. It eases my mind. I'm still a wife, even if I can't bear to live with 'un, nor he with me."

"Doing...?"

Margaret looked at her coldly and then undid the lacing which held the neck of her unbleached robe together. She pulled out a fold of the garment under it. "Come here and feel this."

"Oh, no!" said Liza as her finger and thumb told her the miserable truth. "Not a hair shirt. Oh, *Mother!*" She tugged the fold out farther and looking below, saw the pricks and scratches on Margaret's skin. "Oh, why, why? He's not worth it. Don't do this to yourself, *please!*"

"I'll do it while I live and you've no say in the matter. Don't go tellin' them in Dunster what Herbert did. That's between him and me." She pushed Liza's hand away, tidied her clothing and did up the lacing with fingers that fumbled. Then she turned her head away, to resume her contemplation of the outside world. "Go away. I can't talk long to anyone. It's too much effort."

"But...Mother..." Liza was at a loss.

"Go away!" said Margaret.

The abbess took Liza's arm and drew her gently out to the

gallery, closing the door after them. "Sister Honoria, the lay sister who looks after her, will bring her midday meal soon. She often sits with your mother, although she says they talk very little because Mistress Dyer seems to have no energy, no spirit. We do what we can. We pray for her and with her. I have told her that it may well be sin to give way so to melancholy, and that she cannot take her husband's sins, whatever they are—she won't tell us that—on herself. But she only says she's doing what she must. Come."

They walked back to the steps and went down them. "You are welcome to dine with us," the abbess said. "But it might be better not to try to see your mother again. I promise you she is safe with us."

"But—something's wrong with her!" Liza expostulated. "You said she wasn't sick, but…"

"She isn't, in the usual sense, but I know what you mean. I have seen it happen before. No one can explain it. Mostly to people growing older, but not always. They fall into a lethargy and there is no getting them out of it. Some physicians say it is a thing of the body, some say it is of the mind and some call it an affliction sent by God, and perhaps they're right. But no one knows the cure. Sometimes people recover, sometimes not. We will look after her as long as she needs it, that I can promise."

"I brought things. They're in our saddlebags. A mutton ham and some money and a big round cheese. Please keep them and use them and let her have a share without telling her where they came from."

As they walked back across the cobbles to the nuns' house, side by side now, the abbess turned her head and for the first time, she smiled. "We will do that. Don't fear for her. We *will* take care of her."

"Thank you," said Liza miserably. She added, "I'm travelling back by way of Dunster, where my brothers and my sister live, to give them what news I can. At least I can say that she's safe— if no more."

The sticky heat dissolved into a downpour as they started for Dunster, and lasted for the two days of their journey. On open hillsides they rode with heads bent against the west wind and the rain blowing in from the sea; in the lanes, the mire was hock deep and the ponies were splashed with mud above the girth.

"We're goin' to arrive wet through and with news about as cheerful as this here weather is," Higg said as at last they emerged from the woods above Dunster and crossed the packhorse bridge where once Liza had quarrelled with Christopher. "I'm that sorry about your mother, Mistress Lanyon. Only maybe she's better off there than in Washford. A busy workshop and a man like Dyer, all jolly and hearty, mightn't be best for someone that just wants to be quiet. Though I'm not sure," said Higg doubtfully, "that we shouldn't have called at Washford to give Master Dyer news of her. He's her husband, after all."

"No, Higg! I don't want to go near Master Dyer. Master Richard deals with him when it's necessary, but I can't bear the thought of even seeing him in the distance," said Liza angrily. "If he wants to know how his wife is, let him go to the abbey himself! If it hadn't been for him and his dishonesty, she'd be happy with him now."

"Well, the illness might have come on her anyhow," said Higg mildly. "Who's to know? It could be the abbey's the best haven."

"I hope you're right," Liza said, pulling her cloak more firmly around her. She glanced anxiously at Higg, who had sneezed twice since that morning. He was a healthy man normally, but he still had the cough he had acquired during the epidemic, and he had had several feverish colds since then, when he'd had to keep to his bed in his cottage. She hoped he wasn't going to fall ill now.

Liza had been at Allerbrook now for over twelve years and had visited Dunster very rarely since her marriage, but the woolly, unmistakable smell of the overfull Weaver household, the clack of looms from the weaving shed at the back and the usual air of domestic confusion still meant home. The moment she set foot in the house, she could hear one of the menfolk upstairs complaining that he wanted to change into a clean shirt and hadn't got one, and a protesting female voice, pointing out that things weren't yet dry from the wash. "It b'ain't ideal drying weather, now, be it, zur?"

The sound of the argument made her laugh. It welcomed her as much as the smiling faces of her family. Yes, this was her home, even though her parents were no longer here, even though Aunt Cecy was among the first to greet her, and her first words were "Well, Liza, you look fine and healthy and I'm glad to see it, but still only the one daughter, I hear?"

However, someone had called her brother Tommy from the weaving shed and he came to her rescue, although for a moment she hardly recognised him. She had missed her father's funeral, being still abed after Quentin's birth, and had last seen Tommy when he was only fourteen. He was twenty-one now and disconcertingly like his father. He, however, knew her and seized her in a delighted hug. "Liza! We thought you'd forgotten us! Oh, we're glad to see you."

"I've been visiting Mother. The news isn't happy, I'm afraid.

But first, we need to get dry and warm. Higg here has been sneezing and we're both wet through."

"Elena's here in the house. She and Laurence are supping here tonight. She'll look after you. I'll take care of Higg. Come in, man. I'll get someone to take those ponies down to the stable and rub the mud off them. They look as if they've been rollin' in it! You get that cloak off—God's teeth, it's drenched, right enough. There'll be mulled ale before you've time to turn round. We've news of our own that's not so cheerful, either, but that can wait. *Joss!*" He turned to shout up the stairs, where the altercation about shirts seemed to be getting noisier. "Help yourself to one of my shirts—we're the same size! And stop makin' such a to-do. Liza's come to see us! That's Joss, one of Laurence and Elena's boys," he added to Liza. "Not a boy now—he's grown up since you last saw him. Well, let's get you and Higg here dry and settled."

Before long the whole family, including cousin Joss in his borrowed shirt, had gathered in the big main room to drink mulled ale and exchange news. Liza told them of Margaret's strange malady, though she did not mention the hair shirt. Her mother had said she was not to tell the Weavers why she had really left Herbert, and Liza would not disobey her. Besides, even to think of her mother in that self-imposed discomfort was anguish and she knew she couldn't speak of it without crying.

"The nuns seem to be looking after her as best they can," she said. "Now, tell me where my brother Arthur is."

"That's the thing we've got to break to you," said Tommy. "When all the trouble broke out, the lord of Dunster Castle, Lord Pembroke, I mean, sent someone round to do some recruiting. Or conscripting, rather. He took Arthur, and another of

Laurence's sons—the youngest one, Dickon. Twenty-seven, he was. Good job neither of them was married. They didn't leave widows and children crying for them and that's something. I'm sorry, Liza. They were killed in the fighting before Pembroke was captured. There's a lot of families in Dunster that have lost men. We didn't send word to Allerbrook because the news was all muddled at first. We kept hoping maybe it was wrong. We didn't get firsthand word until a Dunster lad came home a month ago."

"Arthur—dead?" She had not let them see that she wanted to cry for her mother, but the tears pricked now, for her brother. "Oh, *no!*"

"Aye." That was Great-Uncle Will, still in his familiar chair although by now he was over eighty-five. "Tommy's your dad's heir now, Liza."

"Better not send word to St. Catherine's," said Liza. "It would do Mother no good to hear of it. Oh, this cruel war! My husband's away, too, though we've heard he's alive, but when he'll come home I've no idea!"

"More mulled ale for you, my girl," said Tommy. "Try not to be too sad. The lad who came home said he saw Arthur die and it was quick. One sword slash and it was over. Let's hope it was the same for Dickon."

"I'm glad of that," said Liza in a strained voice, and did not repeat what Richard had once told them, that people reporting such deaths always said they had been quick, whether it was true or not.

Laurence and Elena were both at supper and Liza thought that although they were of course not young, they looked older than they really were. They had lost two sons now to the fighting between Lancaster and York and grief had left its mark.

The supper was generous and as good in quality as ever it had been under Margaret's skilled guidance. Higg, who had been given dry clothes from the skin outward, while his own steamed in the kitchen, partook like everyone else, although Liza noticed that he didn't seem to be eating much.

"Aren't you hungry, Higg?" she asked, leaning forward to speak to him down the table.

"Seemingly not so very, Mistress," Higg said. Or rather, croaked.

"Higg! What's wrong with your voice?"

"I'm sort of husky, Mistress. It'll be the damp that's done it, I daresay."

Liza got to her feet and walked down the table to put a hand on his wrist. It almost burned her fingers.

"You have a fever! You should be in bed."

"How is he?" Liza asked next morning, encountering Tommy as she climbed up to the attic room where Higg had been put to bed.

"Not too well, Liza. Go in and see for yourself. Elena's brewing him a draught—she's handy with herbs. Horehound and honey, she says, for his throat and feverfew to cool him."

Liza went on and into the room, not without a shiver because although it was so many years ago, this was the very room where she had been not only imprisoned but beaten. But the memories fled when she saw Higg lying on a pallet, his face flushed and his breath coming harshly.

"Sorry, Mistress. Can't talk much."

"Elena will bring you something. Then you must try to sleep."

He was warm enough; coverlets had been placed over him and

the weather was sunny again. If only it had been sunny on that two-day ride! "I'm sorry I dragged you on this journey. But we shall get you well again and I'll stay here until you are. I'll send a message to Allerbrook to explain."

Higg looked at her unhappily and coughed. When he had finished coughing, he said, "Wish Betsy were here. Can't 'ee send for Betsy?"

Liza found Tommy at the foot of the attic stairs, waiting for her to come down. "He shouldn't be left alone," she said.

"He won't be. We'll see someone watches by him. How do you think he is?"

"Very ill. He wants his wife. Tommy…"

"We've a customer staying at the inn and setting off today for home—and that's in Hawkridge. Allerbrook's hardly out of his way. I'll ask him to take a message."

"Thank heaven," said Liza, "that the shearing's over and we've got the hay in."

"There's my sensible sister! And now," said Tommy, scanning her thoughtfully, "I think you've had misery enough, what with our mother, and hearing the news about Arthur and Dickon, and now all this worry about Higg. We'll look after him. You go out and walk the way you did before you were married. I remember even though I was so young! Take the air and leave Higg to us. I'll see that word goes to Allerbrook, never fear."

"I still like to walk," Liza said. "At Allerbrook, when I have a little time to myself, I go walking on the moor and I enjoy gathering bilberries there when it's the season. Yes, I'll go out. Just for a while."

The air was fresh after the rain, as though the two wet days had washed the air clean. If she were not so anxious about Higg, walking through the village would be a delight and it was pleasant even as things were. She knew her family could be trusted to give Higg the best of care for an hour or so. Stepping out briskly, Liza made her way through the narrow street around the foot of the castle, and wandered on over the crossroads where the track came down the castle hill and continued on to Alcombe.

She had set out with no particular aim but her feet, as if they knew where they were going, took her down West Street, and turned off across the flat little bridge over the mill leat, which had been made before William the Norman ever set foot in England. She walked on beside the gurgling water in its narrow channel, passing the mill, its wheel turning slowly in the leat which farther on rejoined the Avill River. Crossing another small bridge, she found herself turning into a tiny path on her left. It led into a dell that earlier in the year would have been full of bluebells. It was just a grassy place now, with a few daisies and yellow dandelions in it.

On the far side was a fallen tree, not the one on which she and Christopher had once sat, but very like it. It wasn't recent, though, for its bark was gone, exposing the smooth grey wood below. Being sheltered by overhanging trees, it was also dry, despite yesterday's rain. It was just as good a seat as the other had been and a man was sitting on it now, studying a book. The sun had laid a shaft on his head, as if deliberately. He had a tonsure, but it was ringed with thick, springy hair the colour of fire.

It was as though she had known he would be there and had come to meet him.

"Christopher?" she said.

CHAPTER TWENTY-FOUR
LOVE AND DEATH

C hristopher stood up, closing his book. "Liza!"

They stood for a long moment, speechless, until he said hesitantly, "It is Liza, isn't it? It's been so long…."

"Of course I'm Liza. Have I changed so much?"

"No. Hardly at all. It's just that…I come here quite often. I think I do it so as to sit and read in a place where the memories would keep me company. But now the memory has become real and taken me by surprise. What brought *you* here?"

"I think I was looking for memories, too. Or did I know you'd be here? I can't tell. My feet just brought me."

"How are you? You're married, of course? Yes, I can see your wedding ring. Are you happy? With—Peter Lanyon, is that the name?"

"Yes. He's kind and I'm fond of him. He's away at the war now."

"And you pray for his safety every night?"

"He is safe. We know that now. He just hasn't been released from service. But yes, I prayed every night and every morning until the fighting was over," said Liza.

She walked across the dell and they sat down, side by side, on the log. Christopher put his book down at his feet and turned to her. "I'm glad things have gone well for you. Have you children?"

"A daughter, four years old. Quentin, we called her, after my grandmother. I had...some bad luck with children."

"Some families do, and no one knows why. I sometimes think God doesn't want the human race to multiply too fast."

"Are you still at St. George's?" Liza asked.

"No. I'm back in the castle now, chaplain to the steward and servants there. When I first left the priory I thought, perhaps now I can make some enquiries—find out how you were. But I kept hesitating, wondering if I should. I'm a full priest now. I have been for years."

"Yes. I supposed that would happen. Is the castle very different, without the Luttrells?"

"The castle is a disgrace!" said Christopher with energy. "That's how it always is when landlords stay away. I've urged the servants to attend to their duties better, but I'm not the steward and the man who is is bone idle. The land is nearly as bad and so is the village. So many roofs in need of repair! You're visiting your family, I suppose? Are they well?"

"Not all of them." Liza began to explain. With kindness in his eyes, Christopher listened to her account of her mother's illness and the deaths of her brother and cousin, and now of Higg's illness, too. She did not mention Herbert Dyer's dishonesty but kept to the story her mother had chosen to tell, of a desire to retire from the world and take refuge in an abbey. Christopher asked no awkward questions.

"Everything hasn't gone well for you, after all. You have many troubles," he said. "I am sorry. I will pray for Higg's recovery."

"Christopher, are you happy as a priest? Was it the right thing for you after all?"

"I suppose so. I've given myself to it. Sometimes I think that what I took to be a call, back when I was a boy, was just a case of a passionate youth looking for somewhere for passion to go. Like a river seeking the sea. I'm not sure I found the right sea in the end, no. But I have done my best. There's no going back, Liza. Not for me, or for you."

"No, I know. I'm glad we've met again, though. Oh!"

"What is it?"

Liza was looking at his left hand. "You still have my ring. You're wearing it on your little finger."

"Yes. I had it on a chain round my neck while I was in the priory, but now I wear it openly. No one has ever questioned it."

There was silence while she absorbed the significance of that. "I've often thought of you, you know, wondered what you were doing, whether you were in good health and if...whether..."

"Whether I ever thought of you?" Christopher asked, and suddenly there it was again, that tough grin which had always made her insides turn somersaults. "Well, now you know that I have. As your ring testifies."

There was another silence until Liza said, "I've been over twelve years married and I've no complaint of Peter. And you're a priest. I'm glad we've met again, glad you didn't forget me, but..."

"I know," said Christopher, and stood up, holding out his hand to her. "Come. Let us part as friends and remember each other in our prayers. I am happy to know you're safe, and loved by your husband."

"I wish you well in your efforts to make the castle servants work properly!"

"Hah! Absentee landlords!" Christopher said, and they parted, with a handclasp, an exchange of smiles and one backward glance from Liza as she walked away.

Her step was light and her heart sang all the way back to the Weavers' house, although her mood changed quickly when she got there, for Tommy met her at the door, his normally cheerful young face unnaturally solemn.

"Higg is very unwell indeed," he said. "I didn't use our customer as a messenger to Allerbrook after all. I've sent one of Laurie's boys to Allerbrook to fetch his wife, at once."

Betsy was in Dunster by suppertime that same evening. She was well over fifty now and she was drawn with exhaustion by the time she arrived, on a broad-backed Allerbrook pony from which she toppled rather than dismounted. She refused, however, to sit down or take any food or drink or even remove her cloak before she had seen Higg. Liza took her to the attic.

Higg was lying on his back, his mouth half-open and his face sunken. He was barely conscious and his breathing now was very bad, in spite of all Elena's herbal remedies and the steam inhalations recommended by the physician who had been called.

"He's all dry-skinned. He b'ain't sweating," said Betsy, feeling his forehead. "He did ought to sweat. Higg, can you hear me, love?" His eyes half opened and a weak hand stretched out to her. Betsy seized it. "You got to sweat. It'll mean being very hot but it's best for 'ee. We'll put more covers on 'ee and see if that does it, that and this June weather."

"If only we hadn't been caught in that rain," said Liza desperately. "I feel it's my fault."

"He could of got wet through out in the fields, just the same," said Betsy. "He often has, only it never used to matter. Thirty-five years we've been wed. Oh, *Higg!*"

Her face creased suddenly, and Liza put an arm around her. "We'll get him through. Come. Let's fetch some more covers."

Elena helped to carry extra rugs up to the attic and spread them over the patient. "I'll brew some more medicines and fetch another bowl of hot water. The physician gave us something to put in it, some sort of balsam, he says it is, to clear the chest. And I've an ointment to rub in."

"And water," said Betsy. "He should have water. Feverish like that, he'll have a thirst. Have you got well water?"

"Yes. I'll fetch a jugful. Now, you take off that cloak and come down for some supper, even if you eat it quick. You've had a long journey. You can sleep up here if you want. We'll put another pallet down. But one of us'll be here and awake all night. Don't worry."

The warm June night descended, with stars in a sky so clear that the recent downpour seemed unbelievable. The window was closed against draughts and a candle was set on the sill to light the vigil.

Betsy, wearied beyond bearing, slept on the second pallet alongside Higg's, while Liza sat up, relieved by Elena at half past three in the morning. From time to time they gave Higg water to drink, or doses of Elena's medicine, and Elena, coming on duty, brought a towel and a basin full of hot water mixed with the physician's aromatic balsam. Deftly she sat Higg up so that with his head under the towel to keep the steam in, he could breathe the scented vapour.

Liza returned in the morning after a snatched breakfast. She found Betsy and Elena sitting one on either side of him, their faces anxious. "Has the fever broken yet?" she asked.

Miserably, Betsy shook her head.

It went on all that day and all the next night. Betsy kept vigil that night, refusing to rest although Elena was there with her. At daybreak both of them took some hurried food and then collapsed into exhausted sleep while Liza, who had slept, took over. This, the third day of Higg's illness, wore wretchedly on. Hot and dry, drawing breaths that sounded as though they were rattling over shingle, he lay and tossed but no sweat came. Toward evening, Tommy went to fetch the parish priest.

The last rites were spoken over Higg, who managed to croak some weak responses. The priest was still there when Higg, who had been propped up on pillows to ease his breathing, was seized with a paroxysm of coughing and could not stop. It grew worse and worse and his eyes became huge and dark as he fought for breath. When he began to cough up blood, spraying the covers and the wall beside him, the priest said, "Take his wife away," and Liza, though Betsy resisted her, somehow persuaded her out of the room and kept her out until it was all over.

When he had been tidied by some of the other women and moved to another room where there were no bloodstains, Elena and Liza took Betsy, weeping, to say goodbye to him. She clung to his hand and called his name as though still hoping that he would answer, and it took some time before they could coax her to leave him. They took her to the bedchamber Liza was using,

where they induced her, though still with difficulty, to eat something, and gave her a drink of honeyed wine which Elena said
would help her to rest. Then they put her to bed and stayed with
her until she slept.

Liza shared the bed with Betsy that night, and when they both
woke in the dead hours of the night, shared her tears.

In the usual course of events, Higg would have been buried
in Clicket, with people who knew him well to gather at the
graveside. As it was, he was laid in the churchyard of St. George's,
and few of those present knew him at all. There were plenty of
them, however. The Weavers turned out in force and so, in
neighbourly solidarity, did many other Dunster folk.

"Well, he went off with an escort I'm proud of," Betsy said to
Liza when the funeral refreshments, arranged in the Weavers'
house, had been consumed and the crowd had gone. She had
got over her tears and borne herself with dignity all through the
ceremony, though Liza saw, with sadness, that overnight she
seemed to have grown bent and lined. "Now we'll have to go
home, I suppose. Can't leave Kat and Roger and your father-in-
law to manage all alone."

"Father-in-law was talking of bringing in the two younger
Hannacombe boys," Liza said. "They're old enough to be useful."

Betsy sat heavily down in the window seat of the Weavers' big
room. "I can't do the ride tomorrow, not so soon. I've got to do
it sometime but I'd be that thankful for another day, to get my
breath back, like."

"Of course you shall have another day," said Liza. "Spend
tomorrow how you like. Sleep, or walk in the garden, whatever
you want. My family won't mind. We'll go home the day after."

The weather, as though that one rainstorm had cleared the air of trouble, had since then remained pleasant—warm without being hot. In the morning Betsy went back to the churchyard to stand for a while beside the filled grave. "I want to be near 'un. Can't help thinkin' he'll be lonely when I go home."

Liza went with her, but sensing that Betsy wanted to be alone, said that she would go for a walk by herself and call at the churchyard on the way back, to see if Betsy were still there. "We can go back to dinner together," she said.

"All right. Just let me be. I want to cry a bit on my own."

"I'll come back soon," Liza said, and moved away toward the churchyard gate into West Street. Presently she reached the lane by the mill leat and once again, she took the track toward the dell. Once again, it was as though her feet were choosing where she should go.

And once again, Christopher was sitting, reading, on the fallen log. As before, he stood up as she came toward him, and another shaft of sunlight shining from behind Liza's head turned the ring of springy hair around his shaven poll to the colour of flame.

"I hoped you'd be here," Liza said and her voice shook, so that he came to take her arm and steer her to the log, to seat her on it.

"Liza, what's happened? Something is wrong. I can tell."

"Higg died. We buried him yesterday."

"Ah. Yes, I wondered. I visited the monks yesterday—some of them are my friends and I wanted to see how their herb garden did now that I'm not there to look after it—and when I left them, I passed the churchyard and saw that a burial was taking place. I suppose it was his. I'm sorry."

"He was kind. He was always kind. When I first went to Allerbrook—that's the name of our farm—I felt so strange, so far

331

from home. He made me a carved wooden platter as a gift, my first Christmas. His wife, Betsy, is kind, too, and she's heartbroken. She's sitting by his grave now. She didn't want me to stay with her. They'd been married for thirty-five years. We tried so hard to save him. We tried and tried but…"

"Liza. Dear Liza. Don't you go breaking your heart. You're still too young for that."

"Everyone's dying!" Liza cried out. "My brother Arthur's been killed, and my cousin Dickon and though I know now that Peter is alive, it seems to me that I spent forever wondering if I'd see him again. And my mother…I'm afraid for her! I didn't tell you everything. She's not *herself* anymore. She's turned her back on life while she's still living it. I know she's in good hands. I know I should be more sensible. I'm fortunate in so many ways. I'm alive and well and have a good home and a daughter and Peter will come back. But it's all so dreadful. If I'm breaking my heart, I can't help it. Sometimes one just *can't* be sensible."

"No, I know," said Christopher, and his arms went around her instinctively. She never afterward recalled deciding to put hers around him in turn; they went there by themselves. She and Christopher clung together as they had done in the old days, but more strongly, more intensely. Their mouths locked. He pushed her coif off just as he used to do and his fingers were in her hair and hers deep in the circle of his thick red locks, rejoicing in their texture, their vitality.

The grass in front of the log was short and soft. They slid down to it easily. Liza found herself staring into his eyes, thinking once again how beautiful, how rare was that warm amber brown, those golden flecks. She freed her mouth and said, "We shouldn't, we mustn't, but I need you to hold me. I need someone..."

"And I need you. Liza, my only love, there has never been a day when I didn't think of you. My dear and my sweetheart, we should have been married. We were meant to be married. They shouldn't have dragged us apart."

"There's been too much death," said Liza brokenly. "Just too much."

"I know."

All the time their bodies, driven on by the need to outwit death, to perform the one act which could create life, to fling a challenging gauntlet at the old man with the skull face and the scythe, were finding ways to reach each other. Clothing was pushed aside, untied. As they glided together, a tangle of unspoken emotions blazed into life; all the old desire, all the old frustration at its denial; all the bitter grief and secret rage they had felt at being wrenched away from each other. Their union began with a vigour which was near to violence, with anger in it as well as passion; almost a vengefulness.

The storm passed, dissolving into simplicity and love; Christopher nuzzling, comforting, murmuring endearments, giving himself as a gift; Liza laughing and crying, clinging and giving herself in reply, seeking to engulf him as he sought to be engulfed.

Never had it been like this with Peter. Peter had given her satisfaction and sometimes enjoyment, but not like this, this fury melting into tenderness, this growing, spreading tree of joy within her and this unbelievable bursting into bloom at the finish; a flowering the colour of fire, which flamed and died softly away, to leave her marvelling.

They lay entangled, holding each other, until at last it seemed

time to get up, to resume their garments and to sit down, won-
deringly, side by side on the dry grey log and look into each
other's faces.

"I didn't mean that to happen," said Christopher. "But…"

"I'm glad it did. Glad. I've wanted it to happen ever since…I
think ever since we met at the fair. Do you remember? Oh,
Christopher, how can I go back to Allerbrook now? Though
I must," said Liza, bewildered. "I can't, but I must. There's
Quentin, my daughter. I've a life there. And…you must go back
to the castle. There's no way forward for us. There was just
this…this one morning."

"It's real, you know," said Christopher. "What I feel for you.
It always was. It's as though it comes from outside, drawn up into
me as a tree draws up sap from the earth. Today it burst into leaf
and blossom."

"You see it as that? I had such a picture in my mind just now,
when we were together!"

"Did you? It seems we think together. Our minds must be
linked. I believe they would be linked even if one of us were
removed to Cathay."

"I shall have to remove to Allerbrook soon. Darling, I must
go. How long have we been here?"

"I don't know. Half an hour? Most of eternity?"

"Do I look dishevelled? Am I fit to be seen?"

"Your coif isn't straight and there's mud on your face!"

"There's mud in your *hair!*"

They parted, clasping hands once more in farewell, looking
at each other with longing but managing, bravely, to smile. Liza
made her way slowly back up West Street, wondering how it was
possible to be filled with loss and sorrow but also to be insanely

happy, all at once. She found Betsy still sitting alone beside Higg's resting place.

"Betsy, please come. I'm sure that grass is damp, out in the open like this." *The grass in the dell wasn't damp. It was cool and soft and a perfect bed for lovers. Don't think about that!* She helped Betsy up, took her arm and led her out of the churchyard by the main gate.

"Where did you walk to?" Betsy asked as they went.

"Oh, just down to the river. I stood there awhile and looked at the water. One can watch flowing rivers for hours, though I don't have much spare time to watch the Allerbrook, of course."

"We won't have much spare time now Higg's gone, Mistress."

"No," Liza agreed, "I don't suppose we will."

They walked on, arm in arm, two unremarkable women with their plain headdresses and workaday dresses. One of them was still in a nightmare of bereavement and the other had just been to heaven and back, but no one would have guessed it.

Christopher, returning to the castle, knew that he should be racked with guilt. He had betrayed his vocation, his priesthood, his celibacy. Shame should be drowning him. Instead, he felt as though strength and energy were pouring through him. Liza was gone. They might never meet again. But they *had* met; just once in their lives they had met as fully as two human beings ever could and he was glad, glad, *glad*. Whoever thought he should feel guilty did not know what living was.

The castle's state of neglect struck him anew as he went into the hall. He had made repeated attempts to stir the servants up, but Master Hilton never gave him any support and they always slid back into their old ways before long. Eventually he had given up. This, he suddenly decided, was going to change.

Catching sight of the steward, Christopher advanced on him. "Master Hilton!"

"Ah. Father Christopher. I have been looking for you. I have heard of a most interesting devotional book for sale, which—"

"Never mind that now," said Christopher. "There's something I want to say to *you*. The Earl of Pembroke is dead, but he has heirs. One of these days, a new landlord may well descend on this castle. What do you imagine he will think of it?"

"I don't understand," said Hilton disdainfully. He had sought the services of Father Christopher, but since Christopher's arrival, he had sometimes wished he'd chosen differently. There was something positively crude in Christopher's energy. Priests were supposed to be gentlemen and they should be quiet, refined, devoted to prayer and worthy conversation. Priests shouldn't stride about pulsating with red-headed vitality. It was not the way either a man of the cloth or a gentleman should behave.

Christopher, on his side, eyed the elegantly dressed Hilton with annoyance, wondering how a man so plainly fastidious in his person could tolerate such squalid living conditions.

"What he or they will think," said Christopher, kicking the mouldy rushes at his feet, "is that these rushes stink, that the hangings are rotting and no one has as much as brushed them, let alone repaired them, for the last hundred years. That every floor in this place needs a broom and every cooking pan needs some sand and a whole lot of elbow grease, and every table and settle and chest needs a taste of beeswax! The only decently kept room in the castle is the chapel! The rest is something a half-witted peasant wouldn't want to live in!"

"My good man, I've said to you before, you're here to lead us in prayer, not to set us a housewifely example! You have no authority to speak to me in this fashion."

"Authority? Well, if necessary, I can and will write to Pembroke's family and report the lax way you perform your duties. I expect they'd be interested, whoever read the letter. I've got another form of authority, too."

"Which is?"

Christopher grinned. Liza would have recognised that grin. "I'm not taller than you are," he said sweetly. "But I'm stronger and sturdier than you. It's probably due to all the gardening I did at the priory." He flexed a biceps and regarded it complacently. "I advise you to cooperate with me."

CHAPTER TWENTY-FIVE

A MATTER OF A DOWRY

"So once again," said Agnes Sweetwater bitterly, "I am not good enough. It's always the same. They come and look me over, as though I were a mare they might want to buy. At times I expect them to look at my teeth and feel my legs! And then comes the little matter of money—and land."

Walter Sweetwater regarded his daughter unhappily. She was a good girl, with no foolish, romantic notions. She was a Sweetwater through and through—cool grey eyes, bushy brown hair which her maid had to thin out and shave at the front, a build that would one day turn to flesh but not, please God, until after she had produced a flourishing family of brown-haired, well-built, cool-eyed youngsters. Unluckily, before she could start producing the family she needed a husband, and the kind of man he wanted for her always expected more dowry than the Sweetwaters could provide.

The ladies' solar at Sweetwater House was upstairs, at the southwest end of the building, with windows on three sides, providing views of farmland, river and village. It possessed a wide hearth, comfortable, cushioned seats, a table and some shelves to hold such things as lutes, packs of cards, workboxes and a backgammon set. The beamed ceiling was high and the light was good. The room was big enough for a dozen ladies, but at the present time it was used by only four, for Agnes Sweetwater's mother had been dead for a year or more, and two girl cousins who had lived with the Sweetwaters for a time had been retrieved by their parents and married off. Married well, moreover. Their parents had been more skilled at such negotiations than the Sweetwaters were, it seemed. The remaining four were Baldwin's kittenish wife, Catherine, Agnes herself, and their maids. Catherine, head bent over her embroidery, was keeping out of the conversation and her maid was not there, but Agnes's woman, Maude, was seated by her mistress.

"I am sorry for your disappointment," Walter said awkwardly. He was never quite at ease in the feminine surroundings of the solar. They always made him want to be out practising martial skills on his warhorse, or else in the fields discussing sheep with Edward Searle. "Young Northcote is half a Carew and both families are rising in the world and have an eye to gain, it seems. They want land. I would settle land on you gladly if I had it to spare, but I haven't. You liked Giles Northcote, then?"

"Yes, Father. I did, as it happens."

Maybe his daughter wasn't as free of romantic nonsense as he had supposed. Her voice was sad and the maid gave her mistress a worried glance. Maude was attached to Agnes and had done much to comfort her during the sad days after the death of his wife. She was also pockmarked and gossipy and he didn't, personally, like her much, but when Agnes did marry, Maude could go with her and then he wouldn't have to see that pitted face about the place anymore. If only there were a way to bring this marriage off!

"Do you think Giles took to you, as well?" he asked.

"I think so, yes," Agnes said.

Well, and why not? Agnes had good health, clear skin and a pleasant smile. Any young man might find her attractive. But Giles Northcote, like Agnes, was only twenty-one and his parents expected him to do as he was told. If Agnes's dowry were not up to standard, he would be told that he couldn't marry her and he would have no say in the matter.

If only that damned Peter Lanyon hadn't got to Gloucester's side with his confounded horse so quickly at Tewkesbury. If only Walter Sweetwater had got in first!

Three days overdue, Liza thought. She had checked over and over again, counting on her fingers, but there it was. Seventeen days ago she and Christopher had made love in the dell at Dunster, and seen, in their minds, an image of a flowering tree. The flowers, it seemed, had seeded.

Had Kat or Betsy noticed anything? Neither of them now needed the cloths which younger women required at regular intervals unless they were carrying, and Liza looked after hers discreetly, soaking used ones in a lidded pail of salt water which she kept in a corner of the kitchen, changing the salt water night and morning, wringing out cloths when the salt had done its work and putting them in a pail of clean water, and finally, when it was all finished this time around, boiling the whole lot with some

soap and drying them on some bushes at the back of the farmhouse if the weather was good, or around the little hearth in her
room if not.

Liza didn't think that the other women had realised the long
gap since last time. Betsy was too sunk in her grief to notice
anything at all and Kat was distracted by anxiety about Betsy.
Neither was much good at keeping track of time, anyway. If
either of them did mention it, she would say that all the distress
over her mother, and Higg, and the news of her brother's death
had upset her. That would stave off disaster for a while.

But what then? Discovery was bound to come in the end unless nature released her. That was possible, even likely, given her
history. But if nature failed her...

So many times she had prayed to God, to the saints, to let her
carry a child to term. Now she must pray that she would not
and that she would lose it soon enough to pass the matter off as
a normal course, keeping secret the pain and the violence of the
bleeding. If nothing happened...

If nothing happened, then there would be no shelter anywhere, no hope, no future. She would be cast out by the Lanyons
and the Weavers alike, perhaps paraded through Clicket as a
whore. She would do better to make some excuse to go out on
a pony one day, and ride to the distant coast, where there were
cliffs, and cast herself into the sea.

Meanwhile, she must appear as normal as she could. It was
natural that she should seem downcast, of course. Seeing her
mother in such an unhappy state *had* distressed her; so had the
news about Arthur and Dickon, and so had Higg's tragedy.

"But life goes on," Richard had said at breakfast, only that
morning. "No use looking so dismal, my girl. Death's always

with us. If it isn't war, it's illness and if it isn't illness, it's accident. Will Hudd managed to be down with a fever when the Sweet-waters were mustering, so he didn't have to go off to fight, but then what happened at the very next haymaking? He gets careless with a scythe and takes the top off his left forefinger. Life's full of trouble. I've got those two Hannacombe lads—Eddie and Jarvis—coming before the harvest, by the way. You'd better think about where they're to sleep."

Liza spent much of the day planning for them. They could lodge with Betsy, which would give her something to do. She need not feed them; they could have meals at the farmhouse. Betsy, approached on the matter, was *agreeable,* if agreeable were the word for mere acquiescence.

"Just as you say, mistress. Just as you say." Every word that Betsy spoke sounded like a clod falling on a coffin. It would be an even chance whether the young Hannacombes brought cheerfulness back to Betsy, or Betsy's sorrow crushed their youthful high spirits forever. Even Peter's lively dog Rusty looked depressed when Betsy was about.

Liza tried to laugh about it with Richard. It was a huge effort, but he said with approval, "That's better. You sound more like yourself. You're a sensible wench."

Sensible. That word again! Her parents had reared her to be sensible; then one day at a fair in Dunster a redheaded young man had noticed that she didn't like seeing Bart Webber being ex-hibited as a cheat, and there went common sense, wiped out of existence like food stains from a dish. She'd tried to be sensible over the matter of Herbert Dyer, and look what had come of that! But if only she'd been sensible seventeen days ago in Dunster! Maybe tomorrow...

On waking next morning, she checked herself. There was nothing, except a tightness in her stomach and a slight sense of nausea.

Eighteen days since she and Christopher had been together. Four days overdue.

"I've heard some pretty gossip down in Clicket," Richard announced, arriving back from a foray into the village to meet Sim Hannacombe and Will Hudd in the White Hart and discuss details of whose barley was going to be reaped first when the time came. He sauntered into the kitchen, where supper was giving off fragrant smells. "What's this? Pottage with fresh meat in it?"

"Chicken," Liza said. "That hen that seems to have stopped laying. I decided we'd better eat her. I've put her in a stew and cooked cabbage to go with her and there's fresh cheese and dumplings, too." *Sound cheerful, Liza. Why, oh why won't nature set me free when she's done it so often before?*

"Get it on the table, and I'll tell you my tale," Richard said. "Betsy, leave scraping those pots and come and help me off with my boots, and don't burst into tears this time because you'll never take Higg's boots off for him again. Mourning's one thing, but it can't go on forever."

"He's not been gone a month," said Betsy resentfully, though she wiped her hands and went to help him as he sat down by the hearth.

"It feels like a year. Never seen such a lot of long faces in all my life. You ought to be happier, Liza. We know that Peter'll be home one of these days. Thanks, Betsy. Just let me get some supper inside me, and then I'll tell you my tale."

A few minutes later, breaking bread into his stew, he said, "It's more than one tale, as it happens, but they're both about marriage. Gilbert Lowe was in the White Hart today, in a vile temper. That put-upon daughter of his, Martha, well, for all she's not far short of forty, she's run off with a sheepshearer, a widower fellow, about her own age. Gone off with him to Barnstaple, where he comes from, and wed him, too, all right and proper, and left Tilly Lowe to do all the work of the house unless Gilbert loosens his purse strings and takes on a maid or two. Whole tavern was laughing, except for Gilbert!"

"Well!" said Liza, determinedly showing the interest that would be expected. "I never would have thought Martha would have so much spirit! But you said there was more than one tale?"

"Indeed there is. Before Gilbert came in with his long face as though his girl were dead instead of wed, the talk in the Hart was that the Sweetwaters have had another try at marrying off their girl, Agnes, and been turned down again. Same reason as before—her dowry's too small. Adam Turner said they aim too high, and I reckon he's right."

"How did all that come to be known?" Liza asked. "Who spreads the Sweetwater business round the tavern?"

"Agnes has a maid with a tongue that wags like Rusty's tail— or at least like Rusty's tail when he hasn't got it between his legs because Betsy's making him sad. We all valued Higg, Betsy, but he did die cared for and with a priest at hand and that's not so for everyone."

It hadn't been so for a girl on Castle Rock, years ago, but better not think of that.

Betsy, on the verge of weeping, rose and went to the kitchen, banging the door after her. Richard looked after her and sighed.

"I suppose she'll get over it one day. Getting back to my story—
Agnes Sweetwater's chatty tirewoman is partial to a tankard of
ale now and again and that's the way word gets round the White
Hart. It seems that the man they had in mind is a Northcote—
they're a wealthy Devon family—and he's related to another one,
the Carews. His people want land as part of the dowry, but
though Walter has more than just Clicket and the farms round
here, he still hasn't enough going spare and he can't afford to buy
more. That'll be the third time the girl's been said no to." He
sounded pleased about it.

"Well, I be sorry for her, if you're not." Kat didn't care for
Richard's ruthless attitude to Betsy's grieving and seized the
chance to argue. "'Tweren't her fault that her men went huntin'
and crashed into your dad's funeral. It's no good thing for a
wench to be left unwed, like a dusty old bowl on a potter's shelf
that no one wants to buy. Martha Lowe was lucky to escape.
Another couple of years and she'd have been past praying for.
Agnes Sweetwater's got as much right to a good man as any
other, and once 'ee've got one, it's the best thing in the world,
even if it don't last forever." She gave a kindly glance toward
Roger, who was so stooped now that his nose was almost in
his pottage. "Better to have and lose than never have at all."

"As long as you don't lose too soon." Betsy, returning from
the kitchen with a dish of dumplings, sighed heavily. She put the
dish on the table and set about providing little Quentin with
some stew and a chopped-up dumpling.

"I'll have some more stew," said Richard, ignoring her. "It's
good. Who'd have thought that hen would be this tender? What's
the matter, Kat? You've gone rigid like a standing stone out on

the moor. Pass the stew to me, can't you? What are you staring out at the farmyard for?"

"Look!" said Kat, and at the same moment Liza, who had also risen to see what had caught Kat's eye, let out a cry, abandoned her own food and ran for the door into the yard.

A moment later, exclaiming joyously, she was in Peter's arms, even though one of them had Plume's reins looped around it. Peter, in turn, was clutching his wife as though afraid she might vanish if he let her go.

"Liza! My sweet Liza, I've missed you so very very much."

"And I you," said Liza, holding him just as tightly. "And I you!"

"Let me put Plume in the stable and see to him, then I'll be with you. I'm not tired. I've got used to riding for hours on end, but Plume's feeling it, poor fellow."

Richard came out to greet his son and help with the pony. By the time they came in again to the stew, which Betsy, looking more animated than she had in weeks, had hurriedly heated again, they had exchanged a good deal of news. Peter condoled with Betsy, shaking his head at the place where Higg used to sit. "And I'm sorry to learn of the troubles in Liza's family. Maybe a bit of good news will help—well, Father, tell them what I told you just now, out in the stable."

"No, you tell it, boy. It's your story."

"I've been in battles," said Peter. "Two big ones especially. I'm lucky to be still alive but here I am, none the worse except for a nick or two that healed easy. That's by the way. I was made to go with the Duke of Gloucester's men—"

"Who'd he be?" Kat asked.

"King Edward's youngest brother, the loyal one. The one in

the middle joined Warwick at one time, though I think he's back supporting his own kinfolk now. That's not the point. I didn't take Plume into the field. I fought on foot, to start with. But in one battle, in a lot of muddle and a thick fog, I got hold of a big horse, got myself put amongst the mounted soldiers. But in the next battle I saw Gloucester's horse fall under him and I gave him mine. He was grateful. That's why I'm late back. After the king had won, he and Gloucester went to London and I had to go as well, and be there at a ceremony—in front of the Tower of London, it was—where rewards were presented to men who'd pleased the king or Gloucester during the war. I had an award! The deeds are in my saddlebag. I've shown them to Father."

"Two farms and a village, just to the south of the moor." Richard couldn't contain himself after all. "We'll get the rents for all of them."

"It was a parcel of land someone left to Gloucester," Peter said. "It's good land, too. I visited it on my way back. It's all let to tenants, but I am the landlord. I have the freehold."

"Freehold…" said Richard thoughtfully. "You know, that's making me think…. Betsy, bring out your best elderflower wine and we'll drink to Peter's reward, and we'll drink to what we might do with it, too." His mouth curved in a satyrlike smile which startled Liza because it looked so alarming. "If you do as I say, boy, like a good son should, maybe poor Agnes Sweet-water'll get her man after all, but if she does, her father'll be beholden to me for it and oh, how he won't like that!"

"But are you really going to agree? After all, the award's yours, not your father's," Liza said when she and Peter were at last alone. She was glad to see him come into the bedchamber, for he hadn't hurried, and when she looked out the window, wondering where he was, he was chopping firewood in the farmyard with excessive violence, though there was plenty of firewood and no need for a man, who had come home only that day from fighting battles, to create more. She was perplexed.

"I won't have much say in the matter," said Peter dryly. "But it will keep him happy, if it works." He was stripping off his hose and shirt as he spoke. The light of the long summer evening streamed into the room. His body, kept muscular from continual riding and frequent fighting, was in fine trim. Even to Liza, with the splendour of Christopher's body still fresh in her memory, this man was beautiful. It seemed that she loved them both, though differently.

There was a sheen of sweat on his skin, from his efforts with the chopper. He found himself a linen towel and rubbed it dry. "*If* it works," Peter said, "we'd be free of the Sweetwaters. No more landlords! I wouldn't mind that, I admit. We'd own Allerbrook outright. Allerbrook can be sold—that's been so for a good century, since the boundary of the Royal Forest was last moved. You can't buy property inside the forest, of course, but that doesn't matter to us now. We can purchase Allerbrook if the Sweetwaters will sell."

"And your father wouldn't need their permission to build the new house he wants so much," said Liza. She hesitated and then said, "He's very serious about it. While you were away—well, I know he gave it a lot of thought."

"And drew plans. I know. He showed them to me," said Peter.

"Yes," Liza said. "And I know he's afraid that if he had to ask them, the Sweetwaters might say he wasn't to build anything that could challenge their own house."

"Exactly!"

"But Peter, you don't *want* a fine new house and I don't think we need one, either."

"Quite right, but Father thinks otherwise. He talked to me and brought out those plans of his while you were doing your evening chores, and I saw just how determined he is. In fact, I'd say that slightly crazed would be nearer the mark! All the same, there *is* sense in breaking free of the Sweetwaters. What Father wants to do is to keep the village and one of the farms I've been granted, and sell the other farm, the bigger one, and then make an offer for Allerbrook. There's a chance that Walter Sweetwater will sell, because he needs money so badly. With it, he may be able to provide Agnes with enough dowry. Father said he and I could share ownership. We won't have to pay rent—or for the right to eat rabbit—and the Sweetwaters couldn't order any of us to follow them to war, ever again, either!"

"I see that. But—oh, I wish your father didn't keep calling you *boy*. You're not a boy. You're—what—over thirty, and you've just come back from a war and been rewarded for your service!" Liza found that her indignation on his behalf was entirely genuine.

"He likes to feel he's the master," said Peter. He spoke quite calmly but then, as though a surge of rage had overtaken him, hurled the towel away, to land in a heap on the floor. "He *has* to feel he's the master. Damn him, damn him! Do you remember the time he went away to war and I was the master of Allerbrook while he was gone? I did well, I know I did. Did he ever say thank you? Did he ever say as much as well done, thou good and faithful son? Did he? *Did he?* No, he bloody well didn't. It was *Out of the way, boy. I'm back now, I'll take charge.* I'd looked after the place for two years but all of a sudden I was supposed to accept that I knew nothing and he knew it all. Liza, there are times when I think I hate him!"

"Oh, Peter!" said Liza inadequately.

With a groan, he sat down on the edge of the bed. "I didn't mean that. Well, maybe I hate him some of the time. He takes after his own father. I remember *him* well enough! It's best if I let him have his way. One day I'll come into my own and meanwhile, letting him pretend I'm still a boy is a small price to pay for peace. When I feel angry with him, I can always go and chop firewood, and put some effort into it!"

"So that's what you were at just now! I saw you from the window."

"Er...yes." Peter laughed, rather awkwardly. "Yes. He's made me angry today, that's true enough. What the Duke of Gloucester has given me is rightly mine and my father's laying claim to it, as near as makes no difference. But I decided not to quarrel with him. I'd rather my wife and child lived in a peaceful household, my love."

"Yes. You think your own thoughts in secret," said Liza. "I understand."

If anyone had gone in for secret thoughts, she had.

Peter had become calm once more. "If Walter Sweetwater's really desperate for money," he remarked, "there's a real chance he'll agree to sell—after a bit of cursing. And there's something else. I've told Father, and now I'll tell you. It's how we decided which farm to keep and which to turn into money."

"What do you mean?"

"I mean," said Peter, "that one of them, the one we mean to keep, isn't just a farm. The Duke of Gloucester did well by me." He smiled, remembering the moment when the deeds were handed to him by the sparely built young man who had known danger and responsibility from an early age, whose right shoulder was a little too big for the rest of him, whose face was lined before its time, but was now lit by a smile of gratitude. The smile widened his thin mouth and gleamed in his hazel eyes, making him almost handsome.

"There's a stone quarry on that piece of land as well," Peter said. "And a profitable one. As I said, I've visited the place." He frowned. "Of course, Father said that when he builds his house, a stone quarry of our own would be useful! Slightly crazed, as I said. But the quarry ought to be a good source of income and perhaps Father won't go on with this notion of building a house, not when he really sees how much it would cost. He'll still have to do a deal of saving and it'll take years, and perhaps by then he'll have changed his mind. Meanwhile," he said, standing up in order to turn back the coverlet, "I'll chop firewood when I feel the need, and keep him happy."

"Well, it's for you to decide," Liza said, pulling off her own clothing. She slipped into the bed. "Peter, I'm so very very glad to see you back."

"I've ached to *be* back, sweetheart."

He came to her, eager and hungry, pulling the covers right off to look at her and then pouncing joyfully, to meet with a response which made him laugh aloud and shout her name and roll across the bed with her, kissing her frantically. Later, the tiredness of the long road from London finally overtaking him, he fell asleep with his nose pushed into her shoulder and Liza, holding him, silently sent up prayers of gratitude to heaven.

She was safe now. If the child within her prospered, no one, least of all Peter himself, would question its parentage. It would be the child of this night; what else? Even if anyone took to counting on their fingers, and they wouldn't, they would take it for granted when the baby came that it had arrived a little early and there was nothing odd about that, not with Liza.

She was a hypocrite, faithless, a liar, a deceiver, an adulteress, probably damned, probably destined for hell. She might well die in bearing this child. That would be heaven's revenge.

But the baby, if it were born and lived, would be safe and so would her good name. Peter had come home in time.

"Buy Allerbrook?" howled Walter Sweetwater, stamping up and down his hall. "Freehold and all? Those damned Lanyons! First of all Peter Lanyon wrecks my chance of getting a reward out of Gloucester and now…"

"We can't do it." Baldwin was as angry as his father. He stood staring out the window, at the hill and the combe above Clicket. He blocked the light from the window like a thundercloud. "It's unthinkable. They just want to thumb their noses at us! We know that Richard Lanyon wants to build himself a big house! Most of Clicket knows—he talks about it in the White Hart. If he gets his hands on Allerbrook, he'll do it! We won't be able to stop him. No one has a bigger head than a prosperous peasant!"

"If we sell to him, would there be enough?" Agnes asked.

Her father and brother turned around. She had been sitting in a window seat, listening, with Catherine beside her.

"What?" said Walter.

"If we sell them Allerbrook for the best price we can get, could we buy enough dowry land to please Giles Northcote's family?"

"There's no question of it!" Baldwin shouted.

"My dear loving brother, it isn't for you to say. Father?"

"You really do want to marry Giles Northcote?" said Walter. "I mean, *want* him?"

"That isn't the point!" Baldwin bellowed.

"Shouldn't it be considered?" said Catherine. "My dear, did you not *want* to marry me?"

"What? Yes, of course I did, my Kitten, but there was no bar, no difficulty. No one asked me to insult my family for your sake."

"But is it such a dreadful insult? They want to buy something from us for a fair price, that's all. And look what it would mean to Agnes!"

"What it could mean to all of us!" Agnes's head was high and her voice proud. "It is not *only* that Giles Northcote and I liked each other when we met. The Northcotes are a good family and so are the Carews, from whom his mother comes. They mix with people in high office. If Giles and I have children, they would have the chance of good marriages. They might go to court. Our sons might be appointed to good positions. So might you, Baldwin! All that, just for Allerbrook!"

"I wish I'd had the sense to find Peter Lanyon and kill him in the fog on Barnet field!" said Baldwin furiously.

"I want to marry Giles Northcote," said Agnes obstinately. "And I think he wants to marry me, and I don't think any of you would regret it. Father, I wouldn't urge you to this if I didn't believe that! If Giles Northcote were a stable boy, I wouldn't ask to marry him, even if he were as pure as a saint and as beautiful as an archangel! I know my duty. But this is a *chance* for us—if there's enough money. Would there be?"

"There could be...yes. I have some in my coffers that I could add and if Catherine will agree—for I wouldn't do this without her agreement—we could part with one of her dower farms...."

"There are four altogether. Two could go," Catherine said at once.

"That's generous. They could be sold and with that money, and some of my savings and whatever I get for Allerbrook, I could buy an estate worth having," Walter said. "There's one in Devon that would do. I heard of it while I was with the king. It may well be for sale. The owner and his heir were both killed at Tewkesbury."

"No!" shouted Baldwin. "Think of the income we'll lose! Rents from two farms as well as Allerbrook! *No*, Father!" Catherine opened her mouth to speak again, but he glared at her and she stopped. "This isn't your business!" Baldwin snapped at her. "Keep out of it!"

"I'll go to the solar," said Catherine. Looking exactly like a dignified kitten, she slipped off the window seat, but before she left the hall she put a kind hand momentarily on Agnes's arm.

Baldwin saw it. "Women!"

"You were crazy for Catherine," said Walter coldly.

"Yes, you were! And now you want to stand between me and Giles just for spite against the Lanyons!" Agnes shouted. "Because that's what it is. We can live without the rents. We could gain much more than we lose! Which is more important, anyway? Your quarrel with the Lanyons or the future of this family and *my whole life?*"

"Stop that! Shouting like a woman selling yarn in a market! I don't expect my sister to raise her voice. Ladies should be soft-spoken, gentle."

"Father!"

"Your sister cannot remain unwed much longer," Walter said seriously to his son. "As for the Lanyons...I detest them as much as you do and the loss of the rents will be a nuisance, but I can see the advantages of this marriage. No, Baldwin. If this makes you lose your temper, then go out and ride your horse till it founders, or get a couple of the stable boys to fight a round or two with you, bare fisted. That'll take the fury out of you. I've made my mind up. I don't like it either, but I am responsible for settling Agnes in life and we could indeed gain from a link with the Northcotes and the Carews. Those two families are very much on their way up. I'll sell."

"And that upstart Richard Lanyon will be digging the foundations of his house before we know it," said Baldwin indignantly.

"Not he," said Walter. "Allerbrook will cost him enough to keep him short for a long, long time. I'll see to that!"

Allerbrook was indeed expensive. Even with the profitable quarry (of which Walter was comfortably unaware), the new Lanyon house might never have come into being at all if nature hadn't taken a hand.

PART THREE

STORM DAMAGE
1480–1486

CHAPTER TWENTY-SIX
BOULDER

"I want to go out!" said Nicky crossly. He was sitting on a chest-cum-settle under one of the hall windows, expressing his view of the weather by kicking the front of the chest. A squall of wind rattled the window and Liza, going to it, saw that it wasn't properly latched. She raised the latch, intending to secure it with a firm push, and the gale tore the window from her grasp. Rain blew into her face. The moors were invisible, lost in the cloud and the downpour, and the sound of the swollen Allerbrook deep in the combe came with it, audible even from here, so high on the hillside.

Nicky kicked the chest again as she snatched the window back. She slammed and latched it and turned a stern face to him. "Stop that. Why are you not at your books? Did Father Matthew give you nothing to study until your next lesson with him?"

"I've done it," said Nicky. There had been no need to send

Nicky away to school as Peter and Richard had been sent, not with Father Matthew in the village and willing, at Richard's request, to give Nicky private lessons three times a week. "He gave me some Latin to put into English and some sums and they're all finished. And now I want to go out and I can't!"

"Well, I don't order the weather, and if you went out in this, you'd probably drown," said Liza with vigour.

"Father and Grandfather went out in it this morning! So did the Hannacombes!"

"They're grown up and they had to fetch the animals in and even at that, Roger didn't go. He says he's too old. Kat came over to say he was staying in the cottage, and we sent her back to him. I've never seen such weather. It's just as well this is November and the stock's not out on the moor, except for the pony herd, and they seem able to find shelter from anything. I'd like a walk on the moor but I can't have one. Why don't you make another try at learning to weave?"

"I hate sitting at a loom. It goes clatter, clatter, clatter and every moment's just like the one before and it's dull."

"And you're clumsy. You break threads and I'm always afraid you'll break the loom, as well."

Nicky laughed, and Liza, unable to help it, laughed with him.

It was always happening. She would try, for his own good, to be severe, to tell him he must study his books or be patient about bad weather, be a good child, like his sister, Quentin—who was at this moment in the workroom, busy at the loom, weaving the first piece of cloth she had ever made completely by herself.

Quentin was hardly ever disobedient. She was a responsible little girl with a gift for soothing people. Once or twice, when Peter had been angry about something and marched out to vent his fury by chopping wood or digging a ditch with ferocious energy, Quentin had gone out to him and restored his good temper simply by being there and chattering to him about some everyday matter.

Nicky was the wayward one, and Liza knew she ought to be firmer with him. But then Nicky's astonishing resemblance to Christopher would overwhelm her with love as though a great wave had broken over her, and if he came to her for comfort because his father had rebuked him, she would give him an apple or a honeycake because she couldn't bear that little snub-nosed, freckled face to look unhappy. Wayward he might be, but he was affectionate, too, which made giving in to him all the easier.

She was thankful that none of the Lanyons had ever met Christopher and that in the present Weaver family, there was no one now who knew him except as a distant figure occasionally glimpsed in church. She shocked herself sometimes by admitting privately that it was just as well that her parents, who actually had met him, were both gone.

It was six years now since Margaret had finally taken to her bed in the guest house at St. Catherine's and slipped out of life. Liza had mourned her deeply, but was also relieved that Margaret had never set eyes on Nicky and now never would. There was only one source of danger left, and that was the risk that one day, somehow or other, Nicky and Christopher would be seen together by a member of the family. There, she must hope for the best and pray, although it seemed unlikely that God and his angels, or even the merciful Virgin, would collude in hiding her guilt.

Yet her path of deception had certainly been marvellously smooth. Nicky had been born, as far as Liza could calculate, a few days later than he should have been; certainly no one had ever questioned that he was the result of her reunion with Peter. He had emerged straight into a patch of spring sunlight, and that had been the worst moment because there on his newborn head was a tuft of hair as red as fire.

Whereupon Betsy had said, "Look at that! Mistress, didn't you say when Quentin was born, and the master said to name her for your grandmother, that your grandmother was carrot-haired? This one's going to be more like her than Quentin is!"

"Yes," said Liza faintly. "Yes, he will. There was a little red in my mother's hair when she was young and there's just a glint of it in Quentin's, in some lights."

"Maybe he did ought to be named for your side of the family, Mistress."

"Yes," Peter said, when his opinion was sought. "Call him after your father, Liza. Didn't my father suggest that once?"

Never, for a moment, had there been suspicion. Yet every time she looked at Nicky, Christopher was there again for her, fiery hair, shapely eyebrows, eyes the colour of amber or sweet chestnut—quite unlike her own soft brown ones or Peter's Lanyon eyes, which were so dark that from only a short distance away they looked black. He had Christopher's dear snub nose and even a cluster of freckles on his square little chin.

Christopher was still, as far as she knew, at Dunster Castle. She hadn't seen him since that day in the dell and probably would never see him again, for she didn't go to Dunster now. Nicky occasionally did, because his father had decided when the boy turned eight that he was old enough to be taken along when wool was delivered to the Weavers. Sometimes he had stayed there for a week or two, helping to wash fleeces at the river, and being instructed in the craft of weaving, though his Dunster relatives, like Liza, all agreed that he had little aptitude for it.

Liza was uneasy at the idea of Nicky and Christopher being in the same village, but she knew that he should get to know his mother's family. This was a gamble she must accept. For her, Nicky's resemblance to his father was a blessing. He kept Christopher's memory green for her. Christopher lived in her mind, unknown to all others, a quietly flowing underground river. It was enough.

She wished the Allerbrook were flowing more quietly. The noise of it worried her. The wind was increasing, too, and when she peered through the window glass she saw that still darker weather was approaching from the west. Something worse was on the way.

The door to the kitchen swung open and Peter came in, wrapped in a blanketlike robe and rubbing his hair on a towel. The robe was one of a set created by Liza after Higg's death. In farm life, people were always getting drenched in bad weather but she didn't want anyone else to die as Higg had done, and she had woven and sewn a set of thick robes for the purpose of getting wet bodies warm and dry in a hurry.

"What a day! Betsy's put our clothes to dry and the Hannacombe boys are wandering about in a couple of your woolly gowns, looking like a pair of monks."

"I don't see them as monks!" Liza said. "I've been meaning to mention this to you. Quentin's thirteen now. She's growing up. What do you think about Eddie Hannacombe? Your father mentioned the idea once. When Quentin's seventeen, say. Eddie'll be about twenty-six by then. Jarvis is younger, but I'd prefer Eddie. He's is quiet and responsible and Jarvis already has a bit of a name for flirting among the village wenches."

"Father mentioned it to me as well, not long ago. As a matter of fact, Eddie's in the workroom now, talking to Quentin. They're good friends, those two. I fancy the idea will appeal to them. Well, I'm agreeable if they are—and Sim, of course. And yes, it should be Eddie—you're right about Jarvis, I'd say. We could arrange a betrothal party soon, I think—when the rain stops. I've seen plenty of wild weather, but I've never seen rain like this in my life. We've lost a sheep. The bog on the ridge has overflowed and there's a torrent down the hillside out in front of the house, and a sheep lying on an outcrop in the middle of it. Must have been caught and swept away when the water came over the edge."

"I hope it's the only one," Liza said anxiously.

Nicky, who had now climbed up to stand on the window seat so that he could look out, said, "Oooh! Look at that cloud! I've never seen one like that before!"

Liza went to look and was alarmed. The dark weather from the west was now an advancing inky mass that seemed to be wiping out the world below it. "Nicky, go and fetch Quentin, and take her to Betsy in the kitchen and ask for honeycakes. She made some yesterday. Say I said you could both have one. Go along now."

As soon as Nicky had gone, she turned to Peter. "That sky's frightening. There's no thunder. But—*look* at it."

"There's nothing we can do about it," Peter said. "But there's nothing to be afraid of. There's been a house here for centuries. The stock's safely in now, all but that sheep. It'll pass and meanwhile, we're safe, too, in here. We'd better have some candles. It'll be as dark as night in a moment."

They were lighting candles when the monstrous cloud reached

them, taking the last of the daylight, and the wind and rain suddenly doubled. The windows streamed as though water were being poured down them by the bucketful. A mass of water tumbled down the chimney, putting out the fire with a noisy sizzle and causing Liza to spring around in alarm, taper in hand. Then, her eyes widening, she cocked her head and said, "What's that?"

"Nothing," said Peter calmly. "It's just the wind. It…"

A fearful roar and crash from outside interrupted him. The very walls of the hall, stout as they were, shuddered. A chorus of frightened cries rose from the kitchen and the door to it crashed open. Eddie came in at a run with Quentin and Nicky. Eddie and Quentin were both pale with alarm though Nicky, by contrast, had gone red with excitement.

"What's happening?" Liza rushed to meet them. "What…?"

"Mistress, it's terrible! There's water in the back of the house—"

"Right inside!" Nicky squealed.

"And a great big tree's come down with it!" Quentin was clearly terrified.

Jarvis Hannacombe arrived in haste, and his normally stolid pink face was also unwontedly pale. "It's the bog on the ridge— I think! It's overflowed in a new place, close above here. It's pouring down the hillside like a new river. It's—"

"It's in the dairy!" screamed Betsy, lumbering in at the nearest approach her aged legs could make to a run. "There's filthy water in the dairy! The window's burst in and so's the outer door! A tree came down and smashed them in! It's sticking its branches through into the dairy and the apple store up above. And there's water in your parlour, Mistress!"

Incredibly, as they stood there exclaiming, the wind and rain strengthened yet again. A shower of slates hurtled off the hall roof. From the stable, faintly audible through the din, came frightened whinnying.

"I'm going to look at the damage to the rooms in front," Peter said. "Betsy, Liza, stay here with the children. You lads come with me!" He beckoned to the Hannacombes and they all hurried off through the kitchen. Quentin ran to her mother and stood trembling in the curve of Liza's arm but Nicky shook himself free and ignoring his mother's protesting shout, ran after the men.

"Quentin," said Liza, "be good and stay here. It's all right. It's just a loud noise and a lot of rain and some damage to the front of the house, and it's let water in. But I must fetch Nicky. Betsy, take care of her!"

Lifting her skirts, she sped off through the kitchen and almost collided with Richard, who had been upstairs and had now rushed down, to stand aghast at the door into the dairy. "Where's Nicky?" Liza panted.

"I don't know. Wasn't he with you?"

"Nicky!" Liza shouted. "Where are you? *Nicky!*"

"The whole front of the house is flooded!" Peter came striding back through the workroom with Eddie and Jarvis behind him. "I've never seen anything like this before, never!"

"God's teeth, nor have I!" Richard gasped.

The dairy was several inches deep in brown peaty water, but it was on a lower level than the kitchen, with two steps down to it, and so far, the kitchen and its adjoining larder had escaped. But wind and rain were now driving in through the broken window and the shattered door and the thing that had done the damage, one of the shallow-rooted trees from the hillside above the farm, was thrusting vicious twigs and branches in through the holes. The inrush of water had knocked over a table where a row of pans had stood, full of cream which was setting. The pans were afloat in the water, and a milky swirl was all that remained of the cream. Several cheeses, swept from their shelf by an intrusive tree branch, wallowed dismally beside them.

"Where is Nicky?" Liza wailed. *"Nicky!"*

Her redheaded son appeared in answer, in the doorway from the storeroom next to the dairy. "Isn't it exciting? The tree's trying to get in!"

"Nicky! Come here! No, don't wade across through that water. It's disgusting! Go round by the workroom but then come to me at once! What do you mean by running off...?"

There was a renewed roar and rumbling from outside and Nicky, not obeying orders but plunging excitedly knee-deep into the flooded dairy, kicking pans and cheeses aside, made toward the broken outer door. *"Look!"*

They did look, and Liza cried out. The worst of the cloud was passing and grey daylight was returning to the stricken world. Even from the inner side of the dairy, they now had a view of the landscape beyond the smashed outer door and what they could see was terrifying. High on the slope above the farmhouse, a great boulder, one of the outcrops which dotted the hillside, had been torn loose by the flood from the overflowing bog. It was rolling, bouncing, straight toward the house, and another surge of water was coming with it, as though the uprooting of the boulder had released it.

"Nicky!" Liza screamed.

But Nicky, wildly excited, did not even hear her. Eager to see better, he splashed right into the broken doorway, clinging to the doorpost.

Peter and Liza shouted his name again, in unison, and started forward, stumbling down the submerged dairy steps, but Eddie Hannacombe, younger and quicker than either of them, brushed past and threw himself across the room. In the brief seconds before the boulder arrived, he grabbed Nicky, picked him up bodily and hurled him back across the room toward Peter and Liza. Liza flung her arms around him, and Peter, grabbing her arm, dragged them both back up the steps into the kitchen. Eddie waded after them, the skirts of his thick robe spreading out around his knees.

The boulder struck.

The kitchen survived because the inner walls of the old farmhouse were as strong as the outer ones and the outer ones took the brunt, slowing the monstrous missile down. As it was, the dairy's outside wall shifted under the impact and then gave way in a tumble of rubble and stone slabs. The huge rock, crashing through it, crushed the tree as though its sturdy trunk were nothing but a twig and then fetched up against the far wall while the flood that came with it poured across the dairy in a murky brown wave and on into the kitchen, knocking everyone there off their feet.

Like the boulder itself, however, it had lost impetus on the way through the dairy and they scrambled back to their feet, choking and spluttering. And then clung to each other in terror as they saw a second boulder coming. It thundered into the front of the house farther along, striking the parlour by the sound of it, and the entire building shuddered. Then there was stillness except for the sloshing of water.

In the kitchen, though soaked and terrified and standing in two feet of water, everyone was still alive. But Eddie Hannacombe had not been in the kitchen when the boulder hit. He had still been wading across the dairy and had been caught between boulder and wall. They found him there, his body crushed and his head lolling, the blood flowing out and staining the water all around him. The only consolation was that he had probably died at once.

CHAPTER TWENTY-SEVEN ⚭

THE RISING HOUSE OF LANYON

News found its way around the moor in the days that followed, news of farmhouses and cottages swept completely away; of villages flooded by rivers which had always hitherto been friendly brooks; news of sheep and cattle, ponies and wayfarers, caught and drowned; of meadows under water which had never been flooded before; of uprooted trees, of landslides, of peat streams which had changed their courses.

The Lanyons swept the water out of their farmhouse and considered the damage. The outhouses around the yard were unscathed and so, because it was on higher ground, was the hall. The cottages were safe, too. Kat and Roger had crouched, petrified, by their hearth, but their sturdy stone walls had stood firm in the wind and rain, and only their thatch would need repair. Betsy's cottage, sheltered by a spur of hillside, was altogether untouched.

The farmhouse itself, however, had been badly hit. The rooms facing the yard had survived, though their floors had been flooded, but the second boulder had smashed right into the parlour and also destroyed the rusty hinges of the disused front door. The front of the house was a wreck, the upper storey sagging dangerously on unsteady beams, and the thatched roof half gone.

Worst of all was the death of Eddie Hannacombe, and among the most urgent tasks, as well as the most distressing, was his retrieval and burial. Once the water had been swept out, Peter took Plume down the mired path through the combe to see the carpenter and the sexton and bring a coffin back, strapped to Plume's back. The carpenter usually had one or two in readiness and Peter returned two hours later, bringing not only the coffin but Father Matthew, who did his best, offering physical aid as well as prayer, to help them through the horrible business that faced them.

To do it, they had to clear away the rubble of the smashed dairy wall, and then hitch their own and some borrowed oxen to the boulder to drag it away, and even at that, the men, including Father Matthew, had to add their strength to the ropes. Then they lifted the crushed thing that had been Eddie, laid him in the coffin and placed the lid over him, in haste.

The burial was the next day. When the pitiful remains were safe in the churchyard, the Lanyons turned their attention to Nicky.

Since the disaster, no one had said much to him. He had been given jobs to do and had done them, but it had been made unsmilingly clear to him that the adult world was merely dealing with more immediate matters before it dealt with him. Once he found Quentin crying in the workroom, and gathering from her tearful explanation that she was grieving for Eddie, he cried, too, and said he was sorry, and Quentin, surprisingly, actually attempted to

371

comfort him rather than the other way around, saying that she knew he hadn't meant any harm, that it wasn't his fault. The only friendly words he heard during those frightening days were hers. Everyone else, his mother included, was chilly and remote.

The morning after the funeral, Nicky found himself in the hall, facing what amounted to a tribunal.

Liza had dreaded this moment, though she knew it was coming. She knew that Nicky had been in the wrong, but her heart ached for him.

"He's still only eight," she had said that morning when Peter and his father told her in detail what to expect. "I've made it clear to him that he's behaved very badly, but it was just ordinary naughtiness, after all. It was bad luck that it led to something so awful."

"Nonsense!" Richard barked. "He ran off when you told him to stay with you in the hall, and he ran to look out of the dairy door instead of coming back to you when you called him. He ignored you when the very tone of your voice should have told him that it mattered. He knows that Eddie saved him and was killed in doing it. He knows what death means. He saw Eddie's body. I made sure he did! He's been spoiled, Liza. We've all spoiled him, myself included. We've all been so overjoyed to have a Lanyon son."

"I agree," Peter said. "I'm sorry, Liza, but it's true. No one's ever raised a hand to him. He's never been more than mildly scolded. But what sort of man will our son be if he doesn't learn to behave while he's still young enough to learn?"

"I suppose you're right," said Liza unhappily.

If only he didn't look so like Christopher. Oh, my poor little Nicky. All this for just only a moment's disobedience. Every boy has those. Father-in-law and Peter both did in their time—I'd take an oath on it!

But Eddie is dead. I can't deny that.

The table had been pushed out of the way. Liza sat in a window seat, with Quentin and Betsy. Betsy sat grimly, with folded arms. Quentin, on the other hand, looked nearly as frightened as Nicky. Nicky himself stood in midfloor, confronted by a stern row of men: his father, his grandfather, Roger, Jarvis Hannacombe and Sim, father of both Eddie and Jarvis, who had come over for the occasion. There was an ominous air of formality.

His father recited his misdeeds to him, much as Richard had recited them to Liza, and reminded him of the tragedy to which they had led. "What have you to say?" he asked at the end.

Nicky looked from one face to another, finding no comfort anywhere. He looked toward his mother, but her gaze was on the floor. Betsy's face was like flint. Quentin was watching him with huge, worried eyes but her obvious fear only made him feel worse. "I'm sorry. I only wanted to see what was happening. I just wanted to look. I didn't mean…"

"Because of you," said Richard, "as we have just pointed out, Eddie had to snatch you from the path of that boulder and it caught him. You saw what it did to him. It could have been you. Eddie saved your life. And died for it."

"But I didn't mean to hurt Eddie. I didn't think…"

"Nevertheless," said Richard, "you were responsible for his death."

Just as the Sweetwaters were responsible for Deb Archer's death; just as I was responsible for the death of Marion Locke. Never mind that they didn't mean it, that I didn't mean it. They killed Deb and I killed Marion and that's the truth. And Nicky killed Eddie and he's got to know it.

None of that could be said aloud, not to Nicky and not to

anyone else, but it put an implacable look on Richard's face and made his voice as hard as rock.

Nicky's mouth was trembling. His knees had begun to shake. Something dreadful was going to happen to him, though he didn't know what.

"I didn't mean…" he said again. His voice faltered. Then he saw his father glance toward the table and he saw the riding whip that lay there.

Quentin had followed that glance as well and cried out, "Oh, Father, no, please. Nicky's only little. He couldn't have known—"

"Liza," said Richard, "take yourself and your good kind daughter away. There is no need for either of you to witness this."

"Oh, no, don't, please!" Quentin jumped down from the window seat and ran to Nicky's side, but Peter picked her up bodily and carried her back to Liza. She kicked and struggled and then, as he thrust her into Liza's arms, burst into tears.

"Take her away, Liza. Go on."

"Come, sweetheart." Liza, herself trembling, set Quentin on her feet and with an arm about her, steered her toward the door. "Don't cry so. We can't change anything and we mustn't stay here. We'll wait upstairs."

"Eddie was as good as a son to me," said Betsy grimly. "Cheered me up in the days when I was that miserable over Higg. I'd sooner stay here."

The two main bedchambers were now suspended perilously over space, but the ones at the back of the house were usable. When Quentin and Liza were in the one farthest from the hall, with door and windows closed, Quentin said, "Mother, did you and Father have some idea about…about me and Eddie one day?"

"Yes, dear. We did." Liza sat down on a stool. "How did you know?"

"I liked Eddie. He often came to talk to me when I was spinning or weaving—and once or twice I saw you and Father notice it and smile. It made me wonder."

"You're a sharp little thing! There was talk of it, but Eddie's gone now, Quentin." Had the child cared very much for him? Well, she was still little more than a child, after all. "He died very bravely," said Liza, doing her best to say the right things. "There'll be someone else, one day. You're still very young and you'll stop thinking about him in time. Try not to blame Nicky. He didn't realise what might happen, and at this moment he is learning to do as he's told, and learning the hard way." Liza herself knew how hard a way it was.

"I know." Quentin nodded a serious brown head. "He's so unhappy about Eddie. I've talked to him. I told him it wasn't his fault. Only, Mother...I don't like Jarvis so much."

"Oh!" This at least was easy to deal with. Liza drew Quentin to her and put an arm around her. "If that's what's worrying you, put it out of your mind. We don't think Jarvis would be suitable either. You would never be asked to marry someone you didn't like, anyway."

No, indeed you won't. And if there's someone you really want, one day, I'll do all I can to help you. I know what it's like.

Despite the shut doors and windows, sounds were escaping from the hall. "Oh, no!" said Quentin miserably. Liza held her closer still and sat with bowed head until at last there was the sound of a slammed door, and then feet were running up the stairs, accompanied by a pitiful wailing. Nicky, tears streaming down his freckled face, burst in and rushed to clutch at Liza.

"Father beat me! Why did you let him? Grandfather *held* me, held me down...Betsy and Jarvis and Master Hannacombe watched and they were...they were *pleased*. I'll never forgive them, not any of them! It wasn't fair!"

"It was fair," said Liza. She spoke gently, but as she did so, she detached his hands and held them while she looked into his reproachful golden-brown eyes. Christopher's eyes. "Eddie died because of you. I am sorry for you but it was for your own good."

"No!" screamed Nicky, and sobbed more wildly than ever.

"Yes, Nicky. I mean it."

Nicky, in answer, wrenched himself away from her. He would have run from the room, except that Quentin, slipping from her mother's arm, caught hold of him and pulled him to her.

"Oh, Mother, you said it yourself—he never meant anything dreadful to happen. He never meant Eddie to be hurt. I know he didn't." Her voice shook as she said Eddie's name, but her arm around Nicky was gentle. "Hush, Nicky. Mother, can I use some of your salves to help him?"

"Yes, of course you can. You're a good girl." Liza stood up. "I'll leave him with you for a while. The salves are in my chest— the elderflower ointment's in a little glass pot and the yarrow and woundwort one is in the earthenware box. Quentin will look after you, Nicky. I must go to your father."

She found her husband alone in the hall, sitting by the table with his head in his hands. "Peter?"

"That was the hardest thing I've ever had to do," he said. "My own son. It was as though I were hurting myself. Where is he now?"

"I've left him with Quentin. She's taking care of him. She's very fond of him. She was fond of Eddie, but she has sense enough not to blame Nicky. We're lucky in our daughter. Nicky will be all right soon. Don't think about it anymore."

With a shaky smile Peter said, "Did you give him an apple or a honeycake?"

"No. Not this time."

"Wise of you. Oh, dear God," said Peter miserably, "I want to be proud of my boy. But why did I have to do that to him to make him into the son I want?"

Liza, for a whole tumult of reasons, had no answers and simply, silently, held him fast.

The day after that, while Nicky, lying on his stomach, stayed in bed and Quentin continued to minister to him, Liza joined her husband and father-in-law as they went around the property, discussing how best to repair it.

"It looks," said Richard, "as if I'll have to go in for some new building whether I like it or not, so I've been looking in my coffers and talking to Peter here about the yield from that quarry. We've been saving the rents all these years, too."

"We'll certainly have to build something," Peter said, "but I think we can repair the old house. After all, this is a farm and we're not lordlings."

"I don't agree, boy," said his father. "What do you think I've been saving *for*? Seems to me that fate's telling me to get on and build the fine house I've dreamed of. I was putting it off, thinking of the expense, but I reckon we can do it if we want to."

"I don't want to," said Peter frankly.

"Well, I do. We can demolish what's left of the old house bit by bit, as we go along, and use the stone—the way we did with the stone from that old cottage when we had the hall built. We won't put the new place where the old house is—a flood that can happen once can happen again—but behind the hall, where it's higher. The ground there is flattish for quite a way before the hill rises again. I've plenty of ideas. I've been working them out for years. Come with me."

Peter caught Liza's eye and rolled his eyes in annoyance but Richard, oblivious, marched them both into the hall and began to expound on his ideas.

"You know my plan always was to have the hall as a part of the new house. We can lift the roof higher and put bedchambers over the top with windows looking out of gables, like the ones at Sweetwater House. It'll look fine. And perhaps instead of leaving the outer door of the hall in a recess as it is now, we could have a little porch jutting out, with another small gable over the top, to match the ones over the hall. And see, come here and look through this window…there's room enough between here and the hillside for a couple of wings, going off at right angles…."

"Father, what *is* all this going to cost?" said Peter, aghast.

Richard ignored him. "One wing can have the kitchen, dairy and cider press in it and we'll make a spiral staircase going up to an apple store and servants' rooms above. Liza will need more help in the house—I realise that. The other wing can lead from the other end of the hall—over here…."

He led the way, gesticulating. "We can have a workroom in this one, on the ground floor—or two rooms, a study for doing accounts and a room for weaving, if you like, Liza—and some spare bedchambers above. We'll have a straight, wide staircase here, in this corner of the hall, going up to the spare rooms and a door leading into the workrooms below. And I think—yes, come this way, back to the other end—I'll have a chapel built onto the hall with a little tower above it...."

"Father!"

"We'll put stained glass windows in the chapel," said Richard, unheeding, "and Father Matthew will come and say Mass there once in a while and Liza, you can have a parlour or a solar, as the Sweetwaters would call it, above the chapel, looking out across the combe to the moor. The tower can have battlements at the top, just like the Sweetwaters have...."

"Father, this is absurd!" Peter was really angry now. He moved in front of Richard and stood there, hands on hips, glowering. "We shan't have a coin left to call our own at the end of it and what's it all for? Just to show off, to score off the Sweetwaters! All we really need is a house to replace the one that's been damaged."

"Don't argue with me, boy. I'm master of Allerbrook and I know what I want and I mean to have it!"

"No!" Peter, by now, was shouting. "No, we don't need this and we shouldn't waste money on it. I've hoped, all these years, that you'd just forget this idea! Well, I've decided to stand my ground, just for once. The money you're proposing to use will come mostly from that quarry, and that's *my* quarry, presented to me by Richard of Gloucester for *my* services on a battlefield. You've no right to be so free with it and for such a useless purpose. I am telling you—"

"You'll tell me nothing, boy. You'll do as I say or leave Allerbrook."

"Oh...*no!*" whispered Liza, pulling at Peter's sleeve.

"If I leave Allerbrook," said Peter dangerously, "I'll take with me the deeds to that land with the quarry on it."

"I think not," said Richard. "Sons should do as their fathers tell them and any property that comes into this family is for me to control. The deeds are locked up in my personal chest. I put them there long ago. It was after we sold that other farm to get the Allerbrook freehold. You left them out on the workroom table and I put them away. I told you I'd put them away safe. You never questioned it."

"They still belong to me!"

"To us," said Richard. "Now let be. You're upsetting Liza here. She don't want to be made to leave Allerbrook, do you, Liza?"

"No, I don't!" Liza stared at him, wide-eyed with alarm. For the first time, it struck her that in spite of everything, Allerbrook, once so alien, once nothing but a place of exile from Christopher, had somehow become home. "No, of course not! *No!*"

"And nor does Peter here, not really, do you, boy?"

Peter ground his teeth.

"I need my fine house," said Richard. "I've saved every penny I can, these nine years past. I've drawn plans and then torn them up and drawn new plans. I tell you, the whole thing's been growing in my head. Peter will like it well enough once it's built. Oh, yes, you will, boy. Before I'm done, I'll put those damned Sweetwaters in the shade for good and all."

"I despair of you," said Peter. "No, I don't want to leave Allerbrook, and since you're my father, I can't fight you. But before God...!" He left the sentence unfinished and strode away. Presently Liza heard him chopping firewood, with all the vehemence and fury he could not direct against Richard.

CHAPTER TWENTY-EIGHT 🌀

WHIRLIGIG

"So there it is," said Walter Sweetwater to his son and grandson, finding them in the stable yard when he came in from exercising his horse. He dismounted and handed his reins to a groom. "I've just been up Allerbrook combe to see for myself, and yes, Richard Lanyon's finished his house and there it stands. Bah!"

"Well, we knew what he was up to. I've taken the odd glance at it myself," Baldwin said. "Though not lately. I hoped it would all come to a stop, that Lanyon would be standing below when a lump of badly placed masonry fell off the wall, or at least that he'd run out of money halfway."

"He managed it quicker than when he built the hall, by a good bit!" said Walter irritably. "Though no doubt he had his troubles. Last time I caught sight of him, I saw his hair had gone white. I've also heard he's had a noisy quarrel or two with his son about the cost. Peter Lanyon seems to have more sense than his father. It must have taken every farthing they've got. But he's done it. There's smoke rising from the chimneys and I saw a couple of windows open."

"I wonder what the inside is like?" said his sixteen-year-old grandson.

"My dear John, I doubt if we'll be invited in!" Walter said. "They don't challenge us when we ride across Allerbrook land, but I've seen a few dirty looks from men in the fields. It still feels weird, knowing it isn't my land anymore. I made sure today that I got a good view of the outside of the house, anyhow. It's an imitation of ours—gables, crenellated tower and all."

"I'd heard that," Baldwin said. "From Denis."

Denis Sawyer, the stocky, quiet-spoken former archer who had replaced Geoffrey Baker as steward after Towton, drank regularly in the White Hart. Unlike the talkative Maude, who had now gone away with her mistress to Agnes's married home, he didn't gossip about Sweetwater business. What he did do was listen to other people gossiping, and then report what he heard.

"I sometimes think I'd like to sit in a corner of the White Hart and watch Denis collecting news," Walter said. "I think he sits there, quiet as a cat at a mouse hole, paws folded and ears twitching. But—" he grinned suddenly "—I wonder if he picked up this titbit? Gables and battlements or not, the front rooms upstairs, under the gables, look straight onto the farmyard, complete with hens and a cattle byre and a very good view of the pigsty. Likely enough they're the best bedchambers. I suppose you could say it has a comic side to it!" He glanced around him. "Where is Denis now, by the way? Not back from Dunster market yet? Your Catherine will be wanting her new cloth and her spices, Baldwin."

"They're not urgent. No, he's not back." Baldwin, scowling, was not interested in Denis, cloth or the household supplies of pepper and ginger. "Whatever the Lanyons can see from the windows, that house is like a glove thrown in our faces. One day, one of us will pick up the gage."

John said mildly, "Does it really matter? They're not our tenants now so why should we care what kind of house they build for themselves?"

His seniors regarded him with irritation. He was a Sweetwater as far as his solid build was concerned, but he had Catherine's dark hair, and his well-shaped blue eyes were hers, too. He also had something of her sweet-natured temperament, which was becoming in a woman but completely unsuitable in a Sweetwater male.

"He's an upstart," said Walter. "It doesn't do to have peasants saying they are gentlemen and gentlemen forced into penury." The amount he had spent to get Agnes married and the means by which he had acquired it would rankle for the rest of his life. Also, the Sweetwaters had gained nothing from the marriage. Agnes had become wholly a Northcote and had brought no valuable contacts or lucrative posts within reach of her blood relatives. She wrote to them now and then; that was all.

"A man should stay where God has put him," said Walter virtuously. "Social whirligigs are unhealthy. They make plain men restive, and who will till the fields if the labourers think themselves too grand?"

"That whole family has pretensions," said Baldwin furiously. "I hate the Lanyons. One day, our chance will come."

"But…" John was clearly about to express a point of view not in accordance with Sweetwater tradition. His father and grandfather, recognising the symptoms, turned to him frowning, but the threatening argument was disarmed by the clatter of hooves as Denis Sawyer rode in, followed by a groom leading a well-laden pack pony.

"Ah, here's Denis," said Walter, not altogether displeased by the interruption. He was now fifty-six, and sometimes, to his own annoyance, felt wearied by things which in the past had stimulated him, and his dislike of the Lanyons was on that list. Heartily as he loathed them, he no longer had the energy to do more than abuse them verbally, and he didn't like family disputes, either. Baldwin was the one with the violent passions now.

"Sir!" Sawyer began to talk while he was still in the saddle. "Sir, there's news! It's running through Dunster like fire in peat. There's not much doubt that it's true! King Edward is dead!"

The news was brought to Allerbrook by Ned Crowham, who rode from his home on purpose to tell them. "Because you live so far from anywhere—I wondered if you'd heard," he said as they welcomed him in. "I don't visit you often enough myself. It's twenty miles of wilderness and I feel I'm travelling to the moon. In winter I don't even try. It's only when spring arrives that I can face the thought of it. Isabel the Second sends her kind greetings," he added with a smile.

Except for putting on yet more weight he was still, at nearly forty-four, recognisably the Ned Crowham he had been at nineteen when he came to George Lanyon's funeral, even though he had long since lost his own father and was now Sir Ned Crowham of Crowham in east Somerset, and had added substantially to his family estates through a couple of wealthy marriages. His first wife had died young of a wasting sickness, leaving him with no children but in possession of the valuable Dorset manor which had been her dowry. His second wife had presented him with three sons and another valuable manor in Nottinghamshire. He travelled a good deal between the three counties where he owned land.

As it happened, both his wives had been named Isabel, for which reason Ned usually referred to his present spouse as Isabel the Second. He was still fond of a joke, though he took life more seriously now that he was a man of property and had served at court. On his occasional visits to Allerbrook, both Peter and Liza had noticed how, now and then, if some political subject arose in conversation, his eyes would become expressionless and his face very still, as though he were thinking over things that he knew but did not wish to share.

He had come to share knowledge this time, however, and when Peter said, "But how did the king die? What happened? He wasn't an old man," Ned knew the answer.

"He went fishing, got wet, caught cold, was gone in a week," said Ned. "Spring weather can be treacherous. Ninth of April, that was the date..." On the verge of taking a seat, he turned away and went back to the door, pushing it open. "Listen!".

"What is it?" Peter came to his side.

"Church bells, down in Clicket. Father Matthew is tolling a death. The news was hard behind me, clearly."

"I'll send Nicky to tell my father. He and Jarvis are out seeing to the lambing. Where's Nicky?" Peter asked as Liza, who had gone to fetch food and drink, came back into the hall with a tray.

"In the stable cleaning harness with Hodge. I'll give him the message."

"Oh, send Hodge and let Nicky finish his work." Peter took

his friend's arm and led him back to the comfort of a seat by the fire. "Hard work's good for him. How do you like our new house, now that it's finished, Ned? We've got extra people to help us run it, too."

It wouldn't, Liza knew, be wise to say as much to Richard and she never had, but the two years and four months it had taken to bring the new Allerbrook House into being had, in her opinion, been two years of purgatory.

It had been bad enough at the beginning, when they just lived in the few habitable rooms of the old house. They were squeezed for space even though they cleared a barn to use as a dairy, and the ominous creaking every time they trod on certain upstairs floorboards which extended into the damaged rooms at the front had worried her badly. It was impossible to hold any gatherings or even invite the Hannacombes to dine. But as time went on, things became still worse. Richard had held to his plan of knocking the old house down bit by bit in order to use the stone. He had decided to buy from the quarry he had used when building the hall, rather than bring supplies in from Peter's, partly because it was a better match in colour, and partly to save on transport costs.

"Though five miles is quite far enough," he said. "And stone's costly to start with. We'd better not waste our ruined farm-house."

They could not knock the farmhouse down and simultaneously live in it, and before long the Lanyons had been obliged to camp—there was no other word for it, Liza said bitterly to herself—mostly in the hall. She arranged beds at one end, pushing tables and seating to the other. The place still looked congested, especially as her loom had to be put in the hall, as well. No guests could be asked there, either.

The process of demolishing the farmhouse was difficult, too, for the massive walls could be broken only by levering the stones loose one at a time, with crowbars. Or, as Peter said grimly, by a boulder crashing down a steep hillside with a flood to help it on its way, but they couldn't conjure that up to order.

The masons were not a problem. When the hall was built, they had been accommodated in the farmhouse; this time they took lodgings in Clicket. Once again, however, there were hitches with the waggons which brought the stone. No wheels came off this time, but the brakes on one waggon broke on a steep downhill stretch of track and the driver prevented a bad accident only by turning his ox team and urging them up a bank. The waggon stopped but toppled sideways, spilling half its load. Neither the oxen nor the men in charge were harmed, but once more there was a long delay while repairs were carried out. Richard's curses when he heard of it bordered on the blasphemous.

When the work was finally finished, Liza ventured one complaint, half a joke. "The air's still full of stone dust and sawdust. I doubt I'll ever get it out of the linen, or even out of my lungs!"

There was a grim truth behind the jest, for Roger never did get the dust out of his lungs. He and Kat, of course, had their own cottage, but they were often at the farmstead and the haze that continually hung over the site made Roger cough. Before the new house was finished, he took to his bed and died of a choking phlegm. Kat, after a few angry words flung at Richard's head, went to live with a married daughter in Lynmouth.

"I'll stop on," Betsy said. "I've been here so long I don't want to move. But it seems to me that 'ee've paid for this here house with lives, Eddie's and Roger's, and it'll bring bad luck in the end, mark what I say."

"Don't talk nonsense!" Richard barked, but added that he knew the house and farm couldn't be run with so few people, and ordered Peter to find two more men and two more maidservants. "We've room for them now that we've moved in, as it were."

It was September, the time of year for hiring fairs, so Peter went to one and came back with two farmhands called Hodge and Alfred, and a pair of jolly young sisters named Phoebe and Ellen.

Alfred was stolid, amiable, a sound worker and not given to wenching, but Hodge and Phoebe were now married, of necessity, since Hodge, far from being stolid, was good-looking and silver-tongued, and almost the first thing he did at Allerbrook was to get Phoebe with child.

"Bad luck, like I said" was Betsy's comment.

"Bloody careless," said Richard, and Jarvis Hannacombe, who—because the girl preferred another swain and passed her condition off as his responsibility—had narrowly escaped enforced matrimony with a lass in Clicket, put on a prim face and said, "Not the right thing at all, fouling his own doorstep, like."

"He's good with the sheep," said Richard, "and Phoebe's a wantwit to let it happen. But she's handy with a broom, I'll say that for her. They can have Kat's cottage, and no more talk of bad luck, Betsy, if you please!"

The new Lanyon household had shaken down together and they had been in their completed new home now for a week. To Liza, it was an immense relief.

It was even possible, she thought, now that life was returning to normal, that everything else would return to normal, too.

Maybe Nicky would even become his trustful, affectionate, if sometimes disobedient self again.

The beating after the death of Eddie had been reinforced at times by further beatings from his grandfather. Peter took no part in these but did nothing to prevent them, either. "My father may be right. I just don't want to do it myself," he had said to Liza when she protested.

The outcome was that Nicky had now become more or less what Richard and Peter wanted him to be—respectful, hard-working and courteously spoken. Only Liza was aware that the loving side of his nature seemed to have died. He rarely laughed these days, and sometimes she had seen him do something she thought he had learned from Peter (who had demonstrated it frequently after arguments with his father about the expense of the new house), which was to chop wood or do some other physical task with furious violence, as though to relieve a secret rage.

Well, the news of the king's death ought to distract all of them. "What will happen?" she asked when she returned from sending Hodge with the message.

"The king's elder son is in Ludlow, up in Shropshire," said Ned. "He will be brought to London and crowned, I suppose. Richard of Gloucester is the Protector of the Realm until the prince comes of age. He's in Yorkshire, but I imagine he'll be sent for. There may be trouble."

"Why trouble?" Peter asked. "The succession's clear enough."

"Gloucester will control the country and Gloucester loathes the queen's family, the Woodvilles," said Ned simply. "And they've got half the good posts in the kingdom. They've also had charge of the elder prince until now. His maternal uncle, Anthony Lord Rivers, is his guardian. It's an interesting state of affairs. Let us hope it doesn't lead to fighting."

★ ★ ★

"If it does lead to fighting," said Herbert Dyer to his son Simon, "you might have to go. You're only thirty-five. We'd better pray for peace. I don't like these rumours that the Woodvilles tried to keep control of the king's person."

"Gloucester seems to have dealt with them. The queen's in sanctuary, one of her sons has fled the country and her brother Lord Rivers is under arrest. Though I don't suppose Prince Edward is any too grateful for that," said Simon. "Rivers looked after him in Ludlow. However, if it comes to the point and the Protector calls for extra men, I'll do my duty, as all honest men should."

It was a sour joke, understood only by the two of them. Since Richard's ultimatum, years ago, their workshop had been so extremely honest in its dealings that Herbert Dyer and his son had acquired a shining reputation for miles around. They had been complimented on it often and publicly. On the whole, it had been worthwhile, since it had brought in business enough to compensate for the money that virtue had lost them.

But Herbert, lying at night in his solitary bed, missed Margaret so intensely that he rarely spoke of her, because to do so made the wound of her loss throb so very badly. He would never forget the bitter words with which they had parted. To his life's end, he would regret the things he had said to her, and shrink from remembering the things she had said to him. It had been the interfering Lanyons' fault. He would never forgive them for dividing him from Margaret.

Nor would either he or Simon ever forget or forgive the threat that Richard held over them. Simon's wife, who knew nothing of the threat or what had led to it, sometimes heard them make sardonic jests about honesty and was often puzzled. She remained puzzled to the end of her days, for they never told her the truth.

★ ★ ★

News usually reached Dunster Castle promptly. The son of
the Earl of Pembroke who had died before Barnet and Tewkesbury were fought, another William Herbert who was now Earl
of Huntingdon, took marginally more interest in the castle than
his father had. He had never set foot in the place, either, but he
styled himself Lord Dunster and he recognised a political crisis
when he saw one and wished to be prepared for trouble if it
came. That meant preparing any castles which happened to be
in his charge.

When he learned, firstly, that Richard of Gloucester had
executed Lord Rivers, the young king's maternal uncle and erstwhile guardian, and then, astoundingly, that someone (rumour
pointed fingers at Gloucester himself and also at Robert Stilling-
ton, the Bishop of Bath and Wells, a diocese which included
Dunster itself) was casting doubt on the lawfulness of the late
king's marriage and therefore on the legitimacy of his two sons,
Lord Dunster sent his orders. These were accompanied by money
with which to carry them out and a squad of men to reinforce
the skeleton garrison at Dunster.

The castle was to be put into a state of defence, with cross-
bows and cannon; the storerooms were to be filled with non-
perishable food, the walls were to be checked and trees which
might help an enemy gain entrance were to be cut down. Father
Christopher and Miles Hilton, who had been in charge of the
castle hitherto, and to some extent still were because they knew
it thoroughly while the captain of the new garrison did not,
found themselves extremely busy.

On the day Christopher had so graphically pointed out the
shortcomings of the castle maintenance, adding the fact that he was

strong enough to put pressure on Master Hilton in a most direct and physical manner, Hilton had been furious. However, time and some diplomacy on Christopher's part had eroded this somewhat.

"I don't mean that *you* ought to get behind a broom or take to mending tapestries," Christopher had said reasonably. "Only that you ought to make other people do it."

As it chanced, a few months after that Hilton found himself a wife, the bright young widow of a Dunster woodworker. The woodworker had been much older than she was, well established in his trade, and of a saving disposition. Dying, he left her with a coffer full of silver. On her side, Mistress Anne Fry was accustomed to keep her house neat and when she joined her new husband at the castle, saw no reason that shouldn't be kept neat, as well. Mistress Anne had done a great deal to smooth the friction between priest and steward.

Now, while the political news turned into a whirligig, with power spinning from boy king to Woodvilles to Richard of Gloucester, Christopher and Hilton worked in double harness in something like accord. Both were equally horrified when, at length, a messenger on a tired horse clattered up the long slope to the gatehouse to announce that the Duke of Gloucester was now King Richard III and that the young ex-king Edward and his brother were lodged in the Tower of London out of the public eye, and King Richard's coronation would be on July 6.

"There'll be risings, sooner or later," said Hilton as he and Christopher stood on the walls looking out over Dunster High Street and watching the everyday traffic below, of people on ponies and people on foot, coming and going. For all his idle airs, Miles Hilton was politically sharp enough. "Boys turn into men. The princes have been dispossessed and they won't forget it and nor will

a good many others. A party will gather round them as they grow
up. There are still Woodvilles in influential places and they'll lead
the way. Trouble's coming, for sure. That is, *if* the boys grow up."

"You mean...but they're King Edward's sons!" Christopher
was scandalised. "Gloucester was always faithful to Edward.
Loyalty Binds Me is his motto."

"King Edward's dead," said Hilton. "But Gloucester may
prefer to stay alive, and if there were to be a successful rising on
behalf of those boys, I doubt if he'd live long. Besides, he's inured
to such things. King Henry VI died very conveniently, after
Tewkesbury. Very conveniently. Nothing could have drawn the
She-Wolf's teeth as effectively as that. All her wars were to put
him back on the throne so that she could be the power behind
it, and in the fullness of time, behind their son. But the son was
killed on the field, and as for King Henry—do you remember
the proclamations? That he had died of displeasure and melancholy? No one believed a word of it. King Edward only let the
French king ransom *her* because she could do no more harm."

"Yes. I heard that she died a year or so back," Christopher
said. "As King Louis' pensioner, and apparently it wasn't much
of a pension. But the boys would be a different matter. Dispossessed kings are likely to turn into dead kings—that's what you
mean, isn't it?"

"Yes, I do. Those boys are lodged in the Tower. What if
something happened to them there? Who, outside it, would
know exactly what? No one knows for sure what happened to
the other royal brother—George of Clarence—the one who kept
betraying King Edward. He was shut in the Tower and supposed
to have drunk himself to death on Greek malmsey, but how does
anyone know?"

"It's horrible," Christopher said. "Those two boys have done no wrong, apart from being born to a king who died before they were old enough to fight for themselves. Their poor mother!"

"Ah, well. Some people still remember the Earl of Desmond's two little sons," Hilton said sardonically.

"But these boys weren't responsible for that!" Christopher drummed his fingers on top of the wall, and then sighed. "There'd be public fury if word got round that the boys had come to harm, but without a rival to put up against King Richard, what could anyone do? There are no Lancastrian claimants left."

"But there are," said Hilton.

Christopher was startled enough to step back from the wall and turn to the steward in astonishment. "Are there? Who?"

"Well, there's one, anyway. Descended from John of Gaunt, Edward III's third son. It's a senior line to the house of York. His mother's Margaret Beaufort, Gaunt's great-granddaughter." Hilton seemed to have royal genealogy at his command. "That line's been attainted and cut out of the succession but attainders can be reversed—by law or by force. The last Lancastrian's got royal blood on his father's side, too, though not English blood."

"But who are you talking about?" asked Christopher.

"Did you ever hear about Catherine of France, queen to King Henry V? When he died, she married a Welsh minstrel called Owen Tudor. She was a French princess by birth. The Lancastrian claimant is her grandson. He's in France now, in exile. Henry Tudor, that's his name."

CHAPTER TWENTY-NINE

HEATHER, GORSE AND HENRY TUDOR

The news that England was now ruled by King Richard III rather than King Edward V, caused both surprise and disapproval at Allerbrook.

"Can it really be true?" Liza wondered. "If it is, then he's stolen the throne from his brother's children!"

"That's what's being said in Dunster, and they get their news from the castle and the priory." Richard, primed with information, had just returned from a visit to Dunster.

"If the children aren't lawful…" said Liza doubtfully.

"Bah! All this gossip that the old king had a precontract before he married his queen!" said Richard. "That's been used as an excuse often enough when someone wants to break a marriage, but as an excuse it's never been all that good." Peter had tried to lay claim to it once, he remembered. "Both the parties are dead," he said, "and the only witness, seemingly, is this Bishop Stilling-ton. Bishops have been bribed before this."

"I can't see Gloucester wanting to snatch power and bribing his way to it," protested Peter. "I've met him. I think…"

"Power goes to men's heads, boy," said Richard. "Gloucester was generous to you once, but you weren't standing in his way! Well, he's got the crown. I wonder if he can keep it on his head. There've been rumblings already, from what I hear."

They heard more before long. Ned Crowham might say they lived out in the wilderness and might as well be on the moon, but the years of peace under King Edward had made it easier for news to travel. Time had brought a sense of security, giving people the confidence to move about because they no longer feared they would ride straight into a battle, or be cut off from home by one.

The roads had grown busy with travelling merchants and wool buyers, itinerant pedlars, tooth-drawers and strolling players, and the ships sailing into Bristol Channel ports came from every-where from Plymouth to Palestine. These travellers carried news with them. Sometimes it seemed to be borne on the air like dan-delion seeds, spreading through the population even before well-connected families had heard it from contacts at court and given it to priests like Father Matthew to announce.

"I can see what happened, I think," Peter said, returning one July evening from a fair in Dulverton, where rumours were cir-culating briskly. "The dowager queen's family, the Woodvilles, apparently tried to hold on to the person of the young prince so as to rule through him. Richard stopped that, and there were exe-cutions. Well, one of them was Prince Edward's favourite uncle! People are saying that if the boy had been crowned, the first thing he'd have wanted when he was old enough to take power—and it wouldn't have been long—would have been his uncle Richard's head on a nice silver platter, and *that's* why Gloucester stepped in and took the crown himself. It was self-defence, not ambition."

"Well, it's no business of ours," his father said. "A bit of peace and stability, that's what we all need. And plenty of demand for stone," he added. Despite the cost of the new house (and Peter's dire predictions that they would all end up as beggars), the quarry was doing so well that the Lanyons had been able to afford some extra land, in Hampshire this time. Two farms and a village stood on it, and the rents would repay the price of it in due course. Meanwhile, the quarry went on making money. "I told you so," said Richard to Peter, rather too often.

The name of Henry Tudor was spoken in rumour quite frequently and at one point was more than a rumour. Baldwin Sweetwater in fact rode off once to join the defence of the south Devon coast after Tudor had tried to land in Dorset, been driven off and was then said to be approaching Devon. But the attempt failed and Baldwin came home without having drawn his sword. Tudor had been repulsed; the Duke of Buckingham, hitherto King Richard's friend, had tried to raise a rebellion to support Henry Tudor and had been beheaded for his mistake. The trouble faded away.

For the time being.

Two years after the crown had been placed on Richard of Gloucester's head, Henry Tudor landed in earnest.

The day the news reached them, the Lanyons were immersed in a private combat of their own. Unintentionally started by Liza.

It was August 13, and sunny. Crops were ripening and the

cattle grazed contentedly, enjoying the warmth on their backs; every lane was edged with musty pink foxgloves and the moorland glowed with the purple and deep gold of heather and gorse in full bloom, patched here and there by the paler gold of the long moor grass, rippling in the breeze.

Peter and Richard, coming into the hall one morning, found Liza there already, staring at a patch of sunlit panelling and frowning.

"What's amiss, Liza?" her father-in-law asked.

"I was thinking that I wished we had just one tapestry to hang on that wall. There are merchants in Dunster who sell them."

"Not tapestries, not yet," said Richard. "The Sweetwaters don't have much in that way, I believe, so we needn't either. First of all, I want that panelling replaced by something better, with carving on it, and I still haven't managed the stained glass I want for the chapel."

"Well, if we ever do have tapestries," Peter said, "let us have some lively colours. The hues of the moor are worth seeing at this season. The heather's as purple as an emperor's mantle, and the gorse is bright gold. Let's have those."

"God's teeth, what poetic marvellings!" Richard snorted. "Heather? Emperor's mantle? Bright gold gorse! Since when did any of us have time to stand about like gape-mouthed images, gawping at things like that! Tapestries will have to wait!"

Over the years Liza had grown very used to acting as a buffer between her husband and his father, though it was sometimes a tiring business and she was glad that she had kept her health, although she was nearing fifty, and thick around the middle despite her active life. "Perhaps one day," she said pacifically. "What kind of carving had you in mind, Father-in-law?"

Peter cut in before Richard could answer. "Since we *do* have this fine house, though I've always said we didn't need it, we may as well do justice to it. And I'd like to decide something once in a while and not be shouted down. This is my home, too, and Liza's!"

"I've told you before—don't lower your antlers at *me!*" retorted his father. "In this house, I'm the one who says."

"Or shouts," said Peter coldly. "Or strikes."

"Oh, so that's what this is about, is it? So I gave my grandson a reminder or two when I caught him slipping off after he'd been told to help Hodge cut back those brambles. He came running to you, did he?"

"No. I saw, from a distance. You went too far. It wasn't a reminder or two, it was more like a reminder or twelve."

"Don't get clever with me."

"Oh, *please!*" said Liza.

They continued, however, to stand glowering at each other and in the end she decided to seek peace in her workroom. This sort of thing had happened more often of late; it was as though Peter was losing patience after holding himself in for years, and as though her father-in-law's wish to rule his son as if Peter were still a boy was growing on him, like a bad habit.

She never reached the workroom, however, for Quentin, who had been outside collecting eggs, rushed suddenly into the hall without her egg basket, breathless and alarmed. "The beacon on Dunkery's been lit! There's smoke going up!"

"What?" Richard was out in the yard in a moment, the rest of them at his heels. Quentin was right. To the northwest, from Dunkery's purple crest, a column of smoke was pouring into the blue sky.

"But why…what's happened?" said Liza.

Peter said, "I can hear hoofbeats!"

Half a minute later Ned Crowham came in at a gallop, threw himself off his horse and said peremptorily, "It's a call to arms. You've seen the smoke? There go the church bells in Clicket. I was at home in Crowham and a messenger reached me late last night, from my place in the Midlands. Henry Tudor's landed in Wales, with an army. He's marching on to England. I'm gathering my able-bodied tenants and I thought of you, as well. Peter, will you come and bring a man or two with you? We'll have to be quick. Come back to Crowham with me now!"

"You're going? Just like that?" Liza said. "But…"

"I must. Listen—we wouldn't have this house, wouldn't be able to afford half the things we have afforded, but for Gloucester, that's King Richard now, and what he did for me after Tewkesbury. I have to go," Peter said. "Jarvis says he'll come, as well. He's a good shot at the butts. Hodge and Alfred can stay here—someone must get the harvest in. Besides, Hodge is married with two children now and Alfred's courting a girl in Clicket. But I'll come and so will Jarvis. What do you say, Father?"

"Yes, you'd better go, and take one fellow with you at least. Liza, stop standing there looking as if someone's banged you on the head, and go and put his things together. I'll look for the old sword and helmet for you, Peter."

"What's happening? Is it a war?" Nicky, who had been in the fields, ran into the yard. "I saw the smoke from the beacon!" He looked in wonder at Ned and his sweating horse.

"Not for long," said Ned. "King Richard will see the Tudor off if he has men enough. Your father and Jarvis are coming with me. The king's at Nottingham and that's where we're going."

"Can I come? I'm big enough to fight. I've got a bow of my own now and a dagger, too!"

"Certainly not!" Liza, turning to go indoors as Richard had bidden her, swung around again in a swirl of skirts and clamped a hand on her son's shoulder. "You're far too young! Ned! Peter! Say something!"

"King Richard was riding about raising help for the king when he was younger than this lad is," Ned remarked. "And we always have boys looking after the baggage. He could be useful."

"*No!*" said Liza passionately.

"I agree. He's too young," said Peter. "Go inside, Nicky, and help to find my war gear."

"But I don't want to be left here with Grandfather!" Nicky shouted.

"Oh, so that's it! Well, you'd find a battle a lot more frightening than your grandfather is," Peter said frankly. "You stay home and practise doing as you're told. Go and help your granddad. *Now!*"

"Why didn't you leave us alone?" said Liza furiously to Ned. "Why must Peter go? He's not a tenant of yours, or anyone's! The Sweetwaters will go, I expect, but we don't have to follow them now!"

"I'm not following them," said Peter. "I'm following Ned, if you like, but it's out of gratitude to King Richard. I never wanted this house, but our prosperity made it possible and yes, I do like the prosperity. Well, it's due to him. Now, Liza, don't let your face crumple like that. Let us get my packing done."

It had happened so fast that Liza felt giddy. One moment they had been arguing about tapestries. The next, Peter was wearing a helmet and a sword, saddling Plume and saying farewell. Plume, though old, was still very much alive, unlike Magpie, who had died a year ago. Richard had a new horse now, another piebald, called Patches. Peter, however, was content with his pony and didn't intend to go into battle on horseback anyway. Jarvis, he said, could take one of the other ponies.

That suited him, Jarvis said. It looked to Liza as though Jarvis regarded the whole expedition as an adventure, an interesting break from his normal routine. Peter said goodbye with a grave face, but when, saddlebags bulging, the two of them rode away with Ned Crowham, Jarvis went off smiling.

They were gone, and who was to say when they would ever eat at the Allerbrook table again? Peter was forty-six now, not a young man anymore, not as fit for fighting as he was. Richard was irritable, probably because he was worried about Peter though he wouldn't actually say so.

Quentin was tearful and Nicky, angry because he had been left behind, sulked all evening and she made him go to bed early to keep him out of Richard's way.

She and Quentin went to bed not long afterward. Whether Quentin slept or not, Liza didn't know, but she herself did not. The long, slow hours of darkness went by and she hoped that Peter was at least in a comfortable bed in Crowham this night. She missed his presence, the comfort of his body next to hers. They no longer made love frequently; as the years went on, their daily work drained them more and at night they were usually content to embrace briefly and then fall asleep, but they gave each other company. The empty place beside her ached.

She began at last to drift toward sleep but then woke, abruptly, to find the world dark and silent, and yet with the certainty that she had been roused by a noise. The dogs weren't barking, but they had been out all day and were now asleep in the kitchen. She sat up, listening. Yes, the hens were cackling. Something was wrong. Flinging off her covers, she went to look out the window.

She and Peter had one of the best bedchambers and, as Walter Sweetwater had so disparagingly remarked, it overlooked the farmyard. As she pushed the window open, the noise from the henhouse grew louder. At the same moment, the window in the neighbouring gable opened and Richard's white head peered out of it. He noticed her and turned toward her, pressing a finger to his lips and then pointing.

Liza, peering accordingly, saw a slinking shadow close to the henhouse and then, momentarily, the brush of a fox showed in the moonlight. Glancing sideways, she saw that Richard had disappeared, but even as she looked, she saw a crossbow protrude from his window instead. He took aim and loosed the bolt. The Sweetwaters had said that he didn't aim as true as he used to do, but he was as good a shot over short distances as he had ever been, and the fox had come unwisely close. There was a screech from below and something flopped out of the shadows into the moonlight, twisted, cried and then lay still.

"I'll go down and finish it off if need be," said Richard, sticking his head out again. "Go back to bed."

Liza went back to her couch and this time slept, until she was awakened early in the morning by Quentin anxiously shaking her. "Mother—wake up! Please wake up!"

"What is it?" Liza sat up again. It was just dawn and time to milk the cows, but that was work, these days, for Quentin and Ellen. Liza allowed herself a little longer to rest in the morning now.

Quentin's face was worried. "Mother, I went out with Ellen to see to the cows, but as we passed the pony field I couldn't see

Nicky's pony, Sunset! Sunset's the only bay pony we have just now, and it wasn't there! I sent Ellen on to fetch the cows and I went to the harness room. Nicky's saddle and bridle are gone, as well."

"What?" Liza was already out of bed. "Have you looked in Nicky's room?"

"Yes, I did that at once, as I came in, before I came to you. His door wasn't quite shut. I called but he didn't answer, so I looked in. I don't think he slept in his bed last night and his clothes weren't there! You know how he just tosses them across a stool."

Memory flooded back. The sound that had woken her had been mixed up with a dream and only now was she recalling the dream, a muddled fantasy of searching for Peter through a strange, dark house. He was always ahead of her, sometimes in sight, but she couldn't catch up and he kept going through doorways and shutting doors in her face.

Nicky, creeping out, had left his own door ajar for the sake of quietness, but he must have shut the harness-room door after fetching his pony's tack. In the hushed moonlit night, the sound had carried. And then the fox had come and upset the hens, providing another explanation. Meanwhile, Nicky had got away.

"But where can he have gone, Mother?" Quentin was asking.

"I would guess," said Liza, "that he's gone to Crowham. He could be there by now. Is your grandfather awake? I think he'll have to go after Nicky."

In the big stable yard at Ned Crowham's manor house, horses were being groomed and saddled, armed men were talking in clusters and the air was full of a sense of departure. Isabel the Second and her women servants were walking among them, offering stirrup cups. Isabel was pale, but she came of a family whose menfolk went to war as a matter of course, and she knew how to seem cheerful. Ned would have his way, she knew. He wanted to fight and had gathered men to go with him, and all she could do now was wait for news and his return, if return he did.

They were all astonished when a solitary redheaded figure on a very tired pony rode in through the gate, paused to look around and then spurred his pony over to where Peter and Ned stood in conversation, and said, "Hullo, Father, Master Crowham. I've come to join you after all."

"What?" Peter stared at him in horror. "Nicky, what are you doing here? How did you get here? Your mother never gave you permission. I know she didn't!"

"No, I slipped out at night and just rode here. Are you setting off today? Can I have something to eat before we go? I'm awfully hungry."

"You must be tired, too," Ned said. "Can you face a day's riding after a night with no sleep? We're going north to join William Berkeley, Earl of Nottingham. I've land in his earldom and he's my natural leader if there's war in the Midlands. We'll find you something else to ride, because even if you can keep awake all day, you can't ask the same of your pony."

"Ned! What are you talking about? He must eat and rest and then go straight home!" Peter said indignantly. "Haven't you got some older man here, who isn't going with us, who could take him back? Nicky, how dare you behave like this? What your mother and your grandfather will say I dread to think. Come. We must speak to Mistress Crowham and—"

"He'd certainly better snatch some food," Ned said. "We shan't be riding for half an hour or so. There's time."

"What are you talking about? We're not taking Nicky!"

"And I don't want to go home. Grandfather will be angry."

"You'll see angrier men on a battlefield! I told you as much before! Why didn't you listen?" Peter thundered. "Ned, he's not to come. I can't understand why you seem willing to take him!"

"You may understand presently," said Ned, and to Peter's astonishment, that curious, closed expression which he had sometimes noticed before on Ned's face, when some matter of state was being discussed, was there again. His friend's blue eyes were blank and even chilly. "Oh, yes." He put a hand on Peter's shoulder. "I have a reason. Nicky could be very useful. I'll do my best to see he comes to no harm. But there are other boys of his age coming with us. A lad should start learning men's business as soon as he's old enough to understand it. We'll take him along."

Richard came back in the evening on Patches, leading Nicky's pony, but with an empty saddle.

"They'd already left Crowham," he said as soon as he came into the hall. "They'd ridden away long before I got there. The pony was tired and they wanted to go fast, so they'd given Nicky something else to ride. Isabel told me. I hadn't a hope of catching up. But he'll be all right! The boys stay behind to guard the baggage when an army goes into the field. Nicky will come back all right and he'll find me waiting for him."

The unspoken message was *but Peter may not come back.* Richard's face, under his snowy hair, was drawn with worry but not for Nicky. Liza on the other hand was terrified for them both and fear made her flare into anger. "Why didn't Peter send him home? *Why?*"

"God knows. I don't," said Richard, sitting down on the nearest seat and presenting his dusty boots to be removed. Liza brushed tears from her eyes and helped him off with them. If Peter were to walk in at that moment, she didn't know whether she would run to him or throw something at him. What if she lost both husband and child?

Suddenly and quite unexpectedly, she was seized with a need to get away from Allerbrook. It was home now, had been for many years, but without Peter it lacked human sympathy. She needed her kinfolk. She wanted to go to Dunster and be with her own family again, with people who would sympathise. She knew Richard was afraid for his son and grandson, but she knew, too, that he would never seek comfort, or give it, either, and she was frightened as well and could have done with comforting.

As she returned to the hall, Richard expressed a wish for some cider. Liza fetched it, carrying the tankard to him with a smile of deceptive sweetness. After all, if she were to visit Dunster, she would need her father-in-law's permission.

CHAPTER THIRTY

THE RED DRAGON

"No!" said Peter. "I can't believe what you're saying, Ned. I've met Gloucester—King Richard. It's just rumour, wicked tattle, and it's no reason to…what you want us to do is treachery, don't you understand? I can't and I won't. Nor will Jarvis."

"Jarvis Hannacombe, I have no doubt, will do what you bid him."

"Then I shall bid him stay with me and fight on the side of the king of England and the house of York. I'll take him and Nicky and leave this inn at once. We'll find the Earl of Nottingham and—"

"Inform him that there's a little detachment of forty men under Sir Edward Crowham, occupying the Sign of the Azure Dove outside Leicester, and they intend to slip off to join Henry Tudor tomorrow morning? I'm sorry, Peter, but I think not."

"You…!" Peter looked about him. They were outside in the innyard, where Ned had brought him, saying that he wanted a private word. The rest of the company, two score or so strong, were inside the inn, which they had virtually commandeered, eating a late supper and drinking ale. The only guests at the inn who were not part of Crowham's following were a small party of tumblers, who were seizing the chance to earn a few pence for entertaining the rest. The light was fading and candles gleamed within the hostelry. Beyond the stone arch of the gateway the dusty road was empty, and opposite were quiet meadows.

They were still some miles short of Leicester, where the king and his lords were, but Ned had halted them here because he said the men must be fresh for the morning. He had sent just two galloping ahead to Leicester and they had returned to say that the royal army would march westward from the city in the morning to meet Henry Tudor, who had advanced through Wales.

As Peter had at first understood it, William Berkeley, Earl of Nottingham, was with the king and his was the banner Ned proposed to follow. They could cut across country tomorrow and join him during the march. Baldwin Sweetwater and his son, John, who had overtaken them on the way, had been pushing on faster, and were probably with him in Leicester already.

But now...

"I don't think you've been listening to me," said Crowham. "Do you think I do this lightly? Don't you know me better than that?"

"I've known you, or so I thought, since I was ten and now I feel I've never really known you at all!"

"King Richard," said Ned, in the very patient voice of one who has tried to make the same point fifty times, without success, "or the Duke of Gloucester as I prefer still to call him, has murdered his brother's sons to keep himself safe on his throne.

He was supposed to be the Protector of the Realm, but he has had the boy who should have been King Edward the Fifth assassinated and the younger brother, too. He put them in the Tower over two years ago and they haven't been seen since. On Exmoor you may hear news but you're still off the main track and you never hear all of it. Every London tavern has seen grown men shed tears, thinking of the fate of those two lads."

"I don't believe it. I will *not* believe it!" Peter struggled for words, remembering the tired, prematurely aged face of the man to whom he had given his horse at Tewkesbury, and the smile in Gloucester's hazel eyes as he'd handed over the deeds which had created Allerbrook's prosperity. "I understood why he had to take the throne—but this! I *can't* believe it. He was devoted to his brother King Edward, and the princes were—are— Edward's sons! His motto was loyalty!"

"Not any longer, I think," said Ned.

"Well, I shall stay loyal! I tell you this, we Lanyons owe him too much to abandon him for a…a…rumour."

"It's more than a rumour. Where *are* those boys? No one has heard or seen them for two years. And Richard, they say, sleeps ill at night."

"I daresay, with filthy slanders being spoken about him and his own troubles. We heard that his wife and his son had both died. That's enough to keep anyone awake at night."

"The elder boy, Prince Edward," said Ned, "had good reason to hate his uncle Gloucester. After the old king died, the Woodvilles tried to snatch power and oversee the boy's crowning. Once the crown was on young Edward's head, the Protectorship would legally have lapsed, though a new one would have had to be set up until the lad was of age. The Woodvilles by all accounts

meant to make sure that the new Protector was one of themselves, and not Gloucester. To stop that, Gloucester beheaded the
boy's Woodville uncle, Anthony Lord Rivers, because he was the
head of the Woodville family. No doubt he thought he was
doing the right thing, but Rivers had been the prince's guardian
and there was affection between them. I've been to court, close
to the heart of things."

"Believe it or not, I've heard all this, as well!" Peter protested.
"I understood why Gloucester took the throne. If the prince
became king, he probably wouldn't have left his uncle Gloucester
alive for long. I realise *that!* But he didn't become king, did he?"

"You haven't thought it out properly. The boys would grow
up—no doubt the younger one would have backed up his
brother—and supporters would inevitably gather round them.
That could start another civil war. I daresay," said Ned coolly,
"that Gloucester felt he had no choice but to rid himself of them.
In his place, I might even have done the same. But I'm not in
his place and I don't greatly care for the murder of young lads
who can't protect themselves."

"And I can't believe it, not of the Gloucester I knew."

"Really? He and King Edward certainly got rid of old King
Henry," said Ned. "And of their own brother Clarence, I suspect.
None of those were young boys, of course, but they were all
helpless prisoners and if you ask me, King Henry was weak in
the head. King Richard is much more used to such things than
you are. You're only used to killing pigs."

"I was at Tewkesbury," said Peter firmly. "And I intend to be
at this battle and *not* on the side of Henry Tudor."

"You will fight for Henry Tudor," said Ned, and now there
was nothing at all left of the Ned Crowham who had been

Peter's schoolfellow. A plump, joke-loving, layabed chrysalis had cracked open and out of it had stepped a lethal, subtle dragon-fly. "You will," he said, "because if you do not, you may never see your son Nicholas again."

"*What?* Are you out of your mind, man? What do you mean, I may never see Nicholas again? He's here in the inn. What the devil are you talking about?"

"A number of my men have a regard for you—I've noticed it. If you go to Leicester to join William Berkeley and Gloucester—"

"The king!" said Peter savagely.

"Berkeley and *Gloucester,* some of them might slip off, as well. Also, you'd deliver a warning and the rest of us might be inter-cepted. I won't have it, Peter. I won't see swords denied to Tudor and extra soldiers going to Gloucester's side. They would strengthen the hand of a murderer, and Tudor has need of swords—and archers and axemen. His forces are too small, even though the Earl of Oxford has joined him now. His stepfather Thomas Stanley may decide to back him up, but Richard is holding one of Stanley's sons as hostage. It's plain enough that he doesn't at all mind making war on mere boys!"

"Neither do you, by the sound of it! What did you mean about Nicky? Tell me!"

"If he prevails," said Ned, ignoring this, "Henry Tudor has sworn to marry the Princess Elizabeth of York—the princes' sister. I suppose you didn't know that. That will unite his line to that of King Edward. York and Lancaster will lie down together in peace at last—literally."

Ned smiled his old familiar smile, now horribly out of place. "Nicky is no longer in the inn," he said. "I had him removed an hour ago. You will not know where he is until the battle is over.

When it is, whatever the outcome, provided you accompany me to Tudor's camp, he'll be sent home. He'll be safe, even if we are not. But you must buy his freedom by lending your sword arm to the Red Dragon."

"To the what?"

"The Tudor's standard is a red dragon. If you refuse to fight beneath it…"

"You…you…" Peter could not think of any epithet which did justice to this. "You talk of young boys being murdered or held hostage by Richard, but in almost the same breath you threaten to kill Nicky! Nicky's a young boy—he's only thirteen! He—"

"I'm not going to kill him! Don't be a fool. I own ships. Three of them, to be precise. They ply in and out of Dorset, where I also have land. If you fail me, Nicky will be taken to Dorset and sent to sea as a ship's boy. He may flourish or he may not, but it's no easy life for a lad fresh from loving parents, on a peaceful farm. My people in Nottingham have had their orders and will see that Nicky is taken to Dorset or sent home in accordance with my wishes—and your behaviour. Whether I live or die, and whether you live or die. Our fates will make no difference."

Peter's sword was at his side. He drew it instinctively, and then saw that after all, he and Ned were not quite alone in the innyard. Four figures came out of the shadows by the stable and seized hold of him.

"No, Peter," Ned said. "You will not harm me. You will sleep tonight on a wide pallet that these trusty fellows will share with you. If you stir, so will they. They are Crowham men. I've known them all my life and they're the best of human watchdogs. They will see that you don't come near me. They won't stop you from slipping out of the inn. They won't even stop you from collecting Jarvis and taking him with you. But if you do, you know what will happen."

The curse that Peter now pronounced on Ned was comprehensive, and most men would have flinched from it. Many would have stepped backward, crossing themselves or making the sign against the Evil Eye. Ned Crowham did not move. "I mean it," he said. To his men, he said, "Watch him. You know what to do." With that, he turned away and walked back into the inn.

"Now, better just come along and take some supper and get some sleep," said one of the watchdogs amiably. He had a Somerset voice, burring and good-natured, tending to turn *s*'s into *z*'s. His advice actually sounded like *take zome zupper and get zome zleep.* It was an accent Peter had heard all his life; indeed, it was his own, though his was not so marked. To hear it under these circumstances was like seeing Dunkery Beacon turned upside down and balanced on its summit.

But there was Nicky. His son and Liza's and the only son that Allerbrook had. He went into the inn.

It was very difficult to believe that this was happening. What on earth, Peter asked himself despairingly, was he doing here, marching among the foot soldiers behind the stars and streams of the Earl of Oxford's banner, about to fight against Richard of Gloucester, for Henry Tudor? How had he ever been dragged into such a position?

Because Nicky, confound him, had never learned to do as he was bid, not even under the heavy hand of his grandfather. Because Nicky had run away to join the army and was now Ned's captive and the lever by which Peter was to be forced to fight where Ned wished.

It was the second morning after the confrontation at the inn. Ned had marched them all out at daybreak, leading them westward across rolling country. Dusk was falling when they reached an encampment, where cooking fires burned and there were tents with banners flying above them. The stars and streams of Oxford flew over one tent. Over another, and the sight of it sent a thrill of sheer horror through Peter, was a scarlet dragon. To Peter, it was the enemy, the banner of Treason. And willy-nilly, Ned was leading him and Jarvis to it.

Jarvis understood the situation, but was bemused by it. "This b'ain't no way for a friend to treat a friend," he had said as they rode. "Nicky bein' made a prisoner, and by Crowham. That b'ain't right."

"No, Jarvis, it b'ain't right at all," Peter said. "But it's happening."

"I'm with you, sir, wherever you go, whoever you fight for, but if we all come out of this, maybe Master Crowham and me'll have a reckoning one of these days."

"I might get in first," said Peter grimly.

But the fighting was still to come, and he had been forced, so far, to do Ned's will. At the camp, Ned had gone to present himself at the Tudor's tent and presently Henry Tudor himself came out to inspect the reinforcements Ned had brought.

Peter, seeing him close to, was startled. Tudor, although he was wearing a breastplate and a sword, didn't look even remotely like a warrior. He was certainly nothing like Richard of Gloucester, who, though not big, was tough and muscular.

Gloucester had had a determined air, too; there had been resolution in that careworn face. Henry had the face of a conscientious clerk and the beginnings of a scholar's stoop and looked somewhat bewildered, as though he, as well as Peter, were wondering how in the world he had got here. He thanked Ned Crowham for bringing him forty more men, and his thanks were so heartfelt that they verged on the undignified.

"We've got to fight for *him?*" Jarvis whispered in Peter's ear.

"Looks like it. Be quiet," Peter growled in reply.

They had been assigned to the Earl of Oxford, whose name was John de Vere. Peter was a competent archer but Oxford had enough archers, apparently. Peter had retained his sword, but his bow had been given to someone else and in its place he had been presented with a fearsome weapon called a poleaxe. It was long, like a pike, and sharply pointed, and a few inches from the point a blade, savagely sharp and with an edge six inches long, jutted out from one side. A smaller but equally disagreeable blade with teeth like a saw jutted out from the opposite side.

Henry had a mounted escort on good chargers but ponies weren't wanted, and he had been able to leave Plume in safety. Now he and Jarvis and Ned's other men were marching with Oxford.

Ahead of them was a hill, which the man beside him had said was called Ambien Hill. It was occupied now by the king's army and Oxford was leading them toward it. He had sent archers on ahead and already their shafts were flying toward the foe, who were retaliating. Suddenly a cannon boomed. Cannonballs crashed into their midst and a crossbow bolt struck the man who had told Peter the name of Ambien Hill. His blood, hot and stinking, splashed up into Peter's face and screaming broke out all around him. Cursing, sidestepping, he clutched his poleaxe more tightly and felt the sweat of fear on his brow and temples and running down his spine.

Henry Tudor was keeping back. With his mounted escort he was behind them, on another hill. Farther back still and slightly to the right, with a distinct air of not belonging to either faction, was a mounted force in scarlet, the followers, Ned had said when they all set out that morning, of Thomas Stanley, Henry's stepfather.

A front line from the king's army had started downward toward them, flourishing a standard with a silver lion on it. "Norfolk," shouted Ned over his shoulder. "He's leading the charge! We have to deal with him first!"

He slowed down and Peter found himself striding up alongside. "We'll engage in a moment," said Ned rapidly. "It's too late for you to change your mind so I can tell you now—I've put Nicky in the village of Stoke Golding, in an inn called The Seven Stars. He will be returned to Allerbrook after this, even if you fall."

There was no time for more. They were almost face-to-face with Norfolk's men now. Both forces halted. Curses and taunts were exchanged; weapon hafts were pounded on the ground. Peter shouted with the rest, thinking of the man who had fallen to the crossbow bolt and those who had been struck by cannonballs. He couldn't see them as enemies now. Like it or not, he was their comrade. He had become a Lancastrian, regardless.

A trumpet rang out and the advance began again. The arrows and the cannon fire had ceased, because in a moment, friend and foe would be indistinguishable.

The two lines met.

Up on Ambien Hill, in the mounted reserve, Baldwin Sweetwater said to his son, "It looks as if we won't see any action today. The peasantry's going to see to it on foot."

"It just looks like a mess to me," said John.

Peter, caught up in the collision between Norfolk and Oxford, would have used stronger words than *mess* to describe what was happening. It was a vile chaos of kill or be killed. Trumpet calls from both sides kept drowning each other out and since many of the men in Oxford's following seemed to be Welsh, their captains were bellowing orders in the Welsh language, causing confusion because the English couldn't understand them and didn't therefore know what their Welsh allies were supposed to be doing. The Welsh were probably having the same problem in reverse.

Peter lost sight of Ned Crowham, lost sight of Oxford's standard. People collided with him. Blades rang on his helmet. A furious man, his face distorted with rage, attacked him with a sword and Peter swiped with his poleaxe, taking his assailant in the throat and thankful that the poleaxe had a longer reach than the sword had.

The cry went up that the Duke of Norfolk was slain. Peter found himself in the midst of a melee around Norfolk's body. There was one moment when he had a clear view of Ambien Hill and there, high above, saw King Richard, the sunlight flashing on a gold crown worn over his helmet, seated on a white charger, watching. Suddenly he was alongside Ned again. They could see the Stanley forces, in their vivid livery, also watching the conflict, but keeping aloof.

"Buggers want to see who's winning before they join in!" Ned gasped, wiping sweat out of his eyes and wiping blood into them instead from a gash on his arm.

On Ambien Hill a trumpet spoke and Baldwin Sweetwater said, "Action after all!" as their section of the mounted reserve started downhill to help Norfolk's men. They were halfway down when a squad of crossbowmen rose up, apparently from nowhere, and a hail of bolts drove them back. John Sweetwater, uninjured but struggling with a frightened horse, lost sight of Baldwin for a moment. Then his father reappeared beside him, still in the saddle, but with the armour over his left arm smashed and blood seeping through. "You're hit!" John shouted.

"Flesh wound!" Baldwin shouted back. "I'll live!" Another shower of crossbow bolts swished into the air, but the horsemen had veered out of range by now and the bolts fell short. Glancing back, the Sweetwaters caught sight of the king on his white courser. The king, however, was no longer merely watching. "God's teeth!" gasped John. "Look at that!"

Down in the melee, Norfolk's son had taken over command from his fallen father. He was fighting with the fury of an ancient Viking berserker. But a handful of Norfolk's followers had panicked and were fleeing, and with Ned and others, Peter found himself in pursuit. Before they had time to realise it, they were on the outskirts of the fighting, in the open, with a solid phalanx of armoured Yorkist horsemen bearing down on them from Ambien Hill. Just in time, Ned grabbed Peter's arm and threw them both down under a bush, with a hillock between them and the charge.

It missed them and tore past to slay with fine impartiality the men who had been fleeing and those who like Peter and Ned had been chasing them. Then, as though going on an outing after finishing a few dull chores, they made for the scrimmage around Norfolk's fallen body and plunged in, weapons swinging.

Peter, crawling out from the bush and peering around the hillock, glimpsed a flash on the hill above, looked upward and, like John Sweetwater, gasped at what he saw. The king was on the move. With a small squad of men behind him, he was riding down the slope of Ambien Hill, gathering speed, turning it into a charge, aiming straight for the opposite hill where Henry Tudor still sat, an onlooker, among his mounted guard. There was less than half a mile between them.

"Is that King Richard?" gasped Ned, crawling out beside Peter. "Has he gone mad?"

The king and his followers were clear of Ambien Hill already, and Henry's guard were starting down to meet them. The Stanley banner—it was a white hart, like the name of the Clicket tavern— was moving, too, and the red-jacketed Stanleys were following and not, it seemed, to attack the Tudor forces. Swords out, lances lowered, bellowing war cries which reached Ned and Peter faintly despite the roar of the fighting behind them, the Stanley contingent was thundering headlong straight toward King Richard.

The din of the struggle between Oxford's men and the Yorkists crescendoed. Peter and Ned, suddenly and guiltily aware that they ought to be in it, began to run toward it. A charger whose rider had fallen broke away in panic from the struggle and came galloping toward them. It saw them at the last minute, veered away, all but lost its footing, regained it and then skidded to a stop, sweating, trembling, white-ringed eyes rolling and ears flat back. It tossed its head and a rein swung, lashing Peter's arm. He caught hold of it. "Steady! Easy! Easy now!"

He saw Ned looking at him, and realised why. He could get away if he wanted to. He could scramble astride this gift from heaven, cock a snook at Ned and be gone from this arena of horror. He knew where Nicky was now, after all.

But he had lost sight of Jarvis and he couldn't leave him behind, couldn't, somehow, even leave Ned Crowham. A man didn't run from a battlefield, at least not until the Retreat was sounded or all his fellow soldiers decided to run, as well. Ancient instincts, forged in battles through countless aeons of time, forbade it. You stood by your comrades, even if you didn't like them, even if you'd been forcibly co-opted into their midst.

Peter had hated his previous experience of battle chargers. He was about to fling the animal's reins to Ned, who was more used to such things, when, veering around as the horse sidled and dragged him with it, he again caught sight of King Richard's sally and suddenly understood. Richard of Gloucester had chosen to settle the outcome in the most ancient and formal of ways, by single combat with his challenger. He was trying to reach Henry Tudor, to cut him down personally.

At that moment King Richard and his men crashed into Henry's guard. The Stanleys had farther to go and deceptive dips in the ground had slowed them down. They were still on their way. Peter could see the crown flashing on the king's helmet, see Richard's arm rising and falling as he plied his battle-axe like a man hacking his way through a forest. Or a man possessed by a demon of rage. If he could get through, then the invading Tudor would be cut down for sure. But he wouldn't get through; he couldn't, not through so many; no man could...

At Tewkesbury, Peter had given Richard of Gloucester a horse and Gloucester had given him riches in return, and in Peter, a loyalty had been forged which could not now be wiped out, not even for Nicky.

He could not leave the battlefield, but he couldn't go on fighting for Lancaster either. Once more he would dedicate a loose horse to Gloucester's service. He was in the saddle. The horse, steadied by the familiar feeling of weight on its back and strong hands on its reins, let him turn it and put it into a gallop. Peter drove in his heels, crouched over the tossing mane and grasped his poleaxe as though it were a lance. He was only one man and he would probably do nothing more than get himself killed but he would die with Gloucester, and Nicky must take his chance.

As he put the horse to the slope, he could still see Richard ahead, still fighting, still alive. He spurred on, in among Richard's followers whose charge had been checked by the head-on collision with the enemy. At the same moment the Stanleys arrived, bursting into the confusion, trying to get at the king. King Richard, with bitterness, had recognised his betrayal. Peter could hear him shouting *"Treason!"* over and over again.

A man beside Peter shouted a warning and he ducked just in time as a Stanley sword swept through the space where his head had been. The warning had been given in a voice with a distinct west country burr and he wondered briefly whether the Sweetwaters were in King Richard's escort, but he had no time to think about it, for at that moment King Richard fell. He saw the gold-crowned helmet vanish beneath a tide of scarlet Stanley jackets. And saw the blades that rose and fell with hideous intent.

Then Peter's horse trod on a still-living body, plunged away with a squeal, tangled its feet among the legs of a dead horse and went down, throwing Peter to the ground headfirst. His helmet, already badly battered, failed him and fell off. There was an explosion of light and pain mysteriously combined into one sensation and then oblivion.

He came around to find someone shaking him. He tried to

raise himself, but a bad-tempered blacksmith was wielding a fourteen-pound hammer inside his head and his stomach felt queasy. He sagged back. A Welsh voice above him said, "He's coming to. Who is he now, for the love of God? He has no red Stanley jacket, but he's not one of Richard's—proper armour they have, all of them. Horse is his, though. See, he still has a foot stuck in a stirrup." He felt a hand on his ankle, releasing it from something. "Here, fellow, up you come. What's your name?"

For one dreadful moment he couldn't remember. Then his sense of identity came muzzily back. "Peter." He got it out with difficulty. "Lanyon."

"What's that mean, bach? Who are you?"

Another voice, English this time, said, "I think he's that lunatical fellow we saw tearing across on horseback just before Richard fell. Speak up, man! Who's your commander?"

They had hauled him into a sitting position. The demonic blacksmith redoubled his efforts and his stomach heaved. The two men stooping over him seemed enormous and threatening. He struggled to focus his blurred eyes. He seemed to be still where he had fallen. He could see Ambien Hill and fighting still going on below it, and close to him, all around him, were dead men and horses. He could smell blood. It was everywhere, congealing in pools and rivulets, a hell of butchery.

Men were moving about amid the carnage. He saw a group tearing battered armour off a body only a few yards away, tumbling the corpse as they did so. For a moment he saw its face. Its helmet was half off and the golden crown was gone, but he knew those features; even stained with blood and grey with death, he knew them. It was King Richard.

"Who are you?" Hands on his shoulders were shaking him, to get an answer out of him. The hammer in his head almost made him scream.

He ought to say he was Richard's man, and face whatever vengeance that brought on him, but if Peter Lanyon had an aching head, he also had a hard one. He might annoy his father by marvelling poetically at golden gorse and purple heather, but at times he was very much his father's son. Gloucester was dead and no longer needed his allegiance. Where was the sense in dying for a corpse, in sacrificing his son for an empty gesture? He'd sooner stay alive and go home with Nicky.

"I was with…Earl of Oxford," he said mumblingly. "We were in a battle. That way." He made a vague gesture toward Ambien Hill. "I saw…Gloucester trying to get at Henry Tudor. There was a loose horse. I got onto it and tried to get here to help." At the last moment he left it ambiguous and didn't say who, precisely, he had wanted to help, but he had used a fuddled voice and he had already spoken of following Oxford, and nobody queried it. "Got here but…my horse fell. Can't remember anything else."

"He's one of ours, bach," said the Welsh voice. "Give me a hand with him. Best get him to a tent."

"Thank you," said Peter faintly, and was then very very sick.

CHAPTER THIRTY-ONE

FRIENDS UPON A BRIDGE

I'm getting too old for riding, Liza told herself as her pony carried her down the final stretch of track around the hill which formed the southwest end of Dunster Castle's private chase. She rarely rode these days and now every bone ached.

Richard refused to admit that he was anxious about Peter and Nicky but he quite clearly was and at first he was unwilling to let Liza visit her family. He'd finally agreed after two weeks of persuasion.

"I can see you're fretting. But harvest's not far off—don't you be gone long, now."

"I won't do that," Liza promised. She was glad to set off, for she found it wearisome to be constantly in Richard's company without Peter there, even though when Peter *was* there, she often had to mediate between them. She was happy to be returning to these familiar surroundings. Nearly there now. Here was the path around the edge of the Luttrell chase, overhung by trees as ever, and here was the turn to the packhorse bridge and there was the bridge, with the Avill flowing serenely beneath.

She and Alfred, who was with her, used the ford below the bridge and let their mounts drink from the stream, while a couple of horsemen riding toward them and already on the bridge finished crossing it. It was too narrow for horses to pass each other. Then they rode gently on, through the village, into the broad cobbled North Street where the stalls in the middle of the road were still doing business. Alfred, who came frequently to Dunster, since he often escorted the wool clip there, leaned from his saddle as they came level with the Weavers' house, and took her rein.

"I'll take the ponies to the Weavers' pasture, Mistress, and walk back. You go on in. You'll be tired, I reckon."

"Thank you, Alfred." She got down, stiffly. Their arrival had been seen; doors were opening on both sides of the street and there was Laurence coming across from his house, with Elena hurrying after him, and there was Aunt Cecy—*dear heaven, is Aunt Cecy still alive? She must be over eighty*—at the opposite door. She was swathed in black, except that her headdress, a curious affair shaped like the door of a church, had white beads around its edge. Within it, her face had a grim expression and her greeting was characteristic.

"Well, well, Liza! What brings you here?"

"It's good to see you!" Laurence himself must be about seventy and Elena not much younger and they both looked tired and old. Laurence had lost most of his hair, except for a few grey wisps. But unlike Aunt Cecy, he and Elena were smiling in welcome. They embraced Liza joyfully.

"Nothing's wrong," she said, "except that Peter's gone to the war and Nicky's gone with him. But…"

"Oh, my dear! I wondered why Nicky wasn't with you," Elena said. "Come. Let's go inside."

Aunt Cecy moved aside to let them pass. "If you've come for the funeral, my girl," she said sourly, "you're too late."

Liza stopped short. "The funeral? What funeral? Whose?"

"Dick, my husband. Died nine days back and buried a week since," said Aunt Cecy. "It comes to us all. Well, come in, no need to stand there."

Liza and Elena followed her indoors. The house, to Liza, now seemed both familiar and strange. Familiar because there were the same rooms, with the same furniture and the same woolly smell, and from the kitchen, the sound of an argument. A mislaid crock of butter was causing recriminations. Faintly, just as always, she could hear the clack of looms.

But Dick, Cecy's husband and Uncle Will's son, was gone, and Uncle Will too had departed. He had died at eighty-seven. Richard had brought her the news, after a visit to Dunster. The corner where he used to sit looked empty. This was the house that she remembered, yes. But...how odd. She really *had* put roots down at Allerbrook. What was it she had once heard Betsy say? She had been lying with her eyes closed after the birth and death of poor little Jack. *Where she rears her family, that's the place a woman calls home.* Quentin and Nicky had both been born at Allerbrook. Her other relatives were here in Dunster, but her home was not.

Her relatives, however, were gathering eagerly around her. Many of them had changed: grown up or grown older. Her brother Tommy was very much a family man now, with a sensible-looking wife called Susannah, and two small children. They were all full of sympathy when they heard that both Peter and Nicky had ridden away with Crowham, and that Nicky had gone after his father.

"No one's gone from Dunster this time," Laurence said. "And a good thing, too. If only this battle can be the last one. It's high time it was settled once and for all who's going to sit on the throne." His lined face became suddenly red with anger. "The whole of England is sick to the stomach of their squabbling and the way they take our sons and use them and never bring them back. It's a disgrace!" He stopped, breathless.

"Gently, my dear," said Elena, looking at him worriedly. She turned to Liza. "We lost Laurie and Dickon to the wars and now Jem's dead, too, though not through war. He got something wrong with his innards two years back." Liza nodded sadly. Richard had brought that news to her, too. "We've still got Luke and Joss, for which we're grateful, but we don't forget," Elena said.

"Yes, there's death enough without battles creating more. I say it's a bitter shame that folk can't live their ordinary lives in peace," said Laurence. "All we want to do is weave our cloth, bring up our families, look after our homes. But are we ever left alone to get on with it? No, we're not, and more shame to those who call themselves our betters and take our sons away."

"When little Joanna there was baptised," said Susannah, pointing to her five-year-old daughter, "our priest was sick and the castle chaplain came to the church to do it—Father Christopher." Susannah, clearly, had not been told about Liza's past indiscretions and to judge from her casual tone, no one had stared at the priest and exclaimed that he was exactly like Nicky Lanyon. Liza herself gave no sign that Christopher's name meant anything to her, though it had gone through her like a crossbow bolt.

Susannah was continuing. "He gave a little homily afterward, congratulating us, and he quoted a psalm. *Like as the arrows in the hand of a giant, even so are the young children*—that's what he said. Well, that's just how the great men have been treating ordinary folk like us. They just want our lads as arrows to be used and spent. It's true!"

"No one took Peter and Nicky," said Aunt Cecy. "Peter's a free man and from what Liza here says, Nicky just ran off as silly boys do. Nicky *is* a silly boy. We've tried to teach him weaving when he's been here, but he's that mutton fisted he'd break threads even if he was making chain mail. But Peter's no better, going off like that. Men have no sense. If they get spent like arrows, half the time it's because they've spent themselves."

Aunt Cecy had decidedly not mellowed with age. Before supper was over, Liza was beginning to think that she had better not stay too long. Not only was Dunster somehow unfamiliar, but also, she had come to be soothed by the company of her family, only to find that all the news seemed to be unhappy and Aunt Cecy's contributions to the talk were anything but soothing, and no better for being oblique.

Aunt Cecy did not actually say outright that if Liza had had more authority over her son, he would not have defied orders and run off after his father; she merely said that nowadays young people lacked respect for their parents and that parents should insist on it more. Nor did she remark outright that Peter and possibly Nicky as well could be killed. Instead, she asked who would inherit Allerbrook after them, and then added that it was a great pity that Liza hadn't had a good healthy family of boys.

The Weaver family as a whole was used to her and most of them seemed hardly aware of her comments, while those who were, such as Laurence and Elena, tried to change the subject or rephrase Aunt Cecy's remarks for her, in a kinder form. This usually failed, as Aunt Cecy, more than once, said, "No, that's not what I meant," and then repeated her remark in the original wording. Long before the end of the meal Liza was wondering why Aunt Cecy had not been banished to retirement in the guest house of some convenient women's abbey. She understood now why her mother couldn't tolerate life with Cecy after her father's death.

As they left the table, Susannah put a hand on her arm, and said, "Please don't mind Aunt Cecy. She's unhappy without her husband and he hasn't been gone two weeks. She's bitter but she doesn't mean it. She's old and doesn't realise that she upsets people."

Her brother had married a likeable woman, Liza thought, glad for him. She gave Susannah a smile. And wondered if her aching bones could endure riding back to Allerbrook the very next day.

Next morning, as the Weavers gathered just after daybreak to take their breakfast of bread and honey, cold meat and small ale, the talk turned to the state of Dunster harbour.

"If it goes on silting up at this rate, Dunster will end up two miles inland and someone will be planting wheat where the fishing boats are moored now," Tommy grumbled.

"That's right enough." Joss, the younger of Laurence and Elena's two surviving sons (though he was no longer young but was now a widower aged forty) was a weaver and had moved across the road, as he put it, to live with his loom. "No one's even trying to do anything about it. The big ships can only get halfway in these days. Minehead's not much better. Porlock, Lynmouth and Watchet'll all end up more important."

"Dunster'll do well enough," said Aunt Cecy. "Everyone

comes here to buy cloth and yarn and fleeces, too, and there are good roads for the packhorses, in and out."

"That's not the same as having a good harbour," Joss objected.

"From all I've heard, if this Lord Dunster as he calls himself—"

"Pembroke's son," said Tommy aside to Liza.

"If this Lord Dunster," said Aunt Cecy, more loudly, "wants the harbour dug out, he'll put up all our rents to pay for it and even then, from what I've heard, the sea'll bring trouble in faster than any gang of men could dig it out."

"Nonsense," said Tommy robustly. "There's a whole garrison up at the castle, doing nothing most of the time but swagger round the village eyeing up the wenches. That there harbour could be dug out for the cost of a few spades and an ox team."

"You think so? They're soldiers and they'd say digging and ploughing, whether it's fields or a harbour, is beneath them. It's only for common folk like farmers," said Aunt Cecy, achieving further depths of tactlessness. "I've lived a long time," she added. "There's always changes, and never for the better as far as I can see."

"Oh, be quiet, you croaking old raven!" snapped Tommy.

Tears appeared in Aunt Cecy's weak blue eyes and Susannah said mildly, "My dear, Aunt Cecy is in mourning."

"Well, I'm sorry," said Tommy. "But…"

He left the sentence unfinished. However, when breakfast was over, Liza grew restless. The kitchen wrangle about the mislaid butter still seemed to be continuing and this time she found it not amusing, but tiresome. Neither Richard nor Peter would have tolerated such a haphazard atmosphere at Allerbrook and Liza now discovered that she, too, found it irritating. She didn't think she could bear the journey back so soon, but she couldn't stay within earshot of Aunt Cecy a moment longer.

"It's a sunny day," she said. "I want to walk round the village."

"You were always one for walking," said Aunt Cecy. "And no one ever knew who you met or talked to."

"I just liked walking," said Liza coldly.

She left the house and set off along North Street. As she went she took note of changes. She knew none of the people she saw. They were all younger than she was, a new generation, and their clothes were different. Hers had changed very little; on a farm in the midst of the moor, no one followed fashion. But now it seemed that women wishing to appear well dressed had adopted fuller gowns and shorter headdresses, and that the young village men were going in for the kind of elaborate caps which once had been the prerogative of folk like the Sweetwaters. They seemed to like a lot of pleating in their tunics, too. Liza began to feel dowdy.

But the sunshine was pleasant; even the castle towering up at the end of the street looked more hospitable than grim. She followed the lane around the foot of the castle hill, turned into West Street and presently took the lane to the packhorse bridge. The trees were in full and heavy leaf, meeting above the river and rustling softly in a light wind.

She stopped on the bridge to look down at the water, and gazed at her reflection in it, wondering if she had really become dowdy. Since the Lanyons now had a fine house, they ought to dress accordingly. Weaving for long hours was tiring these days. Perhaps she should buy some good cloth in Dunster and get some modern patterns for gowns.

The water rippled into rings as a trout came up. When the ripples settled, there were two reflections in the river. She swung around. "Christopher!"

Like her, he was older. The fire had died in his tonsure, although it was not grey but had faded from flame to sandy, though a few traces of the original flame colour remained. There were lines in his face. But the rest was the same—snub nose, freckled chin, amber eyes smiling and, resting on the parapet beside her own, shapely hands with sandy hairs on them. It was a little surprising that at Joanna's baptism no one had noticed his resemblance to Nicky, but the church was often shadowy, and a man always looked different in full priestly vestments.

Astonished at seeing him, she gazed at him in wonder and he laughed. "There's no magic. I never go to the dell now. It has…memories of something I value very much but know must never be repeated. I come here instead. I come nearly every morning and linger for a while. We argued here once, but it was only because we were so much in love and knew we had no hope of marrying. Do you remember?"

"Of course I remember."

"If you came out walking, on any day when it's not raining, at this time and came to this bridge, you'd be almost sure to find me here. Just as once you'd have been almost sure to find me in the dell. As I said, there's no magic."

"How are you? I heard you were still at the castle. You…you baptised a child in my family not long ago."

"Ah. Yes, I did. I wondered if any of the Weavers would remember our—escapade. But if so, they didn't mention it. You were mentioned, though. I heard you had a son."

"Yes. Named Nicholas after my father. We call him Nicky."

Does he know? Shall I tell him? Liza did not know what to say until Christopher said, "Is he with you? You are visiting your kinfolk, I suppose."

"Yes. But Nicky isn't here. He and my husband…they've both gone to the war, to fight for the king."

"Your son as well? How old is he?"

"Thirteen."

He might work it out from that, but he showed no sign of doing so, and Liza's racing heart had quietened. She would not tell him. It would disturb his peace, and he did seem peaceful; reconciled, at least. She said again, "How are you? Are you well—happy?"

"You know, I think I am. I live at the castle and hold services for the servants and the men in the garrison. I have conducted weddings for some of them, given the last rites to others. Sometimes I run errands here and there."

"If you're really happy, then I'm glad."

He leaned on the parapet, looking down at the water. "It's a quiet life but not dull." He paused and then said, "I ride out quite often on the errands I mentioned. As far as Withypool, sometimes. There's a woman in the castle who sweeps and dusts and she has parents there. They're old and not well and she sends them comforts by me, and money when she can spare some of her wage. I add a little to it. I like the old pair. He used to be the Sweetwaters' harbourer, before he got too old. Faulkner, that's their name. I do jobs about the cottage and garden for them because they're both lame. Liza, you must be very anxious, with your husband and son away at the war, but apart from that, I hope your life is good."

"Yes. I think it is."

There was a silence. Then he said, "It's over, isn't it? The storm and the passion. No more lightning in the air between us. No more agony. I just feel I am standing on this bridge beside a very old friend."

"So do I. As though we hadn't really been parted all this time. As though we'd been together often, only I've forgotten it, as one forgets dreams. Oh!" A wave of guilt had poured over her. "I shouldn't say such things! Not with Peter and Nicky both in danger. I don't know if I shall ever see them again. Aunt Cecy— did you see Aunt Cecy at the baptism?"

"Was she the very elderly lady with the sharp tongue?"

"Yes! She was hinting last night that they might both be killed, and I hate her for that but it's true and I should be thinking of nothing but them. Yet I'm standing here with you and saying… thinking…feeling…"

"You are talking to a friend. I am sorry for your fears and I wish I could reassure you. All I can do is pray for you and for them."

"I'm going home again tomorrow, if I can bear the thought of the saddle. I can't face staying near Aunt Cecy!"

There was another silence, until at last he said, "I pray for you anyway, every single night. I am happy. *My* life is certainly good. Yet there's something missing and always will be. I shall always miss *you,* Liza. I always have. I can't help it."

"I know. I feel the same. Exactly the same."

"There's another dell," said Christopher, "half a mile, perhaps, from the packhorse bridge the Sweetwaters built on their land, on the Allerbrook side. It's lonely, well off the track. It doesn't grow bluebells but there are foxgloves there. I found it one day when I was coming back from the Faulkners and tried to take a shortcut to Washford. I needed to call on the monks there with a message from the steward. He arranges to buy fleeces from the monks, to be turned into cloth by a Dunster weaver—not one of your family. It's to provide livery for the garrison."

"Yes?" Liza was puzzled.

"My shortcut wasn't a shortcut at all. It was a sheep track and it wandered in all directions, but I found the dell on the way. The sheep path turns off the main track just by a standing stone, a small one, the only one in that part of the moor. Liza, I visit the Faulkners every second Tuesday and I'll be there on Tuesday of next week. In the afternoon, if the weather is kind, I may go out of my way and take a rest in that dell. I'll be there every Tuesday fortnight, given fair weather."

"Should you be saying this to me?" said Liza.

"Perhaps not, but aren't we old enough now to be—just friends? It would warm some part of me that has always been left chilled, if we could once in a while meet and talk, just talk. Would it be so wrong? Friendship is a happy thing."

Liza did not know what to answer. The words *some part of me that has always been left chilled* had come home to her. Within her, too, was something that had longed for warmth, for comfort, and never had its wish granted, a secret poor relation longing to hold out its hands to a hearth fire but forbidden to draw near.

She said nothing and he did not ask for an answer. He kissed her before they parted, but just in kindly fashion on the forehead, and then walked away, but he glanced back, just once. He wanted to see her again and she wanted to see him. The old longing for each other's company had not faded, although now it was no longer physical. They didn't want to make love, only to be together and talk, but yes, they did want that. It hadn't changed. And he hadn't been able to stop himself from offering them a way.

She knew even before she had turned to go home that as long as the skies were dry, she would be in that other dell next Tuesday.

CHAPTER THIRTY-TWO
COMING HOME

Peter was too giddy to walk, but the owner of the Welsh voice took charge of him. He found himself being carried to a tent in the Tudor encampment. Someone gave him something to drink and he fell asleep. When he woke in the evening he felt easier, although his head still throbbed and when he gingerly fingered it, he found a tender lump.

It was another full day before he could stand up without the world swimming around him, but he told the Welshman who had helped him that he ought to get word to his leader, Sir Ned Crowham, who was one of Oxford's captains, and this called forth some startling news.

"The Earl of Oxford's gone to Leicester with King Henry. Leicester's the nearest city and the king's making a triumphal entry." The Welshman gave Henry Tudor's new title without a flicker of hesitation. He grinned. "Richard of Gloucester had a crown on over his helmet. King Henry has it now. He'll ride into Leicester in style, indeed he will. But the earl set some sorting out in hand before he went. Well organised is John de Vere, and King Henry, too. He made lists of names—all his lords and captains and most of their followers. If you're Peter Lanyon… that's what you said?"

"Yes, I am."

"Did you have a man along with you, by the name of Jarvis Hannacombe?"

Peter sat up more sharply than was good for him, but he ignored the thud of pain in his skull. "Yes, I did! Is there news of him?"

"It is not good news," said the Welshman sympathetically. "Nor is there good news of Crowham. They're both dead."

"Oh, dear God."

"Crowham was found lying on his back with his breastplate smashed in, and a wound in his chest. Hannacombe was facedown on top of him, with his head half off and a bloodied dagger in his hand. Looks as if he threw himself on top of Crowham when he fell and tried to defend him, only Crowham's wound was mortal already. Meant something to you, did they, Crowham and this Jarvis Hannacombe?"

"Yes," said Peter, feeling his mouth shrivel as he said it, as though he had taken a gulp of verjuice. Ned Crowham was a friend who had turned into an enemy. What he had meant, in the end, was as bitter as any crab apple. But Jarvis was a country lad who hadn't cared a straw for York or Lancaster. He'd come because Peter had told him to and, perhaps, for the sake of an adventure. And died for it.

"It was an honourable end," said the Welshman, kindly enough, seeing Peter's face. "For them both."

"I'm sure it was."

"And you had a pony in the horse lines. One of your comrades knew which one it is and he's taking care of it. He was pleased you'd been found alive."

Peter said, "I must get myself on my feet. Are we free to go home, or not?"

"If you want. We're all small fry and you're walking wounded. But a whole lot of men have gone to Leicester, following the king. You come from the southwest, don't you?"

"Yes."

"Not many of you in the fighting," said the Welshman. "But there were two in Gloucester's pack, that came across to try and kill King Henry. Father and son, they were. They're prisoners. They'll hang."

"What? What are they called?" said Peter.

"Brecher, that's the name, so I heard."

Not Sweetwater, then. He detested the Sweetwaters, but he didn't want to think of either Baldwin or John pinioned, terrified, swinging and choking on the end of a rope. He was surprisingly glad it was neither of them. "Poor devils," said Peter, and lay back once more, closing his eyes.

He heard the Welshman leave the tent, and let himself release a sigh of thankfulness that he had had the sense to lie at the right moment. Otherwise, he would probably have found himself hanging beside that luckless father and son.

As it was, he was alive and free. Where had Ned said he would find Nicky? In a village called Stoke Golding, at the sign of The Seven Stars. He must get there as soon as he could. He wouldn't need to search for Jarvis as well, not now.

Had young Hannacombe really died trying to defend Ned

Crowham? Jarvis had been angry on Nicky's behalf. He had said that one day he and Crowham might have a reckoning. In the confusion of the battle, thought Peter as he lay there, physically weak but privately seething with impatience, had Jarvis seized his chance and made Crowham pay? Very likely, but he'd never know for sure.

The Seven Stars inn at Stoke Golding was the most unpleasant hostelry he had ever seen. It was a rickety timber building that looked as if it might fall down at any moment and the groom who offered to take Plume did so with a slouch and a scowl which caused Peter to insist on stabling and unsaddling the pony himself. The stable was dismally dark and badly needed mucking out, but while he was seeing to Plume, he realised that the animal in the next stall, a chestnut pony, about fourteen hands, with white socks and a blaze, looked familiar. Surely it was the pony Ned Crowham had given Nicky to ride when they set out from Crowham's manorhouse.

With, Peter observed in alarm, an empty manger and a coat that hadn't been groomed for days. He began to feel afraid. He had taught Nicky to take care of his pony. Why hadn't he?

You cared for your horses before yourself, or even other people's horses if necessary. He put fodder in the chestnut's manger as well as in Plume's before he went hurrying into the inn. It was as bad inside as outside—gloomy and smelling of mice and mildew. He stood, nostrils twitching, in a cobblestoned room with a sagging wooden ceiling, and shouted until the landlord came, a thin man with an air of despair about his bent shoulders and watery eyes, as though life had long since defeated him. Oh yes, he had a boy called Nicky here. Brought in by three elderly fellows two days back. *Marched* in was what it looked like, with one of them holding the lad's arm good and hard.

They'd paid in advance, he said, a week's money for each of the four, and the old men had watched the boy like cats watching a mouse hole. Looked as if they thought he'd run away. In fact, he had an idea they had him tied to the bed in the room they'd taken. "Not my business," said the landlord when Peter wanted to know why he hadn't offered Nicky any help. "Thought maybe he'd done something wrong."

"Well, are they still here?" Peter demanded.

"Not the old ones. They came from up Nottingham way. Someone brought a message to them, about the battle and how the Tudor had won the day, and then they were off. Just left the boy behind, as he'd fallen sick...."

"Fallen sick?" shouted Peter. "Where is he?" He wanted to grab the landlord's bony shoulders and shake him.

"Up there," said the landlord, pointing to an unreliable looking staircase. "Something wrong with his stomach." Peter went up it two at a time. It made his head thump again but he didn't care.

Nicky was in a tiny room under the thatch, lying on a straw pallet beneath a grubby coverlet. If he had been tied up at first, he wasn't tied now but the place was filthy and the contents of a bucket by the bed stank horribly. Nicky's hair was soaked with sweat and his eyes had the look, both filmed and bright, of fever. But he struggled to sit up when Peter came in.

"Father! I thought I heard your voice but I'd been dreaming...I thought I'd dreamed that, too.... It really is you? Father, I'm so sorry. I shouldn't have come after you. Please don't be angry! I couldn't help being brought here. I couldn't..."

Relieved and panic-stricken both at once, Peter strode across to the bedside. "I've found you and that's all I care about. But I had no notion you might be sick! I know you couldn't help being captured. Ned Crowham died in the battle, by the way," he said.

"I know. There was a message for the old men that brought me here—"

"On Ned Crowham's damned orders!"

"Yes. The message was about the battle, but the messenger said Crowham had been killed. Then the old men said they wanted to go home, and I could go home, too, when I felt ready, but they didn't want to stay here till I was well. So they just left me. They came from Crowham's Nottinghamshire place, I think."

"What's wrong with you?"

"I've got a fever and I keep being sick. I think it was the salted pork the second night here. It tasted funny. The old men didn't have it—they had pottage. I tried to get away, Father, I really did, but they gave me no chance. I was roped to the bed at first, until I got ill…." He gagged suddenly, and reached in haste for the bucket.

"I'm not surprised. This place is a disgrace. Now, listen. I'm going into the village to fetch some clean, fresh milk and wholesome food for you. And I'll find someone to make you up a cooling draught. Don't worry."

It took Nicky over two weeks to recover. Not wanting to move him while he was still so feverish and liable to fits of nausea, Peter ordered the inn's only maidservant to clean the attic room and change the bedding, while he himself scoured the district for trustworthy victuals. He compelled the landlord to prepare them under his eyes. He also found a village woman with a name for making medicinal herb infusions, who supplied a purge and a febrifuge. The purge made Nicky wretched for several hours, but it seemed to clear his system. After that, the cooling medicine took effect. His fever dropped and he began to eat again, while Peter groomed Plume and the chestnut and bullied the groom into cleaning the stable and feeding its occupants properly.

Ned Crowham had at least done one thing right. He had not expected his followers to bring their own subsistence money as some men did, but had paid them. Peter could buy what he needed—oats for the ponies as well as food for himself and Nicky.

There came a day, at last, when he could pay their bill, put saddles on the two ponies and, with Nicky, leave thankfully for home.

Henry Tudor, in a sense, was home already.

He had been firstly an exile at the French court and then an adventurer trying to seize the estate of England by force, with backing from French troops and a handful of English Lancastrian nobles and some Welshmen who owed allegiance to his Welsh ancestry, but with very little real support in the land he wanted to conquer. All this had turned him into an impressive-looking but privately petrified armoured figure sitting motionless on a large horse and glad of the ironclad fence of French and Welsh knights in front of him.

They had destroyed his enemy for him and he had metamorphosed again, this time into a triumphant new king, riding into Leicester, meeting dignitaries, getting to know those English lords who had fought for him but had hitherto not met him personally, presiding over meetings and banquets, sending out proclamations to announce the outcome of Bosworth Field all over the land, and also attending a few hangings, which he didn't enjoy though he kept his countenance and didn't look away.

This was followed by another triumphal march to London, and a formal reception with entertainments and more banquets. Here he ordered new silk shirts and embroidered doublets, had his hair washed and trimmed and purchased a new cap of soft velvet to put on top of it. His plate armour and helmet were, he trusted, laid away for good and he hoped he would never have to hang a sword from his belt again as long as he lived.

In London he was reunited with his mother, Margaret Beaufort, whose descent from Edward III was his strongest claim to the throne. He also had his first meeting with King Edward's daughter, Elizabeth of York, having summoned her from the north, where she had been living. He had sworn to marry her, to unite at last the warring clans of York and Lancaster, and was relieved to find her a pleasing girl, quiet and biddable. He did not wonder whether they would ever come to love each other. Henry wasn't accustomed to love.

Now, at last, in the quarters he had been given at the house of Thomas Kemp, the Bishop of London, he had embarked on the business and administration side of kingship and that was his true moment of homecoming. Living in tents, marching and riding, warfare and physical danger were not at all to his taste; nor was he truly at ease with ceremonies or making speeches or thinking of pretty things to say to young women. Desks full of papers and parchments, the scratching of quill pens, deferential clerks in decent black gowns, offering him things to sign and seal; this was the world where he belonged.

"Men who stood by me should be rewarded," he said to one of the chief clerks. "And a few examples should be made of the major figures who stood against me. Gloucester was a usurper and never a legitimate sovereign and to fight on his side was an act of treason."

Several stacks of parchments were on the desk in front of him. He picked up a set, leafed through it, hesitated and then removed one or two sheets before shaking the remainder into tidy order and handing them to the clerk. "These estates are to be confiscated and we require the necessary documents to be drawn up, ready for our signature after Parliament reopens at the end of October."

"There should be no difficulty, sir. There is sufficient time."

"Such confiscations will of course require an Act of Parliament before they can go into effect." Henry's voice was formal. "We trust that the act will go through smoothly. We have made notes on each of these pages, suggesting the dates by which the present occupants must leave. Time must be allowed, of course. We are not a barbarian. These, on the other hand…"

He reached for another set of parchments. "These concern families which are to be rewarded or, in some cases, reinstated. For instance, this one refers to a Lady Elizabeth Luttrell, whose husband was killed fighting for the Lancastrians. She was ordered out of her home at Dunster Castle in Somerset. The castle and its estates are to be restored to her and to her son—Hugh Luttrell. He must be grown up by now. Again, the documentation must be prepared for my signature. And these…"

He paused, frowning, considering yet another pile. The chief clerk waited. "These are small ale, as it were," Henry said. "Minor gentry who fought for Gloucester, but did so of their own choice and not because they were tenantry who had to follow their lord. We don't wish to persecute them too savagely but on the other hand…although these properties aren't large, the sale of a fair number would add up to a useful sum, and the exchequer needs money. War is expensive. We will consider each case with care. But we do need to make a profit," he added thriftily.

★ ★ ★

For Nicky and Peter, the journey home was slow, for Nicky was still not strong. It was a week before, at last, they saw the track underfoot turn from brown to the familiar pinkish-red, and Exmoor's hills rose before them and the people to whom they spoke used the familiar accent of home.

"The very air smells different," Peter said, and was grieved anew for the two unknown westcountrymen, the Brechers, who would never draw a breath of it again. The Sweetwaters might well have fallen in that last conflict; but that was better by far than hanging.

"Are you sure you ought to ride yet, with your arm not healed?" Walter Sweetwater said to his son.

Baldwin, whose left sleeve still bulged with the dressing beneath it, merely snorted. "I'm well enough. It's taking time to mend, but Catherine's comfrey ointment is doing its work. I rode all the way back here! And now Blue Lyn needs exercise again."

"But you were feverish when you came home." Catherine had brought some mending into the hall because in the morning the light was better there than in her solar. "You should take care," she said with concern.

"I'm well enough now, Kitten!"

"I wish John could go with you," said Catherine doubtfully.

"So do I, but as John is out heaven knows where, training a hawk, he can't," said Baldwin testily.

"At least he came back safe. I was so thankful to see the two of you home again, even though you were wounded. I prayed for you every morning and every night, believe me. You don't know what women suffer when men are away at war."

"You don't know what we suffer on the march or on the field," retorted Baldwin. "You at least can sleep warm and safe while we try to get to sleep in draughty tents or out on the ground, under the sky at times! It was our duty to go and yours to keep Sweetwater House in order till we came home. That's the way life is. And now I'm going to take the air."

As she watched him ride out of the courtyard, Catherine said, "I think his arm still pains him. It makes him irritable."

"It's more than that," said Walter. "I think I should warn you. There's been a rumour. I heard it when Giles Northcote called on us yesterday. He didn't go to the war but he has well-placed friends who did, who fought for King Henry and went with him to London. He is planning heavy fines for families that supported King Richard, and in some cases, confiscations of land. It's possible that we are on his list."

"Oh, no!" said Catherine, horrified.

"I hope the rumour's not true, but only time will tell. Oh, and the Lanyons won't be on the list. We heard, just before the battle at Bosworth, that Ned Crowham was going over to the Tudor and taking all his followers with him, Lanyons included. There were some travelling tumblers in the same inn as Crowham and his companions, two nights before the battle. They overheard them talking, it seems. Anyhow, they turned up in Leicester next day with information to sell to the Earl of Nottingham. They didn't reach him soon enough for anything to be done, but word got round. So we can assume that even if the Lanyons were important enough to be robbed by Henry, they won't be, whereas we might. *That's* why Baldwin is so angry."

"But…we only fought for the reigning king!"

"This man Henry Tudor," said Walter, "seems to be fond of

money. According to Giles, he has an abacus where other men have hearts. He'd rather shuffle papers and count coins and wield a pen than ride in battle with a sword in his hand. King Richard at least died fighting! Henry never struck a blow. I can't blame Baldwin for his short temper. I'm badly worried myself. But at least his wound is much improved, for which we must both be thankful to you."

"But if we lose our home, John will lose his inheritance!" Catherine cried. "The rumour can't be right. Men can't be called traitors if they fight for an anointed king!"

"I wouldn't place any wagers on it," said Walter Sweetwater grimly.

CHAPTER THIRTY-THREE

FOES UPON A BRIDGE

"Nearly home now," Peter said to Nicky as they left the town of Dulverton, where they had crossed the River Barle, and set off northwestward through the moorlands.

"Your Plume knows he's going home," Nicky said as the ponies lowered their heads to tackle a steep rise. "Look at the way his ears are pricked."

"Of course he knows it," said Peter. "He can smell it!"

They rode steadily onward, over a hillcrest thickly grown with bracken and then by way of a winding pebbly track down into a valley wooded with oak and beech, to emerge beside Walter Sweetwater's packhorse bridge over the small river at the boundary of the Sweetwater land. Nicky fell back, because it was too narrow for them to ride across abreast.

Stepping onto the bridge, Plume tossed his head and whinnied and Peter turned to call over his shoulder that he reckoned his mount was saying, "Nearly home!" in the language of horses.

But before he had framed the words, there was an answering whinny, and out of the trees on the other side of the bridge rode Baldwin Sweetwater, astride a big blue roan stallion.

By rights, since Peter was already on the bridge and the nearest ford was some distance away, Baldwin should have drawn rein and waited for him to finish crossing. Instead, to Peter's surprise and indignation, Baldwin came straight on.

Baldwin himself could not have said clearly why he didn't follow established custom and allow right of way to the rider already on the bridge. All he knew was that within him there was a seething anger, like a lidded pan boiling over a fire, and that he longed, somehow, to relieve the pressure, to let the lid blow off. His wounded arm had been badly infected and though Catherine's treatment was gaining ground, it still had pus in it and it throbbed when he tried to use his left hand. On top of that, the warning his brother-in-law, Giles Northcote, had brought yesterday, that the Sweetwaters stood in danger of a heavy fine or even confiscation of their land, had outraged him.

It hadn't helped that Giles, though outwardly sympathetic, had been unable to hide his smugness when he admitted that no such threat hung over his own family. He had kept out of the war, and his property, including the estate that formed most of Agnes's dowry, was safe. Giles was proving a good husband to Agnes, who seemed, judging from her letters, to be well content, but he clearly considered himself to be a wiser man than either her father or her brother, as well as several social rungs above them. Baldwin would very much have liked to encounter Northcote on that bridge, and force him to leave it backward.

He had, however, recognised Peter Lanyon, and failing Giles, a Lanyon—any Lanyon—would do nicely as a substitute. The Lanyons had gone Lancastrian along with Ned Crowham, so no one was going to take their home away from them. What if the Sweetwaters were compelled to leave their fine house while the Lanyons stayed in untroubled possession of theirs? They were nothing but peasants who thought themselves equal to him, and that was an impertinence.

He did not mentally put any of these things into words. They merely boiled inside his head, in bubbles that came and went, but one thing did emerge plainly and that was that he was damned if he would draw rein and let Peter cross that bridge in peace.

Peter was already two thirds of the way over. Baldwin, however, rode onto the bridge at his end, blocking the way, and halted. So did Peter. Across the intervening space they glowered at each other.

"Lanyon," called Baldwin, as one who identifies the face of a foe. "Go back, if you please!"

"Why? I was on the bridge first!" Peter retorted. Not long ago he had actually been glad to think that Baldwin and Walter had escaped from Bosworth, that they were not the two west-countrymen who had hanged for supporting their crowned king. Now all his normal dislike of the Sweetwaters and his resentment of the things they had done to his family surged up in him. He sat still, Plume's reins in his left hand and his right hand placed aggressively on his hip.

"Just go back!" Baldwin barked.

"No, it's my right of way. I'll be across and out of your road in a matter of seconds. Back off yourself, Sweetwater!"

To turn on the bridge would be difficult if not impossible, but though two thirds of the bridge was a long way for a horse to back, any pony bred wild on the moor, as Plume had been, could get out of trouble tailfirst if necessary. Baldwin's mount had only just set hoof on the bridge. Either could have moved out of the other's way quite easily. Neither did so.

There was a pause, during which the fury inside Baldwin mounted, wiping out, for a moment, not only the throb of his wound but even the memory of it. Here, at last, was the thing he wanted: an enemy with whom he could engage, hand to hand, as murderously as he chose. Suddenly, violently, he swung himself to the ground, removing his sword belt, which he tossed over his saddle. He walked toward Plume.

"Get down and fight it out. Put your weapons aside. I'm not crossing swords with you. That's the way gentlemen settle their accounts and you're merely a peasant with feet too big for his boots. Besides, it wouldn't be a fair fight," he added disagreeably. "I've had real training in arms and you have not."

"So courteous," Peter said coldly. "Such knightly manners, just like your grandfather had." He glanced over his shoulder. "Nicky! Get down, tether your pony and come here. Take charge of Plume and my weapons."

Nicky obeyed but looked worried. "Father! Should you?" he asked as he came forward to take Plume's bridle.

"I'm going to, anyway," said Peter, handing his sword and dagger to Nicky. The Earl of Oxford had given his bow to somebody else and the poleaxe was probably still lying on Bosworth Field. He hadn't seen it since the moment he was knocked out. "Take those, and move Plume back."

"You Lanyons always did think far too much of yourselves. This is where I show you your place," said Baldwin, and launched himself.

It should have been a fairly even contest. It was true that Baldwin had been trained in arms and he was the younger of the two by some years. Peter, however, had spent his life plodding behind ploughs, herding stock on horseback, cutting down trees, shearing sheep, scything corn and slaughtering pigs. Had Baldwin not been injured, they would have been virtually equals.

Peter, unaware of the injury, assumed that they were, and Baldwin had briefly forgotten his wound. Both threw their strength into the fight. It was all in a confined space, the narrow width of the bridge. Blue Lyn, accustomed to human beings fighting one another, stood solidly. Plume, already being coaxed backward by Nicky, flattened his ears and backed faster, dragging Nicky with him. Baldwin's preference was to use his fists, Peter's to wrestle. Nicky tried to soothe Plume, but was himself nervous, afraid for his father.

The combatants made little noise, beyond grunts, until the moment when Baldwin's right fist on Peter's chin sent Peter reeling backward and Baldwin tried to follow it up with his left. Then the wound in his left arm blazed into agony. He cried out and his arm dropped. At the same moment Peter recovered himself and leaped forward again, grabbing for Baldwin's arms and closing powerful fingers right on top of the injury.

In the brief struggle that followed, Baldwin's curses sent birds flying in alarm from the trees. Somehow he broke that agonising grip, wrapped his arms around Peter and tried to heave him backward over the parapet of the bridge. Peter, savagely resisting, once more unknowingly closed his fingers over the wound and Baldwin, one arm suddenly paralysed, could not stop him from turning them both over so that now Peter was on top.

They hung, struggling, half over the parapet and the ten-foot drop below. The parapet was grinding into Baldwin's back and his left arm was useless. Peter, realising this though he didn't understand it, used the edge of his left hand to chop at Baldwin's right arm, momentarily paralysing that, as well. Twisting aside, he tried to shove Baldwin over and Baldwin, shaking life furiously back into his right arm, clutched at Peter and swung his legs up to encircle Peter's calves. For one terrible moment it seemed that they must both go into the river.

Then Nicky let go of Plume and ran to Peter's aid, yanking Baldwin's crossed ankles apart, seizing Peter's feet and dragging him back. Baldwin finally slithered from under his enemy and fell, his heavy body hitting the water with a loud splash while Nicky hauled his father to safety.

"You shouldn't have done that, Nicky!" Peter said, gasping, as he sat down with a thud on the floor of the bridge.

"You could have been killed. I wasn't going to let you be! And he started it! Oh, *Father!*"

Peter got up and looked over the bridge. The river was fairly deep, certainly sufficient to break a fall. It wasn't lethally deep, however, and it was mercifully free of boulders. Baldwin, dripping, had got to his feet. His right hand was clutching at his left arm above the elbow. He stumbled to the bank, but seemed unable to climb it. He stood there, head drooping, thigh-deep in cold peat water. At a run, Peter left the bridge.

"Here." He slithered down the bank, grabbed at Baldwin's right elbow and hauled. Baldwin swore and shouted at him, but Peter merely retorted, "Don't be a bloody fool. What do you take me for?" And as Baldwin was now too shaken and hurt to resist, Peter succeeded in dragging him up to dry land again. Once there, however, his opponent angrily wrenched himself free.

"I'm all *right*. I've got wet, that's all."

"Then go home and get dry!" said Peter, and went himself to fetch Baldwin's horse. By the time he had brought it, Master Sweetwater had pulled himself together. He glared at Peter, face suffused with angry crimson under an interesting array of red bruises from Peter's fists. He snatched Blue Lyn's reins, although Peter noticed that he seemed able to use only his right hand, and tried to mount. He was so awkward, his left arm evidently useless, that Peter gave him a helpful leg up, which produced more curses. Once up, he gathered his reins in his right hand and rode off without ceremony, going back the way he had come, leaving a trail of drops from his wet clothes like a spoor behind him.

Plume had backed himself right off the bridge and into the comforting company of the chestnut. Their owners went together to get them. "I think Master Sweetwater hurt himself, falling," Nicky said.

"It looked like it," Peter agreed as he mounted, somewhat stiffly.

"What about you?" Nicky asked with concern.

"Only bruises and scrapes. He'll have made for home by the straightest track, I suppose. We'd better use a different one! If he's hurt, he might slow down and I don't want to overtake him."

"All right," said Nicky, getting into his saddle.

They took a path they knew would bring them home, although it wasn't straight, since it was a sheep track and meandered a good deal. Plume was still upset, tossing his head and pulling. He cantered ahead until a sharp drop in the ground ahead slowed him down. The path led down into a cup-shaped hollow thickly grown with golden moor grass, with the soft red of fox-gloves here and there.

It was dry and sheltered, a pleasant place, and others clearly thought so too, for it was occupied. A bay horse and a mealy-nosed moor pony, both saddled, were grazing quietly on the farther bank, tethered to the same small bush. Close to them, a man and a woman sat on the grass, side by side. They were not young and they were not making love. His arm was around her and she was leaning back into it as though against a pillow, but it was in a most companionable fashion. They had the air of friends, content to sit together.

Peter halted his pony and looked at them. They saw him and looked back, their eyes widening in shock. They stood up, just as, with a thudding of hooves, Nicky rode up beside his father and halted there.

Peter stared across the dell at the man with whom his wife Liza had been sitting, in that attitude of such hateful intimacy and peace. He turned his head and looked at his son.

His world ended.

CHAPTER THIRTY-FOUR

FALLING APART

So it has happened, Liza thought. She watched Peter as he looked, again and again, from Christopher to Nicky and back, and stared at her husband's face, and knew that the long deception was over. There was no escape now. Without warning, not giving her even a moment in which to prepare, the truth had sprung from the grass to confront them all. She felt the blood drain from her face, knew that her very features had shrivelled.

Nicky and Christopher themselves, as yet, only looked puzzled. Well, how often did Nicky gaze into a mirror? Presumably Christopher, as well, saw his own reflection only rarely. But they, too, were seeing Peter's horror as he glanced between them and understanding had begun to dawn.

Peter felt as though the breath had been punched out of him. The stranger at Liza's side was in middle life, and what was left of his tonsured hair (*tonsured*—dear God, Margaret had said that

Liza had once been in love with a priest of some kind!) was mostly a faded sandy, but there were a few traces of the original colour and they were a blazing red, just like the red of Nicky's hair.

Nor was that everything; far from it. The well-defined eye-brows, the unusual golden-brown eyes were identical. There was something dreadfully familiar about the shape of the man's left hand, which had been curved around Liza's shoulder. Peter's eyes, drawn to the little finger by the silver ring which encircled it, recognised that shape at once. Familiar, too, were the planes of the face, the snub nose, the freckles—faint, as freckles usually were in older people, but there—the strong chin, *and even the cluster of freckles on the chin.* Nicky had them, too. This was Nicky's face, as it would be, half a century hence.

The awful silence had to be broken. Liza, with a dry mouth, took it upon herself to break it. "This…this is…is Master Christopher Clerk," she said. "We met by chance." She heard the defiance, the lie, in her own voice. "We are friends, that's all," she said desperately.

"This is the man you once tried to run away with?" Peter asked coldly. Liza, shivering, put a hand to her mouth to stop herself from uttering a wail. Tears sprang into her eyes.

"You, I take it, are Master Peter Lanyon?" said Christopher.

"Yes. You had your arm round my wife. Not for the first time, I think." There was a silence. Then Peter said, "Nicky was born as soon as was even remotely possible after I came back from Tewkesbury. I suppose you were carrying him already, Liza, my love. You must have been so relieved to see me ride in. In fact, now that I look back, you were."

Christopher had grasped the full situation by now. His wide

eyes were fastened on Nicky's face with an aching intensity. "But…" he said. And then stopped.

"You are a priest," Peter remarked.

"Yes." Christopher recovered himself. "Priests are men, you know."

Before he could stop himself, Peter had remembered Father Bernard and the tales about the parentage of Geoffrey Baker. He passed a hand across his face, and touched the places where Baldwin's fists had landed.

"Peter," said Liza, "what's wrong with your face?"

"It doesn't matter."

Nicky had not been as quick-witted as Christopher. "I don't understand," he said. Peter turned to him. It hurt, far more than the bruises did. He had loved Nicky, for himself as well as because he was an heir for Allerbrook. He had sold his integrity at Bosworth to protect this boy—and on that bridge, not half an hour ago, this son of his had seized his feet and saved him from crashing headfirst into the river. Only, it seemed now that Nicky was no son of his at all. It felt as though something inside him were being slowly dragged apart by oxen pulling in opposite directions.

Sooner than fling himself out of his saddle to hammer his fists on the ground and scream, sooner than abandon all pretence of dignity, he took refuge in extreme formality.

"Nicky," he said politely, "let me introduce you. This is Christopher Clerk, your mother's lover and your natural father. Ride over to him and shake his hand. He is entitled to courtesy from his son."

Once more Christopher opened his mouth and then shut it again, this time without even uttering one syllable.

"Peter," Liza pleaded. "You can't…it isn't Nicky's fault…!"

"I haven't said it is. I have only suggested that Nicky should show respect to his father, as is proper."

"I still don't understand," said Nicky hopelessly.

"Let the boy alone," said Christopher sharply. "If...even if I really did sire him, and I admit that he looks as if I did, you are still his father, sir. You have reared and educated him all these years. He looks like a fine boy and I thank you for your care of him." He looked at Liza. "I'll go now, unless your husband wants to knock me down. He can do so if he wishes. I won't object."

It was an invitation that Peter almost accepted, but the fight with Baldwin, coming so soon after Bosworth, had drained that kind of violence out of him. Besides, the misery of this moment, of the loss, at the same moment, of both wife and son, was too great to be assuaged in such a commonplace and useless manner.

"Just go," he said. "Mount your horse and leave. But tell me first, where is your home?"

"Dunster Castle. I'm the chaplain there."

"And a splendid example of priesthood to all your flock, I feel sure. You will see me there before long. For the time being...just go."

Christopher turned to Liza and held out his hand. "Farewell," he said. "With all my heart, I mean it. Both halves of the word. Fare well."

"And you, you fare well, too," said Liza.

They clasped hands briefly. Peter watched but did not interfere. They let each other go. Christopher picked up a cap which he had put down on the grass beside him, clapped it on his head, went to the bay horse, attended to stirrups and girth, mounted and touched his heels to his horse's sides. With a scramble of hooves the bay climbed out of the dell. A dark tail flicked as he vanished over the top and then horse and rider were gone.

"You had better get on to your pony," said Peter to Liza. "And we'll go home."

"Father, what's happening?" pleaded Nicky. His eyes were wide and frightened but Peter, looking into them, no longer saw the eyes of his son, only those of his rival, the man Liza had loved before she married him, and, it seemed, had never ceased to love, through all the years between.

"I'm not your father," he said sharply. "Haven't I just said so?" The horror mixed with the dawning comprehension in Nicky's face did touch him then, and he spoke more quietly as he added, "Your real father has just ridden out of the dell. You are his living image."

"You are out of your mind, boy!" Richard shouted at Peter. "Beat her and throw her out, the whore!"

"If you call Liza a whore again," said Peter, "I shall punch you on the nose."

He had called her that himself at first. After riding home in stony silence, the three of them had ridden into the yard, where Alfred, who was forking old straw out of the stable, had started to exclaim in welcome. Cutting him short, Peter had dismounted, gestured for Liza and Nicky to do the same, ordered Nicky to help Alfred see to the ponies, seized Liza's arm and hustled her into the hall. Then, throwing her into a window seat so that he could stand over her, he let his rage explode into cursing and accusation.

Liza, staring at him with huge, frightened eyes, said nothing until at last, when the need to breathe had made him pause, she said tremblingly, "I'm making no excuses. I love you, whether you believe it or not—"

"Oh, yes! It's easy to believe, of course!"

"But I loved Christopher before I was married to you and... some things just don't die."

"I wish *I* had died! I wish I had died at Tewkesbury or at Bosworth! Anything so as not to find out what I found out today!"

"We met by chance not long ago and...then we met twice in that hollow, to talk. Only to talk, as friends."

"Friends! You were more than that in the past! Once, at least!"

"Poor Nicky," said Liza, and that was the moment when he came nearest to striking her.

But at that moment he realised that his father had come in, presumably from the fields, since he was in dusty working clothes. He was listening from the doorway. Now Richard, turning crimson, burst into fury as well, hurling terrible invective at Liza, and would certainly have attacked her, except that at that moment, something in her terrified, tearstained face, had a startling effect on Peter.

Ever since being hit on the head at Bosworth, he had had occasional headaches. They were growing fewer, but the force of his emotions now had brought one on and it felt like a jagged crack in his skull, through which an unbearably bright light was pouring. That light seemed to illuminate pictures inside his brain. They were pictures of Liza, his Liza: Liza in his arms, Liza weaving, cooking, tossing hay, laughing, crying, nursing babies; Liza young, Liza growing older and broader around the middle...*Liza*. Part of his life, which was unimaginable without her. And she wasn't a whore. She was *not*. It made no sense. The word didn't fit Liza, not *Liza*.

As Richard strode forward, his right hand upraised, Peter seized his father's arm. "Liza! Go to a spare bedchamber and bolt yourself in! Go! *Quickly!*" Liza slid from her seat and fled to the stairs, and as she did so, he saw Quentin staring, horrified, in the kitchen doorway. "Quentin, go and look after your mother. Take food to her and whatever else she needs!"

Then he dropped Richard's arm and went out, passing a scared-looking Nicky, who was just coming in, without even glancing at him. He went up to his own bedchamber and lay on the bed and although he was a grown man in middle age, he cried.

It went on, the misery and wretchedness, for three interminable days. The loss of Jarvis, over which everyone grieved, made the misery worse. Peter spent one whole day with the Hannacombes, talking about him and condoling with them. Otherwise, he worked on the farm but took meals alone in his room, making Betsy and Ellen, who by now knew all about it, bring food to him there. He avoided the children, though he sometimes saw Quentin looking at him anxiously. Glimpses of Nicky's white, closed face appalled him, because he didn't know what to do about it. He turned away.

He tried to avoid his father as well, but couldn't do so entirely and whenever they met, Richard would break into another stream of fury against Liza, demanding that Peter throw the whore out of the house.

Now, as the third day neared evening, Richard, coming face-to-face with him in the hall, had attacked once more, striding about, storming and threatening, his face scarlet and an engorged vein pulsing in his temple.

And now, to his own surprise, Peter found that the fury inside him was directed more at Richard than at Liza. All his life he had lived in his father's shadow, obeyed him, allowed himself to be addressed as *boy*. Now Richard was trying to tell him how to deal with his own wife, and that was enough. That was private territory.

"If you call Liza a whore again, I shall punch you on the nose."

"You dare to threaten me for telling the truth?" Richard bellowed at him.

"Yes. You call her a whore, but what was Deborah Archer? You remember Deb?"

"Of course I remember Deb! My poor Deb that the Sweet-waters as good as murdered! She was a widow! Her husbands, both of them, were in their graves. That's different! I won't have that woman here for one more night! I won't...!"

"Liza isn't a whore," said Peter. "I called her that at first but I know it isn't true. All these years! So many years. I can't throw them away."

"Send her home! I keep telling you! Send her back to Dunster!"

Peter said, "Do you remember Marion Locke?"

He hoped the name might induce his father to pause for a moment. He didn't expect it to bring Richard's outraged pacings to a complete, frozen halt. "Yes, I do! A fisher girl you had a fling with, in Lynmouth! She ran off with someone else!"

It was hard for Richard to get the words out. He had never broken free of Marion's haunting memory and now, forced to speak of her—worse, to lie about her—he saw her again in his mind and heard her, as she fell backward into the mist....

Only with an effort could Richard keep from raising his hands to grip his temples, to crush her memory out of his head by force.

"I was mad for her," Peter said, "and even after she'd gone...I still didn't want to marry Liza. Only, I had to marry someone and so I agreed to it, and did my best. But maybe...I can... *just*...imagine what it was like for her, since she, too... If I were to meet Marion again, even now..."

He had never spoken of it, but three years after his marriage to Liza he had made an excuse to be out on the moor all day, had gone to Lynmouth and asked if the *Fjord-Elk* was expected to dock there any time soon. Someone directed him to a harbourside tavern where men from another Norwegian ship were drinking, though the ship was not the *Fjord-Elk*. "They might know something about her. She's not been here of late."

And one of the Norwegian sailors had known something. The *Fjord-Elk* had been lost at sea, with all hands, just two years before. If Marion had gone away on her, she was probably in Norway, maybe as a widow, maybe married to a second husband, maybe not married at all but making a living as a whore. He had tried not to think of her again, but had never been able to keep the resolution for long at a time.

"It's different for women!" Richard shouted. "And there's Nicky to tell you why! Most people know who their mother is, but if women aren't honest, how can men be sure their children are their own? Get rid of her!"

"If Mother goes to Dunster, or anywhere else, I go with her." Quentin had joined them. Peter looked at her, thinking that she at least was an unmistakable Lanyon. The beechnut hair and the apple-blossom skin were Liza's but the dark eyes, the shape of the face were entirely his own. He saw, too, that she had left childhood behind. She was a young woman now, eighteen years old, and she was courageous.

"She lies on the bed in that room all day, sobbing," Quentin said. "Grandfather, I don't believe she's any of the horrible things you've called her, but that doesn't matter, not to me. She's still my mother and if no one else will help her, I will."

"You can't leave unless your father and I say so!" shouted Richard.

"You can't chain me up forever," said Quentin reasonably. "And if Mother and I are both gone, who'll see to the accounts?" She looked at Peter. "Oh, *Father!* Are things never to come right again?"

Her voice had always had a calming quality. The crimson faded somewhat from Richard's face. Awkwardly Peter said, "Quentin, I'm sorry. I hate seeing you distressed." He turned to Richard. "For years and years Liza and I have dwelt in peace together, even though we were not each other's first loves. I wish her to stay. I want to mend the breach...."

Quentin's soothing tones could achieve only so much. Richard lost his temper again. "I repeat, you're out of your mind! Look how she's deceived us all! Going for walks on the moor! We thought they were harmless. I wonder how many times she's *really* met this red-haired lover of hers? I wonder how many others there've been besides him!"

"There have been *no* others! Of that I'm sure."

"Oh, are you indeed?"

"Yes, I am! I *know* Liza. As for the red-haired lover, I intend to visit Dunster Castle and see that Christopher Clerk leaves the west country and never returns. I also intend to keep my wife, and I would remind you, Father, that Liza is *my* wife and not yours. It's for me to say."

"Very well," said Richard grimly, quietening down once more but this time becoming, in the process, somehow more menacing, more alarming than ever. "But I'll tell you one thing, boy. If I have to tolerate that woman here, there's one thing I *won't* stand for. Try making me and you'll regret it. Listen to me!"

"It's not right. None of this is Nicky's fault. Please, Father, please, please think again," Quentin implored him, but Peter, accosted as he sat at the study table, only shook his head and sanded the new will he was preparing.

"No, my dear. Nicky is not my son or my father's grandson and he can't inherit the Lanyon property. There, sadly, my father is right and he had no need to threaten to disinherit me as well if I argued. Allerbrook and all the rest of our property will be for you instead. You'll be an heiress!"

"I don't want to be an heiress! I'll…I'll…give it away to Nicky when the time comes. I will!" said Quentin passionately.

"You'll be married by then, I trust," Peter said, "and your husband won't let you, not if he has any common sense."

"But Nicky! What will he do? How will he live, where will he go? It's *Nicky,* Father! *Nicky!*"

"I know. Quentin, my dear girl, I'm not going to abandon him just like that. I shall ask him what he wants to do with his life and help him as far as I can. I know I must do that."

His head was aching again. He found it intolerable to be in Nicky's presence. Every time he looked at the lad, he seemed to see him double—the Nicky he had always known as his son, with an interloping stranger weirdly superimposed on top. But Nicky had followed him to war, and on that packhorse bridge Nicky had saved him from, at the least, a disagreeable accident. And if he had thought of Nicky as a son all these years, Nicky had regarded him as a father. None of these things could be thrown onto the midden. They were reality.

"He can't be the Lanyon heir, but he won't be flung out to starve, Quentin, my dear. I will explain to him. Don't tell him yourself. Leave it to me and to my father. But now I have to go to Dunster. I have one last item of business to deal with."

★ ★ ★

"I have been expecting you," said Christopher, showing Peter into his room at the castle. It was no more than a small stone cell with the plainest of furnishings and coarsely woven blankets on the narrow bed. The only touches of luxury were a prie-dieu with a very beautiful silver crucifix above it, and two or three books on a shelf. By the look of them, they were printed, Peter thought. Father Matthew had a printed Latin Bible in the church at Clicket and Peter had handled it sometimes. A man called Caxton had brought the art of printing to England, Father Matthew said. Printed books were precious.

Christopher offered him a stool, but Peter remained standing. He was studying his rival, wondering what it was in this unremarkable tonsured individual that had so enchanted Liza. Even as a young man, he hadn't been that handsome, surely. Well, Nicky wasn't going to be particularly handsome and Nicky was a good enough comparison. Too good. Practically identical! "Do you know why I've come?" Peter said.

"To make sure I'm thrown out of Dunster Castle, I daresay. Well, rumour says that Lady Luttrell is to return soon and she may not want me here in any case. I daresay she hasn't forgotten the trouble I caused once long ago. I was already making plans to leave. Believe me, I have no wish to disturb Liza's life, or yours, any more than I already have."

"You can hardly outdo the disturbance of finding that I've been saddled with another man's son!"

"I had no idea," Christopher said. "None at all. Liza never told me, never sent me word. She just…did her best, I expect, for you and for the child. What else was she to do?"

"She's no concern of yours now. When do you intend to go? And where?"

"I leave tomorrow. I have already informed the bishop's office that I wish to give up this chaplaincy and seek a new position somewhere in northern England. I told part of the truth. It is on record that as a deacon I behaved in a most unfortunate way and I said that by chance, the woman concerned had crossed my path again and I thought it best to put a distance between us."

"And that was accepted?"

"Yes. I spoke to the bishop's deputy, as a matter of fact. This is the diocese of Bath and Wells, and the bishop's Robert Stillington, the man who stood up in council just after King Edward died and said he was sorry to upset everyone just as they were planning to crown the young Prince Edward, but young Prince Edward wasn't legitimate. He almost put Gloucester on the throne himself! He's now in London, attending King Henry's council and no doubt earnestly promising his utter devotion to the Lancastrian dynasty."

"And has bigger fish on his line than your bygone sins anyhow? I take it," said Peter, "that you have never confessed what must have happened fourteen years ago!"

"No. I prefer to trust in the understanding of God rather than men for what I did, the day I started Nicky on his way into the world. I know his name," said Christopher quietly, "because you more or less introduced us, the day we all met. Liza and I…we came together only that once, by the way. Liza was in distress. There had been deaths—a man called Higg, and also some of her relatives…"

"I don't want to hear. Don't tell me. It's as well you're leaving," said Peter. "If you'd tried to stay, I would have gone to your bishop myself and told him what you've done. Even if I had to go to London to find him. I'd have made him listen!"

"You need not worry. I'll be away from here tomorrow and I go of my own free will. I am sorry, Master Lanyon, for the hurt I have dealt you. I shall never see Liza again, though I shall remember her in my prayers."

"I would rather you didn't."

"Master Lanyon, *please*...if you can forgive her, do so. She's worth forgiving."

"That I know. You may leave her with me in safety."

"And Nicky?"

"Just pack your belongings and go away from here and save your soul. Nicky isn't your concern any more than Liza is. Good day."

Liza, hearing Peter's voice outside her door, hesitated before unbolting it, but after all, the moment had to come. She could not stay here forever. Already she had stopped crying, because even tears ran out in the end. She had lain, unwashed and weeping, for days on end, only nibbling at the food that Quentin brought her, but sooner or later something would have to change, sooner or later this dreadful catastrophe must be resolved in some fashion, though she couldn't imagine what. Peter's request for admittance was the signal that the time of change had arrived.

She was afraid of him, though, and as he came into the room, he looked bigger and darker than she had ever known him and his face was hard as she had never seen it before. She quailed. Peter, studying her, saw the fear in her eyes. He didn't like to see it. She was still Liza.

Quietly he said, "It's time to come out, Liza. We can't go on like this for the rest of our lives."

"But what is to happen?" Liza was so frightened that she had to push the words out as though they were swimming against a tide. "Your father wants me to go back to Dunster, I know. I've heard him shouting it! But my family might not take me in. I suppose I shall have to go to the nuns at St. Catherine's, as my mother did."

The thought was intolerable. At the time of her marriage she wouldn't have believed it, but Allerbrook, now, was home. It was *home.* To be cast out of one's home was one of the most bitter things in the world. How had her mother been able just to abandon hers?

"Do you want to leave?" Peter asked.

"No! Of course not! Oh, if only it hadn't happened! We... Christopher and me...we'd only met to talk, as friends. That was all. There was just that one time, years and years ago..."

"Maybe it was just once and maybe not...."

"It *was!*"

"He's going away. He'd decided to do that even before I turned up at Dunster Castle and told him to leave Somerset or I'd make him."

"Make him? How?"

"I meant to use the threat of reporting him to his bishop. Though as the bishop's attending the royal council just now, I'd have had to chase him to London. But there's no need. Your Christopher is leaving Dunster and going to the north. He's out of your life, and that's the end of it. As for us, Liza, stay here if you want to. We've had many good years together and I don't want everything falling apart, no, I don't."

"What does your father say to that?"

"My father," said Peter sharply, "will accept what I decide. This time it's my business, not his, and I will be a man and not a boy."

"Yes. I see." A faint hope had awakened in her. Peter's face was still strange to her, though—expressionless, remote. She was still afraid. "But...Nicky?" she ventured.

"Nicky's home is here and I will help him to...to find a calling to suit him. I have loved Nicky. I still do, in a way. But he can't inherit Allerbrook or any other Lanyon property, not now."

"Are you revenging yourself on me through Nicky?" Liza asked miserably.

"No. It isn't revenge. It's simply that...he is not a Lanyon. Is he?"

"He has lived all his life as a Lanyon. He must feel like one," said Liza. "Have you told him? Does he know?"

"Not yet. Father and I are going to a lawyer in Dulverton tomorrow to make sure that our new wills are properly worded and sign them with witnesses. There must be no mistakes. Once that's done, I'll tell him. And now..." He stood up, holding out his hand to her. "Come. There's work to do. There always is, on a farm."

"All right," said Walter Sweetwater to the physician he had fetched, personally, from Dulverton. "I can see by your face what you think. I suppose I already know it."

"He's under forty and he's strong. There is hope. But..." The physician, himself an ageing man with a straggly white beard and legs which felt stiff after riding ten miles over the moor, at speed, with Walter Sweetwater urging him on all the way, let the sentence die away, unfinished.

"He only took a chill after falling into a stream," said Walter, almost pleadingly. "He told me he had been thrown from his horse, but I could see he had been in a fight. His face was marked as only fists could mark it. In the end he admitted it. But he's had fights and fallen into streams before."

"Not when his body was still full of bad humours from a battle wound," said the physician. "And the wound has worsened since the fight, as your daughter-in-law says." He looked back toward the door of Baldwin's bedchamber, which was half open. Catherine was there, sitting at the bedside. They were speaking quietly so that she wouldn't overhear, but there was no need to worry about Baldwin overhearing. He was asleep, breathing harshly through a chest which sounded as though it were full of liquid.

"The wound probably opened again during the fight," Walter said.

"I daresay. A chill on top of that, from riding home in wet clothes, perhaps some impurity in the water of the stream—as a physician I have seen such things before. I have told Mistress Sweetwater how to make my special draught for fighting fever. But..."

Again, the sentence died away.

"He is the best of sons," said Walter bitterly. "But always a hothead. When I got him to tell the truth, well, the fight he was in—he started it. It was on a narrow bridge. Another man, someone he doesn't like, was halfway across, coming the other way, and instead of waiting for him my son ordered him to go back. It would have meant backing the pony a long way. The other man was entitled to refuse, and he did and Baldwin insisted on fighting him for right of way and tried to throw him over into the water. But in the struggle it was Baldwin who went over."

"Yes, I see. And with that wound still giving trouble...well, keep him warm and try to induce a sweat. There is poison in his blood, a black and evil earth humour, but sweat may bring it out. Though..."

"I know," said Walter. "Send for a priest. My grandson has already gone to get Father Matthew."

When the physician had left, Walter went back to Baldwin. Catherine looked around. Her kitten face was very pale. "It was such a foolish thing. An argument about precedence on a silly bridge!" She let out a sudden sob, as much of anger as distress. "What a stupid thing to die for!"

"He may not die. He's strong," said Walter, but there was little hope in his voice. "I dislike the Lanyons so much," he said, "that once I'd have been in sympathy with Baldwin simply because of that, but now—I'm getting old, my dear. It is a stupid thing and it's his own fault. I know."

Nicky sat in his window seat, as he had done the night he ran away to follow the man he thought was his father to Bosworth. He was waiting for the house to sink into slumber. He had laid his plans more carefully this time, as he now knew that when he ran off on that occasion, his mother had heard the harness-room door close. Sunset's bridle and saddle were already hidden under a bush in a corner of the ponies' paddock. No one would hear anything this time, indeed they wouldn't. He was taking Sunset, not the chestnut pony Ned Crowham had lent him. Peter, who had never forgiven Ned for forcing him to change sides, had not returned the chestnut to the Crowham manor house but had sold it and given Nicky the money. Nicky therefore had funds and he was taking those as well.

He had made a fool of himself, of course; thrown away his dignity. He shouldn't have screamed and raged like that when his father...no, Master Peter Lanyon...chose to honour a Sunday morning by telling him that he was no longer the heir to Aller-brook. The news had taken him by surprise. In fact, he had never really thought about being grown-up and living on after his father and grandfather were gone, and inheriting all that they had owned, except for a dowry for Quentin.

But once it was explained, then he knew how much he cared for Allerbrook and how much he felt that he belonged here. It was cruel to do this to him, cruel to blame him for what his mother had done. He had said that, shrieked it almost, flung himself at Father—no, Master Lanyon—tried to cling to him, tried to *make* things go back to where they were, when this man was truly his father and he was the son of the house and…

Master Lanyon had detached his grasping hands, not roughly, but firmly. He had said something about helping Nicky to find another future life, even made suggestions about it. Would Nicky like to learn to weave properly, or be apprenticed to Herbert Dyer, or to a merchant? Nicky, sickened and furious, had turned away and run crying out of the room.

No, not dignified. He was old enough to behave better. His world had fallen apart, but he shouldn't have fallen to pieces himself. At his age, he knew, the dead king, Richard III, had had a man's work to do, raising arms for his brother. It was time for Nicky, too, to become a man. He would need help, and yes, he would have to find a new future, but the Lanyons would have nothing to do with it.

His real father couldn't help him. He was a priest and he'd gone to the north of England, so his mother had said. But Nicky still had a real family, after all—his mother's folk in Dunster. He didn't understand how his mother could have broken her marriage vows, but she was still his mother; the affection she had given him all through the years was still a warmth in his memory, which was more than could be said for his grandfather's harshness. And after all, whatever else she had done, she had given him life.

That much he did understand. Working it out, painfully, through sleepless nights, he had recognised that he was glad to be alive and could hardly, therefore, turn in fury on those responsible for his existence. That would be unjust, and he knew injustice when he saw it. Grandfa—Richard Lanyon—had demonstrated it for him, all too plainly.

The house was silent now. Father Matthew had made sure that he could read and write competently and he had penned a letter in which he explained why he was going and where. He laid it on his bed and weighed it down with an empty candlestick. He picked up his cloak and a bundle of belongings he had made ready, and tiptoed to the door. Letting himself out, he made his way noiselessly down the stairs, into the hall, and unbolted the outer door. The dogs in the kitchen sensed him and he heard them stir, but they knew his smell and didn't bark.

Like a shadow he slipped away from the house and into the pony paddock. There had been some rain during the day, but the tack he had left under the bush had been protected and was dry. Sunset greeted him with a snort but came to hand willingly enough. Nicky saddled him and mounted. The sky was clear, as it had been the first time he ran away, and once again there was a moon, though only half of one. But it was enough.

He turned his back on home, and rode away.

CHAPTER THIRTY-FIVE

A SENSE OF ABSENCE

Tommy Weaver was an early riser. On this shining late September morning, which had a faint smell of frost in the air, he was out of bed at first light and hurrying downstairs in dressing robe and slippers to heat some shaving water, while Susannah still slept. Having roused the fire and set the water pot on the trivet, he said good-morning to the maidservants who by then were coming downstairs, too, and went to unbolt the front door.

Sitting on the doorstep, a riding cloak huddled around him against the early chill, was his nephew, Nicky Lanyon from Allerbrook.

"Nicky! What on earth...?"

Nicky stood up, shivering. "Can I come in, Uncle Tommy?"

"Of course." Tommy stood back. "But what are you doing here—when did you come? And why? What's happened?"

"I've run away," said Nicky, stepping into the main room as

Tommy closed the door after them. "No, that's wrong." He turned to face his uncle and Tommy saw that he was at the stage of growth when a boy's body begins to elongate, to stretch toward manhood, and the contours of his face begin to settle. He had always thought of Nicky as Liza's little boy, but this youth had ridden with an army and been held prisoner. His boyhood had been left behind at Bosworth. "I didn't run away," said Nicky. "I chose to leave, and it's not the same thing. But I need shelter somewhere and time to think, so I came here, to my mother's family. Will you let me stay, until I can decide what to do next?"

"Of course we'll let you stay, but why did you run...leave home? What's amiss there?"

There was a silence. Then Nicky said, "It'll upset you, Uncle Tommy, if I tell it all. Maybe I'd better not. I was the son of the house and should have inherited Allerbrook and all that goes with it, but I've been cut out of Master Lanyon's will. But it's not my fault. I've done nothing wrong, I promise. Please can we let it go at that?"

"No, we can't—don't talk nonsense!" Tommy barked. "Now, look here...oh, for the love of heaven, look at you, you're frozen. Sit down. *Sit,* I said. Don't stand in the middle of the floor like a tombstone in a churchyard! Wait." He strode through the door to the kitchen and after a few moments reappeared with a tankard of ale, a chunk of bread, a knife and a pot of honey on a tray, while behind him a maidservant ran up the stairs, calling Susannah's name.

"They're frying some bacon. They'll bring it in a minute." He pushed Nicky into a settle and pulled a table within his reach. "Get some food inside you. My wife'll be down in a minute and

I'm going to fetch Cousin Laurence. Whatever it is you're scared of saying is a boil that needs lancing. I can see that, if you can't. He'll help."

Leaving Nicky to his breakfast, he went across the road at a run, still in his robe and slippers, to pound on the door of the opposite house. He returned once more within a very short time, with both Laurence and Elena. They, too, were early risers and he had found them up and dressed, though Elena's grey hair was only roughly combed and she hadn't put her coif on, and both of them were startled and bewildered by what he had to tell them.

Susannah, also bareheaded, though she had pulled on a gown and overgown, was with Nicky when they arrived, talking to him while he ate. The bacon had been brought and he was obviously ravenous. He rose to greet his cousins, but Laurence told him to sit down again and finish eating.

"Then tell us what's brought you here. It must have been something serious to bring you riding through the night."

With Laurence's arrival, family authority had come into the room. Tommy looked at him gratefully and even Nicky seemed steadied by his elder cousin's presence, though when he had gulped his final mouthful, his first words were, "I can't explain properly. None of it makes sense. I can't stay at Allerbrook and I don't know what to do. I don't want to *say* things."

"I think there are things you will have to say," said Laurence calmly. "For one thing, Tommy says your father has disinherited you but it isn't your fault. Whose fault is it, then?"

"Nicky," said Susannah, "if you've done something to make your father angry, or he thinks you have…well, whatever it was, try to tell us about it. Please. Has it been a…a mistake? I can't believe you've done anything as dreadful as all that."

"I didn't do *anything*. It wasn't like that." The food had made him feel warmer, but the presence all around him of his elders, though reassuring in one way, was also thrusting him back toward his childhood. He had begun to feel like a little boy again, and worse than that, a little boy close to tears. The night ride had been not only cold, but frightening.

He hadn't felt like that the night he ran off to join his father on the way to war, because then he had ridden across open moorland, in bright moonlight. This time the moon was waning and rose late, and the last part of the ride had in any case been through the woods above the village of Timberscombe, farther up the Avill Valley than Dunster was.

No moonlight came through the dark trees that met above his head and although he kept telling himself not to be afraid, that there was nothing to fear, every gruesome tale he had heard in his childhood came back to him. On dark nights, ghosts and witches and demons might be abroad. Anything might be lurking in the shadows to either side. He had felt sick with the long-drawn-out dread by the time he came at last across the packhorse bridge and into the safety of the sleeping village. And after that, after turning the pony into the Weavers' paddock and leaving the tack in the shelter they had built there for the animals, and walking back to their house, he had had to sit on the cold doorstep for what seemed like an eternity.

"I'm sorry," he said. "I'm tired. I rode nearly all night. The pony's in your field, Uncle Tommy. It was still night and I didn't want to wake anyone up, so I sat on the step till morning."

"*Nicky!*" said Tommy protestingly.

"Is it a girl? Have you got a girl with child, even at your age?" asked Laurence.

"Oh, surely not!" Elena put a hand over her mouth.

"No, I haven't!"

"Nicky," Laurence said, "you must tell us! Someone else in your family will if you don't. One of us will ride out there and ask!"

Nicky gave in. "Father...Master Lanyon...says I'm not his son and Mother's been shut up in one of our spare rooms, crying all the time. Quentin took food to her. She's come out now, but she walks about like a ghost, not speaking. Not even to me, though when she sees me, she starts to cry again. And hardly anyone ever speaks to her. Master Lanyon says my real father's someone called Christopher Clerk—"

"Christopher Clerk?" said Laurence. "Him!"

"Yes. Coming home from the war, we came on him and Mother together, sitting in a hollow on the moor, and I look just like him and so I'm not a Lanyon and I can't inherit Allerbrook and...I don't want people to know about my mother. I didn't want to tell you!"

"Oh, dear God!" said Tommy.

Susannah, practical and acute, said, "You can rely on us for one thing. We'll keep your secret. Now that we know what really happened. Won't we?" She looked appealingly at the others, who nodded.

"We'll never tell anyone," said Laurence. "You came here because you weren't happy at Allerbrook. We'll say that. Your grandfather's a hard man. Anyone who's met him knows it. Don't worry."

That same night, in the candlelit sickroom at Sweetwater House, Walter and Catherine tried to quieten Baldwin as he tossed and struggled to breathe, and then saw him lapse into silence and coma and the harsh rattle of approaching death. In the unsteady light Walter's eyes met Catherine's across the bed. "I think I should wake John."

Catherine picked up Baldwin's hand and then the tears began to run, silently, down her face. "There's no life in his hand," she said. "He can't feel me. Baldwin, I'm here. Can you hear me? It's your Kitten!"

Walter left the room, but met John just outside the door, out of his own bed already, a cloak thrown around him. "I just woke and felt as if..."

"Yes. He's going, I think. Come in."

Others followed him, wakened, it seemed, by the same instinct which had roused John: the steward Denis Sawyer, Catherine's maid, Amy. They gathered at the bedside. After a time, the painful breathing grew very faint and there came a gap so long that for a moment they thought it had stopped. Then came another gasp for air and Catherine thought wildly, "I'm still married. I'm still Baldwin's wife. My husband is still alive."

Baldwin, loud, arrogant Baldwin, had not always been an easy man to live with, but he had never ill-used her. They had lived their parallel lives, meeting at board and bed and on social occasions; otherwise keeping to their own worlds. Baldwin had his horses, his hawks, his hounds and his weapons; Catherine oversaw the household, plied her needle and tended her herb garden. She had been restful; he had been protective. It had worked.

The worst criticism he had ever made of her was when he remarked once or twice that it was unlucky that she had had a difficult time bearing John and never thereafter conceived again. Even then, he qualified it, every time, by adding that John was healthy; no one could say she hadn't done her duty and provided an heir. She had been content as his wife.

Some minutes later, she knew that she had become a widow.

"Well, he can't stop here," said Aunt Cecy flatly, sitting very upright despite her eighty-two years and behaving as though she were in charge of this family conclave in the big room at the Weavers' house. "It b'ain't decent."

"It's not for you to say!" snapped Laurence. "If it's for anyone, it's for Tommy and me. None of this is the boy's fault. He's Liza's son and there's no doubt about that!"

"Yes, and what's Liza? A strumpet! She tried to run off with that man when she was a girl and now it seems she's had him after all, and Nicky's the result. Bad blood will out, my boy!"

"Since I'm over seventy, I'm not going to be called a boy by you or anyone else," said Laurence, turning red as he always did when he was angry. "Nicky's a boy, though, poor lad, and he's brave in his way and he's Liza's son, no matter who fathered him. Tommy, what do you say?"

"I agree. I don't want to see Liza ever again, but Nicky himself is a different matter. Susannah agrees—don't you, Susannah? And what about you, Cousin Elena?"

"Nicky's not to blame, but I'd rather not see Liza again either," said Susannah. "She might be bad company for our Joanna."

"I've always felt a bit sorry for Liza," Elena remarked. "Seems to me that maybe she and Christopher Clerk really loved each other. He might have found a way to free himself from the church or else, well, there's many a priest has a comely house-keeper, or an arrangement with a woman somewhere, and many a priest that has nieces or nephews, so-called, and everyone knows they're really his, but no one comments. Maybe we should have let her go."

"Never!" said Tommy, outraged. "This is a respectable family. We'd never tolerate such a thing. We gave her a decent marriage to a decent man and she should have been grateful."

"And once you're wed, you're wed," said Aunt Cecy. "Tommy's right. What's she got to complain of, I'd like to know? Living in a fine house now, b'ain't she, highly respected and all the rest of it? Yet she goes and behaves like this! I call her a strumpet and I don't want that boy of hers here. Besides, what use is he? *He'll* never be any good on a loom."

"That," remarked Laurence's son Joss, who was among the most gifted weavers in the family, "is true enough. Put Nicky in front of a loom and…well…"

They all nodded and, in some cases, sighed. The mayhem that Nicky could wreak on even the simplest piece of weaving suggested not so much ineptitude as some kind of perverse imagination.

"No, he'll never make a weaver," said Laurence. "But he's old enough to be apprenticed to a trade. We just have to find one where he won't cause muddle and confusion. Where is he now?"

"At the field, looking at his pony," said Elena.

"He's an active lad," said Tommy. "There's a merchant I know in Lynmouth—he takes cheeses and iron and leather goods abroad and imports things like silk and brocade and foreign wines and dyestuffs. Brings in dyes for Herbert Dyer—that's how I met him. Once when I was in Lynmouth I went into an alehouse, and there they were. If he's willing to take on an extra apprentice, that might suit Nicky."

"What's his name?" Laurence asked.

"Owen ap Idwal. He's a Welshman, but he married a

Lynmouth girl and settled there so as she could be near her kin. He sails with his ship sometimes, does his own selling and buying. Nicky might get a chance to travel and I somehow fancy he'd like that."

"He's got to be settled somewhere," Susannah said. "He mustn't be turned out to wander. But I think it's best if he doesn't stay here."

"It would be encouraging wantonness, to take him in," said Cecy stiffly. "But find him an apprenticeship, by all means. And there's no need to ask him what he wants. He ought to be glad of anything."

Several members of the Weaver tribe exchanged secret glances. Aunt Cecy would never grasp that she wasn't the head of the household. They had learned to see the comic side of it.

To have Blue Lyn saddled and take him out for exercise was all that Walter Sweetwater could now do for Baldwin. The house was full of weeping, but there was a dreadful sense of absence, too. Baldwin's hectoring voice was so very much not there; far more so than if he were merely hunting or hawking or even gone to a war.

It always seemed unnatural for a child to go before a parent, though it was common enough. Agnes and Baldwin had not been the only children that Mary had borne him. There had been two other little boys, both dead of childhood illnesses before their fourth birthdays. Baldwin, though, had thrived, had lived to manhood, married and had a son, had ridden to battle and come back alive. He shouldn't have died of a mere chill and a wound that ought to have healed—was healing, until he got into the fight, which reopened the wound, and fell into the river, which gave him the chill.

Now he was being washed and laid out by the womenfolk and his father couldn't bear to stay indoors and Blue Lyn was fretting in his stall. Baldwin would have wanted someone to exercise him.

The horse, sidling and restless, needed a good gallop on the moors to take the itch out of his hooves, but to begin with, Walter guided him toward the fields of the home farm to the west of Clicket, a little patchwork of meadow and barley fields like a patterned coverlet, lying smoothly over a couple of low hills and stroked by some gigantic hand down into the deep crease between them.

Walter was making for the meadow where his sheep, which had been brought off the moor for the winter, were now grazing. The flock would have to be moved in a day or two. Edward Searle had told him that sheep should never stay on the same pasture long enough to hear the Sunday church bells ring twice. The pasture would grow rank with their droppings if they did. Out on the moor, they usually moved themselves.

"Folk think they'm foolish things, sheep," Searle had said, "but that's just because they're creatures of the flock and like to be together. It looks as if they just do what the sheep alongside is doing, and can't think for themselves, but you'd be surprised, once you get to know 'un. It's a wonder to me, just as much now as it ever was, that when I've had to separate lambs from their mothers awhile, as we do at shearing, and then turn the little ones back into the flock again, the way lambs and dams know each other. To us, the ewes all look alike and the lambs all look alike, and sound alike, too, but *they* know. It's a marvel, that's what it is."

Edward Searle had understood and loved his woolly charges and in the end had died among them. His heart had stopped when he was out in a meadow with them, wanting to look at a ewe that he said seemed sickly. His son Toby had found him, just lying there in the grass, quite quiet and peaceful. Toby was a skilled shepherd, too, not quite as tall and impressive as his father, but shaped in a similar mould all the same and devoted to his work, and his eldest son Edmund, who was grown up now and worked with his father, followed the same pattern.

It had been something of a joke with Baldwin that when Toby married, the bride he brought home from nearby Withypool had pale curly hair, a bleating little voice and yellow-brown eyes very much like those of a sheep. Baldwin had said things. Baldwin had a broad, not to say crude, sense of humour....

And now Baldwin's father, trotting Blue Lyn along the path beside the sheep meadow, found his eyes stinging. He would have sold his soul at that moment to hear Baldwin laughing in his loud way at one of his own rude jokes.

What roused him from his sorrow was actually the sound of noisily bleating sheep, and as he came in sight of their meadow he saw what had happened. There was a bramble bush at the far end of it, and one of the ewes had got her fleece caught in the thorns. The rest were gathered around her in an anxious semicircle, bleating in sympathy. Spurring Blue Lyn to a canter, he hurried to the gate, pulled up and dismounted. Tying his horse's reins to the gatepost, he went in and made for the scene of disaster.

Which really was a disaster. He had seen it happen before. Sheep clearly did have sense and feeling enough to be concerned if one of the flock was in trouble, but why in the world they didn't have sense enough not to try conclusions with bramble bushes in the first place, he could never understand. Edward Searle had overestimated their intelligence in some ways. There were some ripe blackberries on the bush and the ewe had probably tried to get at them, but didn't these creatures *know* they had fleecy coats that caught on thorns?

He was wearing gloves, since the day, though clear, was not especially warm, but they weren't very thick. This, thought Walter as he began an attempt at rescue, was going to be difficult. It would have helped if the ewe had cooperated, but she was already frightened and when he took hold of her, she began to struggle, entangling herself more thoroughly than ever and kicking him hard on the knee. The oaths he let out did nothing to calm her. He tried to get a prickly branch out of the wool on her shoulder and as he had feared, the thorns went straight through his glove and drew blood, causing him to swear again.

"Need help?" enquired a voice from beyond the hedgerow that separated the pasture from the lane. Walter, still half-crouched in order to hold on to the ewe, glanced around but could see only a brown woollen cap and part of a forehead above the bushes.

"I'd be glad of it!" he called, and heard whoever it was encourage his horse into a canter, going along to the gate. A moment later the newcomer was running back through the field to join him and another pair of hands, not gloved but strong and leathery from outdoor work, were there beside his, bravely tackling the brambles. "If you'll hold her still, sir, I think I can get this branch loose...."

"Here." Belatedly, Walter remembered that as usual, he was carrying a dagger. He pulled it out. "Cut the fleece free where it's caught the worst. Keep still, you damned stupid animal! I think she thinks I've come to turn her into cutlets. So I will, my girl, if you kick me again!"

The other sheep had drawn off to a little distance but were still watching, from time to time emitting anxious baas. Walter, who now had both hands free for the task, gripped the ewe so that she could no longer struggle while his unexpected helper eased some of the prickly stems away and sliced through the fleece where there seemed no chance of disentanglement.

At last they both stepped back, to let the freed ewe bound past them and rejoin her friends, who greeted her with a different note in their bleating, of welcome and relief, before they all flowed away in a woolly stream, which slowed down as it got out into the field, spread apart and stopped to graze.

"My thanks." Walter turned to look at his companion, whom he now recognised. "Good God! Peter Lanyon! What brought you past here?"

"I was up on the moor, looking at our pony herd, and I came back this way, meaning to take a tankard in the Hart before I went home. Er...Master Sweetwater, my farmhand Alfred was in Clicket early this morning." Peter spoke cautiously. "He went to see Father Matthew. He's to marry soon. Father Matthew told him about your son and when he came back, he told me. I am very sorry for your loss. Please believe me."

"Baldwin said it was you he fought and you who shoved him over the bridge into the water."

"Yes." The monosyllable was quiet but not apologetic. "Do you know exactly what happened on that bridge, Master Sweetwater?"

"I know what Baldwin told me." Walter's eyes were like dull pewter.

"And what, exactly, was that?"

"He challenged your right of way. He admitted that it *was* your right of way. But if only you'd backed your pony as he asked!"

"He didn't ask. He ordered. I was nearly across that bridge. When I wouldn't back, he challenged me to fight and I took the challenge. Would you have backed, Master Sweetwater?"

Walter stared at him, shoulders tense with dislike, and then let them sag. "No. I would not. I can't like you, Peter Lanyon, though I must thank you for your help just now, but I am not a dishonest man. It's true. In your place, I suppose I would have done as you did."

"It ended with Baldwin going over the parapet into the river, but only because he tried to push me over first. I fought back, but I was only saved because my…my boy Nicky was there and ran to me and caught hold of my feet." It was painful to speak of Nicky. "I went down," Peter said, "and helped your son out of the water. I told him to go home and get dry. I have heard now that he had a wound from Bosworth, which opened in the struggle—the White Hart is a cauldron of gossip—but I didn't know of it then. I am sorry it happened, but I didn't try to kill him, or want to."

There was a silence. Then Peter said, "After Bosworth, I heard of two westcountrymen, a father and son, hanged at Henry Tudor's orders because they had been at King Richard's side when he fell. I wondered at first if they were Baldwin and his son. When I heard that it wasn't so, I was glad. I wouldn't have wanted such a thing to happen to them."

"Baldwin was a fool to pick a fight when he was injured. I know. So do you. You haven't said it, but I can see you thinking it."

"If you say so, Master Sweetwater. But when I offer my condolences, I mean them."

"If I'd realised straightaway that it was you just now, I'd have told you to go to perdition and leave me to deal with my own sheep."

"And I'd have ignored that and come to help anyway. For the sake of the sheep," said Peter.

"Bloody Lanyons. Always a thorn in our sides, like bramble in a sheep's fleece."

"I sometimes wish," said Peter, "that we could just be neighbours. Will it offend you if I am in the churchyard when Baldwin is buried? I would mean it respectfully, but I won't come if you object."

"I won't object. Just don't be noticeable," said Walter. He sounded tired and Peter, looking at him, saw that the lines in his face told the same story. "I grow weary of feuds," Walter said. "And people clack their tongues in the White Hart and laugh about us. Baldwin will be buried on Wednesday morning, the twenty-eighth. It will give time for me to send word to his sister. She may wish to come. Just about everyone for miles will be there. The Lanyons may as well join in. If your father allows!"

"I shan't ask his permission," said Peter.

Peter had left his pony tied to the other end of the gate where Walter had left his. They walked stiffly back together, loosed their mounts, nodded to each other, got back into their saddles and parted. Peter, forgetting about the tankard of ale, rode home, thinking.

He did indeed feel sorry for Walter's bereavement and he knew why. Last night Nicky had left home, although this time he had also left a note and they knew where he had gone. Richard had forbidden anyone to go after him and with sorrow, both Peter and Liza had agreed that perhaps this was best. But it was the reason Peter had saddled Plume and taken to the moor this morning. Nicky had been his son for so long, had saved him at the bridge and yet had had to be rejected. Now he had rejected Peter in turn. Nicky was lost and it was a dreadful thing to lose a son. The sense of the boy's absence hurt so much.

CHAPTER THIRTY-SIX
EXTRAORDINARY CHANGES

Quentin Lanyon loved her family. It came naturally to her. Her parents and brother were dear to her and if her grandfather was dictatorial he was nevertheless still her grandfather and it was normal for people to love their grand-parents. It did not occur to her to question these things.

One day, she supposed, she would have a husband and children and would love them, as well. Beneath all this, like the hidden foundations of a house, was the assumption that all her family members loved each other.

This foundation had occasionally shuddered—for instance when Grandfather was harsh with Nicky—but always, hitherto, peace had been restored in the end. She had never envisaged a state of affairs where love would cease altogether, where the family would be split into factions, with her mother ostracised and tearful and her brother no longer a member of the family at all. It was beyond her comprehension.

At the beginning, when Liza had shut herself into a spare bed-chamber and Quentin had looked after her, Liza, sitting tearfully up when her daughter brought food to her for the second time, had wiped her eyes and made an attempt to explain.

"Have they told you everything, Quentin? Do you know what's happened, about Nicky and all?"

"Yes. I overheard some of it, anyway." Quentin spoke awkwardly, unsure what her mother expected her to say.

"I wish I could make you—or someone—understand. I care so much for your father. But Christopher—Nicky's real father is called Christopher—well, I met him before I was married and, well, it may happen to you one day and then you'll know. No one it hasn't happened to can *ever* know. You meet a man and he isn't specially handsome or clever or wealthy or...or anything that makes him different from a thousand others, but you look at him and the world turns upside down and it never turns back again."

A girlhood memory came back to Liza as she spoke, something she rarely thought about now, though when Quentin was a child, she had told her about it. "Do you remember, when you were about twelve, one January night I pointed out the constellation of Orion to you? That magnificent pattern, stamped on the sky?"

"Yes. You said you'd marvelled at it when you were a little girl yourself. But..." Quentin was now more puzzled than ever.

"Well, sometimes a man can stamp his image into your mind like that, and there it is, for always, blazing and beautiful. It's like being put under enchantment, only it isn't enchantment, it's love, and if it's real, it doesn't die. We should have married, though if we had..."

Quentin, trying none too successfully to understand what Liza was talking about, felt embarrassed by these confidences. They matched nothing in her experience and besides, it was as though she were the one with authority and her mother a pleading child, and that wasn't natural. But the hollowed pallor of her mother's face would have touched far harder hearts than hers. She put her arms around Liza, who said, "If we had married, you would never have come into being and I'm glad you did. Nothing's simple. But years ago—fourteen or so—I met Christopher again and once, just once, we gave way. And then Nicky was born."

"But the other day...?" Quentin prompted, puckering her brow, wanting to understand, although it was like trying to make sense of a very unfamiliar dialect.

"The other day we met in a dell on the moor, just to talk, to sit side by side as friends do. It was the second time we'd done so." Liza paused, finding herself unable to describe the quality of those two companionable meetings. She and Christopher had indeed done nothing but sit together and talk, of everyday things. He had told her of his work at the castle; a marriage service he had conducted recently at which the groom had got his responses muddled; and how he and the new Mistress Hilton had between them persuaded the steward to have the castle completely cleaned—"spring-cleaned, except that it was summer"—from battlements to basement.

She had talked to him of the farm and the cows, telling him how, since ceasing to be Sweetwater tenants, they had acquired a bull of their own which had chased Hodge twice, and how they had once more replaced their ram, this time with a crossbred animal which had the superb fleece of his predecessor but not the enormous horns and outsize skull.

She could not find words for the quality of those conversations, the comfort of them, the pleasure of talking so easily, without the hint of fear which her father-in-law always inspired in her and without the distortion which was slight but always there with Peter because they had not chosen each other and would, left to themselves, have both chosen differently. All she could say was, "When people grow older, Quentin, that's how it is. Just to sit and talk is enough. All the rest is in the past and long ago. Except..."

"Except that there's Nicky?" said Quentin, still puzzling it out.

"Yes, there's Nicky. And your father caught us, sitting in a dell, and Nicky—I've always known it—is Christopher all over again. There's no mistaking it, not when you see the two of them together."

Here at least was something she could grasp. "If only," said Quentin passionately, "Father hadn't taken that sheep path. If only you hadn't been right *in* his path!"

"Then no one would ever have known. I'd have taken my secret to my grave with me, darling, and who would have been harmed? Your father would have gone on thinking he had a son, and Nicky, one day, would have had Allerbrook and what would it matter?"

"Grandfather says it matters." Quentin's voice was not accusing, only bewildered. "He keeps on saying it, and thumping tables with his fist. He keeps saying that Nicky isn't a Lanyon and has no right to Allerbrook."

"Has he said that in Nicky's hearing?" Liza's voice broke, once more, into a sob. "Oh, poor Nicky!"

"Not yet, but I think he's going to. Father says I'm not to warn Nicky—they'll tell him themselves. It isn't fair," said Quentin roundly. "Lanyon or not, the farms have to be looked after by someone and why can't people just leave things alone and be happy?"

"No, it isn't fair, but that's the way it is." Tears slipped from Liza's eyes, quietly but relentlessly. "I don't know what's going to happen to me, darling. I may have to go away, go to St. Catherine's like my mother did. I don't want to go. It's strange. When I first came here, I thought I'd never get used to it, never call Allerbrook my home, but it's home now, has been for years and…and it'll break my heart if I have to leave it. Only…"

"If you go away, to Dunster or St. Catherine's or anywhere else, I'll go with you!"

"You're a dear girl, Quentin," said Liza. "The only one not to pass judgement on me."

Quentin shook her head, not in denial, but because she didn't know how to explain that she couldn't pass judgement because she didn't understand what it was she would be judging. She could not imagine being so enchanted by a man that the world turned upside down. All she could do was believe that it had happened to her mother, because her mother, whom she loved and trusted, had said so.

"I'm very glad you were born," said Liza, attempting once more to dry her eyes, "and I'm sorry to be burdening you with all this."

"You're my mother," said Quentin. "And that's that."

Only that wasn't that, because that phrase suggested finality, a settling of a problem, and the problem didn't look like ever being settled. Nicky had indeed been cruelly disinherited and although Liza had now emerged from the spare room, she crept about the house like a shadow and no one except Quentin spoke to her much beyond necessity. Betsy pursed her lips and turned away whenever Liza entered the kitchen and Ellen imitated her. Richard literally pretended that she wasn't there, even when she was handing him his dinner. His temper was very short these days, and he seemed to become crimson and breathless when provoked.

Peter did try sometimes to talk to his wife, but his voice was always stiff, as though he were forcing himself. They were sharing a bedchamber again, but Quentin knew that one of them was sleeping in a truckle bed. And now, this morning, they had found Nicky's letter and knew that he had gone. Liza, mouth trembling, said, "I hope my family will help him. He's only thirteen."

Richard said, "It's just as well. He's none of mine and I'm glad to see the back of him. I hope he doesn't try to come back, because if he does, I won't have it."

"I don't agree," said Peter. "He's only a lad. We've been his family since he was born and..."

His father brushed him aside. "He's got a family, a real one. I mean the Weavers and he's had sense enough to go to them. If any neighbours get nosy, we'll just tell them he preferred the Weavers to us and left at his own wish. The Shearers aren't that nosy, anyway," he added, swinging the conversation determinedly away from Nicky. "That was a surprise! Who'd have thought Martha would reappear with her sheep-shearing husband and apply for the tenancy when her dad died? I hear she leads old Tilly a miserable life. Revenge for being used as a maidservant when she was young, I suppose."

From then on, it seemed that Nicky's name was not to be

mentioned in the house. Richard cut anyone short who spoke it in his hearing. The news that Baldwin Sweetwater was dead, probably because of the encounter with her father on the bridge, was just one more wretchedness.

Now, helping her mother to sweep old rushes out of the hall before strewing fresh ones, in Quentin's sore heart something new had taken root—a sturdy little seedling of rebellion. The atmosphere in the house was so turgid with rage and misery that it could almost have been cut into slices with a cheese knife. The rest of her family seemed ready to live like this forever, but Quentin was not. The Quentin who had once kicked and cried in a vain defence of Nicky, had pleaded for his right to inherit Allerbrook, was pleading and kicking and crying again, inside her mind. Something must be done. She didn't yet know what, but *something*...

Liza, listlessly sweeping, seemed to lose heart. She stopped, leaned her broom against the wall, and said, "I must tell Betsy what to make for dinner. Your father likes mutton ham so we could have that, and finish the stew we had at supper yesterday.... Your grandfather hates waste...."

She was constantly making offerings of food, trying to make the angry men of the house less angry by giving them the things they liked best to eat. Quentin could have wept for her. Liza went toward the kitchen and Quentin, putting her own broom aside, followed, just in time to hear Liza explaining that the stew should be finished at dinner today, and hear Betsy reply, "Yes'm," and then, mouth primmed, turn her back and continue stirring a bowl of batter with a wooden spoon.

"I can't bear it," said Liza. *"I can't bear it!"*

"And what might that be, ma'am?" Betsy enquired in a mumbling voice and still with her back to Liza.

"This. You. As though I were a leper. Sometimes I think I'll slip out one night, as Nicky did, only I'll go to the barrow on the ridge, or maybe to the barrows on Winsford Hill. It's higher and colder there. I'll lie down in the night chill and the dew and let myself die. They say there are ghosts at the barrows. I'll be one of them then, and maybe they'll be kinder to me than you are!"

"Well, would 'ee now?" Betsy still wouldn't turn to her. "Add one mortal sin to another, would 'ee? Well, well, no surprise in that, I suppose."

"Oh, Betsy! How can you—after all these years?"

There was a sob in Liza's voice, and with that, the seedling of rebellion in Quentin shot up to full height in the space of half a second and burst into furious bloom. Darting forward, she seized Betsy's arm and swung her around. The wooden spoon scattered yellow drops in all directions. "Don't turn your back on my mother and sneer at her like that, you smug, self-righteous old *prune!*"

"What?" Betsy spluttered.

"You heard what I said! You watch your manners or I'll make you!"

Ellen, tending a pot at the fire, turned around and gaped while Betsy, outraged, flourished the spoon menacingly. "You watch your own manners, my wench. I don't talk pretty to trollops and—"

"It's *my mother* you're talking about!"

"Trollop I said and trollop I meant! Passing off a bastard as the son of the house—"

"Mistress Lanyon," said Quentin savagely, "is *still* my mother. As for Nicky, that happened fourteen years ago and for all those fourteen years you've worked for my mother and she's the same

woman now that she was all that time! Don't you dare call her a trollop again!"

"I'll call 'un what I like and I won't talk to—"

"Why not? You used to talk to Father Bernard and he was supposed to have had a son. You talk to my grandfather and I know all about him and Deb Archer, because Kat told me about them. You talked to Deb, too, apparently! So you'll treat my mother with respect and—"

"You should be ashamed! Standing up for a trollop—"

Quentin lifted her right hand and administered a box on the ear which sent Betsy staggering. She threw her spoon down, clutched at her ear and began to howl. "Quentin, don't!" Liza gasped. "Betsy's over seventy. You mustn't do that!"

"Why not?" Quentin screamed. "I'm sick to my stomach of living like this...you creeping about, afraid of everyone...people glaring and saying things or else *not* saying things...Betsy making holier-than-thou faces and turning away from you...I hate you, Betsy, you self-satisfied old besom, how dare you, how dare you? And don't you look at me like that or I'll hit you again! I won't have this...this feeling in the house, I won't! Nicky's been driven out but I'm not going to be driven out, and nor is my mother if I can help it and I'll stand up for her if I choose!"

"Quentin, Quentin...!" Liza was astounded. It was as though her sweet daughter, whose temperament hitherto had seemed perfectly in tune with her apple-blossom complexion, had undergone an extraordinary change into a wildcat.

"Come, Mother," said Quentin, turning to her. "Let's go back and finish the rushes. And you two, Betsy and Ellen, you can just do as you've been told. Mutton ham and stew for dinner and see that it's a good dinner and serve it up with pleasant faces. If that batter's for honeycakes, we'll expect them at supper, also served with a smile, do you hear?"

"Yes, I wouldn't mind seeing some pleasant faces myself," said Peter, walking into the kitchen. "I'm astonished, Quentin," he said. "I never thought my girl was such a termagant." To her surprise, he smiled at her. "In these difficult days, Quentin, I've felt better every time I've looked at you and heard your gentle voice. And now, when all of a sudden it isn't gentle, you've made me feel better still! Thank the saints you're here."

He hadn't looked at Liza. His eyes were on his daughter. "I can't hold it against you that you love your mother. It's right and proper, I suppose. I came to tell you, and you, Liza—" he turned to her at last, quite calmly "—that we all have an invitation. To Baldwin Sweetwater's funeral."

The change in the air was noticeable when dinner was eaten. Betsy and Ellen, while Quentin's dark eyes watched them with an ominous glitter, made approximately ordinary conversation. Liza, warmed by her daughter's championship, talked a little, too, instead of eating in silence with her eyes on her platter, as she had done since she left the spare room. Peter made reasonably normal replies.

Richard was the one who resisted most strongly. "I hear you've been throwing your weight about, young Quentin. Wouldn't be getting a bit full of yourself, would you, maid? Perhaps it's time we got you married."

"I will be happy to marry any suitable man you find for me, Grandfather," said Quentin. Her tone was one of sweet compliance. "But," she added, still in the same honeyed voice, "I couldn't go further than a betrothal until I felt sure that my mother was safe."

"What do you mean, *safe?* Has anyone hurt her? Though you don't mind hurting our Betsy, I hear."

"There's more than one kind of hurt," said Quentin. "When I know my mother is happy and…and…valued, and when I know that Nicky is all right, too…"

"Nicky's name isn't to be mentioned under this roof. He's no grandson of mine and I'll thank you to forget he ever breathed."

"Nicky is my brother," said Quentin. "I couldn't forget him if I tried. I will marry as you choose, but, as I said, only when I know that both my mother *and Nicky* are well and happy."

"Speak to me like that again, girl, and you'll be sorry."

"Lay a finger on her, Father, and *you'll* be sorry," said Peter, and Liza looked at him with gratitude, while Ellen, ignoring Betsy's attempt to frown at her, smiled. Suddenly the battle lines were redrawn. Liza had acquired supporters. Only Richard and Betsy now were ranged against her. They were ranged against Quentin, too, which Liza hated to see, but Quentin herself was obviously unmoved by it.

"I seem to be outnumbered," said Richard. "It's a sad day."

"If it's wrong to love my mother and my brother," said Quentin, "I'll confess the sin to Father Matthew next Sunday."

"You'll have a clever answer once too often one day," said Richard, "when your doting father isn't here to protect you!"

Peter, changing the subject with an air of determination, said, "Are you coming to Baldwin Sweetwater's funeral, Father?"

"No, I'm not. I wouldn't go to any burial of theirs except to dance on the grave," said Richard unpleasantly. "You go, if you want, you and Liza and Quentin. You'll feel awkward and so you should!"

★ ★ ★

Autumn was coming. The nights had grown cold and the day of Baldwin Sweetwater's funeral was overcast, with cloud flowing in from the west and a whisper of rain on the wind. The gathering in the church and then in the churchyard was well wrapped up against the weather.

It was a big gathering, however. Most of the village of Clicket was there, and all the tenant farmers were represented. It was easy enough for the Lanyons, who did indeed feel awkward, to lose themselves in the crowd. They stood back as the coffin was carried to the waiting grave, with Father Matthew leading the way. Six men of the Sweetwater household, including Denis Sawyer, were Baldwin's bearers. The Sweetwaters themselves walked behind: Walter, bent shouldered as no one had ever seen him before, Catherine swathed in a black cloak and holding the arm of her son, John, Agnes Northcote and her husband, Giles, pacing side by side.

John attracted some attention, since he was now nineteen and an only son, but not yet betrothed. There had been approaches made by and to the Sweetwaters, but none of the girls had pleased him enough, or his parents either, and now the growing rumours of the new King Henry's intentions toward his predecessor's supporters had made offers dry up. But something must surely be settled soon, all the same. It was time. Speculation about John had featured in the White Hart lately and it was featuring again, even here at his father's funeral.

The coffin had reached the grave and was being lowered into the earth and Father Matthew had begun the words of the committal. Only those close by could hear him, because the wind blew his words away, but they all knew what he was saying.

The Lanyons found themselves nearby, edged there by chance in the crowd. Catherine, releasing John's arm, had moved toward Walter and spoken to him, and Walter, bending his head toward her, had replied. They seemed to be trying to comfort each other. John had drawn apart. Quentin found herself suddenly very sorry for him. He looked lonely and very miserable. She knew him by sight, though she had never spoken to him. All the Lanyons said that Baldwin had been an unpleasant man, but his immediate family had apparently cared about him.

Quentin wondered sympathetically how she would feel if it were her father in that coffin, and then, on impulse, she moved forward, slipping between the people just in front of her, until she reached John Sweetwater's side. He glanced around at her, and looking into his face, she said quietly, "I am so sorry. It must be a sad thing to lose your father."

"He died in his bed, and shriven," John said. "It could have been worse. But thank you for your kind words. Who are you, by the way?"

"Quentin Lanyon."

"Oh. Peter Lanyon's daughter?"

"Yes." It occurred to Quentin that John no doubt knew all about the encounter on the packhorse bridge, but even though Baldwin's death had been largely his own fault, his son might not accept that. Perhaps she had been unwise to come up to him like this and speak to him. "I—I'm sorry," she said again. "I mean... I'm a Lanyon...." She looked away.

"It's all right." John's voice was harsh. "No one would blame *you,* anyway."

"Please..." Quentin would have liked to turn and run, but with the coffin ropes just being drawn up and Walter going forward now to toss a clod of earth onto the lid, and people all around with heads bowed in prayer, she couldn't. "We're all sorry," she whispered.

John was still studying her. Taking courage again, she once more turned to look at him. She saw that he was not quite a typical Sweetwater. He had the burly build, but his hair was dark instead of brown, and though it was wiry, it wasn't bushy. Also, instead of the chilly grey Sweetwater eyes, he had good-natured blue ones. Timidly she smiled at him. She meant it as conciliation, an assurance that even though she was a Lanyon she really did feel for him. She had no idea how her smile lightened her face, and made her dark eyes sparkle.

Unwillingly at first, and then more openly, John smiled back.

You meet a man and he isn't especially handsome or clever or wealthy or...or anything that makes him different from a thousand others, but you look at him and the world turns upside down and it never turns back again. It's like being put under enchantment, only it isn't enchantment, it's love, and if it's real, it doesn't die.

That was what her mother had said and now it had happened to her, as well. So this was what it was like—this yawning ache, this wish to *know* this young man, to seek out and become acquainted with every corner of his mind, understand his every thought and touch every last inch of his body. Yes, of his body. She wanted carnal knowledge of him. Father Matthew sometimes spoke of carnality in his Sunday homilies, warning his flock against it, even within marriage. Father Matthew was wrong! She wanted to slide her fingers through that dark wiry hair, press herself against John Sweetwater and investigate every curving muscle, bury her nose against his skin and inhale his scent; open to him and let him come into her and be one with her. *This* was what it was like.

His smile was fleeting, though it had remarkable charm. She could not tell whether it meant that he felt as she did, and she doubted it. He was unhappy; she had said something kind; he had perhaps noticed that she was young and nice-looking. He probably considered that her father had killed his. In any case, Lanyons and Sweetwaters were traditional enemies and no doubt he looked on Lanyons as socially beneath him. She could only let her soul be seen in her eyes, and hope, and pray, and yearn.

CHAPTER THIRTY-SEVEN

PROPOSAL

"It was none of my doing!" Herbert Dyer was defensive and indignant. In his sixties, with his beard now grey, he was not as bluff and self-confident as he had been. These days, he rarely went to meet incoming ships, because long hours in the saddle, or out in a coastal vessel amid the wind and spray, now wearied him. However, Richard Lanyon, though at sixty-five he, too, showed signs of age, was still capable of being intimidating when he was angry. He was angry now.

"And I don't believe it was Simon's either, intentionally," Herbert almost gabbled. "It was an error, just a mistake. We do have customers who want cloth dyed with that costly scarlet that's made from a sort of insect in some far-off eastern country. Lady Elizabeth Luttrell, for instance. Now that she's back in Dunster Castle, there's been an order from her. She wants velvet that colour for her son's bed hangings. Simon makes out the bills, but it's a tedious task and it's never been his favourite. I daresay he was tired and just accidentally went on charging the same rate when he finished a bill for someone who ordered the expensive dye and started on bills for people who'd had less costly colours. And *I'm* tired of you poking into my business and looking for trouble!" he added with an attempt at aggression.

"I daresay you are. But I've done it regularly for years and you know why. You've a lot to lose, let me remind you," Richard said, taking Herbert's arm and steering him farther across the drying yard, to make sure that no one in the workshop could hear them. There were no flapping cloths to get in their way on this November day; it was too cold for outdoor drying. Cloth had to be hung inside the workshop. "You've a reputation," said Richard, "for good work and honesty. Why gamble with it?"

"I didn't, and nor did Simon."

"I think he did, whether you knew it or not. Like father, like son."

"Simon's a fine man. I was so thankful when he came back safe from Bosworth and—"

"May you go on feeling thankful for him. Now listen, Dyer, this is the first time you've slipped in all these years and I'm not vindictive. But if it happens again, I'll set the Watchet constable on you. I mean it. This set of bills hasn't been sent out yet. The ones with the overcharging must be made out again, correctly. You understand?"

Herbert looked at him. "I could kill you sometimes, Lanyon. I've often wanted to, when again and again you come prowling and prying into things that ought to be private to me and Simon."

"You'd have been publicly disgraced long ago if I hadn't," said Richard coolly. "You won't want to house me tonight," he added. "I'm going home by way of Dulverton, so I'll leave now and stay the night at Cleeve Abbey. It's in the right direction."

"I see," said Simon Dyer grimly to his father. "Everyone else does it now and again. It makes up for the bad payers. But we mustn't. *We've* got to be as virtuous as angels in a world where honest profits never make a man rich. That fellow Lanyon is the worst, nosiest interferer that was ever born."

"I hate him," said Herbert morosely. "I hate all the Lanyons, but mostly him. I reckon his son and Liza were his pawns when they came here prying that time, that's all. Richard's the one who's stood over me all these years, and it's Richard I blame for destroying my marriage. Margaret was a good woman and I could have made her happy, if I'd had the chance. I'd do Master Lanyon a bad turn any time."

Cleeve Abbey made its guests comfortable in an austere fashion. The guest house had neither wall hangings nor floor rushes, but the straw-filled pallets were clean. Similarly, the food, though plain, was plentiful. Richard ate and slept satisfactorily, made a donation to the abbey funds in the morning, had an interesting discussion with the abbot about sheep breeding and then started out for Dulverton, a long ride and a long route home, but Liza had asked him to visit Dulverton to buy some salt and a supply of candles.

The weather was cold and the moors misty, but the monks rose early and so did their guests. It was still only noon when he trotted Patches into the busy little town, where the clatter of looms was as persistent as it was in Dunster. Like Dunster, it had a cloth exclusive to itself.

It also had a town crier. As he rode toward Fore Street, its principal thoroughfare, he heard the jangling bell and the powerful voice of the crier announcing a proclamation. Touching his heels to Patches's sides, he caught up with the tail end of the crowd of townspeople who were following the bell toward the church. They all halted as the crier reached the churchyard gate and stood there, once more ringing his bell, until he was sure he had assembled the best possible audience.

Then he made his announcement.

Richard had to put a hand hard against his mouth in order to keep from laughing. Oh yes, this was news indeed. It was the best joke he'd ever heard. Thank God Ned Crowham had made Peter change sides at Bosworth.

He dined in Dulverton and bought good supplies of salt and candles, hiring a mule to carry them. It was coming up to the time of year when they would need candles in the evening and soon, too, they would be slaughtering pigs and salting the bacon. As he rode on home, going slowly because of the mule (pack animals were always a hindrance, which was why he hadn't taken a pack pony with him from home), he thought about the town crier's news. Halfway home, an interesting idea came into his head. He couldn't, straightaway, be quite sure about it. Perhaps it would be too expensive—or perhaps his family might object so strongly that they would stand shoulder to shoulder and actually defy him. But it was certainly an idea. That would put those arrogant Sweetwaters in their place, once and for all, and it was time that young Quentin learned that young women ought to know their place, too, and not spring like mad things to the defence of faithless wives.

★ ★ ★

So this was love, thought Quentin. This was what it felt like to be enthralled by a man. Enthralled. Placed in thralldom. Placed under tyranny. That side of it was something her mother hadn't mentioned.

John Sweetwater haunted her. He walked invisibly by her side wherever she went. The image of him standing alone at his father's graveside, and his face and his smile when she spoke to him were as vivid in her mind as though the printer William Caxton had used her brain as a sheet of paper. They hung in the air between her and the real world. They were probably in her dreams, except that she usually forgot her dreams in the morning.

Hitherto, she had been an industrious girl, helping in the house, caring for cows and poultry, spinning and weaving. Now, although winter was setting in, bringing heavy mists, or else cold winds that hissed across the heather and made the dry bracken rustle, she suddenly began to make excuses to walk or ride on the moor or go down to Clicket.

Finding the excuses wasn't difficult. Liza, as though trying in some way to make reparation for her past, had taken to being charitable. Down in Clicket, Deb Archer's former maid Allie was now a widow and in need. Her only son had gone to sea and Allie made out as best she could, keeping geese and chickens and growing vegetables. Liza sometimes made gifts to her of bacon or butter.

Sometimes, too, she sent small gifts to Tilly Lowe at what was now the Shearers' farm. In old age, Tilly had become pathetic, bullied by Martha and Martha's husband, Andrew, and sometimes by their sharp-featured fourteen-year-old-son, Philip, as well. They were a hardworking family, but impatient and parsimonious and grudged giving houseroom to Tilly, who was lame and trembly but struggled to justify her dragged-out existence by shelling peas and twirling a spindle.

"All three of them shout at her and I've seen her crying over it," Liza said indignantly when Richard protested that she was giving away too much. "And I'm sure they don't give her enough to eat. Now, you take these oatcakes to her, Quentin, and this flask of elderflower wine, and see the others aren't by when you give them to her. They'll grab the things for themselves if they get a chance."

Liza, often busy and no longer comfortable on a pony or as fond of walking as she used to be, frequently asked Quentin to be her messenger, and Quentin, these days, was more than willing to go. She went with eyes wide open, scanning the world around her for glimpses of John Sweetwater. Quite simply, she yearned to see him again, if only from a distance.

Now and then, she was lucky. Once she saw him out on the moor, cantering along on a fine black horse with bridle and scalloped reins of crimson, and carrying a goshawk on his arm. Once, visiting Allie in Clicket, she saw him ride through the street and turn in through the archway to the Sweetwater stable yard. They were glimpses to treasure, to add to her tiny store of mental pictures of him.

She had nothing else. She dared not seek anything further. She ached to be with him, to talk to him, but was afraid to search him out. He would not understand. Even if he responded, it would probably not be in the right way. She was not very old, but she wasn't foolish. When young men like John Sweetwater talked of love to girls like Quentin Lanyon, they did not talk of marriage, and Quentin knew it.

She must yearn alone, and endure, and hope for a miracle. And try not to be glad that after all she had not been betrothed to poor Eddie Hannacombe, because that meant being glad that Eddie was dead, and that would be very wrong.

The third time she encountered John Sweetwater was again in Clicket, when she was taking more gifts for Allie. "A length of green cloth this time, and a ham," Liza said, packing the basket. "She doesn't get much chance of eating meat and last time you went, you said when you came back that her gown was patched. There's cloth enough here for a new one."

Quentin had delivered the presents to a very thankful Allie, had stayed for a while to help sort some of the eggs from Allie's hens, and then said goodbye. As she stepped out again, she saw John riding past. This time he saw her, too, recognised her and smiled. Overcome, Quentin bobbed, smiled back, and felt herself turn scarlet. John, appearing not to notice this, bowed slightly toward her, lifted his black velvet cap about half an inch off his head before putting it back and then trotted on toward his home.

Quentin was left with hammering heart, wild exhilaration at having this new, precious vision of him and fury against herself for behaving like a wantwit, going red and giving him a silly, timid smile when she should have been dignified, given him a polite nod and a gracious, friendly smile as a great lady, an equal of his, would do.

John, riding back to the stable, was amused. She was a pretty thing, that Lanyon wench, and kindhearted. It was a pity that he couldn't pursue the acquaintance, but he didn't want to start up the feud between the families again. It seemed to have faded now, a very odd result of his father's death, considering the circumstances, but this was evidently the way that Grandfather Walter wanted it. The old quarrel would certainly be stirred up, though, if he seduced a Lanyon girl. No. Better leave her alone.

He rode into the stable yard, and found the grooms rubbing down two strange horses. "Have guests arrived?" he asked, swinging a leg over the saddle cantle.

"Royal messengers." One of the grooms left his task and came over to him. It was John's custom to see to his horse himself, but this time the reins were firmly taken from him. "They're with your grandfather now, sir. You may be wanted."

John raised his brows, but took the hint and went in. Denis Sawyer met him in the door to the great hall. "I'm glad to see you back, sir. There's grave trouble. Your mother's beside herself and your grandfather's well nigh in tears."

"What in the world...?" Snatching off his cap, John hastened through the entrance vestibule and into the hall. Walter was in his usual chair by the hearth. The fire crackled cheerfully and the hall was quite warm, but Walter was huddled and shivering, as though he had been stricken by winter, while Catherine was walking in distracted circles, wringing her hands. Other servants, including Catherine's maid Amy, were in the hall, too, standing in clusters, many of the women sobbing.

Also present and apparently quite unmoved by the anguish all around them were two dignified men, dressed alike, in practical dark clothes. One of them turned as John came in, and he saw the red dragon of Henry Tudor embroidered on the man's doublet.

"Who is this?" said the man, as though this were not John's own home and John himself the son of the house.

"My grandson," said Walter. "Whose inheritance you have come to steal. John!"

"What is it? What's happening?"

"They're going to take our lands away!" said Catherine on a wail. "The king sent them! We fought for King Richard, but they say it was treason and they're going to take the Sweetwater property! There'll be nothing left but my dower lands! They're letting us keep those, but we used two farms to make up Agnes's dowry!"

"So that's just the two farms in Devon left," observed Sawyer. "Both with tenants. One lot of tenants and their rents must go to make room for our household."

"Yes. It's true," said Walter. His ageing fingers gripped the arms of his chair and his knuckles showed white. "We've to be out in a week. Our estate will be sold to feed the royal treasury. The sale is being proclaimed now, today, in Dulverton, in Dunster, in Exford, in Minehead, in Porlock and Lynton and Lynmouth— everywhere! We're ruined."

"Well, I'm sorry for them," said Quentin across the supper table. Liza looked at her anxiously, and wished her daughter wouldn't be so downright. It might make Richard angry. Richard had not forgiven Quentin for trying to protect her. He showed it every day, in half a dozen ways—by ignoring his granddaughter, or ordering her about as though she were a slave, or snapping at her for absurdly small reasons: a dish set down with a very slight rattle, a draught when she opened a door, a tear in his hose that she hadn't mended even though he hadn't told her it was there.

And today, all day, he'd been in a very curious mood. She had observed it because pouring rain had kept them all engaged on indoor jobs. He was withdrawn, thoughtful, and she had once or twice heard him humming to himself as though he were thinking of something pleasant; yet she had also caught him glancing at her and at Quentin in a way that worried her. It was hard to define, but it looked like triumph. As though he were planning something that he would like and they wouldn't. It would be better, she felt, if Quentin didn't provoke him now.

And Quentin had managed to do just that. Richard was glowering at her. "You're a fool, girl. You're sorry for everyone. You used to be sorry for Nicky when he asked for a hiding and I gave him one, and you'd probably be sorry for a felon at the end of a rope even if he'd driven your sheep flock away in the night, stolen your purse and had his way with *you*. Too softhearted for your own good, that's you, my girl."

"I was glad myself when I knew that the Sweetwaters weren't going to be hanged by Henry Tudor," Peter remarked.

"I daresay. Just because I don't want them dead doesn't mean I want them prosperous. Betsy, give me another fried trout. Plenty to go round, now that Alfred's moved in with his in-laws in Clicket. Don't know where Hodge got them from, but I'd wager it was out of a stream on Sweetwater land. It usually is. I wonder what Walter Sweetwater's eating for supper? I doubt he'll notice the taste, whatever it is. I'm a happy man tonight. Oh, that was a grand moment in Dulverton when I heard the crier give out that the Sweetwater lands were being put up for sale."

"They've been given so little time to leave!" said Quentin. "Imagine how we'd feel!"

"Will you hold your tongue, Quentin? No one wants to know what you think. Fact is," said Richard, slightly diverted by this interesting topic, "we're lucky it *wasn't* us. Peter here fought for Lancaster at Bosworth, by mistake, so to speak, but anyhow, there he was, on the winning side. The Sweetwaters fought for the house of York. This new king, Henry, he's dating his reign from the day before Bosworth. Sharp practice if ever I heard it, but I gather he likes money," said Richard.

For a few moments they ate trout in near silence. Only near silence, because oddly enough, between mouthfuls, Richard seemed to be humming softly to himself again. Liza watched him covertly and nervously. There was something in the wind, most certainly there was, but what?

Then Richard, having mopped up the last of the fish juice with bread, swallowed it, wiped his mouth with the back of his hand and declared, "I've got something to say. I've been thinking it over for a while now and I reckon it can be done, and it's high time Quentin here was married. I've settled on the man."

There was a staggered silence, until Peter said, "Just a moment. I am Quentin's father and—"

"And I'm *your* father and the head of this house. Just be quiet and listen," Richard barked.

Liza looked at Quentin, whose eyes were terrified. Under the table she reached out and took her daughter's hand. Everyone waited for Richard to go on.

"I'll have to make a few enquiries," Richard said. "The dowry's important. It's the heart of the matter, as it happens. First thing I've got to do is buy up the Sweetwater lands."

"The...*what?*" said Peter, flabbergasted.

"When I heard the announcement in Dulverton," said his father, unheeding, "there was a name given, an official of some sort, who's in charge of selling them off. Can't remember offhand what that name was but it should be easy enough to find out. I reckon we can do it. Sell off the land we bought with the proceeds of the stone quarry..."

"*My* stone quarry," said Peter sharply.

"...and maybe some of the farmland that goes with the quarry as well—not the quarry itself, of course—and very likely it would come to enough, with a bit added from our savings. I've been at your abacus, Liza, when you weren't looking."

His household stared at him, goggle-eyed. Quentin's fingers tightened on Liza's.

"But why buy the Sweetwater lands?" said Peter. "If we're going to give a dowry to Quentin—and we will have to one day, I agree there—why not just give her the farms you're talking about selling? Oh." He snorted. "To upset the Sweetwaters, I suppose, by getting hold of what used to be theirs. I see."

Richard gave him a complacent glance. "Quite. We really can do it. You always thought that building this house would bankrupt us, boy, but look how we're flourishing now! It didn't drain us the way marrying Agnes Sweetwater to a Northcote-Carew crossbreed drained *her* family. And after they'd wrung out a dowry for her, they hoped Agnes's in-laws would put Baldwin forward to be Sheriff of Somerset or Devon or something of that sort, but it never happened. She took the husband they bought for her and that was that. How do I know? Folk talk, in the White Hart and every other tavern and at every market."

Liza said, "And who is the man?"

Richard smiled. "John Sweetwater. And then we hand the family back their land, or some of it anyway as Quentin's portion. Coals of fire on their arrogant heads. Oh, how I'll enjoy their faces, trying to smile at the wedding feast."

"No!" Letting go of Quentin, Liza shot to her feet and her protest came out in a shriek. "You can't do this! I won't see Quentin sacrificed, thrown off, thrust into that family—*that* family.... Well, I hope they won't accept her. I hope they'll say no..."

"Sit down, Liza! Stop screeching! I reckon they'll say yes," said Richard. "They love their land and they'll want it back, at any price they can afford, and they can probably afford young John. Besides, what will they lose? He'll get a nice-looking wife and a family in time, I hope. It'll be a good enough bargain from their point of view."

"Yes, and what kind of life would Quentin have among them? Do you think they'd be kind to her—a Lanyon in their midst?" shouted Liza, still on her feet.

"Maybe not, but it's no more than she deserves, the way she's behaved."

"No!" Liza was crimson with fury. "Head of the house or not, you *can't do this!*"

"No, by God, he can't! You're right, Liza!" Peter roared. "I won't stand for it, do you hear, Father? You've gone too far this time. Quentin isn't going to marry John Sweetwater and that's the end of it!"

"Just a moment," said Quentin.

They turned to her, all of them. The fear had gone from her eyes. She was quite calm and indeed, smiling slightly. "I seem to remember," said Quentin, "not long ago, promising to marry any suitable man you found for me, Grandfather. I suppose that Master Sweetwater is suitable—at least he comes of a well-bred family. I only want to be sure that my mother will be well treated. Please say that she will. And then, if you so order it, I'll gladly marry John Sweetwater. If he'll have me."

Liza's mouth opened again, but this time no words came out. Peter clutched at his hair. "Quentin, you don't know what you're saying! You needn't fear for your mother, that I'll promise anyway. You don't have to marry a Sweetwater to buy her safety. You *can't* marry a Sweetwater! Not you! You're the best thing that ever came into this house! There have been times...so *many* times, when I don't know what I might have done, except that every time I looked at you or heard your voice, I felt calmer, more reasonable. I could bear things. And I want you to be happy!"

Richard, however, had thrown back his head and burst out laughing.

PART FOUR

RECONSTRUCTION
1487–1504

CHAPTER THIRTY-EIGHT

SETTLED IN LIFE

To Quentin, the birth of Johnny, as they nicknamed tiny John to distinguish him from his father, was a wonder and a revelation. It was as though she had been waiting, all her days, for the moment when her very own child was put into her arms, perfect, bawling, a little, adorable, dependent being for whom it would be her privilege to love and care.

Unlike her mother, she had quickened at once and Johnny had arrived swiftly and easily, on New Year's Day, 1487.

Much more swiftly and much more easily than her parents' consent to the marriage had been won, certainly. For Richard's scheme, tossed across that supper table, had torn the family apart nearly as thoroughly as the discovery of Nicky's true parentage. It had even torn people apart within themselves.

Peter's outrage across the supper dishes had gone on and on. He had thundered repeatedly that they would be stripping themselves of land, virtually giving it away to the Sweetwaters, and for what? For *what?* How could a Lanyon hope to be happy, married to a Sweetwater? He pounded the table so that platters jumped and beakers spilled and only by getting hurriedly onto her feet and leaning on the table with all her weight had Liza stopped him from overturning it in his fury.

While all the time her grandfather Richard had laughed, saying that after all, Quentin was a granddaughter to be proud of, a real Lanyon. "She's wiped my eye properly. But it won't get you out of it, young Quentin. You'll keep your word and go through with this. Understand?"

"Yes, Grandfather. I understand," said Quentin demurely.

Whereupon Peter had burst out again, this time so wildly that Quentin, aghast, turned white and began to cry, which caused him, briefly, to check himself.

Until Richard turned to Quentin and said, "You mean it, do you? If I can get their land and house and their agreement, you'll wed John Sweetwater and carry some of their property back to them, a gift from us, the Lanyons they have so much despised?"

"Yes, Grandfather," said Quentin, shakily, which he misinterpreted as fear of the marriage rather than distress at her father's rage. "I will. I mean it. I will do as you bid."

Whereupon Peter lost his temper again and crashed out of the house, and on returning, refused to speak to his father.

Meanwhile, Quentin, well aware that from her grandfather's point of view, marrying her to John Sweetwater was retribution for defending her mother, had decided to be circumspect. But that evening, in a private conversation with her parents in their bedchamber, she told them that at Baldwin's funeral she had met and spoken to John Sweetwater and liked him. And was perfectly prepared to marry him.

"And it would please Grandfather so much, though I think perhaps we shouldn't tell him that John and I have met and that I took to him," she said, drawing her parents deftly into a conspiracy against Richard.

Peter flung up his hands, exclaimed that women were impossible, and left the room. Shortly afterward, he could be heard furiously chopping firewood. Her mother, scanning Quentin's face, said, "There's more than you've told me, isn't there? I don't, I can't, like the thought of this, but you already care for this young man, I think."

"Yes," said Quentin. "Yes, I do."

"*That* way? The way that…I told you about?"

There was a silence. Then Quentin said, "Yes. That way."

"I always swore," said Liza, "that if you fell in love like that, I'd try to help you. I know how it feels. But I never guessed the man would be a Sweetwater."

"I think John isn't quite like the other Sweetwaters. Mother, I mean it. I really want to marry him and I don't think he *dis*likes me."

She knew nothing of the stormy arguments that followed, between her parents, out of her hearing, when Peter declared that his entire family appeared to have taken leave of their senses, and her mother said that the plan had its good points; that if anyone could win the Sweetwaters over, Quentin could, and since the girl was willing, well, it would at least keep Richard sweet. To which Peter more than once replied that he didn't want to keep his father sweet; he felt more like killing him.

What finally overcame Peter's resistance was partly the fact that

Richard, though still chilly toward Liza, now became very pleasant toward Quentin, which was certainly a blessed change. Along with this was a weird but increasingly strong feeling that young as she was, Quentin knew what she was doing.

"Very well," Peter said at last, having summoned her once more to his and Liza's room. "I think you're crazy, all of you, but if you really want this marriage, Quentin, then all right. I agree! Although," he added, "I still hope my father changes his mind."

Richard didn't change his mind. Richard, like a charging bull with head lowered and nostrils snorting, plunged straight ahead. He went to Dulverton to discover the name of the right man to contact and then to Dunster, where he found a messenger in the shape of one of the young Weavers. Peter, wearily, gave consent to the sale or exchange of those items of property which had his name on the deeds. An urgent letter went to London and a deal was struck.

His grace King Henry VII is pleased to accept the lands listed in your letter in simple exchange for the house known as Sweetwater House, in the parish of Clicket in Somerset, the village known as Clicket and the following Somerset farmlands of the Sweetwater estate....

The big joke, said Richard, chortling and fairly shining with satisfaction, was that the Lanyons could never have managed any of this but for the generosity, years ago, of the man who became Richard III. Perhaps it would be as well if King Henry never found that out!

After that, he prepared another letter, this time for Walter Sweetwater, who had mournfully taken his family to stay with Agnes and Giles Northcote until he could eject the tenants from one of Catherine's dower farms. Sweetwater House was empty except for Denis Sawyer and a couple of servants who remained as caretakers. Sawyer was the messenger this time. He was a long time returning, and when he did, came straight to Allerbrook.

"There was a fine to-do," he said dispassionately, sitting in the Allerbrook hall with a tankard of cider in his hand. Denis Sawyer was not emotionally attached to the Sweetwaters, and the uproar caused by Richard's missive seemed to amuse him. "I'm sorry I was so long over it, but Master Sweetwater's got possession of one of the dower farms and he'd left Mistress Agnes's home to move in. Quick work! I had to follow him and his family there. It's too small for them, considering what they're used to. They have to live as their tenants did—no hall or solar, just one big kitchen that counts as their main room, and a tiny parlour that's hardly used because they have to work. They don't have many farmhands, and in the house Mistress Catherine's only got one girl and a handyman to help her, so she's busy with the cooking pots most of the day and Master John has to see to the animals. They all came into the kitchen to talk over that letter, though."

Sawyer grinned and held out his tankard as Liza offered him a refill from a jug. "Master Walter can't get used to the lack of space. There he was, striding about and clutching at his temples and bumping into things and tripping over people's feet and wanting to know what Master John was about, courting a Lanyon girl on the quiet and had he got her with child—was that what this was all about?

"And there was Master John saying no, he hadn't, and wouldn't, but she was a pretty maid and things had been better lately between the Lanyons and the Sweetwaters, hadn't they? Master John said a man could do a lot worse than marry Quentin Lanyon and there was no denying that it would put them all back in Clicket where they belonged and the tenants they'd thrown out so as they could move into this hen coop of a place would be able to come back. And they needed the rent...."

"Is the answer yes or no?" snapped Richard.

"Oh, it's yes," said Sawyer. "Master Walter might curse and swear and say that things being better was just on the surface and so on, but..."

Here he paused, thinking it better not to quote Walter's comments that the Lanyons weren't gentry and had always hated the Sweetwaters and even if Peter wasn't to blame for Baldwin's tragedy, he, Walter, would still be happy enough to do Richard Lanyon down and Richard would probably push him, Walter, over a bridge or off a cliff if he got the chance and he wouldn't sell his son to a Lanyon even to get his own property back.

"Mistress Catherine cried," he said, "and said that if John liked the girl and she was willing, and it would get them all home into the bargain, how could he *think* of turning the proposal down, and then Master John said he was going to marry the lass anyhow. He fancied her and he wanted to get the family property back, and he didn't need any man's consent...at one point they were all shouting—or crying, in the lady's case—at the same time. I never knew a pack of strolling players make a noisier scene."

"But what if Master Walter makes her life a misery, if she goes to live at Sweetwater House and he's there!" said Liza, her brow furrowed with worry. "She's obedient enough—" Liza had well understood that it would be better not to reveal Quentin's secret passion "—and I can see that the idea has advantages. It's a good marriage in its way. Only, Master Walter still resents us, at heart!"

Quentin, however, said, "If John and I can't live with him, we'll have to find somewhere else. But perhaps he'll get to like me, when he's used to me. I'm not afraid of him."

Peter, by then, had given in, because his entire family seemed ranged against him. "But if it goes wrong," he said to Quentin, "if you're miserable, you just come home again. We'll protect you. If it goes awry, we'll get you out of it, if we have to bribe the Pope for an annulment!"

The wedding took place the following March, and was conducted by Father Matthew at the parish church (since even Richard had recognised that it would be tactless to insist on celebrating it in the chapel at Allerbrook House). It was hardly a merry occasion. Walter scowled all the time and Liza, though dry-eyed, couldn't smile, while Peter refused to attend at all. It was Richard who placed Quentin's hand in that of her bridegroom.

There was an awkwardness, too, when the couple were at last alone. Until they were brought together at St. Anne's in Clicket to make their vows, Quentin and John had in fact exchanged very few words and never in private. They had spoken to each other at the graveside, and they had had brief conversations when John and his grandfather came to Allerbrook for the betrothal, and after that, on two occasions, when John visited her and they had made a little conversation. Always, someone else had been present. As she stood beside him in front of Father Matthew, his nearness made her heart turn somersaults, and yet he was virtually a stranger to her.

Throughout the wedding feast, though they sat next to each other, and during the dancing later on, which they had to open, John made only a few conventional remarks to her. "Will you have some more meat? I'll beckon the page." "Your dress is very fine. Pale pink looks well on you." "It's time to start the dancing." He smiled at her now and then and she smiled back, but she was too nervous to initiate any conversation of her own. Now that it was too late, she was saying to herself, *If I'd said no, and been strong about it, my parents would have backed me up, and between us, we might have withstood my grandfather. But I agreed. Of my own free will, I agreed. What have I done?*

When, at last, they lay uneasily side by side in the darkness of a curtained bed in Sweetwater House, however, she took herself in hand. The basic good sense which she had inherited from Liza, albeit alongside the contradictory ability to fall headlong into love at five minutes' notice and stay there for life, told her that she had no choice. She had made this bed herself and had better set about making it comfortable, or at least not complain if it wasn't.

She cleared her throat and then said gently, "This marriage was my grandfather's idea, but I was content with it. I wanted to give you back your own, or as much as I could. I know you haven't got quite all of it since we've kept Rixons Farm, but you've got Hannacombes and Shearers back, and Clicket and your home farm and this house and at least you're home again. I was so very sorry about...about everything. And I liked you. Just being sorry couldn't help you on its own."

For a long moment there was no response from him and her skin seemed to freeze. Then he rolled over and she felt his arm move across her. "You are kind and pretty. If only property and...and...the way our two families have wrangled all these years wasn't mixed up with it...."

"But could we ever have been married at all, unless property and...and the old quarrels...were mixed up with it?" said Quentin in a down-to-earth fashion.

There was another lengthy silence. Eventually, she added, "I will do all I can to see you don't regret it. Can we not put the old quarrels into the past?"

He laughed a little. Then he said, "Talking of quarrels—tell me, why did your brother leave Allerbrook? Was that over a dispute of some sort? All Clicket was buzzing about that, but no one ever had an answer."

Quentin decided to keep to the story Richard had insisted upon, and for the sake of trying to make interesting conversation, invented some extra details. "Yes, there was a dispute. Nicky didn't like the life of the farm. Getting up at first light and always being out of doors even in the freezing cold or the rain—it didn't suit him, and my father and grandfather were angry."

"Oh, I see. Not a typical farmer's son, then?"

"Well, no," said Quentin, sensing a covert jeer at her family's social standing but sensing, too, that John did not realise it was a jeer at all, still less that it was also a jeer at her. "He will make his way," she said. "I expect one day he'll be richer than any of us."

"Well," John said, "I have to admit that my family is richer now than it was when we all woke up this morning. But we haven't quite ratified the treaty yet, have we? I suppose it's time we did."

He rolled himself on top of her. There in the curtained darkness, nature spoke to them. By morning they had invented pet names for each other. Tentatively, quietly, a genuine friendship had begun.

At breakfast, Quentin greeted Catherine and Walter with courteous affection, and then there was a pause, while she looked shyly from one to the other, and waited for an answer. She had been well aware that yesterday, in church, Walter had glowered all the time. Later on, surrounded by wedding guests, he and Mistress Catherine had made an effort, had gone through the motions of courtesy and uttered suitable words of well-wishing, but how far had they meant them? Today she would find out just how welcome they intended to make her.

Catherine gave her a small, cautious smile. Walter stared at her, cleared his throat and then, for a few moments, was silent.

The wedding feast had been held at Sweetwater House instead of at the bride's home in the usual way. Walter wanted it so because somehow, to have it at Allerbrook would be an extra Lanyon triumph. The Lanyons agreed, for a reason they didn't mention to Walter, which was that Peter had objected violently to the idea of holding the wedding celebrations under the Lanyon roof. So Sweetwater House it had to be, which was nearer St. Anne's church, anyway.

On the way back from the church to the house, Liza Lanyon had come to Walter's side.

"Master Sweetwater, may I speak to you?"

He scarcely knew her, but she was now his grandson's mother-in-law and social proprieties sometimes had the strength of fetters. He could hardly say anything other than "Yes, of course."

Liza, with a hand placed on his arm, brought them both to a halt so that she could stand facing him. Pleasant brown eyes looked into his.

"I expect," said Liza quietly, "that this marriage isn't altogether to your taste. But somehow or other, Quentin has become enamoured of your son. Master Sweetwater, Quentin is a good girl and will make a good wife, if you will…if you will give her a chance. Whatever you feel about the Lanyons, please be kind to Quentin. Please."

She did not, as Richard would have done, add that if he were not kind, he would have the Lanyons to deal with. There was no threat in her face or voice, only appeal.

"Mistress Lanyon," said Walter, "I am not a knight, but I could have been, had I gone to war and won my spurs on the field as my father did. I still try to follow the knightly code of behaviour. I do not pursue feuds with women."

Sir Humphrey Sweetwater, knight or not, would probably have set out to make Quentin's life wretched and not thought twice about it, but Sir Humphrey had died at Towton a quarter of a century ago.

"If your daughter fills her place as she should," he said, "she will have nothing to fear from me, and my daughter-in-law Catherine has a very sweet temper. Quentin will be quite safe with us."

"Thank you," said Liza, and gave him the smile which had long ago captivated a red-haired young deacon.

Now he sat in the hall he had been able to come home to only because of this dark-eyed Lanyon interloper, and saw that the timid smile she was offering him was her mother's smile all over again. He drew a deep breath and said gruffly, "I give you good morning." And then, "I hope you will be happy with us. Be seated." He had to drag the words out of himself, but drag them he did.

"What should I do today?" Quentin asked. "I've brought my spinning wheel with me. It's in the baggage we sent here yesterday."

"You can send it back to Allerbrook!" said Walter. He almost snapped, but not quite. "You're a lady now," he said, more gently.

"Sweetwater ladies don't spin and weave. They see to the herb garden, instruct the maids and the cooks, maybe make marchpane fancies. Or they embroider. Mistress Catherine here is making covers for settle cushions. Perhaps she'll let you help with that. Eh, Catherine?"

"Yes, by all means," said Catherine, and, since she had now been in effect given permission to smile properly, did so.

Inch by inch, over the next few weeks, Quentin created for herself a niche in the household, and blew on the small fire of affection she and John had kindled on their wedding night, until it grew into a bright blaze. When she declared that she thought she was with child, Catherine embraced her, and Walter, after a hesitant moment, gave her a kiss and said, "You must take care of yourself, my dear."

The battle was won. The first fruits of victory were made apparent on the day when, about to set out hunting, Walter remarked quite jovially that if they took a deer today, they'd send some venison to Allerbrook, seeing that the Lanyons were family now.

And when, triumphantly, she presented them with Johnny, it seemed that the peace treaty between the Lanyons and the Sweetwaters was not only ratified but renewed. Life from now on, Quentin thought joyously, would be a sunlit, happy upland, like the moors on an August day, when the heather and the gorse were out and the larks were singing.

"We're not much worse off for giving Quentin her dowry." Richard, having led Liza and Peter into the hall because he said he wanted to show them something, stood in midfloor, rubbing his hands together in pleasure. "We kept Rixons for ourselves and now we've got all of the rent the Hudds pay us. And we still have the quarry. Very satisfactory. I think we'll have this plain old panelling ripped out at last and something better put in. We talked of that before, didn't we, but then the war came and we never got round to it. Let's get round to it now. There's a fashion these days for Tudor roses. They'd look handsome."

"Tudor roses?" asked Liza.

"Yes. King Henry's married King Edward's daughter Elizabeth and that's Lancaster marrying York. The white rose and the red rose have come together. The Tudor rose is half white and half red. We could have roses carved into the panelling and then coloured. I've spoken to the carpenter in Clicket already, when I was in the village yesterday. He'll come tomorrow to measure up. He's got a good wood-carver working with him these days. New panelling, good seasoned oak, with a Tudor rose in the middle of each panel, painted red and white. That's what I'll have in here, and new carved fronts for those window seats, too— more Tudor roses, to match."

"He hasn't asked me what I think," said Peter, addressing the roof beams. "He's just decided on his own. Again. And if anyone *should* ask me what I think, I think it's pointless and a waste of money. Whatever you say, Father, it'll take time to rebuild our savings. It's as well the quarry is still flourishing! I don't want to see more good gold and silver being spent on this house. From the start, it was pointless and a waste of money!"

"Nonsense!" Richard barked.

"We're *farmers!* It's land we should value, not Tudor roses in the panelling! And if we'd never built this place, we'd still be on the old terms with our neighbours. They think we think we're above them now! The Shearers almost look the other way when they come across us—Liza's charity to Tilly only matters to Tilly—and one of the Hudd boys took his cap off to me in Clicket the other day. I don't like it. It's embarrassing."

"Well, *I* like it," said Richard. "Take heart, boy. When we can afford it, you can decide what to have in the way of stained glass for the chapel. That'll be next." Peter's disgusted expression seemed to amuse him. "Then we'll have the tapestries I recall you once went all poetical about. It's odd," he added thoughtfully. "If the Sweetwaters hadn't gone hunting the day of my father's funeral and crashed into the procession, it's quite possible I'd never have built this house at all. How very strange."

"It might not have happened either if the stag had run in a different direction," Peter retorted.

Life as an apprentice with Owen ap Idwal in Lynmouth actually suited Nicky Lanyon very well. He had not forgiven his family for casting him out; he would never forgive them, as long as he lived. But nevertheless, it was a fact that life with Owen ap Idwal was more exciting than life at Allerbrook and about a thousand times more exciting than sitting at a loom in a weaving shed at Dunster.

For one thing, it didn't mean staying in Lynmouth all the time. The town at the foot of the towering cliffs was very small, and from its sister town of Lynton at the top of the same cliffs it looked as though the great walls of rock were crowding its thatched and slate cottages into the harbour. But the harbour and the ships that came and went were the heart of the place. And as Nicky soon discovered, Owen ap Idwal sometimes came and went with them, on his own ship, the *Fulmar,* and so on occasion did the boys he was training in his trade. Before Nicky had been with him for a year and a half, he had travelled to Venice and back twice.

Owen ap Idwal himself was short, dark and possessed of a crackling energy. He normally went up the creaky stairs in his house two at a time, leaped from the *Fulmar's* deck to the quay and back again instead of stepping sedately, bolted his food, tossed drink down his gullet rather than savouring any of it, and unpacked goods at full speed, slashing wrappings away with the sharp knife he always carried, and cursing in Welsh if the knife didn't cut through them at the first slash.

Sometimes he cursed the boys as well, or even cuffed them, but there was no ill humour in it and to Nicky, after his grandfather's attentions, these occasional clouts were nothing at all. The ones handed out to the boys, the maids and her young daughter by Owen's thin, busy and short-tempered wife, Constance, were harder. Their two eldest daughters were married and gone and their son acted as the captain of the *Fulmar,* but their youngest girl, Gwyneth, who was only ten ("She came as a surprise," Owen had once said jovially) was still at home and there were two maidservants. The maidservants claimed that Constance was capable of being in half a dozen places at once and always for the purpose of finding that someone had done something wrong.

"One speck of dust on a girt old tabletop or one crumb on the floor, or else you stop mopping or beating eggs just for half a minute to chatty, like any maidens might, and there she be, all of a sudden, when you thought she was up in the attic annoying the rats!" they said.

Neither hated her, though, and Gwyneth loved her, because Constance, in her busy-brusque way, could also be kind at times and she was good to the maids if one of them were hurt or ill or needed time off for some right and proper reason, such as visiting genuinely sick parents, or courting.

"A wench has to have her chance with the lads," she would say quite tolerantly, and it was said that she and Owen had given very good wedding gifts to previous maidservants who had married.

The goods that Owen handled were interesting, too, though the cheeses he carried for export had such a powerful smell that the first time Nicky sailed with his employer, the nausea that plagued him on the first day had more to do with the reek from the hold that plagued him on the first day than did the motion of the ship.

But he liked handling the soft, cured hides: calfskin, deerskin, pigskin and the stout leather made from adult cattle. He admired the ready-made leather boots and gloves, fringed and embroidered, which Owen also took abroad, and was fascinated by the variety of things that could be made from iron.

"It's good iron, lad," Owen told him. "There's a mine or two near here, so there's not much cost for transport. I get things made by a blacksmith in Lynton." Sometimes he took Nicky and the other three youths he was training up to Lynton to watch the smith creating fire irons and rakes, bread ovens and plough-shares, hammers, chisels, currycombs, nails and buckets and chains.

Life at sea, once he had got over the sickness and learned how to sleep in a hammock and to believe that however wet and cold one got in bad weather, seawater wouldn't give him a chill, appealed to Nicky, too. He was an active boy and on his very first voyage learned how to manage the sails as well as any sailor.

Venice, the city which seemed to grow out of the very sea, amazed and enthralled him, and the goods he found himself handling on the way home gave him new cause for wonder. There were bales of gleaming silk, kegs of spices, which unlike the cheeses smelt aromatic and exciting, and earthenware jars of dyestuffs from lands so far away that they were to him little more than legends.

For all his resentment against his family, he would have said he was well settled in life. He would finish his years with Owen ap Idwal and then, he hoped, work for a similar merchant, for pay, until such time as he could set himself up in business. The Weavers had said they would help.

He was seventeen, well grown, that day in the late summer of 1489 when, returning with Owen from another voyage to Venice, he stepped onto the quay at Lynmouth and found himself face-to-face with Herbert Dyer.

CHAPTER THIRTY-NINE
TAVERN TALK

Nicky stopped short. He couldn't recall the name of the bearded elderly man with the good clothes and the square build, but he felt he had seen him somewhere before.

"Surely I know you, sir?" he said. "Are you here to see Owen ap Idwal?"

"Yes, I am. My son engaged him to bring dyestuffs in for me and word reached me that the *Fulmar* had been sighted. I had a fancy to be here to meet her when she made her home port. I've not ridden to Lynmouth for years, but suddenly thought I'd do it once more, before my limbs entirely seize up with age. And yes, I think we have met somewhere before, but I can't remember where. What's your name?"

"Nicky Lanyon, sir."

"Nicky Lanyon! So this is where you went! I heard that you'd left Allerbrook. The Weavers told me. I am Herbert Dyer."

"Oh! Yes, of course. I should have known you at once! I am sorry."

"Well, you haven't seen me since you were a boy. We met a few times at the Weavers' house in Dunster, when you came there as a lad, with your father. You've been travelling on this ship?"

"I'm apprenticed to Master Owen, sir. The Weavers arranged it. I visit them now and then, but obviously not at the same times as yourself. I haven't been there at all lately."

"There have been changes. Lady Elizabeth Luttrell and her son Hugh are back in the castle and Hugh Luttrell's been getting both Dunster and Minehead harbours dredged out. One day, your master's ship may tie up at Dunster quay. Does Master Owen suit you?"

"He would say it matters more if I suit him! But yes, it's a chance to see the world. We've just come back from Venice."

"The Weavers said you'd been thrown out after a family dispute, though they didn't say what sort of dispute."

"It wasn't a pretty business, sir," said Nicky awkwardly. If the Weavers had kept the truth from Dyer, then he wasn't going to reveal it. His mother was still his mother. It was and always had been Richard Lanyon he blamed for his exile. Dyer put a hand on his shoulder.

"I'll ask no questions. I know Master Richard is a hasty man and domineering, if you don't mind me criticising your family."

"No, I don't mind," said Nicky, pugnaciously enough to send Master Dyer's eyebrows rising toward his hairline. Nicky was himself surprised to realise how deep the wound of separation from his home and family had gone. This chance meeting had touched the scar and made it sore again. He would not now go back to live at Allerbrook for any consideration, yet he sometimes thought, *I'd like to visit, see my mother again. I miss her. Only, I can't face the thought of seeing Richard Lanyon.*

"Master Owen is below, sir," he said. "Shall I take you to him? You will want to examine your goods, I take it."

"Yes, and pay for them. Then I must organise their transport— by boat to Watchet and then packhorse to Washford, it'll be, as usual."

"I know all the boatmen here. Do you use the same ones each time? I can arrange the transport for you."

"Can you? Well, I'd be grateful. After that, perhaps we could have a drink together in a tavern, if your master will allow."

"Yes, he lets his older apprentices go to taverns." Nicky wasn't sure that he wanted to drink with this man from the past, whose conversation had already made him homesick, but it wouldn't do to refuse an invitation from one of Owen's clients. "Thank you, sir."

Dyer smiled. *A lad with something against Richard Lanyon.* He had responded by instinct to that pugnacious note in Nicky's voice. A young man who had reason to resent Richard Lanyon was someone with whom Herbert Dyer would probably get on well. "I'll take pleasure in buying you some ale, if Master Owen agrees," he said. "The Harbour Inn will do."

The Harbour Inn was a low-ceilinged cavern, badly lit, in which the sawdust on the cobbled floor wasn't changed often enough. However, the ale and cider were good, and in cold weather there was always a good fire in the hearth. When Nicky and Herbert went in, they found it crowded. Two other ships had arrived on the same tide as the *Fulmar,* and many of their crew, having furled the sails, unloaded the cargo and scrubbed the decks, were now taking their ease in the inn.

There were a number of locals, too. Nicky and Herbert squeezed between two benches full of men who smelt of fish and seemed to be discussing a mackerel catch, and found themselves a double settle close to a bald individual with tufts of greying hair over his ears, who had a small table and a stool to himself, possibly because he didn't merely smell but positively reeked of goat. Herbert gave their order to a serving girl, and then turned to Nicky.

"Tell me about Venice. That's a fine adventure for a boy brought up at Allerbrook and never going farther afield than Dunster."

A little while later, when the girl had brought their ale and the level in the tankards was going down, Herbert said interestedly, "If you don't want to tell me what went amiss between you and your family, well, as I said, I won't question you. The Weavers were obviously willing to help you and I'd trust their judgement. I suppose you fell out with your grandfather. You needn't tell me whether I'm right or not, only I know him!"

"Well, that was more or less the way of it, Master Dyer. I don't want to go back to the farm. I just feel I was done out of something that was properly mine," Nicky said.

"Didn't your father stand up for you?"

"No," said Nicky shortly, thinking that, odd as it seemed, he still thought of Peter Lanyon as his father and Richard as his grandfather and probably always would, however much he loathed those two self-righteous grown men who had victimised him, a boy of only thirteen, for something that was no fault of his.

"Overborne, I suppose. Well, as I said, he's a harsh man, is Richard Lanyon." Herbert shook a disapproving head. "His father was the same! Has it come out in you, I wonder? You don't have Lanyon looks, but maybe one day you'll be a merchant and rule your household like a tyrant king."

"I hope not, sir," said Nicky. "I value my own freedom. I'd try not to bully others out of theirs. If I'd stayed, I'd have had to marry where I was told, while now, when I meet a girl I like as I hope I will one day, I can please myself."

"If you'd stayed you probably would have had to marry to order," Herbert agreed. Their tankards were empty and, picking them up, he waved them at the girl, signalling for refills. "Did you know that before your father was wedded to your mother, he wanted to marry a girl from this very port but wasn't allowed to?"

"No—did he? A girl from Lynmouth? I never heard that."

The girl brought a jug and gave them more ale, for which Dyer paid, ignoring Nicky's attempt to do so. "It's true enough," he said, "though that time your grandfather may well have had the right of it, because I heard that the girl ran off with someone else anyway. She wouldn't have been a sound, decent wife like your mother."

"No," said Nicky, keeping his voice neutral. "Obviously not."

"As a matter of fact," said Dyer, enjoying himself, "it seems the wench was pleasing—hair like a pale gold mist, Richard Lanyon told me, or something of that kind. Marion Locke—that was her name. He even had a notion—he let this out to me once—that he might marry her instead and wipe his son's eye well and truly."

"He *didn't!*" Nicky, in the act of lifting his tankard, thumped it back onto the table. "Oh, no! He *couldn't!* That's outrageous!"

Herbert Dyer looked at him. *Good God. I shoot a longshaft into the air and phutt! It hits the target dead centre. I've had the weapon I need in my hand all these years and never knew it.*

"Well, he did. I don't suppose Peter Lanyon knows, to this day, though. I'd love to see his face if anyone ever told him. I don't somehow feel it's something he'd forgive, even after so long and even if the girl did run off. In his place, I wouldn't forgive it."

"My grandfather…" Nicky began.

"Will get his deserts one day, I've no doubt of it." *There, that'll do. The seed is planted. Best not overdo it.*

"He always wants to look bigger, more important than he is," Nicky said, ruminating. "That's why he built that great big house that I won't now inherit. And he does domineer over people, yes. I wonder if that's why the girl ran away! Perhaps she couldn't bear the thought of being married to him. Maybe her family thought it would be a good idea and were urging her to it. I wonder if she ever came back to them?"

"I don't think he ever approached them," said Herbert. "From what he told me, she ran off too soon."

"He shows off," Nicky grumbled. "He never used to ride moor ponies, you know. He liked horses that stuck in people's minds. When I left, he had a showy piebald…."

"Patches. And before that, another piebald called Magpie."

"When I was very small, I saw the horse he had before Magpie—Splash it was called. It was old by then, out at grass," Nicky said. "It was the weirdest-looking animal I ever saw—a sort of dapple grey, but the dapples were a very dark grey and there were some very big ones, and they ran into each other and overlapped as though the horse had had ink splashed on its hide. I've never seen another horse like it."

Unexpectedly, the goat-scented man with the tufts over his ears suddenly turned toward them. "Here! Do you mind me speakin' to 'ee? I couldn't help hearin' 'ee and I thought to myself, I did, that's a funny thing. That's a very funny thing, that is."

"What is?" asked Herbert, slightly annoyed by the interruption and making an effort not to hold his nose as the rank odour on the other man's clothes wafted toward him.

"Talkin' about a 'orse that looked like it had dark grey splashes all over it. I saw one like that once, but only the once, and I'm thinking, would it be the same 'orse? It were hereabouts, years back. Well, I say hereabouts. It were in that there Valley of the Rocks, up atop there, nigh to Lynton."

"When would that have been?" Nicky asked, not very interested but polite to an older man out of habit.

"Ah. Long time back. I were only a lad of fifteen, herding my goats in the valley, I was. I'm well on the wrong side of forty now. Don't know what, exactly. Never keep count of time, I don't."

"I suppose Master Lanyon could have been there for some reason or other," said Herbert. "Why shouldn't he be?"

"Ah, but he were with a wench! Pretty thing, too. I had good long-sight in them days." The goat-scented one sighed. "Didn't I hear you say summat just now about a girl with hair like a pale gold mist and him thinkin' of weddin' her? Could have been the same wench. Like a cloud round her head it were, catching the sun in glints. Sort of thing a lad like me would look at, and none of it kept decent under a coif. And the way of walking she had…aaarh!"

His audience regarded him with dislike but also with increasing interest. "And they were in the Valley of Rocks together?" Nicky said.

"Yes. Came in on the horse, with the girl behind him. There

were a dog, too, black-and-white. Never seen any of 'em afore, I hadn't. They got down and left horse and dog nigh the valley entrance and walked on. Argifyin', by the look of it. She jerked away from 'un at one point and she were shakin' her head, but he yanked her back and started walkin' her up that path round Castle Rock. You know it?"

"No," said Herbert Dyer, but Nicky said, "I know it. We go up there sometimes, me and the other apprentices, on sunny days when we've got some time off. It's fun to climb about up there."

"Well, she didn't think it fun, by the look of it," their informant said. "They'd started up the path when all of a sudden he swings round and gets hold of her arms. Looked like a proper disagreement, it did."

"And then?" asked Nicky.

The goatherd shrugged. "I didn't see no more. I thought it were all a bit funny, but I had me goats to see to. There was one limpin' like and I wanted to catch 'un and see what was wrong and anyhow, just about then a girt mist started rollin' in from the sea. Cleared a bit later, it did, just as I finished seein' to the goat. I went down to my old hut to eat a bite out of the cold and I see the 'orse and dog was gone. They'd come down and taken 'em, I s'pose. I remembered, after, 'cos the 'orse was that queer-coloured and I'd have liked to know what the man and the girl were quarrelling over, but I were only a lad myself. I never told no one, not until now."

"What are you drinking?" asked Nicky, leaning across Herbert for the purpose. "Can we get you another?"

"Cider, it be. Don't mind if I do. Like I said," said the goatherd, clearly taking pleasure in his audience, "I never told no one. But I thought about it, many a time. Leaves pictures in the mind, that sort of thing does. Queer-lookin' 'orse, and that girl with all that there pale hair and the way she moved…that were come-hither if ever I saw it. Aarh!"

The last syllable was positively lascivious. Nicky caught Herbert's eye and they exchanged speaking looks, but nevertheless, Herbert signalled to the serving girl and requested a pint of cider. The goatherd raised his existing tankard and drained it in an appreciative toast to them, and then startled them by changing his tone of voice completely.

"It was queer, that's what it was. That's why I never spoke of it. It were like a sort of dream, not real somehow and…well, it gave me a sort of funny feeling. Like it wouldn't be lucky to talk about it. I were only a lad and there were something about that day, an' those two quarrelling and that there mist drifting round—it must of caught them up there. Felt weird. That mist even scared me a bit, swirling round so as I could hardly see my feet. It were a queer sort of day altogether, see?"

"Yes," said Nicky as the cider arrived and Nicky, this time, succeeded in paying for it. "Yes, I do."

Later, as they emerged into the sunlit afternoon, Herbert remarked, "What an odd story that was. I wonder if he really did see your father's sweetheart quarrelling with your grandfather?"

"Not improbable, if he meant to separate her from my father. He went to see her, maybe."

"In the Valley of the Rocks instead of in Lynmouth?" Thoughtfully Herbert stroked his beard. It was unlikely that there was anything more in this than a chance meeting and a fleeting argument, long ago. Maybe Richard actually had proposed to the girl, been turned down and preferred not to say so, to pretend instead that he'd never had a chance to ask her. That fitted the Richard that Herbert Dyer knew.

"Have you ever seen your Allerbrook family since you left?" he asked.

"No. I don't think they'd want to see me, either."

"It's time you tried to make it up," Dyer said. "You're a young man now with a future and a trade. You won't be going there to beg. You've proved you can make your way in the world without them. It's time you went home and showed them! Your mother would like to see you, of that I'm sure—so well-grown as you are. Why don't you go?"

Nicky paused uncertainly, looking toward the quay and the *Fulmar*. "I suppose I want to, in a way, but..."

"You should. Well, think about it. We'd better part company here. I've a long ride home and I don't go fast, not at my age. I've left my horse at a stables." He clasped Nicky's hand in farewell. "If you do go, and happen to mention this odd tale we've heard, best not mention my name, if you can help it. But in your place, I must say I'd be curious. I'd want to see Richard Lanyon's face if I asked him about it."

He nodded and walked away, well pleased with himself. The seed might well have fallen on stony ground but on the other hand, Nicky was young, which usually meant indiscreet, and he was still angry. The thought of asking his grandfather upsetting questions and giving his father upsetting information might well appeal to him as much as it appealed to Herbert Dyer.

CHAPTER FORTY
KICKING A PEBBLE

The day that was to end in chaos began gently, with a grey cloud spilling soft drizzle over the moors and hiding Dunkery from view, until the gathering power of the August sun lifted the vapours away, and the sunlight sparkled on a well-washed landscape.

"Nice drop of rain," Richard said with satisfaction, encountering Liza in the farmyard as they both returned from tasks outside. "Now, if only God sends us dry weather when it comes to the harvest, we'll do well. How's Primrose doing, Liza? You've been working hard on her."

"I've taken her to the pasture now," Liza said. "That teat is working now. I kept at it and kept at it and I think she's going to be quite all right. I must go and see to the bread."

She went indoors to help Ellen. Richard watched her go, thinking that most households would have packed her off to a nunnery but that it was just as well that he and Peter hadn't. When it came to things like difficult lambings and cows with mastitis, and making bread, she was incomparable.

And all the more these days, for Betsy was gone, carried off the previous winter by a sudden chill and lung congestion, and neither Ellen nor the two other maids who now helped her could match Liza's skills. Oh well, time brought changes of all kinds. Word had come from Dunster the year before that Laurence and Aunt Cecy, too, had passed away, Aunt Cecy very quietly in her bed one night, Laurence with mysterious pains and bowel bleeding, and then a sudden collapse. Nothing stayed the same forever. Not people and not even righteous indignation.

Liza, if asked, would have agreed that the unhappy relationship between herself and the Lanyon menfolk had changed, though it had been slow, and didn't even now go very deep.

Quentin's outburst had begun the process of reconciliation and Liza, thereafter, had fairly toiled at it. It was not a matter of forgiving or forgetting; only of raising a new edifice on the ruins of the old one. She knew she must never transgress again, by even the faintest degree, by as much as a single wistful reference to Nicky or by ever mentioning Christopher's name or by any unexplained absence for as much as half an hour. Buildings raised on top of rubble were never quite solid.

Throughout the past four years, though she and Peter had at length begun once more to share a bed, they had never coupled, but a new partnership had gradually been forged as they talked to each other of everyday, necessary matters to do with the work of Allerbrook. They had not stood side by side as parents at Quentin's marriage because Peter refused to attend it, but they had been there as grandparents at the christening of her son.

Betsy had never quite thawed, but Betsy was gone and Ellen, more impressionable and more concerned, in any case, with her forthcoming marriage to the cowman from Rixons, had been willing to make friends again. In fact, Liza sometimes suspected that Ellen was secretly rather excited by the wild romance in Liza's past.

If only, Liza sometimes thought, she could sometimes hear news of Nicky. No messages ever came to her from the Weavers, though they had let Peter know that he had indeed gone to them and later, that he had been apprenticed to a Lynmouth merchant. Peter had told her that much. But that was all. They had not mentioned Nicky again even to Peter and certainly not to her. Her family had cut her off. Unless Nicky himself one day contacted her, he was lost. She prayed that he was happy, but was afraid to speak his name and could not, therefore, ask Peter to find out for her.

Meanwhile, the morning had turned bright, and there were loaves to shape and put in the bread oven, and a capon to put on the spit for dinner. Phoebe and Hodge's small son would come to the farmhouse soon to turn it. Phoebe and Hodge believed in training their children to be useful early in life and they had already begun showing their four-year-old daughter how a spinning wheel worked.

She was in the kitchen, sorting eggs into dozens and putting them into small baskets, ready for Clicket market, when she heard Pewter, the young dog they had recently acquired, barking loudly and then Ellen, who had been out in the yard fetching water, came to say that Master Nicky had ridden in.

"Nicky!"

"Yes, ma'm. All the way from Lynmouth. Oh—here he is!"

And there indeed he was, her Nicky, a young man now, hair

as red as fire, chestnut eyes glowing, coming toward her to greet her with a hug.

"I've got permission from my master. I said it was time I visited you. I hired a nag in Lynton and started out early. The nag," said Nicky, "is lazy and slow but it's got me here. It didn't even shy when that lurcher you've got in the yard started baying."

"Pewter's new. He doesn't know you. We've got two new sheep-dogs, too, Hunter and Trim. They're out with Peter and his father now—they're moving some sheep. Alfred's about somewhere."

"He's seeing to the horse. I passed Sweetwater House on the way here. Odd to think of Quentin living there. The Weavers let me know about her marriage. Is all well with her?"

"Yes, it seems that it is. The match is turning out well," said Liza. "And I'm as thankful as I can be, let me tell you. I say so in my prayers."

"I can believe it." He held her at arm's length and looked at her, smiling, glad to see her at last. He had felt unaccountably nervous on the ride. After all, he was the victim, who had been thrown out though he was innocent of any wrongdoing. If he met with any rudeness from the men who had disowned him and cast him forth, well, he had something to say that might well cause them to turn on each other. He carried it like a concealed knife. He might use it or he might not, but they had more to fear from him than he from them. He hoped they had been treating Liza well. "Am I welcome?" he asked.

"Of course you are! Come into the hall," said Liza, happily abandoning the eggs. "Ellen, bring some cider!"

She led the way to the hall. Nicky followed, frowning a little. His mother looked older, he thought, and thinner, too. Just what kind of life had she had since he left?

The question received a reply within the next two minutes, for just as Ellen came in with the cider, Richard and Peter returned for dinner. Nicky, accepting his tankard, raised his head as he heard the voices of the men who had for thirteen years been his father and his grandfather. Ellen had put down her tray and hurried out to tell them of his arrival. He could hear her explaining. Then the two of them came into the hall. Peter looked merely anxious. But Richard's face was cold and it was he who spoke first.

"And what are you doing here? We thought we were rid of you for good, you young cuckoo! If you've come to ask to be taken back…!"

"Oh…!" said Liza, shrinking. All trace of nervousness left Nicky at once and anger took over. He stepped in front of Richard and stood facing him.

"You have no right to speak to me like that. I never did you wrong, and now, let me tell you, I need nothing from you."

"Really?" said Richard.

"Yes, really! I am apprenticed to a merchant seaman in Lynmouth and in time, the Weavers are willing to help me set up for myself. I have a future, and I call myself happy. I've been to Venice three times now. I'm here to see my mother, nothing more. A reasonable thing for a son to do, don't you think?"

"Your mother doesn't need to be reminded of you and nor do we!" said Richard. "I thought we were rid of you for good!"

"Father, please!" said Peter. "Nicky is blameless and I have feeling for him, if you have not. I was glad of you, Nicky, that day on the packhorse bridge. Father, it's hardly a sin for him to want to see Liza. Let us be hospitable as we would be to any guest! I would like Nicky to join us for dinner."

Liza, evidently taking courage from this, said, "There's plenty of food. I'd like him to eat with us, too."

"Very well," said Richard. "This once. But let it be understood, young man—you chose to walk out on us and as far as I'm concerned, you're not welcome to walk back. So it's only this once."

Fury clenched in Nicky's guts. *So that's how it is! On the way up the combe I thought about the things Dyer and I heard from that goatherd in Lynmouth, but I thought I'd see what kind of welcome you gave me before I decided whether to mention them or not. Well, I've made my mind up now!*

Liza smiled at him and without a word fetched out the best pewter dishes and the silver salt which the Crowhams, long ago, had sent in celebration of the newly built hall. Richard scowled but made no comment.

Nicky, prudently, filled his stomach first, while answering his mother's questions about life with Owen ap Idwal, and the voyages he had made on the *Fulmar*. Peter and Richard were silent, neither interrupting nor attempting to join in. Ellen and Alfred and the two young maids, who were all at the table as well, were clearly conscious of family tension, and were also quiet. The gladness with which Liza had greeted him was now dimmed, like sunlight through a grimy window. She was herself aware of it. She could not properly enjoy his company, with Richard's disapproval filling the air like a disagreeable smell. Nicky sensed it, too, and knew that his mother dreaded Richard's anger. Oh yes, she had been allowed to stay, but she had not been forgiven. Not by Richard Lanyon, anyway. It hardened his heart still further.

When his mother ran out of questions and his stomach was safely laden with capon and raisin pudding, he turned to Richard.

"I heard the oddest bit of gossip the other day. Did you once think of getting married again, Master Lanyon? To a girl called Marion Locke, only she ran off with someone else instead?"

"Who told you that? They have it wrong, anyway," said Liza. "That was Peter, before he and I were betrothed. The girl you almost married was called Marion, wasn't she, Peter?"

"Yes. Marion Locke. That's right. But…" Richard had turned dusky crimson and Peter was looking at him curiously. "What's the matter, Father? It's just a bit of garbled gossip. I can't think how Nicky got hold of it."

"It was something I heard in a tavern. I believe this Marion Locke lived in Lynmouth," said Nicky, keeping it vague and remembering that Herbert Dyer did not want his name mentioned.

Richard, however, was already thinking about Herbert, and with loathing. *I let it out to that man Dyer and he talked, God curse him. He does business in Lynmouth at times. I might have known! She still haunts me. I think she gets into my soul and takes over my tongue. I still dream of her at times. She's using Nicky. I feel hot and my heart is pounding. Why did this…this little human accident have to come here and…?*

"I'm angry, that's all!" he barked. "Don't stare at me like that, boy! I don't like being gossiped about, and garbled gossip's worst of all!"

"But there was more than that," said Nicky, wrinkling his brow in a thoughtful frown. "The girl had cloudy yellow hair, hadn't she?"

"Yes, but what of it?" Richard snapped. "I saw her once, when I called on her parents to put a stop to the business of her and Peter. That's how I know."

"But at the time, you had a very odd-looking horse, called

Splash. I saw him myself, when I was a tiny boy and he was a very old horse, out at grass," Nicky said. "I was talking to a man in a Lynmouth tavern…"

"About me?" demanded Richard.

"Why not? I talk to whoever I like about whatever I like," said Nicky. "I'm not your grandson now, remember? I spoke of this girl Marion and I spoke of Splash and what he looked like and a fellow sitting nearby overheard me. He said that once, when he was a boy herding goats in the Valley of the Rocks, he saw a horseman come into the valley on a horse just like Splash, with odd-looking splodgy dapples, running into each other. He'd never seen a horse with a coat like that before and never saw another after. The man had a girl behind him, and she had hair like a pale gold cloud.

"He was almost poetic," said Nicky, enjoying his erstwhile grandfather's suffused face and glassy eyes. "They got down and left the horse—and a black-and-white dog—at the valley mouth and walked on to Castle Rock. I know the valley, so I know where he meant. They were quarrelling."

There was a silence. Then Richard said, "What's this rigmarole?" in a quiet voice which was somehow more alarming than when he was shouting.

Peter, however, was frowning. "I remember Splash and I never saw another horse like that, either. And Marion's hair…*did* you ever meet her in the Valley of the Rocks, Father? God's elbow, you surely didn't…." Richard's face now was purple, and Peter's eyes were widening. "It can't be true. You *didn't* have ideas of courting her for yourself! Did you?"

"Of course not! This is all a tarradiddle. I can't think…"

"Nicky," said Liza, distressed, "did you make this up because you are still angry at being disowned?"

"No, Mother. What I've said is what I heard. Truly."

"He's lying!" shouted Richard. "He's…!" There were beads of perspiration on his forehead. He stopped, gasping for breath, and half came to his feet, clutching at the edge of the table. Then he let go with one hand and jammed his palm against his chest. "I…"

He couldn't get any more words out. He staggered and fell, and might have pulled the table over except that Alfred and Nicky grabbed hold of it in time, and Richard's fingers lost their grip. Just as Liza sprang up and rushed around the table to help him, he crashed to the floor.

"Father-in-law!" Liza dropped to her knees beside him. "What's the matter? Oh, someone help me sit him up! What's *wrong?*"

Nicky was on his feet, too, appalled. It was as though he had kicked a pebble, and sent a landslide roaring down a hillside. Ellen and Peter had joined his mother at Richard's side and were lifting him into a sitting position, resting his back against the nearest wall.

"Can you not stand, Master Lanyon?" Ellen asked in concern. Richard, still pressing his hand to his chest, only shook his head. Sweat poured down his engorged face and his eyes were terrified. They sought Peter's and he struggled to speak but could only make gobbling sounds. Blobs of spittle appeared on his mouth.

"I'm here, Father. Take it slowly."

Somehow, Richard dragged a breath into his body and used it to force words out. "Not…slowly. No…time. Going to die. Priest."

"You're not going to die. People don't just die, like that, over dinner," said Liza in resolutely cheerful tones. "Take deep breaths."

"Going to *die*. Got to…get shriven. Can't die…with such a sin on me. Can't…"

"Father Matthew do say anyone can hear a confession if there b'ain't no priest handy," said Alfred. "Heard him tell us that, one Sunday. Master Lanyon, you ease your mind now, and then you'll likely feel better. Just to me, if you like, not bein' family. Might be easier."

"Doesn't matter…shan't be here to worry…aaah!" It was a moan of pain and he hunched forward, holding his chest as though he thought it might break apart. "Got to say…she wants me to say…she won't go away till I do…be waiting for me…"

"Who?" asked Alfred. "Who, Master Lanyon? Who is she?"

"Marion."

"Marion?" Peter burst out. "What are you saying, Father?"

"Wanted her…for me. Wanted…make her your stepmother." An awful rictus on Richard's face appeared to be a kind of grin. "Met her…in the valley. Walked her up Castle Rock. Asked her to…marry me…she wouldn't. Quarrel. Mist blowing in. Didn't mean it." His voice was fainter, as though his strength was going. "Caught hold of her. She broke away. Couldn't see…cliff edge. She…"

"She went off Castle Rock?" said Peter in a low voice. "Is that what you're saying? You…you killed her?"

"Accident. Didn't mean…" His voice gave out and his head fell back. He slid down the wall and let go of his chest, to strike feebly at the air with two clenched fists, before he slumped into unconsciousness. They shook him, shouted at him. Then Liza snatched a little silver spice tray out of the Crowham salt and held

it in front of his lips. No mist appeared on it. He was no longer
breathing.

Alfred, shaking his head, tested for a pulse in Richard's neck
and sat back on his heels. "He's gone." He looked up at Peter.
"I'm that sorry, sir."

"Sorry?" said Peter. "You may well be. I'm not. I can't
believe...oh, no, *I can't believe...!*" He sprang to his feet and
stood there, staring down at his father's body. "Oh, carry him to
his room. Put him on his bed! Alfred, Nicky, just do it! I won't
touch him! I'd sooner touch pitch...or eat muck from the
midden!"

"Peter..." Liza went to him and put a timid hand on his arm,
but he shook her off.

"All my life," he said, addressing not Liza but the hall in
general, the table, the roof beams, the red-and-white Tudor roses
on the panelling, the leaded windows, the rushes on the floor,
"*all my life* I've given in to him. All my life he's been the one
who says. I'm fifty years old and he still called me *boy!* He wanted
a big house—I had to see our substance wasted on it. To get the
substance to begin with, I was to marry for money while he
indulged himself with the girl I wanted!"

"Peter!" wailed Liza.

"And when she wouldn't play his game," he shouted, "he
killed her! He bloody well killed her and let me think she'd run
off with another man! Let everyone think it!"

He flung away from them all in a frenzy of released rage, hammering a Tudor rose with a fist, kicking another on a window
chest and shouting, shouting in repetitive fury.

"*All my life* he's had his way, never mine, never mine! He's de-
spoiled our property for this house, like an old stag lying in a

cornfield, crushing what he's lying on and eating everything within reach. Like the Sweetwaters riding across crops when they chase the same old stag! I was the one rewarded on a battlefield, but he took my reward from me and used it to suit himself. *We'll do this with it, we'll do that.* As though it were his! Always saying he's right, he knows best, he's the only one who should have a say! Calling me *boy* when I was a grown man and never a word of thanks when I looked after Allerbrook while he was away fighting—never a single word of praise! And all the time, all the time, he *killed Marion Locke!*"

"Peter!" Liza protested. "*Peter!* It was all long long ago and—"

"She'll never be long long ago for me. I loved her. *I loved her!*"

"And I loved Christopher Clerk!" Liza shrieked. "And now I see why! He wasn't a Lanyon!"

If anything could seize his attention, that would, but he didn't even seem to hear. "I hate this house! It's built on her bones! I'd like to burn it down! I will burn it down!" Peter bellowed, and would have made straight for the kitchen, where there was a fire, except that Liza got to the kitchen door first and stood with her arms spread wide, and Nicky and Alfred returned at that moment from laying Richard on his bed.

"I see," said Peter, glaring at his wife. "I'm still not to have my own way. Not ever, even at my age. No say in my own daughter's marriage, no say when money was cast away to build this house, or when land was cast away to the Sweetwaters! I thought I had a son once, but then I found I didn't even have that!"

"Peter, stop this, stop it!"

"Master Lanyon...Father...I still think of you as that...please don't. I never thought...I never expected..." Nicky was pale with horror.

"If he weren't dead, I'd like to kill him. I'd like to kill myself! I want to tear this place to pieces!" And once again he was hurling himself around the room, kicking and punching at the panels and the window seats.

"Nicky," said Liza frantically, "there's only one person I know of who can quieten Peter down when he's angry, and that's Quentin. He cares more for her than for anyone else in the world. She's at Sweetwater House...."

"I know. Shall I fetch her?"

"If you can. Get your horse and ride down the combe as fast as you can manage. Be careful bringing her back—she's expecting again and not far off her time. But don't lose time either. Go, Nicky, go!"

CHAPTER FORTY-ONE

A DUTY TO LIVE

Nicky's hireling resented being dragged away from the manger Alfred had filled for him, and he tried to bite, but Nicky saddled him, mounted and drove him ruthlessly down the track through the combe, reaching Sweetwater House in a matter of minutes. Once there, his demands to see his sister were so peremptory and loud that Quentin herself, slow-moving now with the bulk of her second baby, heard him shouting in the courtyard, looked out of the solar window and came down to meet him.

"There's no time to lose." Nicky had not even dismounted. "Your grandfather's collapsed and your father's running mad and your mother thinks only you can calm him. It's serious! It's *urgent*. Quick, get up on this horse. Use the mounting block. Sit sideways behind me and I'll get us back to Allerbrook as fast as is safe. Come *on!* I'll explain as we go!"

"What's all this? Who are you? Where are you taking Quentin?" John ran from the house, with Walter, who these days was getting very rheumaticky, hurrying after him as best he could.

"He's my brother, there's trouble at Allerbrook, they need me to help," said Quentin rapidly. She hadn't seen Nicky for years and couldn't think where he had sprung from, but his frantic voice and the appeal in his eyes were enough. She was already perching sideways on the hireling's back, and was still finishing her explanation over her shoulder as Nicky urged the horse back to the archway.

"But you can't—" John was running alongside. "You mustn't…"

"I can. I must. Follow me if you like! We might be glad of you!" said Quentin, a new, decisive Quentin, one whom John had never seen before, and with that she was gone. The horse, his nose once more pointing to the manger from which he had been so summarily dragged, began for once to pull, and Nicky actually had to check him, so as not to jolt Quentin too much.

"What's wrong at Allerbrook?" Quentin demanded as they made for the combe. "How did you come to be there? I'm glad to see you, but…"

"Listen and I'll tell you."

By the time he had enlightened her and answered her astounded questions, they were at the top of the combe and turning toward the house. Hearing cries and thumpings, he risked a trot to get them quickly into the yard, where he pulled up sharply, while the horse, with good reason, whinnied and sidled.

Everyone except Peter was out in the yard. Ellen and the other two maids were clinging together, terrified. The dogs, all three of them, were running about, barking and yelping. Alfred was at the top of the porch steps, pounding on the door of the hall, while Liza, banging on a window and trying to see through it although it was so high that even on tiptoe she could only just peer over the sill, was screaming for Peter to let them in. And ominously, frighteningly, there was a seeping of smoke from the edges of the door, and the smell of it was in the air.

"He's in there!" Liza cried as Nicky jumped down and turned to help Quentin off. "He's setting fire to the hall and he's shut himself inside! He kicked Alfred from behind and threw him, *threw* him out of the door, and then he picked Ellen up and tossed her after Alfred like a…a piece of rubbish, and then pushed me and the other girls out, too, and Richard's dead and he's upstairs on his bed…!"

"The inner doors! From the kitchen, the workroom! The upstairs door to the spare bedrooms! What about those?" Nicky demanded.

"No use! He's bolted them all. I saw him! I could just about see! Even the upstairs door! I saw him run upstairs and do it. We can't get in!"

"Then find me something to break the front door down! Alfred! Hurry! Hurry! Anything!"

"Ah!" said Alfred, and abandoning his efforts with his fists, ran for the shed where the tools were kept, reappearing a second later with a gigantic hammer in one hand and an axe in the other, which he thrust at Nicky. "This any good?"

"Yes. Go for the hinges!" yelled Nicky. "Ellen, Quentin, get that horse away before it hurts itself or someone else!"

Ellen had pulled herself together and gone to help Quentin with the frightened horse. The two of them led it away toward the pony field, while Nicky and Alfred struggled with the door.

It was not intended to withstand such treatment and yielded quite quickly, breaking away from its hinges and falling inward. Smoke billowed out, and behind it there was fire, which flared up at the inrush of air, licking up the panelling and dancing along the floor where the rushes had been kindled, bursting into a blaze where Peter had piled wooden furniture to help it along. Peter himself, soot stained and livid, tried to attack them, but Liza, shrieking for the maids to help as well, joined in and between them all, they were a match for him.

"And no man kicks me from behind and gets away with it, not even you, Master," said Alfred grimly, grasping one of Peter's arms and helping to drag him out to safety.

"But the house, the house!" Liza screamed as flame ran across the rushes, pursuing them.

"It won't burn that easy, not all that good stone," Alfred said. "Get buckets, quick, Mistress, while we lock this madman up! And get these here dogs out from under my feet!" The lurcher, Pewter, seemed to think that Alfred was attacking Peter and had planted himself in front of them, barking furiously.

"Oh, Father, whatever is the matter with you?" Quentin and Ellen reappeared and at the sight of Peter struggling against his captors, Quentin cried out in distress. She also made haste to get hold of Pewter's collar, which brought her in front of her father. Seeing her seemed to bring Peter partly to his senses.

"Why are you here, Quentin? You're almost at your time! Nicky, if you did this...!"

"I sent him, you fool, because there's a faint chance you might listen to her!" Liza shouted. "You won't listen to anyone else! Ellen, take that dog from Quentin and shut it in somewhere! And the others!"

Ellen came running to deal with the dogs. Liza was already hauling a bucket from the well. Peter tried to break free from his captors, but they wrestled him to the shed where, long ago, Liza had seen her first pig carcase stripped of its bristles, thrust him inside and bolted the door. "Here!" said Liza, pushing the bucket at them as they ran back to her, and clattering a second one into the well.

Hoofbeats announced the arrival of reinforcements. After no more than a few minutes of distracted argument, John and Walter Sweetwater had saddled up and followed. They came headlong into the yard and pulled up, the horses sliding on their haunches. John leaped and Walter slithered to the ground, both exclaiming, "What the devil's happening here?"

"Where's my wife?" John shouted. "Quentin, put that bucket down! Have you gone clean out of your head?"

"God's teeth, John, the house is on fire!"

Hard behind them, attracted in from the fields by the sound of shouting, came Hodge, on foot, grasping a billhook. John and Walter, whose horses were edging nervously from the smell of smoke, promptly threw their reins at him, and with a shrug and a bewildered shake of the head, he led them away to add to those in the pony field.

Ellen, having shut the dogs into the tool store and sped back to join the firefighters, was too distracted to see the two new arrivals as anything but merely two new pairs of hands. She thrust a full bucket straight at Walter.

"What's this? What's this? What are you giving me this for?"

"She thought you might be thirsty! Oh, go and throw it on the fire!" shouted Liza. Walter's mouth opened in astonishment, but he suddenly grasped the need and bore the bucket to the hall as fast as he could limp. John seized Quentin, pulled her into the gateway, sat her down with her back against the gatepost, ordered her curtly to stay there and not move, and then joined in.

Alfred had been right to say that the hall would not burn easily. The panels and the floor were of seasoned oak, nearly as hard as iron, and there were still no tapestries. The pile of benches and stools, with cushions thrown in, was ablaze in midfloor, but there was no shortage of buckets, which were always needed for carrying food and water to stabled animals or getting bristles off pigs. With nine of them at the task, once Hodge had rejoined them, the flames were put out. There were dark stains on the walls and floor and window chests and a few on the roof beams and much of the furniture was lost, but the hall was still there and the damage could be repaired.

At the end of it all, Quentin rose and went to the door of her father's makeshift prison and talked to him through it. Presently, she came to the hall where the others were all busy pulling the piled furnishings apart and prowling about with buckets, looking for signs of smouldering, to say that she thought it would be safe to let him out.

"I knew you would manage him," Liza said thankfully. "He was beyond me, or I wouldn't have sent Nicky for you. If you're sure it's safe, set him free and bring him into the house. But only if you're sure."

Quentin, warily, went back to the shed. "Father? Are you all right? Please be all right. I'm so worried about you."

"There's no need to worry. There's nothing wrong with me."

"If I let you out, you won't...do anything dreadful again, will you? Please promise."

"No, I won't. I'm in my right mind now. Don't be afraid, my girl."

Quentin drew back the bolts and Peter emerged. He was trembling and looked sick. "Oh, my poor Quentin! What have I done? I think I was possessed."

His rage had gone out, like the fire. Quentin, talking gently to him, led him into the house and across the hall to the parlour. The others, still working, looked away. In the parlour she coaxed him to sit down, and a moment later Liza and Nicky joined them.

"Ellen will get us some cider," Liza said. "We've all got dry throats. The fire's out, though. Everything is going to be all right."

She said it calmly and even felt that it was true, though in his rage, Peter had uttered things which would be hard to forget. It had been wounding to hear his declaration of love for the unknown Marion, but in a way, it had eased her own bad conscience. If he had truly, all along, felt for Marion what she had felt for Christopher, then it was no wonder that they had never, quite, been able to form the bond a married couple should, and just how virtuous would Peter have stayed if Marion had been still alive and had one day come back to him?

The Sweetwaters, sooty, water-splashed and sweating, had finished in the hall and came in carrying full tankards and followed by Ellen with a trayload of more. John and Walter both looked angry.

"Just what did you think you were doing, Nicky Lanyon," John demanded, "dragging Quentin away up here, in her condition, into the middle of this?"

"Her father was in such a state. He'd learned something… something that upset him very badly," said Liza. "He wanted to set fire to the hall. Well, he did! Quentin's the only person we thought could quieten him." She looked around. "Quentin, you…where's she gone?"

"She was here beside me and then she suddenly went out," said Peter dully. "Just now."

"Ellen, go and find her!" Liza commanded.

Ellen set down her tray and disappeared. She was back in a very short time, her face frightened. "Mistress Lanyon…Master Sweetwater…I think the baby's on the way. She'm walkin' about in the kitchen but I think she did ought to be upstairs, in a bed-chamber. I—"

"But it's early!" John shouted. "It's two weeks too soon!"

Peter and Nicky both sprang up.

"If anything happens to her…" Peter looked horrified.

Nicky, shakily, said, "We needed her here, but perhaps it was too much for her…" and then sat down again, his face stricken.

"You went because I sent you, Nicky," said Liza. "I'm sorry I had to send for her." She turned to Peter and her voice was pitiless. "It was all I could think of, with the house about to burn down and hers the only voice you were likely to heed. If anything goes wrong now, it will be partly my fault, but mostly yours!"

"Yes, his," said Walter savagely, and pointed a quivering fore-finger at Peter. "And if my son's wife dies, I will kill him."

"Blessed Mother, intercede for her!" pleaded Ellen tearfully, down on her knees beside Quentin's bed. "Dear Lord, wilt thou not bring forth that which thou hast formed?" It was the fourth time she had uttered the ancient prayer for women in travail. The only response was another moan from Quentin and Ellen's tears flowed faster. "Ellen!" Liza said desperately. "Get up! More hot water, more cloths to wring out in it, more chicken broth and make haste."

"It's gone on too long, Mother." Quentin, weak and exhausted from twenty-four hours of constant pain without result, clutched at Liza's hand for comfort and then cried feebly as the anguish rose again. "I'm going to die. I just wish it could be over."

"You're *not* going to die," said Liza. "*Ellen! Broth!* And water and cloths!"

"I've got the chicken broth." John and Walter had ridden headlong back to Clicket, and an hour after that, John had reappeared with his mother. Catherine Sweetwater had taken charge in the Allerbrook kitchen. She had come into the room carrying a bowl. Ellen, still sobbing, got to her feet and passed her in the doorway. "At least those two maids of yours had the sense to start making the broth straightaway," Catherine said. "Now, what's all this about dying?"

"I'm going to," said Quentin, exhausted. "Can't manage it. Can't make it come."

"You've got to do it, and you've got to live. It's your duty," said Liza, wiping her daughter's wet forehead and smoothing back the soaked brown hair which had been plastered across it. "Because if you don't, your grandfather-in-law swears he'll kill your father. John didn't argue, either. Quentin, my darling girl, listen, it's up to you now!"

It's up to me. Her mother had no idea, Quentin thought as another pain twisted her guts into knots, what that phrase meant. It always seemed to be up to her. She had had to fight for her mother after Bosworth—make Betsy behave, get her father and grandfather to soften their anger. She had been the only one who

really fought for Nicky. She had done that twice. She hadn't succeeded, but no one else had as much as tried.

She had eventually reconciled her father—more or less—to
her marriage; within that marriage, much as she loved John
Sweetwater, she had had to work to call forth an answering love
from him, to make terms with Walter. And she had been the one
Liza sent for in desperation when her own father was overset and
dangerous. Now she must live when it would be much easier and
more comfortable to die, because if she didn't, all hell would
break loose all over again. Walter Sweetwater would renew the
old feud, this time with lethal intent.

Sometimes she thought she had spent her whole life trying to
coax other people to be reasonable. Now here it was again. She
must live, or else. She was tired of it. Let them get on with it.

"No," she said wearily. "I'm going to die. I want to. I can't
fight anymore."

"Rubbish, of course you can. Don't you dare give up now,"
said Catherine. "There are a few things we haven't tried yet.
Mistress Lanyon, is there any pepper in the house?"

"I can't go on. I can't. Whoever's made threats, whatever
they've said, I can't do anything about it!" Quentin wailed.
"Why am I supposed to try? Why must it be me who has to stop
people killing each other? Why do I have to be called because
Father's trying to destroy the house? Why must it fall on me? No,
I don't mean that, exactly, but…"

"Come. If you can make jokes, you're not dying," said Catherine, presenting her daughter-in-law with a spoonful of broth.

"Not making a joke. Just a mistake," said Quentin, and then,
seeing that however accidental, it had indeed been a joke, unexpectedly laughed. The laugh collided with a violent contrac-

tion and turned into a cry, but as Catherine Sweetwater remarked afterward, laughter could be as good as a noseful of pepper and a few hearty sneezes for getting things to move. Five minutes later Ellen returned with the hot water and the cloths to find that a very small but very noisy girl-child was in Liza's arms and Quentin, however tired, was still very much alive.

"Elizabeth," said John Sweetwater. "We settled, if the babe were a girl, that she should be Elizabeth, for you, Mistress Lanyon, and for our queen, Elizabeth of York. It's a good Yorkist name," he added with a glinting smile full of such charm that Liza, for the first time, understood why Quentin had so improbably fallen in love with this young man. "But Quentin? You are sure she will come through?"

"Quentin is sitting up and taking broth," said Liza. "I'm rather sorry that Master Walter didn't come back with you from Sweetwater House. I would like a few words with your grandfather, John. Quentin will come through. In a few moments you can see her and your daughter. When you go home, tell Master Walter that we will hear no more talk of revenge and murder!"

"He may not have meant it," said John.

"I rather think he did," Liza told him. "Though I'd have done all in my power to stop him. I'd have made the parish constable arrest him for disturbing the peace with threats if I had to. One thing our new King Henry has done is introduce a little more law into the land."

There was a brief, tense silence. John Sweetwater's face darkened and in that moment he was wholly a Sweetwater, with as much arrogance in his eyes and the tilt of his chin as there had ever been in Sir Humphrey's.

"My late father, Baldwin Sweetwater," said John, "did not think that women should interfere in men's business."

"If Master Peter Lanyon were harmed, do you really think either Quentin or I would agree that it was nothing to do with us? That our bereavement wasn't our business? Come, come, Son-in-law," said Liza, and then, realising that she sounded exactly like her own parents, "Let us have a little common sense!"

Again there was a moment of tautness during which Liza's attempt to be reasonable strove in midair with the time-ingrained pride and the violent traditions of the Sweetwaters. She held John's eyes and almost held her breath, as well.

And then he laughed. "Quentin would think her father's death, or mine, come to that, was very much her business and I expect she'd say so. She's strong-minded, is Quentin. I saw it when she answered your call and got up behind Nicky without a second's hesitation. I pray she'll never take such a risk again."

Peter had taken no part in their exchange. He had a stunned air, as though too much had happened too rapidly for him to take in. He looked around him, at the damaged hall. "I can't believe I caused this. And I still can hardly believe that my father—"

"The burial will be tomorrow," said Liza, cutting him short. It would be better, she felt, if they didn't discuss the transgressions of Richard Lanyon. She had already told the rest of the household that whatever they had heard at that horrible dinner table had better be forgotten.

John remarked, "I think the stonework here will always carry those dark stains, but surely the woodwork can be restored?"

"Yes. It will be. I'll see to it," Peter said rather shortly, turning to him at last.

A silence fell. There might well, in the future, be a good many silences, Liza thought. There would be times when for this or that reason, conversation would veer in dangerous directions and have to stop, or change course. Walter Sweetwater and the Lanyon family would hardly be able to look each other in the face for a very long time, while both she and Peter had said things to each other which could never be forgotten but should never be mentioned again, either.

She'll never be long long ago for me. I loved her. I loved her!

And I loved Christopher Clerk and now I see why! He wasn't a Lanyon!

No. Let those dreadful, truthful, telling phrases be lost in time and silence. They must not be repeated. Nor must the scorn in *I sent him, you fool, because there's a faint chance you might listen to her! You won't listen to anyone else!*

There was one thing she must ask him, though. "Peter…"

"Yes?"

"Nicky is outside just now, attending to his horse. He'll go back to Lynmouth after the funeral. I would like it if he could visit me again, now and then. He is my son, after all." She held his eyes steadily as she spoke.

Here was another of those difficult pauses, in which the thirteen years during which Peter had believed Nicky to be his own son, and the moment when Nicky saved him from Baldwin, came to the minds of both Peter and Liza, though in John's presence they could not possibly be mentioned.

Peter was also having thoughts of his own which he knew it would be best not to utter. *I'm free now. I hated my father the day I tried to burn this house down, but now I need not even hate him. I'm even free of that. He can't control me anymore, and as for Marion…I suppose he's paid for her now.*

And because his father was gone, Peter need no longer deny those thirteen years of affection between Nicky and himself, an affection which had been strong enough to make Peter change sides at Bosworth, and bring Nicky running to his aid during the fight on the bridge. In a calm voice, he said, "But of course I'm agreeable. Naturally Nicky may visit."

John glanced at the two of them and looked as though he wanted to ask questions, but did not. The reason Nicky had left home would remain forever a Lanyon secret.

Catherine appeared at the door. "John, you can see your wife and daughter now."

CHAPTER FORTY-TWO

TOKEN

"Nicky! I'm so pleased to see you. It's been over a year!" Liza's voice was crackly now, like her weathered old skin or the creak in her joints when she moved. She was close on seventy, and felt it.

Nicky, on the other hand, was thirty-two and in his prime, a successful young merchant who had married the daughter of his former employer and now lived in Lynmouth with Gwyneth and their two little sons and had lately acquired a ship of his own.

He did not know, as he stood in the hall at Allerbrook looking at the panelling and window chests and Tudor roses, all of them carefully restored long since, that even now, when his mother was old, the sight of him made her inside turn over because he looked so like Christopher Clerk. He saw, however, that she was—as always—delighted that he had come visiting, and he gave her Christopher's tough grin, which was more of a reward than he dreamed.

"I had a good ride over the moor," he said. "Your crops are ripening well, though I think you've had deer in the barley again. You'd better have a word with the Sweetwaters' harbourer and see if he can't set the hounds on the miscreants."

"Yes, I'll tell Peter. How are your family?"

"All well—now. Gwyneth is as lively and merry as her father still is. The boys have had measles, but they've come through safely. They're good lads most of the time," said Nicky, "and even when they're not, I don't beat them. They both take after me and they might not forgive me."

There was a brief silence, one of the silences that Liza had foreseen when Richard died and Quentin's daughter was born. Nicky had never forgiven Richard for his beatings or for casting him off, and look what had come of that long bitterness. After a moment she said, "Did you call on the Sweetwaters as you usually do, and see Quentin?"

"Yes. I found her in the dairy with Elizabeth, making clotted cream. The Sweetwaters have never quite succeeded in turning our Quentin into a lady," said Nicky, grinning again. "Johnny told me that last year, at harvest time, she made him arm himself with a scythe and go out reaping with the rest of the parish!"

"I know. We had him here, taking his place in the line across the field. Her husband doesn't mind," Liza said. "John claims that his grandfather Walter was very interested in his sheep and used to go about sometimes with Edward Searle. He's happy enough to see his son and daughter learning to be practical. Walter approved, too—Catherine told me. Peter and I never spoke to him again, nor he to us, after the day of the fire until the day he died, but he valued Quentin. It was for her sake that he threatened Peter! It was all very complicated. Well, the old feud died with him."

"Thank God it died. Can I have another look at Quentin's window in the chapel?"

They went to the chapel together. It was not large, but like the rest of the house, it had been enhanced during the fifteen years since the fire, at Peter's expense. The day he made up his mind to embark on improvements for the hall and the chapel had been one of the rare occasions when an area of silence, hitherto as pristine as untrodden snow, had acquired just a few footprints.

"I've been thinking, Liza. You know, I'm quite proud of our house now. Father was right. We didn't end up dressed in rags and begging for alms in Clicket or Dulverton, did we?" He had never before made even an oblique reference to the day he had tried to burn down the house and even now, Liza silently noticed, Marion's name was not mentioned. It never would be. "We've prospered well after all," Peter said, "and I find I have land enough to content me. There are a few things I'd like to add…."

So tapestries now adorned the hall and the sun made coloured patterns on the floor of the little chapel when it shone through the stained glass of the windows Peter had installed. The first to be put in was known as Quentin's window.

"It's a thank-you to her," Peter had said. It showed an angel, whose face bore a certain resemblance to that of his daughter, standing before a building with arms outspread, denying entrance to a man who held a flaring torch aloft.

"That was a terrible day," Nicky said as they stood together, looking at it. "When the fire happened, I mean."

"Yes. Yes it was. Nicky, do you want to see Peter? He's out with the sheep—he's sixty-five but as able to get about as ever he was. He'd be sorry if he missed you. He likes to see you these days."

"Poor Peter. I still sometimes want to call him Father, you know. Now I'm grown up myself, I can see what a muddle he must have been in."

"He was. He'd loved you as a son for thirteen years and he wanted you to go on being his son and when he found that you weren't, he didn't know what to do with the love," Liza said, and then looked astonished. "I've known that for years and never put it into words before. Fancy that!"

"I'll see him—of course I will. But I want to give you something first, privately. Beside Quentin's window is as good a place as any. I think she understands you and even understands about…"

"She does." He had paused, but Liza, making a cautious footprint or two on another stretch of silent snow, finished his thought for him. "She fell in love with John just as I did, long ago, with your father."

"Here," said Nicky, and drew a small packet from inside his doublet. "I sailed north recently, to collect a consignment of copper for my first voyage abroad in my own ship. Which is lying in Dunster at the moment, by the way. The Luttrells are maintaining the harbour very well. But while I was in the north, I made some enquiries. I've seen my real father."

"You've seen Christopher! He's still alive?"

"Yes, though he's frail. I knew that he'd gone to the north. You told me that, back then, when we first found out…about everything."

"I remember. Peter told me and I spoke of it to you, before you left home."

"I've thought for years that I'd like to find him, if it wasn't too late. I'd only seen him once, and hardly under ideal circumstances. I did find him, but I think I was only just in time. He said himself that he didn't think he'd got much longer. He's still a priest, though he has a younger priest with him who does most of the work of the parish. They have a church in a Yorkshire village. He was happy to see me, very happy, and pleased to have news of both me and you. He gave me something for you. Here. Better not say he sent it, perhaps. If Peter asks, say it was a present from me. He won't mind that. My fa…I mean, Christopher said that as the end of his life couldn't be far away, he wanted you to have this, as a token of his lifelong prayers for you."

She took the packet and opened it. And then looked at what it had contained, marvelling, holding it in one palm and turning it over with her other hand.

It was a patterned silver ring.

AUTHOR'S NOTE 🙟

The origins of this book lie far back in time. It was, I think, the year 1959, and I was only about twenty-two on the day when, during a morning ride in Somerset, on the edge of Exmoor, I turned my horse onto a path halfway up the side of a narrow valley, with pine trees growing up from its floor.

I hadn't been there before. Later I learned that the pines were on average 150 feet high and were among the tallest trees in Great Britain. On that morning they almost made me giddy. The path was level, roughly, with their halfway point. When I looked down, my eyes followed their slim trunks to the ferny ground far below. When I looked up, I could see them stretching far above me, tapering toward the sky. It was staggering. It was also exhilarating; another splendid thing I had discovered about a district which had fascinated me since I saw it first at the age of eleven.

I was not yet a writer, but I knew I would be one day. On that morning, looking at those pines, I knew that I wanted, intended, was determined, one day, to write a book with Exmoor and its surroundings as a setting.

It was many many years before the right opportunity and the right theme presented themselves. And then, one day, long after I really had become a novelist, my agent telephoned me and said he knew I had always wanted to write a novel based on Exmoor. Well, it looked as though the chance had come. There was a publisher who was interested in a historical novel with an English regional setting.

The House of Lanyon is the result. Nearly every place it mentions is real, except for Allerbrook and Clicket. These, like the characters, are fictional. There is no such house as Allerbrook; indeed, there is no manor house of that type anywhere on Exmoor. Where I have placed both village and house there is in reality nothing but moorland and isolated farms.

The name of Clicket is genuine. At one time there really was a hamlet called Clicket on the outskirts of Exmoor. It was however a very small community, nothing at all like the prosperous village I have described in the book, and it wasn't in the same place. I believe it was abandoned sometime in the nineteenth century. It seemed a pleasant idea to use a genuine Exmoor name, that's all.

To save Exmoor enthusiasts the trouble of noting references to places like Dulverton, Withypool and the River Barle, getting out their Landranger maps and trying to work out where Clicket ought to be, I will tell them that it is approximately (I won't be too specific) between three and five miles west of Tarr Steps, the curious granite slab bridge across the Barle. Allerbrook House is a mile away from it, high up in a combe which is also fictional. I have simply and ruthlessly planted village, house and combe where I wanted them to be. Writers of fiction do that kind of thing.

Oddly enough, there is no reference in the book to a valley with tall pine trees in it, but the memory of that morning's ride was with me all the time as I wrote *The House of Lanyon*. I have loved writing it. I hope it will give pleasure to readers, too.

Valerie Anand
November 2006

THE FISH LADDER

THE FISH LADDER

A Journey Upstream

KATHARINE NORBURY

BLOOMSBURY

NEW YORK · LONDON · OXFORD · NEW DELHI · SYDNEY

Bloomsbury USA
An imprint of Bloomsbury Publishing Plc

1385 Broadway	50 Bedford Square
New York	London
NY 10018	WC1B 3DP
USA	UK

www.bloomsbury.com

BLOOMSBURY and the Diana logo are trademarks of Bloomsbury Publishing Plc

First published in Great Britain 2015
First U.S. edition 2015

ISBN: HB: 978-1-62040-995-4
ePub: 978-1-63286-001-9

Library of Congress Cataloging-in-Publication Data has been applied for.

2 4 6 8 10 9 7 5 3 1

Typeset by Hewer Text UK Ltd, Edinburgh
Printed and bound in the U.S.A. by Thomson-Shore Inc., Dexter, Michigan

To find out more about our authors and books visit www.bloomsbury.com. Here you will find extracts, author interviews, details of forthcoming events, and the option to sign up for our newsletters.

Bloomsbury books may be purchased for business or promotional use. For information on bulk purchases please contact Macmillan Corporate and Premium Sales Department at specialmarkets@macmillan.com.

To Jean Norbury and in memory of Fred Norbury
with boundless love

Fish ladder (noun):

A structure that allows the natural migration of fish around an obstacle, such as a dam. Most fish ladders consist of a series of pools, arranged in low steps (hence the term *ladder*) that the fish swim and leap up to reach the open waters on the other side. The velocity of water falling over the steps has to be great enough to attract fish to the ladder, but it cannot be so great that it washes them back downstream, or exhausts them to the point of inability to continue their journey upriver.

PART I

It is no small pity, and should cause us no little shame, that, through our own fault, we do not understand ourselves, or know who we are. Would it not be a sign of great ignorance, my daughters, if a person were asked who he was, and could not say, and had no idea who his father or his mother was, or from what country he came?

Teresa of Avila

Font del Mont

'The theme for the summer is following watercourses from the sea to the source.'

It was the first day of the holiday and my nine-year-old daughter Evie reached for her journal. She transcribed my statement, and then underlined it, and in doing so turned it into a title. Beyond her a dozen crows, visible as sooty flecks, spiralled above Garn Fadryn's summit cone.

'What's a watercourse?' she asked.

'A watercourse is the path that water follows. It can be anything from a trickling stream to a mighty river.'

'What about the source?'

'The source is where it comes from.'

'Like a spring?'

'Maybe,' I said. 'It might be a pool, or a spring, or a crack in a rock. I've never really thought about it.' Evie looked at me, then put down her pencil.

'How shall we begin?'

★

This is the story of how I set out, often in the company of Evie, on a series of walks, or journeys. Our pastime began as a coping mechanism, a device that would get us through an otherwise blighted summer. Coping, because I had been pregnant the previous winter, but had lost my baby in the spring.

There had been tension in our household from the day a pink line appeared on the plastic wand of the tester kit. I was delighted, excited, and felt blessed. My husband, Rupert, was anxious. We had been living in Barcelona because the euro was weak against the pound, although that was already changing. Evie was thrilled, and wrote a poem called 'My New Brother', that was put up on the wall at school, but Rupert and I argued most days. I was nauseous, often sick, which I welcomed as a happy sign. Statistically, because of my age, I had a fifty per cent likelihood of miscarrying. But I was sure it would be all right.

When I felt the fizz of life slow down I stayed in bed, put my feet up, convinced myself the child was growing, although everything felt different from how it had with Evie. It was as though I carried a somnambulist, a sleeper, even now, when sleep was the natural state. Yet this rest was deeper, profound, dreamless. And then, one day, the baby's heart just stopped. My doctor tried to persuade me to have the miscarriage induced. But I loved him – I was sure the baby was a little boy – and I didn't want him to leave me. So I decided to let him rest as long as he would.

Most days I walked on Tibidabo, the rumpled mountain at the back of the city. One morning, after dropping our children at school, my friend Olga and I picked our way up one of the many narrow paths to join the track along the ridge – the Carretera de les Aigües – Olga swearing under her breath, and vowing to give up smoking, tucking her long hair behind her ear. Tibidabo was covered in pines, figs and prickly pears, populated with wild boar and herds of lost sheep and, occasionally, FC Barcelona footballers, training on the unpaved road above Camp Nou, as well as scores of joggers and morning walkers, some with dogs or baby strollers, and Lycra-clad cyclists wearing bug-eyed goggles. Swallows whispered in pulsing clouds. Cicadas creaked and buzzed. Despite the forest, the hill was bright, because the Mediterranean Sea, which was tacked like a veil to the hem of the city, acted as a vast reflector, and bounced light into all but the darkest gullies, driving out the shadows. At this time of year the mountain was dense with desert flowers, century cactus, scrubby pink roses, flat yellow poppies, the blue fluff of rosemary. Olga pointed out the places where, later in the year, mushrooms might be found, and wild asparagus in its season, bitter and thin as samphire.

At Tibidabo's southernmost ridge there was a freshwater spring, the Font del Mont, or spring of the mountain. It could be accessed by a road up the back of the hill, and every day a line of elderly Catalan men wearing wide braces and orthopaedic shoes, and leaning on gnarled sticks – for digging mushrooms – formed a line at the spring with their plastic water carriers. A stone cairn had been built over the spring and the water directed through a steel pipe where it spilled into a polythene ice-cream carton before running, profligate, onto the ground. Dogs that had run ahead of their owners formed a shifting community about the carton, tails wagging dust. The men waved us to the front of the queue to come and refill our water bottles, eyes darting to the smooth bump of my belly. We asked them if there was anything special about the water, if it contained healing properties. The old men looked at us as though we were mad, and laughed. 'It's water,' they said, 'and it's free!'

When we got back to Olga's house her mother was waiting

with a casserole of veal, eggs and peas. She spoke to me in Catalan, which Olga translated: 'Darling, you must keep up your protein. And replace your fluids.' At home, I stocked the fridge with isotonic drinks, enough to run a marathon.

The baby left my body in his own good time, almost a month after his heart stopped beating. We were at home when it happened, Evie asleep, Olga's number propped by the telephone. Rupert was in London for the premiere of a film, an adaptation of one of his books. There had been no way of knowing when it was going to happen; life couldn't and shouldn't stand still.

When summer came, and brought with it the realisation that our baby should have been with us, have been in my arms, warm and cuddly and smelling of sunshine, I found that I was struggling. It wasn't the first time that, grieving, I had found things hard; not the first time that the world had closed around me in a tight, hard sphere. I had been so afraid when it happened the first time that I declared, on my recovery, that I was more afraid of madness than of death. Although it turned out, in the end, that this was a luxurious boast, a terrible falsehood, and I would have the opportunity to revise my view entirely. So, because I had a daughter, and I had to be strong for Evie, I searched for something that would keep the air breathable, the sound of the wind audible, the smell of a bonfire or the smart tang of sea salt sharp on my lips and tongue. That might shut out the possibility of – depression is such a vague word – stasis. That would shut out the possibility of everything standing still, as it had stood still once before, when I was sad, and I never wanted to go back there, ever again.

So I came up with the idea of following a river from the sea to its source. The idea came to me in a roundabout way, which I will share with you, and for a long time I failed to achieve it. Indeed, the plan unravelled so fast that it very soon came to include anything with a watery theme. But I found, as the summer progressed, that I had accidentally embarked on a journey to the source of life itself. Not an abstract journey, or a metaphorical one, about who we are and what we're doing here. A literal one: a journey to the source of this, particular, life. Because, although my childhood had been a happy one, and my adult life fulfilling, if not particularly exceptional, or notable from the point of view of achievement, there had been a slight unorthodoxy about my beginning.

I had been adopted as a baby, brought into our family because my parents wanted to have a second child, and my mother had been unable to carry one after giving birth to my brother. I hadn't stopped to think about this in many, many years, although, at one level, I had always been aware of it. But for some reason, perhaps connected with, or triggered by, this new lost baby, I started to dwell upon this mystery. Of who I was, and where I'd actually come from. Of whom we speak when we talk about *our family*. And it turned out, as the weeks rolled by, and became months, and then years, that I discovered that there were places, empty spaces, *places in the heart*, that I simply hadn't imagined could exist.

Swimming Pool

On a huge hill,
Cragged and steep, Truth stands, and he that will
Reach her, about must and about must go

John Donne

The idea, of following a river from the sea to its source, had its origin between the pages of a novel – *The Well at the World's End* – by the Scottish writer, Neil M. Gunn. Unfortunately I no longer had this book, because I had given it to my friend Sofia, in Barcelona, just a few days before we returned to Wales for the long summer holiday.

At Evie's international primary school Sofia was, without doubt, the richest mother, being married to one of the wealthiest men in the world. We met when she overheard me complaining to Evie's teacher about an apparently armed man who had followed the children's bus to the swimming pool. Miss Linda had looked thoughtful. Bodyguards were the new black. One of the Russian families had one. Also one of the Bulgarian families, though theirs was more like a footman and doubled up as a chauffeur. A gentle-looking woman in a tracksuit then stepped forward and said that it was she who employed the guard, and she apologised for the fuss. A diamond the size of a penny glittered on her finger. The woman insisted that she thought it was better for all the children that there was a bodyguard outside the school, and I had been unable to think of a response.

In spring the knots of security already looped around Sofia pulled tighter. Her father-in-law stepped down from control of their family business, which was a bank, and Sofia's husband, with a minimum of fuss, slipped into his father's shoes. The daily walk to the school gates was accompanied by a huddle of walkie-talkied ex-marines and black-clad secret policemen. While the arrangement was clearly unsatisfactory, it was also short-lived, for during the course of the summer Sofia and her family would leave Barcelona for their own country, where the net of security could better enfold them, and the children would go to school in a four-wheel drive.

Shortly before she left, Sofia invited some of the mothers from the school gates over for supper. I was one of them. I pressed the buzzer by an electric foot-gate and her head of security asked me to state my identity and articulate the purpose of my visit. Overhead, a three-quarter moon competed with the intruder lights of the house. When the gate opened I stood outside the front door while the guard phoned Sofia, who confirmed the information I had given him. He admitted me to the hallway and opened a second door. I passed beyond him into a stylish, austere room where a glass table was set with damask napkins and ornate heavy silver. A centrepiece of unfamiliar flowers with beaded stamens, delicate as sugar, dropped ochre dust onto the table; it was like the powder on the wings of moths.

Beyond the table the women from the school gates sat talking on two low sofas. Sofia waved a greeting, the phone still in her hand. Behind her French windows opened onto a wooden deck. There was a swimming pool, filled with anthracite shadow. The reflection of the houselights crackled over its surface, illuminating bits of twigs and insects. The water looked cold despite the heat. It shivered with the vibration of the filters. Sofia had once invited me to come over and swim with her, and I had bought a black Calvin Klein bikini, the most expensive swimsuit I had ever owned, but the swim had never materialised, and now, I supposed, it never would. There was a tennis court, its bubble-gum surface speckled with pine resin and littered with fallen needles. There were swings and a climbing frame for the children. A high, bougainvillea-draped wall promised both shade and privacy. A slip of tyres and the hiss of brakes indicated the proximity of traffic lights on the other side of the wall. A magpie clattered in a tall pine and a blue-black feather curlicued to the ground. The place was reminiscent of a cloister, although a curiously secular one.

Inside the room the women sipped champagne from crystal glasses. A Lebanese butler attended to our needs. My eyes kept snagging, returning to his features, because he reminded me of a famous English actor. Eventually I asked him if they were related.

'Who is Steven Berkoff, Señora?' he replied.

The girls had fallen over themselves to give Sofia something to remember them by: a Hermès scarf. Gucci anything. Fleur de The Rose Bulgare, a perfume said to have been created by the House of Creed for the actress Ava Gardner, who fell in love with Frank Sinatra, Old Blue Eyes, in Tossa de Mar, an hour's drive from where we were sitting. I had had no idea what to give.

The most special thing that I had discovered that year had been the book I have already mentioned, *The Well at the World's End* by Neil M. Gunn. It told of a well 'whose water is so clear that it is invisible: when the two lovers first find it, they think it is empty . . .' I had told Sofia about the novel, and she made me promise to write down what it was, and who had written it, and instead I gave her my copy. I gave Sofia my book because there was no time to buy another, and I was glad, because I had passed on something good.

And yet.

The Well at the World's End tells the story of a journey. The protagonist goes alone into the wild places of Scotland and tells anyone who asks that he is searching for the well at the world's end. His name is Peter Munroe, which may or may not be a play on *Peter the rock on which I will build my Church* and *munro*, as in a Scottish peak over three thousand feet. He is a successful academic, although now at the end of his youth. His wife's beauty is beginning to fade. Their only child – like that of Gunn himself – was stillborn. He is motivated by an indeterminate, and bittersweet, longing; the anticipation – were he to fail to act on this impulse – of something like *chagrin*, in the sense of both sadness and disappointment.

He is unable to articulate this feeling with any adequacy beyond the idea of the well. So he sets off into the wildest parts of the country, and finds adventure both in the land and in those he meets, discovering all kinds of different things about himself. Truth hovers at the corner of his vision, sometimes flickering in the landscape just ahead of him, sometimes appearing to one side of his path, only to disappear when he looks at it head-on.

In my heart I knew that Sofia would never make such a journey, even should she want to. It would mean bodyguards and chefs, servants and tents, tables and chairs and a four-wheel drive, cameras and digital surveillance. It would be like being on location with a heavily armed film crew. Sofia could never do it. But I could. My relative lack of wealth and absolute anonymity gave me a different kind of freedom. And the more I thought about it, the more I became determined to undertake Peter Munroe's journey, although I couldn't have explained why. I, too, had reached the end of my youth. I, too, had lost an unborn child. These were, possibly, the only points of connection between me and the fictional hero; but maybe that was enough. I certainly shared a sense that there was something beyond my grasp, something out of reach, and perhaps the idea of a secret well was as good a way of expressing it as any.

After Sofia left I tried to buy a new copy of the book, but discovered that it was out of print. In the three months since I had found it, *The Well at the World's End* had, quite literally, disappeared. I found a society associated with the writer, who was himself long dead. I communicated with people in his home town. I wanted to know if the journey described in the novel was real and, if so, where was it from and where did it lead? Did the places mentioned in the book exist? Was there a well that had inspired the writer? The general view was that the journey was real, that there had been a well, and that Neil Gunn had filled his kettle at it, but that no one, for the life of them, could remember where it was. Mr Gunn's nephew, Dairmid Gunn, was the one most likely to know, but he was away just now and no one knew how to contact him. I set the idea of the well to one side.

Gunn had written another book called *Highland River* and I was able to track down a 1975 paperback. It arrived a few days before

Evie and I flew to Britain for the holidays. I didn't have time to read it before we left, but I opened a page at random:

'And what will you do with yourself?'

'Oh, I'll knock about and fish and that . . . Though actually I do have one small idea — I intend to walk a certain river to its source. It's a thing I have wanted to do for a long time. That's all really.'

'Not a pilgrimage?'

'Hardly!'

'You mean that it is — slightly?'

I stared at the words *one small idea*, and felt their weight as they passed beyond my retina, a stone disappearing into a pool, aware already that something had happened, was happening, alive to the new disturbance. *I intend to walk a certain river to its source . . . It's a thing I have wanted to do for a long time.*

So had I, though I had forgotten all about it. I remembered a geography lesson, my hair tied in plaits, my front teeth crossed. *The water table*, ladybirds beetling over the scarred varnish of my desk: they had got into everything that summer. Flicking their ruby bodies to the safety of the inkwell so I could liberate them at break-time, hiding them from the naughty boy who tugged out their lacy wings, so he could race them and they wouldn't fly away. Understanding that I had drifted, the words *porous* and *igneous* before me in looping chalk, but it was too late to ask what it all meant. I had missed hearing the part about where the water started, and the diagram in the textbook offered nothing. If I got a detention the ladybirds might die.

★

I closed the book, ran my hand across the cover, its aged paper smooth as chamois. I read the description on the back:

> *The Highland river with its dark brown pools and sudden rushing shallows is a magical playground for little Kenn and his fellows. Here he battles for salmon with home-made hooks . . . With no conscious aim beyond satisfying the hunting instinct, Kenn's journey up the river becomes a thrilling exploration into its source and the source of himself.*

I turned it over and studied the picture on the front: a photograph of a brown river, descending purposefully over flat slabs of rock, a few farm buildings in the foreground, some bluish hills beyond. The river was a real river. It was called the Dunbeath Water.

I slipped the book inside a suitcase.

When Evie and I arrived in the UK, we went first to our family home in Cheshire. Rupert had stayed in Barcelona to work on his book, and he would come out in a few weeks to visit us. I looked up the Dunbeath Water on a road map. It was very far away. And it really didn't look like much. About fifteen miles long, hunched in the top right-hand corner of Scotland, it was just a little way short of John O'Groats. There was no spring or loch marked on the map, no source or well – it simply vanished, a thin blue squiggle into a dazzling white page. It was in the middle of what appeared to be the emptiest part of the British Isles. I tried to find a better map, an Ordnance Survey map. But this seemed always to be missing whenever I was in a bookshop. And then I realised that to follow this river from the sea to the source I would have to make a return trip of around fifteen hundred miles, for a journey on foot of perhaps thirty. I decided that we would start closer to home.

Humber

If you look at it on the map Spurn Point appears as a bent hair-pin, slightly to the right of Hull, curving out into the North Sea and then back on itself. What it is, is a spit of land, of sand, of shingle, that separates the wide mouth of the Humber from the formidable North Sea. Towards the tip there is a lighthouse, which has fallen into disuse because the spit, every quarter of a millennium, breaches, and the whole thing starts again. Beyond that is a lifeboat station; it too awaits abandonment. Spurn is felt to be nearing the end of this particular incarnation. There is a road along it, made of flat square tiles, and the spit, sinuous as a cat, shifts constantly under it, so the road has to be remade, rearranged, in a new place, wherever the spine of the land finds rest.

I had just kissed Evie goodnight.

'Where are you going?' she asked.

'I'm going to Spurn Point.'

'Where is it?'

'It's on the other side of the country. Pretty much in a straight line from here. I'll be back tomorrow afternoon,' I said.

Evie arranged Jerome, a stuffed dog, next to her pillow.

'I thought we were going to the cottage tomorrow.'

'I know. We can go the next day,' I said. 'Will you and Grannie be all right on your own?'

'Yes!' she said. 'We're going to do baking.' She glanced at me sideways along her cheekbones. 'Sing long-and-winding?' I held her hand and began to sing 'The Long and Winding Road' by the Beatles. By the time I reached the end, Evie was asleep. I tucked a curl of hair behind her ear, then bent to kiss her forehead, rested my face next to hers. I listened to her breathing for a while.

I had always wanted to walk to the lighthouse, and Mum had encouraged me to go. I hadn't been alone all year, other than for the handful of hours when Evie was in school. Mum and Evie only saw one another in the holidays. Spurn Point formed the top lip of a river mouth, so it even fitted in with our holiday theme. Although the Humber wasn't a river one could follow from sea to source. Strictly speaking, the name referred to the estuary. There had once been a freshwater river, a long time ago, when the ice had first begun to melt. But the River Humber had been displaced by the rising North Sea, and today the name describes the confluence of the rivers Ouse and Trent, joined later by the Ancholme and the Hull.

By midnight I had still not made up my mind to go. I sat on the end of Mum's bed, the two of us drinking tea.

'If you set off now,' she said, 'you'll be there for sunrise.' Her pale eyes were as blue as forget-me-nots. The bones of her hands in mine felt frail, yet pliant as feathers. She was eighty-one. A lovely lady, and an impassioned wanderer; Mum wouldn't have hesitated for a moment. So I kissed her soft cheek, and laughed, and went out into the summer night, made black by the glow of the street lamp. There was no need for a map. I started the car and headed east, past Manchester, towards morning.

Crossing the central ridge of the Pennines felt exciting – the M62 was the highest motorway in England – the journey surprisingly swift. But then the road passed along the northern bank of the Humber. In Hull the docks spilled on, mile after mile. I began to wish I'd brought a map. Although I knew where I was going: to the place that separated the sea from the river. If I followed the river, I'd get there. And yet . . . I hadn't thought the place would be so far beyond the city.

A flat landscape opened to the east, definite against the imperfect darkness. I passed through a hamlet: picturesque, sleepy. A triple-stretch white limousine parked jauntily on the village green. A farmyard crammed with Romany caravans where a wooden windmill powered the nodding head of a life-sized puppet clown. A nuclear power station. Wind farms. The detritus of extremities. I thought of Dungeness, where the filmmaker Derek Jarman spent his final years in a black pitch shiplap cottage, and dragged a garden from the blue-grey shingle as his once keen eyes foundered, then failed. There is a photograph of him as a smiling Canute, wrapped in a cloak with a necklace made of fishing floats, pitching himself between the land and the sea, ordering back the waves. Or perhaps it was King Lear. A fighter, against the dying light, the creeping sea. Despite the echo Dungeness seemed far away. Smaller, and harder. There was a softness about this new landscape, a vastness, which I had not anticipated.

I reached the village of Easington, and the signs for Spurn Point itself. There was a car park, although to use it seemed extravagant, given that there was no traffic, but I did so anyway. Next to the car park was a mobile-home park. I locked the car, went back, checked it. Was irritated with myself for doing so. It was, after all, not yet two in the morning. Who would come here now? I walked through farmland, past a number of houses, and was surprised by how many lights were on. I hadn't thought the place would be so populated, and had imagined that those who did live here would be sleeping.

I tried to suppress a panic, a rising fizz of anxiety. I felt sure it was to do with the unexpected proximity of so many other people, and the consequent vulnerability of walking alone out to the point. It was like walking the plank. I had acknowledged the possibility of meeting the odd birdwatcher, though at that time of year, and in a place so remote, I had believed it to be unlikely. And yet, behind the pulled curtains, I felt eyes fixed on television sets, sweating cans of chilled lager warming in the summer night. Young mothers with sleepless children, shift workers, the very old. I sensed their wakefulness.

Headlights approached: a police Range Rover. It stopped and the occupants – dough-faced, currant-eyed – peered at me; I raised a cautious hand. What were they looking for? Smugglers? Suicides? Vice? They seemed satisfied that I was none of these although did not reciprocate my wave. They drove on, out towards the point.

Where the arm of sand first lifted out from the body of the land – so that both the river and the sea became visible – there was a collection of prefabricated huts, of corrugated iron and precast concrete. A number of cars were strewn, rather than parked, outside them. There was an old BMW, its chrome lines glinting, its windows misted from within. One of the buildings, a Nissen hut, seemed to have been a café serving visitors to the point, but the signs looked old and abandoned. Yet the cars implied that someone still lived there, that there were other inhabitants of the fringe. My plan had been simply to walk out across the spit, to the tip, where the river met the sea, and then lie down, somewhere beyond the lighthouse, and sleep. I had thought that I could spend the following day there, exploring, absorbing, before going back to Mum's. But I hadn't comprehended how little darkness there would be. None, in fact. There had been a shadowing, a filling in, soon after midnight, but since then the sky had gradually lightened. At first dark blue, it was now streaked with lighter bands. It was easy to see the pale curves of sand ahead, the colours slowly emerging, like those in a developing Polaroid. The police passed by again. In just a few minutes they had completed the journey that I had driven through the night to undertake.

I walked over to the river mouth. Its shore was flat and fecund, green marsh, brown mud. There was a popping sound, as though a hundred mouths sucked bull's-eyes. Marsh gas, I supposed. And the Humber. As wide and real as death. A few miles upstream a single-span suspension bridge joined Lincolnshire with the East Riding of Yorkshire; it was a popular place for suicides. I wondered if any of them floated out this far, had washed up on this shore. I was afraid to look at the water, afraid of what I might see. A bloated dog, pale limbs like chair legs pointing at a sightless sky. Or worse.

My unease was accentuated by a sound, and one so distinctive that I would have known the place if I were brought back blindfold. It was a deep vibration, a plainsong, a confluence of many voices. At first I thought it was an accident formed by the architecture of the air, by the river-wind running against the sea-wind. And that may have been so, but in the paleness of the night I could see the instrument in which the notes were caught: the electricity poles that ran out to the lighthouse, and the cables strung between them. Any electrical current that passed through the wires was silent, or at any rate its gentle hum suppressed below the song, which was ceaseless, low, continuous as madness.

I turned away, and walked over to the other side of the spit, to the beach.

The more space I put between myself and the wakeful inhabitants of the mainland, the better I felt. The sea shone pearl-grey, opaque, and the sky lightened above it with a bloom as soft as a plum. Sunrise seemed imminent but I knew it wasn't for another hour. A rusted raffia-and-metal chair retrieved from the sea and set up on the sand attested to the presence of fishermen, or birdwatchers, but not now. I liked being alone. I settled into my gait, happy that mine were the first footprints in sand as new as snow.

Over the years there had been attempts to stop the spit from breaking, to protect it from the combination of long-shore drift and the river's passage that formed it, destroyed it, and will form it again. These various schemes now presented themselves as so many abandoned works. Ballast, in concrete blocks. The ribs of groins, each one made from a single tree, the bars of a giant cage along the shore. The horizontal planks had long since washed away, or been removed, as the futility of what they were attempting became apparent. The remaining upright posts had the gravitas of gods, each one as thick as a man, and twice as tall. I thought of Easter

Island, the unseeing heads that guarded the land. Or the skeleton of a Viking ship, its king and cargo turned to ash. I was delighted by the place, forgot about my fear, and was still running about between the forest of posts when the sun lifted out of the sea, orange into an indigo sky. I was surprised by the warmth as it lit my face. As though a stranger had reached out and touched me, in greeting, or reprimand. And shadows! Long, spidery shadows. Suddenly, to the right of me, I saw my own. Tall, and spectre-thin, my long hair blown sideways, my arms incidental above endless scissor legs. And suddenly my face was wet, tears from nowhere, my shadow. My shadow! I stood between it and the sun, it flooded from my feet along the earth and, for a little while, I knew I was alive. This moment, these moments, of recognition, they come so rarely; without hindsight, without forethought. Time passing even as we enter it.

I became accustomed to the day, relished the light wind, the turning tide, the water easing back. And now, outlined by the shadows, I could see each beach-combed fragment, each piece of rope, of driftwood, old toy, bit of net, and pram. Absolutely nothing unexpected. And then a ruin! A cottage, a bothy; without roof, or doors, or windows, half sunk into the sand. It must have been built on the spit, when the spit was somewhere else, and as the snakelike course shifted, the house, long abandoned, had ended up on the beach, disappearing under the water with each spring tide. I explored the bothy, its rooms cobwebbed in sand, but I wanted to get on and it was tiring, walking on the beach, my feet sinking with every step. I headed into the low dunes and was thrilled by snapdragons and sea holly, convolvulus and sea pinks. Saxifrage, pink – everything pink. *Rosa rugosa* flourished, arching sideways like a bramble, self-seeded from someone's garden; and then a yellow star-shaped flower, hypericum. I was enchanted with the softness of the landscape.

I saw the lighthouse. Something from a children's tale. And then I saw him. The man. At first I thought he was fishing. He stood, or rather acted, halfway between me and the lighthouse. I couldn't be sure of his age. I didn't want to get close enough to look. He could have been anything between twenty-five and fifty. I realised he hadn't seen me so I dropped into the long grass, aware suddenly how tired I was. He looked like Frank Auerbach, the painter, thick-set, wavy hair, energetic, strong. And yet he ran at the sea like a dancer, stopped – almost on tiptoe as his arms flew forward – and then hugged himself, ran back, but backwards, never once taking his eyes from the sea. He picked up a rock, ran again at the water's edge, hugged the rock to his chest, and then hurled it. It was this movement, I now saw, that I had mistaken for casting, for fishing. He was throwing. His arms fell, free of their burden, and he paused to see where the stone had landed. It was in the water. But he was still only for a moment. He seemed to rail at the sea, lift his arms in despair, or supplication, then run again, repeating his strange dance. And then again, another rock, hugged to the water, thrown, watched, the same backward, erratic movement. Every so often he reached the sea empty-handed, seemingly because he hadn't found an appropriate stone in the time he allowed for each circuit, and that's when the arms flew outwards, followed by the hug.

I was curious, yet afraid of him. I tried not to think about Virginia Woolf's novel *To the Lighthouse*, that told the story of a family and their holiday intention to visit a lighthouse; but they didn't actually get there until the First World War had happened, and some of them were dead, and the children grown up, and it was all too late. I had no desire to pass this man to reach my destination. And I was so very tired. The dunes were full of indentations, clearings among the sea holly and marram grass, protected from the wind. Keeping one eye on the man, I moved behind him in an arc. A dusty green car was parked by the road, at my side of the lighthouse, and I thought it likely that it was his. The only footprints on the beach had been my own. There was a track leading from the road to the beach, between me and the car. There were no footprints in the dunes. So he'd either driven here, or walked, but either way he hadn't come over the ridge of dunes, or along the beach, which left the road, and the riverbank, as the spit was only a few yards wide at that point. And he was a creature of the most compulsive habit.

I retreated back into the dunes, keeping more or less equidistant from the track, the beach and the road, and scooped a hollow with my fingers in the warming sand, at the place furthest from where I felt he was likely to pass. I lay down in it, curled up, foetal. I could not see anything but grass and sky. I was below the lip of the dune. I could not see the man. Which meant, I supposed, that he couldn't see me.

The soft sand blew constantly. I closed my eyes. I remembered an event a few weeks earlier when I had met up with Rupert in London. We were staying in a hotel and I had woken early. I had walked over to the window and, while Rupert slept, had watched the hard summer light pick the shadows from the street below, first drawing detail, brickwork, cobbles; then bleaching it, until everything glowed and hazed with the promise of heat. I had watched a man come out of a mews house, as though to leave for work: he wore a suit, a flare of white indicating his shirt, too bright to see if he wore a tie. He had a cup in his hand, which surprised me. And then I realised: he was a smoker. I imagined a child in a high chair at a kitchen table, the mother or au pair in attendance. As he lit the cigarette, everything about him seemed to come together, his very atoms coalesced, formed a cloak about him, a swirl of testosterone. I watched him relax into himself, becoming a man, and for a while I had remained there, curious.

Later, I had walked past the house and seen that it wasn't a home but an engineering consultancy. This made more sense of his distraction, his abstraction, and also of his desire for the cigarette – when you want something, and you can't have it, there is tension inherent in the situation. I wondered what had happened to this man on the beach, what had brought him to this place, this erratic dance, this compulsion. But I was unable to hold the thread. Sleep worried at the fabric of my consciousness, loosened it, pulled at it before lifting it, so that it blew and dipped across the sand like a child's favourite blanket, carrying my thoughts away with it.

I woke up an hour or so later. The satiety only sleep can give. Sand covered me in shallow drifts; my hair was full of it. Warm in the hollow basin, heavy-lidded. I sat up. Cautious. I was incredibly hungry. I had brought food with me, but I was already ill at ease, and would remain so until I knew where the man was.

I walked to the tip of the dune, bending forward to reduce my height, the lighthouse to my right, the beach to my left and ahead of me. And there he was, still throwing rocks. I caught now the O of his voice, no words, the wind had shifted. It was as though nothing had happened (nothing had happened). Perhaps he was a little slower, but not much. I wondered, for the first time, how long he'd been there. Did we arrive more or less together? Or had he been there all the while that I drove, over the Pennines, along the estuary, under the deepening sky? But I didn't really want to know, not now, possibly not ever. I wanted to be free of him, away. I was very much afraid of him, afraid of his unquiet mind, and I felt this fear coiling in my intestines.

My heart pulsed at the base of my throat; my mouth was dry. I was still so tired. One hour's sleep was not so much and I was jittery with adrenalin. We were three miles into the North Sea, the murderous estuary to the west. At some point the man was likely to leave — I had hoped this would happen while I slept, leaving me to follow him, leisurely, off the peninsula. But no, it would be he who followed me. I didn't believe he had come along the beach, but the sand was too slow, and tiring at best, exhausting to walk along. The road would be in full view of him. In spite of this I decided to remain visible — he seemed settled for a while — and make distance. When I reached the road of tiles, I ran.

Because most of me suspected the man to be harmless, I could not find the necessary edge. My fight-or-flight-mechanism was folded, resting, just below the surface, and I could not access it. I was irritated that I was running away from a place that I had come so far to see. I simply could not believe the literary irony of not getting to the lighthouse, which was wonderful, full-bodied with black-and-white hoops, like an Everton mint, its decommissioned light held in a liquorice cage with diamond sugar panes. I knew that, if I was a man, and I was ten years younger, I probably wouldn't care. I was irritated that my long blonde hair and slight frame rendered me vulnerable, unexpected. I wished I'd brought a hat.

A hare appeared; huge, brown, with unmistakable black ears, the slightly devil eye. It seemed so large that it filled the road. I stopped.

Quite unperturbed, it loped off in the direction of the river. Had it come from the beach? What a thought. And I was happy — suddenly everything was all right. If I hadn't run away from the madman, I would never have met the hare. I followed it. The river-bank, so recently a place of terror, seemed, under the warm sun, quite lovely. The light on the water rendered it accessible, possibly this was also an effect of the receding tide. Even as I watched, a cargo ship entered the river mouth, brightly coloured and flat as cardboard, bound for Hull and full of purpose. On the far bank, impossibly far away, was a town, rows of towers and cubes, some-thing made on a children's TV show, from matchboxes and toilet rolls. Not Hades, but Cleethorpes.

I walked along a narrow track through short bright grasses following the path of the hare. Every so often it reappeared before me, in exactly the same aspect, facing west, towards the river. Its hazel eye seemed to appraise me, before it turned once again and loped off, apparently as tame as a cat. Suddenly all around me were oystercatchers. I heard them before I saw them and laughed out loud when I did. They floated like an articulated carpet, like some-thing from *Arabian Nights*, washing over the sand and onto the riverbank, pouring through grass, across the track, opening to circumvent a stone, or a bit of wood, and closing around it on the other side, their shifting pattern hovering above a movement smooth as castors. And their funny, chirruping, pulsing whistle — soft as mechanical birds'. I supposed they had gone to the river, because quite suddenly they disappeared, and it was as though they were never there.

I saw a fisherman ahead of me. Broad-shouldered, yet slender. My eye was drawn by the movement of his back. I could avoid him, he hadn't seen me, but I was not afraid. I continued to walk along the path. He was reeling in his line. He glanced at me and nodded. There was a smile implied in the gesture and humour in his expression, although that could just have been an effect of the sunlight, his eyes half closed against it. I returned the greeting, inclining my head fractionally, a Japanese quality to this silent exchange of nodding courtesies. I thought of the willow pattern, the blue-and-white plates, although they were from China and the figure on the plate carried a whip. The fisherman looked at the tip of his rod, and fiddled with it, the movement slightly exaggerated; I had probably surprised him. I knew that he was checking the whereabouts of the hook, and that this was for my benefit. So I looped behind him, allowing him room to cast. I walked on without looking round.

The hare had gone, the riverbank was not my demesne, so I made my way up to the road, then retraced my steps along the beach, towards the mainland.

I was curiously disappointed as I passed by the prefab buildings. It seemed silly, now, to have been afraid, to have abandoned my journey. I found the car. Noticed immediately that one tyre was low, and liquid seeped from underneath the engine. I reached down, touched the liquid; it was clear and had no smell. Water. That was something, then. I glanced at the wheel on the front driver's side, examined the tyre. It was soft, but not too bad and there was no obvious damage to it. I listened, but there was nothing, no hiss of air. The cap had been removed. So. Not a puncture. I opened the door and reached for a bottle of water; it was misted with condensation. I flicked the switch that released the bonnet. With one hand I held the bottle as I drank, long, slow, cool. With the other, I raised the bonnet. I flexed my foot against the bumper, watching for the movement of the water in the radiator reservoir.

It seemed OK. I checked the container that fed the windscreen wipers. Tipped the rest of my bottle into it.

A man appeared. I hadn't heard him approach and there was no sign of a car but, at this point, nothing surprised me. He was about sixty, heavy set, wearing baggy denim dungarees and a pair of Crocs. No socks, no shirt; indeed, he appeared to be naked beneath the dungarees, the sides unbuttoned to reveal pale flesh, but he wore a navy-blue-and-white bandana around his head, Hell's Angel fashion. Presumably to hide his encroaching baldness if the few wispy tufts that were visible were any indication of what was underneath. A large pair of binoculars hung around his neck, gold sovereign rings gilded the fingers that rested there. A twitcher.

'Someone's let your tyres down,' he offered, surprisingly well informed. 'And there's liquid coming out of your engine.' The pitch of his voice was light but nasal and this, in combination with his elongated Hull vowels, created an incongruously effeminate effect in such a big man. I noticed a large hooped earring.

'I think it's from the air conditioning,' I said. He was standing in the long grass at the side of the car park, and seemed unwilling to step onto the tarmac.

'That's good,' he said. 'Well. I can see that you're on your own, so I'll leave you in peace. Not disturb you.' And he set off in the direction of the beach. I smiled to myself, trying to work out what he'd have said if I'd had company, but was nonetheless touched by his gentle grace, and the implied understanding of what it is to be alone. I looked around me. How many pairs of eyes? What a curious place. I got into the driver's seat. I was about to turn the key in the ignition when I saw the hare again. Or rather, a hare. It was cropping grass on the bank ahead of me in more or less the place where the man had stood a few moments earlier. The word *psychopomp* formed in my mind. Meaning spirit guide.

I turned the key. The hare looked up at the sound, enquiring, deer-like, but unruffled. It went back to pulling at the grass. I put the car into reverse, and left.

Mersey

Mum unfolded a sheet of newspaper and spread it on the table in front of us.

'I'd like to see this; I'm certain Evie would enjoy it.' It was half of a page cut from the *Liverpool Daily Post* and showed a photograph of a figure on a beach. There was a seagull standing on its head. The headline read: *Fate Of Iron Men Decided Tonight*, although the cutting was a few years old. It referred to Antony Gormley's installation, *Another Place*. Evie peered briefly at the picture, then went back to taking the order for breakfast on a spiral-bound waitress's notepad. I said I'd like toast, as it was the only thing she felt comfortable making, and she disappeared into the kitchen.

'Are you sure they're still there?' I asked.

'I should think so,' said Mum. 'I don't think anyone will move them now. We could have a picnic. And see anything else that you think might be of interest.' I looked at Mum and then back at the newspaper cutting.

'Anything?'

'Anything that you think we might like to see.'

I wondered how long Mum had been waiting for this moment. 'It's very close to the Convent,' I said. 'Did you know that?'

'Well, I remember you'd said it was somewhere near there. If you wanted us to have a look at it we could.' Mum had that slightly too wide-eyed expression that she always wore when she had an ulterior motive, or was planning some kind of surprise. Evie came back in with the toast.

'Would you like to go on a picnic?' I asked her.

'You said we were going to the cottage today.' Evie was frowning. This was true.

'What if we go to the cottage tomorrow? We can spend another day with Grannie.'

Evie agreed to the picnic, although warily, as though uncertain whether or not she had been cheated. She helped us to make sandwiches, pack apples, find the chocolate. We filled a flask, containing more chocolate, and then the three of us set off for Liverpool.

I parked the car close to the beach. Tall fences and razor-wire barriers marked one edge of the car park. On the other side were the docklands. Empty metal cranes clustered over cargo containers that were heaped like giant boiled sweets. Dunes the colour of sackcloth spilled beneath the fence, flowing north in rumpled bolts, until the coast bent them out of sight. Ahead of the dunes, in the river mouth, was a wind farm, but the blades were still. There was a boating lake, an oval lagoon, but it was empty. The only thing that seemed to move was the coarse, springing grass that grew all around us and pulled, tentatively, against the wind as though taking part in a tug-of-war. I felt edgy, as if I was on display, a Master of Ceremonies, although of what I couldn't say. Even the fact that we'd brought sandwiches seemed significant, somehow indicative of a need for self-sufficiency, a desire to remain apart. I tried to push the feeling away from me and enjoy the day for what it was. A picnic, after all, was an adventure; but Evie, for reasons of her own, became uncooperative, insolent, and would hardly move from the car. Suddenly Mum, who had been tapping ahead with her walking stick, turned on Evie.

'This isn't about you, this is Mummy's special place, and you are spoiling it!'

I looked at Mum. *Mummy's special place.* I was oddly thrilled to hear Mum fight my corner, even against my daughter. Even so, we couldn't get Evie out of the car park. She wrapped herself around one of the few trees planted to act as a windbreak. I was aware of the pressure inside my head. Eventually I snapped:

'Stop it! Stop it! Stop it!' while trying to recall if it was illegal to shout at your children in England, or just bad form. We glared at one another.

'This is a magic place,' I said, feeling as if I was falling down a hole. 'On the other side of the dunes is a portal to another world.' Evie looked unconvinced. At the edge of the boating lake signs the size of postcards read: *Beware of Blue Green Algae. Do Not Touch the Water. Danger.* About five hundred yards away – painted brightly and hedged in with shrubs to protect it from the wind – was a children's playground. It had snagged at the edge of Evie's vision and, I finally realised, was the cause of her dissent. Beyond stretched the dunes, characterless and dull, over which the calico sky was drawn down like a blind, a lighter area overhead denoting the position of the sun. We had to pass through the dunes to get to the beach. The playground was the only thing Evie could see that was of interest to her. But she had liked the word *portal*. I wasn't sure why I'd said it. I wondered if Evie knew what it meant, or if I did, for that matter. It had sounded vaguely sci-fi, indicative of travel.

'Look,' I said. 'Just come with me through that gap in the sand and you'll see. If you don't like it we can come back and go to the playground.'

'You promise?'

'I don't need to promise. You know it's true. In fact, we can go there anyway. Just come with me and Grannie first.'

A boardwalk led to the gap through the dunes. I wondered who swept it, who maintained the space, and how often they needed to do it.

Portal.

Evie let go of the tree, her eyes lingering briefly on the upright posts of the playground, the only brightness in the muted land-scape, then looked towards the dunes with as much apprehension as though she were going for an injection. Mum was already half-way there, the steadfast click of her walking stick on the wooden path a tortoise challenge to Evie's hare. Evie let go her breath then ran after her.

I walked behind them, aware of the push of the wind from the north, and caught up with them as they came to the gap. On either side of the pathway the dunes were fenced in, grown over with spiky grass and lilac sea holly. There were more signs saying: *Erosion, Keep Off*, which Evie ignored, running to the top of one dune and scudding down the other side. Mum and I walked through the gap, the three of us arriving at the same time, each of us surveying the beach.

Another Place is an installation of one hundred life-size casts of the artist Antony Gormley, although it took us a while to see them. Gradually the immobility of the figures intensified before the shift of the sea and the slowly revolving sky. The metal men became apparent, one by one, stretching into the distance. Their rows disappeared into the grey water, neither waving nor drowning. Mum, with a gentle smile, absorbed the fact of them. Evie saw one, pointed, and ran to it, and then another, and then quite suddenly became aware of the extent of them, realised that they were all around her, and that the beach was dominated by them. She stopped running, and turned back to me, her laughter breaking free.

When I first came here, the 'Antonys' were new, austere, automaton-like. I was surprised how little time it had taken to soften them, rust rising to the surface of their cast-iron skins in a patina that looked like lichen. Their extremities had eroded, were becoming vague. Some of them were buried knee-deep in sand while others stood on previously hidden plinths. There was an echo of the upright timbers of Spurn Point, although they lacked the physical function of the groins, and were entirely without altruism. Yet they seemed united by a resolution to remain between the sea and the land. I stood next to one of the metal men and tried to follow his gaze. Looking out to sea. My task this summer, the task I had set myself, was to look back. To turn my back on the sea, on what it might mean, and walk back on myself. Out there was another place, the whole of life not lived, and, at some point, although very distant, I hoped, was death. But I didn't want to look at the setting sun, or even the rising sun, as it dropped into or lifted out of the sea. I had unfinished business to attend to.

★

Taliesin was a poet whose story is told in *The Book of Taliesin*, one of the sacred texts of Wales. Before he was a poet he was an ordinary boy whose name was Gwion Bach. Late one night a great lady, who was also a witch, took Gwion from his parents' house. The witch had a son who was both dull-witted and ugly. She wanted wisdom for her child so that he might be made welcome at court, and also to compensate him for his appearance, about which she could do nothing. But she could do something about his stupidity, for there was a famous spell, which she made. The spell had to be stirred for a year and a day and the first three drops, when it was ready, would bestow the Grace of Inspiration. The rest would turn to poison. So because her son was lazy, as well as dull and ugly — and anyway grand people never do these things for themselves — she took Gwion from his parents' house so he might stir the cauldron night and day.

The witch told Gwion, in no uncertain terms, that he must never taste the spell. But on the last day, which was the first day of the second year, three drops of the boiling liquid spat onto Gwion's thumb, and burnt him. He was so hurt, so shocked, and so very, very tired that in his confusion he forgot about the witch's words and put his thumb straight into his mouth to soothe it, thereby tasting the spell intended for her son, and in one vast, eternal, tiny instant, Gwion became wise. He knew, without being told, everything there was to know. And the first thing he knew was that the witch would kill him.

He ran away from the castle as fast as he could, the cauldron exploding behind him. But the witch, who was gathering herbs, felt the betrayal as surely as though a great door had closed far beneath her. She came after him. When he saw her, Gwion turned into a hare, and ran. But she became a dog, a great grey long-limbed hunting dog, and she followed the hare and turned him until there was no land left for him to cover.

So Gwion became a fish, and he slipped through the reeds into a lake, where he hid from her. But the witch became a she-otter, all needle teeth and oily pelt, and she chased Gwion all around, until he jumped from her, became a bird, and flew.

She turned into a hawk. No sooner had Gwion gained the blue heights than he saw her beating over him. He caught sight of her curving talons, saw her wing feathers fanned like knives, and heard her *arr-wah* cry. He watched as she retracted her wings, the wind spiralling a tunnel around her, its voice caught humming and whirring through her feathers, and all the time she came falling, faster and faster still until the fear in his heart was so great that he felt it must burst. Yet at the moment that she reached him and righted herself, her wings releasing the song of the wind, her thorny toes clasped air.

Gwion was dropping away from her, a golden grain of wheat, too fine for her scissored feet to hold.

He came to rest in a barn, amid a heap of grain.

The witch became a black hen, high-crested, with yellow claws, and she scratched at the grain; Gwion's terror was so great, and at last she found him. Ate him. She could feel that he was inside her, and she was glad.

But Gwion wasn't dead, although he was at the end of his strength. He knew that he was inside the witch, and used all that he had left to make one final shift. He became a baby. He grew inside her into the most beautiful child the world would ever see. The witch determined to kill him as soon as he was born. But when her time came upon her, and she looked at the lovely little boy, she knew she couldn't do it. So she threw the baby into an old leather bag, and tossed it into the sea.

There was a poor man fishing at the mouth of a river. He had caught nothing all day long and had decided, very sadly, to go home. Just then he saw the leather sack, which had caught against a pole in the weir, and he fetched it, and opened it. He took the boy ashore, this special golden child, and lifted him gently onto the back of his horse, heaping up the blankets, all he had with him, to make a bed. And of course the man and his wife had no children of their own, so they kept him, and they loved him, and called him Taliesin. Which means: Radiant Brow.

As the child grew up he told astonishing tales. His voice was as pure as water, and he became a famous bard, singing at the court of King Arthur, and other things, which we don't need to know.

What matters for this story is that the life of Taliesin, the only life he knew, began at the mouth of a river.

The first time I came to this place was by accident. Or rather, the first time that I came here knowingly. I had been to the read-through of a play. I was tired and cramped from being indoors, my eyes sticky from staring at the page. I had longed to walk on a beach. As Liverpool is a port it seemed obvious that if I headed north then sooner or later I would find one. So I had left the writer, the cast and the director, with their curling sandwiches and their vending-machine coffee, and had driven from the City Centre, past the Cunard, East India and Exchange buildings until the seafront gave way to the fragmented, potholed road, cracked and meandering, which ran alongside the docks. My car hugged the walls and fences and the razor-wire security until finally the road opened out, the city became residential again, and I saw a sign: *Antony Gormley's* Another Place. And because I didn't know about the metal men, and had forgotten about wanting to be on a beach, I grew curious, and I followed the signpost, and it brought me here.

Now, I had been adopted as a small child and I knew little of the circumstances of my birth. Mum and Dad had told me that I was conceived as the result of an *indiscretion* during my mother's engagement, and that my mother had married her fiancé shortly after I was born. But – and there was always a *but* – the condition for this gesture, this saving from disgrace, had been the giving up of the evidence, the discarding of the cuckold's horns. I remembered asking if that meant I was a bastard, as I had been called the name at school, my cheeks more pink with worry over using a bad word before my parents than any possible revelation about what the word might mean, and then Mum saying that 'illegitimate' was the proper way of saying it, though I wasn't, not any more, because they had adopted me. That was the story that Mum and Dad told me, one night, when I was eleven years old, after I had finally plucked up the courage to ask. We never discussed it again. How, or where, it had all taken place, there was nothing written down, other than the district of my birth, unavoidably preserved on my birth certificate along with the name of my birth mother and a thin blue line, a hyphen, that represented my father.

So on that day I had come to the beach for what I presumed was the first time in my life and found it familiar. In fact I was overwhelmed by the idea – not just that I had been there before – but that I had been born there.

★

A few years ago salmon were found in the Mersey for the first time in two hundred years. The fisherman who found Taliesin hoped for salmon, which is why there was a pole in the weir. A net was strung across the river mouth, at the place where the river meets the sea, to catch them as they returned to their breeding grounds. Before they stopped coming, when the effluent pouring into the rivers made the water too dirty to sustain them, salmon were common. In *The Water-Babies*, Charles Kingsley tells of a petition from the children in an English workhouse begging not to be fed salmon more than twice a week. In days gone by this magnificent fish was considered food for the very poor. It still is: Alaskan tinned salmon even now cross the seas to Africa, complete with a book of recipes, the shelf-life of a can, six years.

In addition to being their breeding grounds the high pools to which salmon make their way are also, for the most part, their graves. As the disintegrating bodies of the parent fish fragment and float back towards the sea they sustain the tiny smolts. It is a curiously sacramental death. Birth. Dark there, under the sea, the cool fresh easing towards them, the late spring floods bringing a scent, a peaty memory, diverting them from their diet of prawns. How do they know when to respond? What calls them?

On that day, I'd had a sense. I'd felt a pull, a draw, as though something were listening. I'd felt it in the space around me. It was so strong that I had turned in my tracks, away from the shore and away from the Antonys, and walked back, towards the land. Later, I wondered if the cleaning up of the Mersey had contributed to my feelings on that day. I wondered if I was able, finally, to perceive something that until then the dirty water and chemical spill had smothered. Drowned. Or perhaps the time just happened to be right; everything in alignment, a coincidence.

So I had walked towards the children's playground, the one that had so captivated Evie. There was an ice-cream kiosk, and two ladies waddled towards it along the same boardwalk path, a young girl between them in a green crocheted dress, a matching hat, her eyes wobbling behind thick lenses. Above and behind them hundreds of knots whirred in their two-tone winter plumage. The knots vanished briefly, then reappeared, with the slight tilt of a Venetian blind as their underbellies, which were the colour of the sky, made them momentarily invisible, although the air still crackled with their passing.

'Excuse me,' I said, 'is there a hospital around here?'

'There used to be,' said one of the ladies, and pointed through a gap in the sea wall. 'It's just up there.' It was a convent, they told me, and the sisters still lived there, but it wasn't a hospital any more. Quite grand, it had been, a sort of private nursing home.

'I see. Thank you.'

I followed their directions and came to the house. Inside the hallway was a brass plaque dedicated to the Sisters of Mercy, *who have cared for the sick in this place for over one hundred years*. No longer a hospital, but a guest house with a reception, which was empty. There was a bell, which I chose not to ring. Behind the desk there was a door into the main house, with a Yale lock. But it was on the latch. I eased inside.

The house opened around me, and grew larger, or perhaps I grew small in relation to it. There was a rectangular stained-glass window above a staircase; I felt certain that I knew it, that I had seen it before. I found a chapel, and what I took to be a baptismal font although it could have been a holy water stoup. A grille divided the house from the nuns' residence, and a few aged sisters sat in the pews, white as doves, tucked into prayer. An electric candle stand illuminated a painted metal relief of Our Lady, and I thought of school and Physics, the simple circuits and fairy-light bulbs.

'Can we help you?' As I turned and walked back into the hallway I almost knocked over two of the sisters.

'Oh! Yes. I'm sorry. There was no one in reception.' The sisters waited. One of them was about my own age, while the other was ancient, the crown of her veiled head barely reaching the shoulder of the younger nun. I found myself thinking of a pepper-pot.

'I was wondering if it might be possible that I was born here?' The nuns seemed unfazed by the question.

'Yes,' the younger one replied, 'it is. In fact, if you were born in a hospital, in this part of Liverpool, then there was nowhere else. What's your name?'

'We can look up your records,' said the older nun, 'though I'm sorry that they're not of the best.'

'Actually, I was adopted as a child, and my name has been changed, but I know the name on my birth certificate: Marie Therese', and I mentioned a surname. The two nuns lifted their arms in unison, white puppets acting surrender.

'Sister Marie Therese!' they both said. I looked over my shoulder, thought perhaps someone was standing there. There was nobody.

'Sister Marie Therese?' I asked.

'Yes,' the older sister said, and turned to the younger woman next to her.

'Could Sister Marie Therese help me?' I asked.

'Yes,' said the older nun.

'Can I meet her?'

'No,' said the younger sister. 'She's died, ten years ago. But we know who you are.'

And as we stood in the hallway they told me the story, finishing one another's sentences, of the midwife who had been left, quite literally, holding the baby and of the mother who had fled the hospital. The younger sister seemed to be as familiar with the details as the older nun who had witnessed them. The midwife's name was Sister Marie Therese and she had taken charge of me, and looked after me, and kept me until a home could be found for me. 'She baptised you and she gave you her name.'

Whether this was Sister Marie Therese's own name, or one that she had taken on entering the Convent, I didn't think to ask. There was no time for me to register any feelings about the discovery, and loss, in under a minute, of my namesake. The idea, the fact, that I had one.

The sisters were gentle, animated. They seemed to be not at all surprised by what was happening, no matter how unlikely. They took an almost childlike pleasure in the continuance of an inter-rupted narrative. They showed me the room where I had slept, the cupboard where my nappies were stored, and where the baby food was kept. They showed me the room where I was born, which was now an office. Grey-metal filing drawers belched disorganised paperwork. I noticed a heavy glass paperweight with the three-tiered crown and crossed keys of the papal coat of arms. A tree filled the window. 'It would have been here already on the day of your birth. It would have been the first green thing you saw.'

I had got the idea that this must have been a Catholic mother-and-baby home, and presumed my story to be a common one. But no! The sisters were even a little put out by the suggestion. It was a hospital, a private nursing home, just as the ladies on the beach had said it was. Why was I trying to reduce this extraordinary circumstance, to render it commonplace? The sisters would have none of it; I was the only one, Sister Marie Therese's baby.

There were more sisters now. They didn't stop what they were doing, the internal pathway of their lives adhering to a proscribed invisible order, but they looked, pausing briefly in their steps. Word had gone about: 'Tis Sister Marie Therese's baby, and she's come back to us!' I felt their curious eyes, their kindly faces, those who had joined the Convent in more recent years seemingly as familiar with the story as the older nuns. I had a sensation of being contained within a mechanism. My unveiled hair and dark clothes, which trapped the scent of the outdoors – of wet leaves, of sea, of woodsmoke – seemed brash among the detergent white of their habits. I felt hot, faint. A smell of bleach and polish, which I had noticed on entering, now felt pervasive, oppressive. I asked if there was a garden and yet I didn't want to be an inconvenience; but the sister who had become my guide said I wasn't disturbing her. She worked in the local hospice and her working day had ended. I found her at her leisure. A nun's leisure: I realised how little I knew about the working of this order, any order. But I understood, or thought I did, that she had come here at this moment to be of help. Some of the older nuns were well into their eighties, and it would be getting time to prepare the evening meal. I had the impression that she remained, on the pretext of being social, to share, and thereby lighten, their burden.

She opened a door into a garden, adjuring me to stay as long as I wished. We could have tea, if I liked, when I was finished.

A dream. Clouds, talc, soap, milk. A veiled woman dressed in white, turning slowly towards me. I always woke before I saw the woman's face and felt that, if I did see it, I would die. Yet here she was, the veiled woman, made of concrete and painted glossy white. Green-black moss covered one side of her nose. It frosted the beads of her rosary. Lichen bloomed about an enigmatic smile. Pots of shrivelled geraniums clustered around her feet and her dress was spattered in compost, displaced by a watering can. But there was another part to the dream, another fragment: a real woman, a blue coat over the whiteness, her hair a pale blonde flag. The flag of hair had blotted out the light as she bent down to lift me from my pram. Summer tar, cracking wood, the peppery scent of tomatoes. Glasshouses, row upon row of them. This woman, bending down to me, I had assumed she was my birth mother. The smell of washed linen and, beyond her shoulder, the glasshouses, and that green hot reek of tomatoes. I know exactly where I was the first time I articulated this memory, the only time I told it to somebody else. I was in Bluebell Wood catching minnows with my cousin, Susan, string handles tied about the necks of our jam-jars, the silver fishes jabbing at the thickened glass, jerky as compass needles. I thought perhaps my cousin might have known the lady. I thought the lady might have been my mother. I can't have been more than four because after that we moved away from the village, and never went back to Bluebell Wood.

But as I turned away from the concrete statue I found myself looking at the glasshouses, row after row of them, the wooden frames splintered, the panes all but gone, and I realised that the woman in my dream with the flag of pale hair was not my mother, but a sister, probably Sister Marie Therese, and that the beloved face, which had always eluded me, was hers. Not hair, then, but the veil; the crisp white cotton of the Augustinians.

'I've made some tea!' It was the sister who had become my friend, and I followed her back into the house, the sunlight folding as we entered the panelled hallway. Her name was Maria, but before she joined the order it had been Katherine. My name had been Marie, but had then been changed to Katharine. I was born in the Convent and had then gone out into the world. Sister Maria had given up the world in order to enter it. We laughed at the inverted symmetry of our lives, our names. Sister Marie Therese had been Maria's special friend, and had cared for her as a novice, had cared for both of us.

'She prayed for you every day of her life,' she said, and I had no idea what to do or say so simply sat there, the teacup slipping across the yellow saucer until the sounds of the kitchen and a smell of frying onions made me conscious that I should be on my way.

When I left we exchanged addresses. Sister Maria said that this was my first home, and that I would always be welcome here. Later she wrote to me with a photograph of Sister Marie Therese and a baby, although she couldn't be sure if it was me.

The newborn Taliesin had regarded his discovery in the river mouth by the poor man as a most propitious event. For the man. For though he was only one day old Taliesin miraculously spoke, chastising the man for being sad over his empty net, adding that in the time of need he, Taliesin, would be worth more than three hundred fish. Later he spoke to the poor man's father, and gave the most colourful account of his provenance:

> Into a dark leathern bag I was thrown,
> And on a boundless sea I was sent adrift;
> Which to me was an omen of being tenderly nursed,
> And the Lord God then set me at liberty.

Taliesin was one for whom the cup was decidedly half full. The wondrous story of his life, which – after all – he wrote himself, has survived for fifteen hundred years. He was without self-pity as he acknowledged, and slid over, his humble origin as Gwion. The pathway from lost boy to mighty bard was bright and packed with adventure, for which Taliesin took all of the responsibility and all of the credit, although he thanked God for his release.

I too began my life at the mouth of a river. I had found a missing piece in the broken vase of my history, accounting for the lost months of my babyhood. I had been born in this place and now, by chance, I had returned. It was as though I had been given a coat that turned out to be a perfect fit without ever having realised that I was cold. I found it hard to remember that the gift was new, and that yesterday, or even an hour ago, I didn't have it.

Yet, at the same time, I had stumbled on heartache. I had no recollection of a loving birth mother who had given me up against her will. I had no more fragments. The shard of memory I had conserved, of a woman looking into a pram, was not of her. When she married she became as carefully hidden as Gwion's grain of wheat, her husband's name as common to the Welsh as John Smith is to the English. I had never found her and no one, as far as I knew, had ever looked for me. The day of her wedding was the day of my adoption. I presumed she was aware of this. When Anne Boleyn was executed, upright, on her knees, with a fine French sword, her successor, Jane Seymour, was trying on her wedding dress. Which was yellow. Not quite the image of the English rose that has been so carefully handed down. Perhaps if she'd lived long enough she'd have shown her colours.

This sounds bitter. It is. Although I felt no ill will – the opposite in fact. I was thankful from the bottom of my heart for my existence, although not to her, the gift of life unintentional, abortion illegal. But in her desire for anonymity, be it conscious or feckless, my birth mother had also hidden me from my natural father, and I could not tell what hurt the most, the two things rushing against one another, noisy, confluent. All I could see, from looking in the glass, was that I was most likely of Celtic origin. And even that could not be certain, although I have always passed for such.

I was sorry not to have known my foster-mother, Sister Marie Therese, but it was her goodness, and an unexpected sense of my own completeness – or rather normalcy – that I took away with me that day. The rest I left on the shore; a life I could have known, but never did, its myriad possibilities suspended.

We walked along the beach, Evie making zigzag tracks in the sand, which I did my best to follow. Mum came behind us with her stick, her footsteps and the circular divots made by her cane running in a median line between our undulating ones, and I thought of sine waves and Aboriginal paintings. One of the Antonys was wearing a cardigan, another a scarf, one had a pair of socks on his hands, while another had a Tesco bag tied about his wrist. We sat on a concrete wall and ate our lunch, wind tickling the greaseproof paper. You had to chew the brown bread and crumbly Cheshire cheese for a while before it became something tasty, melded into something good, and Evie just munched the middle out of her sandwiches and discarded the crusts, impatient with the process. The tide was coming in. Some of the Antonys slipped below the waves, their clothes loosening.

Evie was the first to reach the playground.

'Grannie,' she called, 'there are four swings!' A man dressed wholly in red, including a prize-fighter's belt and a scarlet baseball hat from which stiff dreadlocks protruded, stalked past us in the direction of the shore. Two workmen in Day-Glo overalls ate ice cream. One photographed his 99 cornet with his mobile phone while the other, holding an ice-lolly, laughed. Two robust identical orange-haired boys scaled monkey bars. Their mother was pale, with dark smudges under her eyes, as though the twins had sucked the goodness from her. We stopped for ice cream at the kiosk by the playground: *Soft Ice-Cream Sold Here. Lolly Ices. Cold Cans. Slush. Hot Drinks. Popcorn. Candy Floss & More.* Then, ice creams in hand, we made our way back over to the swings. Mum laughed at the sign that said only children under the age of fourteen could use the playground, and then graciously, but firmly, ignored it. She used the hook of her walking stick to bring one of the swings within reach, and then Evie held the seat in place while Mum manoeuvred herself onto it. Evie and I then sat on the two swings flanking her, and the three of us rocked to and fro, gazing seaward, eating our ice creams. Mum wore a woolly hat to keep her hair from the wind. She laughed when she caught me looking at her.

Mum had always been an enigma to me. Throughout my child-hood she had remained unfathomable. When I was Evie's age, possibly younger, Mum would bounce light from a compact mirror around the living room, swearing it was a fairy, and when I tried to touch the flickering image she snapped the compact shut and, laughing, dropped it into her handbag. It took me for ever to realise it was a trick. It was only now that Dad had died that Mum was starting to afford tightly angled views into herself, although she remained very difficult to read. She had an easy love of simple things, like swings, and ice cream, classic novels. Walking through wet leaves. Driving. She was uncomplicatedly happy. I had never seen her cry. It was her extraordinary engagement, her zest for life, that had drawn Dad to her, that drew all of us. I had always known that Mum wasn't my 'real mother' and, for a long time, as a child, I had tried to make sense of our relationship, the word *mother* connoting something both formal and alien to me. For some reason Dad had been exempt from this sense of 'otherness'. Perhaps because no one mentioned the possibility of my having another father, so for a long time he was the only candidate. It was only as an adult that I had grown curious about the man whose identity remained hidden, concealed behind the hyphen on my birth certificate.

Mum and Dad had met when they were children. Dad lived in a Cheshire village, defined by a Norman castle, in a community divided by Church and Chapel. Mum lived a couple of miles away, in the industrial township of Runcorn, but they had attended the same primary school. Mum left school at sixteen, and all I really knew about her early life was that she had once run a hundred yards in 11.4 seconds, that her mother was the District Nurse, and that her father had a car with white wall tyres. Most of the stories, although it was Mum who told them to me, were about Dad.

He had proposed to her when he was twenty-four, and Mum was twenty-two, at the top of Tryfan, in Snowdonia. On a clearer day the mountain might just be visible, across the estuary, from the playground where we now found ourselves. Certainly, if you look the other way – north-west from the summit of Tryfan – you can see Liverpool Bay. It is a deceptive and formidable mountain. Mum would tell how she and Dad had skipped up the Heather Terrace, a prettily named, if scant, footpath, through the eponymous heather, that was pocked with steep drops down to the valley. At the summit were two stone monoliths, about ten feet high, known as Adam and Eve. After agreeing to become husband and wife, Mum and Dad had held each other's hands, and then leapt from one rock to the other, a distance of just over a yard. Then, apparently, they got lost in mist and almost walked off a precipice on their way back down.

I followed Mum's gaze as she drifted with the swing, now moved only by the breeze. I wondered if she realised that Tryfan was across the estuary. A few summers earlier, at Mum's request, Rupert and I had carried Dad's ashes back to the mountain, passing them between us, taking it in turns, and then tipped them out and left them, blowing furiously between Adam and Eve.

When Evie was ready to leave the playground Mum asked if we might visit the Convent. When I first told her that I had found the place by chance, she had simply said, 'Well, we always knew you were a Catholic,' and this had silenced any further discussion. This trip to the beach, this picnic engineered by Mum, was something new, and unexpected. We set off in the direction of the house.

The sisters were welcoming, just as before. *You're the one that was born here? Marie Therese? Come in!* I glanced at Mum but she didn't react to the use of the discarded name. When Sister Maria explained to Evie that this was my first home, Evie suggested that we all move in. Mum seemed wholly at ease as she chatted and laughed with Sister Maria and the older nuns. They talked about recipes for fruit cake. When it was time for us to go Evie crammed her pockets with biscuits.

Careful directions from Sister Maria brought us to a cemetery. It was within a field, far enough from the sea to prevent the water from permeating the graves. A cluster of yew trees, poisonous to the cattle, creaked safely inside the walls. The sisters' plot was in the farthest corner, and marked by two large headstones. I scanned the memorial list of names and stopped at *S. Marie Therese Fay, Canoness of the Augustinian Order*. Evie made a shrine from things she had brought from the beach: bottle tops and razor shells, bladderwrack and sea cabbage. Stones. We planted sedum, careful not to crush its squashy leaves and winking suns. We hoped it took. Mum clapped her hands to bring warmth back to her fingers, then took Evie's hand in her own. The flat sky lightened marginally as the sun slipped beneath the cloud line. We told a decade of the rosary, and then went home.

Afon Geirch

Evie wiggled a forefinger through the widening gap at the top of the car window. She was striving to point something out to me and she couldn't express herself fast enough.

'Look, Mummy! Look!'

Three fox cubs bounced down the hillside, hot loaves knocked out of their tins. As I slowed the car to a stop they righted themselves. A wire fence, tufted with wool, acted as a buffer against a roll into the road. Their faces heaped together, as neat as party sandwiches. After appraising the car and the two of us inside it they circled back where they had come from, ululating, warbling, snout to brush, repeatedly glancing behind them, the next shunting tumble not far off. We marvelled till the cubs were lost – it was over before there had been time to steal a picture – and when they were gone there was just the Jew's harp buzz of the wind in the grass and the dropping notes of skylarks. We had stopped the car on the natural border to the Llŷn Peninsula in the midst of three peaks known as the Rivals, which gives a combative and brotherly ring to the Anglicisation of Yr Eifl, meaning the strides. Below us, at the bottom of the hill, was Nefyn Bay.

Evie called this place the Misty Moor, after a line in a children's prayer: *Matthew, Mark, Luke and John, hold my horse while I leap on, hold him steady, hold him sure, till I win o'er the misty moor.* She called it that because the Rivals were usually covered in cloud, even on the hottest days, though on this day the sky was clear but for the odd tugged wisp smoothed over the tops. The island of Anglesey was visible to the north, Cardigan Bay and the mountains of Mid-Wales to the south, and the Wicklow Mountains, across the sea in Ireland, stretched out like a knotted string on the western horizon. Behind us, to the east, the cantilever of Yr Eifl's peaks gated off Snowdonia. Ahead, the road spooled towards the volcanic cone of Garn Fadryn. Somewhere on Garn Fadryn's flank, very small, not yet visible, was our cottage. The Llŷn Peninsula floated before us, towing its islands with it, the sea and the sky continuous, indistinguishable one from another.

We pulled up outside the cottage, one of four houses on a cross-roads. Tony, who lived in the house opposite to ours, waved from the armchair in his glass porch. He spent most of his days, and nights, in this armchair, a tank of oxygen at his side. I was about to speak to him when Evie clambered over the rendered wall on her way to our front door.

'Be careful!' The wall had a crack in it from top to bottom and had split into free-standing halves. The pieces gave perceptibly whenever anyone vaulted it. According to Tony it had been like that since the summer of 1984 when, thirteen miles beneath the mountain, the European Plate had eased its position relative to the Mid-Atlantic Ridge. The subsequent earthquake had measured 5.4 on the Richter Scale and remains the most significant seismic movement on record in the British Isles. It had rattled teacups and crumpled chimneys as far away as Liverpool. There was some debate about whether or not ours was one of them. When I first bought the cottage, which is a traditional two-room bothy, the inglenook fireplace was concreted in. I asked a local builder to try to reveal it and Tony had come over in his vest and slippers to watch the work and have a beer. There was no foundation to the house, only mud beneath black tiles. A few inches below the surface an underground stream ran out from the centre of the fireplace and on through the only bedroom. The stream was visible, outside, at either end of the cottage, where it ran clear beneath rusted grilles. The newly revealed inglenook and chimneybreast dominated the room.

'You want to watch that,' Tony had said. 'It started shifting after that last rumble. That's how come it was rendered in.' Tony leaned against the mantel and gently scratched his belly with the hand that wasn't holding the bottle. Geraint, the labourer, looked up from the hole that he had dug in the floor. It was filling up with water from the stream, which no longer ran clear. His spade hit something hard. Emlyn, the builder, climbed down into the hole and the two men eased up a pillow of granite from the centre of the fireplace. It belched free of the mud, they curled their arms beneath it, staggered with it, lurched and slipped towards the door, as though carrying a newborn calf. There was an uneasy moment.

'That's the foundation stone,' offered Tony.

'What?' asked Emlyn.

'It'll fall down now, for sure.' Tony shifted his footing to get a better look in the hole.

'You want to mind you don't fall in,' Emlyn said. 'My insurance won't cover it if you do because you're not supposed to be here.'

'Well, I'll come back when you've put the floor in. Thank you for the beer, flower, *Diolch yn fawr!*' and with that Tony shuffled out.

The men persevered. Over the next few days they dug a footing, more than two hundred years after the house was raised on the turf from *random rubble*, which is a technical term in the building trade meaning *anything that comes to hand*. They accommodated the stream within a layer of gravel, and a membrane, and covered it all in concrete. They built a wooden cabin bed for me, and a ladder up to the crog-loft for Evie. The chimney was restored and the stream, visible beneath the grilles at the sides of the house, regained its former clarity. The 'foundation stone' remains, where it was dropped, in the garden.

I lit a fire. Even though it was June there was a chill to the stones. The house had been empty since Easter. Over lunch we discussed our project, our plan to find the well at the world's end by following watercourses from the sea to their sources.

'Can we count the Mersey?' asked Evie.

'I think so,' I said. 'I don't think it has to be the same river that we follow, as long as we eventually get to an end.' Evie thought about this, then nodded her agreement. We could count the trip to the Mersey Estuary as an exploration of 'sea'. Evie wrote an account of the picnic in her journal. She drew a picture of the beach with the Antonys.

'What should we do next?' she asked.

'I think we should follow the river that comes out at Cable Bay,' I said. 'We could go now, and see how far we get.' Evie pressed her lips together. Having just arrived at the cottage she was loath to go out again, but after the two-hour drive from Mum's I wanted, dearly, to stretch my legs, uncoil my spine. I put some chocolate and water and a couple of apples in a rucksack. The purple-and-white wrapper caught her eye.

'Can we eat the chocolate now?' she asked.

'Let's have it when we get there.'

'Can we eat some on the way?'

I glanced at her. 'How about we open it when we get to the beach?'

Evie slipped down from the table. 'All right.'

Cable Bay is the nickname given to a curved beach near our home. Its name in Welsh is Abergeirch, which means the mouth of the River Geirch. A rusted metal pipe runs down to the sea, alongside the Afon Geirch, supported on concrete blocks. All kinds of local stories account for the function of the pipe. One of them involves a telephone cable running under the sea to Ireland and it is this that has given the bay its nickname. The place nearest our home where the road meets the sea is called the Bwlch, so that was where we headed for.

Bwlch means pass, or valley, and it is a natural cut through the sandy cliffs, a place where boats can be ferried from the beach on trailers tugged by tractors. The shelter it gives from the wind makes it a natural oasis and its banks were stacked with montbretia, the orange lilies dancing over pliant, strap-like leaves, racing along the paths like a Pentecost. Lanterns of green and blue hydrangea ballooned against red and purple tutus of fuchsia. Roses made a scaffold for the softer plants and gave them substance against the wind.

The beach was the reason I had bought the cottage in the first place – or rather, Rupert had bought the cottage. It was his extraordinary wedding gift, funded by a film deal from one of his books, *so I will know where to find you when you wander.*

I had first come to the beach when my father was dying. We had planned to come on a family holiday – everyone knew it would be the last – but at the last moment Dad felt he wasn't well enough. Evie was still a baby, and she and I came anyway. My brother and his family had gone ahead, and Dad had waved us off. His eyes, that were sometimes the colour of slate, on that day shone blue.

'Goodbye, my darlings!' He had stood on one leg outside their house, and raised his walking stick in a yogic salute, Mum standing anxiously behind him, her hands hovering at each side of his body. As I turned the car onto the main road I could still see him in the rear-view mirror, wobbling, happy, laughing. His smile seemed to say, *Go on, my darlings: anything is possible!* Yet the reverse had felt true. I had pushed my sunglasses up the bridge of my nose to cover my tears before glancing at Evie. Like Dad, she too was laughing, constricted by the baby seat, her blue anorak with pink roses rucked above the straps where she'd turned to keep his gaze.

When we had arrived in the Llŷn I was unable to settle. I could see no beauty in anything. The hills were too low, the sea was too grey and the sand was a characterless expanse. The cliffs were unstable. Two hours' drive away Dad was dying; in a few weeks I would never see him again. Yet I was on holiday, collecting shells.

But despite this the location drew me, and after Dad died I found myself returning. On some days the sea's surface wrinkled like elephant skin; on others it had the opacity of emulsion paint. Sometimes it was as clear as camomile tea, and Evie and I watched the hard ridges of sand below the water from the tops of the cliffs, pointing out the banks of bladderwrack, blue mussels and barnacle beds. The beach, too, rearranged itself, its skirts lifting to reveal clay, pebbles the size of tennis balls, shark's eggs, which were really dog-fish spawn, hard rectangular pouches with spiralling tentacles at the corners. Chips of red jasper, fists of granite, a cormorant's skull, smooth as a pen, a spider crab's pimpled shell, fishing floats, a knot of polyprop rope.

Once, when the tide was low, we found some big square stones. A fisherman said they were the foundations of a castle. A house, near the place, was known as Hen Blas, which means the old place, or perhaps the old palace, and this seemed to be all that was needed to verify the tale. The fisherman said that a minstrel, on his way to a feast, had been warned by a fairy that he met at Nefyn Fair not to sleep at the castle, so he'd slept under a hedge, had moaned all night, but by dawn all the guests had been murdered, and the minstrel was the only one who was saved. But a few weeks after the fisherman told the story the sand came back and the castle, or jetty, or harbour wall, or whatever it had been, vanished.

One icy March the beach was dotted with clams. They pulled themselves across the frosted sand with a single orange digit. Evie and I followed their monorail tracks, trying to remember the words to 'The Walrus and the Carpenter'; shouting sing-song, over the wind. We'd picked them up, and taken them home, and then eaten them, every one.

The beach was a book that fell open. Each visit was a different page. I could not read it, neither could I leave it.

Cable Bay was on the north side of a finger of land, and the two beaches were back to back. 'Our beach', as Evie called it, Porth Dinllaen beach, was sheltered, but Cable Bay was hit by norther-lies, and was rugged, and rocky. Porth Dinllaen had once been a contender for the location of the Dublin car ferry, but the contract had gone to Holyhead, on Anglesey. The beach, as might be supposed from this, edged a wide natural harbour. There was a pub at the water's edge, the Ty Coch, meaning the red house, and Evie tugged at my hand as we passed it – *Not now, Mummy!*

We looped around the headland, stopping to open the chocolate, and then clambered down onto a pebbled beach. In years gone by geologists had come from all over the world, as far away as Hawaii, wearing hard hats and dangling silver hammers, and specimen bags.

'Daddy says it's got some of the oldest rocks on earth,' Evie said, as though she had been reading my thoughts.

'Really?' I asked.

'I don't know. I think so. It might have been Daddy. Or it might have been somebody else.' I smiled, because I'd meant the stones. Folds of rock, red and blue, heaped like futons across the gravel, spilled in a stream from Garn Fadryn's cone, cooled into blocks by the sea. Or maybe the sea came later. A blue pebble caught my eye; I bent and picked it up. It looked like a beetle with red lines to mark its wings, as though it were crammed with fire; like the tadpoles of glass called Prince Rupert's drops that explode if you snap their tails. I closed my hand around the stone, its surface so smooth it felt soft. It nestled in my palm. *Basalt* is a satisfying word, glassy and seismic-sounding, and I wondered if it might be the right one. Other rocks rose like giant molars, umber and black, yawning from the beach. I thought about the tectonic plates and the rumble under the ground, 5.4 on the Richter Scale. I glanced in the direction of the hill, as though Garn Fadryn herself might answer.

I lay down on the pebbles and closed my eyes, lulled by the sound of the sea through the stones. Each retreating wave was an apnoeic gasp, gravel lungs filled with water, drowning without panic.

Time held me green and dying,
Though I sang in my chains like the sea.

The lines popped out of nowhere. They were by Dylan Thomas. I opened my eyes.

I must have fallen asleep. I raised myself onto my elbows and scanned the beach for Evie, my heart scrunching like a ball of baking foil.

There she was, at the edge of the sea, the yellow smudge of her blonde hair bright against the monochrome shore. She was throwing stones at a piece of driftwood. It was rotted and fragile. She pelted the driftwood until it broke, coming apart in pieces like bread on the water. A few yards beyond her charcoal birds, their blunt wings lifted, heads tilted back, vied for the shrouded sun on a rocky islet. The outline of the cormorants formed a mandorla around Evie; she was illuminated like a medieval saint. The sun was veiled behind a haze of cloud and showed as white as the moon, although the dark stones beneath me held the heat. I was confused by this, the warm stones, and the sun-moon, the time and the season slipping. But then Evie turned and looked for me, the driftwood crusts of no more interest to her, and I raised an arm, and could sense her smile, and suddenly she was running towards me, her head angled down, her arms straight at her sides, the small stones skittering at her feet.

A promontory crowned in sea pinks marked the edge of the beach. Cable Bay was the next inlet. The sea churned and gurgled through uneven channels. So we followed a footpath above a seam of grass in an oblique traverse across the cliff. From the top we were able to follow rough steps down to the river mouth.

At the back of the beach the sea had formed a bank of heaped-up pebbles, and the river pooled behind it, forming a kidney-shaped lagoon. Beyond the pool the Afon Geirch looped tightly between banks and beaches. It meandered through a deep wide gulley, back into the land, with sandy cliffs on either side. Montbretia lined the gulley walls, just as at the Bwlch, but where the sand ran to clay the orange flowers gave way to the first uncurling ferns, heads lifting uncertainly from their nests of bracken like hungry pterodactyl chicks. The rusted pipe, that may or may not have once held a cable, and was more likely to have carried sewerage, maintained a straight course towards the sea, the river winding under it.

At the place where the stream was widest there were stepping stones, although they were so steep, and so smooth, as to be unusable. They looked like tortoises. A few yards beyond them a thatch of phragmites reeds and bulrushes partially concealed the water. Between the rushes and the stepping stones was a wooden footbridge carrying the pilgrims' path that led to the tip of the peninsula. We stood on the bridge, and peered into the flow, shading our eyes with our hands.

'Look!' Evie said. 'Fishes!' And there in the darkness were the tails of trout, four of them, all in a row, their position sustained by a ripple of fins, and betrayed by the odd flick of a tail. I turned around and looked upstream and found myself staring at a heron. The fountain of white feathers springing from its breast seemed close enough to touch, its gold eye cold as glass. It was so still it could have been a decoy.

'Evie,' I whispered. 'Look!' And she gasped, we were all three taken aback, bird and people alike, but the heron had no intention of giving up its place, in thrall to the small fat trout.

We left the bridge and continued upstream. Partly because of the thick vegetation, and partly because of the marshy nature of the riverbed, there was no obvious way along the bank. Keeping the stream to the right, we followed it at a discreet distance, clambering to the top of the gulley, which formed a V-shaped cut in the land. On our side of the stream was a links golf course. Fields fringed the opposite bank. But the path across the golf course veered away from the water and into a sunken footway, a path from a time long before there was a golf course – a green lane, a holloway – spun around with gorse and blackthorn so that it formed a prickly tunnel adjacent to the stream. When we reached the end of the green lane the water was over to our right. At the edge of the golf course was a barbed-wire fence. We turned and went back to the footbridge and tried following the stream on its western bank. The western path went through a farmyard, towards the village of Edern, and again it bent away from the water, which now seemed to form a boundary to the farm, and was fenced in with barbed wire on both its banks. The houses of the village clumped ahead of us. I had read somewhere that Edern was the last village in Britain where fairies were seen. An old lady had apparently left a cake out for them, each week on baking day. She had done this until the 1950s. I started to tell Evie about it.

'Mummy?'

'Yes?' Evie was tired, her face smooth, pale despite the sun, the usual animation of her features still, folded away like birds' wings. 'Come on,' I said, 'let's go back.'

We retraced our steps, and broke out the remains of the chocolate, and resolved to try again. We would pick up the stream a bit closer to its source, somewhere on the shoulder of Garn Fadryn. But not today.

★

As the summer unfolded, this became something of a pattern. We would pick up a river along the coast of the Llŷn and follow it as far as we could. But there was always a fence, or a field, or someone's garden, private land, or a bull: something that could not be easily got around. Several of the rivers were enclosed, like this one, with barbed wire along both banks, so that the riverbed was the only pathway. In other places the fence might cross the stream itself. As the land rose higher water skipped through gullies, bouncing and slipping over rocks and stones, between banks that grew ever more deeply ferned. Occasionally we came across oases of vegetation, watercress and duckweed, nourished to frenzy by the fertilisers that washed off the land. The streambeds were difficult to ascend safely or with comfort. The enclosure of the land was constant, and uniform, and it forced us to go back, or around. It seemed impossible to trace a watercourse without wire-cutters and secateurs.

'What are they frightened of?' Evie asked, and I had no answer for her.

Ffynnon Fawr

At its western tip the Llŷn Peninsula is like a pointing hand; a solitary finger gesticulates a warning against the Irish Sea, at the place where the tides converge, and this place is known as the Swnt, or Sound. Sometimes the sea is calm, but when the tides turn the slabs of water heave alongside one another to create whirlpools and vortices, currents that are legendary. A hill crouches on the south side of the headland, cloaked by heather and stubby gorse that forms a pretty, but prickly, mantle. Below the hill, running to the edge of the land, is an apron of baize-like grass and this flourishes, protected from the worst of the weather, kept short and neat by sheep. In the centre of the green-baize apron is all that remains of St Mary's Church, now a rectangle of four low banks with a half-moon on one of the shorter walls, a ghost of the semicircular apse, although the whole thing has long since, centuries ago, grassed over. Occasional loose stones spill through the banks and people use them to write their names, or make symbols, or the sign of the cross – the round grey rocks on the short green grass encouraging a game as aimless yet seemingly addictive as the idle rearrangement of fridge magnets.

Each summer our family come to the headland for a picnic, and Evie and her cousins use the almost perfect rectangle for a slightly too large wicket, the natural ha-ha created by the grassed-over walls serving as their boundary. At the edges of the green apron, where the land meets the sea, there are cliffs, striated with red jasper and capped with a yellowish, ochre-coloured crystal, peculiar to this place. The children know to stay well back from the drops. There are no beaches in the immediate vicinity, and on clear days the children perch within the safety of the crags and watch the shifting currents below. Often they see seals. Sometimes they see fishermen checking lobster pots at the base of the cliff. And, almost always, they see the island, Ynys Enlli.

We have never been to the island although we've looked at it often. All we know of it is the fin of its mountain, the huddled ruins of its abbey. On rough days we have watched the waves break white as sail sheets against an inchoate shore. On clear days we have seen the sun fall full over its back, bleaching it pale as sea-glass. Once, when the haze was slight, we saw Jules Verne's green ray, were surprised by it, as a last curve of coloured light became visible in the sea air. It flared, acidic lime, almost fluorescent, for the smallest moment, before the sun dropped into the sea, leaving an unlikely crème de menthe afterglow.

A tree grows on the island – an extraordinary tree – seeded, it is said, from the pip of Merlin's apple. The apple that he discarded as he turned away from a wicked enchantress; growing hard, his power drawn from him, he was turned to stone by her, and only his bones remained. The bones are said to lie inside a cave and a child could reach for them, could feel for Merlin's bones, if only they knew where to look.

In our garden, pushed into the hedge, there is another tree, although it's more like a bush, being round like a spider's nest with no obvious trunk, just spindles of leaf-covered wands which in late summer are studded with lemony, pink-striped fruit. Our tree was propagated by a local horticulturist from this one twisted parent, the oldest apple in Europe, the oldest apple in the world, which has evolved beyond recognition into a clattering wooden net, as vigorous as a vine, braced against the thin soil and burnt salt winds of the island. Twenty thousand saints are buried alongside Merlin, and possibly also King Arthur, for Geoffrey of Monmouth maintained that it was Avalon, after *afal lon*, meaning lane of apples in Welsh.

But our business was not with the saints, or with the apples, or with the king and the wizard and his bones. We had come to the headland, to Anelog, and we were searching for St Mary's Well.

When Evie and I arrived we found everything enclosed, improbably, given the June day, in mist. The road was discernible, although only just, and when it ran to grass I stopped the car. There was nothing to see – no hill, no apron of land, no island. Cool and white, we inhabited a cloud; it was a curiously muted world. We left the car and began to walk in the direction of the cliffs. Our eyelashes and hair filled with beads of moisture that ran down our faces like tears, both delighting, and frightening, Evie. She was sure that a space had opened in the mist around us, and that this space was following us, which unnerved her. I tried to explain the idea of visibility, the idea of cloud density, and that we were able to see a little way ahead, and also a little way behind, but she could not comprehend it. Why were we able to see where we were going but not where we had come from?

'How do you know where we are?' she asked.

At first we had followed a drystone wall but after a while that came to an end. I heard the muffled sound of the stream that ran to the zawn, to the place in the cliffs where we might climb down to the well, though I could not see it. By moving fractionally to our left we would meet the mantle of heather and gorse that covered the hill, and this would also suffice as a guide, so I pointed it out to her.

The gorse and heather brought us almost to the edge of the zawn. It seemed to be an impenetrable chasm and Evie's eyes were wide with wonder. She had remembered an incident with a football the summer before, when her cousin Connor had kicked it over the cliff.

'You mustn't bring the other children here. It isn't safe, do you understand?'

'Your secret's safe with me,' she said, as though I had just told her I had robbed a bank. She could not believe she was going to climb down into the place where Connor had kicked his ball, and I had declared it lost.

At the edge of the cliff a pocket opened in the mist or, as was more likely, we were below it. Rising air currents from the sea maintained the space. We followed the trickle of water, which we had found again, and the path, which sloped steeply down. Below the cliff edge there was a moss-filled gully, skittering to stones, before the way ran to nothing over red and yellow rock. It looked, at first glance, as if there was no safe way down, a sheer drop into the sea. But by scrambling carefully sideways we were able to pick out handholds cut into the rock and reach the base. A narrow cleft led deep into the cliff face. We had to brace our feet on either side of it, because the sea rushed in beneath us, making bridges of our legs. At the end of this passage, almost inconsequential, and revealed by the ebbing tide, was a pool. A rope of water fed the pool from above and about this flow, by an odd trick of the light, the rainbow colours of the spectrum were gathered. The pool itself, the sacred well, was no bigger than an upturned hat.

St Mary's Well is known locally as Ffynnon Fawr which means the big well. It is said to have been consecrated by Mary herself when she visited the headland, presumably in the Dark Ages, because that's when all the indeterminate and exciting things seem to have happened. It is said to have been the last watering place for the medieval pilgrims before they made their way, or attempted to make their way, to the island, because for a long time three trips to the island netted the same number of indulgences as one return pilgrimage to Rome. This may all be true, although there are many other springs along the coast and it is much easier to launch a boat from the long sandy beach two miles away, in the village of Aberdaron. One of the reasons the well was deemed to be special – which sufficed as a miracle in the eyes of the medieval pilgrims – was because its salt water would turn, at certain times, to fresh. The poet R. S. Thomas, who was the Vicar at Aberdaron, described it in his poem 'Ffynnon Fair':

> *They did not divine it, but*
> *bequeathed it to us:*
> *clear water, brackish at times,*
> *complicated by the white frosts*
> *of the sea, but thawing quickly.*

The transformation is in fact no more than a conjuror's trick, a natural sleight of hand. The salt water of the pool, left full by the departing tide, is slowly displaced by spring water. Yet local legend has it that if you fill your mouth with well water, climb back up the cliff, and run three times around the ruins of St Mary's Church – and can do this without swallowing a drop – then your dreams, your wishes, will come true.

We looked down at the pool. I hadn't told Evie about the wish. The skeleton of a seagull, the odd feather clinging to its fanned and broken wing, pointed to the well. I thought about Allardyce, the rotted human compass in Robert Louis Stevenson's *Treasure Island*, its bony arm pointing dramatically, if no longer accurately, to the place where Flint's treasure might be found. A traveller called, appropriately, Ieuan Lleyn, who visited the Llŷn Peninsula in 1799, described entering 'St Mary's cave, in which is a well dedicated to Mary, and many other papal relics, such as the hooves of Mary's horse and the likes. As the place was steep and scary I tried to come up . . . as fast as my hands and feet, nay even my teeth would take me!' My own eyes were becoming accustomed to the milky half-light in the narrow space beneath the pulsing ceiling of mist. We were in a natural chapel whose walls of black stone rose sheer behind the pool. I made out what at first appeared to be a skull, but in its perfect roundness turned out to be a fishing float, one of the small buoys used to mark the lobster pots. There were bits of bone and driftwood, a plastic gallon container and a nylon orange net; all wedged deeply between tall wet splinters of rock. The rope of water, with its fans of gathered rainbows, spilt down into the pool. Any papal relics intended to remain here would have needed fixing in place with iron pins drilled into the rock, as securely as any mooring, if they were to withstand the twice daily onslaught of the sea which must entirely flood the passage. It seemed more likely that Lleyn had found the remains of an animal that had slipped over the cliff. Sheep droppings were visible on the ledge above our heads, over which the spring water splashed, the dark turds kept moist upon cushions of bright green moss and interspersed with tufts of wool. I had no desire to hold this water in my mouth, or anywhere else, my anxiety over hygiene interfering significantly with my capacity for wonder. I glanced around us. I felt certain that this couldn't be the right well. But if we were in the wrong place, so too had Ieuan Lleyn been, when he came here in 1799.

Evie, recognising by some unspoiled instinct holy water when she saw it, dipped her fingers into the triangular pool and dabbed her forehead with it, the water trickling down her nose, and this felt like a happy compromise, for although I seemed unable to free myself from a pervasive anxiety, almost nausea, I was relieved of the necessity of having to share it with her.

As we turned to begin the rocky climb back I was caught by a memory, raw as the day it retrieved. A spring afternoon in Barcelona. Three months earlier. Returning from the clinic. There had barely been time to collect Rupert from his office, for him to drive me home, and then for him to collect Evie from school. I had been adamant that I did not want to see anyone.

I'd heard them first, outside the front door. Green parrots were squabbling in the palm tree on the other side of the road. I couldn't make out what Rupert and Evie were saying above the parrots' squeaky-toy din. I had no idea what to expect, no idea what he had told her. When the door opened Evie spilled in with the sunlight, her face half full of wonder.

'Can I see the picture, Mummy? Of the baby?'

I could not believe he had not told her. I was absolutely unprepared for this, particular, moment. 'There is no picture, my darling. You see, the baby's died.' Her face. His half-turned body. Not looking at me; looking instead at the keys in his hand, the edge of his anger, the heat of his shame. I could not believe what we were doing.

'Where is it?' she asked.

'It's here.' My fingers touched my swollen belly.

'And it's died?'

'That's right.' She paused, still assimilating. 'Does this mean I'm not going to have a baby brother or sister?' I had tried to think of a decent lie, a euphemism, something that would make it all right. I was unprepared, defenceless before the truth. We all were.

It was dark in the hall after the door had closed.

'Can I watch TV?' she asked.

'Of course.' Evie slipped past and I could not be bothered even to recriminate. The damage, for what it was worth, was done.

I tried to fold the memory, reduce it. But it clung to me, sticky, insistent.

We made our way out of the channel on stepping stones while seawater funnelled beneath us. The waves hissed and foamed like the froth that slips over the rim of a beer glass. It was a cushioned world, opaque as cataracts, and the mist, when we reached it, was as dense as before. We pulled ourselves up the rocks towards the path. I followed Evie, remaining behind her in case she slipped. I pointed out handholds to her across the red and yellow stone, and helped her to place her feet in footholds, until I heard the crunch of little stones beneath her shoes and knew she had regained the path. I heard a sibilant trickle, a mischievous chatter as the stream spattered over gravel, and the white cloud once again pressed around us. The only colour was in the bright moss, visible once more at our feet.

Evie was delighted as the stream became apparent and then dumbfounded as it disappeared again. I pointed out to her the path, made plain by thick vegetation, of watercress, thistles, spiky marsh grass and sphagnum moss that indicated the water's journey. She listened: the mist was thicker and whiter now; the silence seemed to stop up our mouths. And then a sound, quiet as an indrawn breath. The water. She didn't want to talk. She was intent, like a spaniel, following a scent.

And then she saw it.

A round pool, a bowl of clear water, as wide as her arm's length, as deep as her knees. At first it appeared still and we saw fine sandy gravel on the bottom, the occasional green weed. Tightly coiled water snails, small as seeds, bright as jewels, encrusted the straight walls and heaped against the stems of weeds. Somewhere below the surface where the spring fed the well these images bent, the refraction attesting to the pulsed movement. Around the pool were signs of pilgrimage. Flat stones marked its edge and at one point they were drawn into a lip, the run-off that formed the stream. The grass around the well was flattened, muddied by many feet, and the stones had been grouted in to keep them stable. On either side were long sticks where someone had lifted green algae from the surface, and this was now browning in the air. Evie noticed and peered for more pea-green discs. She tried to pull a young fern, to act as a scoop, but the fronds came off in her hand, leaving the stem bent, but still attached.

'Will you help me, Mummy?'

There was a bluff, hardly that, a winged mound behind the water, where we counted pink saxifrage, primroses – no longer flowering – a yellow flower – tormentil – and purple foxgloves, whose tall rods screened the well. Beyond the bluff the heather and gorse and new ferns led back towards the drystone wall where we had begun our journey. I told Evie about the legend – the running round the church, the wishes. A veil seemed to pass across her eyes. The white mist pressed closely all around us, and I saw that she had no need for the miracle. All she wanted, she had before her. She took her water bottle, emptied it out, and then filled it from the silent well. She studied the contents, held them up, and asked me to reaffix the lid. Then, suddenly a child again, she put out her hand for me to hold, and we left.

I no longer knew what to wish for.

Health and happiness, I think. Nothing more.

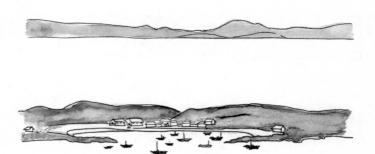

Traeth Porth Dinllaen

Two weeks after the Spanish school holidays started, in an explosion of fireworks for the Feast of St John, the British school holidays began. The first to arrive on the beach at Porth Dinllaen, in early July, were a handful of Scottish children. They were closely followed, a week or so later, by children from the British independent schools. Finally, almost a month after we had got here, the state-educated Welsh and English children joined the beach party. Now, in early August, the rock pools which had been Evie's exclusive domain became, at low tide, cluttered with warriors armed with plastic buckets and Day-Glo fishing nets. The older children carried spools and lines. Bits of bacon or gooey winkles served for bait.

Evie's preferred method for luring crabs was with a nylon drawstring bag, one that had come in a box of washing powder, and was intended for use with the detergent. She placed a boiled potato, soaked in bacon fat, inside the bag, then attached this to a hook and line. I had snapped the barb off the hook with a pair of pliers and now watched as a brick-red crab, a pointillist crown etched onto its shell, nipped the potato with a bone-coloured claw. Evie transferred the crab into a bucket of seawater with a careful sweep of her arm. A number of children clustered about; they exuded a mixture of excitement and awe, curiosity and envy as Evie tried to shake the crab free of the bait with determined, jerky movements, finally taking it between finger and thumb and slowly twisting it until it released the potato, its nut-cracker pincers open, pointing skyward.

The rock pools formed a narrow peninsula that bisected the curve of the bay like an arrow drawn over a bow. At its sea-facing tip the stones were caramel-coloured and smooth, the barnacles and seaweed polished away and stopped from coming back by scores of feet and bottoms, giving easy access, a slide if you were brave enough, to a plunge pool that opened, in its turn, onto the bay. Evie and the crab were surrounded by admirers. I watched her for a while. She looked up at me, and smiled, and I pointed at the bay, and then at the rock pool and mouthed *You stay here!* She nodded, widening her eyes in an *as if!* gesture, her hands opening like flowers, and I slipped into the mermaid pool. I swam between two rocky islets known as the Oysters, then pushed into the open water, registering the drop in temperature as a spiral around my body, the cold digging into my arms and neck like cheese-wire. I swam a tentative breaststroke until I located a ribbon of warmth, then stretched out into freestyle. The surface of the water was criss-crossed with these warmer paths, as wide as carpet runners, a reminder that the Gulf Stream ran near by.

We were waiting on the beach for Rupert, who was coming to join us for a week. The previous night, while Evie brushed her teeth, I had told her of the visit. She stood in front of the bathroom mirror, singing 'I Don't Care if the Sun Don't Shine' by Mack David. Toothpaste foamed over her chin, and dropped onto her foot. I was glad I hadn't told her sooner. Later, she had gone to the swing at the end of the area of trimmed field that was our garden, because it was the only place near the cottage that had any cover, and she had phoned Rupert. She twirled around with her arms about the ropes, the phone pressed to her ear. Behind her was Garn Fadryn's triangular cone, the first of the heather glowing like coal. Rupert must have said something about wanting to catch mackerel because she'd laughed, and said: 'Actually, Daddy, we're all a bit mackerelled out.'

The mackerel had arrived a couple of weeks ago. Our friend Mike had bought an old fishing boat, and he and his friend Anthony took us to the edge of the bay. A family of seals balanced on exposed rocks, their bodies curved like smiles, their heads and flippers raised to catch the sun. Evie had drawn fish after fish with a line and spool, no bait, just a spinner. She held the line between her thumb and forefinger and knew at once when she had a bite. A cheeky herring gull, following the boat, swooped down and nipped one of Evie's mackerel behind the gills as she drew it from the water, and she had handed me the spool, saying: 'Faster, Mummy!' She was determined not to give up her prize. Anthony was a surgeon, and he showed her how to lift the fish heads through ninety degrees, killing them softly with a quiet 'pop', and Evie was fascinated, and solemn. She wasn't comfortable about removing the hook. Later Anthony showed her how to gut them, placing the tip of his knife at the opening in the belly, pushing out the insides with his thumb, and washing the fish in seawater.

One evening I had a phone call from Endaf, a local builder. He had caught more than he could eat and asked if we would like some of them. I drove down to his house with a carrier bag to find him sitting on a deckchair in the garden, a plastic crate at his feet. A monkey-puzzle tree towered over us.

'How many do you want?' he asked me.

'Oh, just enough for supper. Two.' He frowned. 'Three?'

'Ah, take more than that. You can freeze them.'

'I don't know, Endaf, that's very kind. Twelve?' and he had nodded as I started to pick up the fish one by one.

'Oh for God's sake don't count them!' he said, and disappeared into the house. When he came back he held a black refuse sack, and he filled it with handfuls of fish. When I got home I waved to my neighbour, Joan, and she took half of them. The rest I stuffed into our little box freezer.

As the days rolled by we barbecued mackerel in salt, pan-fried them in custard powder, poached them in milk and wild dill collected from the shore. Evie stuck fish heads into a stargazy pie that neither of us felt like eating, and we smoked them on shavings of apple wood and then whipped them into paste, with crème fraiche, and lemon, and pepper. Even hearing the word *mackerel* now made me queasy. We were at the *sleek and glossy* phase of our holiday, it happened every year, when our blood became more fish oil than iron, our hair and skin soft and shiny despite the constant exposure to salt.

Later, after the phone call, we read *Swallows and Amazons* together. Evie squealed with delight at the part where the boy Roger swam with one foot on the bottom, because she too 'swam' with one foot on the bottom, and I could sense her, in that moment, resolving not to. We were curled up in the big cabin bed, and I had said that she could sleep there, for tonight, although tomorrow she must go back to the crog-loft, to her futon nest of cushions and pillows, to the place where adults never went, because the ceiling height precluded it. At some point in the night her hand reached out, her palm flat against my neck. And then she shifted and pushed both feet into my solar plexus, to the place under my ribs where she had grown. She smelled, mysteriously, of peaches.

Evie kept asking when we were going to the airport. She seemed unable to retain the information that we weren't. My friend Bronwen was arriving at Liverpool at the same time as Rupert, on her way to visit her parents in North Wales. She had offered to give Rupert a lift, and would stop over for one night.

Keeping to my warm ribbon, I swam across the harbour. A flat tender was moving towards the beach. Ken, who owned two fishing boats, which made him important in the life of the village, stood in the middle of the tender, his hands on his hips, while another fisherman sat at the back of the boat with his hand on the tiller. I stopped by one of the mooring buoys, treading water, and lifted my arms so they could see me.

'You want a lift?' asked Ken.

'No, I'm all right. I just didn't want you to run me over.' I held onto the side of the boat with both arms. My legs drifted beneath it. I was trying to remember what Dad had told me about the fluid mechanics of flat-bottomed boats, and vortices in shallow water. Dad had been an engineer. Dad would have known what was happening. A cloud covered the sun and a breeze lifted the hairs on my forearms into barbs, wet hair flicking across my mouth. Ken allowed me a head start before re-engaging the motor. A current had wrapped about me, or the tender had drifted into it, and for a moment I appeared to be going nowhere. When I reached the far side of the harbour I touched the sea wall. My hand was splayed like a starfish. I noticed the way the orange lichen spread like rust over the rocks above the water, and how the stones beneath the waterline were indigo. And then I noticed the white band where my wedding ring should have been. I put the hand quickly back into the water, took it out again, and re-examined it.

The ring had gone.

I didn't allow any thoughts to form about this discovery but turned quickly and went back the way I had come, including the detour through the current where Ken's boat had been. The ring had come from Tiffany's in New York. It was made of twenty-two princess-cut diamonds and weighed about four and a half carats. Rupert had given it to me when Evie was baptised. We didn't get married until Evie was five, when we found ourselves travelling through Las Vegas. We had used the ring as a wedding ring because we had forgotten to buy another. And anyway, I didn't want another ring.

Rupert would be here in a matter of hours.

When I reached the rock pools I stood in the shallow water by the place where I had entered the pool. I looked again at the white band around my finger. The noise of the children, the waves and the wind was shut out by a growing anxiety. Rupert would read this as a sign, I was sure of it. An indication of how I valued our relationship.

I had lost the first ring he ever gave me within a few hours of receiving it – also, as it happened, on a beach – in Mexico. We had searched for that ring for over an hour, but the shell-white sand had swallowed it. I stared at the toffee-coloured Welsh beach, unable to believe what I had done. At the rock pool a group of children was gathered around a young girl in a sarong, who was covered head-to-foot in wet clay, her hair dreadlocked into ropes. It was Evie. She was pointing to a place beyond the rock pool where a squashy seam had been revealed by the tide. The sun broke through a tear in the cloud and a movement on the sea floor distracted me. I bent down, my chin just below the water. Dancing rays and spots of light were bouncing around a barely discernible shadow-circle, like a child's illustration of the sun. It was the ring! It must have come off my finger as I entered the water. I would never have seen it, against the sand, without this coincidental, actual sunburst, that bounced white light through the stones. I reached for the ring and the sea filled my ears, covered my head. It was as hard as a drawer full of knives. I stood up, looked at the ring, brushed away the sand. Then I pushed it over my fattest, middle, finger.

When Evie noticed me standing in the shallow water she grinned, and the clay, which had dried into a ghostly mask, crackled like the face of Methuselah, and I was incredibly happy, and yet also afraid, although I couldn't, in that moment, have said why.

At four o'clock the fishermen began stacking crates of blond whelks onto acrid, flat bed trailers. There were spider crabs for the Chinese restaurants in Manchester. Some lobsters nosed about beneath a net, litmus blue and lively. The fishermen dragged the trailers off the beach behind rusted Massey Ferguson tractors that hummed with a metallic riff. Evie spotted Rupert and Bronwen almost as soon as they passed through the Bwlch, tall figures in urban travel clothes, their city shoes incongruous on the sand. I imagined the trapped, reconstituted air of the plane escaping as their coats flapped in the breeze. Evie had already tucked in her chin and was running as fast as she could towards them.

When I reached them, Rupert and Bronwen were laughing. Behind them, at the Bwlch, a crowd of people were clustered around a Land-Rover. Gulls hopped and shuffled inquisitively along the ridge-tiles of the nearest cottage. Evie's eyes were round and two little waves at the top of her nose indicated a frown, despite her joy at seeing her father. Bronwen was holding a plastic carrier bag.

'They were four for a pound,' said Rupert. Of course, of course, today had been the Mackerel Race to raise money for the RNLI, when anyone who had a boat set off at the crack of a starting pistol to catch as many mackerel as they could in just three hours. Evie was staring into the pungent, slippery bag as though it contained the head of a seal.

Later, we all lay on a woollen blanket in the garden, our eight legs making a star-shape, our heads clumped together on cushions. The charcoal on the barbecue was turning to powder, although it gave off more heat than ever. White wine knocked the edge off the night. Cold blades of grass tickled my ankles and feet.

A solitary flash caught my eye. As though someone had drawn a chalk line then erased it. I looked at the place where it had been, and saw a second streak, fading, even as it passed. Soon they were coming every few seconds, the Perseids, they happened every

August. High above, behind the shooting stars, was the Milky Way, and it really did look like a glass of spilled milk, thrown across the sky, and sinking into velvet. We stayed outside as long as we could, laughing and pointing at the stars, until the blanket and cushions grew damp with condensation, and the cold drove us indoors. We made up the cabin bed for Bronwen. Evie disappeared into the crog-loft, into her tangled den of pillows and toys, and arranged herself so she could see the fire. Rupert and I slept in a wooden shepherd's hut in the garden.

The next morning I woke before dawn. I pulled on a sweater and a pair of jeans and sat on the steps of the shepherd's hut, aware of the shift as the darkness began to fade, my eyes adjusting from night to day vision. Because we were in the west, the sun was up a good while before it finally appeared over Snowdon. It was cold in Garn Fadryn's shadow. The stars dimmed, then disappeared, till only Venus, the morning star, was left. I liked to watch the sky brighten behind the Garn although I could not see the summit, still enclosed in its envelope of mist. Locally the hill is known as Madryn, from *modron*, meaning mother.

I had tried to prepare for this visit by Rupert. I felt soft, closed, like a soap bubble. Before Rupert arrived my friend Mike had lent us a wooden dinghy. It was painted Baden-Powell blue and was called the Mirror. Whether Mirror was its name, or described the kind of boat, I didn't know, and hadn't wanted to show my ignorance by asking. I had been fascinated by the noise the water made as we cut through the waves, the ripple of the wind against her blood-red sail. I had become accustomed to small sounds, to not talking, and not touching, or being touched, other than in my day-to-day contact with Evie, and now Rupert was here. Over the next two weeks we would laugh, love, and argue. There would be a chink of glasses. A rectangle of light stretching over the garden as we kept ever later nights. I would become a half of something, or rather, a third. For some reason I was unsettled by this. The arguments that had railed over the baby, the possibility of the baby, the things that had been said, that could not now be unsaid lay between us like a badly made rope bridge upon which I dared not trust my weight.

The realisation that our baby should now be in my arms spilled and stuck to the surface of my mind, garish as white paint flung across a road, as difficult to remove. I felt more fiercely alone, perched on the wooden steps, Rupert sleeping behind me, Bronwen and Evie in the cottage, than I had ever felt when I was actually alone.

There was a hip flask full of damson gin in the shepherd's hut. I reached for it and removed the lid, took a sip of the clear liquid, garnet red, flecked with fragments of blue-black fruit skin, which were ticklish on my palate, like tea leaves. I had made it with my brother, John, three years ago on my birthday. We had gathered the damsons from a tree in his garden that is no longer there.

I tiptoed into the cottage, heard a movement.

'Bronwen, are you awake?'

Her voice came from the other side of the wooden panel that separated the bedroom from the living room: 'I am.'

'Shall we go for a swim? It's high tide in less than an hour.'

'Brilliant!'

We left a note and headed for Lifeboat Bay, a secluded beach at the tip of the headland. As we walked the sun lifted behind us, and the mist over Garn Fadryn grew lacy. In front of us the sea and the sky were merged into a single sheet. Blue as smoke, soft as silk. Lifeboat

Bay was exactly what it said it was: home to the RNLI station. The water looked still, although warning signs discouraged swimmers, advising them to keep off the concrete ramp. Strong currents pulled just off the point. We ignored the signs and dived from the ramp, into sea that was as limpid as oil, and as cool as the light. The earless wet-dog head of a seal peered at us from beyond the current.

A radio was playing. And there was litter on the beach. It was still only five o'clock. I was about to say something when Bronwen caught my eye and pointed, bright water falling from her outstretched arm. An untidy head had lifted from the foreshore and a young man stared at us, incredulous. I watched him trying to assimilate the populated nature of his wilderness experience: two women and a seal eyeing him from the middle of the bay. He started to pick up beer cans and discarded clothes, watching us as though we were the police. I felt for him; my own experience at Spurn Point was still fresh and perplexing to me.

As the sun lifted higher we could see through the water to sand-coloured crabs betrayed by their shadows and squid-like pulsing seaweed. A darting shoal of little fish, camouflaged against the sand, was momentarily visible as it changed direction. The surface of the water had seemed sheer when we entered it – but I could now see that it was speckled with flies, leaves and dust motes caught in a vast meniscus.

The night before Rupert returned to Barcelona we visited our friends Peter and Jackie in their cottage on the beach. We ate lobsters, caught by Ken the fisherman. The usual debate about how best to kill the lobsters had fizzed around the beach like gunpowder. For the most part we were all agreed on the 'freezer method', which meant putting the lobsters in the deep freeze until they were drowsy and then dropping them, dribbling, into boiling water, which we believed to be 'humane'. My friend Lucy had trained as a chef in France and she advocated stabbing them in the back of the head with a knife, but Peter had tried this and missed the spot, or maybe he hadn't, but the lobster had clattered to the floor, and then set off in an erratic dance, the knife waving like a metronome, frightening the children and dissipating the appetites of the guests. But in time the shells had turned from dusty blue to scarlet, and now lay empty, as did several bottles of wine. Evie had fallen asleep, and was tucked up in a bunk bed with her cousin Lauren. After Rupert and Peter crashed through a chair, their high spirits reducing it to kindling, the three of us set out in Peter's rib for the middle of Nefyn Bay, so we could see the phosphorescence in the water. Jackie was visible as a bright point on the sand, a funnel of light from her torch reminding us where the shore was. Every so often I looked back at her. She must have been walking up and down the beach, because the tiny funnel moved first one way, and then the other, with tiny erratic jumps indicating her footsteps. We were all so drunk I was amazed she'd had the foresight to think of this. Beyond the bay were some of the most treacherous waters in the British Isles. Both the sky and the sea were black. But in the bay, tonight, the water was calm. Rupert and I trailed our arms in the inky sea, the cold fit like opera gloves. The glow of phosphorescence illuminated us, our arms and fingers were green. It lit up Peter's face above the tiller and frothed behind the propeller in ghostly, cheerleader pom-poms. Beyond the little boat, the starless darkness pressed about us.

The next day Evie and I waved Rupert off from Liverpool Airport, his smile disappearing as he passed through to Security, leaving an imprint fading in the air, a moment of brightness, an impression of light, and then he was gone. People swarmed around us, holding plastic zip-lock bags and their hand luggage. Walking back to the car we picked our way through the holidaymakers as they surged about us, arriving – tanned and tired, or departing – pale and anxious. As Evie and I began the two-hour drive back to the cottage I found myself thinking of the Canadian pianist, Glenn Gould, whose recording of Bach's Prelude and Fugue from *The Well-tempered Clavier* is on a satellite headed for the end of the galaxy. Gould believed that there was a ratio between the time one could spend in company, and the time it subsequently took to recover from it. Our days in the Llŷn had, ordinarily, a sequestered quality about them. But the recent weeks had been packed with company. This was a good thing, we were cushioned in friendship – but suddenly I too had a yearning to travel, to move on, to go somewhere else. It was a sensation that I knew well. It was the same hankering after remoteness that had brought me to the Llŷn Peninsula in the first place.

Caherdaniel

Our departure from the Llŷn Peninsula happened almost straight away. Less than a week after Rupert had returned to Barcelona, I received a phone call. Evie and I were walking along the sand, Evie scouting for skimmers, when the phone buzzed and I recognised an Irish prefix, although not the number. It was my friend Sean:

'It's Pamela.'

'What's the matter?' Pamela had often been unwell; she'd had a string of operations. Evie had found a stone. She held it up to show me, then threw it, and it skipped in lively arcs across the waves.

'It's serious, man. She's on life support. They're turning it off tomorrow.' I looked at the phone in my hand, and then put it back to my ear.

'Are you in Belfast?'

'I'm in Tralee. Can you get here?' I stared at Evie; the sea stretched behind her like tarpaulin. A black-and-white collie-dog was dancing alongside her; he clearly thought the stones were for his benefit.

'Yes,' I said, 'I hope to be . . . I'll be there when I can.'

I wasn't quite sure how I got Evie off the beach, but suddenly we were driving back to Mum's house, two hastily packed overnight bags behind us. I tried to book a flight from Liverpool or Manchester but neither Mum nor I had a computer. It was almost impossible by phone. Sean rang again and I realised I wasn't going to make it to Tralee. I focused my energies on the funeral, which was to be held in Limavady, County Derry. Mum took Evie to her cousins' house, and I booked a morning flight to Belfast.

I had first met Pamela the day that I turned thirty. I had held a birthday party, and over a hundred people came to a sunlit ballroom in Earls Court Square. I had been due to leave in a couple of weeks for a new job, in Belfast. Senator Mitchell's Peace Process was just about to begin, and I was going to play my part developing grassroots drama among the divided communities, as a script editor with BBC Northern Ireland. The party was a send-off as well as a celebration. There had been an enormous table covered in tea-lights that joined the dots between vases stuffed with cow parsley, which Rupert and I had gathered that afternoon from Brompton Cemetery. An armada of half-filled glasses floated, bubbles blinking between the fingers of gesticulating hands. At a certain moment the voices rose, and then relaxed, becoming a part of something whole, and the room filled with a sudden expansive loudness. I had never really had a party before, certainly not one on this scale, and I watched with wonder as the glow-worm constellations of tea-lights asserted themselves before a slow, but eventual, sunset. There were some unexpected faces, friends, I supposed, of friends, and one in particular caught my eye, or rather my ear, because it was the sound of laughter that made me turn my head.

In the 1990s London people always wore black, occasionally white, although there was a season they'd all worn brown, and while this undoubtedly widened the palette, it hadn't left much of an impression. Pamela was wearing an aquamarine linen shift, her red hair smooth as a helmet. She was like something from antiquity, classical and rare, and when our eyes met she began to move across the room, pulling her companion by the arm.

'I know, I know –' I caught her voice, the sing-song, soon-to-be-loved Limavady tilt. 'I hope you don't mind but I *had* to come, I was talking to Jackie here and it all just sounded . . . so *lovely*.'

On my first Thursday in Belfast Pamela telephoned me: *Just pack a bag and take it with you tomorrow, then come up to the house after work.* I had been wary as I set out from the new city. The Union flags and the tricolour kerbs of the different tribes perplexed me, and the fortified police station at Dundalk unnerved me, with its razor-wire fence and bulletproof glass. I had driven over the Glenshane Pass, and wondered at the heather beginning to shine against the dark, underlying peat. From Limavady I followed Pamela's directions: *Find the low bridge and then continue up the lane, you can't miss the house.*

No, I couldn't miss the house. I turned into a driveway between crenellated turrets to gaze, at the end of a long lawn, into rows of windows that reflected the evening back to me. Walworth was a large, fortified plantation house. I had heard of such a thing but never troubled to imagine it. The façade was grand and appeared to be Georgian, but turning the corner into a yard I found a cluster of other dwellings, including a cottage that stuck out in an L-shape. Clearly those who the house had been built to protect, who had come to 'plant' the land, had not ventured very far from its cover. In spite of the unquestionably Protestant nature of the estate an Ulster flag waved from a pole on the lawn.

When I walked into the kitchen I had found a small, wiry woman, muscularly building a fire in an enormous grate. I assumed this was Pamela's mother, and held out the flowers I had brought with me. The woman took them and put them in a vase and called: *Mrs Brown, there's someone here for you*, and an elegant woman of indeterminate age appeared in the kitchen, holding out both her hands in greeting. *Hello, I'm Noreen, you must be Kate; Pamela said you were coming.* We had eaten supper in a long panelled dining room where I counted eight grown-up children including Pamela, some with lovers and children of their own. I was trying to figure out who they all were when Noreen caught me looking.

'Brian is my second husband,' she said. 'We have four children each, well, Brian also has a fifth, Felicity, but she isn't here tonight. Actually, she grew up in England,' Noreen nodded. 'She's got young children.' As the wine spilled, and the night yawned, a story began to come together. Noreen and Brian had been lovers for years. Both of them had young families, both had despaired of their marriages. One night, Noreen's husband Arthur had appeared at the door of the house and set about Brian with a blackthorn walking stick, beating him to the ground and cracking two ribs.

'You had to hand it to him,' Brian said. 'She was a woman worth fighting for, and I dare say I deserved it!'

Noreen wore a large emerald ring and I asked her how she came by it. She had been holidaying with her family in the Far East and Brian – unable to part from her – had followed them and even stayed in the same hotel. He had bought the stone and given it to Noreen when Arthur's back was turned. Of course she couldn't wear it or even declare it at Customs, so she re-entered the country with the emerald hidden. She smiled at the recollection, and glanced at the ring as she talked: deep as sea-glass, and spilling dark light, it was clustered around with diamonds.

They had both divorced and eventually married when Noreen's youngest child turned eighteen.

I began to spend most of my weekends at the house. Even my parents and an aunt came to visit. Brian always seemed especially interested in me. We had something in common, he had rapidly gleaned: I was an adopted child. He had given his firstborn up, although the decision had been both against his wishes and out of his hands. A few years ago he had paid a private detective to find his daughter. She had been born to his first wife, but before they were married, and convention or scandal didn't allow them to keep her. The baby had been given in adoption to an English vicar and his wife, and they had called her Felicity. As it happened the vicar had recently died and Brian appeared at just the right moment. He brought Felicity to Walworth, with her husband and little daughter, and she met the unruly family that were her kin.

This was the dream that I had never dared acknowledge, and for Felicity it had come true. I glowed in the warmth from Pamela's family, like a stray dog drawn to a fire. To me they were beautiful, wild, generous, hilarious, glamorous, and good.

Noreen told me one night of a home movie that had gone missing at the height of the Troubles, when Brian was a leading defence lawyer representing various Protestant paramilitaries, despite his Catholic business interests. The film was of the family playing Cowboys and Indians. Brian had worn a feathered chieftain's headdress and stripes across his cheekbones. Noreen was a squaw. The children were everything in between and at one point Brian's eldest son had surfed down the kitchen staircase on an ironing board, devastating both the ironing board and the stairs. Brian roared at the thought of MI6 or the IRA or the Army or whoever had pinched the film scratching their heads at the tomfoolery.

I had longed to be a part of it — and in a way, of course, I was. But I also longed for such a story to open — for me. In part, this yearning stopped me from revisiting the house when I left my job in Ireland. I had driven away from Walworth, for what turned out to be the last time, the morning after the 1997 General Election. The Labour Party had taken power in a landslide victory with a majority of over two hundred seats. Brian had placed a rollover bet. He was especially interested in proportional representation, and he won fifty thousand pounds that night. I drove past him in the grey first light. I was due to be in Belfast at nine, and Brian was asleep. He was sitting very straight on a wooden bench beneath a tree, and a soft rain was falling. His glasses had misted over, and his two Irish wolfhounds lay at his feet, the fine rain sticking to his hair and their coats so that all three figures seemed adorned with pearl hairnets. For me, in the years that followed, other things came up: Evie was born, my own adopted father fell mortally ill, and I didn't return to Ireland until Evie was almost two years old, when we came for Pamela's wedding. And now, seven years later, I had come again, and this time it was because Pamela had died.

She had been swimming in the sea off Caherdaniel in Kerry with some friends. It was in a river mouth, as it happened, where the Atlantic breakers surged against the downward stream, and at high tide you could bodysurf through a channel into the shallow water of the river. Pamela was struck by a headache and had come out of the water, walking to a house above the beach. She was staying with the same friend who had introduced us to one another, all those years ago. Pamela had said something about going to make the lunch. But her headache grew worse until soon she could not speak. Her husband, John, was with her, and she lost consciousness looking into his eyes. An ambulance brought her to Tralee. Noreen took a taxi from Limavady. As many of Pamela's friends as could get there in time gathered around her bedside, and then her life support was switched off. The cause of death had been an aneurysm. That, at any rate, was the story that I pieced together when I eventually got to the house.

I missed the funeral. I had missed my flight from Liverpool to Belfast because I fell asleep in the bath, and the next flight wasn't until noon. By the time I got to Walworth the mourners were streaming home. The family and Pamela's closest friends were gathered at the house. I passed Arthur standing in the yard behind the house, a glass, half empty, in his hand. He was talking with someone who was inside the kitchen, but he made no move to enter. In the living room of the cottage where Pamela had lived were two wooden trestles where her body had lain in an open coffin. The room was filled with flowers, many of them cut from the garden, hydrangeas, roses, marguerites, lilies. They surrounded the place where Pamela had been. Her husband John was sleeping, and the voices in the cottage were subdued. Towards evening someone commented that the room felt cold. People supposed that it would be all right to light a fire, but felt they'd better wait till John woke up. I went back into the big house where Noreen was moving among the mourners, gracious, outwardly calm. The emerald glinted on her finger, there were more at her throat and wrist. She held a cut-glass tumbler of dark liquid, which I supposed to be brandy. I grew vaguely anxious at the thought of meeting Brian. I still hadn't seen him, and I wasn't sure what my reception would be. But when he saw me, his face opened into the same wild smile, and he said:

'Did you ever find your father?'

'No,' and it was my turn to smile. More than ten years had passed since Brian had first asked me that question, but I had never even learned my natural father's name or, as Brian saw it, my own.

'I'm so sorry,' I said.

'What about?' asked Brian.

'Well, Pamela —'

'Ah. Death slides off me like water,' he said. 'I've seen enough of it to last a lifetime. What have you been doing with yourself?' I told him about my summer plan to follow a Scottish river from the sea to its source and how I had so far failed to get off a beach in Wales. Until now.

'Book Five!' he roared.

'I'm sorry?' I said.

'Of *The Odyssey*. "But Hermes did not find great-hearted Odysseus indoors but he was sitting out on the beach, crying, breaking his heart in tears." Odysseus spent nine years crying on a beach before the gods remembered where they'd left him. Only then could he fulfil his destiny.'

'And what was that, Brian?' asked a passing mourner, a glass of wine in each of her hands.

'To go home, to his family, to his sheep and his pigs.' Brian's hand came down on the mourner's arm, the ash from his cigarette toppling. 'What else is there?' The question didn't seem to need an answer and the young woman smiled and moved on. 'Kate, where are you staying tonight?'

'Oh, I have an early flight from Belfast,' I started, but Brian patted my shoulder.

'You must stay here, of course.'

Later, when the wine and spirits had been replaced by tea, and the sad tales by poetry and song, I slept on a long leather couch in Brian's study, where the housekeeper made up a bed for me, protesting that she could find me *a proper bed* if I wanted one. But I was where I wanted to be, behind the sign on the door that said: *Piss off I'm busy*. I watched the fire burn to nothing as the sun diluted the darkness and I felt something, some spirit, flow through the house, binding us, and holding us all together.

When I got back to Wales I was disconsolate. Evie was still at her cousins' house; she'd been invited to stay for the week. I was alone at the cottage. I thought about a conversation I had had with my friend Liz, who lived near Berwick-upon-Tweed.

'If Evie's in Chester why don't you come over? I mean, you're just on your own down there.'

If I were to visit Liz in Berwick, as she had suggested, then I would have reached Scotland. The journey I had told Brian about, the abandoned trip to find the source of the Dunbeath Water, re-presented itself, shadowy, but real. I walked down to the beach. The wind was blowing in a cool flat block, and I pressed my back into the harbour wall for shelter. A man was also leaning on the wall and I didn't notice him until he spoke to me.

'You love it here, don't you?' he said. I realised that he was one of the fishermen, and that I had never actually heard him speak before.

'Yes,' I replied, and I found myself trying to explain the feeling that just being there gave me; and the odd sense of breathlessness whenever I thought of it, like an ache underneath my ribcage.

'It's love,' said the fisherman, 'I feel it myself.' I was amazed. In part because I hadn't thought one could feel such a thing for a place, and in part because I hadn't recognised the symptoms. Which seemed a tragedy. As I walked back along the beach I picked over the unexpected conversation.

Love. I wasn't sure about it. But the feeling of longing, or yearning, for something not quite discernible that could almost be nostalgia. A sense that was as acute as hunger, or homesickness, but not necessarily for a place that one knew. Something elusive, unquantifiable, and yet − in its very depth and poignancy − as compelling as desire.

When I got back to the cottage I telephoned Rupert, who agreed that there didn't seem to be a word for it in English. But Rupert spoke German. He said:

'Try *Sehnsucht*.'

'But what does it mean?' I asked, and Rupert found it difficult to reply. It's made from *Sehnen*, he said, meaning yearning, and *Sucht*, which means addiction, but *Sehnsucht* conveyed more than simply an addictive yearning. I waited on the telephone while he tried to find a better meaning. He said: 'C. S. Lewis describes it as: "That unnameable something, desire for which pierces us like a rapier at the smell of a bonfire, the sound of wild ducks flying overhead, the title of *The Well at the World's End* . . ." '

'You're joking,' I said. 'Did he really say *The Well at the World's End?*'

'Yes. It's a book.'

'I know what it is . . . Look, I've got to go.'

I called Liz straight away. I packed a sleeping bag and a thermos flask, as well as a hip flask, *just in case*, and carried them out to the car. I then turned the car round so that it faced downhill. In the morning, before the sun had reached around the Garn, or pushed aside the blanket of mist, I closed up the cottage. Liz lived just the other side of the Scottish border; I could be there by the end of the afternoon.

Skell

I retraced my route over the Pennines from the early days of the holiday – this time in daylight – under the warm August sun. The moors looked hazy, the heather at the cusp of flowering, with a promise of lilac fire. When I reached Yorkshire, I headed north. The previous day Liz, on whose coat-tails I was following, sent me a text: *Just passing the Angel of the North, he is so big and strong!* And he was. I gasped when I saw him, another Antony Gormley metal man, part Titan, part spitfire, dark as mahogany. The Angel stood on a smooth mound between two carriageways of the A1 and I pulled up the car in a lay-by-cum-car park next to him. Oddly, like the metal men at Crosby Beach, the Angel faced the opposite direction to the one in which I was travelling. Children gathered around his feet and perched on them, eating sandwiches, or having their photographs taken.

The mound reminded me of Silbury Hill, the so-called Neolithic burial mound in which no burial chamber has ever been found. A well at its base, called Swallowhead Spring, floods the River Kennet – at certain times – around the hill, to form the shape of a pregnant woman made of water. Much has been made of this, not least by me. On the winter solstice before Evie was conceived I made my way across the monochrome plains of Wiltshire. I ignored the barbed wire and the warnings to keep out and passed through a gap in the fence. When I reached the top I crouched beneath a tearing wind and shelterless sky, and as the white sun rolled into soft clay, I emptied my heart:

Give me a child!

But on this northern mound, between the two carriageways of the A1, there stood an angel, and he resembled nothing so much as the angel standing guard outside the gates of Eden – now a blasted wilderness – to keep prying eyes away from all that remained of the tree of life. Which would make the garden, now a wilderness, Scotland.

The Irish *Metrical Dindshenchas* are packed with stories about our relationship to the land. They tell how certain features of the landscape were called, or forced, into being and describe how they came to be named.

There was once a High King, a god, called the Dagda. Strong and tall, he was a warrior, and a hunter, a skilled musician, a storyteller, a lover.

A lover.

In *The Well at the World's End* Neil Gunn tells of a goddess who went to seek a well in the land beyond our own. It is called the Well of Elcmar, after its guardian, a water god. Boand, the goddess, was Elcmar's wife. Everyone was forbidden from approaching the well except those who were charged with its care. It was said to be impossible even to move before the water without incurring injury, and that the eyes of anyone attempting to look into it would burst. So what was Boand, *fair and white-limbed* — according to the *Metrical Dindshenchas* — *soft-blooming, and with perfect eyes*, doing there?

> *Hither came on a day white Boand*
> *(her noble pride uplifted her),*
> *to the well, without being thirsty*
> *to make trial of its power.*

Another version of Boand's story says she approached the well in the hope of finding knowledge, so she could learn how to conceal her infidelity. For that most capable god the Dagda was her lover, and she wanted to know how to hide this, as well as the child she had borne him, from her husband.

The Dagda did everything he could. When he and Boand began to make love, before dawn, on that first lovely day, he held the sun in the sky for nine whole months, so that in the space of their coupling their child was conceived, grew full-term inside her, and was born before sunset. And while this great feat of love-making continued, throughout the whole of this very long day, Elcmar was diverted by the most ludicrous of errands. Aengus, the love child, was magnificent — of course — and grew up to become the god of love himself. The affair was not so easy to conceal.

Or perhaps Boand was just curious. It was, after all, the fountain of knowledge. Yet even as she walked about the well, *heedlessly,* according to the legend, *three waves roared out of it,* one for each circuit that she made. One can more or less put money that she walked anticlockwise, or wicken way. The first wave *broke off her foot,* the second *took out her eye,* and the third *shattered her hand.* Boand rushed to the sea, in order to escape further blemish, and so that none might see her mutilation. But the waves followed her and drowned her. The water kept flowing from the well. And this water, this river, was named after her, and we now know it as the Boyne. Yet, while the River Boyne preserves Boand's name, fourteen other rivers – including the Euphrates, the Tiber, the Jordan and the Severn – were all said to have come into being when Boand upset the well. Even the River Tigris, which flows through paradise itself.

> *Every way the woman went*
> *The cold white water followed*
> *From the Sid to the sea (not weak it was),*
> *So that thence it is called Boand.*
> *Boand from the bosom of our mighty river-bank,*
> *Was the mother of great and goodly Aengus,*
> *The son she bore to the Dagda – bright honour!*
> *In spite of the man of this Sid.*

With thoughts of the Dagda and poor drowned Boand nudging at one another inside me, I got back into the car.

I continued on my way, the Angel receding in the mirror. I found him wonderful and saw in him a good omen, if any omen were needed. I felt as though I'd passed through a gateway, and that my journey had begun for real. I found myself thinking about *Another Place*. The Angel was made of iron, as were the Antonys at Liverpool. In the old tales iron is said to be abhorrent to the fairies, the people *of this Sid, aes sidhe*, meaning the hill dwellers. According to the fairy tales this is because the nails of the cross were made of iron. A more prosaic reason might be because the Celtic people brought it with them, or rather, brought the skill to work it. It represented, in the plough, and the sword, and the horseshoe, the displacement of a different way of life.

The Celts believed that the Otherworld was parallel to our own, and that you could step into it, or through it, at certain times. Only particular things, like a tree half covered in leaves, or a field full of black-and-white sheep, indicated that you were there at all. You had to look out for the signs. You had to know them.

The lay-by had been on a slip road, and I discovered that I couldn't get back to the A1. Somehow I had made an error, and was running parallel to my route. While I was wondering how to rectify this I saw a sign for Fountains Abbey. Many years ago I had worked on a film in which the abbey had been used as a location. I had been in the cutting room, in London, and was enthralled by the film rushes as they came in from the lab. I had held the 16mm film up to the window, saw the replicated images of green grass, a golden river, the lacy ruin of the church itself, each cube of sunlight separated by a frame bar, like dozens of emerald cut stones. So I followed the sign, and drove towards Ripon, presuming the abbey to be near by. But it wasn't. After half an hour travelling through undulating fields, I still didn't seem to be moving. The thickly clouded sky was silver, with the very high contrast of a black-and-white print. Hand-tinted. Bruised. The mustard stubble of the fields looked brittle. The road, which was featureless, seemed to absorb, rather than reflect, the sky, its surface flat, and suit-grey. I couldn't see anything ahead except an isolated copse and cylindrical wheels of baled hay where the wheat had been recently harvested. I began to consider turning back, but the road wasn't wide enough.

Just as I was feeling that I must have taken a second wrong turn, I entered the town of Ripon. After meandering for a few more miles, a sign for the abbey appeared. A perimeter wall bound an estate, and there were signs for Studley Royal Water Gardens. The abbey and the gardens seemed inseparable. I followed signs to a National Trust car park and entered, without paying. Doing my best to remember where I'd parked, I followed more signs to the abbey. I was hungry. I hadn't eaten since breakfast, and it was now early afternoon. I had an apple in my bag, and some chocolate, but I didn't want to stop and get them out. I ached from driving and needed to keep moving to ease the stiffness in my spine and hips. I was aware that I was on my way to visit Liz, and that I had told her I would be with her mid-afternoon. I missed Evie. We were probably together for three-hundred and fifty-five days of the year, and this unexpected week was feeling like an eternity. I was halfway through the third day.

The night before we had left the cottage Evie had been reading in her bed in the crog-loft. She crept down the ladder. Her eyes had a storm-washed look. Something tragic had happened.

'*Pony Club?*' I asked – her book: one of the ponies had been ill – and she nodded. I put down what I was reading. She climbed into the bed. I turned off the light, and opened my hand on the pillow. Evie eased her face into it. We lay there, her face resting in my hand, my palm slowly filling with hot tears, until her breathing changed, and she fell asleep.

Something seemed to pass through the room. There was a tightening among the shadows, a splintered movement in the fire. I must live a long, long time, and stay well, remain strong, until this passionate creature can find her feet. Perhaps some of Rupert's unyielding hardness – his brilliance, his discipline, his ability to focus on his work – might balance the tidal nature I had given her.

Lighthouse. Storm. Love.

I found the entrance. It was inside an eco-spacecraft welcome centre full of pencils with rubbers on the end, postcards, fudge, and CDs of wild birdsong. There was a fast track painted onto the floor – like an IKEA showroom – for Trust members. I followed the arrows, but the guardian of the gate, a sour-looking lady in a Barbour coat and Wellingtons, stopped me. She embodied what Wilkie Collins called 'that state of highly respectful sulkiness which is peculiar to English servants'.

'This is for members,' she said.

'Yes. Of course.' I showed her my green card. She peered at it. Hard.

Unable to find anything wrong with the card, the woman handed it back, then sucked in her cheeks and flicked her eyes towards the gate. I felt that she was disappointed not to be able to send me to the end of the extensive queue meandering towards the ticket desk.

I spent most of my year in Barcelona, where I communicated in the most basic Spanish. The rest of the time I lived in the Llŷn Peninsula where Welsh was spoken by seventy-five per cent of the community, but I was, so far, unable to follow it. I was protected from day-to-day grumpiness because all nuances passed me by. It was like living in a religious order that had taken a vow of silence. I was cushioned. If I did wish to communicate with any level of sophistication, it tended to be with friends or family. All other human interactions were pared to a minimum; Ockham's Razor had become a way of life. The downside of this was that when I found myself surrounded by my increasingly abrasive countrymen, and understanding every word of it, I felt as though I was missing a layer of skin.

'Thank you,' I said, smiling, and pocketed the card.

I set out across open ground, still following the IKEA-style footpath, and feeling oddly coerced, as though my freedom had been curtailed. There were more notices, they were everywhere, making suggestions regarding route or destination: *The Banquet House is now open*, and an arrow. My phone rang. Liz was in Newcastle – where was I? She was going to be another couple of hours. Time was suddenly on my side and I no longer felt obliged to hurry. But a sense of anxiety had accompanied me since I left the car. It had begun to emerge as I crossed the yellow fields, growing out of the feeling that I was lost. And now I felt put out by my interaction with the gate-keeper, who was the first person I had spoken to on this journey. It had been an interchange bereft of human kindness, and quite without welcome. It was the third time I had been alone, entirely alone, since my miscarriage. The trips to Spurn Point and to Pamela's funeral had been the others. I felt empty, my arms long and elastic. I had no one to look after, nothing to hold.

I followed the footpath downwards through a wood. Tall trees closed over me, wrapping me in green light. The air was cool. There was a quality of stillness about the place. A wood is usually crisp with sound, a place of constant movement: the gentle oscillation of the trees, the card-pack shuffle of leaves, the dry voices of twigs as they mutter and grate. There should have been a lifting cry of birds, the klaxon *haw!* of rooks, the snap and skitter of squirrels through the canopy – something to indicate the presence of the countless creatures that I knew were there. Yet there was nothing. I felt as though I were in an empty hall. The leaves rested against one another like papers on a desk. They could have been that way for years.

The footpath persisted, directing my steps. It descended to a valley and opened onto a vast manicured lawn. The River Skell curled through the lawn and past a water mill. The silence gave way to a murmur of voices, the vibrant hum of a souk. Before me was the shell of Fountains Abbey, out of all proportion to the trees among which it stood. It was like an emaciated creature trying to stand, but without enough muscle left on its bones to enable it to complete the action. The empty window at the end of the nave yawned out of the valley floor. Broken walls were capped in sky. It was something from another age – another perception – but it could as easily have been from the future as the past. I tried to imagine the abbey rising from the forest floor. The original church would have been made of timber – hand-hewn blocks of stone fitted around it, facilitated by a wooden scaffold. I wondered who had dreamed the building. How many generations of how many families had made this church their whole life's work?

A few years ago, while driving from Las Vegas to Denver, Rupert, Evie and I had stumbled across a ghost town, called

Bannack, in Montana. It had been founded in 1862. The school desks with their cast-iron fittings remained in the abandoned classroom, a blackboard was still affixed to the wall. A fragile roundabout, made of wood and metal, tilted in the playground, and we played on it. There was a grand hotel in the French style, with wood-burning stoves and a bread oven. There was a Wild West saloon bar with louvred swing-doors. Yet grass poked through the gaps in the boardwalk and filled the main street to knee height. The only sound was the ruffle of wind as it tested the blades and tousled the seed heads. The jail was a rough log cabin. The only people ever to have been executed were the Sheriff – a notorious outlaw who hoodwinked the people into electing him – and his deputies. They were hanged without trial from a gallows pole built especially for the purpose. We found this pole, lying in pieces, partially hidden amid the long grass. At first I mistook it for a telegraph pole. In its first five months Bannack was said to have produced $500,000 of gold that was ninety-five per cent pure – the equivalent of over $10,000,000 today – with a population that grew from four hundred to three thousand in the same span. But when the gold ran out the town was abandoned, almost overnight, the whorehouse and saloon silent.

Fountains Abbey was abandoned when Henry VIII dissolved the monasteries, its abbot, prior and thirty monks paid off with handsome pensions. But now it was part of a curiously polished theme park, with cafés and facilities and the heavily signposted footpath. It swarmed with people. One couple, holding hands, stared up at the carcass of the church. Then, quite suddenly, they embraced, sobbing into one another's arms, the rough bark of their cries flat against the stillness of the trees. I pulled my sunglasses down onto the bridge of my nose, conscious that I was staring. I wondered if they were descended from one of the masons who had built the church. Perhaps they were going to get married. Maybe someone had died.

There is a children's film about an articulated bin that saves the planet after pollution forces the Earth's inhabitants to go into space. In the spaceship the people become obese and diabetic, and develop osteoporosis while eating junk. But the bin, which has found a plant, brings them back, so that they can go forth and multiply, and fill up the planet once more. Only this time, one has the impression, they will be a bit more ecologically aware.

Fountains Abbey felt like a stepping stone towards such a future. The manicured footpath ensured wheelchair access and an easy passage for baby buggies. Yet its primary purpose felt like the fulfilment of a Health and Safety directive, an attempt to reduce the risk of litigation. I had never seen so many super-sized people. A young girl walked towards me, her face as glorious as an angel's. In the middle of her brow was a ridge of flesh, her smile disappearing into dimples. I imagined the size of her heart. Visitors were encouraged to shuffle along the neat path, and to stop for cake, or ice cream. None of us were encouraged – or even free – to wander at our leisure, to poke about, or climb. To sleep overnight, or to have an adventure, to camp among the cold old stones.

A tour was about to begin. A group clustered about a man who held a shepherd's crook over his head. I watched, perplexed, neither in nor out, the guide's words thrown like a net.

The community at Fountains was established in 1132. Thirteen rebellious monks, longing to live a simple life, were taken into the protection of

Archbishop Thurston of York. He granted them this valley, uninhabited, thickly overgrown and 'Fit, rather,' as the Revd. A. W. Oxford put it, 'to be the lair of wild beasts than the home of human beings.' It is a perfect place for a community – remote and secluded – protected in its wooded valley from the winds of the Yorkshire Dales. The valley was formerly known as Skelldale, from the Saxon skel, meaning spring, and Old English dael, for valley, and refers to the many springs that rise in the woods. This woodland, and the steep sandstone cliffs of the valley walls, also provided the raw materials for construction. It seems likely that the Skelldale springs originally gave the abbey its name: St Mary of Fountains. The name 'Mary' derives originally from the Hebrew, Myriam, which itself means strong water. Or it may be an allusion to the 'fountains of living water' promised by Christ to the Woman of Samaria. Three years after they arrived, in 1135, the Yorkshire monks were embraced by the Cistercian order. The abbot of the great abbey at Clairvaux at that time was called St Bernard de Fontaines, so Fountains might have been named after him, as the monks doubtless received much help from Clairvaux. The coarse white habit of the Cistercians is made from undyed fleece and, with time, and the assistance of a community of lay brothers, the monks became wool merchants, and fabulously rich, as seems to be the way with austere orders, the Franciscans being another obviously wealthy example, despite being founded on a rule of poverty. The lands of the monks at Fountains extended to the Lake District on one side, to Teesside on the other . . .

It occurred to me that if I stayed I might learn something helpful, something about the nature of sacred wells. I had been interested to learn that Myriam meant strong water. Mary, Maria, Marie, would seem to come from the Latin *mare*, meaning sea. The lines on my palms form the shape of an M and as a child I used to look at my hands, and wonder at the mystery locked in the letter. The secret reminder of my name before my adoption: *Marie*

Therese, permanent as a tattoo. But I couldn't keep still, or bear the proximity of so many people. I made my way, alone, through the ruins of the church. High up, at the apex of a window, was an angel. On the external face, in the reverse position, was a carving of a Green Man. He seemed surprised by the foliage issuing from his mouth and encircling his furrowed brow. It was as though he had meant to speak, but the alacritous vine prevented it. On the surface the message seemed clear enough. The Christian angel was on the inside of the church while the pagan deity was out in the cold. It was surprising he had survived at all. And yet the ancient gods are often near at hand. The Dagda was said to be the father of St Brigid of Kildare. Characters change their names and shift their histories, but their archetypes remain, dense with lived experience. They rise up like grains of gold, glittering, from the silt.

The guide, and his group, wandered back into earshot.

One of the first poems written in English – found carved into an Anglo-Saxon cross – is called 'The Dream of the Rood', meaning rod, or upright post. In the poem, the Rood tells how it came to be felled, separated from its fellow trees, and forced to play its part in the crucifixion. The Rood is an object of veneration because, without it, the Passion could not have taken place. The tree sang: 'They drove me through with dark nails. On me are the marks, Wide-mouthed hate dents.'

Iron into wood. A tree that sang. I wondered, vaguely, about the relationship between mystical Christianity and trees. There was an early medieval Irish/Welsh alphabet known as the ogham script, whereby each letter corresponded to a tree. St Joseph was a carpenter. And the Rood, yes, well, that was a tree. Books were made of paper. I felt I had bitten off more than I could chew, although the idea of a mutually beneficial relationship between woodland and people didn't seem far-fetched as a place to start. A very holy priest

I once knew, Father Tony Storey, planted over four thousand trees during his lifetime – rowan, hazel, oak and birch – the trees of the English forest. 'The two most important things in life,' he maintained, 'are to love, and to plant trees.'

I walked beneath the Green Man, moved beyond him. I was back on the lawn, which was clipped, like shearling fleece, for as far as the eye could see. The river had been diverted in this section of the valley and ran as straight as a zipper. The footpath passed on either side of the Skell. There was a bridge next to a ruined house. Beyond that, like a selvedge, neat woodland hemmed the valley. I crossed the river and turned back on myself, facing the way I had come, but on the opposite bank.

And then I saw it.

The prissy path, which had so irritated me, was in fact a garden footpath. The grass had been clipped because it was indeed a lawn, and the crumbling abbey a giant folly. The whole valley had been landscaped into a surreal vision: the Studley Royal Water Garden.

The river ran in a liquid avenue down the centre of a formal garden in the neoclassical style. At the end of the valley it was dammed into a bean-shaped pool. I felt like a pantomime character to whom the audience had been shouting: *It's behind you!* The cupola of a temple was visible above the trees. I abandoned the church and the abbey buildings and followed the river – or rather the canal – downstream. It was swollen and brown, spotted like a seal. On either bank a tidemark of sweet wrappers, bottles, cans, leaves and grass cuttings marked the place where the river had flooded – a Hansel and Gretel trail – parallel to the water's edge. The greensward, which ordinarily should have been the bank, veered out of sight beneath the water. A slow-moving scum covered the surface and I thought of Maxpax hot chocolate, a powdered drink popular in the 1980s that always came out watery, the dried milk never quite dissolving but floating in viscous bubbles. The footpath on my side curved away from the river, passing into woodland. People crowded the opposite bank. I contemplated cutting through the wood to the furthest extent of the garden, where I might be able to cross the river, and then walk back, on the other side, beyond the surging people. But I seemed incapable of leaving the Skell. I hugged its shore, as though following an invalid, waiting for someone to fall. Two blond children played on the far side. They threw sticks into the water. One of the sticks was sucked under the surface, disappearing into a scummy whirlpool. My anxiety followed it, dipping like a mallard, and reappeared, all but unseen, downstream.

When the river opened out onto the bean-shaped lake, it became apparent I was in the wrong place. The bank was wet, and slippery. I made muddy prints as I circumvented the water, windmilling my arms in an attempt to remain upright, the soft mud beneath the grass deceitful as ice. After a while I came to a bridge, and joined the proper path. The river-canal, as it left the lake, was ruler-straight. A right-angled bend afforded a glimpse of further pools, but the footpath again forsook the bank for the trees, and this time I followed it. A bird, as big as a pheasant, but bald-looking, crossed my path. And then two more — the first wildlife I had seen — but they weren't like any bird I knew. A tree rose above me, tall, very tall, a Scots Pine. I thought of Winnie-the-Pooh, and Christopher Robin, and the bees.

I had met a man over the summer, on Porth Dinllaen beach, who told me his father once had an affair, and that a child had been born of it. This child had been adopted. It was a little boy, and he was never named. The man and his brothers and sisters knew him only as Christopher Robin. The man's sister had left a message on the Adoption Contact Register and this said, quite simply: *Searching for Christopher Robin.* But if he had never been named, how would he know that it was him?

In Ireland Brian had asked me if I had ever found my natural father. All I knew him by was the hyphen on my birth certificate. In order to learn his name I needed first to locate my mother. Over many years my searches had turned up nothing, beyond the date and place of her wedding. I had made that discovery after hours spent riffling though the marriage records in St Catherine's House, in London. But after that initial, hasty victory, the trail ran cold. My searches were sporadic. For the most part I didn't think of it, but from time to time I would find myself looking. In the 1980s I leafed through phone books, in later years I scanned the electoral register. For a while I had been employed as a professional researcher, and had access to a number of databases. But there was never a note for me, or a message from a private detective, although I left messages for her, in all the obvious places – the Adoption Contact Register, and also in some of the less obvious ones – with the current owners of the farm that had been given on her marriage certificate as her home address. In 1792 Georgiana, Duchess of Devonshire, was forced by protocol – for which she didn't much care – and her husband, who told her that he'd prevent her from setting eyes on her legitimate children ever again if she didn't cooperate with his demands, to give up the baby daughter she had borne to the future Prime Minister, Charles Gray. The child, Eliza, was raised by Charles Gray's family. Georgiana visited her daughter in secret whenever she could, and gave her small gifts, although she never revealed her identity or was able to give her money. The Cavendish family later destroyed many of Georgiana's letters, embarrassed by the scandal confirmed in them. But a poem made its way into Eliza's effects. It ended:

> ... *should th' ungenerous world upbraid thee*
> *For mine and for thy father's ill*
> *A nameless mother oft shall assist thee*
> *A hand unseen protect thee still.*

I reached my own hand towards the tree, aware of a pain between my eyebrows, an aching heat behind my eyes. A flat weight, hard as a coin, pushed into my sternum. It is a common theme in the stories of displaced children that their absent parent thinks of them, that they somehow continue to care for them, and keep a flame burning through the years of separation. The Greek myths are full of tales of gods who softened the paths of their demi-god children, who in turn grew into heroes: Theseus, Perseus, Achilles, Helen of Troy. When I was a child Mum told me that my birth mother had been unable to keep me, but that she loved me, and that she had done the very best she could by me. In which case, why had she never contacted me? I was fighting to control my breath, to smooth the contours of my face, but I couldn't. So I sat on a low wall at the edge of the manicured path, and wept for all that Christopher Robin means.

On the other side of the wood, the footpath rejoined the canal. Ahead was a sort of aquatic ha-ha, which must once have been a waterfall, but about ten yards short of it the river had been diverted.

The naked mechanism of the man-made watercourse was visible, the paved and slimy riverbed, the sluice gates, and the iron wheel that moved them. I thought momentarily of a mechanic's garage, a car raised up, the unexpected aspect of the vehicle's workings, and was taken aback by the crack in the façade, the realisation of impermanence, and artifice.

I crossed the empty riverbed at the place where the waterfall had been. A lake was to my left, inhabited by nodding swans; there was a café, but I wanted nothing. I continued to follow the riverbank and passed beneath a bough of yellow honeysuckle, shot with indigo, the petals curled like fingers or little traps, the glossy stamens sore. They were the first flowers I had seen in the garden, but I didn't stop. I regretted it immediately, and went back. The scent was hardly discernible in the dying flowers, but the piquant rot of an early autumn gave an unexpected subtlety. The impression of colour, of lightness, was instant.

Suddenly I saw beauty. A child shook his bag of sweets for the sheer pleasure of hearing the sound. And because it confirmed that the contents were still there. And still his. I stopped worrying about why the English ate so much, and acknowledged that I was starving. The footpath opened onto a round pool, separated by a pea-green walkway from other, crescent-shaped pools. The water was tea-coloured. A pink temple, fronted by Doric columns, knelt above its own immaculate reflection in the gold August sunlight. A statue of Neptune rose before the temple, trident in hand, his face turned away, his gaze angled along his cheekbones. I felt as though I had stumbled upon some intimacy, that my appearance had somehow disturbed the god. I imagined those who were here before me, long ago, now long dead. This was a place for laughter, lovers, whispered trysts.

There was a shifting movement through the trees, a blown warmth, soft as a kiss. I stood still, and looked about me, not sure what I expected to see. The surface of the tea-coloured lake wrinkled; the immaculate reflection scattered. But just as quickly as it had appeared, the pocket of warm air passed by. The water settled. The reflection began to piece itself together. A hush rolled over the woodland.

Tummel

Ten-year-old Dexter sat on the floor outside the bathroom while I lay in a claw-footed bath. My big toe was wedged inside the tap, hot water funnelled round it. I twirled a champagne flute between finger and thumb, and watched it mist and clear. Steam rolled in bales about the panelled walls, the wood forming a buffer against the cold stone beneath.

'Kate?' The voice came from the other side of the bathroom door, below the level of the doorknob.

'Hello, Dexter.'

'Are you all right?'

'I'm fine, darling. Are you?'

'Is there anything I can get you?'

'No. Thank you. You don't have to sit outside, Dex. I'll come down very soon.'

'You're all right . . . I'm OK here.'

Later the three boys quizzed me while their father, Chris, made supper. Liz and I sat opposite one another at the kitchen table, working our way down the rest of the bottle of champagne.

'Where are you going?' asked Angus.

'I'm going to follow a river.'

'Which river?' said Elliot.

'It's called the Dunbeath Water.'

'Will we see you again?' asked Dexter.

'Yes. I'll come back this way.'

In spite of living just inside the Scottish border, none of the boys had been to the Interior, as they called it. They told me it was full of mountains, forests and lochs. There was a lot of golf. And it rained – all the time.

'Where are you going to sleep?'

The next morning Liz and the boys heaped me with gifts. There was a well on their land and Elliot, the oldest boy, brought me eighteen litres of spring water. Dexter and Angus made me sandwiches. I didn't see Chris. He was up at the farm, harvesting. As I got into the car Liz leaned in with a half-full bottle of Rioja that we had opened the night before.

'You might want this in your hip flask,' she said. At the end of the drive I turned and looked back at the house. The three boys waved to me from the upstairs windows, their bare feet dangling beneath blond sandstone sills.

The Forth Bridge was exciting. The fields and hills of Scotland unrolled like a rope of silken handkerchiefs tugged from a magician's sleeve. I had reached the A9 that wound from Perth to Wick. All I had to do was follow it and I would come to Dunbeath. After a couple of hours the road, which had been hugging a river, took me through a town. A sign read: *Pitlochry Welcomes You In Blood*. It seemed very visceral. And then I realised that the sign said: *In*

Bloom, and referred to the baskets of flowers that lined the streets and hung from lamp-posts along the riverbank. There was a Fish Ladder marked on my map. Incongruous images flourished in the space between the otherwise familiar words. I parked the car and walked down to the riverbank.

The water was fast-flowing, shallow, pebbled. Dark trees reached from either bank as though attempting to touch. The air smelled of wet leaves. I could taste malt. A distillery was on the other side of the river. I was slightly hung-over from the champagne and Rioja that I had drunk with Liz the previous night, and the fumes from the distillery triggered waves of nausea. I began to walk in the direction of the fish ladder. I had an image in my head of utilitarian tanks, rising in even steps, industrialised and smooth, each filled with glittering salmon, bright as aluminium. I envisaged the fish leaping up through perfect waterfalls alongside a shining dam.

The reality was different. The fish ladder was indeed comprised of concrete tanks, thirty-four of them, and they did rise in uniform shallow steps. But they were blackened with moss and slime. The water screamed and boiled. Signs warned of: *Strong undercurrents, Danger of drowning, Water level may increase significantly at any time.* Some of the tanks were larger than others, resting places for the fish. One of the tanks contained a viewing chamber. It was a dingy room, dripping and cold. I thought of submarines. The sound of the water was all around me. A wall of thickened glass opened into the tank but it was grimed over on the inside, the interior difficult to make out. A chute about the width of a barrel funnelled water from the tank above. A second chute exited on the other side. A fallen branch turned and span, buffeted by the flow; trapped in a cycle, it would remain there until the waters broke it. I felt sick. There were no fish in the chamber.

Dad had been an engineer. If he had been here today he would have explained what we were looking at, described the fluid mechanics of the tank. He could have lifted away the fear that clung to me in wisps. Dad would have found the viewing chamber wonderful. And also the dam that was behind it. I imagined him chuckling at the simplicity of a vision that gave electricity to thousands of homes by the simple act of bricking up a stream. It was like a halter thrown over the head of a horse. As for the fish, displaced by the illumination of the Highlands? Well, of course, they must be helped. The fish ladder was an engineer's dream.

I turned away from the viewing chamber. The hydro-electric power station was between the fish ladder and the dam. In front of me a section of the river had been fenced across to stop debris from being drawn into the turbines. A man with iron-grey hair in a blue woolly jumper was looking over the metal rail, and he was pointing to something in the water. I realised he was speaking to me.

'Sorry?' I said.

'They'll not turn against the flow.' He was talking about the salmon. 'If they slip through these rails they get trapped.' They were young fish, mostly, he told me, coming back after just one winter at sea. Or cock fish, slimmer than the spawn-packed hens.

I looked down. There was a salmon. Every so often it jumped, its head black against the slate-coloured water, its grey eye cold as a pearl.

'Why's it black?' I asked him.

'The longer the salmon are in fresh water, the darker they get. The silver colour you get at the supermarket is caused by something called guanine; crystals laid down beneath their scales. It protects them while they're at sea.'The salmon also had a breeding livery, he told me, of russet and gold.The few that survived and returned to the sea were known as black salmon, or kelts, yet they began to change colour as soon as they left the breeding grounds, swiftly rebuilding the armour that would shield them from the corrosion of the salt. It was mostly females who survived; as soon as they had spawned they turned, ravenous. Salmon rarely ate on their upward journey. Even so, only around one in five of them would return to the sea. But the males stayed in the high pools, fighting among themselves, seeking out fresh females until their lives were spent.

The man told me that his job today was to free the fish that were caught in the turbine pool, to open the gates in the metal grille, and try to flush them out.The thin black salmon leapt again. I studied it for a while.

The Celts believed the salmon had all come from a well.The same well Boand provoked by walking around it widdershins. Nine hazel trees encircled it; their fruit contained all knowledge. As the hazelnuts ripened and dropped into the water the salmon that lived there ate them. As a result of this they embodied all the wisdom of the world.

When the well rose up, and Boand drowned, the salmon were washed out to sea. Not one of them remained.To this day they are trying to return.The spots on a salmon's back tell the number of hazelnuts it has eaten. Not all salmon are wise. But if you can catch one, and roast it, then the first three drops of spitting fat will confer all the knowledge in the fish. The rest, alas, is poison. One of the best-known versions of the story is that of the Irish hero, Fionn mac Cumhaill.

Fionn, which means the Fair One, was a young man, and hungry, and wandering in the forests near the River Boyne. A Druid, called Finegas, known as Finn the Seer, had waited seven years to catch a salmon. That afternoon he had succeeded, and was roasting it on a spit. He saw Fionn, and asked him to oversee the cooking, making sure not to eat any of it, while he went to attend to something else. But three drops of fat spat from under the crispy skin and landed on Fionn's thumb. He put the injured digit into his mouth, and acquired all the knowledge of the world. He carried the salmon to Finegas who immediately noticed something different. There was a brightness to the boy, an alacrity, that hadn't been there before.

'Have you eaten of the fish? the Druid asked.

'Well, no,' said Fionn, 'but I did burn my thumb and I put it straight away into my mouth.'

'Ah,' said the bard, 'then the knowledge is yours.' He handed the fish back. From that time on, if Fionn had a problem, all he had to do was suck his thumb and the answer would present itself. The Druid explained to Fionn that the knowledge always found its way to the one most deserving of it. For his own part, he would wait another seven years, and try again.

I walked towards the power station. There was a museum that told the story of the fish ladder, and a cool humming room that housed the turbines. The first fish ladder had been designed, and patented, by a miller called Richard McFarlan, in New Brunswick, in 1837. He had designed the ladder to circumvent the dam at his water mill. The museum also told the story of the electrification of the Highlands. I tried to picture the workers, the men who had come from all over Europe, in the strange, disjointed months and years after the Second World War had ended, to dam the River Tummel and raise the loch behind it. I sensed the caress of rough cotton shirts, and fabric stiff with sweat. The blistering pinch of hobnailed boots. Scratchy trousers, lice and wool, dirt and ice, the cracked-bell ring of a pickaxe.

On the tiled exterior wall was a bronze memorial relief of a kindly, but sad-looking man. The portrait was executed in profile and the artist had shown no mercy in depicting both the softness beneath his chin and the almost monastic severity of his pate. An unpunctuated script read:

SIR EDWARD MACCOLL 1882–1951
ENGINEER AND PIONEER HYDRO-ELECTRICITY
SCOTLAND

It was a muted dedication: nine words, two dates, no frills. But the dam spoke. The nine dams of the Tummel Valley Hydro-Electric Scheme. One for each word of his epitaph. It seemed that MacColl had died just before the opening of the Pitlochry Station, and instead of a party with bunting, and a band, and tea and cakes, there had been the respectful unveiling of this monument.

I felt I should move on. I walked back through nodding trees to the car. After a very few miles I saw a sign for the village of Killecrankie. We used to come to Scotland, Mum, Dad and my brother, for two weeks every summer, when we met up with my grandparents, aunts, uncles and cousins. One year we had visited the grave of one of Dad's graduate students. I seemed to recall this being in Killecrankie; but when I got to the village the cemetery was unfamiliar, so I called at the local Heritage Centre, thinking I might ask if there was a second cemetery. But the staff all came from Eastern Europe. Not one of them knew the village, other than as a bus stop on their way to work. I passed a café. A conversation in the kitchen caught my attention. Two ladies, well into their middle years, were in loud and animated discourse with a young man. He was tall, and slim, with black hair and liquid eyes. Neither of the women reached higher than his shoulder. From a string about his neck hung a spiral-bound notepad with a pen pushed through the wire. His hands moved with grace and precision creating pictures, like charades. I realised that he could not hear, although he could lip-read, and that they could not sign. When the women were unable to understand his mime the young man wrote, instead, and the ladies, one at each of his elbows, peered down at the notepad. He caught me looking, and I felt invasive but he grinned, curling his fingers around the idea of a cup and then lifting it briefly towards his mouth. I nodded.

When he came over to my table I told him I was looking for a cemetery, and I described the jigsaw bits of memory I had retained. The cemetery was down a long straight track. It formed a perfect square, and was flanked by trees. I couldn't remember if there was a church. The young man nodded and opened the notepad, and put it next to me on the table. He drew a square, filled it with crosses, then drew two huge trees and a straight road that ran up the centre. 'Yes, that's it.' He wrote: *Blair Atholl*.

In less than half an hour I had found it.

I walked along the track, which separated fields full of bullocks. I passed beneath the sheltering trees, which had now grown vast. The track had been grass in my memory, but had now been tarmacked over. A stream chirruped along one wall, a wood closed off the back. I hadn't remembered the cemetery being so close to the road.

Iain MacMartin was killed, very early one morning, in a motorcycle accident, while returning to the university after the Easter holiday. He was working towards the completion of his doctoral thesis. Although it was over thirty years ago his sister, Miss MacMartin, still wrote to Mum each Christmas. I knew I was in the right place. I remembered Miss MacMartin telling us that the coffin had been carried on a grocer's cart. This detail had seemed important at the time, as though the young man had been transported on a gun carriage. There had been a piper. It was only a small place, and I began systematically to search the headstones. But, try as I might, I could not find his name.

A fine rain began to fall, and I was aware of the lightness of its touch. I recalled having my face washed as a child, the softness of the cloth, the gentleness of the hands, yet here was no kindness, no unkindness; the caress without feeling or intention. A brown buzzard eyed me from the adjacent field. It shifted from a gatepost to the grass, before lifting away, peevish.

Iain MacMartin. I looked everywhere, searched every headstone, searched again. There were Robertses, Robertsons, McFarlanes, Macfarlanes, Shantos. I observed how connected many of the names were. I thought of Robert Macfarlane, and his book, *The Wild Places*. It was Robert who first told me of *The Well at the World's End* and introduced me to the writing of Neil Gunn. I thought about Richard McFarlan of New Brunswick, who had patented a fish ladder in 1837. I became intrigued by the idea that one might come from somewhere. Or perhaps, rather, that one might know where that somewhere is. All around me, lying side by side, were kinsmen. A field of them.

★

Rupert and I had been together for twelve years before Evie was born. A surgical investigation revealed the architecture of my Fallopian tubes to be imperfect. I might fall pregnant naturally, but it was really very unlikely. If I were to have *in vitro* fertilisation, then the obstacle presented by the damaged tubes would be bypassed. We met with a fertility specialist. The benefits of IVF were obvious: we might have a child. But the disadvantages, too, were concrete: it was expensive both financially and emotionally. It would take up a lot of our time, possibly over several years. There was a significantly increased risk of cancer in women who received the treatment relative to those who did not. Whether this increased risk was connected to the reasons for referral in the first place, or whether it increased as a result of the treatment itself, was not clear. After a while the doctor asked us if we would consider adoption. Well, yes, I said, adoption was a possibility. But I was an adopted child myself. Whenever a baby was born, or a family idio-syncrasy discussed, or if an old photograph came to light, then I had always stepped back – by which I meant that I would get up and move – deliberately maintaining a respectful distance from what I perceived to be the genetic hum in the room. I had done it since my earliest childhood. If I didn't move fast enough then there would always be someone who could, and generally did, point out the impossibility of the baby, or great-aunt, or whoever it was, ever looking like me, or me like them. What for others might be a moment of shared history was, for me, an ongoing reminder of my charity status.

My grandmother used to fascinate me with the stories of Dad's ancestors. Of Faithful Norbury, the sixteenth-century groom, who was 'elevated beyond his station to his mistress's bed', which gave a whole new slant to the family motto: *Regi Et*

Patriae Fidelis. Of William Norbury, converted from the liquor to Methodism by John Wesley himself, who then paced the county for the next forty years with a suitcase of sermons written in minute cursive script and carried by a 'half-wit lad', who had never been known to leave his side. Or of Roger de Bulkeley who had changed his name to that of his Shropshire land: *Norbury*, meaning a northern town or fortification. Genealogy allows us to construct our identities from our own myths and legends, to know who we are, and where we have come from. Or we can use the stories as a starting point for where we might like to go, a legacy to be built on or rebelled against. Sara Maitland describes the tradition of storytelling as 'a very fundamental human attribute, to the extent that psychiatry now often treats "narrative loss" – the inability to construct a story of one's own life – as a loss of identity or personhood.' The stories I had inherited were fascinating, but they weren't mine. I had never met anyone who shared my blood, or who looked like me. There was no genetic starting point from which I could begin my narrative. I didn't even know my nationality.

In answer to the doctor's question, then: I didn't, in the first instance, want to adopt a child, because I was lonely. Not superficially so, not lacking in friends or loved ones. Cosmically. I felt, I had always felt, dizzyingly adrift. I realised that this might be regarded as a poetic conceit, or even a form of vanity, but it also happened to be true.

The doctor then told us that when he was a little boy his own father – a GP – had abandoned his mother, abandoned both of them. The word *divorce* was never mentioned, at any rate he had no recollection of hearing it, and his mother did not remarry. Each birthday and Christmas a present arrived, purporting to be from his father, but the doctor recognised the writing on the package to be that of his mother. Even as an adult he could not bring himself to discuss the subject with her. Shortly after his mother died an aunt had contacted him. She told him that his father was buried in the graveyard of St Mary's Priory in Abergavenny. The doctor was unable to describe his feelings in that place. He realised that he had followed in his father's footsteps, and had clung to what little he knew of him – his profession. Our doctor had facilitated the conception of hundreds of children – their photographs covered the wall behind him. He had four daughters of his own, and several grandchildren. He said: 'I am personally acquainted with the loneliness of which you speak. In my own way, I have sought to fill the void.' He had noticed that a disproportionately large number of people who were adopted, relative to the normal population, presented themselves for fertility treatment. In other words, either adoptees with impaired fertility had a greater desire to create a child of their own than non-adopted people in the same circumstance, or adopted people were proportionally more likely to encounter difficulties conceiving than the non-adopted population. He had even written a paper on the relationship between unexplained infertility and shame, in which shame might be defined as the sense that one is different from other people and therefore, at some level, *not right*, and not worthy to continue one's line, in a very literal, physical, way. This perception, of being different, was sufficient, he believed, to explain infertility. The American psychologist Nancy Verrier has written about the way in which the brains of children who have suffered separation trauma might differ from those of children who have not. Others refer to 'attachment disorders' and these are both, perhaps, ways of describing what the fertility doctor had observed. Adoptees inherit a complex legacy.

Returning to this graveyard, to this wet afternoon, it seemed fitting, or at least ironic, that I who came from nowhere that I knew of – before the Convent – was unable to find the one person I was looking for, and even that was someone – no longer living – who I'd never known in life. I wondered if I had misremembered his name, Iain MacMartin, and if it was an Anglicisation from the Gaelic. Or if it perhaps referred to the little blue bird, the martin, the one with such a long migratory path.

> *Where trouble melts like lemon drops*
> *High above the chimney tops*
> *That's where you'll find me . . .*

The words of 'Over The Rainbow' began to revolve, in unexpected spirals, inside my head. They were accompanied, like the hiss of an old 45, by the drip and crackle of the rain.

> *And the dreams that you dare to . . .*
> *Why, oh why, can't I?*

One of the graves was marked by a wedge of granite. There was no name. It was flanked by two jam-jars of freshly pulled heather, tight clusters of magenta bells. It was a wild place, made tame. I stopped and crouched down next to it and for those few moments drew my dead about me, my own lovely darlings, those whose arms had enfolded me, those small enough to hold in the palm of my hand – Dad, Pamela, my lost baby. Neither Dad nor my miscarried child had a grave that I might visit. Pamela had been buried, but I arrived too late to visit the churchyard. The following morning I had left, in a rainstorm, and though I had driven past the cemetery where Pamela was lying, I had been too afraid to stop. I didn't want to look at the flowers, and the mud, and know that she was under them.

The rain in this Highland cemetery was becoming heavier. It found a way inside my collar, down my sleeves, it flattened my hair against my skull and in wet curls against my neck. I carried my dead in a net, a clattering catch of bones, of promise, of might-have-been. I knew that I had to leave them, free them, free myself. Yet something was interfering with the resolution of my grief, complicating it. Dad had been dead for almost eight years. I felt as I had the day I accidentally found the Convent where I had been born, as though there was a truth, close by, if I could but see it. But the beginner's luck that graced me then had gone. I could perceive this truth in the flickering landscape, like watching television without an aerial, an incandescent image beneath the cloak of rain; but I was either looking too hard, or not hard enough. In part I had not been honest. I did not begin this journey on behalf of Sofia, the girlfriend to whom I gave my copy of *The Well at the World's End*. I came here because I wanted to. There was no other reason. But I couldn't understand what motivated me on my not quite random, yet only loosely guided, path. I turned away from the unmarked granite and as I did so four words, cut into a nearby stone, caught my eye: *Glad did I live*. I was puzzled by the brevity, the baldness of the statement. The inscription felt like a gauntlet, a challenge, requiring something from me.

Early on the last day of Dad's life, I had gone into the room where he was lying. Outside, a Japanese maple tree flapped, ragged, in the wind. I had looked at the scarlet, tenacious leaves, wanting to point them out to Dad. Then realised it was too late. There would be no more trees. I rested my head on his chest. He appeared to be unconscious, and yet I could sense his anxiety, a steady fizzing below his skin, beneath his ribs, at his core.

'Dad?' I ran my fingers over his, put my mouth close to his ear. 'Remember . . . The first law of thermodynamics states that energy cannot be destroyed. Or created. It can only change its form.' I watched his face: it was opaque as alabaster in an unlit room, the deep cold already separating us, drawing us further apart. For all intents and purposes, Dad was in a coma. And yet, in spite of this, he smiled.

Glad did I live.

Newton's first law, of which Dad was also fond, states that an object will remain in a state either of rest, or of uniform motion in a straight line, unless compelled to change by the action of an external force. For me to be able to look back on my life, and to know those four words to have been true, I had to alter my course.

Garry

For the rest of the afternoon I travelled ahead of the weather, the A9 before me, companioned by the River Garry. The dark sleepers of a railway line were laid out as neat as pickets. All three paths – road, rail and river – ran in parallel across the plain that divided the Am Monadh Liath, the grey hills, from the Am Monadh Ruadh, the red hills – the Cairngorms.

The previous night, at Liz's house, I had toyed with the idea of abandoning the journey to Dunbeath. It was still a day's drive away. I had lingered over a map of this plain, looking for a river that might replace the Dunbeath Water. The River Garry was a tributary of the Tummel, which was itself a tributary of the Tay. It had its source in Loch Garry, which in turn was fed by three other rivers. Strictly speaking the Garry didn't run from the sea to a source, but rather it formed a part of such a journey. The River Spey did travel from the sea to its source, Loch Spey in the Corrieyairack Forest, and it also ran across this plain. This new idea was tempting. I had a connection with the River Spey, because we used to holiday next to it when I was a child. I had even caught my first fish in it. However, I was already many miles inland, the Spey ran alongside a road for much of its length, and I wanted to walk from a river mouth. Also, the idea of actually reaching Dunbeath was becoming concrete. I found I couldn't even look at the surrounding hills because I did not wish, as the result of an accidental glance, to develop an idea that might divert me from my intention. I was well aware that I could spend happy hours, if not days, in the Cairngorms. So I kept my eyes at the level of the road, and glanced only occasionally at the river. But at the turn-off to the village of Dalwhinnie, I noticed some buildings, small as matchboxes. Beyond them the mountains rose in lilac slopes.

I stopped the car in a lay-by and got out. I leaned on the boot and listened to the *clatter-clatter-clatter* of a magpie. I watched it lift up and then alight behind each car that passed, picking at something red and furry that was mashed into the tarmac. Overhead, clouds were combed out like wet hair. Rain covered the western side of the plain like plastic sheeting, sealing off the direction I had come from. The weather front that encompassed me in Blair Atholl was getting nearer. I had no map and no adequate protection from the elements.

I had another reason for wanting to continue my journey, beyond these practical considerations. I wanted, just for once, to complete something I had started. My life was cluttered with abandoned projects: degree courses, film scripts, houses, journeys. My head was noisy with unanswered, or only half-formed, questions.

I had made a reservation at a hotel in Grantown-on-Spey. From Grantown it was a just few hours' drive to Dunbeath. I got back into the car.

Spey

A buzzard perched on the *Welcome* sign in the small Highland
town of Grantown-on-Spey, its head angled down and
sideways. Its eye peered into my own, a bright pulse of
contact as I drove by. My reservation was at the same hotel where
our family used to holiday each summer, although it was decades
since I had been there. We had first returned to Grantown because
my brother John, aged fifteen, had won a local golf tournament,
and Dad thought he should have the chance to defend his title.
After that we just came back because we liked it. After meandering
up and down the side roads, running parallel to the main street, I
eventually found the Springfield Lodge Hotel.

Its wide gravel drive had given way to a car park, with white
lines painted onto pitted asphalt. There had been a croquet lawn at
the back of the hotel, with bent rusted hoops, but this, too, had
disappeared, beneath a development of executive homes. Previously
the grounds had felt exotic, in a *Secret Garden* kind of way, with
clipped yew hedges and rhododendrons. Now the place had a
hunched, suburban feel, and the word *conference* formed in my

mind. But for the most part the house was familiar to me. I walked through a set of double doors to see a walnut writing desk. I recognised the Victorian glass display case that still housed a – possibly depleted – collection of hand-tied fishing flies. Watery sunshine reached the lobby through the open doors of adjoining rooms, and the half-lit fishing flies bristled, iridescent, over their hooks.

I had often wondered how fishing flies worked. The man I had met at the power station in Pitlochry had told me that returning salmon starved themselves, sustained only by the fat of their sea-years. So why then would they be attracted by a fly? Perhaps it was a reflex that made them snap at the disturbed water surface. Or maybe the flies that fell into the river didn't count as eating, too few and far between to constitute a meal. Perhaps the fishing fly was the salmons' last temptation, a pretty feathered demon with a curved steel tail, complete with a vicious barb. Its sole purpose to distract them, perhaps fatally, from their journey upstream. As a child I used to watch the goldfish in our garden pond use their mouths like hands, to examine anything that was of interest to them. Possibly salmon took the fly in order to discover what it was. I had placed my own hands on the glass case but lifted them, suddenly conscious of my fingerprints, when I realised that a woman was staring at me.

'Can I help you?' she asked.

'Yes, thank you, I have a reservation,' and I gave her my name. The woman peered at the computer screen in front of her. She seemed slightly puzzled.

'Is everything all right?'

'I'm not sure,' she said. 'I have you down for tonight and for two days hence but not tomorrow. Is that right?'

'Yes,' I said, 'I will be spending tomorrow night outside.' I told her about my plan to follow the Dunbeath Water to its source.

'My goodness! Do you want me to hold the room for you? It's forecast rain.'

'No. Thank you.' I would need to check out early though. I asked the woman if I could have breakfast at seven. She smiled, and held a key towards me.

'You can. Good luck if I don't see you in the morning. Callum will take your bag to your room.'

I couldn't see anyone who might have been Callum so I picked up my holdall and made for the stairs. I thought about asking the woman if she knew who had made the fishing flies, but she was peering closely at the computer screen. Its milky reflection shone in her spectacles.

The hotel had seemed vast in my recollection, but was in fact no more than two floors of rather grand rooms beneath an attic of smaller bedrooms which our extended family of grandparents, parents, aunts, uncles and cousins, together with me and my brother, must pretty well have filled. The only other guest I remembered was Mr Kenneth Yields, an angler who always took his holiday in the same fortnight as us. Mr Yields had helped me land my first brown trout, when I was eight, which the kitchen staff had cooked for breakfast. My brother had eaten it while I watched on, preferring the hotel's thin, brittle toast and hand-curled butter.

The staircase ascended between landings of polished wood with well-worn carpet runners. A row of heavy white-painted doors, the numbers stencilled in black gloss, opened onto the stairwell on each of the first two floors. My own room was at the top of the house. I put my bag inside the door and went back down the stairs. I still hadn't bought an Ordnance Survey map for tomorrow's journey. I also wanted a bivouac bag, which was a weatherproof cover for my sleeping bag. The shops would be closing in less than an hour.

There was nowhere in Grantown that had what I wanted, so I drove back to Aviemore, fifteen minutes away. In Blacks they had not heard of a bivouac bag, *a what?* And I was surprised, and also worried by this, because I hadn't brought a tent. But in the last shop I entered, pushing past the proprietor as he turned the card in the window, I found what I was looking for. The man didn't seem to mind about the time.

'Now,' I asked, 'do you sell maps?'

'I do,' he said. 'Where are you looking for?'

'Dunbeath, in Caithness. I want to follow the river there to its source, so I need a map with all of it on.' He found a map of Dunbeath and opened it out so we could check it had the river on it. I had been driving all day, and I needed glasses, but my first impression was that most of the page was blank. I thought perhaps some of the colours hadn't come out.

'Do you mind if we move it closer to the window?' I asked. The shopkeeper carried it as though it were an origami swan's nest and laid it in a rectangle of sunlight. This initially bleached the paper further, but my eyes were becoming accustomed to the whiteness. It was the right map.

At one corner of the sheet was a wedge of blue: the sea. Along the coast ran the A9, long and lovely, and pink as bitten candyfloss. The fishing town of Dunbeath was there, and the knotty blue squiggle of the river. To begin with there were woods on either side of the strath, a few buildings, some ruins – *Old Sheilings, Burnt Mound, Standing Stone*. But that was all. Much further north there was a forest, in green, and some terracotta web-like contours. The white areas must have been moorland, and yes, there were blue tufts, hard to see and discreet as fallen eyelashes. It was a bog. As the contours snagged together where the land began to rise I made out clusters of blue spots, half the size of sequins and as random as spattered ink, and the words *dubh lochs*.

'What are dubh lochs?' I asked.

'Black water,' said the shopkeeper. I had no idea what he was talking about. 'Sometimes they are only a few feet across but the waterhead is like a sponge, it's full of holes. Stay away from them, and use a stick to measure depth, even if it looks like a puddle.'

I felt a flicker of fear behind my pubic bone as though an oil-lamp, containing my essence, had been knocked.

'It's all right,' I said, 'I'm going to be following the river.'

I traced the blue line as it coiled and bent over the folds in the page, through the slowly rising landscape. As it wound higher it was joined by tributaries. When that happened its pathway grew deceptive, labyrinthine, the lines of water as evenly balanced as fingers on hands, so that it was not clear which stream led to the source. There was no loch, no thumbnail oval, just a petering out among the scattered pools in a frightening lonely emptiness. Had I seen the map two months ago, when I began my journey north, I would never have come this far. I wasn't certain whether the new knowledge was an advantage, or if I would have been better driving to Dunbeath without a map and simply following the water. I hoped that when I found the place where the tributaries joined the river that the right path would become apparent to me. The shopkeeper had been kind, but he wanted to go home. I thanked him and left with the map and the survival bag, and headed back to Grantown-on-Spey.

Woodland pressed almost to the heart of Grantown. Beyond these woods was the river. As there were still a couple of hours before supper I decided to walk down to the Spey. A sign directed me to a footpath, curtained on either side in green-black firs, so that I had the sense of being in a corridor. After a while the trees became more spaced and in the lighter places the needle-deep ground choked into life. The summer bilberries had gone, the blackberries were not yet ripe. Gold lichen tufted quartz boulders stained to copper by the peaty soil. Toadstools pushed through moss. The forest scent was pungent; a soft sweet churchy resin over mushroom over mulch. Falling leaves drifted like confetti through the trees, the first messengers of a change in air pressure, the front that I had remained ahead of, yet had followed me all day long.

My memory of the river was of smooth black water travelling between green banks, the fish clearing the water in deep pools below the bridge. There had been occasional sandy coves, child-sized beaches, where I had constructed dams and captured elvers to use as bait. My eel-trap had been a wine bottle with a hole drilled in the bottom, a piece of Mum's nylon stocking stretched over the neck. I would lay the bottle among the gravel of the shallows in the path taken by the elvers. A piece of bacon fat lured them through the hole in the base and, because they only swam in one direction, they became trapped against the stocking at the top. I never did have the heart to put a hook through them. Each one was returned to the river, but not before I had stared at them for the longest time. The smoky bottle of undulating eels was as fascinating and mysterious as Aladdin's magic lamp. But as I came out of the woods on this August afternoon I was greeted by a swollen, opaque, drowning river, matted with daisy-filled weeds. It was an Ophelia river that heaved against heavy, muddied banks. I remembered the debris that had littered the submerged banks of the River Skell, and the water churning through the tanks of the fish ladder at Pitlochry. I realised, finally, that I was looking at the work of weeks of rain. It was so strange, after spending the summer in the sun, on the Llŷn Peninsula, which had been safe within its own microclimate. Tales of floods throughout the country, and newspapers showing ducks swimming under deckchairs had reached us, on our Welsh beach, but had felt unlikely, queer as fairy tales.

I tried to find the place where I had caught my first trout. I was seven years younger than my brother, and was often left behind when he and my cousins, who were all of a similar age, went on expeditions. Sometimes, Mr Yields would take me fishing. I recalled, at the end of one such afternoon, my auntie Marge making her way towards the water's edge in a PVC cream mac, approaching warily, yet sassily, in inappropriate heels, her smile a vermilion streak, her unnecessary sunglasses glinting in the pale light. Mum and her sister Marge shared Scottish/Welsh descent. Mum was the Scot, with the light brown hair and soft blue eyes of her grandmother. Mum was gentle, her features delicate, finely boned. She was at home on the moors, in the mountains, outside. My aunt was tall, yet voluptuous, with raven hair, and took after her great-grandfather, a Welshman called Ifan Evans. I felt certain I had seen a photograph of Marge as a young girl wearing a tall Welsh hat, a wool shawl pulled tight around her shoulders. But by the 1970s she was most at ease with a cocktail in her hand, fingers curved around a highball glass, her nails signalling red for danger. For the very first time it struck me that this occurrence might have been unusual, Auntie Marge coming down to the river, and she and Mr Yields wandering off, leaving me to oversee the rods. *Now you watch the lines . . . Keep your eye on the float . . .* and then they would come back a while later. I remembered sheltering from the rain in a wooden fisherman's hut, alone. Alone! A few days before the fishing trip with Mr Yields, my grandfather – who always carried a pearl-handled knife, ostensibly for cutting apples – had carved our initials and closed them in a heart on one of the upright posts of the hut. I had occupied myself, while I waited for Auntie Marge and Mr Yields to come back, by inking in our initials with a biro. Spots of rain had dropped through the water's surface, making circles as big as my head. Each round band had merged with the next, forming patterns as dense as chrysanthemums. The river hadn't felt dangerous to me then, not like now. It would never have occurred to me to go in, or to follow the adults. I had made a prop from a forked twig, to support my fishing rod, and devoted myself to my cave art, my private act of vandalism.

At a bend in the river I came upon a wooden shelter. It had been extensively patched and repaired. There was no sign of a heart and arrow. I turned the memory, questioned it, for in truth it seemed unlikely. But I was cold, the rain was coming fast behind the wind, which was rising, so I left the river, and hurried through the skittering forest.

By the time I got back to the hotel I was soaked. I walked up the wax-polished staircase, feeling the burnt-caramel oak of the banister rail, its textured grain sticky beneath my wet hand, and at a right-angled bend met another splintered recollection, bright and translucent as film. I had a sudden clear image of myself crouching on this first-floor landing, my hair unkempt, the laces of my damp pumps dirty as worms, and watching in fascination through the wooden rails while my uncle, who was a jazz musician, and had the floppy hair and angular cheekbones of Chet Baker, raised one hand in warning, and argued vehemently across the stairwell – presumably in full hearing of everyone, because the space would have amplified the sound – with the waistcoated and tweedy figure of Mr Yields, who blinked, and polished his spectacles, but nonetheless stood his ground. *I don't need you to teach my wife how to fish!*

The first time we came here Mr Yields had Mrs Yields with him, but in subsequent years he always came alone. On that first occasion I had assumed Mrs Yields was his mother because their children hadn't come with them. Possibly they didn't have any. Her lilac-tinted hair billowed in a wispy cloud over an apricot twinset and pinkish pearls, the colour matching the plastic arms of Mrs Yields' spectacles. My only memory is of her reading in the drawing room one evening, and folding a soft leather bookmark into the spine of her novel, adjusting the glasses on her nose, as my uncle and cousin appeared laughing in front of her, resplendent – as they saw it – in chest waders. They were going out to fish, beneath the bridge, at night. Mrs Yields didn't seem to find anything funny about a man and a boy wearing waders in a drawing room, and this had made them laugh even more.

In subsequent years, Mr Yields had told us, his wife went to stay with her sister because she claimed that the Highlands didn't agree with her. I developed the idea that Mrs Yields was an invalid, a word that meant nothing to me, but sounded exotic, although of limited interest. I imagined it involved having breakfast in bed, only all the time. I had seen *Rear Window* by Alfred Hitchcock in which the invalid wife is chopped up and put in a trunk. But I think I may have made the invalid part up because I couldn't see why anyone would want to stay behind when they could have been on holiday in Scotland. With us.

I tried to make sense of the memories. I searched the numbered doors for clues. As I did so one of them opened and a woman stepped out. Before the door closed again I glimpsed a double bed and behind it a casement window. A man was sitting on the bed, pulling on a pair of socks. The bed and the casement were familiar to me. I was sure that I had a recollection of Mr Yields sitting on the edge of my aunt's bed, framed by this same casement window, or, at any rate, one very like it. Auntie Marge often suffered with her lungs, but why would Mr Yields be sitting on her bed? Yet I remembered standing in the doorway, looking at them both, my aunt beneath a gold-coloured eiderdown, her fever spent, drifting in and out of sleep, but still wearing lipstick. Mr Yields had been engrossed in the newspaper crossword and had remained perfectly motionless, his pipe tucked into the corner of his mouth, although he raised his eyebrows in greeting when he saw me standing there, the pipe momentarily slipping.

One of the reasons we know so much about the Celts is that the Romans wrote about them when they came to Britain. Cassius Dio, a Roman chronicler, noted a British woman's response to an acerbic remark made by the Empress Julia Augusta: 'We fulfil the demands of nature in a much better way than do you Roman women; for we consort openly with the best men, whereas you let yourselves be debauched in secret by the vilest.' It occurred to me that my aunt, for whom I would have flown to the moon had I been able, may well, in her prime, have been a fine example of her race. Although they are both now deep into their eighties my uncle remains devoted to Marge, and she in her way to him, despite a slightly hysterical decade of divorce when it was never really clear who the wronged party was. They never remarried, but grew slowly back together, in the same way that bark heals around initials carved in a tree. A stroke, some years ago, slowed Marge down, softened her. But she still sees no reason to elucidate the myths that have grown with her, shrouding her like brambles. I commented recently on a photograph of her youngest son, taken when he was a little boy, struck by his bright blue eyes and Viking looks in such contrast with the black hair of his siblings.

'Where on earth did he get that hair?' I said, realising, only as the words left my mouth, what I'd done. But her eyes crinkled mischievously.

'Do you think the time has come to tell the truth?'

I stared hard at the photograph. Observed the Chet Baker cheekbones and the mop of unkempt hair. It was a different colour, but that apart, my cousin was the image of my uncle. 'Do you?' I asked, and she had pealed into laughter, saying:

'Now, are we going to have another gin and tonic or will you go and open a bottle of wine?'

I shivered as I turned the key in the door to my room. I put the bivouac bag and the map of Caithness on the bed. The map looked innocuous in its orange and silver covers with a photograph of a lone cyclist. Yet somewhere among its creases was the place where I would be sleeping the following night. Given how cold I was feeling the idea seemed at best unlikely, at worst foolish. I decided to have a bath. Going back into the corridor, I found a bathroom tucked beneath the eaves. I brought the towels from the bedroom and placed them on a Lloyd Loom basket; the cracked floor was ancient lino. I ran the bath using only the hot water tap because a granite chill permeated everything, even though it was August. An art deco mirror above the sink, which was flanked with engravings of angular sea creatures, steamed over quickly. Condensation trickled down flaking tongue-and-groove walls. The water in the bath cooled as rapidly as it filled, the cast iron stealing the heat. I ran the hot tap constantly, the water gurgling into the overflow, until I felt warm enough to turn it off, whereon a protest broke out in the pipes. The rain, which seemed to have set in for the night, rustled at the window, slipped across the slates, and I seemed to lose my grip on time, in this space beneath the roof, the old house becoming a memory box, where recollections matted with dreams.

An hour later I pulled on a pair of jeans and a sweater. I tried to call Rupert, and then Evie at her cousins' house, but there was no cover for my mobile and the rooms didn't have telephones. I took Neil M. Gunn's *Highland River* from my holdall. It described, in the form of a novel, the exact journey I hoped to make the following day.

A table had been set for me in the dining room, silver service, a crisp white damask tablecloth, but I had been alone all day. I suddenly craved the intimacy of the bar. There was a deep Knole sofa, next to an oak coffee table, in front of the fire, so I sat down and ordered a venison salad, followed by salmon. I watched the young barman talking to a German couple about whisky. He was tall, fair and blue-eyed, and exhibited an authority beyond his years. I wondered if he was the absent Callum who the reception-ist had referred to earlier, the one who had failed to collect my bag. The German couple wanted to know if a single malt whisky was better than a blend, and if age was an indication of quality. He answered them knowledgeably, yet evenly, exhibiting no personal preference, nor implying any hint of stigma or qualitative judge-ment, so that while being very well informed about whisky – in the abstract – they did not seem any the wiser, with regard to making a decision, by the time he had finished. His face was as unreadable as a poker player's.

I opened *Highland River*. It had been my intention to read the novel months ago, and yet a part of me wanted to experience the river first hand, rather than seeing it through the filter of the book. As a result of this I still hadn't got beyond the opening chapters. But the Ordnance Survey map had set anxiety fizzing around inside me like a toy train on a loop track. The rain that still landed against the windows in handfuls, now as hard as grain, only served to increase my unease.

The book told how a boy was sent by his mother, early one morning, to fetch water from the well-pool. The well-pool was close to the river mouth, and he disturbed an enormous salmon there, silver and blue-backed. He wrestled with it, and brought it to land.

A curious mood of fatalism comes upon a salmon that has committed its life to a pool. Up and down it will go, round this boulder, by the side of that, turning here, turning back again there, but never making any attempt to leave the known ground. No barrage of stones will drive it forth, however successfully timed. The dangers of the shallows are the dangers of the unknown, of death. If the pool be just deep enough a salmon will pass between swimming human legs rather than be driven forth, and in this restless fashion will ultimately tire out its enemies.

Although drawn by the narrative, I was aware of a subtext, and at some level I was distracted by it, as though I was straining to hear a radio playing in another room. When I glanced up, it was to see the barman removing my plate and asking me if I wanted anything else. He was standing in the space between me and the coffee table. Our feet were almost touching. As if in response to my unspoken discomfiture, he glanced behind him and down at the table, which was heavy, and pressed into the backs of his calves. He shrugged, creating an impression of a vague but deliberate insolence. Well, surely it would have been more orthodox to lean across from the side to clear the table? I put down the book.

'I'd like whisky,' I said, 'but I'll come and see what you have.' I eased past him and walked over to the bar. He was attentive, professional. As before, he gave nothing away. I made my selection, Glenfarclas, large, no ice, but he had several bottles of various ages, and I allowed him to guide me through this second stage. Another young man appeared. The two of them exchanged a few words. The second man was offering to make up my order, and I understood that the shift had changed. My barman placed the heavy tumbler on a tray, accompanied by a jug of water. I slipped down from the bar stool in order to move back to my seat by the fire, but in that moment a couple from the dining room entered. He and I watched as they sat down on the sofa, filling it. The tray was suspended between us. The barman looked from it to me, and his eyes darkened, a momentary flaring of the pupil, as he said:

'Would you like me to bring this to your room?'

Not quite sure that I'd heard him right, I focused on the button that secured his white shirt, the top button remaining unfastened. The skin of his throat was pale and this, combined with the white of the cotton and the fairness of his hair, gave him a slightly studious look, although he exuded a butterscotch warmth. The shirt seemed tight across his shoulders, which were wide, and arched as taut as a bow. His waist was narrow, he was probably a climber, or perhaps a rower, the deltoid muscles pulling a ruck across the line of his shirt, the hand that held the whisky strong. The distance between us seemed to expand, and then shrink, very quickly, back to nothing. I was aware of the planes of his body that were facing mine, and sensed a movement as silent, yet frenetic, as Brownian motion filling the space between us.

I lifted my eyes and met his look, causeway to an unknown land. I was aware of the exquisitely finite nature of the moment.

'I'll take the whisky here,' I said, 'thank you,' and as I lifted the glass the stones of my wedding ring glittered under the halogen lights of the bar. But I kept his gaze, was held by it, and for a few moments felt the promise implied there, the feckless possibility of sudden joy, ephemeral as the smell of hot bread. But then I dipped my head, and turned away, and when I looked again he had gone.

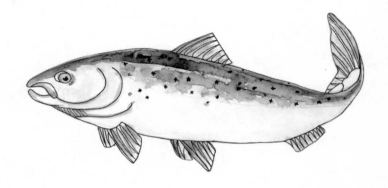

Dunbeath

The A9 curved out above the village of Dunbeath, dwarfing the harbour town beneath it. The road looked like a boomerang placed across an architect's model, and at first I missed the turning, and had to turn back and try again, to find the spiral slip road that curled down to the village. I stopped at the Dunbeath Heritage Centre and collected a tourist map, to complement my OS map, before parking the car close to the river. Above me, the traffic buzzed in a whining Doppler along the seaboard of the Eastern Highlands. Until this moment the A9 had been my path, since leaving Liz's house it had formed my route, yet suddenly it was veering away from me. I stood beneath the road at the edge of a deep crease in the land. In front of me was the sea.

I walked down to the harbour. The sea was blue and silver, striped like a mackerel, and the moorland that skittered into it over sandstone cliffs had the colour and appearance of deer hide. Crimson heather glinted on the wind-burned moor, iron oxide under gold leaf, the mineral pigments pure. Heaped-up pearly clouds covered the sun. I could make out occasional townships, slipped like love-notes into cracks along the coast. There was an almost mythological cleanness about the place, as though I were standing on a stage, these things just props, and a drama was about to begin.

The river mouth was held open, on the southern side, by concrete ballast. On the other side was a jetty wall, and both the ballast and the wall reached into the sea like the arms of a flamenco dancer. Scrubby detritus – a rubber float, gull feathers, old bits of rope, a one-gallon plastic container – garlanded the shore on either side of the dancing arms. A single lonely fishing boat rocked in their embrace. I walked to the tip of the wall, to the very end of the jetty, and looked down into the water. It was almost black. I watched the tide as it pushed into the river, and I found it difficult to focus, to judge distance, or depth, amid the waters' shifting pattern. This was the place, the beginning, or the end, where the identity of the river was lost, or discovered, depending on how you looked at it. I stood quite still following the movement of the water, the movement of my breath, and the sound of my heart and the blood in my ears drowned out the sound of the water. And then the moment passed, and the sky, which had seemed to grow suddenly very close, became once again impervious, a canopy, the sea was before me, the river behind me, the sense of dissolution gone.

I turned to face upstream.

On the opposite shore a man in chest waders, with a black-and-white dog, was tying a feather fly to his fishing line. On my side of the river was a bronze statue showing young Kenn, the protagonist of *Highland River*, resolute, determined, his fingers knotted through the gills of his fish, which was almost as big as he was. A cool breeze pulled at me, returning me, reminding me that the time had come to choose my path. The fisherman and the collie were on the southern bank, accessible by a footbridge. The bronze statue of the boy and the fish were on the other. I chose the statue. I would remain on the northern shore.

In his novel *Christ Recrucified*, the Cretan writer Nikos Kazantzakis describes a group of villagers as they prepare to take part in a Mystery Play. As the weeks slide by the amateur actors make the ancient lines their own, and gradually the villagers begin to exhibit the attributes of the characters they have assumed. As I passed beyond the metal figure, and past neat stacks of lobster pots, I felt as though I, too, was taking part in something, fulfilling a role.

I passed back beneath the viaduct. On the tourist map I had found at the Heritage Centre there was a black dot marked at the edge of the river that indicated the well-pool where Kenn caught his salmon in *Highland River*. I could see an inlet with some stepping stones, but I couldn't be sure if that was it. Maybe the recent floods had concealed the pool. A way-marked footpath crossed under a second, older road bridge that pulled the two sides of the village together. The footpath was clearly in regular use, and the first few hundred yards of the bank were littered with dog turds in every stage of decomposition, which gave this section of the pathway the urban feel of a city park. The fashion for notices that had been so evident at the River Mersey, at Fountains Abbey and at Pitlochry was also a feature at Dunbeath. While the English signs had been full of direction, and even instruction, about what one might – or might not – do, the Scottish signs concentrated on avoiding mishap: *Danger of Death: Keep Off, Danger – Overhead Electric Power Lines – No Fishing, You Cross This Bridge at Your Own Risk. Cast with Care.* Drawings of stick-men in different forms of extremis, hit by lightning bolts, falling into water, illustrated the hazards.

After a few hundred yards a wall appeared, reaching almost to the water's edge. It emanated from a ruin on a raised mound above the riverbank. According to the map this was the site of an ancient monastery and was known as the House of Peace. The stones were green and covered in moss; there was a farmhouse near by, called Ballachly, meaning cemetery. One night, according to the notes on the tourist map, a tributary of the Dunbeath Water had flooded, and the dead had been raised, and then lowered, although not quite in the same place where they had started. The farmer had ploughed the displaced remains back into this field, and was said to have had ill luck from that day on.

A wooden footbridge crossed the tributary burn and a path led to the Dun Beath Broch, marked on both of my maps. I walked on, beyond it, not wanting to be diverted, but the riverbank crackled with reminders of human habitation. A few more yards revealed a hut circle, the remains of a field system was visible on the higher ground. My OS map was dotted with clues: *Chambered Cairn, Quarry (dis), Settlement, Standing Stone, Broch.*

A long wall was bent in a right angle close by the river's edge. Behind the wall was a beech wood, framed in a perfect rectangle. The trees were huge, and their dry leaves chittered and clattered above the sibilant rowans and rustling birch on my side of the wall. A second right-angled bend marked the end of the enclosed beech wood, and small trees pressed closely on both banks of the river. Sunlight was filtered through the tissue-paper discs of hazel leaves. Lichen, ghostly pale, bloomed in the shape of oak leaves, garlanding and silvering the hazels. I pulled a sprig of green nuts from a branch and put them in my mouth, splitting the pliant shells between my teeth. A milky juice spilt from a soft core, tasting of grass, with a hint of wood, and it was like sucking an ice-lolly stick, but without having had the benefit of the ice cream. I reached for another sprig, snapped it off, and was about to repeat the process, but instead dropped it into my pocket. The green nuts, rather than providing a snack, were actually making me feel hungrier than I had been before I started eating them.

The land had been rising gently, and the river bubbled wide and shallow. But now a gorge opened in front of me, its sandstone walls tall as a church. The river opened into a peat-coloured pool, in the middle of which was an island of heaped-up pebbles. The banks on either side were smooth and grassy, but beyond the pool the gorge looked impassable, the red stone rising sheer above the river. I would have to leave the bank, for a while, and follow along the top of the cliff. I sat down and took an apple from my bag. The place was like a cloister, warm and green. The soft banks and quiet pool invited sleep. Brightness bounced off the water as it was whipped into peaks by a passing breeze, before flattening again, smooth as a new-made bed.

A dark fin broke the surface, a black back sliding through sunlight. A salmon! I longed to let my arm trail in the water, to feel the salmon move against my hand. But I was captivated by its appearance of indolence, in awe of its explosive power, and I couldn't move. I found myself wondering about Finan Cam of Kinitty, a sixth-century Irish saint, who was said to have been conceived when his mother went swimming in a salmon pool at night. Both Finan Cam's acuity and his great wisdom were attributed to his aquatic parent. Every so often the fish broke the surface and picked off a fly, leaving ripples as round as plates.

A Scottish tale, from Jocelyn of Furness's *Life of St Kentigern*, tells the story of a Highland queen:

who turned her eyes onto a certain young soldier,
who seemed to her spring-like, with a beautiful appearance . . .
And as a man who was sufficiently ready and inclined for such homage,
he was easily made to sleep with her.

She gave the spring-like soldier a ring, of great value, one that had been a gift from her husband. The young man was not at all discreet, and wore the jewel openly. An informer told the king about the lovers, and the king invited the soldier to escort him on a hunting trip. In the afternoon, when they had eaten, the king suggested they might rest awhile on the riverbank, and so the two of them lay down. The unsuspecting soldier fell immediately asleep. The king saw the ring in his open hand and, although he was sorely tempted to kill the soldier there and then, he removed the ring instead, and cast it into the water.

When the king came home, he asked the queen what had become of the ring he had given her on their wedding day. The queen said she thought that it was in a certain chest, and went off and made as if to look for it. Instead, she dispatched a messenger to the soldier, who sent word back that he had lost the ring. He then remained in hiding. Consumed with jealousy, the king accused his wife of adultery, and had her held under guard. He let it be known that, if she could not produce the ring within three days, he would kill her.

The queen sent a message to St Kentigern, who was living as a hermit on the banks of the River Clyde, begging him to help her. St Kentigern, who had already heard the story, ordered his servant to take a fish-hook to the river and bring him the first fish that he caught. When the servant brought the fish — which was a salmon — the saint opened it and found the ring inside its belly, and he immediately sent the jewel, with his servant, to the queen. Humbled by this quite extraordinary proof of his wife's innocence, and the apparent falseness of his accusation, the king knelt before the queen, begging, publicly, for her forgiveness, and swearing that he would put her accuser to death. But the queen wisely maintained that it was her deepest wish that the king should not harden his heart against the man, but forgive him. She then went to visit the hermit-saint, and made her full confession. She amended her life according to his counsel, *restraining her feet from another such fall.* While her husband lived, the queen never revealed the means by which mercy had been shown to her, but after his death she let the story be known to anyone who wished to hear it.

It seemed natural that St Kentigern should be kindly disposed towards the queen. His own mother, who was also the daughter of a queen, had been thrown from a cliff for conceiving outside wedlock. When that failed to kill her, her father took her to the deepest part of the ocean and set her adrift in a leather coracle beyond the Firth of Forth, without oars, and commended her to the mercy of the sea. She washed up on a shore, near Culross, and made her way to the embers of a fire, which she stacked up with driftwood, and then gave birth to her son. The light from the fire attracted some shepherds, and they brought meat to the mother and clothing for her and her child, and brought them both to the home of St Servanus, who named them, and cared for them, as though they were his own.★

★ As it happened, Saints Servanus and Kentigern lived a hundred years apart, and would never have had the opportunity to meet.

With regard to the unknown paternity of the saint, his biographer Jocelyn of Furness simply remarked:

> *Truly we think the matter absurd to inquire further as to who the sower was and in what manner he ploughed or even planted the earth when, by the Lord's goodness, this earth produced good and abundant fruit.*

Kentigern had lived over fifteen hundred years ago. He was also known affectionately as Mungo, meaning the dear one, or darling. In spite of being a hermit he attracted a great community around him, and this came to be known as *glas cu* meaning the dear green place. His community still thrives on the banks of the River Clyde.

Glas cu.

Glasgow.

Good and abundant fruit.

The salmon tilted in the pool next to me. My eye caught the curve of its back as it broke the surface, and I heard a *clock* as it slipped away.

I climbed up a steep bank clustered in hazels. Below me was the sequestered pool in its chapel. The riverbank had been protected from the wind, but now I could feel a cool damp breeze on my face, although there was no sense of rain. Two red grouse flapped up in front of me, *crack-crack-crack*, their voices like the hinge of a gate.

I stepped out onto a flat, wide world. I couldn't see the sun. The river was tucked away inside the gorge. At the northern and southern edges of the flatness were low rumpled hills. At the peak of one of them a monolith leaned into the wind, as though it were trying to walk. Beyond that, and some way north, were the twirling blades of a wind farm. The gold and chamois peat flows lifted in front of me. Two thin black lines, a Land-Rover track, ran parallel with the hidden river. Occasional low walls split the land into sections. These few features, like delineations on a board game, created an illusion of emptiness more intense than if there had been nothing there at all.

I approached a five-barred gate. According to a sign the land ahead was private. But *pedestrians visiting the cemetery* were welcome. In spite of the word *welcome* there was something off-putting about the notice. Possibly the inclusion of the word *cemetery*. Looking behind me I could make out a large low hunting lodge on one of the hills above Dunbeath. I wondered, belatedly, if I should have asked permission before coming here. But pedestrians were welcome. I climbed over the gate and took out the Ordnance Survey map.

I was standing at the edge of that same area of whiteness, that vast empty page, which had so unnerved me when I saw the map in the camping store at Aviemore. Three towns, Dunbeath, Latheron and Latheronwheel, were linked by the candy-stripe A9. Rivers, hemmed in green, bisected the towns, passing beneath the road and wriggling towards the sea. An intricate patchworked field system skipped along the coast, a lacy trim along the edge of the page. Inland, the map was minimalist. It seemed more so in daylight, and the occasional contours, blue lines, spots and tufts of grass were as mute and inexplicable to me now as when I last looked at them. There was no forest, or anything that might be thought of as a mountain, and no loch beyond the boggy clusters of dubh lochs.

The next feature marked on my map was the cemetery to which the wooden signpost referred, although I couldn't see it yet.

Beyond it was a farm, and these two things were the last signs of human habitation, if a cemetery could be called a habitation, on this side of the river. The only other building was on the opposite bank, about eight miles away, and there was no track to it. It was simply called Poll Roy. On my side of the river, at the far boundary of the farm, there was a footbridge across a tributary, and there, I believed, I could rejoin the river.

I came to a boggy pool at the side of the path. In the centre was a cushion of sphagnum moss and in the middle of the cushion sat a rabbit. It started when it heard my footstep but otherwise did not move. Its nearside eye bulged. It was blind. I thought of the glossy hare at Spurn Point that had loped sparkly-eyed from the shore: my wise and lucky sea-hare. Why do we read good omens into pretty things but are so quick to dismiss ugliness as fancy? With difficulty I ignored the rabbit, and tried not to develop the idea that my spirit guide had left me.

I longed to pass the enclosed land, and be alone. Of course I was alone, I had been all day, but the Land-Rover track, the cemetery and the farm buildings ahead of me were all indicative of regular human visitation. I felt vulnerable, and visible, in much the same way that I had at Spurn Point. Some way ahead of me a wall crossed the path and to the right of it was a chambered cairn that I had seen marked on the map. There was a gate across the track and an animal pressed its face through the bars. From a distance it looked like a goat, all devil horns and slanting eyes, but as I drew closer I could see it was a sheep. More sheep came to the gate and I was not sure if this was a response to my approach, or if they were expecting a visit from the shepherd. By the time I reached them, they were thickly clustered and showed no sign of moving. So I climbed over the gate and pushed my way between them, their sticky wool and unexpectedly bony frames rubbing against my legs. Looking up, I could see the cemetery. It had whitewashed stucco walls and was situated towards the edge of the gorge, over-looking the river below. The cemetery was filled with elegant black and ochre monuments. As the path curved, and my angle of approach altered, the monuments appeared to rearrange them-selves, like the figures on a Bavarian clock. A padlock and chain coiled around iron gates. Below, in the gorge, the river glittered. I felt happy to see it again, as though I had been reunited with a friend.

Sheep pressed into the whitewashed walls, grubby against the pristine brightness. To the sixth-century icon painters sheep repre-sented thoughts. A good shepherd was someone who had control of their thoughts, who could corral them, stop them from wander-ing. Orpheus had been a shepherd. It was shepherds who first saw the divine light of the Nativity. Evie's favourite character in the Catalan Nativity is called the *Caganet*, that is, the Shitter. In add-ition to the Shepherds, the Three Kings, the Angel and the Holy Family, the animals in the byre and the lambs, the Caganet squats, his eyes fixed on the manger, his skirts hoisted around his waist, while he drops an astonishing turd.

According to legend the *Caganet* was one of the shepherds to whom the Angel first announced the Good News, but unfortu-nately he was taken short. Anxious not to miss anything, he positioned himself discreetly at an appropriate distance from the Holy Family and relieved himself, while remaining in a state of wonder and contemplation. The field where he was squatting became fertile from that day forth, and so he has come to embody a number of ideas: the importance of a reciprocal rela-tionship between mankind and the earth — for even as he receives he is giving back – and enlightenment, both physical and spiritual.

Ahead of me were the farm buildings. They were still so far away they looked like Lego blocks. Slowly they grew bigger until the track brought me to the farmyard. The moors lifted away on every side. The house and outhouses were well maintained. I peered through a kitchen window. I thought I might see a mug and a kettle, perhaps a packet of biscuits, or a chair. But there was nothing, the house was quite unfurnished, although there had been fresh hay and animal feed in the barn.

I passed quickly through the farm and after climbing over a stile set into the farthest wall, I was at last on the open moor. The Land-Rover track continued a little way beyond the last field, and then formed a neat loop back on itself, as precise as a surgeon's thread. There were more scattered remains of earlier dwellings, an old cistern filled with farm equipment, and then the footbridge. I had regained the river, and it was smoother now, a curving ribbon, fed by a single tributary. I crossed the tributary with a sense of elation, and was surprised by quite how much my heart warmed at the sight of the water. The river was gently and visibly rising, held in a gentle V in the land. The fear that I had felt when I first saw the map had quite dissipated. While I followed the river I could not get lost. It was as constant and as concrete as a ball of flax. I folded the map away and put it at the bottom of my bag.

Water always takes the easiest path. So, too, do deer, although they are not keen on getting their feet wet. Clear tracks followed the bank of the river, avoiding areas of moss and mud. Smiling, I noticed that the deer also preferred the northern bank. I caught a sudden movement at the edge of my vision, and turned as a vast herd of young stags rustled along the horizon, their antlers drifting like Shakespeare's Birnam Wood.

On the other side of the river was a stone house – I had reached Poll Roy. A waterfall, a low step, was the last of the river's features to be recorded on my map and I had been looking forward to reaching this place. I liked the name – it sounded heroic, like Rob Roy. Poll Roy seemed to be a conventional – if abandoned – farmhouse, but the fact that there was no road to the house felt wrong. It was like Dorothy's home landing out of nowhere on the Wicked Witch of the East, but without the ruby slippers. Glancing down I saw a rusted wire loop encased in plastic. A trap. It was old, and abandoned, but I narrowly missed stepping in a second. I came across two more, the metal nooses shiny. New traps. There was no real danger, although I might have turned an ankle. But the idea that someone might come here unnerved me. I was at least two miles beyond the end of the Land-Rover track. Behind the abandoned house ran a ridge of low hills. I sat down, retrieved the map. Unfolded it. Beyond the hills was a second river, the Berriedale Water, and an unpaved track ran along the side of it. Later the track turned north-east, away from the new river, past a lochan, and then crossed the Dunbeath Water, about three miles upstream from where I was now. I don't know why I hadn't noticed it earlier. It hadn't occurred to me, on my linear trajectory, that one might cut across the hills to get here, and that I was not as remote from other people as I had supposed.

Evening was refracting all around me. I was aware of the cool air in the shadows of the house, the darkness pooling to one side of it. I was affected by its stillness and sense of uncertain abandonment, like that of the farm below. I wondered how it came to be empty, conscious of the legacy of the Clearances, when tenant farmers throughout the Highlands were turned out of their cottages by their landlords, driven to poorer lands, driven to the coast, or to the cities, to America, Canada and Australia, while their homesteads became vast sheep farms. I found that I was afraid, as I had been when I saw the madman at Spurn Point. I had walked about half the length of the river and although I intended to sleep on the moor, I didn't want to meet anyone, certainly not the setter of the traps. Although I was as much unnerved by the spirit of this house as by the thought of any human encounter. I decided to try and reach the track – the one on the map that bridged the river – as quickly as the path allowed. Beyond the crossroads I felt sure I would be alone.

The land was rising, and the river was narrowing, winding and curving between broken peat hags that curled down over me, two or three times my height. I was still following the split hoof marks of the deer that speckled the water's edge. White stones appeared at the bends in the river; other than that the earth was black, the roots of heather forming a ragged fringe along the top of the bank. Traps still appeared, sporadically, along the deer path, so I climbed up to the top of the peat. I could see in every direction, but there was nothing except the moor and the sky, which was as soft and white as the underbelly of a goose. There was no sound; the river, quiet at best, was inaudible from the slight elevation. No feature broke the horizon – either rock or stone or tree. How quickly I might get lost if I were to wander even a short distance from the water! My senses were alternately flooded and starved by the uncompromising austerity of the moor. The dry heather didn't make for easy walking, being rough and uneven, and the peat was deeply cracked. I was aware how frightening the place might appear if one were unable to trust one's senses.

When I was twenty-two years old I met a fortune-teller in Brighton. I had travelled there with a girlfriend, Emma, who had come from Nigeria to begin her Ph.D. in London, and we had taken the rattling train from London's Victoria Station, the grey-green landscape of south-east England obscured by the rivulets that meandered across the window glass. It was November. When we arrived at Brighton the rain had stopped. The sun was like a torch beneath a bed-sheet. A zigzag wind, vigorous as elvers, burrowed into our clothing. There were very few places that offered shelter. We ate fish and chips, and walked along the pier. We sipped afternoon tea from white china cups, and grew dissatis-fied as it cooled too fast. We hunched into Lloyd Loom chairs behind chattering conservatory glass. The glass reminded me of garden cloches and I had an incongruous flash of Beatrix Potter's Peter Rabbit, naked and sorrowful, squeezing chubbily beneath Mr McGregor's gate. Simply being there filled me with panic, the desire to run tempered by enervation – it would be ten years before Brighton became fashionable and we seemed little removed, in our wicker chairs, from the old people gazing from the double-glazed care homes that bandaged the seafront like wraparound sunglasses covering the eyes of the blind.

Emma didn't appear to have noticed, or perhaps the newness of the monochromatic landscape filled her with wonder. Most of what I knew about Africa had been gleaned from a trip to Morocco. It had been an unmitigated disaster, and I was in and out of Africa in less than two days, my girlfriend and I with our inappropriate clothing and short, bleached hair attracting more attention than we either wished for or could cope with. We had spent a miserable night in a cheap hotel in Tétouan, where I saw my first cockroach, heard my first muezzin, and where strange voices muttered outside the door all night, knocking, and calling, *M'm'selles! M'm'selles! Would you like to see the souk?* In the morning we found the very same taxi driver who had brought us there and begged him to take us back to the port. I thought it unlikely that Brighton was having the same impact on Emma. She seemed enchanted by its gentleness, or perhaps its shabby genteelness, her brows arched with laughter, delighting in the fact that we two were there at all. And so I had tried to temper my anxiety, my longing to shrug off the fug of central heating and the cinnamon plastic aftertaste of teacakes. Later we made our way to the slick wet beach where a mêlée of traders struggled against the low season, recessed into the arches beneath the promenade, like cave dwellers, or bees. I wanted to stamp down to the water's edge, to stand before the flinty sea, fill my ears with the sound of the waves, and touch the spattering spray. It was the non-human element of the town that attracted me. But Emma was drawn to the life that hugged the shore, and she wanted to see everything, stop at every stall, and I felt it graceless to suggest that we might part. We passed purveyors of smoked fish, mussels, prawns, jellied eels. Fish and chip shops, with mushy peas, and gift shops with postcards bent into curves by the damp winter air, animals made from glued-together shells and imported from Taiwan. Finally we came across a sign above a door that said: *Professor Mirza, Famous Mystic of the East.* Outside was a sandwich board bearing a large delineated hand. We had stumbled across a palmist.

There was a price for one hand, double for two. The hand you have been dealt, and what you will make of it. The professor seemed ancient, yet his face was unlined. His skin was a warm mahogany, although it had the chalky bloom that an English winter's day gives to everyone. He wore a grey woollen astrakhan hat. I think in part it was a desire to look at the hat that kept me there. Also, it was warm in Professor Mirza's room, and the knowledge that cold legs scurried overhead lent a *Wind in the Willows* riverbank feel to the place. It had the same addictive cosiness that Ratty had shared with Mole. Letters lined the walls. While Emma chatted to the famous clairvoyant I studied the framed and often ebullient commendations from his clients. They included a short, polite note from Lady Antonia Fraser.

I don't remember what the left hand said, other than that I was naturally impulsive and had done little to temper this. But I do remember what he found in the right. I would become a writer – a detail that, oddly, I have only recalled as I write this account. I would live with more than one man. I would have a child in my mid-thirties who would compensate me for the loss of a loved one. I should beware of mental illness at around the same time. I don't recall the rest. I might have listened more, and argued less. I told him I was going to be a filmmaker, I had already met a good man, and I wanted to have many children. Professor Mirza asked for the birthday of my lover. When I gave it to him he began to laugh, for this was not the one – oh goodness, not at all. Beneath the laughter the professor conveyed a firm yet gentle authority. If I would but accept the knowledge, he seemed to be saying, it would be easier for me in the long run, and I could prepare better for the road ahead. After all, why else was I here?

I dismissed the professor's vision, because it wasn't what I wanted to hear. I had wanted to hear about romance and roses, success and plenty, and I was ill-tempered for the rest of the day. I have sometimes wondered if things might have turned out differently had I paid closer attention. Or if they turned out the way they did *because* of what I learned, so that my life became a self-fulfilling prophecy.

Many times in the years that followed I tried to forget what I had heard that day. It had amounted to a fifteen-year forecast. Shortly afterwards I had met Rupert, but the years slipped by and no baby came, and the *child born in your mid-thirties who would compensate you for the loss of a loved one* began to glow, ephemeral, persistent. Sometimes I tried to ignore it. If it was my lot to be childless then I should accept this fact, get on with it, and try to live a different sort of life. Because waiting interferes with living. I hoped, and I feared. I reached for her – I knew it was a she, I even knew what she looked like, down to the blue vein that curled like the tip of a vine from the outer edge of her eye. The prophecy became a hope that both sustained me and controlled me.

Twelve years later, when I was about to begin the IVF treatment that would result in my pregnancy with Evie, Dad told me that he had cancer. It was early one morning, still dark, in November, and he was sitting on my bed, holding a cup of tea that he had brought for me. My lovely father. He said: 'Everything is going to be all right.'

Suddenly it was me who had a vision of the future, of the set of scales in which Dad was balanced next to my longed-for baby. Cassandra was blessed with foresight by the sun god Apollo, and then later cursed by him, so that no one believed a word she said. I didn't want to be believed. There was no one I could tell. And yet

I didn't want to stop it; because I feared, at some level, I had agreed to it. The past grew insubstantial, the present began to seem unlikely, blotted out by a vision of a future in which that which I most desired, and that which I most feared, were – if Professor Mirza's prophecy was correct – about to coincide.

One day, standing in our kitchen, Dad – uncharacteristically, for he was always warm, but not especially tactile in the way in which he articulated affection – wrapped his arms around me, and held me close to him, burying his face in my hair, as though through the act of inhalation he could somehow conserve my essence, imprint it on his soul. I could feel the boniness of his frame, pared by illness, and no matter how close we stood, or how tightly we embraced, the gap between us seemed to be widening, the pockets of air expanding, and then acquiring the solidity of Perspex. Dad felt like a fairy's child that disappears when seen for what it is. I held in my arms a bundle of twigs and feathers, already splintering into dust.

There was a grace period.

The cancer metastasized into Dad's bones when Evie was three months old. He lived another seventeen months during which the two became the closest friends, so that she still speaks of him with affection, even today.

Eight days before Dad died, the day an ambulance brought him home from the hospital, I watched a plane bank into a building. It was on a television in a shop. I was getting a few last provisions before Dad's arrival. The fact that a portable television had been set down next to the cash till was unusual. The staff were clustered round it. I saw matchstick people, clothes fluttering, jump from a collapsing tower. I realised, dimly, that something terrible had occurred, although my only thought was: I mustn't tell Dad – he was such an *Americophile*. He had taught at the University of Princeton, and had charmed us with his tales, of Professor Einstein, and of John Nash, the brilliant mathematician who became quite mad, who wandered the quadrangle, his arms heaped with papers, and whose story was told in the Oscar-winning film *A Beautiful Mind*, which had just been released that summer.

My own beautiful mind was beginning to shift. It was a tent in the desert, full of lovely things, but the sand was getting in as the wind tore at the pegs, loosening the ropes.

After Dad died I had found a torn-off piece of lined A4 paper. It was in a file marked *Kate*, among the school concert programmes and a lock of my baby hair tied with a turquoise ribbon. There were a few lines of poetry, written in blue ink in Dad's beloved, looping hand, and they told of a dream he'd once had. Of how that dream had now come true, and was here, beside him. At first I thought he'd written it himself. Later I discovered it to be a misquotation of some lyrics of a song called 'Long Ago And Far Away' by Ira Gershwin.

In the weeks following the funeral my life began to come apart. We had been living in a cottage that belonged to my brother, John. He had told me that we would be doing him a favour by living in it, through I suspected he had lent it to us so we could all be close to Dad. After Dad's death Rupert and I had intended to move back to our own flat, in London, but the days slipped by.

I had always found solace in walking. It was something Dad and I did together. We had probably, over twenty-five years, followed every single footpath throughout the hills and woodland around our family home. As Dad became sicker I began to walk these paths alone, or with Evie carried in a backpack. But an outbreak of foot-and-mouth disease stamped out all my wanderings. On the day after

Dad's death I drove over the border into Wales. Moel Famau, near Ruthin, was a particular friend. But when I reached Moel Famau the police had closed off the mountain with the same rustling plastic ribbons that they used to mark a crime scene. At home, the public footpaths across the fields, and the woodland tracks, and the hills were all out of bounds. There was nowhere that I could walk, except on asphalt. Six and a half million sheep, cattle and pigs were slaughtered, with over eighty thousand animals being destroyed each week. Smoke drifted from their burning pyres, and the fires lasted for weeks. The foot-and-mouth outbreak would eventually cost the country around eight billion pounds. It cost me my sanity.

The descent began, not with sadness, but with an extraordinary rush of energy. One day I pulled the car into Mum's driveway with over five thousand pounds' worth of goods that I had bought that morning at John Lewis, including a hand-knotted Ziegler carpet, a set of steel pans, and a different-shaped Dyson to the one I already had. I had only gone to buy an iron. Mum came out to the car and asked if I wanted help unloading the goods, but I had simply shaken my head and said: 'It's all got to go back.' I then returned everything to the shop the following day. But quite quickly my high spirits disappeared. After three months I went to see my doctor, convinced that I was suffering from over thirty listed side effects to a topical antibiotic cream and was astonished when he told me I was severely depressed. When I got home, after an indeterminate period of time, for my memory had grown poor, and my ability to concentrate laughable, I looked up the drug the doctor had prescribed for me, and found a set of contraindications not listed by the manufacturer, including suicide and murder. The rock star Michael Hutchence, who a few years earlier had been found dead in his hotel bedroom hanging from a door, was rumoured to have been taking this medication. So had a man in America who murdered his family and then killed himself. I disregarded the obvious fact that both these people were arguably unstable in the first place. But I didn't take the pills. The doctor advised me to cooperate with my treatment before my 'neurotic condition became psychotic'. It was already psychotic. I had seen the devil in the post office and almost caused a car crash in my haste to get away. I noticed that one of my neighbours had the horizontal pupils of a goat. Another lady, I observed, had an extendable neck, her skin like that of a turtle.

I was working on a screenplay at the time, with the Liverpool writer Alan Bleasdale. Because of various hitches the production had slowed down, which was a mercy, so the phone seldom rang. In a moment of lucidity I made a diagram, listing the writer – Alan – the name of the commissioning editor, the broadcaster, the production company, the fact that a director had not yet been appointed, the name of the project and a brief description of the plot, all joined by circles and arrows, so that – if asked – I could sustain a conversation, my forefinger tracing the lines on the paper, which I Sellotaped to my desk.

One morning I found myself staring at the bathroom sink, which was spattered with blood, my hands gripping the sides of the washbasin, a metallic taste in my mouth. Rupert was in the shower, holding his head in both of his hands, weeping. I had no idea what might have occurred, or what I had said, or done. I had deduced that the blood was mine, that it most likely came from a blood vessel in my throat, and that I had therefore, probably, been screaming. I no longer recognised my face in the mirror. In fact, I was terrified of it.

Another day, feeling tired, always so very tired, I decided to make a cup of tea, and then lie down, while Evie had her afternoon nap. I walked over to my bedroom window to close the curtains. In addition to the cup in my hand, there were five other cups, the tea in various stages of cooling, standing in a row on the windowsill. I touched them, the first was tepid, the last only recently made. I watched the sun as it vanished behind our orchard, tangerine and lilac, and I thought it beautiful. The birds had began to chirrup and stir, a last burst of activity before they settled for the night. I listened to the song of a blackbird, the ring-tone of a collared dove. I didn't remember putting the cups of tea on the windowsill. I wondered how long it had taken to make them all. I wondered if it was me that had done it. For the first and only time in my life I understood why suicide might seem reasonable, even sensible, under certain circumstances.

In spite of all this I thought I was doing fine, but could tell from the faces of my friends and family that this probably wasn't so. The fact that I could understand that there was a gap between what I felt and what I saw gave me hope. But I could not trust my senses. Sometimes the walls shifted, or bulged. My greatest fear was that I would go to sleep and wake up mad. Or madder. Evie – the fact that I had to care for her, to feed her, wash her, attend to her every need – was my reason for persevering. She had to be looked after from one moment to the next. She forced me to inhabit the present.

It was a priest who engineered my recovery. I had taken to parking outside the local Catholic church when I went to visit the doctor. The car park was usually empty, except when there was a Mass, and it was easier to negotiate than the crowded surgery car park. One day I knocked on the door of the presbytery, although it had been over twenty years since I had set foot in a church, other than for a wedding or a funeral. The priest invited me inside, and we sat at a table, a glass of water in front of me, while I tried to tell him why I was there.

He looked at me warily, as though at a dog that was known to bite. It was a look to which I had grown accustomed. But the priest was not afraid – of me, or of the condition that I attempted to describe – and this gave me confidence. I found myself telling him how, on the last day of Dad's life, I had watched his spirit leave his body, leave our home. It had begun before dawn. I was sleeping in Mum and Dad's bedroom, a baby monitor at my side, so I could hear Dad breathing in his hospital bed downstairs. Suddenly I was awake, the sound of his voice, the vowel sounds flattened and torn by the monitor. There were no words to speak of. The pain in Dad's bones was almost impossible to relieve. Morphine sedated his mind, but it could not reach into his bones. The day before, I had implored the nurses to leave Dad unwashed, instead of trying to move him, and had smoothed clean linen napkins on either side of his face rather than changing the sweat-soaked pillow. The last word I had heard him utter was *torture*. But now I was too tired to get out of bed. I meant to go to him. I knew Mum was there, resting fitfully in a bed adjacent to his. I could hear her even sleeping breaths crackling through the baby monitor. My sister-in-law, Maria, and I had divided the days and nights into shifts, had taken it in turns looking after Dad, because he didn't want a full-time nurse, none of us wanted a full-time nurse, but I had not slept, other than in brief snatched moments, for five days. I forced myself out of bed and down the stairs, holding onto the wall of the stairwell for support, unable to locate the banister in the darkness. When I got to Dad silence had closed over him, the agony passed for now, his breathing deep and even. I sat next to him and held his hand. Tentatively. Everything hurt. It was the 19th of September

– his father's birthday – and I told him this. I felt that he could hear me. Rupert had shaved Dad's face the previous afternoon, and his skin was smooth and soft. 'No hair on face,' Dad had said. I went to the fridge and opened a bottle of Sancerre. I used cotton wool soaked in cool wine to wash Dad's lips. He could no longer swallow. I cleaned around his teeth and gums with a wine-soaked Q-tip. I poured a glass for myself. It was then that I noticed the light. At first I thought I was mistaken. The light was like the aura around a candle flame, or a street lamp in fine rain. It was orange, and seemed to be emanating from his body. I could only see it from certain angles. As the day uncoiled, the house murmured with people. Dad's breathing remained strong for hours at a time and then, quite suddenly, it would falter, the gaps between each tattered inhalation growing longer. The suspense was extraordinary. Someone brought the Port of Liverpool Tide Table. We consulted the charts, compared the times to the changes in Dad's breathing. 'He'll go out with the tide,' Maria said. At lunchtime we called my brother John, who came from work. But the waters turned again and Dad's strength returned, seamless as the river's bore. So confident were we of his alignment with the water that John went back to work, and returned just before the next high tide, which was due in the early evening. When the tide turned again, Dad's family were gathered about him. Seconds yawned between each breath. The gaps between in-breath and out-breath grew longer. The room had filled with people. At one point there were nineteen of us in the house. The district nurse called by.

'Try to get your mum to leave the room,' she said. 'His love for her binds him to the earth. Even a few moments would do it.' Astonished by the folk wisdom of the nurse, we persuaded Mum to leave Dad's side, on the pretext of having something to eat. John and Rupert took their places on either side of him, and held Dad's two hands. But no sooner had Mum sat down at the table in a room across the hallway, declaring that she had no appetite, than John and Rupert called us back.

As we stood in the doorway a sigh left Dad's body. Mum walked to Dad and took his hand in both of hers. She bent to kiss him, and then sat next to him. There was a terrible sound as my uncle Dennis beat his chest with the backs of his fists, and roared, his head back, mouth open, like a Picasso bull. The room filled with people, they revolved like planets around Dad's awful stillness. Looking down I noticed my own yellow hair, like summer cobwebs, on the floor around the bed. It had been falling out for days. Someone had brought a box of iced buns from the bakery in the village, *for the mourners*. Flipping open the cardboard lid I sat down next to Dad and ate them all. There was a lot of movement in the house, a lot of drinking, tea, whisky, wine. Someone phoned the doctor, the undertaker. Asked if we could keep Dad's body overnight. Yes, we could. I wondered where Evie had got to. Someone had taken her off for the day, but as the hours stretched she had been passed from one friend's house to the next. It was then that I noticed that the orange glow had gone. I wondered if the electric lights rendered it invisible. And then I saw it. No longer emanating from his body, the orange light was now a man-shaped cloud, and it hovered just below the ceiling. I climbed onto the windowsill, and opened the highest window, and then watched as the shape slipped like smoke from a cigarette, into the September sky. That night John slept on the sofa alongside Dad's body. The next day the undertaker came.

The priest looked at me, his fingertips pressed together, making a church of his hands. I wasn't mad, or mentally ill, so far as he could see. He said that if we were Mediterranean it would probably be said that I had *gone mad with grief*. What I had described was not unknown to him. The phenomenon, of a visible aura, wasn't a symptom of psychosis. It had been well documented by the Church over many centuries. The followers of St Francis of Assisi reported just such an orange glow emanating from beneath the door of the saint's cell while he was at prayer. The priest arranged for me to talk to another priest, a Jesuit, and also to a nun, who had trained as both a spiritual director and a counsellor. I don't remember much about this, only that Sister Josephine showed me photographs – of rioting crowds, of deserts, of children, of war, of a river, a fighting bull, and a matador. I began to perceive that there was a world beyond my heartbreak.

I began to cycle, every morning, at dawn, while Rupert looked after Evie. I rode for miles through country lanes. One morning I saw a chubby grey badger slip into a ditch at the sound of my approach. Another day I passed beneath an oak tree heavy with buzzards, and a flock of collared doves, the doves fanned a branch's length from the nine solemn raptors, a temporary truce between them. I saw a family of mute swans at the reed-encircled disc of Hatchmere Lake, the immaculate parents at the side of the road, their muddy-looking cygnets behind them. Often I cycled along the ridged switchback road bisecting the ancient forest of Delamere. I grew back into the world that held me. I learned to reconnect. Gradually I learned to fit.

I stepped back down into the riverbed. It was filled with new grass, brilliant and green, no higher than my foot. I was happy for the companionship of the water. The river was now little wider than a stream, but it was my clue through the labyrinth.

I seemed to have been wandering for hours. I wondered if I had missed the track, which according to the map was about two-thirds of the way along the river's length. Maybe it was a ford, rather than a bridge – and I had passed it, without noticing. The stream was barely more than the span of my arm, and the deer-tracks wandered from one side to the other as the animals sought a straighter path than that of the wriggling stream. I climbed back up onto the heather. A short-eared owl lifted up in front of me with a *he-awe* cry, its black-rimmed eyes as fierce as suns, burning through pale rings, delicate as pansies. The Welsh word for owl means flower-face, after an enchanted woman made from flowers, who was condemned – for her adultery, and for plotting to murder her husband – never to show her face in daylight again. There was no sun now, but neither was it dark, and I tried to dismiss the superstitions linked with the appearance of daytime owls, and to concentrate instead on the fact that short-eared owls are diurnal. After I had passed the spot, the owl returned to its place, and was immediately lost beneath the heather. I walked on. In part I had been unnerved because the owl was sitting on the ground; but there was nowhere else for it – for either of us – to be.

At last I could see the track. It crossed the stream at a bridge made of wooden railway sleepers. There was a square shack with a metal roof and picture windows. As I got closer I saw a kitchen table and some chairs. The stream and the track – two tyre lines across the moor – formed a perfect crossroads. I was still uncomfortable at the thought of being seen. I was too nervous even to put my face to the window of the hut, or to try the door. And yet as soon as I had gone past it, and the stream had curved out of sight of the hut, and out of sight of anyone who might come to it, I felt safe. The transition took moments, not even a minute, because the dwindling stream was now constantly turning, sometimes leaving crescent moons of still water through the gentle cut. There were no more traps. The cleft prints of the deer were for the most part hard and cracked, the black peat baked by the sun. The grass was longer now, and every so often I came across the pressed, indented shapes that marked the place where deer had rested. A golden frog, with a shiny Murano eye, hopped quickly away into the damp grass by the stream.

A hind came down from the moor to drink, her pale face and large ears tuned inquisitively towards me. Uncertain, she changed her mind, and picked her way back onto the peat hag, head pulled back, one eye swivelled in an attempt to keep me in view. And then she turned, and remained there, her ghostly face suspended, waiting for me to pass. She was the first solitary deer that I had come across although I had seen several herds throughout the day.

An eagle. Like the owl, she too must have been resting on the heather, and I heard her before I saw her. When she gained sufficient height to catch the breeze she curled away, black against the still-white sky, which muffled her *pee-oow* call, a white band under her tail attesting to her youth.

It was the time of the evening when the creatures move.

I was relaxed as I walked towards the waterhead, although it seemed extraordinary to me that I still hadn't reached it — the stream was so very narrow. I wondered about settling, soon, for the night, because the boggy water table might not be the most sensible place to sleep. In any case I was hungry. I had apples, chocolate, pumpkin seeds and raisins. And, like *Treasure Island's* Dr Livesey, I carried a block of cheese. I also had the remains of Liz's Rioja in my hip flask. While I was pondering the meal I might make with these things, I heard something.

At first I thought it was an effect of my being alone, a trick my ears were playing caused by the silence of the moor – I wondered if it was tinnitus. But it didn't seem to be coming from inside my head, so I stopped a moment to listen. And as soon as I stopped moving they descended.

Midges!

They filled my eyes, my ears, my nose and mouth with their pointy needle kisses. I breathed them, swallowed them, spat them out, batted at them, and then began to run.

Without ever stopping moving I scanned the ground for somewhere to sleep. A heather-covered ledge had collapsed at the edge of the cut. It was about a yard below the level of the open moor, and yet still a little elevated above the stream. I scrutinised the place as best I could through the stinging cloud. I could see no tracks across it, and found a spot in the middle where I was least likely to be stepped on should a deer descend from the moor in the night. The deer-track along the edge of the stream was around three yards away: I had no desire to find out if *sure-footed as a deer* was a truism.

Having identified my spot, I broke into a furious dance. I pulled off my Wellingtons, pushing them into my bag. I opened out my sleeping bag and wriggled into both it and the bivouac bag before pulling the hoods of both of them over me. I was, mercifully, wearing a muslin T-shirt, and I pulled this over my face like a fencing mask, before killing every one of the horrid little flies that had so comprehensively invaded my bed.

At last it was over. I drank a sip of water from within the safety of the sleeping bag. It was the only one of my supplies that had made it into the sanctuary. I then rearranged the fencing mask. I could feel a space about the size of a fist under my ribs, but hunger was a small price to pay for being safe from the midges. The whole of my body, face and hands stung with their bites. Earlier, as I walked, I had nursed an image of myself sitting by the stream in the long northern night and reading Neil Gunn's book while eating an apple. The electronic-sounding whine was still at full strength, though; I could not even hear the water. And I couldn't see through the muslin fencing mask. In spite of the early hour – it couldn't have been more than nine o'clock – I pushed my body into the heather, which was soft and springy, and didn't even mark the passage into sleep.

A joyful sound awoke me: rain. A light summer rain, but I was warm and dry and the midges were being washed away. When the rain gave way to silence, I peeped out from beneath my mask, then took it off. The darkness was imperfect, and the gentle bubble of the stream replaced the high-pitched hum. A white mist hugged the water, visible as a light area below me. I drifted off.

I felt him before I saw him. It was as though there was a dial in my stomach and an arrow had spun me back to consciousness, accurate and sensitive as a compass. The needle stalled, quivering, in his direction. He coughed and then shifted his footing, and my nose burned with pungent musk. Lying very still, I lifted my face. The stag was standing just behind the crown of my head, his own head held high. His antlers filled the darkness over me; it was like looking at the sky through leaded panes. I could make out the deeper darkness of his body but he was too close, and it was too dark, to see his legs. He seemed unsure about what to do and then, sliding back his head in that tight, reined-in gesture that the hind had exhibited earlier, he delicately stepped down onto the track, and whether he stayed to drink or left immediately I will never know, because sleep once again stopped my senses.

I woke soon after dawn. Thick mist filled the streambed. On either side, in the long grass, cobwebs cast about in all directions, weighted with an early catch of rain. I glanced down at my sleeping bag. I too was covered in a pearly veil. I touched my cheek and my hand came away wet. Even my eyelashes were beaded. I was about to turn over and go back to sleep, wait for the sun to burn it off, when I caught myself. How many times would I ever again wake up alone, at dawn, on a Highland moor? And yet I would sleep the day away!

I took off my clothes and wandered around barefoot, feeling the soft moss and cold peat between my toes. I found a flower which looked like edelweiss, but was really a sprig of sphagnum moss that had dried, rehydrated and then dried again so many times that it had petrified. Stalks of drenched bog-cotton formed an army of white-haired witches, partially transformed into their broomsticks. I got dressed and packed away my bed. I was thrilled to see the place where I had been, the crushed heather dark against the dewy whiteness. I looked up and down the streambed, as though for someone or something with whom to share my excitement at this concrete mark of my existence. But I was alone with the impassive moor. And yet the fact that it was clearly so very much alive reassured me. Made me glad.

I picked up my bag and broke through the cobwebs, feeling certain that the source was close. I smiled at my lack of faith in bringing such a quantity of bottled water to the source of a river.

The stream disappeared into a muddy hole in the ground. Or, rather, it emerged. It hadn't got any narrower. There was no bubbling spring, no crystal well. Just a navel oozing primordial soup: viscous and green. The water seeped, rather than flowed. One half of the damp oval was covered in grass, the height of a finger, preternaturally bright.

There was absolutely nothing there.

I suppose that made sense. That there *was* nothing there. It was the source. Embryonic. The beginning. Although my spirits had sunk when I saw it. I knew that I was fighting to make something out of the discovery, because this was nowhere near the Well at the World's End I'd come to look for. I sat down. I had a flask of hot water, and some sachets of coffee, sugar and milk that I'd taken from the hotel the night before. I made myself a cup and drank it, broke off a piece of chocolate, and all the while gazed at the hole.

The mist blew past in gauzy fragments, sometimes closing, sometimes lifting, and I couldn't really see what lay beyond. I didn't want to move away from the navel. Since reaching the water table the ground had levelled off. I was afraid of getting lost if I left the indentation of the streambed. I was in no hurry to move on.

I took out *Highland River* from my backpack. I still hadn't got beyond the opening chapters. I flicked to the end.

His dismay was vague and ludicrous. From his map-gazing he knew that his river should rise in a loch. He could not have been mistaken . . . And here it was coming out of the earth itself. The realism mocked him.

Vague and ludicrous . . . I took out the map and opened it. I peered at it very closely. There was no loch. I returned to the book.

He went on over the broken ground and came to a round still pool . . . About him the ground was broken and hag-ridden, but he could see he had not yet reached the crest of the watershed. There remained the suggestion of an upward hollow. He came on another small pool like the first. Then another. A primeval no man's land of out-spewings like water-logged shell holes . . . And then all at once before him again was the tiny stream and lifting his eyes he saw the far half of the loch, Loch Braighe na h'Aibhne, the water-head.

I picked up the map again. Stared at it. Yes, the stream *did* disappear, and that could be it re-emerging at the very edge of the page. But there was no loch. I glanced at the back cover of the book as it rested on a peaty knoll. Saw the word *Fiction* in the bottom left-hand corner. Again I scrutinised the map: *Braighe na h'Aibhne* was there, but it described a collection of small pools on the high ground to the south. They looked like a collection of dubh lochs. The book was first published in 1937. Could the loch have disappeared? Was this the result of global warming? Had it sunk into the peat as though through a sponge?

*The mountain of Morven that had been hard and bright all afternoon,
its screes and growths now clearly defined, was gathering about it an
imponderable blue.*

There was no mountain marked on my map, and no mountain
visible before me. I was puzzled by the discrepancies between the
novel, the Ordnance Survey map, and the place in which I found
myself. The mist continued to blow in ragged wisps and I
contemplated turning back. This hole in the ground was of
limited interest, especially after I had read of a hard bright mountain and a non-existent loch, its shores *of pure ground quartz, paler
than any woman's face in any old poet's dream.* I could try to pick up
the stream again, as did the character in the novel, but I was wary
of setting out over the moor now that a danger more real than
the inconvenience of getting lost in mist had occurred to me.
That is, the possibility of drowning in the bog. And it would
mean walking off the edge of my map. I wanted to cry with
frustration.

But I didn't. It was still early in the morning. I was ravenously
hungry. I made a meal of cheese, apples, raisins and chocolate, and
drank the water that I was happy to have brought with me. I
packed away the book and map and sat down on the peaty knoll.
It was a summer morning in August. I unscrewed the cap of my
hip flask and sipped the chilly, slightly metallic, Rioja.

Half an hour later the sun had chased off the mist. The wide
bowl of the watershed became visible for the first time. It was
filled with heather, and pocked with little pools. The land was still
rising, faintly, and there appeared to be a ridge along one edge of
the bowl. I stepped out of the crease that held the river and headed
for the ridge.

I was anxious as I made my way over the open ground, and kept looking behind me for the dip in the land that marked the head of the strath. Every so often I came across another pool, and circumvented it with anxiety. I couldn't find any deer-tracks and this, too, worried me. And then I stopped, because I could hear a sound I had heard before, a sound like an indrawn breath. Water. A sudden diversity of bright vegetation confirmed the path of the stream. It was flowing just beneath my feet, just beneath the ground, towards the place where I had come from. I followed the sound, bent low so I could hear. Soon I could see it: a trickle barely a hand-span in width. It was leading me towards the ridge. I glanced back to the neck of the valley, anxious lest the mist return. But the visibility held. At the edge of the plateau was a fringe of reeds, and I stepped up onto a bank of peat, before stumbling at the sight before me.

A loch!

The loch. Its surface, soft as pewter, mirrored the clouds. Salt-white boulders lined a powdery shore of crystal sand, unmarked and clean, its whiteness stained to the colour of cork by the peat. Nothing disturbed the water, not a ripple, not a fly. I was choked by its loveliness; my senses flooded. As I watched, the low clouds shifted, lifted, and there, beyond the farthest shore, was the slate-green flank of a mountain. So this was Morven! The sky behind the clouds was as pale as a thrush's egg and the surface of the loch took this new palette for its own. I could see the screes, the grassy slopes, the dark outlines of trees and rocks pencilled in by their elongated shadows. But the vision was momentary and a cloud passed over the mountain, cowling the peak, rearranging the features of the slopes, covering up the sun. My eye returned to the loch. Without the bright reflection I could see to the bottom. The powdered quartz continued beneath the water, a few looping tea-coloured tide-marks as it deepened, the occasional shard of bright white rock. Loch Braighe na h'Aibhne. I sat down on the bank overhanging the shore, my feet dangling above the water, not wanting to spoil its surface.

I don't know how much time passed, but suddenly I felt that I must go. I hadn't swum, or drunk the water, or even walked around the loch. I had presumed, when I first arrived, first knew that it was true, that I would swim to the centre, inhabit the water, make it my own, and yet even as my fingers began to tug at my clothes I knew that it was not going to happen. I straightened my clothing. The strongest sense had settled on me, concrete as the mist that covered the mountain, that, if I once disturbed the surface, or entered the water, I would upset a balance both chemical and physical. I didn't even want to contemplate how long it might take before the stillness of the loch could be recovered.

And yet the rain must do it all the time.

I picked up a handful of the quartz sand and poured it into my pocket, over the silky green hazelnuts that I still had from yesterday. I turned away from the loch and retraced the tiny stream, and this seemed straightforward now, despite its passing underground, and it led me back to the funnel of the valley and the muddy oval where the river re-emerged. It was surprisingly easy walking.

I was following in my footprints, and wondering how long they would remain there, when I was struck by the idea that something was passing, or had ended. I tried to push the feeling away from me, and for the most part I was successful, though I was unable to dismiss it entirely. I again passed the place where I had spent the night, but the dew had vanished and the heather regained its shape. There was nothing to suggest I had ever been there.

I disturbed the eagle, still in her place, and was again unnerved by the owl. The deer came and went as they had throughout my trip. There was no sign of the golden frog. A black seabird rose above me and followed me, crying. I supposed it to be an Arctic skua, we were far enough north, and it remained with me for half an hour, adhering to the path of the stream, and then it circled back across the moor, calling, calling, as though I were a fishing boat and we were at sea, and some good might come from following me. Or perhaps it was curiosity, a desire for companionship, the fascination of living things for one another.

I re-entered the part of the river where the traps were set, and paid careful attention to my footing. But my thoughts ran on independently, looping back now to the loch, and to my decision not to swim. Swimming was one of my passions, one of the ways by which I defined myself. Knew myself. I was also surprised that I had not drunk from it. The idea that had brought me here was the idea that there might just be a well at the end of the world, full of wisdom, and answers, and that I might go and look for it. A lot of the stories associated with the well were about forbidden love. The attempt to explain away, or to cover over, children born of what were often single encounters. Even the miraculous story of the birth of Taliesin – born to an enchantress who had swallowed him whole, while he was a grain of corn, and she was a hen – could be interpreted as a ripping yarn to explain away the need to name a father. Why else would his mother have thrown him into the sea? Then there was the paternity of St Finan Cam of Kinitty, he whose mother successfully maintained that she had been impregnated by a salmon — a big fish tale if ever there was one. St Kentigern's mother claimed her son was miraculously conceived, although his biographer Jocelyn of Furness would have none of it, stating firmly that *that which was born in her womb she received from a human embrace*, although he speculated that she may perhaps have *taken the drink of oblivion*, and therefore been genuinely unable to put together, or to believe, what had happened to her.

Isak Dinesen wrote: 'Love, with very young people, is a heartless business. We drink at that age from thirst, or to get drunk. It is only later in life that we occupy ourselves with the individuality of our wine.' Lovemaking is indeed a heartless business for anyone other than the lovers. It annihilates, blinds, burns, bruises, chokes, consumes, crushes, devours, destroys — and I have only reached D. Cupid pierces our hearts with an arrow, orgasm is a little death. Love is not about personal responsibility, or being considerate of other people's feelings. Love is impulsive, compulsive, addictive. Lovers are selfish, and can be infuriatingly self-righteous, so that more or less anything is felt to be excusable if it is done in the name of love. Consequences have never come into it.

> *A secret well there was . . . .*
> *from which gushed forth every kind of mysterious evil.*
> *There was none that could look to its bottom*
> *But his two bright eyes would burst:*
> *If he should move to left or right,*
> *He would not come from it without blemish.*
> *Therefore none of them dared approach it . . .*

The day unravelled slowly and I followed the thickening ribbon until it again became a brook. I passed the almost ornamental waterfall as it stepped past Poll Roy, and saw it fortified by the tributary at the boundary of the enclosed land, where it once again regained the character of a river. I recovered the Land-Rover track, and the road reasserted itself. I experienced a sense of homecoming as I stepped onto it.

At the farm I came across a rabbit: beheaded and gutted, and left out on the path. I wondered if it was the blind rabbit from yesterday, but could read nothing into the blackening mess, except that a ghillie had been there, and had left the carcass to fatten the hawks against the winter. Soon I was able to make out the cemetery, white as sugar on the green-gold moor. The spidery tombstones again appeared to move.

When I was below the cemetery a glint of light drew my eye. Looking at the place where it had been I caught a second flash, as though someone were signalling across the moors. I listened hard, but could hear nothing above the rustle of the wind, the anxious spill of skylarks. I had regained the place where birds sang. And then a bounced movement: a four-wheel drive was curling up the road; I could hear the constricted voice of an engine in low gear. There were two men inside, one dressed like a country gent, the other in a donkey jacket and woolly hat. They pulled up alongside me.

'Good afternoon!' said the country gent.

'Good afternoon,' I replied.

'Are you walking to Dunbeath?' he asked. When I nodded he told me that they were going to play the pipes for an old friend in the cemetery, and that if I'd like to accompany them they could run me back to the town when they were done.

'Thank you, that's really kind. But I've walked all the way from the sea to the loch. If you don't mind, I'd really like to finish the journey on foot. It's only a few more miles.'

'The loch?'

'Yes. Loch Braighe na h'Aibhne.' I had no idea how to pronounce the Gaelic.

'There's a loch?'

'Yes.' And I pointed to the moor. 'Up there.'

'Well, do you know, I have lived here all my life and I never knew there was a loch!' He turned to the other man, and I missed what he said, but I felt a perfect bubble of delight, because I knew that my journey had been special, and I thanked them again, and bid them goodbye, and continued on my path. When I got to the place where the track bent I glanced back towards the cemetery. I watched the two men search for the key and unlock the iron gate. The man in the donkey jacket raised his pipes; but the wind was against them and all I could hear were the summer bees and the river. In less than an hour I had reached my car, but I continued beyond it, beneath the stone bridge and the boomerang-shaped viaduct, past a dozen or so fishermen's cottages. As I approached the harbour I saw two lovers on a wooden bench, caught in the net of their own arms and legs, their noses almost touching. The tips of their fingers wandered, collecting information, each about the other, as much as their senses could withstand. And then behind them, high above the water, came a flick of silver, a comb of falling droplets, and the arching, turning body of a salmon. It must have entered the river mouth, even as I had reached it. *Did you see?* I wanted to cry to the lovers. *Did you see it?* But of course they didn't, their eyes were closed. But I saw, and my heart filled at this coincidental, timely fish.

It was evening when I got back to the hotel. I had walked thirty miles in the last two days. Then driven two hours back. Although

I had felt almost fluid in Dunbeath, my summer body loose as willow, I ached as I walked from the car park to the lobby, my limbs stiffening in the evening chill. One toe throbbed. I suspected I would lose the nail. The young barman Callum entered the lobby, and without saying a word picked up my holdall and headed up the stairs. At the landing he turned towards the grand rooms at the front of the house and I paused, confused, for I was very much aware of our last interchange. My room had been at the top of the hotel. Realising that I was no longer following him, he also stopped, and turned to me:

'They said you'd gone to follow a river to its source. We said *well, if that's the case, then that lassie's going to be wanting a hot bath . . .'*

I suddenly felt like a warrior queen, from long ago, coming home triumphant from a battle. Callum opened the door to what was probably the best room in the house, and put down my bag; he then nodded towards an open door. There had been no bathroom in the old room, just the communal bath beneath the eaves; but I could already see the lip of a roll-top bath and a pile of fluffy white towels.

'Would you like me to set your table in the bar?'

'Thank you,' I said. 'That would be grand.'

Madryn

wo days later, Evie and I returned to our home on the Llŷn. The Welsh and English schools had, for the most part, begun the autumn term, although there were still a couple of weeks before the Spanish schools went back. We decided to pick up the last part of Afon Geirch, the river that ended at Cable Bay, but which we had failed to follow beyond the golf course at the start of the holiday. We left the cottage on foot, and then set off up a bridle path that spiralled around Garn Fadryn. It took us across the lower reaches of the mountain until we climbed over a stone wall beneath the summit cone. The river, which was now a shallow stream, passed beneath the wall in a specially built granite conduit. A bridge of railway sleepers carried sheep and walkers across the waterway. Watercress and sorrel filled the streambed. Evie called the sleepers Picnic Bridge, and we stopped to eat the eponymous picnic that we had, of course, brought with us. Our legs dangled above the water, which gurgled with a domestic, familiar sound, like bath water passing down a drain.

'Do you know something?' said Evie. 'This is my favourite place in the world.' And we sat there, smiling, eating our sandwiches.

A drone of farm machinery floated up from the plain, then stopped. Beyond the plain was the sea, and it was the same soft blue as the sky, the transition marked by a whitish haze. For a brief moment there was silence, broken only by the occasional *mah* of sheep, until a staccato song of squabbling chaffinches drifted on a sudden breeze: two leaning trees were alive with their chatter, I could just make out their little forms. We put away our picnic and followed the stream up the hill. Evie was adept at picking through thistles and reeds and sphagnum moss, and she soon unearthed the source. Rushes like stiff ribbons festooned the ground, and a bent tree partially obscured the spring. A white boulder marked the place where the water began, two other stones were arranged to either side. It felt unlikely that this rock formation was natural. Evie began to clear the area around the biggest stone, heaping handfuls of moss and leaves, beech nuts and pine needles to one side, until she revealed the well, its water cloudy as she churned the bottom, searching out further debris. She looked up at me while she worked:

'We need to bring gardening things and tidy it up properly,' she said. 'What shall we call it?'

I told her about St Madron's Well in Cornwall. It was a rag well, and people left bits of cloth − often ribbons cut for the purpose, but sometimes the torn hem of a shirt or a hastily removed sock − in the hope that their wishes would be granted, their prayers answered. Our mountain was called Garn Fadryn, known locally as Madryn, after the Welsh mother goddess Modron, and we decided, for the sake of harmony, on St Madryn's Well in English, and Ffynnon Madryn in Welsh. Evie asked me for a piece of paper, and a pen, and I gave her a page of my notebook. She then sat down and wrote for a few moments before spearing the torn-out page onto a branch of the bent tree, as though it were a bill awaiting payment.

I wondered what she had written, and watched for a few moments the square of paper. It shivered like a Buddhist prayer flag at a shrine. She saw me looking, and shot me a glance, and her soft grey eyes conveyed a warning. I stepped back. Evie's business was between her and the well, which was already beginning to clarify.

When we got back to the cottage it was evening. After supper and a bath, Evie went to bed. There was a missed call on my mobile, so I went and sat on the swing in the garden to retrieve the message. It was Rupert. He had heard about a hotel along the Costa Brava, it occupied a curving bay, close by the Catalan/French border. It had been built to house some archaeologists during the 1930s when they had unearthed a Graeco-Roman city. He thought that if Evie and I were to come back early, and he were to take a few days off work, then perhaps we could go there, the three of us, and spend some time together before school began.

The last time the three of us had been together in a hotel was when we were married, Evie and I unwinding curlers from our hair in the dawn light, her face absolutely serious as she arranged the snowy folds of my dress, and used her licked finger to clean a line of fine dust from the toe of my white cowboy boot. I recalled the furrow of intent between her eyebrows as she wound uneven pearls around my neck and I fastened Navajo silver beads – her gift from Rupert – round hers. Then she ran out in her raw silk skirts and scarlet ballet pumps to Rupert – with our gift to him of an antique turquoise bolo in her hand – calling: *You mustn't look at*

Mummy till we get there. The soles of her feet had been barely insu-lated against the blistering asphalt footpath. Her excitement at the stretch limousine. Her puzzlement at the empty church. Her delight at our wedding breakfast of sushi. Later, the three of us – lazy as lions – had lain beside the pool, while champagne warmed to the temperature of blood and a golden box of handmade choc-olates ran to liquid.

It was the hottest day on record in Las Vegas.

Stars appeared around the summit of Garn Fadryn. A triangle of darkness marked the peak. I dialled the number, waited for the connection, and then listened for the steady pulse of the ring.

PART II

Is it possible to pierce . . . the dark cloud, even for a few moments, and come on the light, the bubbling well at the end of the fairy tale? Do folk still do it, ordinary people?

Neil M. Gunn

All that I have is a river.

Johnny Flynn

Swimming Pool (2)

was with my friend Eleonora at a café in Barcelona. We were about to collect the children from school.

'There is a big wave coming,' I said, 'and we have to leave before it gets here.'

'A wave? What sort of wave?' she asked.

'A tsunami.'

We collected the children and began our walk to the bus stop. Evie and Matteo, Eleonora's son, climbed onto the fence that surrounded Sofia's garden. Or the garden that had been Sofia's before the summer. Sunlight had split the fence, and I could see through the cracks to the empty pool. The bougainvillea was struggling without water. Dried stalks spilled out of ceramic pots like leftover take-away noodles. The grass was covered in pine cones. Neither of us had heard from Sofia since she'd left Barcelona, though I'd emailed a couple of times.

'It's to do with the banks,' I said, returning to where we'd left off. 'We have to leave while we still can.'

'But you've already left your pretty house!' Her face looked so lovely with her raised eyebrows that I found I was smiling. We had shifted from our eighteenth-century terracotta-roofed house, built around a tiled courtyard, into a tiny flat in a 1970s apartment block, and we lived surrounded by packing boxes.

'It's not enough. I need to go back to London. I need to get a proper job.' A bus came round the corner, and I stuck out my arm, because I couldn't think of anything else to say.

Rupert's livelihood had been shattered by the first hard shock. His American publishers, for the first time in his career, had turned down a book. When the news came we had lain awake all night, holding hands, staring at the ceiling. At about four in the morning Evie appeared in her pyjamas on the terrace that linked our two bedrooms. She tapped on the glass door: 'I can't sleep.' The sky above her head was dense with stars.

Looking overhead he saw that the stars had come out, but why should he seem to see Andromeda, Cepheus, and Cassiopeia? What had become of the constellations of midsummer?

The lines were from a John Cheever story. It was funny what came to mind. I could clearly see Orion's belt. 'Neither can we,' I said, as I opened the glass door for her, and we all three went downstairs and sat around the kitchen table, staring at a pot of tea, and making shrapnel-like toast from the remains of yesterday's baguette.

Rupert had been a writer for almost thirty years. In the UK, the book would win a literary prize. But the prize was a piece of engraved glass. We could no longer afford to pay Evie's school fees, or the mortgage on our home. Every so often I recalled the presentiment I had had as I turned away from the loch at the foot of Morven. The idea that something precious was passing. Had passed. I recalled the headless rabbit on the footpath above Dunbeath. Its rubbery entrails. Presaging what? When Christmas came the three of us went to stay with Mum. Evie and I stayed longer than Rupert who needed to return to his work. In the days following his departure it began to snow. When it was our turn to fly home a taxi took us to the airport in a dawn the colour of unwashed sheets. A man in a luminous yellow jacket waved us away. The airport was closed. The driver turned the slipping car across the hard ridges that marked the edges of other tyre-tracks. I watched his eyes in the rear-view mirror and I felt a fluttering unease.

'I've never driven in anything like this before,' he said, trying to make light of it. He was too young to remember the last serious snowfall.

'Really?' I asked. 'Try not to use the brakes.' His eyes flared in the mirror. Wet flakes clogged up the windshield. He changed down through the gears and we fish-tailed slowly back to Mum's house.

Later that day Evie went sledging with her friend Alice in a sloping field behind their house. I went too, and watched the girls as they shrieked and giggled, bouncing on Alice's scarlet toboggan over snow-filled rabbit holes. Children and grown-ups stood about, laughing, clapping snow from woolly fingers and sharing coffee from a flask. My friend Lucy, who was Alice's mum, offered me a tea tray and I too juddered over the beleaguered rabbit warren and came to rest by a frozen stream at the far edge of the field. But I felt cold, tired and stiff, and I couldn't enter into the spirit of this unexpected extension to our holiday. It wasn't like the surface patina of winter, but an internal ache, that felt colder than the space between the stars. It was as though a plug had been pulled out of my breastbone, just to the right of centre, and my vitality, my life, was passing through it.

In the weeks that followed we began to fold away our Barcelona life. We looked for a new home in London, one we could afford, and a new school, a state school, for Evie. With the help of my brother John, and Evie's godfather Calvin, who paid her school fees, we would be able to stay in Spain until the start of the summer holiday. When the summer term ended we would move to London.

One morning, in late spring, I found myself staring into the bathroom mirror. Despite the sunlight bouncing off the tiles my face looked lined and puffy. A thought presented itself, singular and loud. *You look as though you are dying.* On a Sunday morning at the end of May I noticed a sensation of tightness near my sternum. I massaged the skin. There wasn't anything specific. I worked my fingers into the space between my ribs. There was something, a sort of stiffness, as though chewing gum had been stuck alongside my breastbone. I thought it must be a knot in the muscle. But a week later it still hadn't gone. I made an appointment to see a doctor. She said she thought that it was probably a cyst, but advised me to have a mammogram. She felt fairly certain there was nothing urgent. Sometime in the next three months would be fine. I resolved to see a doctor when we arrived in London.

Innominate Stream

S chool finished. We stayed for the fireworks for the Feast of St John, and then Evie and I flew back to Mum's house, as we had done every summer for the past six years. The three of us meant to spend a week at the cottage, and then I would fly back to help Rupert. Evie would stay with her cousins. The night before we were due to leave for Wales Mum stood outside her house. She was looking at my rental car in the driveway, walking around it, peering through the windows. For some reason she had been adamant that I should hire a car, although God knows I had little enough money, and now, after tapping the roof, she said:

'I think we'll go in my car tomorrow.' I stared at her, unable to fathom her reasoning.

'Well, what do you think we should do with this?' I said.

'We can leave it on the drive until we get back.'

The whole debate about the rental car had seemed bizarre to me, and in order to avoid an argument I went to my room, and started shuffling a deck of cards that Evie had brought with her. Mum was behaving extraordinarily oddly. One card flipped free and slid to the floor. The three of spades. I picked up the card and shuffled again, and then turned over the top card in the pack. The three of spades.

In Tarot, the suit that corresponds to spades is the called the suit of swords. The three shows a scarlet heart with three swords piercing it and rain clouds opening behind it. Black streaks of rain. I shuffled again. The three of spades. I tapped its surface, couldn't resist speculating over its meaning. The first spade, it seemed to me, was the immediate, financial trouble in which we found ourselves. But the second and third pips worried me. I pushed the card back into the centre of the pack, and went to bed, irritated by my superstition.

'Kate? Kate?' It was Mum's voice. I reeled into consciousness, was suddenly wide awake. I listened but could hear nothing more. I disentangled myself from the bed, and ran along the landing to Mum's bedroom, which was empty, the covers thrown back. There was a smell that I could almost touch. Fear.

'Kate?' I looked over the stairwell and there was my little bird, my mother, reaching up the stairs, her eyes spoke where she could not, and I rushed down to her, and helped her to the sofa, her lungs bubbling with liquid. I telephoned 999 and then ran back up the stairs:

'Evie, Grannie is very, very sick and I have called an ambulance, you must get dressed and come down right away.'

Mum waved to us from behind the oxygen mask as she was lifted in a wheelchair into the ambulance. I dropped Evie at my brother's house, and continued to the hospital.

When I got there, Mum was in a bay in Accident and Emergency with two nurses trying to clip heart monitors onto her fingertips. She reached forward, her fingers stretched before her, as though she were trying to find something to hold onto, and pull herself clear of the bed. I touched her hand, but she pushed it away. It was something else that she needed, something more. A doctor appeared at her bedside, and said:

'Prepare for defibrillation.' I was swept aside as a cardiac team gathered around my mother. I saw her fall back on the bed, and her head roll to one side, her hair untidy as a rook's nest. There was a bang, and an electronic whine.

A nurse moved me into a peach-coloured room, with *Bereavement Suite* written on the door.

'It doesn't mean that your mother is dead,' she said, 'but that this is the best place to be while this goes on. There are a lot of people round her.' I heard again the butcher's cleaver bang of the defibrillator behind the door. I telephoned my brother.

When John arrived, trailing Evie and his own family, and we had gathered in the peach-coloured room, the doctor came in to talk to us.

'We have tried to resuscitate your mother three times with the defibrillator, and she has had an adrenalin shot to her heart, but she is unresponsive. Would you like us to continue to try to resuscitate her?' The air in the room seemed to be made of plastic.

'Will she have suffered brain damage?' I asked.

'She has been without oxygen for six minutes, so yes, there will be damage, but what it is I cannot say.'

I looked at John. Mum had never wanted to be revived. She had always been very clear about it. There was a moment where nobody seemed to move, and then one of us must have said something because the door was closing and the doctor had gone. A nurse came in and said that they were preparing Mum's body, taking it to somewhere we could look at it, at her, and would we please wait a few minutes more. I phoned Rupert, and told him that Mum had died. The words sounded very strange to me.

And then the doctor came back. 'This is really very unusual,' he said, his hands raised as though in blessing, 'but your mother's heart has begun to beat of its own accord although she is unable to breathe. We have put her on life support and are moving her to our critical care unit. If there is no improvement in twenty-four hours we will turn off the support. In the meantime we'll try and find out what has caused this.'

Critical care.

I woke in darkness at my brother's house. I was in the spare bed in my nephew Connor's room. He was awake. 'Connor, I'm going to go over to the hospital. Do you want to come?'

'It's OK. I'll stay here and look after Evie. I'll tell the others where you've gone.'

I drove to the hospital and parked Mum's car in the almost empty car park. Trees huffed and nodded. Blue streaks lightened the inky sky. A copy of *Jane Eyre* was tucked beneath my elbow. I made my way through the quiet corridors, their vinyl floors and fluttering fluorescents, and rang the buzzer outside the critical care unit. A nurse admitted me and then rejoined her colleagues sitting peaceably at their station. Mum and two other patients rested, each with their private, internal struggle, each mechanically suspended in a space held open between life and non-life, an opportunity, a place of choosing. Mum was all wired up, with a tube taped to her nose.

There were a lot of pipes. The rhythmic sound of her mechanically controlled breathing was like waves on an artificial beach.

I pulled up a chair and leaned close to Mum's face. Ordinarily she was deaf, and the life support had a range of noises all of its own. I had to lift my voice even to hear myself above it. I read the part where Jane Eyre frightens Mr Rochester's horse and he accuses her of being a fairy. Mum gave no indication of knowing that I was there, but the nurses were very appreciative. After a while, the man in the next bed, who had been in a coma, woke up. There was a choking and whirring as his lungs began to inflate of their own accord, causing a flutter of activity as he fought against the machinery, which suddenly threatened to smother him. Shortly afterwards his wife arrived. He seemed to be trying to say something. His wife translated for him, through his pipes and tubes:

'He wants to know what you were reading,' she said.

'It was *Jane Eyre*.' She looked nonplussed. 'By Charlotte Brontë.'

'He very much enjoyed the story,' she said. Her husband wheezed and rasped. He looked from me to my mum. 'And he wants to know if you're going to come and read again tonight.'

Tonight.

Mum's condition was to be reviewed at four o'clock that afternoon, and if there was no improvement, they would disconnect the breathing apparatus.

'If I'm here, yes, certainly,' I replied.

At some point during the morning Mum's doctor told us that her heartbeat had stabilised, although she was unable to breathe without the machine. He thought she had suffered a thrombosis to her heart, and was almost certain that she would not recover. She had been without oxygen for six minutes before her heart began to beat. It had been damaged by what had happened. He put her chances of recovery at about a million to one. But the medical team agreed that they would postpone turning off the machine until the following afternoon. So Mum was to be given another day. Others came to visit. Evie stayed with the cousins. I went back to Mum's house and collected some personal things. Pyjamas. A photograph of Dad, held in a silver frame. It had been taken on holiday, in France. Feet apart, arms folded. His happy smile as he squinted through bright sunlight at the camera, and at the woman who was taking the picture. He must have been about fifty. I cleaned the glass. It had been Mum's habit to kiss the photograph each night before she went to bed.

When I got back to the hospital and the wide, artificially lit space of the critical care unit, and saw the nurses sitting at their station, it was as though I were looking at it for the first time. I seemed to recognise nothing. Possibly because until this moment I had been focused on Mum, her tiny form, the tubes. Looking at it now, in the middle of the day, it felt more like NASA than a hospital. The intubated patients weren't in space, but they were suspended, several yards apart from one another, each with a bank of equipment and wires maintaining their life on earth. The gasp and bubble of mechanical breath. It took me a while to notice that the man in the next bed, the man who had woken up, and had enjoyed *Jane Eyre*, had gone, and so too had his bed. Only the husk of machinery remained, cracked open like an empty chrysalis. A nurse told me that Mum's condition was stable, but that she was making no effort to breathe.

'She has spent the last nine years waiting to join that man,' I said, and pointed to the photograph of Dad. I had arranged it where Mum would see it if she were to wake. 'You're going to have to try very hard if you want to get her back.' My brother and his wife and I took it in turns sitting with Mum. In the afternoon, the children came too. Evie was fascinated with the tubes. Rupert called from Barcelona. We were already discussing the funeral.

That night, when Evie was in bed, I again returned, alone, to the hospital. I had brought *Jane Eyre* with me, although the empty space where the man had been, and Mum's continued unresponsiveness, made the effort seem pointless. The nurse I had spoken to earlier was sitting in the chair next to the bed. She held Mum's hand.

'Come on, Jean!' she was saying. 'You can do better than that!' When she noticed me standing there we chatted for a moment or two, and the nurse gestured to the photograph of Dad.

'How did they meet?' she asked. I found myself telling her how Mum's best friend had been Dad's sister, and that they had all gone to school together. Dad had decided that he wanted to marry Mum when he saw her playing tennis at the village recreation ground. She must have been about sixteen.

'She was just so *alive*!' he would say.

'What did your dad do?' the nurse asked.

'He was a teacher. At the university. A professor of Mechanical Engineering,' I said.

'You must be very proud of him.'

'Yes,' I said, 'I am.' I had the feeling that the nurse's questions might be in some way therapeutic, though whether intentionally, or accidentally, I couldn't tell. I was very much aware that Mum might hear our voices. So I found myself telling the nurse how when Dad was a boy he had won a scholarship to the local grammar school. I was conscious that I should try to get the story right.

Or more specifically, that the reason I was telling the story at all was in the hope that Mum might recognise it.

Dad had won a scholarship, sponsored by the tannery where his father worked. His grandfather – William – also worked at the tannery. William was a man with forearms like roasted hams, who had been converted to Methodism by John Wesley himself when he crossed the country on horseback.

I looked at the nurse. Then back at Mum. Her face was pale. The breathing apparatus bubbled as her breath condensed in the pipes.

'No, I'm very sorry,' I said. 'That can't possibly be right.' John Wesley died in 1791. Great-Grandfather William must have been born around 1870. I had obviously crossed my wires. I had another go.

From the day of his conversion William Norbury never touched alcohol, and he even turned the other cheek when a fellow-worker struck him. Although, when his assailant hit that cheek also, William had decked him with a single punch to the jaw, saying: 'The Lord said "tha' must turn the other cheek", but he never said owt about what to do if tha's hit on that one.' William had become a lay preacher. He travelled around the county with a suitcase full of sermons, written in a minute, cursive script, and carried by a young man who had incurred some sort of brain damage, but was devoted to William, and would not leave his side. William married and had five children. His first son, Wesley, named after William's hero, had died of meningitis in childhood. The two younger boys had gone into the tannery, where they heaved the stinking hides of cattle into deep salt pits, their sleeves rolled up, rubber boots protecting their legs, their cotton shirts and twill trousers protected by black stuff aprons. This had gone on, day in, day out, until the coming of war in 1914 interrupted a grinding pattern. William remained at the tannery, but my grandfather, Russell, who was the same age as the century, was called up for the fighting. When he came back home again, injured, from France, he was still a teenager. Although his physical injuries healed quite quickly, the war left its mark in other ways. Russell spent four years looking at his face in a mirror, convinced that one side was bigger than the other, and that shrapnel was still embedded in his jaw. Because he was unable to work in the tannery proper, the owner, Mr Posnett, gave Russell a job in the Time Office, where he stamped cards for the workers as they began and ended their shifts. Mr Posnett was often heard to say: 'I saved Russell Norbury's life after the war.' I wasn't sure whether a mind-numbingly dull job in the Time Office constituted saving Granddad's life, or not, but it had certainly provided him with an income. He was plagued by anxiety, although he was always a gentle man, with a fine tenor voice, and was good-humoured about everything except his neuroses.

During the years in which Granddad was unwell, my grand-mother, Doris, worked as a bookie's clerk. She told us of the diminutive jockeys and their bright silks, as the men were weighed in the scales. Throughout the years when Granddad was staring in the mirror, Doris was the only breadwinner.

I stopped again. This, too, seemed far-fetched. What would a Methodist be doing working at a racetrack, and a woman with children at that? And how would she have got there? The nearest racetracks were at Aintree, in Liverpool, and Haydock Park near

Manchester. Without access to transport, they may as well have been on the moon. Maybe Doris had simply worked for a bookkeeper, or a local accountant. Perhaps it was I who had made the leap from bookkeeper to bookie, and embellished it with half-remembered scenes from *National Velvet*, in which a young Liz Taylor won the Grand National, or very nearly did, on a farm horse. My time frame for all these events was, in any case, extremely woolly. The fragments of story pulsed and glowed like lumps of molten ore in mud, scattered over an indeterminate period that was punctuated by hardship and war. The stories were familiar to me. But I had never before laid claim to them, or attempted to share them.

Still, somewhere in the hardship years – that came between the war years – Dad won the Highfield Tannery Scholarship. He had gained, briefly, the highest mark in his year at the village school, but a Methodist had never won the School Prize before, and so the examination papers had to be remarked. This meant Dad now had the second highest mark after a girl called Sheila McKnight, who beat him by one per cent. The school wasn't known for its gender equality, but it was clearly better that the prize went to a girl who was an Anglican, than to a boy from Chapel. This, at any rate, was the view expressed by the Methodists and I was aware that it, too, had a ring of legend about it. But Dad quite definitely won the scholarship. Mr Posnett offered, in addition to the bursary, to buy Dad's uniform and books, his protractor and compass, ruler and pens, his Latin grammar, his dictionary. But the tannery workers declined the offer and instead they had a whip-round. Fred was one of their own. He had all that he needed for the grammar school. Later he obtained a government bursary to study at the university in Liverpool. The tannery continued to support him.

Mr Posnett made it clear that Dad should ask for whatever he needed. Once again, the villagers made sure he was properly kitted out. There were no summer holidays, on account of the war, and after two years he completed his bachelor's degree in Mechanical Engineering. By the time he had graduated, with first-class honours, peace had broken out, erratic and wild, and Dad was never called upon to fight. When he completed his master's, and Mum was twenty-two, he asked her to marry him at the top of Tryfan, a mountain in Snowdonia. Afterwards they jumped between two monoliths called Adam and Eve, almost ten feet above the ground. This was known as the Tryfan step, and conferred the Freedom of the Mountain on all who successfully completed it.

'My goodness, she must have been fit!' said the nurse. I'd forgotten that she was there.

'She was,' I said. 'She once ran a hundred yards in 11.4 seconds. A research chemist, who had been a Cambridge Blue, saw her race at the ICI recreation ground, and wanted to train her, there'd even been talk of the Olympics. But they weren't able to pursue it, on account of the war.'

Mum didn't stir, and when morning came I took Evie to Liverpool to buy her a dress for the funeral. They would switch off Mum's machine at four o'clock. I could wear the same black Nicole Farhi suit that I'd worn at Dad's funeral. After all, I'd never worn it since. But when we got back to the car there was a message on my phone. Mum had opened her eyes. She looked at her nephew, Peter, who had come to hold her hand. Evie took the bag with her new dress in it and squashed it into the glove compartment. We arrived at the hospital at three o'clock, to find Mum sitting up in bed, a cup of tea in front of her, a slice of buttered toast in her hand.

'I really don't feel very well,' she said.

Mum remained in hospital for weeks. While her astonishing and unlikely recuperation unfolded, I moved between her home, the Welsh cottage, our new home in London, and Barcelona. By the end of the summer we had left Catalunya. Evie began the autumn term at a primary school in Battersea, and I finally took the opportunity to have the mammogram that I had postponed at the start of the summer. I hadn't yet had time to register with a doctor in London, so I went to the same hospital in Chester where Mum was still a patient.

The radiographer said: 'That doesn't look like a cyst.'

It was white, the lump, which meant it was a solid mass, and it had tiny arms that shot out like spider's silks, or pincers. It was uneven, and knobbly. Like a crab.

'Does it look like cancer?' I asked. The radiographer paused.

'Yes.'

'Can you think of anything else, in your experience, that isn't a cyst, and isn't cancer, that this might be?'

This time she didn't hesitate. 'No.'

'I have a ten-year-old daughter,' I said. 'I have to live.' The radiographer took a biopsy. The device sounded like the dead-bolt that vets use to kill a horse. I gasped as it nipped the muscle of my chest wall. The area began to swell. Afterwards I sat and waited with some other ladies, all of us dressed in lilac surgical gowns, outside a nurse's room, our day clothes in plastic crates. I couldn't raise Rupert on the phone. I called my sister-in-law, Maria, who happened to be near by, and she came to sit with me.

'I didn't want to come here.' It was a blonde woman speaking, her roots showing wiry and grey. 'I come here from Caernarfon. They said I should do it on account of my mum. She's died of it.' The rest of us were silent. 'I wouldn't have come if they hadn't told me to. I don't want to be here.' A woman sitting next to me leaned forward. She asked the lady from Caernarfon about her journey, asked if it had been difficult to get to Chester, asked her how long it had taken. A nurse brought me tea in a china cup and saucer, and some custard creams on a doily-covered tray. I noticed that some of the other ladies also had trays. The obvious luxury in an NHS hospital made me feel both special and apprehensive. A nurse told me that the result of the biopsy wouldn't be available until after the weekend, but that eighty per cent of women with breast cancer survived it. Rupert and Evie expected me home in London, but the hospital advised me to wait.

I went back to Mum's empty house, but I was skittish, and couldn't keep still. More than one friend said *I'm sure it will be fine* and this seemed strange to me, because what I'd seen on the ultrasound hadn't looked fine. I recalled the way the radiographer had glanced at the nurse, the way the architecture of the room had appeared to tighten.

I packed an overnight bag and took Mum's car. I drove towards the mountains of Cumbria, two hours north of Chester. When I reached the Lake District I drifted west, towards the Wasdale Valley, and parked the car at the head of the deep lake called Wastwater, beneath the buttressed, stubborn flank of Great Gable and the Scafell Massif. I didn't need a map for this place. I knew it better than anywhere on earth. I had first climbed Scafell with Dad, when I was Evie's age, wearing shorts and thin-soled plimsolls, through which I had felt every stone, Dad's big hand wrapped around my little one.

When Dad had been a doctoral candidate his supervisor, Geoff Calvert, built a cottage in the Lake District out of anything that came to hand. The stones were random rubble. The Crittall windows, which were almost as big as the walls, had been salvaged from a hospital in Liverpool. Geoff told his graduate students that anyone who helped with the construction could have a week's holiday, gratis, for life. And so, every summer, we spent a week at the cottage. There were gas lamps in the early days, run off Calor gas canisters. Later, electricity was provided from a car battery. The water passed through a charcoal filter directly off the mountain behind. And there was a bath beneath the kitchen draining board. We went on expeditions in the day, to the mountains, and the lakes, and laughed and played cards at night.

So I had climbed Scafell, on one of those feted summer days, my hand in Dad's for much of the way, though he had carried me back down on his shoulders, not because I was tired, but because I could feel the stones through my worn-out plimsolls, although my brother had teased me mercilessly for being a baby. Afterwards Mum insisted that we drove to Kendal, so I could have some proper walking shoes. I know that the memory was of Scafell because of a great wall of rock that loomed over us, forbidding as a Cunard liner. The rock-wall led to a passage, and the passage was called Lord's Rake. It rose like a ladder, up and down in a diagonal zigzag, and emerged at the summit of the hill. The combination of the wall, which acted as a landmark, and the narrowness of the passage made Lord's Rake a safe route, even in mist, because you could feel your way, and know exactly where you were, even if you couldn't see. A roughly carved cross at the start of the rake marked the place where, on a warm September afternoon in 1903, four young men, all experienced climbers, 'skilful, careful and modest', had inexplicably fallen to their deaths. But Lord's Rake led beyond the cross, obliquely rising through dips and cols, some as narrow as a horse's saddle, and it carried the traveller across, not over, the buttress.

I had returned to the place many times. When I was twenty-three I ran away from a love affair in New York, and had driven from Heathrow Airport in a rented car wearing a Jean Paul Gaultier suit and ice-pick Jimmy Choo heels. When I arrived at Scafell I rummaged in my travel bag, and then stripped in the National Trust car park, climbing the hill in Converse All Stars, my ex-lover's Levi 501s and a man's black cashmere sweater. I had nestled inside Lord's Rake, and had felt safe, held, the cleft of rock filled with gritty snow, my cheek against the stone, the mist beading in my eyebrows and lashes, and settling in my bleached cropped hair.

This time, as I visited the mountain, I was hopeful, despite what I had seen on the ultrasound. I felt strong, although I also felt sick, and though my thoughts were as skittish as a bird's on a twig peeping down at a lash-tailed cat, my heart sang. Wastwater glowed, a chasm of reflected light. There was a bathtub filled with water for the sheep. The September day was bright although the lower slopes of Scafell were veiled in shadow: the arc of the autumn sun remained low. I followed the footpath over a ridge known as Brown Tongue, walking between two nameless streams, keeping to the bank of the southern one, searching for a place to cross. But the stream was in spate, and at the ford it was not possible. I could see the stepping stones, sunk, conserved, beneath a dark slab of bubbling water. The water looked like glass. I decided to keep to the southern stream, and to follow its northern bank. As I walked higher over the humped side of the mountain I entered the natural amphitheatre that characterised Scafell. I could see Mickledore and Scafell Pike, which is the highest peak in England. Tucked away, to one side, was the summit of Scafell itself. I walked for an hour through bilberry and scattered rocks. In early summer Hollow Stones, for that is what this place is called, is a picture-book tapestry meadow, something from the loom of the Lady of Shalott, where only the unicorns are missing. But today it wore a different coat, the green grass caramelised into brown, a wheezy breath as the wind passed over it, some dried-out blackened seed heads. A dog had slipped its owner's leash and trotted excitedly about, rounding up sheep, its sharp bark and their worried bleats hanging in the air about me, revolving like the shapes on a child's cot mobile. I wondered if the owner was close at hand, or if any of the sheep were pregnant. The farmer might shoot the dog if he saw it. All these 'ifs'. White haze made a ceiling for the sound and my anxiety. And then, quite suddenly, I had reached the spring that was the source of this innominate stream. The water spilled from beneath a rock as big as a car.

The rock is marked on A. Wainwright's iconic guidebook drawing of Scafell, and labelled simply: *Big Boulder*. Beneath it is an 'X' and the word *Spring*. On the other side of the stream, the side of the way-marked footpath, the National Trust were building a staircase of rock in the interest of conserving vegetation and preventing soil erosion. The close proximity of this staircase to the boulder reminded me of the A303, which so narrowly misses the monument at Stonehenge, and where the proximity of heavy traffic to the ancient site mystifies spiritual tourists. The spring was choked with litter. This, too, seemed new. Paper wrappers and plastic crisp packets twirled and snagged in a pool the size of a washing-up bowl. Beyond it was the scree slope that led to the rake, and to the cruise-ship wall of rock.

I searched for a place to drink. There was a channel, litter-free, right underneath the boulder. Reaching in I pulled out handfuls of water, metallic, peaty, cold. I drank because I was thirsty, but also because I wanted something. I wanted the water to wash clean the results that I would receive on Monday. I found two acorns and two hazelnuts in my pocket, souvenirs of other walks, and I dropped them into the water. They were the nearest that I had to pennies. I straightened up, stiffly. An old gentleman with two long sticks appeared. He drew level and then walked past me. He picked his way meticulously and energetically, wiping the sweat from his chin, and pushing his false teeth out when he stopped to catch his breath. After about fifty yards he stared at his map, and then at the wall of rock.

'It's there,' I called. 'Just follow the scree.' He nodded back at me, and after a few more minutes' scrambling, a tall stick in each of his hands, his map on a cord around his neck, he vanished. I followed, then, persevering, until I too had entered the rake. I spread my palms over the cross that was carved in the rock, the memorial to the four dead climbers. The old gentleman had gone. The passage was filled with broken stones. Lemon-coloured saxifrage illuminated the monochromes. Splintered rocks leaned inwards, uncertain as old chimney stacks.

> *Where trouble melts like lemon drops,*
> *High above the chimney tops . . .*

There was a whirring sound: *whop-whop, whop-whop, whop-whop* and a black bird flapped by at nose level. I could see the lie of the feathers on its back. A crow. There was a staggered note to the downbeat, which was bouncing off the ceiling of cloud. The cloud looked close enough to touch. I couldn't go on. I sat down for a moment, and then stood up. I told myself that it was the stress of Mum's illness, and of moving house, and the biopsy that had exhausted me, unwilling to accept the possibility of cancer, or rather, that I might be affected by it in this manner, prevented from completing what I had come to do, and I turned, away from Lord's Rake, away from the summit, and went back down the hill by the same route that I had climbed it.

Thames

I had never really got to know the Thames. Even though I had lived in London, on and off, for over twenty years, before moving to Barcelona, I had spent most of that time in Earls Court, and I hardly ever saw the river. But now we lived in Lavender Hill, and I crossed the Thames most days.

We were sitting on the front upstairs seat of a Number 49 bus: Evie, Rupert and I, on our way to an Open Day at one of the secondary schools Evie had chosen. She had only just begun to attend a local primary school, an oasis among the social housing and tangled railway tracks of Battersea. Sacred Heart Primary had chickens in the garden, allotments growing rosemary and chives, chard, sunflowers, sweet peas, sedum and green beans. But she had been there less than a fortnight before we'd had to start thinking about where she might go next. The bus was crossing Battersea Bridge.

'Evie,' I said, 'look at the houseboats!' and I pointed to the pastel-painted boats moored alongside Cheyne Walk. There must have been forty of them, hugging the wall of the Embankment.

Late roses in full bloom nodded around the doorway of the nearest one. The river, at this point, was as wide as a lake.

'Mummy, why do you keep going to visit Grannie, and why is your breast covered in bruises?' I reeled my attention back to Evie. I could feel that Rupert was looking at me, but I didn't meet his gaze. I looked at Evie.

'Because I have breast cancer.'

Her eyes opened wide, her face turned the colour of cream. 'Are you going to die?' she asked.

'Well, yes, eventually, we all are. But I don't know when, and I wouldn't know when if I didn't have cancer. None of us do.' I could see it wasn't the answer she was looking for.

'But are you going to die of this?' Rupert reached for Evie's hand and wrapped it up in his. He looked down at the crown of her hair.

'I don't know, my darling.' The bus had crossed the river and was continuing up Beaufort Street in Chelsea. I glanced back at the coloured houseboats as they slid from view. 'Eighty per cent of women with breast cancer live and I very much hope to be one of them. I've been going to Grannie's because we don't have a doctor in London yet, and I have to have a lot of tests. I'll have to have an operation. It'll be quicker if I have it done in Chester.' Evie seemed satisfied with this, with the idea that something was being done, and turned her attention back to the visit.

The school was like a well-ordered version of St Trinian's. Girls wearing goggles shot home-made aeroplanes out of latticed windows above a statue of the Sacred Heart of Jesus. Evie ran about the frescoed cloister, marvelling at the scarlet ceiling with its white-painted wooden beams, like the inside of the divine chest cavity. 'It represents the belly of Jonah's whale!' a rather strict prefect corrected us, and I was happy about this, because the belly of Jonah's whale seemed an excellent place to receive an education.

We all went to stay with Mum for the surgery, although she was barely out of hospital herself. Evie had a week off school. The day of the operation was the Feast Day of St Francis of Assisi, and Evie lent me her gold medallion of the saint, which I am wearing even as I write. I went into what I had thought would be forty minutes of anaesthetic and woke up five hours later. The sun had gone from outside my window, my throat was sore, my neck stiff from being intubated. Nausea rolled around in sticky bales. I had a recollection of a conversation happening around me, but felt sure the cancer had gone. I felt better, so much better, despite the anaesthetic. Evie and Rupert were sitting at my bedside. The next morning the registrar came to visit me. He told me that my surgeon, Claudia, had removed two lymph nodes along with the prickly tumour. She had kept me under anaesthetic while she waited for an initial analysis of the nodes. They had appeared to be disease-free. Had they been otherwise she would have removed all the nodes in my arm. It was this wait that had prolonged the anaesthetic. The survival statistics were woolly for my particular type of cancer, perhaps because so very few people got it. I was aware that the prognosis was 'generally poor'.

'Claudia has done her very best for you,' he said.

'Yes,' I smiled. 'I know she has.'

★

Claudia referred me to the Royal Marsden Hospital in Chelsea, which was exactly two miles from our house. I was excited by this because I believed it to be the best cancer hospital in the country. For a month I kicked my heels and was impatient with my new doctors. I longed to begin chemotherapy. But the pathologists at the Royal Marsden wanted to perform their own examination of the tumour. And there was the idea that I should recover from surgery. There was tension in this waiting. The cares that had resulted in our coming to London in the first place were not about to go away. Obviously, I still wasn't working, and was not in a position to look for work. Rupert's schedule had been completely disrupted. We talked about selling the cottage. Or rather, Rupert did. I couldn't bear to part with it. One night Evie ran to her bedroom, her hands over her ears, as we argued.

Keeping our house warm became a contentious luxury. For the most part the house was cold. We used the heating when Evie got home and if I had visitors, although the moment the door closed behind them I flicked the control to *Off*. Food also required consideration, not helped by my insistence on buying organic produce, and I perfected the art of making a chicken last three days (roast, soup, risotto). Rupert gave up drinking in order to save money, although insisted that I should drink red wine, because it contained something that counteracted cancer. Our lives were pared back, finely honed, absolutely without excess.

What I could do, and did do, every day, was walk. Early one afternoon, towards the end of October, I set off north through Battersea Park until I reached the wide expanse of the river. I left the park at Albert Bridge, and headed west along the Thames Path. A heron flew low over the water. Brake lights winked along the Embankment on the opposite shore. The bronze water appeared to be still. A cormorant splashed clumsily into the middle of the river. One wing was missing a couple of flight feathers, and I thought briefly of the black and white keys on a piano. And then the cormorant remained there, drifting neither east nor west. As I crossed the road at Battersea Bridge a cyclist slammed into me: *What the bloody hell do you think you're doing?* We landed together, on the pavement, and I caught his smell of sweat and 3-IN-ONE OIL, a rich, metallic tang. He got back onto his bike, muttering under his breath, a red light winking on the back of his helmet, and was on his way before I had even got to my feet. I swung my legs out of the road, anxious to avoid the lunchtime traffic. I was winded, and bruised, but inexplicably energised, glad of the contact with another human being, jolted by the impact of the collision.

I rejoined the footpath. Alongside the river wall, in front of St Mary's Church, a line of single shoes hung by their laces. Plane trees, starved of colour, hissed in the breeze. Behind them, the *tick-tick-tick* of a London cab, the yawn and judder of a double-decker bus. A single scarlet leaf, big as a beer mat, blew to my feet and I bent down and picked it up. It was from a Virginia creeper, sometimes called five-finger, although this one only had three. At its base was a lemon-coloured crescent. I pressed the leaf inside the book I was carrying. Other leaves curled like yellow cigarette papers. I picked one up. Rowan. The orange berries hung in clusters over my head. Some late nasturtiums had put out optimistic watery green discs. Pale roses, like balled-up tissues, nodded on browning stems. I listened to the layers of sound, the cars, the clank of a JCB on the northern bank at Chelsea Wharf, the whine of aeroplanes on their way to Heathrow Airport, the whirr of a child's buggy, and the flat rhythmic tread as his mother sped past me, multitasking, running, walking the baby, all the while listening to her iPod on padded headphones. The child's hair floated like the fluffy seeds of willow herb. I worried about his head getting cold. His fingers opened like daisies as they passed.

At Battersea Railway Bridge I stopped. The bridge needed repainting. Undercoat the colour of marigolds showed through a grey, peeling topcoat. Buddleia, fading with the season, waved between metal arches. A weeping willow nodded, its leaves trailing in the water. In the middle of the Thames was a flat tender, containing two men in Day-Glo jackets. The men seemed tiny, and were pointing into a flurry of circling gulls. The whole scene reminded me of a snow-globe paperweight. Suddenly the gulls stopped circling and settled on the water. They began to drift upstream. One of the men threw something, and again the gulls swirled about the boat. And again they settled on the water, and began to drift upstream.

I watched the river settle into this new direction. The sun was shining, the sky pale blue, and the distinctive chalk-milk, clay-grey emulsion was hidden beneath the reflected sky. Etymologists argue that this colour gives the river its name, although they disagree about exactly how. *Thames* derives from the Middle English *Temese*, which in turn grew out of the Celtic name, *Tamesas*, which probably means dark, while a possible Indo-European, but pre-Celtic root implies muddiness, from *$t\bar{a}$-, or *melt*. The water crackled like a stream of newly minted coins. The river had been quite silent, but now a sound appeared, regular as a heartbeat, and every second or two a wave broke along the shore. Common gulls and mallards trimmed the water's edge, each one no more than a yard from the next. The ducks guzzled the soft mud, the emerald and turquoise heads of the drakes giving a beaded, party look, the white gulls soft as sequins. The female mallards were the same colour as the bank, which was spattered in webbed footprints. A great whirring of cormorants landed in the middle of the river, diving below the water, and reappearing back at the surface, each one always in a different place, like the revolving tin birds in a fairground shooting range. By the time I had regained Albert Bridge the river had settled into its new direction, the water coursing inland in sheets, like newspapers slipping off a press. A man and a woman were arguing. The man was holding a map, and then jabbing in the direction of Putney.

'Tower Bridge is that way!' the man insisted. 'Look at the direction of the water.' The man pointed at the river, and then at Battersea Park. 'That is clearly the Royal Hospital in Chelsea.' From where they stood, the iconic Battersea Power Station, which would surely have helped them orientate themselves, was hidden, tucked out of sight. The woman looked uncomfortable, and tugged at her hair. We were far from the Estuary, and yet there was nothing to indicate, as they and I stood and watched the water, that it might ever have behaved in any other way. When they set off in the direction of the Railway Bridge I said:

'Excuse me.' The man looked surprised, and the woman looked relieved. I said: 'The river flows upstream.'

'What?' he said.

'The Thames is tidal. Tower Bridge is behind you. This is the south bank of the river. In about six hours it will flow the other way.' The man looked at me as though I were mad.

I left the couple squabbling about where they thought they were. But I had had the germ of an idea. If this river, the mighty Thames, could flow upstream, could reverse its direction, twice, each day, then surely it was possible that I could survive my cancer.

★

A month later I walked over Albert Bridge. The sugar-pink and lilypad-green and powder-blue suspension bridge was under repair. The road had been taken up to reveal the rotting iron plates below, although there was still a footpath along one side. Men in steel-toed boots and orange jackets and hard plastic hats filtered the pedestrians, and asked cyclists to dismount. Sparks rained down from a welding torch. There was a smell of sea salt and tar. A cormorant skipped and dived through the current, the same colour as the water. When I got to the Royal Marsden I went round to the Fulham Road entrance and marched up the steps to the front door, although the back door had been nearer. I glanced at the coat of arms in passing. The shield was flanked by an owl and a unicorn. Beneath one of the owl's feet there was a crab. I remembered my little diurnal owl on the moors above Dunbeath. But this owl was the owl of Minerva, Athena, daughter of Zeus, who hatched from her father's head fully dressed with her shield, spear and helmet, her free hand flashing lightning bolts. The goddess of wisdom, healing, and war. The one who helped Odysseus come home.

In the clinical day room I began the long wait of blood tests and examinations, weights and measurements, while my customised drugs were mixed and prepared and a canula fixed into my arm. My friend Tessa arrived before the drugs did. Rupert waited at home to look after Evie. Tessa appeared not to notice the women without hair, the women with open sores, the woman whose face had turned metallic green, the woman who would die within the month. She brought me grapes and started eating them, and then laughed and gave them to me. This wasn't a place where we had ever thought to meet. Over the weeks I learned to accept the kindness of our friends. My sister-in-law Jane took me shopping for daffodil and tulip bulbs so that I would have something to look forward to after the winter. My brother and his family took Evie on holiday. Her godfather Calvin flew from New York. He took us to shows in the West End and brought a blue fox-fur hat to keep my bald head warm and a pair of chocolate-coloured UGG boots for Evie. My friend Rob sent the manuscript of his new book and invited me to give him notes. In thanks for these he gave me a map of Buttermere, marked up in his oddly angular hand, blue ink illuminating valleys and rivers, ridges, places to retrieve my strength. My friend Clare spent two weeks in our home so that Rupert could carry on writing. She cooked, shopped, cleaned, organised the Voewood Festival, and ran her literary agency from our living room. Rupert's brother, Robin, planted roses in the front of our house and his agent, Peter, sent us a hamper that lasted for weeks. And Rupert. Rupert folded his life about me. He brought me books and fresh flowers, and hid his fear behind laughter. When I panicked at the thought of dying surrounded by someone else's wallpaper he painted our bedroom a pristine white. He kept Evie close by his side, walked with her to school every morning, and collected her every afternoon. He cared for me, cared for both of us, steadfastly. Since her own illness Mum was, for the most part, unable to remember that I was unwell, and this made me happier than I could say. Although, during one brief moment of clarity, she had looked at me, and said: *You'll be all right. I can feel it in my waters.*

On my first day in hospital I had been asked if there was a history of breast cancer in our family. I explained that I had been adopted, and didn't know. But as the months shunted into one another, and the year turned around, and again became summer, the question of a family medical history appeared again. For the first time it occurred to me that the reason I had never found my birth mother was because she might have died. My friend Caradoc was also an adoptee. He had written a thoughtful memoir about his experience, called *Problem Child*.

'Why don't you talk to Ariel?' he said. He had taken me to lunch at Sheekey's Restaurant, a treat before I left for Wales with Evie. Ariel was the social worker who had helped reunite Caradoc with his own lost family. He rang her on my behalf. The next day, I spoke to Ariel. There were necessary protocols, like proving who I was, and notifying the relevant local authority, but Ariel gave me her assurance that she would rush these through as efficiently as she was able, given the state of my health. I gave her the information that was recorded on my birth certificate, as well as the name of my birth mother's husband, which I knew from their marriage certificate. Shortly afterwards I met with Ariel. I sat on a sofa in her cool white room and glanced at the piece of paper that she had put in front of me. On it was the name, date of birth and address of my birth mother. She had been on the electoral register all along. As were two half-brothers.

I don't know why I hadn't seen her. It seemed ridiculous how easy it had been. When I got back home I replicated the search myself, and found my birth mother in seconds. She lived about a two-hour drive from where I had grown up. I realised, suddenly, obtusely, bizarrely, that I had only ever looked for her under her maiden name. I couldn't believe, hadn't wanted to believe, it had never even occurred to me – that a marriage that took place on the condition that I was given up could succeed.

It had succeeded. Her marriage had lasted forty years but now her husband, the man I believed had turned me out, was dead.

Ariel wrote a letter to her. At the last minute I panicked. I had the strongest feeling that this might be my only chance to communicate with my mother directly. I told Ariel that I wanted to write to her myself. But Ariel reassured me that it was better this way, that the news would come as a shock, and it was kinder to use an intermediary, and I could see this, so I agreed to it. So Ariel wrote to my birth mother to say that she was researching the genealogy of a client, and had reason to believe that we were related. She included the date, and place, of my birth, along with the name on my birth certificate.

Severn

vie and I decided to make a pilgrimage to the source of the River Severn. What had started as a holiday project now lingered as a habit. It was two years ago that I had followed the Dunbeath Water. No longer just a reason for a journey, the rivers had evolved into a metaphor. Each body of water plaited with the next, twisting first into a bubbling thread, and then into a silver rope. When viewed on a map of Britain and Ireland these ropes formed a net, or a ladder. When I was out walking, the waters became my guide, companion and teacher. They marked a border between different states of being: solid, liquid, air. And they kept moving, were – quite literally – defined by their movement. Heraclitus said that 'no man ever steps in the same river twice, because it's not the same river and he's not the same man.' Woman. Wherever I went, I sought them out, and it seemed fitting that the longest river in Britain should rise just a few miles from my birth mother's house.

Evie and I had been staying at the cottage over the summer holiday. Rupert stayed in London to work. Ariel had still not had a reply to the letter she had sent, but I had noticed that our route back to London passed very close to my birth mother's village, which in turn was near the source of the River Severn. We had booked into a pub in the village of Montgomery. We would visit the source of the river the following day. But when we passed the sign for my birth mother's village we giggled, wondered if we should take a look, decided against it, drove twice round a round-about, and then up and down the same stretch of dual carriageway, before finally pulling into a lay-by and doubling back on ourselves. We decided to make the detour. She lived in an almost inconse-quential village that we missed the first time we passed through it. Her house was at the outer edge of the settlement. The door was at the side, which meant we couldn't see it. The curtains were drawn, although it was afternoon. In the garden was an American-style mailbox. A ticking anxiety circled inside me as finely cali-brated as a Hornby train set. She was in there, behind the door that we couldn't see. I was sure of it. I felt drunk. A notice in the window said: *Say No to Wind Farms.* The previous summer I had been invited to speak at a public inquiry into a proposed wind farm. A car was parked in the drive, and it was the same make as my own. This woman was familiar to me, even from the scant evidence that was visible of her day-to-day life. She spoke to me in a way that I had never experienced. I could feel a hum of recog-nition. Three generations of women were within a few yards of one another. But one of them didn't know it. I wondered if she could feel our proximity.

No one went in or out. Evie and I couldn't stop laughing, although I don't know why. Nerves, I suppose. We discussed what we would do if my birth mother appeared, wondered if we should come back with flowers, and chocolates, and pretend to be

Interflora. I was conscious of my boyish hair, only just returning after the months of chemotherapy. I made myself imagine the possibility that, before the end of the week, we might be returning to this very place, and being welcomed into the house as guests.

Alice Oswald had written a poem called 'A Sleepwalk on the Severn'. A part of it was called: 'mother', and two lines kept recurring to me as I looked at the silent house.

> *I am waiting for an old frayed queen*
> *To walk to that window:*

So was I. The River Severn (Welsh: *Hafren*, Latin: *Sabrina*) takes its name from the ghost of a little girl, murdered by a bitter queen, who killed her husband and then drowned both his mistress and their love child in the river. The child's name was Hafren. After the drowning, the queen permitted the little girl's name to be given to the river. When the Romans came they Latinised it — Sabrina — and honoured the child as a goddess. I thought the lines of the poem must refer to the queen of the story. But the River Severn was also one of fourteen rivers that came into being when Boand upset the Well of Wisdom, and I wondered if the stories might be connected. They were both about illegitimate children.

No one seemed to be coming into, or going out of, the house. We decided to check into our pub.

The next morning we drove past a dammed-up lake through soft green land, which grew greener, and greyer, as it rose. After a while we came to a wooded area with a circular car park and a Portakabin loo. There were some moss-covered wooden sculptures that looked as though they had been made with a chainsaw. Plastic containers indicated the place where leaflets or maps had been stored. Wooden stairs descended into woodland, and there was a slipway for wheelchair users and pushchair access. A number of wooden posts, with different-coloured collars, indicated the choice of footpath one might take. One of them showed a drawing of a young woman with flowing hair and a medieval gown. Stars encircled her head.

'Look, Evie,' I said, 'that must be Sabrina.'

I had told her the story of the jealous queen, and the drowned child immortalised by the river. How the Romans made little Hafren into a goddess.

'That's like trying to make something good out of something horrible,' Evie said. 'How come she is grown-up in the picture?'

'I don't know,' I said. 'Maybe it's not her.'

The Severn appeared, a flash through the trees, quite wide and flowing fast, amber water over slabs of rock. In a short space of time it became very straight, with coppiced woodland along the opposite bank, and it felt vulnerable, exposed, naked in its canal-like straightness. There was very little sound; low cloud cover muted the river. What birdsong there was seemed to come from far away. A plastic chain-link footpath, brightly coloured, of the sort that are found on golf courses, paved the bank on our side. Every so often there were benches. We caught up with a party of walkers, dressed as though they'd been out for Sunday lunch, incongruous on the woodland trail. We almost stepped on a frog.

The land began to rise, through deeper woodland, quite quickly, and the river narrowed suddenly. It meandered, and so did we.

'It's like bees,' Evie said, 'a tail made out of bees!'

In the past, when we had walked, Evie had been the one to slow down, to reach for my hand to help her. But it was me, now, who followed slowly, me who fought to catch my breath. I had still not recovered my strength from the months of treatment. I had been weakened by chemotherapy, my heart had been affected, and I had had extensive surgery just a few weeks before the summer holidays began, designed to reduce my risk of developing further primary breast cancers. I still had limited use of both my arms, and my stamina returned as slowly as my hair. Every so often I had to stop and rest while Evie ran ahead. She stood on a boulder and waved down at me, threw two sticks into the current, one for each of us, and then raced downriver after them. If they got caught she leaned across the flow, poking until the blockage span free. After a while she found a longer branch, which she stripped of tiny twigs, and this she gave me to use as a walking stick. I took it, happy, grateful for its help. Joint pain was an unexpected side effect of hormone therapy, or perhaps a consequence of a chemically induced meno-pause. Whatever the cause, in medical terms, the practical conse-quence was that my feet, knees, hips and spine protested with every step.

We came to a dirt road. On the other side the river narrowed sharply. The way-marked footpath became a well-trodden track next to the stream. White mist drifted like dragon's breath. Our faces were misted in droplets. They filled our eyelashes and beaded our hair. Evie put her hands to her face: *It's so cold!* I couldn't feel it, because my face was numb, and remains so to this day. Another of the side effects of treatment. But I recognised, from my journey to Dunbeath, the proximity of the waterhead.

As the land rose and the source of the river grew closer the foot-path became boggy and wet. Great stone slabs had been set along the path and for once I didn't complain at the intervention. I wouldn't want to walk out across this moor without very concrete guidance. Suddenly, the stream opened out into a high-sided, bean-shaped black lagoon. A post next to the footpath announced the source of the River Severn. I had that same feeling, of staring into primordial soup, that I had experienced at the hole in the ground at Dunbeath. But this hole was the size of a swimming pool. It was walled around by collapsing peat hags. The river flowed quickly, even from this place. I was amazed that it began with such strong purpose.

Evie looked into the pool, but she too seemed perplexed by it. White mist curtailed the view, although a dim path was visible across the moor. The source of the River Wye was just a few miles away. I wondered if the footpath led to it. But that wasn't what we'd come to do. 'Let's go back,' Evie said. Alice Oswald's poem again returned to me:

> *I am waiting for an old frayed queen*
> *To walk to that window:*
> *She who shines like the Moon,*
> *But shits on the walls,*
> *She whose house has no books in it*
> *Or bath.*

> *She who stares at her dead child*
> *And never tidies away*
> *Its rat-eaten cradle clothes . . .*

> *Waiting for whatever hard worked mother*
> *Owns those feathery bones.*

My fingers caught the stone slab and I hauled myself out of the water. My nose, ears, eyes, lungs were choked with it. Pain seared my chest, from the recent surgery, but I felt that I might drown if I let go of the stone. I could hear Evie shriek behind me. I had stepped off the footpath into a patch of water the size of a puddle. I couldn't help laughing, even as I hauled myself free. Everything that I knew, all I had been told, about the hazards of walking in a bog. The peat around the fixed stone footpath had formed a pocket, and this pocket had worked outwards, but mostly downwards, to form a dubh loch as treacherous as any I might have found in Scotland. Practise what you preach, check the depth of any water with a stick, no matter how small the surface. I laughed even as I tended to the tearing pain across my chest.

Evie hovered, anxious. I was glad that I had done it. I was glad that she had been there, that she had learned, with no harm done, that the moors are not to be fooled with. Once it was clear that I wasn't going to die she became a little sterner.

'You're covered in dirt.'

'It's only water.'

'It's very peaty water. What if we see someone?'

'What if we do?' I said. 'They'll just have to make of it what they will.'

We had planned to drive on to London after our walk. But when we reached the car park Evie telephoned the pub, and asked if we could have our room back. When we arrived we had hot baths, and hot chocolate, and laughed at our adventure. The next day, just as we were leaving, Ariel called to say she had received a letter.

I love you.

There has not been one day when I have not thought of you.

I have been searching for you from the moment we were separated.

The fantasy evaporated, even before Ariel started to read to me. Her tone of voice had given it away. Ariel read words to the effect of:

I have been deeply shocked to receive this correspondence. I do not wish to hear anything else about this matter. Do not pass any information about me to your client. I am sorry she wants to know her family but I grew up without knowing my own father and I am certain your client can survive without knowing her ancestry. This really is the most horrible thing that has ever happened to me and I trust I will hear nothing more on this subject. All I will say is I was in Australia at the time, trying to avoid difficulties of my own.

Yours sincerely

And her name. Let us call her, for the sake of this history, Mrs Thomas. This letter is an approximation because the copyright belongs to Mrs Thomas. The piece of paper on which it was written is the property of Ariel because it was to her that the letter was addressed. The irony of not owning this communication, and of not being able accurately to share the story of my life, in order to protect the privacy of my birth mother, is not lost on me.

Ariel wrote again. She told Mrs Thomas that I already knew what information was publicly available about her, which included where she lived. She said that I had approached her through an intermediary out of consideration for her feelings. I was not searching for her out of idle curiosity but because I had been diagnosed with a rare and aggressive cancer, that I had undergone chemotherapy, bilateral mastectomies, reconstructive surgery and that I had a daughter. In order to make the best possible decision for my daughter's future I would like a full medical history of the family. She also said that I sent Mrs Thomas my very best wishes, and I was irritated by this, because I did no such thing.

The reply came quickly. Mrs Thomas said that she felt terrified, and that there was nowhere where she felt safe. But she would tell us 'what was required'. She then told how she had become engaged to *a wonderful man* just before going to Australia. She had hitch-hiked down the length of the east coast picking up work where she could find it. She said that just before leaving Sydney she had had *a quickie* at a party with someone who belonged to a group of people she hung around with, although she claimed not to know his name. She said she didn't know that she was pregnant until her mother realised her condition after her return to the United Kingdom. A flat was rented for her and she was shut away for the remainder of her pregnancy. She said she had given birth under anaesthetic and never saw the baby. *They told me later that it was a girl.* She talked about her husband, the man she said she had betrayed, who had been good enough never to mention *it* in all the long years of their marriage. She did, however, provide a thin medical history and I was happy to find, for Evie's sake, that there had been few deaths through cancer, although several due to acute alcoholism. Mrs Thomas contradicted her first letter, in which she had stated that she did not know her father, by providing details of his and his parents' medical history. Her paternal grandmother, for example, had had the only case of breast cancer in the family, and had survived it. She ended by saying that everyone had rights, even her, and that she wanted to be left alone.

I was struck by her lack of interest, of curiosity. She didn't mention her children. She accepted no social or moral responsibility for her actions. She clearly didn't believe that she had any. I did not believe that she did not know the name of my father. And yet, I felt for her. This woman was, technically, my mother. The tie that had been broken between us is generally regarded as the most powerful bond there is. Certainly, in relation to Evie, that is true. I tried to tell myself that it was not me that Mrs Thomas was rejecting, but a circumstance that had been traumatic for her. I was just an idea to her, and her experience had shaped the rest of her life. One of the two of us had to be the mother, and it clearly wasn't going to be her. I drafted a reply:

Dear Mrs Thomas

My only regret, in approaching you through an intermediary, is that it allowed you to make the first words you said to me a passing reference to 'it'. Had I written to you myself I doubt you would have done this. You say you want to be left alone and, also, that you are terrified. There is nothing here for you to fear. If you truly want to be left alone, then help me, by giving me what I seek.

In your letter you mention rights. I have no right to a relationship with you, or even to meeting you. But I believe I have a moral right to know who I am, and where I come from, and that you have an obligation to tell me what you know. Are we Scottish, English, Welsh or Irish? Norwegian? Sailors or publicans? Gypsies or priests? Are we dark, fair, tall or short? You know the answers to some, if not all, of these things. I invite you to share your story with me, not just the pitiful circumstances of your pregnancy. Let me see something of the fabric of who I am.

Yet this is only half the story. It seems improbable that you neither knew, nor subsequently discovered, the identity of my father. He will

be an old man now — if, indeed, he is still alive — and I would like
to know his name, the colour of his hair, his eyes, what he did for a
living. Was he even Australian? Has it occurred to you that he might
be happy to know he has a child? It need not involve you in any
way.

To go to Australia, alone, in the 1960s, and to travel the length of
the coast, was a brave and wonderful thing to do; you are not so retiring
as you make out.

If you feel unable to help me, then there are other people able to
answer most of my questions. Although it seems unlikely that you have
told your children they have a half-sister.

I wish you well, and send you my best wishes

I wasn't sure if the 'best wishes' were heartfelt or not this time,
and I kept the letter, and fiddled with it, for several weeks.
Mentioning her children was provocative, but I didn't have much
to work with. However you looked at it, I was begging, which was
an invidious position to be in. I decided, in the end, not to send it.
There didn't seem to be any point. What could possibly be gained
from approaching someone who so clearly wanted nothing to do
with me? And anyway, I hadn't been honest. What I wanted was to
set eyes on a human being who was related to me by blood. Not
just Evie. I wanted to meet my birth mother. I was curious about
my half-brothers and I wanted to know the identity of my birth
father. I wanted to extend the rope back into time and see the
genetic tribe from whom I was descended. I wanted to blot out
the loneliness. I decided to write to my half-brothers. But there
was a problem. There were two boys that I knew of, Ioan and
Robert. There were over seventy Robert Thomases in the county
where their mother lived and almost as many Ioans. I downloaded

the addresses of all of the Roberts from the electoral register. I wrote another letter:

Dear Robert
Forgive me for writing to you out of the blue.

I am researching my family history and have reason to believe that I am closely related to a Robert Thomas, born, I believe, in Caernarfon, and living at some time in Montgomery, Powys. I know the approximate age. I also know the names of other family members, so could easily work out if you are the right one. For my own part I was given up at birth, with the absolute minimum of information regarding my identity. It is my impression that other family members have not been made aware of my existence. I apologise, therefore, for the scattergun and potentially unsettling nature of my enquiry.

If I have got the wrong Robert Thomas (and there are many on the electoral register) then think no more of this, and thank you for your time in reading it. Otherwise, if you think you might be the right one, I would be delighted to hear from you.

With all best wishes

I didn't send that either. If I sent the letter, or rather the seventy-five identical letters, to the seventy-five men in Powys who carried my half-brother's name, and somehow found the right one, then Mrs Thomas would likely become my sworn enemy, whereas now she was simply adamant that she didn't want to know me. Any chance I might have had of finding my natural father would be gone for good. And I felt a growing certainty that any good qualities that I might have inherited had not come from her. Other than a feisty spirit, for it was clear from her two existing letters that she was in possession of that. That, and the ability to string a sentence.

Every so often I took out my birth mother's letters, or rather the photocopies that Ariel had given me, and looked at them. The more familiar they became, the less hurtful they appeared. I was all but incidental to them. But it was becoming less and less clear to me what I might gain from attempting to pursue a relationship with the woman who had written them. The only thing that was apparent was that hearing from me had distressed her.

If she had been prepared to meet me even a small part of the way, this story would have had a different ending. In her second letter she had said something about having made one mistake through ignorance, and not wanting to have to pay for it for the rest of her life. But she hadn't made a mistake when she gave me up for adoption. She had done the best that was possible under the circumstances. Her mistake, it seemed to me, was to refuse the hand of friendship, now.

It was checkmate, or maybe it was check, but the next move wasn't clear to me. I folded away the letters, the photocopies of hers and the drafts of the ones I hadn't sent, and I put them in a file marked: *Mrs Thomas*. I put the file in a box in the attic that contained Rupert's genealogy, researched by his late father, scroll after scroll of family trees, describing a meandering line that wandered back to a sea captain in the 1700s.

And then, just after Christmas, I decided to send the letter that I had drafted to Mrs Thomas. Her reply came quickly. She didn't reveal the identity of my father, or tell me my nationality. Only that she had been 'unimpressed' by the sex, which she described as 'a very brief incident'. She said that her maiden name was different from her father's name, because her mother had remarried. She did not say what my grandfather's name had been. She did say she'd

253

had an illegitimate half-brother who her mother referred to as 'a bastard in both senses of that word'. I wondered why she had chosen to include this, particular, turn of phrase.

I wrote to her again. I told her that I wanted to meet her. No one need know. I gave her my word. I would come to her. If she was unhappy, I would leave at once, and she need never see me again. I hoped with all my heart she could agree to this.

A month later she sent her reply. Certain phrases caught. This was 'the worst kind of emotional bullying'. 'You had parents.' 'You are not mine.'

I knelt down and retrieved the letter from where it had dropped from my open hand, and continued to read.

'My mother said that we could live with her, but I was broke, and had no prospects. You were always going to be adopted.' She didn't mention that she was engaged to be married, and about to embrace the comfortable, middle-class life that her husband made available to her, and which sustains her to this day. I was aware that I had hit her as hard as she hit me. I laughed, dryly, at this family resemblance – not grace, or courage, or wit, or humour – but a sheer bloody-minded determination. Her desire to bury the truth of my existence was exactly mirrored by my own desire, my deepest wish, that she acknowledge it.

I never looked at the baby.
They told me later it was a girl.

She who shines like the Moon,
But shits on the walls,
She whose house has no books in it
Or bath.

A secret well there was

from which gushed forth every kind of mysterious evil.

There was none that would look to its bottom

But his two bright eyes would burst:

Every way the woman went

The cold white water followed

From the Sid to the sea (not weak it was),

So that thence it is called Boand.

That night I tried to laugh it off. Mrs Thomas as the Evil Queen. Or maybe it was me. I could no longer tell. I wanted my parent to acknowledge me, my primal scream stuck in my throat. It was never going to happen. But why should it? She'd given up a baby that she didn't want on the understanding that she'd never hear of it again. Why should she cooperate now? Why was what I wanted more important than what she wanted? She had gone into an operating theatre pregnant, and had recovered from the anaesthetic no longer so. At some level, her pregnancy had been aborted. She had never looked at the outcome. The next day I couldn't get out of bed. Rupert must have got Evie to school, and then gone to work himself. I drifted in and out of sleep. At lunchtime I awoke from a dream. In the dream I had been a child again, and I was standing in front of a door, as though waiting for someone to come for me. The door was made of red wooden boards and had been built into the side of a hill. Water seeped constantly from under it. I watched my dream-self stamp in the mud. Later I splashed my arms in it and made palm prints on the chipped red paint, before banging on the door with both my hands. I was certain that behind the door was *the source*. I could hear it, like a waterfall, my origin. But the door was locked and had no handle. All I had was the mud on my feet and hands, now drying in pale flakes on the wooden door. I realised, dimly, that the mud was clay, and that something might yet be made of it, although I couldn't see what.

I got out of bed and went to the bathroom. I stood beneath the shower. Some time went by, I don't know how long, and then I reached for a razor, tested the blades. I shaved my legs, my pubis, my armpits and, finally, my head. The lovely new conker-coloured hair that was just beginning to grow clogged up the plughole, choking it. I turned off the shower and walked over to the mirror before starting on my eyebrows. But when I saw my face in the misted glass, the water running off my nose, a wriggle of diluted blood where I had nicked the skin above my ear, I put down the razor, and reached for a towel.

Afon Rhiw

What is existence
but standing patiently for a while
amid flux? Mostly the fish
nibbled out of my reach.
The fly soared, drying its wings
in the March wind before redoubling
its temptations, offering like life itself
a hook hidden among feathers.

R. S. Thomas

Mrs Thomas had addressed the last letter she wrote to me to *Mrs Kate Connelly*. At first I assumed that she had forgotten my name. Later, I began to wonder if this was her father's name. She had told Ariel, when she provided the medical history, that her father was buried in the Beach Head Cemetery at Anzio, in Italy. The Battle of Anzio, in January 1944, was one of the bloodiest battles of the Second World War. Over thirty thousand men lost their lives on the beaches, in the successful attempt to break through the enemy's defences. This awful fact explained the apparent contradiction between Mrs Thomas knowing her father's medical history, yet claiming not to have known the man himself. He had died when she was a baby. I looked up the war records from the Second World War, searched for soldiers called Connelly who'd died at Anzio. I found one. Thomas John Connelly, a member of the Royal Fusiliers. There was a photograph of his white, slightly crooked tombstone. He was buried in the Beach Head Cemetery.

I wrote back to Mrs Thomas, one last note, on a postcard, with a picture of a lion on it. I mentioned the name on her letter to me, *Mrs Kate Connelly*, and I thanked her – if this was my name – for sharing it. I gave her my word that I would never write to her, unsolicited, ever again. I sent her a copy of 'Ash Wednesday' by T.S. Eliot, because she had turned every word that I wrote to her, had prised out a meaning that I had not intended, and I was no longer confident using words of my own. Let her interpret the poet how she will. After posting the letter I lit a candle. I started a novena for the soul of Thomas John Connelly, who died of his wounds at Anzio. Later, Evie and I researched the name. I bought her a Claddagh ring, with a tiny emerald set in the heart, and we laughed that we were descended from the High Kings of Ireland, of whom the Dagda was one.

Three months later Evie and I were in a carwash halfway between Shrewsbury and Newtown.

'Why are we washing the car?' she asked.

'So we don't draw attention to ourselves.' I drove out of the carwash and reversed into a bollard.

'Mum!'

'I'm sorry.'

'Calm down,' Evie said. 'It'll be fine.' When I had been putting the petrol into the car I had noticed that everything added up to eight. Forty-four pounds' worth of fuel. Four and four is eight. The day of the week and the month and the year came to eight; the clock on the dashboard read: *18:08* which, as well as having two eights in it, also added up to eight as did the cost of unleaded petrol at 134.9 pence per litre. I got out of the car to inspect the damage but there was just a faint yellow streak of plastic melded onto the bumper. There was a 1, a 7, and a 4 in our licence plate, which didn't add up to eight but two of the numbers equalled it and another was half of it.

'Mum?'

I got back into the car. We had driven from London to Wales to watch my half-brother, Robert, play rugby.

After giving Mrs Thomas my word that I would not contact her, I had started to think seriously about my half-brothers. Ariel had not seemed keen to trace them, and I had let the correspondence drift. I had promised Mrs Thomas that I wouldn't tell a soul if she would agree to meet me. But she had declined. I had let three months pass by. Three months, in which she might have changed her mind. But there was nothing. So one Friday evening in March, I sat down at our computer, and typed in my half-brothers' names. I added the village where I believed they had grown up, then pressed *Enter*. But there was another word in the search box.

Rupert had been looking up something to do with rugby, and I had failed to delete this one last word. I was about to repeat the search when my eye was caught by the first entry. It was the history of the local rugby club.

'During the '90s brothers Robert and Ioan Thomas went on to play for the league.'

I started looking for a rugby player called Ioan Thomas. I found a reference to one in a club record, but it was years ago and he had retired. I turned my attention to Robert. Instead of looking at clubs I searched through images of rugby players called Robert Thomas. Dozens of faces flashed on the screen, and in the middle of the first page, as the pictures stilled, my eye was caught by a postage-stamp-sized, passport-style image. A kind-looking, good-looking, smiling man, who had my daughter's eyes. Evie came over and stood behind me.

'That's him,' she said.

He was still playing for a Welsh Rugby Union club. I clicked on the image, brought up the website, studied the upcoming fixtures. There was an away match the following evening. Evie and I packed our overnight bags, got into the car, and drove.

We got to the ground early. There was hardly anyone there. A young man came over and tapped on the window of the car. I glanced over at Evie. She was white with apprehension.

'Is it OK to park here?' I asked. 'We've come for the rugby.'

'Over there,' he said, and he pointed. I had driven into the car park of a building supplier next door to the ground, and the man wanted to lock the gate. The floodlights had still not been turned on.

'This is awful!' said Evie. 'I think I'm going to be sick.' I looked at her, chastened. I hadn't stopped to think how she might be feeling. Although I couldn't have imagined it had I tried. There was no emotional signpost by which we might orientate ourselves, although that wasn't an excuse. I had once again walked off the edge of a map, to a place that was completely unknown. I couldn't articulate my feelings. I had little hope of comprehending hers. I parked carefully, close to the exit, with the car facing towards the road.

'We haven't got the right clothes,' Evie said.

'Sorry?'

'Look at us!' Evie was wearing jeans and a brown leather jacket. I was wearing a green plaid duster coat, cut on the bias. It was three months since I had shaved my head. We didn't look as though we were going to a rugby match.

'We look all right. No one is going to be interested in what we are wearing . . . Would you like to go back home?'

'Yes,' she said, and my heart folded like a shot bird. 'No. I want to stay.' I held out my hand, avoiding her gaze.

'Do you want to wait in the car?'

'I'm coming with you,' she said. We squeezed each other's fingers tightly.

We took up a position in the grandstand. There were seventeen people, including us. One young man opened a sports holdall and removed a club flag, and then another, Welsh, flag, and secured them to the back wall of the stand. A young lad with a 1950s cut to his bright red hair ducked in front of us. The man with the flags took out a radio, and began to tune it. A farmer type with flannel trousers tapped a blackthorn walking stick, as though searching for a hidden panel. They all seemed to know one another. I hoped they would assume that we were supporting the visiting team.

There was a training session in progress for the second team. At the edge of the floodlighting, beyond the boundary fence, a horse ran up and down, dipping its head. And then the players came out. I had read the match reports for the previous games and Robert usually wore 6 or 7. I looked for the numbers. Two men, dark-haired, in their twenties.

'He isn't here.'

'That's him!' Evie pointed. 'Number 8.' He was at the other side of the pitch, overexposed in the milky lights, the turf glowing emerald beneath his feet. His hair was longer than in the picture, and he looked stronger than I had imagined; he talked a lot.

'Ah Ref!'

'If I hear one more word from you, Tommo, it's a yellow card!'

'He is *exactly* like you!' Evie said, and giggled. 'Only a boy!'

After that came a tackle which threw him onto his shoulder. He bounced up, tweaked his sleeve, and ran on.

'But, Evie, they're calling him *Tommo*.'

'It's short for Thomas. There's probably another Robert.' I was astonished and delighted by her acumen and detective skills.

Half time came.

We bought milky tea in polystyrene cups. Evie's hands were shaking, though with cold or anticipation she couldn't say. For the first time I began to see how much this secret uncle might mean to her. I had been so caught up in the journey. But Evie had travelled with me. She had lost the hope of having a brother or a sister, at any rate through me. As a result of the treatment I was as barren as the snow. Chemotherapy had damaged my ovaries. Tamoxifen ensured they didn't recover. I had been caught in an early frost. Mum was the only grandparent Evie knew, and she was as frail as apple blossom. Dad had died when she was one. Rupert's parents died long ago. Although there were cousins on both sides of our family, we were not what one might call a dynasty. We moved over to the centre line, and waited for the players to come back. When they filed onto the pitch the man in front of Robert stopped. He chatted for a few moments to the farmer in the flat tweed cap, now leaning on his blackthorn walking stick. The farmer was standing next to us. Robert looked beyond the hold-up, saw there was no virtue in passing, and waited. Then he looked from one to the other of us. He was close enough to touch. I could feel Evie standing next to me. Neither of us seemed able to move. Robert lifted his eyebrows, as though about to speak, and then he grinned at us. It is impossible for me to articulate how I felt.

When the match resumed Robert kept glancing back in our direction. I felt that, if we hadn't gone when he came out of the dressing room, he would come over and speak to us. I watched him shake hands with the referee, the opposing captain, the linesmen and then, as he approached the edge of the pitch, I took Evie by the hand and we flowed down the steps of the stand. Robert glanced briefly in our direction, but he was still talking, and we left the ground.

We checked into a coaching inn in a nearby town. Evie made hot chocolate for both of us – her first time, scrutinising the instructions on the sachet – and poured a generous glass of sherry for me, from a cut-glass decanter on a lace doily. We talked about having hot baths, talked about getting something to eat. Ate the complimentary biscuits instead and curled, a knot of limbs, into the bed.

★

I had seen my half-brother and he had smiled at me. I was indescribably happy. But he had smiled without knowing who I was. This knowledge munched at my equilibrium like a caterpillar inside an apple. In the weeks that followed I veered over what to do. Nothing? Or something? If so, what? Robert was thirty-five years old. It was possible that he might retire. The last match of the season coincided with Evie's half term.

We decided to go back. On the Saturday morning before we left I wrote a letter.

Dear Robert Thomas

I wonder if you remember, at the match against Llangennech, a woman with short hair wearing a long green coat and a young blonde girl with a ponytail. You smiled at us as you walked onto the pitch. We had driven from London to see if the Robert Thomas who played for Llanbeuno might not be the same Robert Thomas we had been seeking. Your smile confirmed it.

I am aware that this letter will come as a surprise to you.

I am a member of your family who was given up at birth. Eighteen months ago I was diagnosed with a rare and aggressive form of cancer. It was for this reason that I wanted to locate my birth family. In part it was because I knew that a family medical history would be invaluable to my daughter. But, in truth, I ached to set eyes on a blood relative. I have approached the older generation of the family and been told, in no uncertain terms, the past is the past. I am sorrier for this than I could ever say, for that past is my 'present continuous'. I do understand that to have had an illegitimate child in the 1960s was considered shameful; though I had hoped that time would soften this.

I have agonised over what to do because no one goes lightly against the wishes of their blood ties, even if it is against the wishes of someone

one has never met. But you are the only blood family I have ever seen, other than my child, and the questions of what is right and what is wrong are complex.

I beseech you not to judge those who have known of me and, I imagine, never spoken of me. It's possible that only one person now living ever knew of my existence in the first place. I would ask you to think deeply about whether or not to share this letter with them.

I have had no way of knowing if you were the 'right' Robert Thomas. When I saw you across the pitch, though, I knew in an instant it was you. So did my daughter. She said: That's him! Number 8. We have come back now to give you this, having no postal address.

I hope and pray with all my heart that you will view this letter positively. I pray that we can meet as friends. Whatever happens, your smile will sustain me for the rest of my life.

With my very best wishes

Kate Norbury

PS. I am staying tonight at the Dragon Inn in Montgomery.

And I added my mobile phone number.

The last match was another away game, in a quiet village, where the Afon Rhiw, a tributary of the River Severn, was intersected by an aqueduct. We parked next to the aqueduct, among a strip of trees between the canal and the river, and made our way to the ground.

We arrived just a few minutes before full time. When the whistle blew the players walked into the tunnel below the stand. Robert walked past me, but I was transfixed. Evie said: *Mum!* and I handed the letter to one of the players.

'Could you give this to Robert Thomas, please?'

He looked at the envelope. 'Yeah, all right.'

'Thanks.'

And I walked away from him. Evie caught up with me; I could sense that she wanted to run. We went back to the place where we had left the car, among the trees between the river and the canal, and we climbed the bank onto the aqueduct. Below us, along the lane, people were returning to their cars. Soon there was only a handful of vehicles left. Others walked in the direction of a pub next to a bridge across a bend in the Rhiw.

The riverbed, where it flowed beneath the aqueduct, was paved to protect the supports of the structure from erosion. The river rustled as it slipped across the stones. The trees still seemed bare, but the new leaves were rolled tight, and were bright, making the light beneath the bridge an absinthe green. There was a flick of bronze, a stroke, slight, quick as a meteor. A goldcrest. Above our heads stacked clouds unfurled. Evie said they looked like candlewax.

And then suddenly Robert was there, walking down the lane towards the aqueduct, relaxed, in conversation with another man. He was wearing jeans and a shirt, no sign of a letter, either in his hand or in his pocket. He passed beneath us.

'He hasn't seen it,' I said.

'How do you know?'

'Look at him! That isn't a man who has just been told, after running about for ninety minutes, that he has a long-lost relative.'

'Mum! You must have given it to the wrong man! What if it's in the hands of his enemy!'

'Enemy? Maybe the other guy hasn't come out of the shower yet.'

'What shall we do?' she wailed, her hands on either side of her face.

'Nothing. We'll just hang around here for a bit.'

'How could you go to all that trouble and then give the letter to the wrong man?' she said.

'I don't know! Just be quiet, Evie!'

'You be quiet!'

And then my mobile rang. Unknown caller.

'Hello?'

'Hi Kate, this is Robert. How are you?'

'I'm fine, thank you, Robert. Thank you for ringing me.'

'Where are you?'

'We're in the car park.'

'Well, I'm in the pub, and I would ask you to join me, but there are thirty players in here and you've clearly gone to a great deal of trouble. Do you know where the bridge is?'

It was about five hundred yards away. We'd passed it on the way to the ground.

'Yes,' I said.

'Will you meet me there in five minutes?'

'Yes.'

'Great!'

'Thank you!'

I stared at the phone. Stared at Evie.

'Oh my gosh!' she said.

'Come on.' I reached for her hand. We clambered down the embankment.

As we neared the bridge, Robert was talking on the telephone. When he saw us approaching he finished his call, turned towards us, nodding, smiling, then lifted both arms in greeting. We all shook hands.

'Evie, this is Mr Thomas.'

He laughed, 'It's Robert . . . Please. I am your brother.'

I looked at him. That wasn't what it said in the letter. He raised his hand, stilled the unasked question. 'You don't have to tell me who you are,' he said. 'You are the image of her.'

We stood and chatted for a while on the bridge. 'Obviously this is a surprise,' he said, 'but as far as I'm concerned, it's a good surprise.' Evie went for a walk along the river path. We watched her, looking back at us, and she waved, happy. I may have been the image of Mrs Thomas, but Evie had her uncle's eyes. She held up her iPod and gave a thumbs-up sign. My own eyes kept glancing off the planes of Robert's face, his hands, his body. I was fascinated to meet someone who looked like me, but was a man. He seemed extraordinarily relaxed. Did I mind if he asked me when this happened?

'It was before she married your father,' I said.

'He wasn't your father?'

'I don't know who my father is.'

His eyebrows furrowed. 'Ah! She needs to get this off her chest!'

'I don't think she wants to. She was really very clear.'

He sighed. 'I imagine she was . . . My mother, that is, our mother, is a very hard woman.'

'I think I've worked that out,' I said. A space had opened between us, full of the secret darkness of the years. He saw my fear, and closed the gap.

'Look, we don't have to do all this now,' he said, 'this is just the beginning,' and suddenly he was smiling again. But as I returned the smile his own fell away and he said, 'Look, I'm very sorry for everything that you must have been through. But it's all right now.' The smile had already returned.

We met again a few weeks later, on our way up to the cottage for the summer holiday. Evie and I arrived early in a roadside pub, and were looking around for Robert when a man leaned into Evie, passing her a bundle, soft and fluffy, and smelling of milk and fabric softener.

'Mum!' Evie cried, and I leaned forward, folding her arms about the baby, showing her how to hold her in the crook of her arm. Robert sat next to us. We all peered into the bundle. From beneath a blue hood, covered in roses, two round eyes stared out.

'There you go,' said Robert. 'Here's your cousin, Seren.'

'Oh my goodness!' Evie cried.

'It means star,' he said.

'She's got your nose!' I said. When Evie was born her nose had been a mystery. Now we knew whose side of the family it came from. Seren also had Evie's eyes, and the two girls appraised one another curiously. When Evie looked up her face was glowing. Seren seemed at home and kicked her feet. I waited for it to be my turn for a cuddle.

In the days and weeks that followed, Robert and I pieced together a fragmented history. Robert asked me why I hadn't done this years ago. I told him that I had left messages for our mother. I told him that, when the law changed, and birth parents were free to seek their children, I had put my name on the Adoption Contact Register. I believed that she would come and look for me. In fact, I had expected her to appear on my doorstep the very next day. Naïve, without doubt, but these things are the stuff of fairy tale. It's almost impossible to envisage something sensible, because it falls outside ordinary experience. Still, as the days went by, and slipped into weeks, then months, and finally years, my excitement and resolve had dissipated. After ten years I realised that she wasn't coming, and after that it had seemed hard to know what to do. It took a diagnosis of cancer to bounce me into action.

Robert didn't know who Thomas Connelly was. In fact the name meant nothing to him. He did have a grandfather who was buried in the Beach Head Cemetery at Anzio. Of course, in protecting Robert's identity, I cannot tell you what the name of our grandfather is. But I smiled at the thought of Thomas John Connelly, warmed in his journey through the Underworld, surprised by the gift of an unexpected quiver of arrows in the form of my novena. And I laughed as my Irish heritage evaporated. We discovered that Robert's home was more or less on my way home, if I drove to London from the Llŷn Peninsula. Robert asked me how come I had a cottage there. I said that the purchase had been an impulse. I just felt happy there. Why did he ask? Well, no reason, he said. But his father's relatives all came from the Llŷn, and he still had family on the peninsula.

The next time I was in Cheshire I told my brother John about finding Robert. And then I told Mum. She listened carefully to the story. Although she was often confused now, there was a glint of steel about her, a warning, and I knew I couldn't mention Mrs

Thomas. We had never discussed my birth mother since that one night when I was eleven years old, not even when we had all been to the Convent. But Mum was happy to discuss the idea of Robert. She considered the information for a moment and then said: 'Does that mean there's a brother for Evie?' I thought about Baby Seren, her bright eyes and perky nose.

'More or less,' I said. 'More or less.' I hadn't thought of it that way.

They say you should never play cards with the devil because he always deals you a shitty hand. I had mistaken the hand that Mrs Thomas held. I had no idea what the name *Connelly* signified. It could simply be, as I had first assumed, that Mrs Thomas had forgotten my name. Part of me suspected that Mr Connelly was the man she believed was my natural father, the man she had met in Australia, and that she knew more than she chose to tell. But I had given Mrs Thomas my word that I would never to write to her again – unless she approached me first. Robert and Evie bore an extraordinary likeness to one another. I didn't know how long Mrs Thomas had been in Australia, but it did occur to me, watching Robert and Evie together, that perhaps his father was, after all, my natural father, too, and the whole thing had been a terrible mistake. I wondered if, perhaps, I too had travelled – like the martin, the little blue bird – in a long migratory arc that had brought me to a hillside on the Llŷn Peninsula, to what was, quite literally, the land of my fathers.

But the truth was, I no longer really cared. My father, the only father I could ever need or want, was the man who claimed me when I was a baby, the man to whom I had given my first smile, at the very moment that we met, and who had given me his family's name. Who had laid me down on a rug on the living-room floor and said: 'Now, what are we going to call *you*?' My father was Emeritus Professor John Frederick Norbury, OBE, B.Sc., M.Sc., Ph.D., LLB, Fellow of the Institute of Mechanical Engineers, our Fred, the village boy made good, who had won a Highfield Tannery Scholarship and obtained a first-class honours degree by the time he was nineteen. Who had proposed to Mum on the summit of Tryfan, on one of two rocks called Adam and Eve, and then held her hand as they leapt from one to the other. Who had wrapped his hand around mine and walked with me to the top of Scafell, and then carried me back down on his shoulders. Who had returned our family to the same town in Scotland, so that my brother could defend the trophy he had won playing golf there the year before, when he was only fifteen years old. When I began to read Philosophy as an undergraduate and hated it, I had telephoned home at midnight from a payphone at the end of a rain-filled street to tell Dad how unhappy I was. He had got out of bed, and answered the phone, and said: 'Well done, darling, it's great that you know how you feel about this. Now, don't worry about anything, just go back to bed, and we can make some plans in the morning.' Whenever I had gone to the mountains, because I often walked alone, Dad would telephone the hotel, or pub, where I was staying, every day, to ask how I'd got on. He had welcomed Rupert into our family the first moment they had met, already laughing, his arms held wide, even as Rupert climbed out of his car. His grandchildren he called *my shining diamonds*. When Dad entered a room he had the ability to make everyone in it feel special. You could see it in their faces, and I had been told about it often enough. This lovely, kind, irreplaceable man was, in every way, my father, and if I have a sense of loss, it is because he has died, and there isn't a day when I do not think of him.

The Well at the World's End

Rupert and I had gone to a party at the home of the writer Kirsty Gunn when *The Well at the World's End* came up in conversation. Kirsty, it turned out, was a distant relative of Neil Gunn. We chatted about the book, and I told her of my journey to Dunbeath, now three summers earlier, and she asked me: 'Did you visit the well?'

'No!' I said, and told her how I had tried to find out where it was but had eventually abandoned the search, and had followed the Dunbeath Water instead.

'My sister lives in Caithness,' she said. 'I'm certain she knows where it is,' and Kirsty promised that she would write to her straight away. She was sure that her sister would be able to draw a map, there was really no mystery about it. But the reply, when it came, was tantalisingly vague and as fruitless as my earlier searches. The sister had forgotten the exact location of the well, and suggested I contact the Heritage Centre in Dunbeath. I had done that three years ago, too. But I did write again, and the same kind lady I had spoken to then now wrote to Neil Gunn's nephew,

Dairmid Gunn. This time Mr Gunn was not away from home, and he wrote to me by return.

Dear Kate (if I may)
I have been asked by Meg Sinclair of the Dunbeath Heritage Centre to give you directions to reach the well . . .'

It was that easy. Evie and I went together. The road journey, again, took three days to complete. We went first to Dunbeath because I wanted to show her the loch. We stood with our backs to the sea, until a black wave slapped the harbour wall with a crack like a starting pistol. We followed the river until we were high above the town. We passed the cemetery and the waterfall and the abandoned farm and the empty house called Poll Roy. At the farm the wool from a recent shearing clogged the path like sea-foam. We were careful to avoid the rabbit traps. We bent to finger the tangled heads of bog-cotton. Morven, invisible when I had come alone, appeared as a blue wedge on the horizon. The river was the colour of tea. Two pale hinds appeared on the skyline, their leaf-shaped ears revolving like antennae. We slept side by side on the heather. We began walking again just after four the next morning. We saw no birds at all. There were midges. There were *midges*. The only sounds were of the river and our footfalls, the occasional chatter of our voices, and the *swoosh* as we walked through long grass. Mostly, we walked in silence. Once, there was a noise, like a glass of water being knocked over, and a slick black salmon broke the surface of a pool. It made a pattern like a firework before it disappeared beneath the shelter of the bank. Evie stared at the place where the salmon had been. It was the only living thing we had seen all day but for the midges. There was little or no breeze as we followed the river, but above our heads the clouds rolled quickly from the sea, like an autocue of Rorschach inkblots.

We reached the edge of the water table. Clumps of mist in curious shapes appeared like empty dresses. The land was much heavier than when I had come by myself. We had been up to our knees in mud and moss, the peat hags too spongy to be safe, and were now walking barefoot up the streambed. The mist began to press about us, silently stopping up our senses. We perched next to one another on a dryish clump of heather and pondered what to do. The memory of slipping into water that covered my head, on our visit to the source of the Severn, was fresh with me. I couldn't, with good conscience, take Evie across the blasted shell holes between the head of the stream and the unseen loch.

It was as though a blind had been drawn down over our endeavour. It was strange to me how receptive the landscape had felt when I had come here on my own, and how enigmatic, and secretive, it was today. There were no birds, no deer. Only the whine and pin-prick of midges, although the mist – mercifully – had dispersed them for a while. It was like being in an empty theatre between performances. As though the action was happening elsewhere.

'Is this where the well is?' Evie asked.

'No, there's a loch, but we wouldn't see it in this mist. The well is a few miles from Dunbeath. If we turn back now we could find it before nightfall.'

'Let's find the well,' she said.

Later that afternoon Evie reached into the glove compartment of the car and took out Dairmid Gunn's letter and an Ordnance

Survey map. The place Dairmid had described was a few miles south of Golspie. Evie opened the map, and ran her finger down the pink stripe of the A9. We had a grid reference. Evie's finger came to rest on a single letter: W.

Meaning, *Well*.

Evie hated map-reading. We drove up and down the same stretch of road for about half an hour. In Neil Gunn's novel, the well is close to a collection of cottages. The hero has gone to fill his kettle at the well but when he looks at the water it's so clear he can't see it, and so he tells the old woman who lives in the nearby cottage that it's dry. 'That well is never dry,' she replies. We pulled over and I looked at the map. There were two little cubes opposite the 'W' on the map. We'd driven right past them. I turned the car round. The cottages were on a particularly lethal bend in the A9 but they could have been lifted from the book. A band of woodland ran on both sides of the road, and at the northern boundary of the wood, on the opposite side to the cottages, was a lichen-covered wooden gate. We tried to find a place to park. The A9 is the only significant road in that part of the Highlands, and cars fumed like killer bees. I eased the car onto a low grass verge. As I got out I saw a penny. I picked it up and showed it to Evie. She took her bottle of water and emptied what was left of it onto the road.

'For the well water,' she said.

We passed through a wooden gate. A high wicker fence ran alongside a footpath. We could see the woodland between the reeds of the fence, and it seemed to be in a poorly state, black pines leaning against one another. Other trees had been cut down, but not replanted. A chill hung in the air, the only sound came from the creak of the pines, and the occasional buzz from the road. After about fifty yards the path opened out onto a blackened mulchy glade, where a wicker man, wearing a kilt, with a wooden sporran, a tam-o'-shanter and Wellingtons lay alongside an empty stream-bed, pebbled with pine cones and dried leaves. Bronze pine needles covered the earth. The well-keeper scarecrow implied that this was the right place. My heart sank. It seemed as though the well had, after all, dried up. I placed the penny I had found on top of the reclining figure's sporran.

And then I saw it, we both saw it, seemed to notice it together. In a dark bank, a few yards away, surrounded by tendrils of new ferns, was a wooden door. It was made of boards and painted ox-blood red. It wasn't big, more like a cupboard, and on the lintel, in block capitals, had been carved the words:

THE WELL AT THE WORLD'S END

It was similar to the door that I had dreamed about, but unlike that door, which had no handle, there was a ceramic doorknob and a brass bolt. Above the lintel were two chipped enamel cups containing a smattering of pine needles.

We crouched in front of the door.

'You do it,' said Evie. 'Go on.' I slid back the bolt. I was terrified that the well would be empty, filled with broken twigs, like the streambed a few yards to the left of us. I opened the door.

At first I thought that a light had come on. We were looking into a rectangular box, with smooth pale stone sides and a fine whitish sand on the bottom. Looking above it I saw that the roof of the chamber was like a cistern, made of stones the size of apples. A bright fern curled between two of the stones. The water wasn't immediately apparent, but a couple of pine needles that I dislodged on opening the door revealed its surface. The light appeared to be coming from inside the well, and I thought of the words that had inspired our journey: *a well whose water is so clear it is invisible.*

A pulse, like a heartbeat, seemed to move the air in front of us. Without really speaking we fumbled for a cup. Evie passed it to me, and I pressed the cup into the water. A curved meniscus seemed to swell along the rim, to hesitate momentarily before flooding the beaker. I lifted the cup.

'You go first,' she said.

'No, you're my daughter.'

Evie drank off half the water in the cup, and then I finished it. We drank with speed as though we had run a race. It was sweet. Like swallowing light.

A small wind entered the clearing, circling, rising, the trees behind the wicker fence creaking like halyards. We heard the ratchet laughter of crows and then, overhead, a bird with trailing legs flapped slowly above the circle of trees.

'Is that a heron?' Evie asked. The bird flew in an arc.

'No, look at its head. The neck's extended, and it's white. It must be a stork.' The trees were moving around us. The sky had turned porcelain blue. Sunlight streamed to the floor of the glade. The change was so sudden that I found myself laughing, and then a silence fell all about us. A cloud settled over the sun like a dust-sheet. The trees shuffled back into stillness.

'What do you think?' I asked Evie.

'I think the audience is over,' she said.

I closed the door of the well. We hadn't filled our plastic bottle. We walked quickly back the way we had come and as we reached the gate, Evie said: 'Do you feel different?'

I hesitated. 'Yes. Do you?'

'Everything looks clearer,' she said.

We called Rupert to say we were coming home. The journey, as before, took three days. We called to visit Mum. Since her illness her memory had grown extraordinarily patchy and she was surprised to see us, although delighted, and sorry when we had to go. 'Look after yourselves,' she said, 'and ring me when you get home. You children are all I've got!'

'And you're the only mum I've got!' I said.

'And my only granny!' said Evie.

The next night we stayed at the cottage, and then closed it up for the winter. On the third day we headed south through Wales. We drove over mountains and along a tree-lined valley. There was a thunderstorm on the road ahead of us. We passed the signpost to the village where Mrs Thomas lived. I was finding it easier to drive past the turn, knowing that she was there, but suspected that it was never going to be effortless. My phone bleeped and Evie looked at it. It was a message from Robert, he was on his way back from Cardiff. Where were we?

There was a tympanic rumble followed by a bouncing lightning bolt that tore the sky ahead of us into halves. The road was dark, and slick, and shining, although no rain fell. We must have been travelling at the same speed as the storm, because we remained in green light for the whole of our journey, and we counted seven rainbows.

Acknowledgements

I would like to thank the following people: At Bloomsbury, my brilliant and unruffleable editor Alexa von Hirschberg, and the lovely Alexandra Pringle for choosing me; Sarah Barlow, Laura Brooke, Michael Fishwick, Helen Flood, David Foy, Greg Heinimann and fierce-eyed Mary Tomlinson, for helping to make this such a pleasing book. Ariel Bruce for her generosity and for finding my birth family; Joanna Comino for her astute notes and her friendship; Clare Conville for being my nurse, and for feeding me; Jane Coward for her constant friendship and excellent company; Mary Doyle and David Austen for looking after our little family when it all looked a bit grim; Tessa Ettedgui for coming to chemotherapy with me; Robin Farquhar Thomson for insisting that I sing; Sr Maria Goretti and Sr Carmel for remembering the story; Dairmid Gunn and the Neil M. Gunn Literary Estate for being consistently supportive of *The Fish Ladder* and for telling me where the well was; Claudia Harding McKean, and her team at the Countess of Chester NHS Trust, for saving my life; Olga Jubany Baucells for reminding me that Minerva is also the goddess of healing; Caradoc King for suggesting I record my wanderings and being my friend, teacher and agent; Robert Macfarlane for mistaking me for a writer, for introducing me to *The Well at the World's End*, and for his encouragement, advice and friendship; Fiona McNeil, her team, and everyone at the Royal Marsden for getting me through the worst of it; Jean McNeil at UEA for her faith in the project; Calvin Mitchell for his overwhelming generosity, tender concern and concrete support; the Norbury family: Jean, John, Maria, Anna, Connor and Lauren, for everything; Oba Nsugbe for his extraordinary care, generosity, wisdom and counsel; Deborah Orr for keeping me company when we had no hair; the dear memory of Dennis Pinnington for a lifetime of love, friendship and encouragement, and for being my second reader, although he died before he got to the end; Polly Samson, for her infectious laughter and for being my first reader; Sue Swift and David Flusfeder for being such welcoming neighbours; my brother 'Robert Thomas,' for being there.

The following people have helped in ways as various as themselves: Louise Allen-Jones; John Bernasconi; Sharon Blackie; Jared Brading and the staff of Sacred Heart Primary School; Harvey Cabaniss; Cynthia and John Carson; Amit Chaudhuri; Simon Chu; Andrew Cowan; Linda Cracknell; Kristin Dean; Amy Elliot; Johnny Flynn; Lucy Geldenhuys; Kirsty Gunn; Judy Herbert; Clare Jolly; Bronwen Jones; Julian Kenyon; Yuko Komiya; Nigel Langford; Michael Lengsfield; Jackie Lomax; Sara Maitland; Bishop Vincent Malone; Chrissie O'Farrell; Mgr Canon Peter O'Neill; Fr Jordi Padro; Jeremy Page; Gwenna Parry Williams; Georgina and William Petty; Noemi Ranz; Jon Riley; Mary Sackville West, Linda Shaughnessy; Meg Sinclair; Peter Straus; Henry Sutton; Gwydion Thomas; Nancy Verrier; Nicola Waddell;

Stuart Webley; Amy Wellesley Wood; Sharon Wilkinson; Peter Womack; Mildred Yuan.

My special thanks go to Evie Thomson, my daughter, for her sparkling companionship and for the brilliant drawings in the book, and to Rupert Thomson — my friend, husband and soul's companion: where can I begin?

Notes

This book is a work of life writing based on the experiences and recollections of Katharine Norbury. In some cases names of people, places, dates, sequences or the detail of events have been changed solely to protect the privacy of others.

NOTES ON SOURCES

Epigraph to Part I

p. 1   'It is no small pity': Teresa of Avila (translated by E. Allison Peers), *The Interior Castle*, Dover Thrift Edition, New York, 2008. Reproduced by kind permission of Dover Publications Inc. on behalf of the E. Allison Peers Literary Estate.

Font del Mont

p. 7   'Places in the heart': Leon Bloy's words, 'Man has places in his heart which do not yet exist, and into them enters suffering, in order that they may have existence', have been made famous as the epigraph to Graham Green's *The End of the Affair*, although no one seems to know when or where Bloy first published them.

Swimming Pool

p. 8   'On a huge hill': John Donne, 'The Third Satire' from *The Complete English Poems*, Penguin Classics, London 1976.

p. 11   'Whose water is so clear': Robert Macfarlane, personal correspondence, 2009. Reproduced by kind permission of Robert Macfarlane.

p. 13, 14   'And what will you do': Neil M. Gunn, *Highland River*, Penguin, London, 1975. Reproduced by kind permission of Dairmid Gunn on behalf of the Neil M. Gunn Literary Estate.

Humber

p. 16   A version of 'Humber' first appeared in *A Wilder Vein*, edited by Linda Cracknell, Two Ravens Press, Port of Ness, 2009.

Mersey

p. 47   'In a dark leathern bag': *The Mabinogion*, translated by Lady Charlotte E. Guest, Dover Thrift Editions, New York, 2000.

Afon Geirch

p. 56   'Matthew, Mark, Luke and John': This is a version of the English language prayer and nursery rhyme also known as the 'Black Paternoster', traditionally said by children as they go to bed. It has a Roud Folk Song Index number of 1704. It may have origins in ancient Babylonian prayers and was being used in a Christian version in late Medieval Germany. The earliest extant version in English can be traced to the mid-sixteenth century.

p. 61   There are many variants of this story: Jan Morris recounts one in her book *Wales*, in which all the revellers but one drown as the waters rise around a castle, but it also shares a family likeness with the story of Odysseus's revenge on Penelope's suitors, when the hero enters his besieged home disguised as a beggar, then kills the suitors with the help of his son and a trusty swineherd.

p. 63　'Time held me green and dying': Dylan Thomas, 'Fern Hill' from *The Collected Poems of Dylan Thomas: The Original Edition*, New Directions, 2010. Copyright 1945 by The Trustees for the Copyrights of Dylan Thomas. Reproduced by kind permission of David Higham Associates and New Directions Publishing Corp.

Ffynnon Fawr

p. 72　'They did not divine it': R.S. Thomas, 'Ffynnon Fair' from *Collected Poems 1949–1990*, Phoenix, 2000. Reproduced by kind permission of Gwydion Thomas on behalf of the R. S. Thomas Literary Estate.

p. 73　'St. Mary's cave': Ieuan Lleyn (1769–1832), also known as Evan Pritchard, was a renowned bard, poet and writer of hymns. This extract is from a letter to his friend Dafydd Ddu Eryri, 1799. Translation reproduced by kind permission of Gwenllian Jones on behalf of Rhiw.com.

Caherdaniel

p. 99　'But Hermes did not find': *The Odyssey of Homer*, translated and with an introduction by Richmond Lattimore, Harper Perennial, New York, 1999. Copyright 1965, 1967 by Richmond Lattimore; Renewed 1995 by Alice B. Lattimore. Reproduced by kind permission of HarperCollins Publishers.

p. 101　'That unnameable something': C.S. Lewis, Foreword to *The Pilgrim's Regress*, Fount, London, 1998. Copyright C.S. Lewis Pte Ltd 1933. Reproduced by kind permission of The C.S. Lewis Company Ltd.

Skell

p. 106, 107　'Hither came on a day': 'Every way the woman went': *Irish Metrical Dindshenchas*, translated by Edward John Gwynn, CELT, University College, Cork, 2004.

p. 110　'That state of highly respectful sulkiness': Wilkie Collins, *The Woman in White*, Penguin Classics, London, 2007.

p. 120 'Should th' ungenerous world': Georgiana, Duchess of Devonshire, letter to Eliza Gray, from *Verses copied by Lady Charlotte Cholmondeley in her common place book*, c. 1816.

Tummell

p. 133 'A very fundamental human attribute': Sara Maitland, *Gossip from the Forest*, Granta, London, 2013. Reproduced by kind permission of Sara Maitland.

p. 135 'Over the Rainbow': Words and Music by Harold Arlen and EY Harburg © 1938. Reproduced by permission of EMI Feist Catalog, London, W1F 9LD.

Spey

p. 141 A version of 'Spey' first appeared in the *UEA Creative Writing Anthology*, foreword by Andrew Motion, Eggbox Publishing, Norwich, 2012.

p. 150 'We fulfil the demands of nature': Cassius Dio, *Roman History*, published in Vol. IX of the Loeb Classical Library edition, Harvard, 1927.

p. 153 'A curious mood of fatalism': Neil M. Gunn, *Highland River*, Penguin, London, 1975. Reproduced by kind permission of Dairmid Gunn on behalf of the Neil M. Gunn Literary Estate.

Dunbeath

p. 162, 163, 164, 195 'Who turned her eyes onto', 'restraining her feet', 'Truly we think the matter', 'That which was born in her womb': *Jocelyn, A monk of Furness: The Life of Kentigern* (Mungo), translated by Cynthia Whiddon Green, as part of an MA Thesis, University of Houston, 1998, from the Internet Mediaeval Sourcebook, a collection of public domain and copy-permitted historical texts edited by Paul Halsall.

p. 190   'His dismay was vague': Neil M. Gunn, *Highland River*, Penguin, London, 1975. Reproduced by kind permission of Dairmid Gunn on behalf of the Neil Gunn Literary Estate.

p. 195   'Love, with very young people': Isak Dinesen, 'The Old Chevalier' from *Seven Gothic Tales*, Penguin, 2002. Reproduced by kind permission of the Karen Blixen Estate.

p. 195   'A secret well there was': *Irish Metrical Dindshenchas*, translated by Edward John Gwynn, CELT, University College, Cork, 2004.

Epigraphs to Part II

p. 205   'Is it possible to pierce': Neil M. Gunn from a letter to Geoffrey Faber, 1950. Reproduced by kind permission of Dairmid Gunn on behalf of the Neil Gunn Literary Estate.

p. 205   'The Water' by John Patrick Vivian Flynn © Transgressive Publishing Ltd (PRS) (NS). All rights administered by Warner/Chappell Music Publishing Ltd. All rights reserved.

Swimming Pool (2)

p. 208   'Looking overhead he saw': John Cheever, 'The Swimmer' from *Collected Stories*, Vintage Classics, 1990. Reproduced by kind permission of Penguin Random House UK on behalf of the John Cheever Literary Estate.

Innominate Stream

p. 225   'Skilful, careful and modest': from *The Scawfell Accident*, Climbers' Club Journal No 21, 1903.

Severn

p. 243, 246, 254   'I am waiting for an old frayed queen', 'She who shines': Alice Oswald, *A Sleepwalk on the Severn*, Faber and Faber,

London, 2009. Reproduced by kind permission of United Agents LLP (www.unitedagents.co.uk) and Faber and Faber Ltd on behalf of Alice Oswald.

p. 250   'The connection between biological mother and child is primal, mystical, mysterious, and everlasting. Far more than merely biological and historical, this primal connection is also cellular, psychological, emotional, and spiritual. So deep runs the connection between a child and its mother that the severing of that bond results in a profound wound for both, a wound from which neither fully recovers. In the case of adoption, the wound cannot be avoided, but it can and must be acknowledged and understood'. Nancy Verrier, 'Position Statement', www.nancyverrier.com/position-statement. Reproduced by kind permission of Nancy Verrier.

p. 255   'A secret well there was', 'Every way the woman went': *Irish Metrical Dindshenchas*, translated by Edward John Gwynn, CELT, University College, Cork, 2004.

Afon Rhiw

p. 258   'What is existence': R. S. Thomas, 'Mass for Hard Times' from *Selected Poems*, Penguin Modern Classics, London, 2003. Reproduced by kind permission of Gwydion Thomas on behalf of the R.S. Thomas Literary Estate.

p. 279   'That well is never dry': Neil M. Gunn, *The Well at the World's End*, Faber and Faber, London, 1951. Reproduced by kind permission of Dairmid Gunn on behalf of the Neil M. Gunn Literary Estate.

A Note on the Author

Katharine Norbury trained as a film editor with the BBC and has worked extensively in film and television drama. She is a graduate of the Creative Writing MA programme at UEA and a doctoral candidate at Goldsmiths. She lives in London with her family. *The Fish Ladder* is her first book.

@kjnorbury

A Note on the Type

The text of this book is set in Bembo. This type was first used in 1495 by the Venetian printer Aldus Manutius for Cardinal Bembo's *De Aetna*, and was cut for Manutius by Francesco Griffo. It was one of the types used by Claude Garamond (1480–1561) as a model for his Romain de L'Université, and so it was the forerunner of what became standard European type for the following two centuries. Its modern form follows the original types and was designed for Monotype in 1929.